W9-ADO-051

Praise for the Mistborn Trilogy
by Brandon Sanderson

On NPR's Top 100 Science-Fiction, Fantasy Books List

Mistborn

"Intrigue, politics, and conspiracies mesh complexly in a world Sanderson realizes in satisfying depth and peoples with impressive characters." —*Booklist*

"The characters in this book are amazingly believable. Vin is an eminently sympathetic protagonist whose development over the course of the book is beautifully and realistically delineated. The system of magic is exceedingly clever and well-integrated into the complex and plausible world that Vin and Kelsier inhabit. While this is the first in a series, it's an exceedingly satisfying book on its own, and fans of the genre should waste no time picking it up." —*RT Book Reviews*

The Well of Ascension

"This entertaining read will especially please those who always wanted to know what happened after the good guys won." —*Publishers Weekly*

"Vin's struggles with love and power inject the human element into Sanderson's engaging epic. . . . Epic fantasy fans will want to keep following Vin and her cohorts' adventures." —*Booklist*

"Sanderson's hallmark is to take traditional high fantasy tropes and turn them upside down, and he doesn't disappoint here. Vin's a beautifully realized protagonist whose struggles are wonderfully written and, as always, the world-building is unusual and compelling." —*RT Book Reviews*

"All the explosive action any adventure fan could want." —*Locus*

The Hero of Ages

BY BRANDON SANDERSON®

THE STORMLIGHT ARCHIVE®
The Way of Kings
Words of Radiance
Oathbringer
Rhythm of War

THE MISTBORN® SAGA

THE ORIGINAL TRILOGY
Mistborn
The Well of Ascension
The Hero of Ages

THE WAX AND WAYNE SERIES
The Alloy of Law
Shadows of Self
The Bands of Mourning

Elantris
Warbreaker
Arcanum Unbounded: The Cosmere® Collection
Legion: The Many Lives of Stephen Leeds

ALCATRAZ VS. THE EVIL LIBRARIANS
Alcatraz vs. the Evil Librarians
The Scrivener's Bones
The Knights of Crystallia
The Shattered Lens
The Dark Talent

THE RECKONERS
Steelheart
Firefight
Calamity

SKYWARD
Skyward
Starsight

The Rithmatist

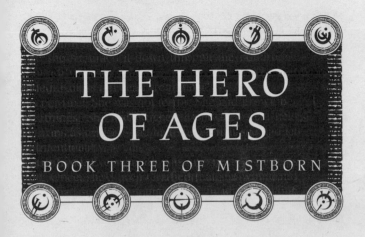

THE HERO OF AGES

BOOK THREE OF MISTBORN

BRANDON SANDERSON

A TOM DOHERTY ASSOCIATES BOOK · NEW YORK

THE HERO OF AGES: BOOK THREE OF MISTBORN

Copyright © 2008 by Dragonsteel Entertainment, LLC

Mistborn®, The Stormlight Archive®, Reckoners®, Cosmere®, and Brandon Sanderson® are registered trademarks of Dragonsteel Entertainment, LLC

All rights reserved.

Edited by Moshe Feder

Tin symbol and spikes by Ben McSweeney originally appeared in the *Mistborn Adventure Game* by Crafty Games, www.mistborn.games. Maps and other ornaments by Isaac Stewart.

A Tor Book
Published by Tom Doherty Associates
120 Broadway
New York, NY 10271

www.tor-forge.com

Tor® is a registered trademark of Macmillan Publishing Group, LLC.

ISBN 978-1-250-31862-6

Our books may be purchased in bulk for promotional, educational, or business use. Please contact your local bookseller or the Macmillan Corporate and Premium Sales Department at 1-800-221-7945, extension 5442, or by email at MacmillanSpecialMarkets@macmillan.com.

First Edition: October 2008
Revised Mass Market Edition: December 2019

Printed in the United States of America

0 9 8 7

FOR JORDAN SANDERSON,

Who can explain to any who ask

What it's like to have a brother

Who spends most of his time dreaming.

(Thanks for putting up with me.)

CONTENTS

ACKNOWLEDGMENTS

As always, I owe a whole lot of people a whole lot of thanks for helping make this book what it is today. First and foremost, my editor and my agent—Moshe Feder and Joshua Bilmes—are to be noted for their exceptional ability to help a project reach its fullest potential. Also, my wonderful wife, Emily, has been a great support and aid to the writing process.

As before, Isaac Stewart did the fine map work, chapter symbols, and circle of Allomantic metals. Sam Weber did such stellar work on the Mistborn trade paperbacks that we requested him for these new, more symbolic covers. His work continues to impress, and I appreciate his vision of the series. Thanks to Larry Yoder for being awesome, and Dot Lin for her publicity work for me at Tor. Denis Wong and Stacy Hague-Hill for their assistance to my editor, and the —as always—marvelous Irene Gallo and Seth Lerner for their art direction.

Alpha readers for this book include Paris Elliott, Emily Sanderson, Krista Olsen, Ethan Skarstedt, Eric J. Ehlers, Eric "More Snooty" James Stone, Jillena O'Brien, C. Lee Player, Bryce Cundick/Moore, Janci Patterson, Heather Kirby, Sally Taylor, Bradley Reneer, Steve "Not Bookstore Guy Anymore" Diamond, General Micah Demoux, Zachary "Spook" J. Kaveney, Alan Layton, Janette Layton, Kaylynn ZoBell, Nate Hatfield, Matthew Chambers, Kristina Kugler, Daniel A. Wells, The Indivisible Peter Ahlstrom, Marianne Pease, Nicole Westenskow, Nathan Wood, John David Payne, Tom Gregory, Rebecca Dorff, Michelle Crowley, Emily Nelson, Natalia Judd, Chelise Fox, Nathan Crenshaw, Madison VanDenBerghe, Rachel Dunn, and

Ben OleSoon. Gamma readers include Deana Whitney, Gary Singer, Ted Herman, Joe Deardeuff, and Bao Pham.

In addition I'm thankful to Jordan Sanderson—to whom this book is dedicated—for his tireless work on the website. Jeff Creer, also, did a great job with the art for Brandon Sanderson.com. Stop by and check it out!

PREFACE

This is the book where I had to prove I could do this—both to myself and to my readers.

During the years that I was trying to break into fantasy, I noticed something about newer writers. There were a lot of great world-builders selling books. There were also a lot of people who could write great chapters, compelling characters, and interesting situations.

I consistently found myself disappointed by the endings of these books, however. Granted, I'll take a book with a weak ending but great characters over the reverse—but I felt that a lot of writers were neglecting this key point of their stories. If I read an epic book, or series, that fully immersed me and took weeks of my time to get through, I wanted an equally epic ending.

With *The Hero of Ages*, I needed to put my money where my mouth was. I'd invested in writing all three of these books nearly back to back, finishing this one before the first one had to go to press. I'd pushed myself this far, and this hard, because I wanted to make sure the last book was appropriately themed with the first two.

But I'd never done this before. I was exploring what was, for me, new territory. I'd written some fifteen or sixteen books at this point, but no series endings. So this book was stressful for me. I so badly wanted to get it right, that when some things went poorly (like Sazed's arc in the rough draft) I felt a lot of pressure to find another path.

At the same time, there was a certain momentum to writing *The Hero of Ages*. Book two was the biggest overall struggle of the three, even if Sazed's arc in this book was the biggest individual struggle of the series. I wrote this book in a fervor, energized by having stopped (briefly) to write the first Alcatraz book. I tried to channel every bit of apocalyptic fantastical idea I'd had over the years, holding nothing back.

I had to stick the landing with this book. For the most part, I think I did. Like all of the Mistborn books, it has a unique, individual focus. It's somehow both a small book and a large one at the same time. One of my pitches to myself for the series was, "Do in three books what other series take ten to accomplish." The way to do this without letting the book get overwhelmed by side stories was to keep the focus on a few main characters—show their world falling apart around them, but keep the attention on them and their struggles.

I'm very proud of the result. I like how intimate it is, despite the epic scope of the series. I like how lean it is. (Though large, it is still half the size of my average Stormlight book.) I like how the world-building ties together and, most of all, how well the three volumes work as a whole. Both as a journey for the characters, and as entries into a deconstruction of the fantasy genre.

Mistborn is my calling card to the world.

16. LAKE TYRIAN
17. LAKE LUTHADEL
18. THE BLACK LAKE
19. RIVER SERAN

20. NORTH SERAN
21. SOUTH SERAN
22. THE RIVER CHANNEREL

THE FINAL EMPIRE

1. LUTHADEL
2. PITS OF HATHSIN
3. URTEAU 4. FADREX CITY
5. TREMREDARE 6. TATHINGDWEN
7. CONVENTICAL OF SERAN
8. MOUNT DERYTATITH, HISTORIC LOCATION OF
THE WELL OF ASCENSION

THE ASHMOUNTS
9. TYRIAN 10. ZERINAH 11. FALEAST 12. DORIEL
13. MORAG 14. KALLING 15. TORINOST

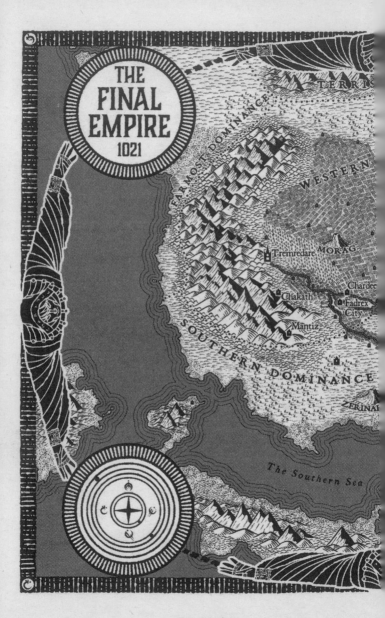

THE
FINAL
EMPIRE
1021

TERRIS

FAR MOST DOMINANCE

WESTERN

MORAG

Tremredare

Chakath   Chardee
                           Fadrex
                           City

Mantiz

SOUTHERN DOMINANCE

ZERINAH

The Southern Sea

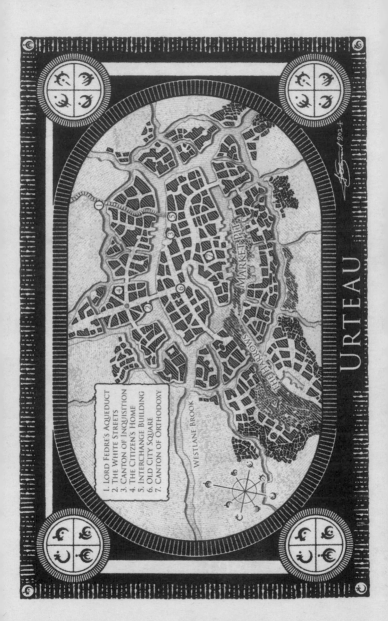

URTEAU

1. LORD FEDRE'S AQUEDUCT
2. THE WHITE STREETS
3. CANTON OF INQUISITION
4. THE CITIZEN'S HOME
5. INTERCHANGE BUILDING
6. OLD CITY SQUARE
7. CANTON OF ORTHODOXY

MARKET PIER

SMOKSVILGEN

WESTLANE BROOK

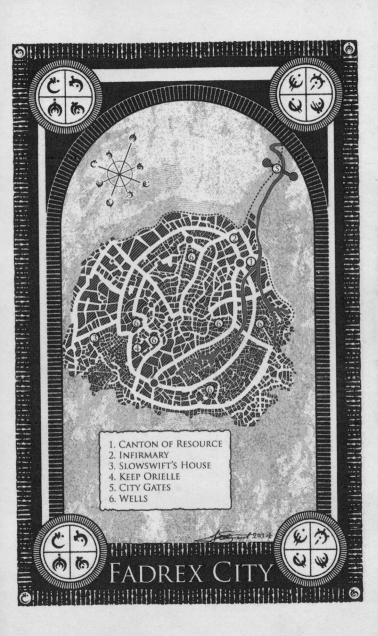

1. CANTON OF RESOURCE
2. INFIRMARY
3. SLOWSWIFT'S HOUSE
4. KEEP ORIELLE
5. CITY GATES
6. WELLS

FADREX CITY

THE HERO
OF AGES

PROLOGUE

MARSH STRUGGLED TO KILL HIMSELF.

His hand trembled as he tried to summon the strength to make himself reach up and pull the spike from his back and end his monstrous life. He had given up on trying to break free. Three years. Three years as an Inquisitor, three years imprisoned in his own thoughts. Those years had proven that there was no escape. Even now, his mind clouded.

And then *it* took control. The world seemed to vibrate around him; then suddenly he could see clearly. Why had he struggled? Why had he worried? All was as it should be.

He stepped forward. Though he could no longer see as normal men did—after all, he had large steel spikes driven point-first through his eyes—he could sense the room around him. The spikes protruded from the back of his skull; if he reached up to touch it, he could feel the sharp tips. There was no blood.

The spikes gave him power. Everything was traced in fine blue Allomantic lines, highlighting the world. The room was of modest size, and several companions—also outlined in blue, the Allomantic lines pointing at the metals contained in their very blood—stood with Marsh. Each one had spikes through their eyes.

Except for the man tied to the table in front of him. Marsh smiled, taking a spike off the table beside him, then hefting it. His prisoner wore no gag. That would have stopped the screams.

"Please," the prisoner whispered, trembling. Even a Terris steward would break down when confronted by his own violent death. The man struggled weakly. He was in quite an awkward position, as he had been tied to the table on top of another person. The table had been designed that way, with depressions to allow for the body underneath.

"What is it you want?" the Terrisman asked. "I can tell you no more about the Synod!"

Marsh fingered the brass spike, feeling its tip. There was work to do, but he hesitated, relishing the pain and terror in the man's voice. Hesitated so that he could . . .

Marsh grabbed command of his own mind. The room's scents lost their sweetness, and instead reeked with the stench of blood and death. His joy turned to horror. His prisoner was a Keeper of Terris—a man who had worked his entire life for the good of others. Killing him would be not only a crime, but a tragedy. Marsh tried to force his arm up and around to grab the linchpin spike from his back—its removal would kill him.

However, *it* was too strong. The force. Somehow it had control over Marsh—and it needed him and the other Inquisitors to be its hands. It was free—Marsh could still feel it exulting in that—but something kept it from affecting the world too much by itself. An opposition. A force that lay over the land like a shield.

It was not yet complete. It needed more. Something else . . . something hidden. Marsh would find that something, and bring it to his master. The master that Vin had frccd. The entity that had been imprisoned within the Well of Ascension.

It called itself Ruin.

Marsh smiled as his prisoner began to cry; then he stepped forward, raising the spike in his hand. He placed it against the whimpering man's chest. The spike would need to pierce the man's body, passing through the heart, then be driven into the body of the Inquisitor tied below. Hemalurgy was a messy art.

That was why it was so much fun. Marsh picked up a mallet and began to pound.

PART ONE

LEGACY OF
THE SURVIVOR

I am, unfortunately, the Hero of Ages.

1

FATREN SQUINTED UP AT THE red sun, which hid behind its perpetual screen of dark haze. Black ash fell lightly from the sky, as it did most days lately. The thick flakes fell straight, the air stagnant and hot, without a hint of a breeze to lighten Fatren's mood. He sighed, leaning back against the earthen bulwark, looking over Vetitan. His town.

"How long?" he asked.

Druffel scratched his nose. His face was stained black with ash. He hadn't given much thought to hygiene lately. Of course, considering the stress of the last few months, Fatren knew that he himself wasn't much to look at either.

"An hour maybe," Druffel said, spitting into the dirt of the bulwark.

Fatren sighed, staring up at the falling ash. "Do you think it's true, Druffel? What people are saying?"

"What?" Druffel asked. "That the world is ending?"

Fatren nodded.

"Don't know," Druffel said. "Don't really care."

"How can you say that?"

Druffel shrugged, scratching himself. "Soon as those koloss arrive, I'll be dead. That's pretty much the end of the world for me."

Fatren fell silent. He didn't like to voice his doubts; he

was supposed to be the strong one. When the lords had left the town—a farming community, slightly more urban than a northern plantation—Fatren had been the one who had convinced the skaa to go ahead with their planting. Fatren had been the one to keep the press gangs away. In a time when most villages and plantations had lost every able-bodied man to one army or another, Vetitan still had a working population. It had cost much of their crops in bribes, but Fatren had kept the people safe.

Mostly.

"The mists didn't leave until noon today," Fatren said quietly. "They're staying later and later. You've seen the crops, Druff. The autumn planting overwintered poorly, and they're all stunted—not enough sunlight, I'd guess. We won't have enough food to make it to the spring planting's harvest."

"We won't last the summer," Druffel said. "Won't last 'til nightfall."

The sad thing—the thing that was really disheartening— was that Druffel had once been the optimist. Fatren hadn't heard his brother laugh in months. That laughter had been Fatren's favorite sound.

Even the Lord Ruler's mills weren't able to grind Druff's laughter out of him, Fatren thought. *But these last two years have.*

"Fats!" a voice called. "Fats!"

Fatren looked up as a young boy scrambled along the side of the bulwark. They'd barely finished the fortification—it had been Druffel's idea, before he'd given up hope. Their town contained some seven thousand people, which made it fairly large. It had taken a great deal of work to surround the entire thing with a defensive mound.

Fatren had barely a thousand soldiers—it had been hard to gather that many from such a small population—with maybe another thousand men who were too young, too old, or too unskilled to fight well. He didn't really know how big the koloss army was, but it was bound to be larger than two thousand. So a bulwark was going to be of very little use.

The boy—Sev—puffed up to Fatren. "Fats! Someone's coming!"

"Already?" Fatren asked. "Druff said the koloss were still a while away!"

"Not a koloss, Fats," the boy said. "A man. Come see!"

Fatren turned to Druff, who wiped his nose and shrugged. They followed Sev around the inside of the bulwark, toward the front gate. Ash and dust swirled on the packed earth, piling in corners, drifting. There hadn't been much time for cleaning lately. The women had to work the fields while the men trained and made war preparations.

War preparations. Fatren told himself that he had a force of two thousand soldiers, but what he really had were a thousand skaa peasants with swords. They'd had two years of training, true, but they had little real fighting experience.

A group of men clustered around the front gates, standing on the bulwark or leaning against its side. *Maybe I was wrong to spend so much of our resources training soldiers,* Fatren thought. *If those thousand men had worked the mines instead, we'd have some ore for bribes.*

Except koloss didn't take bribes. They just killed. Fatren shuddered, thinking of Garthwood. That city had been bigger than his own, but fewer than a hundred survivors had made their way to Vetitan. That had been three months ago. He'd hoped that the koloss would be satisfied with destroying that city.

He should have known better. Koloss were never satisfied.

Fatren climbed to the top of the bulwark, and soldiers in patched clothing and bits of leather made way for him. He peered through the falling ash across a dark landscape that looked as if it were blanketed in deep black snow.

A lone rider approached, wearing a dark, hooded cloak.

"What do you think, Fats?" one of the soldiers asked. "Koloss scout?"

Fatren snorted. "Koloss wouldn't send a scout, especially not a human one."

"He has a horse," Druffel said with a grunt. "We could

use another of those." The city had only five. All were suffering from malnutrition.

"Merchant," one of the soldiers said.

"No wares," Fatren said. "And it would take a brave merchant to travel these parts alone."

"I've never seen a refugee with a horse," one of the men said. He raised a bow, looking at Fatren.

Fatren shook his head. Nobody loosed as the stranger rode up, moving at an unhurried pace. He stopped his mount directly before the city gates. Fatren was proud of those. True wooden gates mounted in the earthen bulwark. He'd gotten both wood and fine stone from the lord's manor at the city center.

Little of the stranger was visible beneath the thick dark cloak he wore to protect himself from the ash. Fatren studied the stranger over the top of the bulwark, and then he glanced at his brother, shrugging. The ash fell silently.

The stranger leaped from his horse.

He shot straight upward, as if propelled from beneath, cloak whipping free as he soared. Underneath it, he wore a uniform of brilliant white.

Fatren cursed, jumping backward as the stranger crested the bulwark and landed atop the wooden gate. The man was an Allomancer. A nobleman. Fatren had hoped those would all stick to their squabbles in the North and leave his people in peace.

Or at least their peaceful deaths.

The newcomer turned. He wore a short beard, and had his dark hair shorn close. "All right, men," he said, striding across the top of the gate with an unnatural sense of balance, "we don't have much time. Let's get to work." He stepped off the gate onto the bulwark. Immediately, Druffel pulled his sword on the newcomer.

The sword jerked from Druffel's hand, yanked into the air by an unseen force. The stranger snatched the weapon as it passed his head. He flipped the sword around, inspecting it. "Good steel," he said, nodding. "I'm impressed. How many of your soldiers are this well equipped?" He flipped the weapon in his hand, handing it back toward Druffel hilt-first.

Druffel glanced at Fatren, confused.

"Who *are* you, stranger?" Fatren demanded with as much courage as he could muster. He didn't know a lot about Allomancy, but he was pretty certain this man was Mistborn. The stranger could probably kill everyone atop the bulwark with barely a thought.

The stranger ignored the question, turning to scan the city. "This bulwark goes around the entire perimeter of the city?" he asked, turning toward one of the soldiers.

"Um . . . yes, my lord," the man said.

"How many gates are there?"

"Just the one, my lord."

"Open the gate and bring my horse in," the newcomer said. "I assume you have stables?"

"Yes, my lord," the soldier said.

Well, Fatren thought with dissatisfaction as the soldier ran off, *this newcomer certainly knows how to command people.* Fatren's soldier didn't pause to think that he was obeying a stranger without asking for permission. Fatren could already see the other soldiers straightening a bit, losing their wariness. This newcomer talked like he expected to be obeyed, and the soldiers were responding. This wasn't a nobleman like the ones Fatren had known when he was a household servant at the lord's manor. This man was different.

The stranger continued his contemplation of the city. Ash fell on his beautiful white uniform, and Fatren thought it a shame to see the garment being dirtied. The newcomer nodded to himself, then began to walk down the side of the bulwark.

"Wait," Fatren said, causing the stranger to pause. "*Who are you?*"

The newcomer turned, meeting Fatren's eyes. "My name is Elend Venture. I'm your emperor."

With that, the man turned and continued down the embankment. The soldiers made way for him; then many of them followed behind.

Fatren glanced at his brother.

"Emperor?" Druffel muttered, then spat.

Fatren agreed with the sentiment. What to do? He'd never fought an Allomancer before; he wasn't certain how to begin. The "emperor" had certainly disarmed Druffel easily enough.

"Organize the people of the city," the stranger—Elend Venture—said from ahead. "The koloss will come from the north—they'll ignore the gate, climbing over the bulwark. I want the children and the elderly concentrated in the southernmost part of the city. Pack them together in as few buildings as possible."

"What good will that do?" Fatren demanded. He hurried after the emperor—he didn't really see any other option.

"The koloss are most dangerous when they're in a blood frenzy," Venture said, continuing to walk. "If they do take the city, then you want them to spend as long as possible searching for your people. If the koloss frenzy wears off while they search, they'll grow frustrated and turn to looting. Then your people might be able to sneak away without being chased."

Venture turned to meet Fatren's eyes. The stranger's expression was grim. "It's a slim hope. But it's something." He resumed his pace down the city's main thoroughfare.

From behind, Fatren could hear the soldiers whispering. They'd all heard of a man named Elend Venture. He was the one who had seized power in Luthadel after the Lord Ruler's death over two years before. News from up north was scarce and unreliable, but most of it mentioned Venture. He had fought off all rivals to the throne, killing his own father. He'd hidden his nature as a Mistborn, and was supposedly married to the very woman who had slain the Lord Ruler. Fatren doubted that such an important man— one who was likely more legend than fact—had made his way to such a humble city in the Southern Dominance, especially unaccompanied. Even the mines weren't worth much anymore. The stranger had to be lying.

But . . . he *was* obviously an Allomancer . . .

Fatren hurried to keep up with the stranger. Venture—or whoever he was—lingered in front of a large structure near the center of the city. The old offices of the Steel Ministry. Fatren had ordered the doors and windows boarded up.

"You found the weapons in there?" Venture asked, turning toward Fatren.

Fatren stood for a moment. Then shook his head. "From the lord's mansion."

"He left weapons behind?" Venture asked with surprise.

"We think he intended to come back for them," Fatren said. "The soldiers he left eventually deserted, joining a passing army. They took what they could carry. We scavenged the rest."

Venture rubbed his bearded chin as he stared at the old Ministry building. It was tall and ominous, despite—or perhaps because of—its disuse. "Your men look well trained. I didn't expect that. Do any of them have battle experience?"

Druffel snorted quietly, indicating that he thought this stranger had no business being so nosy.

"Our men have fought enough to be dangerous, stranger," Fatren said. "Some bandits thought to take rule of the city from us. They assumed we were weak, and would be easily cowed."

If the stranger saw the words as a threat, he didn't show it. He simply nodded. "Have any of you fought koloss?"

Fatren shared a look with Druffel. "Men who fight koloss don't live, stranger," he said.

"If that were true," Venture said, "I'd be dead a dozen times over." He turned to face the growing crowd of soldiers and townspeople. "I'll teach you what I can about fighting koloss, but we don't have much time. I want captains and squad leaders organized at the city gate in ten minutes. Regular soldiers are to form up in ranks along the bulwark—I'll teach the squad leaders and captains a few tricks, and then they can carry the tips to their men."

Some of the soldiers moved, but—to their credit—most of them stayed where they were. The newcomer didn't seem offended that his orders weren't obeyed. He stood quietly, staring down the armed crowd. He didn't seem frightened, nor did he seem angry or disapproving. He only seemed . . . regal.

"My lord," one of the soldier captains asked. "Did you . . . bring an army with you to help us?"

"I brought two, actually," Venture said. "But we don't have time to wait for them." He met Fatren's eyes. "You wrote and asked for my help. And as your liege, I've come to give it. Do you still want it?"

Fatren frowned. He'd never asked this man—or any lord—for help. He opened his mouth to object, but hesitated. *He'll let me pretend that I sent for him,* Fatren thought. *Act like this was part of the plan all along. I could give up rule here without looking like a failure.*

We're going to die. But, looking into this man's eyes, I can almost believe that we have a chance.

"I . . . didn't expect you to come alone, my lord," Fatren found himself saying. "I was surprised to see you."

Venture nodded. "That is understandable. Come, let's talk tactics while your soldiers gather."

"Very well," Fatren said. As he stepped forward, Druffel caught his arm.

"What are you doing?" his brother hissed. "You *sent* for this man? I don't believe it."

"Gather the soldiers, Druff," Fatren said.

Druffel stood for a moment, then swore softly and stalked away. He didn't look like he had any intention of gathering the soldiers, so Fatren waved for two of his captains to do it. Then he joined Venture, and the two started back toward the gates, Venture ordering a few soldiers to walk ahead of them and keep people at a distance so that he and Fatren could speak more privately. Ash continued to fall from the sky, dusting the street black, clustering atop the city's stooped one-story buildings.

"Who are you?" Fatren asked quietly.

"I am who I said," Venture said.

"I don't believe you."

"But you trust me," Venture said.

"No. I merely don't want to argue with an Allomancer."

"That's good enough, for now," Venture said. "Look, friend, you have *ten thousand* koloss marching on your city. You need whatever help you can get."

Ten thousand? Fatren thought, feeling stupefied.

"You're in charge of this city, I assume?" Venture asked.

Fatren shook out of his stupor. "Yes," he said. "My name is Fatren."

"All right, Lord Fatren, we—"

"I'm no lord," Fatren said.

"Well, you just became one," Venture said. "You can choose a surname later. Now, before we continue, you need to know my conditions for helping you."

"What kind of conditions?"

"The nonnegotiable kind," Venture said. "If we win, you'll swear fealty to me."

Fatren frowned, stopping in the street. Ash fell around him. "So that's it? You saunter in before a fight, claiming to be some high lord, so you can take credit for our victory? Why should I swear fealty to a man I only met a few minutes before?"

"Because if you don't," Venture said quietly, "I'll simply take command anyway." Then he continued to walk.

Fatren stood for a moment, then rushed forward and caught up to Venture. "Oh, I see. If we survive this battle, we'll end up ruled by a tyrant."

"Yes," Venture said.

Fatren frowned. He hadn't expected the man to be so blunt.

Venture shook his head, regarding the city through the falling ash. "I used to think that I could do things differently. And I still believe that someday I'll be able to. But for now I don't have a choice. I need your soldiers and I need your city."

"My city?" Fatren asked, frowning. "Why?"

Venture held up a finger. "We have to survive this battle first," he said. "We'll get to other things later."

Fatren was surprised to realize that he *did* trust the

stranger. He couldn't have explained why he felt that way. This was simply a man to follow—a leader such as Fatren had always wanted to be.

Venture didn't wait for Fatren to agree to the "conditions." It wasn't an offer, but an ultimatum. Fatren hurried to catch up again as Venture entered the small square in front of the city gates. Soldiers bustled about. None of them wore uniforms—their sole method of distinguishing a captain from a regular soldier was a red band tied around the arm. Venture hadn't given them much time to gather—but then, they all knew the city was about to be attacked. They had been gathered anyway.

"Time is short," Venture repeated in a loud voice. "I can teach you only a few things, but they will make a difference.

"Koloss range in size from small ones that are about five feet tall to the huge ones, which are about twelve feet tall. Even the little ones are going to be stronger than you. Expect that. Fortunately, the creatures fight without coordination between individuals. If a koloss's comrade is in trouble, he won't bother to help.

"They attack directly, without guile, and try to use blunt force to overwhelm. Don't let them! Tell your men to gang up on individual koloss—two men for the small ones, three or four for the big ones. We won't be able to maintain a large front, but that will keep us alive the longest.

"Don't worry about creatures that get around our line and enter the city—we'll have the civilians hidden at the back of your town, and the koloss who bypass our line might turn to pillaging, leaving others to fight alone. That's what we want! Don't chase them down into the city. Your families will be safe.

"If you're fighting a big koloss, attack the legs, bring it down before you go for the kill. If you're fighting a small one, make certain your sword or spear doesn't get caught in their loose skin. Understand that koloss aren't stupid—they're merely unsophisticated. Predictable. They'll come at you the easiest way possible, and attack only in the most direct manner.

"The important thing for you to understand is that they *can* be beaten. We'll do it today. Don't let yourselves become intimidated! Fight with coordination, keep your heads, and I promise you that we *will survive*."

The soldier captains stood in a small cluster, looking at Venture. They didn't cheer at the speech, but they did seem a little more confident. They moved off to pass on Venture's instructions to their men.

Fatren approached the emperor quietly. "If your count is correct, they outnumber us five to one."

Venture nodded.

"They're bigger, stronger, and better trained than we are."

Venture nodded again.

"We're doomed then."

Venture frowned, black ash dusting his shoulders. "You're not doomed. You have something they don't— something very important."

"What's that?"

Venture met his eyes. "You have me."

"My lord emperor!" a voice called from atop the bulwark. "Koloss sighted!"

They already call to him first, Fatren thought. Fatren wasn't certain whether to be insulted or impressed.

Venture immediately jumped up to the top of the bulwark, using his Allomancy to cross the distance in a quick bound. Most of the soldiers stooped or hid behind the top of the fortification, keeping a low profile despite the distance of their enemies. Venture, however, stood proud in his white cape and uniform, shading his eyes, squinting toward the horizon.

"They're setting up camp," he said, smiling. "Good. Lord Fatren, prepare the men for an assault."

"An *assault*?" Fatren asked, scrambling up behind Venture.

The emperor nodded. "The koloss will be tired from marching, and will be distracted by making camp. We'll never have a better opportunity to attack them."

"But we're on the defensive!"

Venture shook his head. "If we wait, they'll eventually whip themselves into a blood frenzy, then come against us. We need to attack rather than wait to be slaughtered."

"And abandon the bulwark?"

"The fortification is impressive, Lord Fatren, but ultimately useless. You don't have the numbers to defend the entire perimeter, and the koloss are generally taller and more stable than men. They'll take the bulwark from you, then hold the high ground as they push down into the city."

"But—"

Venture looked at him. His eyes were calm, but his gaze was firm and expectant. The message was simple: *I am in charge now.* There would be no more arguing.

"Yes, my lord," Fatren said, calling over messengers to pass the orders.

Venture stood watching as the messenger boys dashed off. There seemed to be some confusion among the men— they weren't expecting to attack. More and more eyes turned toward Venture, standing tall atop the bulwark.

He really does look like an emperor, Fatren thought despite himself.

The orders moved down the line. Time passed. Finally the entire army was watching. Venture pulled out his sword and held it high in the ash-scattered sky. Then he took off down the bulwark in an inhumanly quick dash, charging toward the koloss camp.

For a moment he ran alone. Then, surprising himself, Fatren gritted his teeth against shaking nerves and followed.

The bulwark exploded with motion, the soldiers charging with a collective yell, running toward death with their weapons held high.

Holding the power did strange things to my mind. In mere moments, I became familiar with the power itself, its history, and the ways it might be used.

Yet this knowledge was different from experience or the ability to use that power. For instance, I knew how to move a planet in the sky. But I didn't know where to place it so that it wouldn't be too close, or too far, from the sun.

2

AS ALWAYS, TENSOON'S DAY BEGAN in darkness. Part of that was due to the fact that he didn't have any eyes. He could have created a set —he was of the Third Generation, which was old even for a kandra. He had digested enough corpses that he had learned how to create sensory organs intuitively without a model to copy.

Unfortunately, eyes would have done him little good. He had no skull, and he had found that most organs didn't function well without a full body and skeleton to support them. His own mass would crush eyes if he moved the wrong way, and it would be difficult to turn them about to see.

Not that there would be anything to look at. TenSoon moved his bulk slightly, shifting inside his prison chamber. His body was little more than a grouping of translucent muscles—like a mass of large snails or slugs, all connected, somewhat more malleable than the body of a mollusk. With concentration, he could dissolve one of the muscles and either meld it with another one or make something new. Yet without a skeleton to use, he was all but impotent.

He shifted in his cell again. His skin had a sense of its own—a kind of taste. Right now, it tasted the stench of his own excrement on the sides of the chamber, but he didn't dare turn off this sense. It was one of his only connections to the world around him.

The cell was no more than a grate-covered stone pit barely large enough to hold his mass. His captors dumped food in from the top, then periodically poured water to hydrate him and wash his excrement out through a small drainage hole at the bottom. Both this hole and those in the locked grate above were too small for him to slide through—a kandra's body was supple, but a pile of muscles could be squeezed only so small.

Most people would have gone mad from the stress of being so confined for . . . he didn't *know* how long it had been. Months? But TenSoon had the Blessing of Presence. His mind would not give in easily.

Sometimes he cursed the Blessing for keeping him from the blissful relief of madness.

Focus, he told himself. He had no brain, not as humans did, but he was able to think. He didn't understand this. He wasn't certain if any kandra did. Perhaps those of the First Generation knew more—but if so, they didn't enlighten everyone else.

They can't keep you here forever, he told himself. *The First Contract says . . .*

But he was beginning to doubt the First Contract—or rather that the First Generation paid any attention to it. But could he blame them? TenSoon was a Contract-breaker. By his own admission, he had gone against the will of his master, helping another instead. This betrayal had ended with his master's death.

Such a shameful act was the least of his crimes. The punishment for Contract-breaking was death, and if TenSoon's crimes had stopped there, the others would have killed him and been done with it. Unfortunately, there was much more at stake. TenSoon's testimony—given to the Second Generation in a closed conference—had revealed a much more dangerous, much more important lapse.

TenSoon had betrayed his people's secret.

They can't execute me, he thought, using the idea to keep him focused. *Not until they find out who I told.*

The secret. The precious, precious secret.

I've doomed us all. My entire people. We'll be slaves again. No, we're already slaves. We'll become something else—automatons, our minds controlled by others. Captured and used, our bodies no longer our own.

This was what he had done—what he had potentially set in motion. The reason he deserved imprisonment and death. Yet he wished to live. He should despise himself. But for some reason, he still felt he had done the right thing.

He shifted once more, masses of slick muscle sliding around one another. Midshift, however, he froze. Vibrations. Someone was coming.

He pushed his muscles to the sides of the pit, forming a depression in the middle of his body. He needed to catch all of the food that he could—they fed him precious little. But no slop came pouring down through the grate. He waited, expectant, until the grate unlocked. Though he had no ears, he could feel the coarse vibrations as the grate was dragged back, then its rough iron dropped to the floor above.

What?

Hooks came next. They looped around his muscles, grabbing him and ripping his flesh as they pulled him out of the pit. It hurt. Not the hooks alone, but the sudden freedom as his body was spilled across the floor of the prison. He unwillingly tasted dirt and dried slop. His muscles quivering, the unfettered motion of being outside the cell felt strange. He strained, moving his bulk in ways he had nearly forgotten.

Then it came. He could taste it in the air. Acid, thick and

pungent, presumably in a gold-lined bucket brought by the prison keepers. They were going to kill him after all.

But they can't! he thought. *The First Contract, the law of our people, it—*

Something fell on him. Not acid, but something hard. He touched it eagerly, muscles moving against one another, tasting it, testing it, feeling it. It was round, with holes and several sharp edges . . . a skull.

The acid stink grew sharper. Were they stirring it? Ten-Soon moved quickly, forming around the skull, filling it. He already had some dissolved flesh stored inside an organ-like pouch. He brought this out, oozing it around the skull, quickly making skin. He left the eyes alone, working on lungs, forming a tongue, ignoring lips for the moment. He worked with a sense of desperation as the taste of acid grew strong, and then . . .

It hit him. It seared the muscles on one side of his body, washing over his bulk, dissolving it. Apparently the Second Generation had given up on getting his secrets from him. However, before killing him, they knew they had to give him an opportunity to speak. The First Contract required it—hence the skull. But the guards obviously had orders to kill him before he could say anything in his defense. They followed the form of the law, yet at the same time they ignored its intent.

They didn't realize how quickly TenSoon could work. Few kandra had spent as much time on Contracts as he had—all of the Second Generation, and most of the Third, had long ago retired from service. They led easy lives here in the Homeland.

An easy life taught one very little.

Most kandra took hours to form a body—some younger ones needed days. TenSoon had a rudimentary tongue in seconds. As the acid moved up his body, he forced out a trachea, inflated a lung, and croaked out a single word:

"Judgment!"

The pouring stopped. His body continued to burn. He

worked through the pain, forming primitive hearing organs inside the skull cavity.

A voice whispered nearby. "Fool."

"Judgment!" TenSoon said again.

"Accept death," the voice hissed quietly. "Do not put yourself in a position to cause further harm to our people. The First Generation has granted you this chance to die because of your years of extra service!"

TenSoon hesitated. A trial would be public. So far, only a select few knew the extent of his betrayal. He could die, cursed as a Contract-breaker but retaining some measure of respect for his prior career. Somewhere—likely in a pit in this very room—there were some who suffered endless captivity, a torture that would eventually break even the minds of those endowed with the Blessing of Presence.

Did he want to become one of those? By revealing his actions in an open forum, he would earn himself an eternity of pain. Forcing a trial would be foolish, for there was no hope of vindication. His confessions had already damned him.

If he spoke, it would not be to defend himself. It would be for other reasons entirely.

"Judgment," he repeated, this time barely whispering.

In some ways, having such power was too overwhelming, I think. This was a power that would take millennia to understand. Remaking the world would have been easy, had one been familiar with the power. Yet I realized the danger inherent in my ignorance. Like a child suddenly given awesome strength, I could have pushed too hard, and left the world a broken toy I could never repair.

3

ELEND VENTURE, SECOND EMPEROR OF the Final Empire, had not been born a warrior. He'd been born a nobleman—which in the Lord Ruler's day had essentially made Elend a professional socialite. He'd spent his youth learning to play the frivolous games of the Great Houses, living the pampered lifestyle of the imperial elite.

It wasn't odd for him to have ended up a politician. He'd always been interested in political theory, and while he'd been more a scholar than a true statesman, he'd known that someday he'd rule his house. Yet he hadn't made a very good king at first. He hadn't understood that there was more to leadership than good ideas and honest intentions. Far more.

I doubt you will ever be the type of leader who can lead a charge against the enemy, Elend Venture. The words had been spoken by Tindwyl—the woman who'd trained him in practical politics. Remembering those words made Elend smile as his soldiers crashed into the koloss camp.

Elend flared pewter. A warm sensation—now familiar to him—burst to life in his chest, and his muscles became taut with extra strength and energy. He'd swallowed the metal earlier, so that he could draw upon its powers for the battle. He was an Allomancer. That still awed him sometimes.

As he'd predicted, the koloss were surprised by the attack. They stood motionless for a few moments, shocked—though they must have seen Elend's newly recruited army as it charged. Koloss had trouble dealing with the unexpected. They found it hard to comprehend a group of weak, outnumbered humans attacking their camp. So it took them time to adjust.

Elend's army made good use of that time. Elend struck first, flaring his pewter to give himself yet more power as he cut down the first koloss. It was a smaller beast. Like all of its kind, it was humanlike in form, though it had oversized drooping blue skin that seemed detached from the rest of its body. Its beady red eyes showed a bit of inhuman surprise as it died, Elend yanking his sword from its chest.

"Strike quickly!" he yelled as more koloss turned from their firepits. "Kill as many as you can before they frenzy!"

His soldiers—terrified but committed—charged in around him, overrunning the first few groups of koloss. The camp was little more than a place where the koloss had tromped down ash and the plants beneath, then dug firepits. Elend could see his men growing more confident at their initial success, and he encouraged them by Pulling on their emotions with Allomancy, making them braver. He was more comfortable with this form of Allomancy—he still hadn't gotten the hang of leaping about with metals the way Vin did. Emotions, however—those he understood.

Fatren, the city's burly leader, stuck near Elend as he led a group of soldiers. Elend kept an eye on the man. As the ruler of this city, his death would be a blow to morale. Together they rushed a small number of surprised koloss. The largest beast among them was eleven feet tall, with its skin pulled tight around its oversized body. Koloss never stopped growing, but their skin always remained the same size. On the younger creatures it hung loose and folded. On the big ones it stretched and ripped.

Elend burned steel, then threw a handful of coins into the air in front of him. He Pushed on the coins with his weight, spraying them at the koloss. The beasts were too tough to fall to coins with any reliability, but the bits of metal would injure and weaken them.

As the coins flew, Elend charged the large koloss. The beast pulled a huge sword off its back, and it seemed elated at the prospect of a fight.

The koloss swung first, and it had an awesome reach. Elend had to jump backward—pewter making him more nimble. Koloss swords were massive, brutish things, so blunt they were almost clubs. The force of the blow shook the air; Elend wouldn't have had a chance to turn the blade aside even with pewter helping him. In addition, the sword—or more accurately the koloss holding it—weighed so much that Elend wouldn't be able to use Allomancy to Push it out of the creature's hands. Pushing with steel was all about weight and force. If Elend Pushed on something heavier than himself, he'd be thrown backward.

So Elend had to rely on the extra speed and dexterity of pewter. He dashed to the right, watching for a backhand. The creature turned, silent, eyeing Elend, but didn't strike. It hadn't quite frenzied yet.

Elend stared down his oversized enemy. *How did I get here?* he thought, not for the first time. *I'm a scholar, not a warrior.* Half of the time he thought he had no business leading men at all.

The other half of the time, he figured that he thought too much. He ducked forward, striking. The koloss anticipated the move, and tried to bring its weapon down on his head. But Elend reached out and Pulled on the sword of another koloss—throwing that creature off balance and allowing two of Elend's men to slay it, and also Pulling Elend to the side. He barely evaded his opponent's weapon. Then, as he spun in the air, he flared pewter and struck.

He sheared completely through the beast's leg at the knee,

toppling it to the ground. Vin always said that Elend's Allomantic power was unusually strong. Elend didn't have enough experience with Allomancy to judge that, but the force of his swing sent him stumbling. He managed to regain his footing, then took off the creature's head.

Several of the soldiers were staring at him. His white uniform was now sprayed with bright red koloss blood. It wasn't the first time. Elend took a deep breath as he heard inhuman screams sounding through the camp. The frenzy was beginning.

"Form up!" Elend shouted. "Make lines, stay together, prepare for the assault!"

The soldiers responded slowly. They were far less disciplined than the troops Elend was accustomed to, but they did an admirable job of bunching up at his command. Elend glanced across the ground before them. They'd managed to take down several hundred koloss—an amazing feat.

The easy part was over.

"Stay firm!" Elend yelled, running down in front of the soldier line. "But keep fighting! We need to kill as many of them as quickly as possible! *Everything* depends on this! Give them your fury, men!"

He burned brass and Pushed on their emotions, Soothing away their fear. An Allomancer couldn't control minds— not human ones at least—but he *could* encourage some emotions while discouraging others. Vin said that Elend was able to affect far more people than should have been possible. It was another sign giving credence to the idea that Elend's abilities came from the same source and method as that which the original Allomancers had used to gain their own powers.

Under the influence of the Soothing, his soldiers stood up straight. Again, Elend felt a healthy respect for these simple skaa. Though he lent them bravery, the determination was their own. These were good people.

With luck, he'd be able to save some of them.

The koloss attacked. As he'd hoped, a large group of the creatures broke away from the main camp and charged toward the town. Some of the soldiers cried out, but they were too busy defending themselves to follow. Elend threw himself into the fray whenever the line wobbled, shoring up the weak point. As he did so, he burned brass and tried to Push on the emotions of a nearby koloss.

Nothing happened. The creatures were resistant to emotional Allomancy, particularly when they were already being manipulated by someone else. But when he *did* break through, he could take complete control of them. That required time, luck, and a determination to fight tirelessly.

So he did. He fought alongside the men, watching them die, killing koloss as his line bent at the edges, forming a half circle to keep his troops from being surrounded. The fighting was grim. As more and more koloss frenzied and charged, the odds quickly turned against Elend's group. The koloss still resisted his emotional manipulation. But they were getting closer . . .

"We're doomed!" Fatren shouted.

Elend turned, a bit surprised to see the beefy lord beside him and still alive. The men continued to fight. Only about fifteen minutes had passed since the start of the frenzy, but the line was already beginning to buckle.

A speck appeared in the sky.

"You've led us to die!" Fatren yelled. He was covered in koloss blood, though a patch on his shoulder looked to be his own. "Why?" Fatren demanded.

Elend simply pointed as the speck grew larger.

"What is it?" Fatren asked over the chaos of battle.

Elend smiled. "The first of those armies I promised you."

Vin fell from the sky in a tempest of horseshoes, landing directly at the center of the koloss army.

Without hesitating, she used Allomancy to Push a pair of horseshoes toward a turning koloss. One took the creature in the forehead, throwing it backward, and the other shot over it, hitting another koloss. Vin spun, flipping out another shoe, and shot it past a particularly large beast, taking down a smaller koloss behind him.

She flared iron, Pulling that horseshoe back, catching it around the larger koloss's wrist. Her Pull immediately yanked her toward the beast—but it also threw the creature off balance. Its massive iron sword dropped to the ground as Vin hit the creature in the chest. Then she Pushed off the fallen sword, throwing herself upward in a backward flip as another koloss swung at her.

She shot some fifteen feet into the air. The sword missed, cutting off the head of the koloss beneath her. The koloss who had swung didn't seem to mind that it had killed a comrade; it only looked up at her, bloodred eyes hateful.

Vin Pulled on the fallen sword. It lurched up at her, but also pulled her down with its weight. She caught it as she fell—the sword was nearly as tall as she was, but flared pewter let her handle it with ease—and she sheared free the attacking koloss's arm as she landed.

She took its legs off at the knees, then left it to die as she spun toward other opponents. As always the koloss seemed fascinated—in an enraged, baffled way—with her. They associated large size with danger and had difficulty understanding how a small woman like Vin—nineteen years old, barely over five feet in height and slight as a willow—could pose a threat. Yet they saw her kill, and this drew them to her.

Vin was just fine with that.

She shouted as she attacked, if only to add some sound to the too-silent battlefield. Koloss tended to stop yelling as they entered their frenzy, growing focused solely on killing. She threw out a handful of coins, Pushing them toward the group behind her, then jumped forward, Pulling on a sword.

A koloss in front of her stumbled. She landed on its back, attacking a creature beside it. This one fell, and Vin rammed her sword down into the spine of the one below her. She Pushed herself to the side, Pulling on the sword of the dying koloss. She caught this weapon, cut down a third beast, then threw the sword, Pushing it like a giant arrow into the chest of a fourth monster. That same Push threw her backward out of the way of an attack. She grabbed the sword from the body of the one she'd stabbed before, ripping the weapon free even as the creature died. And in one fluid stroke she slammed it down through the collarbone and chest of a fifth beast.

She landed. Koloss fell dead around her.

Vin was not fury. She was not terror. She had grown beyond those things. She had watched Elend die—had held him in her arms as he did—and had known that she had let it happen. Intentionally.

Yet he still lived. Every breath was unexpected, perhaps undeserved. Once, she'd been terrified that she would fail him. But she had somehow found peace in understanding that she couldn't keep him from risking his life. In understanding that she didn't *want* to keep him from risking his life.

So, she no longer fought out of fear for the man she loved. Instead she fought with an understanding. She was a knife—Elend's knife, the Final Empire's knife. She didn't fight to protect one man, but to protect the way of life he had created and the people he struggled so hard to defend.

That peace gave her strength.

Koloss died around her, and scarlet blood—too bright to be human—stained the air. The ten thousand in this army were far too many for her to kill. However, she didn't need to slaughter every one of the koloss.

She merely had to make them afraid.

Because despite what she'd once assumed, koloss *could* feel fear. She saw it building in the creatures around her, hidden beneath frustration and rage. A koloss attacked her, and she dodged to the left, moving with pewter's enhanced speed. She slammed a sword into its back, and spun, noticing a massive creature pushing its way through the army toward her.

Perfect, she thought. It was big—perhaps the biggest

one she had ever seen. It had to be almost thirteen feet tall. Heart failure should have killed it long ago, and its skin was ripped half free, hanging in wide flaps.

It bellowed, the sound echoing across the oddly quiet battlefield. Vin smiled, then burned duralumin. Immediately the pewter already burning within her exploded to give her a massive, instantaneous burst of strength.

Vin burned steel, then Pushed outward in all directions. Amplified by the duralumin, her Steelpush crashed like a wave into the swords of the creatures running at her. Weapons were ripped free, koloss thrown backward, and massive bodies scattered like flakes of ash beneath the bloodred sun. Her duralumin-augmented pewter kept her from being crushed by her own Push.

Her pewter and steel both disappeared, burned away in a single flash of power. She pulled one of her small vials—of an alcohol solution with metal flakes—and downed it in a single gulp, restoring her metals. Then she burned pewter and leaped over fallen, disoriented koloss toward the massive creature she had seen earlier. A smaller koloss tried to stop her, but she caught its arm by the wrist, then twisted, breaking the joint. She took the creature's sword, ducking beneath another koloss's attack, and spun, felling three different koloss in one sweep by cutting at their knees.

As she completed her spin, she rammed her sword into the earth point-first. As expected, the large, thirteen-foot-tall beast attacked a second later, swinging a sword that was so large that it made the air roar. Vin planted her sword right in time, for even with pewter she never would have been able to parry this enormous creature's weapon. It slammed into her stabilized blade instead. The metal quivered beneath her hands, but she held against the blow.

Fingers still stinging from the shock of such a powerful block, Vin let go of the sword and jumped. She didn't Push—she didn't need to—but landed on the crossguard of her sword and leaped off it. The koloss showed that same characteristic surprise as it saw her leap thirteen feet into the air, leg drawn back, tasseled mistcloak flapping.

She kicked the koloss directly in the side of the skull. It cracked. Koloss were inhumanly tough, but her flared pewter was enough. The creature's beady eyes rolled back, and it collapsed. Vin Pushed slightly on the sword, keeping herself up long enough so that when she fell, she landed directly on the felled koloss's chest.

The koloss around her froze. Even in the midst of the blood fury, they were shocked to see her drop such an enormous beast with only a kick. Perhaps their minds were too slow to process what they had seen. Or perhaps in addition to fear, they really could feel a measure of wariness. Vin didn't know enough about them to tell. She did understand that in an ordinary koloss army, what she'd done would have earned her the obedience of every creature that had watched her.

Unfortunately, this army was being controlled by an external force. Vin stood up straight, and could see Elend's small, desperate army in the distance. Under Elend's guidance, they held. The fighting humans would have an effect on the koloss similar to Vin's mysterious strength—the creatures wouldn't understand how such a small force could hold against them. They wouldn't see the attrition or the dire situation of Elend's men; they would simply see a smaller, inferior army standing and fighting.

Vin turned to resume combat. The koloss approached her with more trepidation, but they still came. That was the oddity about koloss. They never retreated. They felt fear, they just couldn't act on it. But it did weaken them. She could see it in the way they approached her, the way they looked. They were close to breaking.

So she burned brass and Pushed on the emotions of one of the smaller creatures. At first it resisted. She shoved harder. And finally something broke within the creature, and it became hers. The one who had been controlling it was too far away, and was focused on too many koloss at once. This creature—its mind confused because of the frenzy, emotions in a turmoil because of its shock, fear, and frustration—came completely under Vin's mental control.

Immediately she ordered the creature to attack its companions. It was cut down a moment later, but not before it killed two other koloss. As Vin fought, she snatched up another koloss, then another. She struck randomly, fighting with her sword to keep the koloss distracted as she plucked members from their group and turned them. Soon the area around her was in chaos, and she had a small line of koloss fighting for her. Every time one fell, she replaced it with two more.

As she fought, she spared another glance for Elend's group, and was relieved to find a large number of koloss fighting alongside the group of humans. Elend moved among them, no longer fighting, focused on snatching koloss after koloss to his side. It had been a gamble for Elend to come to this city on his own, one she wasn't sure she approved of. For the moment, she was simply glad she'd managed to catch up in time.

Taking Elend's cue, she stopped fighting, and instead concentrated on commanding her small force of koloss, snatching up new members one at a time. Soon she had a group of almost a hundred fighting for her.

Won't be long now, she thought. And sure enough, she caught sight of a speck in the air shooting toward her through the falling ash. The speck resolved into a figure in dark robes, bounding over the army by Pushing down on koloss swords. The tall figure was bald, its face tattooed. In the ash-darkened light of midday, Vin could make out the two thick spikes that had been driven point-first through its eyes. A Steel Inquisitor, one she didn't recognize. She'd deliberately lured him out, killing and controlling his koloss, forcing him to reveal himself. Now she had to deal with him.

The Inquisitor hit hard, cutting down one of Vin's stolen koloss with a pair of obsidian axes. It focused its sightless gaze on Vin, and despite herself she felt a stirring of panic. A succession of distinct memories flashed in her mind. A dark sky, rainy and shadowed. Spires and towers. A pain in her side. A long night spent captive in the Lord Ruler's palace.

Kelsier, the Survivor of Hathsin, dying on the streets of Luthadel.

Vin burned electrum. This created a cloud of images around her, shadows of possible things she could do in the future. Electrum, the Allomantic complement of gold. Elend had started calling it "poor man's atium." It wouldn't affect the battle much, other than to make her immune to atium, should the Inquisitor have any.

Vin gritted her teeth, dashing forward as the koloss army overwhelmed her few remaining stolen creatures. She jumped, Pushing slightly on a fallen sword and letting her momentum carry her toward the Inquisitor. The creature lifted its axes and swung, but at the last moment Vin Pulled herself to the side. Her Pull wrenched a sword from the hands of a surprised koloss, and she caught this while spinning in the air, then Pushed it at the Inquisitor.

He Pushed the massive wedge of a weapon aside with barely a glance. Kelsier had managed to defeat an Inquisitor, but only after a great deal of effort. He himself had died minutes later, struck dead by the Lord Ruler.

No more memories! Vin told herself forcefully. *Focus on the moment.*

Ash whipped past her as she spun in the air, still flying from her Push against the sword. She landed, foot slipping in koloss blood, then dashed at the Inquisitor. She whipped out a glass dagger—he would be able to Push away a koloss sword—and flared her pewter. Speed, strength, and poise flooded her body. Unfortunately, the Inquisitor would have pewter as well, making them equal.

Except for one thing. The Inquisitor had a weakness. Vin ducked an axe swipe, Pulling on a koloss sword to gain the speed to get out of the way. Then she Pushed on the same weapon, throwing herself forward as she jabbed at the Inquisitor's neck. He fended her off with a swipe of the hand, blocking her dagger arm. But with her other hand she grabbed his robe.

Then she flared iron and *Pulled* behind her, yanking on a dozen different koloss swords at once. The sudden Pull propelled her backward. Steelpushes and Ironpulls were jolting, blunt things that had far more power than subtlety. With pewter flared, Vin hung on to the robe, and the Inquisitor obviously stabilized himself by Pulling on koloss weapons in front of him.

The robe gave, ripping down the side, leaving Vin holding a wide section of cloth. The Inquisitor's back lay exposed, and she should have been able to see a single spike—similar to those in the eyes—protruding from between the creature's shoulder blades. However, that spike was hidden by a hard leather shield that covered the Inquisitor's back, somewhat like a sleek turtle's shell, and ran underneath his arms and around his front like a formfitting breastplate.

The Inquisitor turned, smiling, and Vin cursed. That dorsal spike was each Inquisitor's weakest point. Pulling it free would kill the creature. That was obviously the reason for the armor—something Vin suspected the Lord Ruler would have forbidden. He had *wanted* his servants to have weaknesses, so that he could control them.

Vin didn't have much time for thought, for the koloss were still attacking. As she landed, tossing aside the ripped fabric, a large, blue-skinned monster swung at her. Vin jumped, cresting the sword as it passed beneath her, then Pushed against it to gain height.

The Inquisitor followed, now on the attack. Ash spun in the air currents around Vin as she bounded across the battlefield, trying to think. The only other way she knew to kill an Inquisitor was to behead it—an act more easily contemplated than completed, considering that the fiend would be toughened by pewter.

She landed on a deserted hill on the outskirts of the battlefield. The Inquisitor thumped to the ashen earth behind her. Vin dodged an axe blade, trying to get in close enough to slash. But the Inquisitor swung with his other blade, and Vin took a gash in the arm as her dagger turned the weapon aside.

Warm blood dribbled down her wrist. Blood the color of the red sun. She growled, facing down her inhuman opponent.

Inquisitor smiles disturbed her. She threw herself forward, to strike again.

Something flashed in the air.

Blue lines, moving quickly—the Allomantic indication of nearby bits of metal. Vin barely had time to twist out of her attack as a handful of coins surprised the Inquisitor from behind, cutting into his body in a dozen different places.

The creature screamed, spinning, throwing out drops of blood as Elend hit the ground atop the hill. His brilliant white uniform was soiled with ash and blood, but his face was clean, his eyes bright. He carried a dueling cane in one hand; the other rested against the earth, steadying him from his Steeljump. His physical Allomancy still lacked polish.

Yet he was Mistborn like Vin. And now the Inquisitor was wounded. Koloss were crowding around the hill, clawing their way toward the top, but Vin and Elend still had a few moments. She dashed forward, raising her knife, and Elend attacked as well. The Inquisitor tried to watch both of them at once, its smile finally fading. It moved to jump away.

Elend flipped a coin into the air. A single sparkling bit of copper spun through the flakes of ash. The Inquisitor saw this and smiled again, clearly anticipating Elend's Push. It assumed its weight would transfer through the coin, then hit Elend's weight, since Elend would be Pushing as well. Two Allomancers of near-similar weight, shoving against each other—they would both be thrown back, the Inquisitor to attack Vin, Elend into a pile of koloss.

Except the Inquisitor didn't anticipate Elend's Allomantic strength. How could it? Elend did stumble, but the Inquisitor was thrown away with a sudden, violent Push.

He's so powerful! Vin thought, watching the surprised Inquisitor fall. Elend was no ordinary Allomancer—he might not have learned perfect control yet, but when he flared his metals and Pushed, he could really *Push*.

Vin dashed forward to attack as the Inquisitor tried to

reorient himself. He managed to catch her arm as her knife fell, his powerful grip sending a shock of pain up her already wounded limb. She cried out as he threw her aside.

Vin hit the ground and rolled, throwing herself back up to her feet. The world spun, but she saw Elend swing his dueling cane at the Inquisitor. The creature blocked the swing with an arm, shattering the wood, then ducked forward and rammed an elbow into Elend's chest. The emperor grunted.

Vin Pushed against the koloss who were now barely a few feet away, shooting herself toward the Inquisitor once more. She'd dropped her knife—but he'd also lost his axes. She could see him glancing toward where the weapons had fallen, but she didn't give him a chance to go for them. She tackled him, trying to throw him back to the ground. Unfortunately, he was much larger—and much stronger—than she was. He tossed her down in front of him, knocking the breath from her.

The koloss were upon them. But Elend had grabbed one of the fallen axes, and he struck for the Inquisitor.

The Inquisitor moved with a sudden jolt of speed. Its form became a blur, and Elend swung at empty air. He spun, shock showing on his face as the Inquisitor came up, wielding not an axe, but—oddly—a metal spike, like the ones in his own body but sleeker and longer. The creature raised the spike, moving inhumanly fast—faster than any Allomancer should have managed.

That was no pewter run, Vin thought. *Nor was that duralumin.* She scrambled to her feet, watching the Inquisitor. The creature's strange speed faded, but it was still in a position to hit Elend directly in the back with the spike. Vin was too far away to help.

But the koloss weren't. They were cresting the hill, mere feet from Elend and his opponent. Desperate, Vin flared brass and grabbed the emotions of the koloss closest to the Inquisitor. In the moment the Inquisitor moved to attack Elend, her koloss spun, swinging its wedgelike sword and hitting the Inquisitor directly in the face.

It didn't separate the head from the body. It just crushed the head completely. Apparently that was sufficient, for the Inquisitor dropped without a sound, falling motionless.

A shock ran through the koloss army.

"Elend!" Vin said. "Now!"

The emperor turned away from the dying Inquisitor, and she could see the look of concentration on his face. Once, Vin had seen the Lord Ruler affect an entire city square full of people with his emotional Allomancy. He had been stronger than she was, and far stronger than Kelsier.

She couldn't see Elend burn duralumin, then brass, but she could feel it. Feel him pressing on her emotions as he sent out a general wave of power, Soothing thousands of koloss at once. They all stopped fighting. In the distance, Vin could make out the haggard remnants of Elend's peasant army, standing in an exhausted circle of bodies. Ash continued to fall. These days it rarely ceased.

The koloss lowered their weapons. Elend had won.

This is actually what happened to Rashek, I believe. He pushed too hard. He tried to burn away the mists by moving the planet closer to the sun, but he moved it too far, making the world far too hot for the people who inhabited it.

The Ashmounts were his solution to this. He had learned that shoving a planet around required too much precision, so instead he caused the mountains to erupt, spewing ash and smoke into the air. The particles in the atmosphere reflected sunlight and made the world cooler, and turned the sun red.

4

SAZED, CHIEF AMBASSADOR OF THE New Empire, studied the sheet of paper in front of him. *The tenets of the Cazzi people*, it read. *On the beauty of mortality, the importance of death, and the vital function of the human body as a partaker of the divine whole.*

The words were written in his own hand, transcribed out of one of his copperminds—where he had storages containing literally thousands of books. Beneath the heading, filling most of the sheet in cramped writing, he had listed the basic beliefs of the Cazzi and their religion.

Sazed settled back in his chair, holding up the paper and going over his notes one more time. He'd been focusing on this one religion for a good day now, and he wanted to make a decision about it. He had long known much about the Cazzi faith, for he'd studied it—along with all of the other pre-Ascension religions—for most of his life. Those religions had been his passion, the focus of all his research.

And then the day had come where he'd realized that all of his learning had been meaningless.

The Cazzi religion contradicts itself, he decided, making a notation with his pen at the side of the paper. *It explains that all creatures are part of the "divine whole" and implies that each body is a work of art created by a spirit who decides to live in this world.*

However, one of its other tenets is that the evil are punished with bodies that do not function correctly. A distasteful doctrine, in Sazed's mind. Those who were born with mental or physical deficiencies deserved compassion, perhaps pity, but not disdain. Besides, which of the religion's ideals were true? That spirits chose and designed their bodies as they wished, or that they were punished by the body chosen for them? And what of the influence of lineage upon a child's features and temperament?

He nodded to himself and made a note at the bottom of the sheet of paper. *Logically inconsistent. Obviously untrue.*

"What is that you have there?" Breeze asked.

Sazed looked up. Breeze sat at a small table, sipping his wine and eating grapes. He wore one of his customary nobleman's suits, complete with a dark jacket, a bright red vest, and a dueling cane—with which he liked to gesture as he spoke. He'd regained most of the weight he'd lost during Luthadel's siege and its aftermath, and could reasonably be described as "portly" once more.

Sazed looked down. He carefully placed the sheet alongside the many others within his portfolio, then closed the cloth-wrapped board cover and did up the ties. "It is nothing of consequence, Lord Breeze," he said.

Breeze sipped quietly at his wine. "Nothing of consequence? You seem to always be puttering around with those sheets of yours. Whenever you have a free moment, you pull one of them out."

Sazed set the portfolio beside his chair. How to explain?

Each of the sheets in the thick portfolio outlined one of the over three hundred different religions the Keepers had collected. Each and every one of those religions was now effectively dead, as the Lord Ruler had stamped them out early in his reign, some thousand years before.

One year ago, the woman Sazed loved had died. Now he wanted to know—no, he *had* to know—if the religions of the world had answers for him. He would find the truth, or he would eliminate each and every faith.

Breeze was still looking at him.

"I would prefer not to talk about it, Lord Breeze," Sazed said.

"As you wish," Breeze said, raising his cup. "Perhaps you could use your Feruchemist's powers to listen in on the conversation happening in the next room . . ."

"I do not think it would be polite to do so."

Breeze smiled. "My dear Terrisman—only you would come to conquer a city, then worry about being polite to the dictator you're threatening."

Sazed glanced down, feeling slightly abashed. But he could not deny Breeze's remarks. Though the two of them had brought no army with them to Lekal City, they had indeed come to conquer. They simply intended to do it with a piece of paper rather than a sword.

It all hinged on what was happening in the next room. Would the king sign the treaty or not? All Breeze and Sazed could do was wait. He itched to get his portfolio out, to examine the next religion in the stack. He'd been scrutinizing the Cazzi's for over a day, and now that he'd made a decision about it, he wished to move on to the next sheet. During the last year, he'd gotten through about two-thirds of the religions. Barely a hundred remained, though the number was closer to two hundred if he took into account all of the sub-sects and denominations.

He was close. Over the next few months, he'd be able to get through the rest of the religions. He wanted to give each one fair consideration. Surely one of the remaining ones would strike him as containing the essence of truth he was searching for. Surely one of them would tell him what had happened to Tindwyl's spirit without contradicting itself on a half-dozen different points.

But for the moment, he felt self-conscious reading in front of Breeze. So Sazed forced himself to sit and wait patiently.

The room around him was ornate, after the fashion of the old imperial nobility. Sazed wasn't used to such finery, not anymore. Elend had sold or burned most of his lavish trappings—his people had needed food and warmth during the winter. King Lekal hadn't done the same, it appeared, though perhaps that was because the winters were less harsh here in the South.

Sazed glanced out the window by his chair. Lekal City didn't have a true palace—it had been a mere country estate until about two years ago. The manor house did have a nice view over the growing town—which was more a large shantytown than a true city.

Still, that shantytown controlled lands that were dangerously inside Elend's defensive perimeter. They needed the security of King Lekal's allegiance. So Elend had sent a contingent—including Sazed, who was his chief ambassador—to secure the loyalty of the Lekal king. That man deliberated in the next room with his aides, trying to decide whether or not to accept the treaty—which would make them subjects of Elend Venture.

Chief Ambassador of the New Empire . . .

Sazed was not fond of his title, for it implied that he was a citizen of the empire. His people, the Terris people, had sworn to call no man master again. They had spent a thousand years being oppressed, being bred like animals and turned into perfect, docile servants. Only with the fall of the Final Empire had the Terris become free to rule themselves.

So far, the Terris people hadn't done a very good job of that. Of course, it didn't help that the Steel Inquisitors had slaughtered the entire Terris ruling council, leaving Sazed's people without direction or leadership.

In a way, we're hypocrites regardless, he thought. *The Lord Ruler was secretly a Terrisman. One of our own did those horrible things to us. What right do we have to insist on calling no foreigner master? It wasn't a foreigner who destroyed our people, our culture, and our religion.*

And so, Sazed served as Elend Venture's chief ambassador. Elend was a friend—a man Sazed respected like few others. To Sazed's mind, the Survivor himself hadn't possessed Elend Venture's strength of character. The emperor hadn't tried to assume authority over the Terris people, even after he had accepted the refugees into his lands. Sazed wasn't sure if his people were free or not, but they owed Elend Venture a large debt. Sazed would gladly serve as the man's ambassador.

Despite the other things Sazed felt he should be doing. Such as leading his people.

No, Sazed thought, glancing at his portfolio. *No. A man with no faith cannot lead them. I must find the truth for myself first. If such a thing exists.*

"It certainly is taking them long enough," Breeze said, eating a grape. "One would think that after all the talking we did to get to this point, they'd know by now whether they intended to sign the thing or not."

Sazed glanced toward the elaborately carved door on the other end of the room. What would King Lekal decide? Did he really have a choice? "Did we do the right thing here, do you think, Lord Breeze?" Sazed found himself asking.

Breeze snorted. "Right and wrong don't come into it. If *we* hadn't come to bully King Lekal, someone else would have. It comes down to basic strategic necessity. Or that's how I see it—perhaps I'm merely more calculating than others."

Sazed eyed the stocky man. Breeze was a Soother—in fact, he was the most brazen, flagrant Soother Sazed had ever known. Most Soothers used their powers with discrimination and subtlety, nudging emotions at precisely the most opportune times. But Breeze played with *everyone's* emotions. Sazed could feel the man's touch on his own feelings now, in fact—though only because he knew what to look out for.

"If you will excuse the observation, Lord Breeze," Sazed said, "you do not fool me as easily as you believe you do."

Breeze raised an eyebrow.

"I know you are a good man," Sazed said. "You work hard to hide it. You make a great show of being callous and selfish. Yet to those watching what you do and not solely what you say, you become far more transparent."

Breeze frowned, and Sazed got a little stab of pleasure at surprising the Soother. He clearly hadn't expected Sazed to be so blunt.

"My dear man," Breeze said, sipping his wine, "I'm disappointed in you. Weren't you just speaking about being polite? Well, it's not *at all* polite to point out a crusty old pessimist's dark inner secret."

"Dark inner secret?" Sazed asked. "That you're kind-hearted?"

"It's an attribute in myself that I've worked quite hard to discourage," Breeze said lightly. "Unfortunately, I prove too weak. Now, to completely divert us from this subject— which I find *far* too discomforting—I shall return to your earlier question. You ask if we are doing the right thing? By forcing King Lekal to become a vassal to Elend?"

Sazed nodded.

"Well then," Breeze said, "I'd have to say that yes, we did the right thing. Our treaty will give Lekal the protection of Elend's armies."

"At the cost of his own freedom to govern."

"Bah," Breeze said, waving a hand. "We both know that Elend is a far better ruler than Lekal could ever hope to be. Most of his people are living in half-finished shacks, for the Lord Ruler's sake!"

"Yes, but you must admit that we bullied him."

"That's how all politics is. Sazed, this man's nephew sent an army of koloss to destroy Luthadel! He's lucky Elend didn't simply come down and wipe out the entire city in retribution. We have bigger armies, more resources, and better Allomancers. This people will be far better off once Lekal signs that treaty. What is wrong with you, my dear man? You argued all these same points not two days ago at the negotiating table."

"I apologize, Lord Breeze," Sazed said. "I . . . find myself feeling contrary of late."

Breeze didn't respond at first. "It still hurts, does it?" he asked.

That man is far too good at understanding the emotions of others, Sazed thought. "Yes," he whispered.

"It will stop," Breeze said. "Eventually."

Will it? Sazed thought, looking away. It had been a year. It still felt . . . as if nothing would ever be right again. Sometimes he wondered if his immersion in the religions was merely a way of hiding from his pain.

If that was so, then he'd chosen a poor way to cope, for the pain was always there waiting for him. He had failed. No, his *faith* had failed *him*. Nothing was left to him.

It was all just . . . gone.

"Look," Breeze said, drawing his attention, "sitting here and waiting for Lekal to make up his mind is plainly making us anxious. Why don't we talk about something else? How about telling me about one of those religions you have memorized. You haven't tried to convert me in months!"

"I stopped wearing my copperminds nearly a year ago, Breeze."

"But surely you remember a bit," Breeze said. "Why don't you try to convert me? You know, for old times' sake and all that."

"I don't think so, Breeze."

It felt like a betrayal of his legacy. As a Keeper—a Terris Feruchemist—he could store memories within pieces of copper for later withdrawal. During the time of the Final Empire, Sazed's kind had suffered much to gather their vast stores of information—and not only about religions. They had gathered every shred of information they could find about the time before the Lord Ruler. They'd memorized it, passed it on to others, depending on their Feruchemy to maintain accuracy.

Yet they'd never found the one thing they sought most urgently, the thing that had begun their quest: the religion of the Terris people themselves. It had been erased by the Lord Ruler during the first century of his reign.

Still, many had toiled, bled, and died so that Sazed could have the vast storages he'd inherited. And he had taken them off. After retrieving his notes about each religion, writing them down on the pages he now carried in his portfolio, he'd removed each and every one of his metalminds and stored them away.

They simply . . . didn't seem to matter anymore. At times nothing did. He tried not to dwell too much on that. But the thought lurked in his mind, terrible and impossible to banish. He felt tainted, unworthy. As far as Sazed knew, he was the last living Feruchemist. They didn't have the resources to search for any right now, but in a year's time no Keeper refugees had made their way to Elend's domain. Sazed was it. And like all Terris stewards, he'd been castrated as a child. The hereditary power of Feruchemy might well die with him. There would be a small trace of it left in the Terris people, but given the Lord Ruler's efforts to breed it away and the deaths of the Synod, things did not look good.

The metalminds remained packed, carried along wherever he went, but never used. He doubted he would ever draw upon them again.

"Well?" Breeze asked, rising and walking over to lean on the window beside Sazed. "Aren't you going to tell me about a religion? Which is it going to be? That religion where people made maps, maybe? The one that worshipped plants? Surely you've got one in there that worships wine. That might fit me."

"Please, Lord Breeze," Sazed said, gazing out over the city. Ash was falling. It always did these days. "I do not wish to speak of these things."

"What?" Breeze asked. "How can that be?"

"If there were a God, Breeze," Sazed said, "do you think he'd have let so many people be killed by the Lord Ruler? Do you think he'd have let the world become what it is now? I will not teach you—or anyone—a religion that cannot answer my questions. Never again."

Breeze fell silent.

Sazed reached down, touching his stomach. Breeze's comments pained him. They brought his mind back to that terrible time a year before, when Tindwyl had been killed. When Sazed had fought Marsh at the Well of Ascension, and had nearly been killed. Through his clothing, he could feel the scars on his abdomen where Marsh had hit him with a collection of metal rings, piercing Sazed's skin and nearly killing him.

He'd drawn upon the Feruchemical power of those very rings to save his life, healing his body, engulfing them within him. Not long after recharging them and storing up enough health, however, he'd asked a surgeon to remove the rings from his body. Despite Vin's protests that having them within him would be an advantage, Sazed was worried that it was unhealthy to keep them embedded in his own flesh. Besides, he had just wanted them gone.

Breeze turned to look out the window. "You were always the best of us, Sazed," he said quietly. "Because you believed in something."

"I am sorry, Lord Breeze," Sazed said. "I do not mean to disappoint you."

"Oh, you don't disappoint me," Breeze said. "Because I don't believe what you've said. You're not meant to be an atheist, Sazed. I have a feeling you'll be no good at it—it doesn't suit you at all. You'll come around eventually."

Sazed held his peace. He was considered brash for a Terrisman, but he did not wish to argue further.

"I never did thank you," Breeze said.

"For what, Lord Breeze?"

"For pulling me out of myself," Breeze said. "For forcing me to get up, a year ago, and keep going. If you hadn't helped me, I don't know that I would ever have gotten over . . . what happened."

Sazed nodded. On the inside, his thoughts were more bitter. *Yes, you saw destruction and death, my friend. But the woman you* love *is still alive. I could have come back too, if I hadn't lost her. I could have recovered as you did.*

The door opened.

Sazed and Breeze both turned. A solitary aide entered, bearing an ornate sheet of parchment. King Lekal had signed the treaty at the bottom. His signature was small, almost cramped, in the large space allotted. He knew he was beaten.

The aide set the treaty on the table, then withdrew.

Each time Rashek tried to fix things, he made them worse. He had to change the world's plants to make them able to survive in the newly harsh environment. Yet that change left the plants less nutritious to humankind. Indeed, the falling ash would make men sick, causing them to cough like those who spent too long mining beneath the earth. So Rashek changed humankind as well, altering them so that they could survive.

5

ELEND KNELT BESIDE THE FALLEN Inquisitor, trying to ignore the mess that was left of the thing's head. Vin approached, and he noted the wound on her forearm. As usual, she all but ignored the injury.

The koloss army stood quietly on the battlefield around

them. Elend still wasn't comfortable with the idea of controlling the creatures. He felt . . . tainted by mere association with them. Yet it was the only way.

"Something's wrong, Elend," Vin said.

He looked up from the body. "What? You think there might be another one around?"

She shook her head. "Not that. That Inquisitor moved too quickly at the end. I've never seen a person—Allomancer or not—with that kind of speed."

"He must have had duralumin," Elend said, looking down. For a time he and Vin had held an edge, since they'd had access to an Allomantic metal the Inquisitors hadn't known about. The evidence now indicated that edge was gone.

Fortunately, they still had electrum. Poor man's atium. The Lord Ruler was to be thanked for that, in fact. Normally, an Allomancer burning atium—which allowed an Allomancer to see slightly into the future—was virtually invincible; only another Allomancer burning the metal could fight them. Unless one had electrum. It didn't convey the same invincibility, but the immunity to atium that it granted was invaluable.

"Elend," Vin said, kneeling, "it wasn't duralumin. The Inquisitor was moving too quickly even for that."

Elend had seen the Inquisitor move out of the corner of his eye, but surely it hadn't been *that* fast. Vin had a tendency to be paranoid and assume the worst.

Of course, she also had a habit of being right.

She reached out and grabbed the front of the corpse's robe, ripping it free. Elend turned away. "Vin! Have respect for the dead!"

"I have no respect for these things," she said, "nor will I ever. Did you see how that thing tried to use one of its spikes to kill you?"

"That *was* odd. Perhaps he felt he couldn't get to the axes in time."

"Here, look."

Elend glanced back. The Inquisitor had most of the

standard spikes—three pounded between the ribs on the right side of the chest and four on the left; there was no sign of an atium spike, so perhaps this Inquisitor had originally been a Mistborn. But . . . there was one more spike—one Elend hadn't seen in any other Inquisitor corpse—pounded directly through the front of this creature's chest.

Lord Ruler! Elend thought. *That must have gone right through its heart. How did it survive?* Of course, if two spikes through the brain didn't kill it, then one through the heart probably wouldn't either.

Vin reached down and yanked the spike free. Elend winced. She held it up, frowning. "Pewter," she said.

"Really?" Elend asked.

She nodded. "That makes eleven spikes. Two through the eyes and one through the shoulders: all steel. Seven through the ribs: two steel, four bronze, one gold. Now this, a pewter one—not to mention the one he tried to use on you, which appears to be steel."

Elend studied the spike in her hand. In Allomancy and Feruchemy, different metals did different things—he could only guess that for Inquisitors, the type of metal used in the spikes was important as well. "Perhaps they don't use Allomancy at all, but some . . . third power."

"Maybe," Vin said, gripping the spike and standing up. "We'll need to cut open the stomach and see if it had atium."

"Maybe this one will finally have some." They always burned electrum as a precaution, but so far none of the Inquisitors they'd met had possessed any atium.

Vin shook her head, staring out over the ash-covered battlefield. "We're missing something, Elend. We're like children playing a game we've watched our parents play, but not really knowing any of the rules. And . . . our opponent created the game in the first place."

Elend stepped around the corpse, moving over to her. "Vin, we don't know if it's out there. The thing we saw a year ago at the Well . . . perhaps it's gone. Perhaps it left, now that it's free. That could be all it wanted."

Vin looked at him. He could read in her eyes that she didn't believe that. Perhaps she saw that he didn't really believe it either.

"It's out there, Elend," she whispered. "It's directing the Inquisitors; it knows what we're doing. That's why the koloss always move against the same cities we do. It has power over the world—it can change text that has been written, create miscommunications and confusion. It knows our plans."

Elend put a hand on her shoulder. "But today we beat it—and it sent us this handy koloss army."

"And how many humans did we lose trying to capture this force?"

Elend didn't need to speak the answer. *Too many.* Their numbers were dwindling. The mists—the Deepness—were growing more powerful, choking the life from random people, killing the crops of the rest. The outer dominances were wastelands; only the lands closest to the capital, Luthadel, still got enough daylight to grow food. And that area of livability was shrinking.

Hope, Elend thought forcefully. *She needs that from me; she's always needed that from me.* He tightened his grip on her shoulder, then pulled her into an embrace. "We'll beat it, Vin. We'll find a way."

She didn't contradict him, but she clearly wasn't convinced. Still, she let him hold her, closing her eyes and resting her head against his chest. They stood on the battlefield before their fallen foe, but Elend had to admit it didn't feel like much of a victory. Not with the world collapsing around them.

Hope! he thought again. *I belong to the Church of the Survivor. It has only one prime commandment.*

Survive.

"Give me one of the koloss," Vin finally said, pulling out of the embrace.

Elend released a medium-large creature, letting Vin take control of it. He still didn't quite understand how they controlled the creatures. Once he had command of a koloss, he could direct it indefinitely—whether sleeping or awake, burning metals or not. There were many things he didn't understand about Allomancy. He'd had only a year to use his powers, and he had been distracted by ruling an empire and trying to feed his people, not to mention the wars. He'd had little time for practice.

Of course, Vin had less time than that to practice before she killed the Lord Ruler. But she was a special case. She used Allomancy as easily as other people breathed; it was less a skill to her than an extension of who she was. Elend might have more raw power—as she always insisted—but she was the true master.

Vin's lone koloss wandered over and picked up the fallen Inquisitor and the spike. Then Elend and Vin walked down the hill—Vin's koloss servant following—toward the human army. The koloss troops split to make a passage at Elend's command. He suppressed a shiver as he controlled them.

Fatren, the dirty man who ruled the city, had thought to set up a triage unit—though Elend wasn't very confident in the abilities of a group of skaa surgeons.

"Why'd they stop?" Fatren asked, standing in front of his men as Vin and Elend approached across the ash-stained ground.

"I promised you a second army, Lord Fatren," Elend said. "Well, here it is."

"The koloss?" he asked.

Elend nodded.

"But they're the army that came to destroy us."

"And now they're ours," Elend said. "Your men did very well. Make certain they understand that this victory was theirs. We had to force that Inquisitor out into the open, and the only way to do that was to turn his army against itself. Koloss become afraid when they see something small defeating something large. Your men fought bravely; because of them, these koloss are ours."

Fatren scratched his chin. "So," he said slowly, "they got afraid of us, so they switched sides?"

"Something like that," Elend said, looking over the soldiers. He mentally commanded some koloss to step forward. "These creatures will obey orders from the men in this group. Have them carry your wounded to the city. And make certain not to let your men attack or punish the koloss. They are our servants now, understand?"

Fatren nodded.

"Let's go," Vin said, eagerness sounding in her voice as she looked over at the small city.

"Lord Fatren, do you want to come with us, or do you want to supervise your men?" Elend asked.

Fatren's eyes narrowed. "What are you going to do?"

"There is something in your city we need to claim."

Fatren hesitated only briefly. "I'll come, then." He gave some orders to his men while Vin waited impatiently. Elend gave her a smile, then finally Fatren joined them, and the three walked toward the Vetitan gate.

"Lord Fatren," Elend said as they walked, "you should address me as 'my lord' from now on."

Fatren looked up from his nervous study of the koloss standing around them.

"Do you understand?" Elend said, meeting the man's eyes.

"Um . . . yes. My lord."

Elend nodded, and Fatren fell a little behind him and Vin, as if showing deference. He didn't seem rebellious—for now, he was probably happy to be alive. He might eventually resent Elend for taking command of his city, but by then there would be little he could do. Fatren's people would be accustomed to the security of being part of a larger empire, and the stories of Elend's mysterious command of the koloss—and therefore salvation of the city—would be too strong. Fatren would never rule again.

So easily I command, Elend thought. *Less than two years ago, I made more mistakes than this man. At least he managed to keep his city's people together in a time of crisis. I lost my throne, until Vin reclaimed it on my behalf.*

"I worry about you," Vin said. "Did you have to start the battle without me?"

Elend glanced over. There was no reproach in her voice. Only concern.

"I wasn't sure when—or *if*—you'd arrive," he said. "The opportunity was too good. The koloss had just marched an entire day. We probably killed five hundred before they decided to start attacking."

"And the Inquisitor?" Vin asked. "Did you really think you could take him on your own?"

"Did you?" Elend asked. "You fought him for a good five minutes before I was able to get there and help."

Vin didn't use the obvious argument—that she was by far the more accomplished Mistborn. Instead she walked silently. She still worried about him, though she no longer tried to protect him from all danger. Both her worry and her willingness to let him take risks were part of her love for him. And he sincerely appreciated both.

The two of them tried to stay together as much as possible, but that wasn't always feasible—such as when Elend had discovered a koloss army marching on an indefensible city while Vin was away delivering orders to Penrod in Luthadel. Elend had hoped she would return to his army camp in time to find out where he had gone, then come help, but he hadn't been able to wait. Not with thousands of lives at stake.

Thousands of lives . . . and more.

They eventually reached the gates. A crowd of soldiers who had either arrived late to the battle or been too afraid to charge stood atop the bulwark, looking down with awe. Several thousand koloss had gotten past Elend's men and tried to attack the city. These now stood motionless—by his unspoken command—waiting outside the bulwark.

The soldiers opened the gates, letting in Vin, Elend, Fatren, and Vin's single koloss servant. Most of them eyed Vin's koloss with distrust—as well they should. She ordered it to put down the dead Inquisitor, then made it follow as the three of them walked down the ash-piled city street. Vin had a philosophy: the more people who saw koloss and grew accustomed to the creatures, the better. It made the people less frightened of the beasts, and made it easier for them to fight should they have to face koloss in battle.

They soon approached the Ministry building that Elend had inspected upon first entering the city. Vin's koloss walked forward and began to rip the boards off its doors.

"The Ministry building?" Fatren said. "We already searched it. What good is it?"

Elend eyed him.

"My lord," Fatren said belatedly.

"It has to do with the Steel Ministry's direct link to the Lord Ruler," Elend said.

The koloss yanked the door open. Moving inside, Elend burned tin, enhancing his eyesight so he could see in the dim light. Vin, clearly doing the same, had little trouble picking her way across the broken boards and furniture littering the floor. Apparently Fatren's people hadn't only searched the place—they'd ransacked it.

"But none of the ministry's obligators are in the city anymore, my lord," Fatren said. "They all left with the nobility."

"The obligators saw to some very important projects, Fatren," Elend said. "Things like trying to discover how to use new Allomantic metals, or searching for lines of Terris blood that were breeding true. One of their projects is of particular interest to us."

"Here," Vin said, calling out from beside something set in the floor. A hidden trapdoor.

Fatren glanced back toward the sunlight, perhaps wishing that he'd decided to bring a few soldiers with him. By the trapdoor, Vin lit a lantern she'd salvaged from somewhere. In the blackness of a basement, tin wouldn't provide sight. Vin opened the trapdoor, and they made their way down the ladder. It eventually ended in a wine cellar.

Elend walked to the center of the small, untouched cellar, surveying it as Vin began to check the walls. "I found it," she said a second later, rapping her fist on a certain portion of the stone block wall. Elend walked forward, joining her. Sure enough, there was a thin slit in the stones, barely visible. Burning steel, Elend could see two faint blue lines pointing to metal plates hidden behind the stone. Two stronger lines pointed behind him, toward a large metal plate set into the wall, affixed securely with enormous bolts bored into the stone.

"Ready?" Vin asked.

Elend nodded, flaring his iron. They both Pulled on the plate buried in the stone wall, steadying themselves by also Pulling against the plate behind them.

Not for the first time, the foresight of the Ministry impressed Elend. How could they have known that someday, a group of skaa would take control of this city? Yet this door had not only been hidden—it had been crafted so that it required someone with Allomancy to open it. Elend continued to Pull in both directions at once, feeling as if his body were being stretched between two horses. Fortunately he had the power of pewter to strengthen his body and keep it from ripping apart. Vin grunted in effort beside him, and soon a section of the wall began to slide toward them. No amount of prying would have been able to wedge the thick stone open, and only a lengthy, arduous effort would have been enough to break through. Yet with Allomancy, they opened the door in a matter of seconds.

Finally they let go. Vin exhaled in exhaustion, and Elend could tell that it had been more difficult for her than it was for him. Often he didn't feel justified in having more power than she—after all, he'd been an Allomancer for far less time.

Vin picked up her lantern, and they moved into the now-open room. Like the other two Elend had seen, this cavern was enormous. It extended into the distance, their lantern's light making no more than a faint dent in the blackness. Fatren gasped in wonder as he joined them in the doorway. The room was filled with shelves. Hundreds of them. Thousands.

"What is it?" Fatren asked.

"Food," Elend said. "And basic supplies. Medicines, cloth, water."

"So much," Fatren said. "Here all along . . ."

"Go get more men," Elend said. "Soldiers. We'll need them to guard the entrance, to keep people from breaking in and stealing anything."

Fatren's face hardened. "This place belongs to my people."

"*My* people, Fatren," Elend said, watching Vin walk farther into the room, bearing the light with her. "This city is mine now, as are its contents."

"You came to rob us," Fatren accused. "Just like the bandits who tried to take the city last year."

"No," Elend said, turning toward the soot-stained man. "I came to conquer you. There's a difference."

"I don't see one."

Elend gritted his teeth to keep himself from snapping at the man. The fatigue, the draining effect of leading an empire that seemed doomed, put him on edge so often lately. *No,* he told himself. *Men like Fatren need more than another tyrant. They need someone to look up to.*

Elend approached the man, and intentionally didn't use emotional Allomancy on him. Soothing was effective in many situations, but it wore off quickly. It couldn't be used to make permanent allies.

"Lord Fatren," Elend said. "I want you to think carefully about what you're arguing for. What would happen if I *did* leave you? With this much food, this much wealth down here? Can you trust your people not to break in, your soldiers not to try selling some of this to other cities? What happens when the secret of your food supply gets out? Will you welcome the thousands of refugees who will come? Will you protect them, and this cavern, against the raiders and bandits who will follow?"

Fatren fell silent. Elend laid a hand on the man's shoulder. "I meant what I said outside, Lord Fatren. Your people fought well—I was very impressed. They owe their survival today to you—your foresight, your training. Mere hours ago, they assumed they would be slaughtered by koloss. Now they are not only safe, but under the protection of a much larger army.

"Don't fight this. You've struggled well, but it is time to have allies. I won't lie to you—I'm going to take the contents of this cavern, whether you resist me or not. But I will also give you the protection of my armies, the stability of my food supplies, and my word of honor that you can continue to rule your people under me. We need to work together, Lord Fatren. That's the sole way any of us are going to survive the next few years."

Fatren looked up. "You're right, of course," he said, "no matter how much I wish I could deny it. I'll go get those men you asked for, my lord."

"Thank you," Elend said. "And if you have anyone who can write, send them to me. We'll need to catalogue what we have down here."

Fatren nodded, then left.

"Once, you couldn't do things like that," Vin said from a short distance away, her voice echoing in the large cavern.

"Like what?"

"Give a man such forceful commands," she said. "Take control away from him. You'd have wanted to let these people vote on whether or not they should join your empire."

Elend looked back at the doorway. He stood silently for a moment. He hadn't used emotional Allomancy, yet he felt as if he'd bullied Fatren anyway. "Sometimes I feel like a failure, Vin. There should be another way."

"Not right now, there isn't," Vin said, walking up to him, putting a hand on his arm. "They need you, Elend. You know that they do."

He nodded. "I know it. I simply can't help but think that a better man would have found a way to make the will of the people work along with his rule."

"You did," she said. "Your parliamentary assembly still rules in Luthadel, and the kingdoms you reign over maintain basic rights and privileges for the skaa."

"Compromises," Elend said. "They get to do what they want only as long as I don't disagree with them."

"It's enough. You have to be realistic, Elend."

"When my friends and I met together, I was the one who spoke of the perfect dreams, of the great things we'd accomplish. I was always the idealist."

"Emperors don't have that luxury," Vin said quietly.

Elend looked at her, then sighed, turning away.

Vin stood, watching Elend in the cold lantern light of the cavern. She hated seeing such regret, such . . . disillusionment in him. In a way, his current problems seemed worse than the self-doubt he had once struggled with. He seemed to see himself as a failure despite what he had accomplished.

But he didn't let himself wallow in that failure. He moved on, working despite his regret. He was a harder man than he once had been. That wasn't necessarily a bad thing. The old Elend had been a man who was easily dismissed by many—a genius who had wonderful ideas, but little ability to lead. But she missed some of what was gone. The simple idealism. Elend was still an optimist, and he was still a scholar, but both attributes seemed tempered by what he had been forced to endure.

She watched him move along one of the storage shelves, trailing a finger in the dust. He brought the finger up, looking at it for a moment, then snapped it, throwing a small burst of dust into the air. The beard made him seem more rugged—like the wartime commander he had become. A year of solid training with Allomancy and the sword had strengthened his body, and he'd needed to get his uniforms retailored to fit properly. The one he wore now was still stained from battle.

"This place is amazing, isn't it?" Elend asked.

Vin turned, glancing into the darkness of the storage cavern. "I suppose."

"He knew, Vin," Elend said. "The Lord Ruler. He suspected that this day would come, when the mists returned and food would be scarce. So he prepared these supply depots."

Vin joined Elend by a shelf. She knew from previous caverns that the food would still be good, much of it processed in one of the Lord Ruler's canneries, and would remain so for years in storage. The amount in this cavern could feed the town above for years. Unfortunately, Vin and Elend had more to worry about than a single town.

"Imagine the effort this must have taken," Elend said, turning over a can of stewed beef in his hand. "He would have had to rotate this food every few years, constantly packing and storing new supplies. And he did it for decades, without anyone knowing what he was doing."

Vin shrugged. "It's not so hard to keep secrets when you're a god-emperor with a fanatical priesthood."

"Yes, but the effort . . . the sheer scope of it all . . . You know what this means?"

"What?"

"The Lord Ruler thought it could be beaten. The Deepness, the thing that we released. The Lord Ruler thought he could eventually win."

Vin snorted. "It doesn't have to mean that, Elend."

"Then why go through all of this? He must have thought that fighting wasn't hopeless."

"People struggle, Elend. Even a dying beast will keep fighting, will do anything to stay alive."

"You have to admit that these caverns are a good sign though," Elend said.

"A good sign?" Vin asked quietly, stepping closer. "Elend, I know you're trying to find hope in all this, but I have trouble seeing good signs anywhere lately. You have to admit now that the sun is getting darker. Redder. And it's worse down here in the South."

"I doubt the sun has changed at all," Elend said. "It must be all the smoke and ash in the air."

"Which is another problem," Vin said. "The ash falls

almost perpetually now. People are having trouble keeping it out of their streets. It blots out the light, making everything darker. Even if the mists *don't* kill off this year's crops, the ash will. Last winter—when we fought the koloss at Luthadel—was the first I'd seen snow in the Central Dominance, and this winter was worse. These aren't things we can fight, Elend, no matter how big our army!"

"What do you expect me to do, Vin?" Elend asked, slamming his can of stew down on the shelf. "The koloss are gathering in the Outer Dominances. If we don't build our defenses, our people won't *last* long enough to starve."

Vin shook her head. "Armies are short-term. This," she said, sweeping her hand across the cavern. "*This* is short-term. What are we doing here?"

"We're surviving. Kelsier said—"

"Kelsier is *dead,* Elend!" Vin snapped. "Am I the only one who sees the irony in that? We call him the Survivor, but he's the one who didn't survive! He *let* himself become a martyr. He committed suicide. How is that surviving?"

She stood for a moment, looking at Elend, breathing deeply. He stared back, apparently undaunted by her outburst.

What am I doing? Vin thought. *I was just thinking about how much I admired Elend's hope. Why argue with him now?*

They were stretched so thin. Both of them.

"I don't have answers for you, Vin," Elend said in the dark cavern. "I can't begin to understand how to fight something like the mist. Armies, however, I can deal with. Or at least I'm learning how."

"I'm sorry," Vin said, turning away. "I didn't mean to argue. But it's so frustrating."

"We're making progress," Elend said. "We'll find a way, Vin. We'll survive."

"Do you really think we can do it?" Vin asked, turning to look him in the eyes.

"Yes," Elend said.

And she believed him. He had hope, and always would. That was a big part of why she loved him so much.

"Come on," Elend said, laying a hand on her shoulder. "Let's find what we came for."

Vin joined him, leaving her koloss behind, walking into the depths of the cavern as they heard footsteps outside. There was more than one reason they had come to this place. The food and the supplies—of which they passed seemingly endless shelves—were important. However, there was more.

A large metal plaque was set into the back wall of the rough-hewn cavern. Vin read the words inscribed on it out loud.

" 'This is the last metal I will tell you about,' " she read. " 'I have trouble deciding the purpose of it. It allows you to see the past, in a way. What a person could have been, and who they might have become, had they made different choices. Much like gold, but for others.

" 'By now, the mists have likely come again. Such a foul, hateful thing. Scorn it. Don't go out in it. It seeks to destroy us all. If there is trouble, know that you can control the koloss and the kandra by use of several people Pushing on their emotions at once. I built this weakness into them. Keep the secret wisely.' "

Beneath that was listed an Allomantic compound of metals, one with which Vin was already familiar. It was the alloy of atium they called malatium—Kelsier's Eleventh Metal. So the Lord Ruler *had* known about it. He'd simply been as baffled as the rest of them as to its purpose.

The plaque had been inscribed by the Lord Ruler. Or at least he'd ordered it inscribed. Each previous cache had also contained information written in steel. In Urteau, for instance, she had learned about electrum. In the one to the east, they'd found a description of aluminum—though they'd already known about that metal.

"Not much new there," Elend said, sounding disappointed. "We already knew about malatium and about controlling koloss. Though I'd never thought to have several Soothers Push at the same time. That might be helpful."

"It doesn't matter," Vin said, pointing at the other half of the plaque. "We have *that*."

The other half contained a map, carved into the steel like the ones they had found in the other three storage caverns. It depicted the Final Empire, divided into dominances. Luthadel was a square at the center. An X to the west marked the main thing they'd come looking for: the location of the final cavern.

There were five, they thought. They'd found the first one beneath Luthadel, near the Well of Ascension. It had given the location of the second, to the east. The third had been in Urteau—Vin had been able to sneak into that one, but they hadn't managed to recover the food yet. That one had led them here, to the south.

Each map had two numbers on it—a five and a lower number. Luthadel had been number one. This one was number four.

"That's it," Vin said, running her fingers along the carved inscriptions on the plaque. "In the Western Dominance, as you guessed. Somewhere near Chardees?"

"Fadrex City," Elend said.

"Cett's home?"

Elend nodded. He knew far more about geography than she.

"That's the place then," Vin said. "The one where *it* is."

Elend met her eyes, and she knew he understood her. The caches had grown progressively larger and more valuable. Each one had a specialized aspect to it as well—the first had contained weapons in addition to its other supplies, while the second had contained large amounts of lumber. As they'd investigated each successive cache, they'd grown more and more excited about what the last one might contain. Something spectacular, surely. Perhaps even *it*.

The Lord Ruler's atium cache.

It was the most valuable treasure in the Final Empire.

Despite years of searching, nobody had ever located it. Some said it didn't exist. But Vin felt that it had to. Despite a thousand years of controlling the sole mine that produced the extremely rare metal, he had allowed only a small portion of atium to enter the economy. Nobody knew what the Lord Ruler had done with the greater portion he had kept to himself for all those centuries.

"Now, don't get too excited," Elend said. "We have no proof that we'll find the atium in that final cavern."

"It has to be there," Vin said. "It makes sense. Where else would the Lord Ruler store his atium?"

"If I could answer that, we'd have found it."

Vin shook her head. "He put it somewhere safe, but where it would eventually be found. He left these maps as clues to his followers, should he somehow be defeated. He didn't want an enemy who captured one of the caverns to be able to find them all instantly."

A trail of clues that led to one last cache. The most important one. It made sense. It *had* to. Elend didn't look convinced. He rubbed his bearded chin, studying the reflective plaque in their lantern light. "Even if we find it," he said, "I don't know that it will help much. What good is money to us now?"

"It's more than money," she said. "It's power. A weapon we can use to fight." She'd burned up their last bit of atium a year ago, and she'd never gotten used to how exposed she felt without it. Electrum softened that fear somewhat, but not completely.

"Fight the mists?" he asked.

Vin hesitated. "Perhaps not," she finally said. "But the koloss, and the other armies. With that atium, your empire becomes secure. Plus, atium is part of all this, Elend. It's valuable because of Allomancy—but Allomancy didn't exist until the Ascension."

"Another unanswered question," Elend said. "Why did that nugget of metal I swallowed make me Mistborn? Where did it come from? Why was it placed at the Well of

Ascension, and by whom? Why was there only one left, and what happened to the others?"

"Maybe we'll find the answer once we take Fadrex," Vin said.

Elend nodded. She could tell he considered the information contained in the caches the most important reason to track them down, followed closely by the supplies. To him, the possibility of finding the atium was relatively unimportant. Vin couldn't explain why she felt he was so wrong in this regard. The atium *was* important. She just knew it. Her earlier despair lightened as she looked over the map. They had to go to Fadrex.

The answers would be there.

"Taking Fadrex won't be easy," Elend noted. "Cett's enemies have entrenched themselves solidly there. I hear a former Ministry obligator is in charge."

"The atium will be worth it," Vin said.

"If it's there," Elend said.

She gave him a flat stare.

He held up a hand. "I'm merely trying to do what you told me, Vin—I'm trying to be realistic. However, I agree that Fadrex will be worth the effort. Even if the atium isn't there, we need the supplies in that store. We need to know what the Lord Ruler left us."

Voices sounded from the other end of the cavern, and Elend turned. "I should go speak to them," he said. "We're going to have to organize things in here quickly."

"Have you told them yet that we'll have to move them to Luthadel?"

Elend shook his head. "They won't like it," he said. "They're becoming independent, as I always hoped they would."

"It has to be done, Elend," Vin said. "This city is well outside our defensive perimeter. Plus they can't have more than a few hours of mistless daylight left this far out. Their crops are already doomed."

Elend nodded, but he continued to stare out into the

darkness. "I come, I seize control of their city, take their treasure, then force them to abandon their homes. And from here we go to Fadrex to conquer once more."

"Elend—"

He held up a hand. "I know, Vin. It must be done." He turned, leaving the lantern and walking toward the doorway. As he did, his posture straightened, and his face became more firm.

Vin turned back to the plaque, rereading the Lord Ruler's words. On a different plaque, much like this one, Sazed had found the words of Kwaan, the long-dead Terrisman who had changed the world by claiming to have found the Hero of Ages. Kwaan had left his words as a confession of his errors, warning that some kind of force was working to change the histories and religions of humankind. He'd worried that the force was suborning the Terris religion in order to cause a "hero" to come to the North and release it.

That was exactly what Vin had done. She'd called herself hero, and had released the enemy—all the while thinking that she was sacrificing her own needs for the good of the world.

She ran her fingers across the large plaque.

We have to do more than fight wars! she thought, angry at the Lord Ruler. *If you knew so much, why didn't you leave us more than this? A few maps in scattered halls filled with supplies? A couple of paragraphs telling us about metals that are of barely any use? What good is a cave full of food when we have an entire empire to feed!*

Vin stopped. Her fingers—made far more sensitive by the tin she was burning to help her eyesight in the dark cavern—brushed against grooves in the plaque's surface. She knelt, leaning close, to find a short inscription carved at the bottom, the letters much smaller than the ones above.

Be careful what you speak. It can hear what you say. It can read what you write. Only your thoughts are safe.

Vin shivered.

Only your thoughts are safe.

What had the Lord Ruler learned in his moments of transcendence? What things had he kept in his mind forever, never writing them down for fear of revealing his knowledge, always expecting that he would eventually be the one who took the power when it came again? Had he perhaps planned to use that power to destroy the thing that Vin had released?

You have doomed yourselves. . . . The Lord Ruler's last words, spoken right before Vin had thrust the spear through his heart. He'd known. Even then—before the mists had started coming during the day, before she'd begun hearing the strange thumpings that led her to the Well of Ascension—even then she'd worried.

Be careful what you speak . . . only your thoughts are safe.

I have to figure this out, she thought. *I have to connect what we have, find the way to defeat—or outwit—this thing that I've loosed.*

And I can't talk this over with anyone, or it will know what I'm planning.

Rashek soon found a balance in the changes he made to the world—which was fortunate, for his power burned away quickly. Though the power he held seemed immense to him, it was in truth a tiny fraction of something much greater.

Of course, he did end up naming himself the "Sliver of Infinity" in his religion. Perhaps he understood more than I give him credit for.

In any case, we had him to thank for a world without flowers, where plants grew brown rather than green, and where people could survive in an environment where ash fell from the sky on a regular basis.

6

I'M TOO WEAK, MARSH THOUGHT.

Lucidity came upon him suddenly, as it often did when Ruin wasn't watching him closely. It was like waking from a nightmare, fully aware of what had been going on in the dream, yet confused as to the reasoning behind his actions.

He continued to walk through the koloss camp. Ruin still controlled him, as it always did. Yet when it didn't press hard enough against Marsh's mind—when it didn't focus on him—sometimes Marsh's own thoughts returned.

I can't fight it, he thought. Ruin couldn't read his thoughts, of that he was fairly confident. Yet Marsh couldn't fight or struggle in any way. When he did, Ruin immediately asserted control once more. This had been proven to Marsh a dozen times over. Sometimes he managed to quiver a finger, perhaps halt a step, but that was the best he could do.

It was depressing. But Marsh had always considered himself a practical man, and he forced himself to acknowledge the truth. He was never going to gain enough control over his body to kill himself.

Ash fell as he walked through the camp. Did it ever stop these days? He almost wished that Ruin would never let go of his mind. When his mind was his own, Marsh saw only pain and destruction. When Ruin controlled him, however, the falling ash was a thing of beauty, the red sun a marvelous triumph, the world a place of sweetness in its death.

Madness, Marsh thought, approaching the center of camp. *I need to go mad. Then I won't have to deal with all of this.*

Other Inquisitors joined him at the center of the camp, walking with quiet swishes of their robes. They didn't speak. They never spoke—Ruin controlled them all, so why bother with conversation? Marsh's brethren had the normal spikes in their heads, driven into the skull. Yet he could also see telltale signs of the new spikes jutting from their chests and backs. Marsh had placed many of them, killing the Terrismen that had either been captured in the north or tracked down across the land.

Marsh himself had a new set of spikes, some driven between his ribs, others down through his chest. They were a marvelous thing. He didn't understand why, but they excited him. The spikes had been imbued through death, and that was pleasant enough—but there was more. He somehow knew that the Inquisitors had been incomplete—the Lord Ruler had withheld some abilities to make the Inquisitors more dependent upon him. To make certain they couldn't threaten him. But now, what he'd kept back had been provided.

What a beautiful world, Marsh thought, looking up into the falling ash, feeling the light, comforting flakes upon his skin.

I speak of us as "we." The group. Those of us who were trying to discover and defeat Ruin. Perhaps my thoughts are now tainted, but I like to look back and see the sum of what we were doing as a single united assault, though we were all involved in different processes and plans.

We were one. That didn't stop the world from ending, but that's not necessarily a bad thing.

7

THEY GAVE HIM BONES.

TenSoon flowed around them, dissolving muscles, then re-forming them into organs, sinew, and skin. He built a body around the bones, using skills gained over centuries spent eating and digesting humans. Corpses only, of course; he had never killed a human. The Contract forbade such things.

After a year in his pit of a prison, he felt as if he had forgotten how to use a body. What was it like to touch the world with rigid digits, rather than flesh that flowed against the confines of stone? What was it like to taste and smell with tongue and nostrils alone, rather than with every bit of skin exposed to the air? What was it like to . . .

To see. He opened his eyes and gasped, drawing first breath into remade full-sized lungs. The world was a thing of wonder and of . . . light. He had forgotten that, during the months of near madness. He pushed himself to his knees, looking down at his arms. Then he reached up, feeling his face with a tentative hand.

His body wasn't that of any specific person—he would have needed a model to produce such a replica. Instead he had covered the bones with muscles and skin as best he could. He was old enough that he knew how to create a reasonable approximation of a human. The features wouldn't be handsome; they might be a little grotesque. But that was more than good enough for the moment. He felt . . . real again.

Still on hands and knees, he looked up at his captor. The cavern was lit by a glowstone—a large, porous rock set atop a thick column base. The bluish fungus that grew on the rock made enough of a glow to see by—especially if one had specifically grown eyes that were good at seeing in dim blue light.

TenSoon knew his captor. He knew most kandra, at least up to the Sixth and Seventh Generations. This kandra's name was VarSell. In the Homeland, VarSell didn't wear the bones of an animal or human, but instead used a True Body—a set of false bones, human-shaped, crafted by a kandra artisan. VarSell's True Body was quartz, and he left his skin translucent, allowing the stone to sparkle faintly in the fungal light as he studied TenSoon.

I made my body opaque, TenSoon realized. *Like that of a human, with tan skin to obscure the muscles beneath.* Why had that come so naturally to him? Once he had cursed the years he spent among the humans, using their bones instead of a True Body. Perhaps he had fallen to that same old default because his captors hadn't given him a True Body. Human bones. An insult of sorts.

TenSoon stood. "What?" he asked at the look in Var-Sell's eyes.

"I picked a random set of bones from the storeroom," VarSell said. "It's ironic that I would give you a set of bones you'd contributed yourself."

TenSoon frowned. *What?*

And then he made the connection. The body that TenSoon had created around the bones must look convincing—as if it were the original one that these bones had belonged to. Var-Sell assumed that TenSoon had been able to create such a realistic approximation because he'd originally digested the human's corpse, and therefore knew how to create the right body around the bones.

TenSoon smiled. "I've never worn these bones before."

VarSell eyed him. He was of the Fifth Generation—two centuries younger than TenSoon. Indeed, even among those of the Third Generation—with scant exceptions such as Paalm, constantly sent on personal missions by the Father—few kandra had as much experience with the outside world as TenSoon.

"I see," VarSell eventually said.

TenSoon turned, looking over the small chamber. Three more Fifth Generationers stood near the door, watching him. Like VarSell, few of them wore clothing—and those who did wore only open-fronted robes. Kandra tended to wear little while in the Homeland, as that allowed them to better display their True Bodies.

TenSoon saw two sparkling rods of metal embedded in the clear muscles of each Fifth's shoulders—all three had the Blessing of Potency. The Second Generation was taking no risk of his escaping. It was another insult. TenSoon had come to his fate willingly.

"Well?" TenSoon asked, turning back to VarSell. "Are we to go?"

VarSell glanced at one of his companions. "Forming the body was expected to take you longer."

TenSoon snorted. "The Second Generation is unprac-ticed. They assume that because it still takes them many hours to create a body, the rest of us require the same amount of time."

"They are your elder generation," VarSell said. "You should show them respect."

"The Second Generation has been sequestered in these caves for centuries," TenSoon said, "sending the rest of us to serve Contracts while they remain lazy. I passed them in skill long ago."

VarSell hissed, and for a moment TenSoon thought the younger kandra might slap him. VarSell restrained himself, barely, to TenSoon's amusement. After all, as a member of the Third Generation, TenSoon was senior to VarSell—much in the same way that the Seconds were supposedly senior to TenSoon.

Yet the Thirds were a special case. They always had been. That was why the Seconds kept them out on Contracts so much—it wouldn't do to have their immediate underlings around all the time, upsetting their perfect little kandra utopia.

"Let's go then," VarSell finally decided, nodding for two of his guards to lead the way. The other one joined Var-Sell, walking behind TenSoon. Like VarSell, these three had True Bodies formed of stone. Those were popular among the Fifth Generation, who had time to commission—and use—lavish True Bodies. They were the favored pups of the Seconds, and tended to spend more time than most in the Homeland.

They had given TenSoon no clothing. So, as they walked, he dissolved his genitals and re-formed a smooth crotch, as was common among the kandra. He tried to walk with pride and confidence, but he knew this body wouldn't look intimidating. It was emaciated—he'd lost much mass during his imprisonment and more to the acid, and he hadn't been able to form very large muscles.

The smooth rock tunnel had probably once been a natural formation, but over the centuries, the younger generations had been used during their infancy to even out the stone with their digestive juices. TenSoon didn't see many other kandra. VarSell kept to back corridors, obviously not wanting to make too much of a show.

I've been away so long, TenSoon thought. *The Eleventh Generation must have been chosen by now. I still don't know most of the Eighth, let alone the Ninth or Tenth.*

He was beginning to suspect that there wouldn't be a

Twelfth Generation. Even if there were, things could not continue as they had. The Father was dead. What, then, of the First Contract? His people had spent ten centuries enslaved to humankind, serving the Contracts in an effort to keep themselves safe. Most of the kandra hated humans for their situation. Up until recently, TenSoon had been one of those.

It's ironic, TenSoon thought, *but when we wear True Bodies, we wear them in the form of humans. Two arms, two legs, faces formed after the fashion of humankind.*

Sometimes he wondered if the unbirthed—the creatures that the humans called mistwraiths—were more honest than their brothers the kandra. The mistwraiths would form a body however they wished, connecting bones in odd arrangements, making almost artistic designs from both human and animal bones. The kandra, though—they created bodies that looked human. Even while they cursed humankind for keeping them enslaved.

Such a strange people they were. But they were his. Although he had betrayed them.

And now I have to convince the First Generation that I was right in that betrayal. Not for me. For them. For all of us.

They passed through corridors and chambers, eventually arriving at sections of the Homeland that were more familiar to TenSoon. He soon realized that their destination must be the Trustwarren. He would argue his defense in his people's most sacred place. He should have guessed.

A year of torturous imprisonment had earned him a trial before the First Generation. He'd had a year to think about what to say. And if he failed, he'd have an eternity to think about what he'd done wrong.

It is too easy for people to characterize Ruin as simply a force of destruction. Think rather of Ruin as intelligent decay. Not merely chaos, but a force that sought in a rational— and dangerous— way to break everything down to its most basic forms.

Ruin could plan and carefully plot, knowing if he built one thing up, he could use it to knock down two others. The nature of the world is such that when we create something, we often destroy something else in the process.

8

ON THE FIRST DAY OUT of Vetitan, Vin and Elend murdered a hundred of the townsfolk. Or at least that was how Vin felt.

She sat on a rotting stump at the center of camp, watching the sun approach the distant horizon, knowing what was about to happen. Ash fell silently around her. And the mists appeared.

Once—not so long ago—the mists had come only at night. During the year following the Lord Ruler's death, that had changed. As if a thousand years of being confined to the darkness had made the mists restless.

Now they had begun to come during the day. Sometimes they came in great rolling waves, appearing out of nowhere, disappearing as quickly. Most commonly, they appeared in the air like a thousand phantoms, twisting and growing together. Tendrils of mist that sprouted vinelike tentacles creeping across the sky. Each morning they retreated a little later, and each evening they appeared a little earlier. Soon—perhaps before the year ended—they would smother the land permanently. And this presented a problem, for ever since that night when Vin had released the power of the Well of Ascension, the mists killed people throughout the Empire.

Elend had had trouble believing Sazed's stories over a year before, when the Terrisman had come to Luthadel with horrific reports of terrified villagers and mists that killed. Vin too had assumed that Sazed was mistaken. A part of her wished she could continue in that delusion as she watched the waiting townspeople, huddled together on the broad open plain, surrounded by soldiers and koloss.

The deaths began as soon as the mists appeared. Though the mists left most of the people alone, they chose some at random, causing them to begin shaking. These fell to the ground, having a seizure, while their friends and family watched in shock and horror.

Horror was still Vin's reaction. That and frustration. Kelsier had promised her that the mists were an ally—that they would protect her and give her power. She'd believed that to be true until the mists started to feel alien to her, hiding shadowed ghosts and murderous intent.

"I hate you," she whispered as the mists continued their grisly work. It was like watching a beloved old relative pick strangers out of a crowd and, one at a time, slit their throats. And there was nothing at all she could do. Elend's scholars had tried everything—hoods to keep the mists from being breathed in, waiting to go outside until the mists had already established themselves, rushing people indoors the moment they started shaking. Animals were immune for some reason, but every human was potentially susceptible. If one went out in the mists, one risked death, and nothing could prevent it.

It was over soon. The mists gave the fits to about one in six, and only a small fraction of those died. Plus, a person needed to risk these new mists only once—one gamble, and then you were immune. Most who fell sick would recover. That was no comfort to the families of those who died.

She sat on her stump, staring out into the mists, which were still lit by the setting sun. Ironically, it was more difficult for her to see than it would have been if it were dark. She couldn't burn much tin, lest the sunlight blind her—but without it, she couldn't pierce the mists.

The result was a scene that reminded her why she had once feared the mists. Her visibility reduced to barely ten feet, she could see little more than shadows. Amorphous figures ran this way and that, calling out. Silhouettes knelt or stood terrified. Sound was a traitorous thing, echoing against unseen objects, cries coming from phantom sources.

Vin sat among them, ash raining around her like tears, and bowed her head.

"Lord Fatren!" Elend's voice called, causing Vin to look up. Once, his voice hadn't carried nearly as much authority. That seemed like so long ago. He appeared from the mists, dressed in his second white uniform—the one that was still clean—his face hardened against the deaths. She could feel his Allomantic touch on those around him as he approached—his Soothing would make the people's pain less acute, but he didn't Push as hard as he could have. She knew from talking to him that he didn't feel it was right to remove all of a person's grief at the death of one they loved.

"My lord!" she heard Fatren say, and saw him approaching. "This is a disaster!"

"It looks far worse than it is, Lord Fatren," Elend said. "As I explained, most of those who have fallen will recover."

Fatren stopped beside Vin's stump. Then he turned and stared into the mists, listening to the weeping and the pain of his people. "I can't believe we did this. I can't . . . I can't believe you talked me into making them stand in the mists."

"Your people needed to be inoculated, Fatren," Elend said.

It was true. They didn't have tents for all of the townsfolk, and that left only two options. Leave them behind in their dying town, or force them northward—make them go out in the mists and see who died. It was terrible, and it was brutal, but it would have happened eventually. Still, although she knew the logic of what they had done, Vin felt awful for being part of it.

"What kind of monsters are we?" Fatren asked in a hushed tone.

"The kind we have to be," Elend said. "Go make a count. Find out how many are dead. Calm the living and promise them that no further harm will come from the mists."

"Yes, my lord," Fatren said, moving away.

Vin watched him go. "We murdered them, Elend," she whispered. "We told them it would be all right. We forced them to leave their town and come out here to die."

"It *will* be all right," Elend said, laying a hand on her shoulder. "Better than a slow death in that town."

"We could have given them a choice."

Elend shook his head. "There was no choice. Within a few months, their city will be covered in mists permanently. They would have had to stay inside their homes and starve, or go out into the mists. Better that we take them to the Central Dominance, where there is still enough mistless daylight to grow crops."

"The truth doesn't make it any easier."

Elend stood in the mists, ash falling around him. "No," he said. "It doesn't. I'll go gather the koloss so they can bury the dead."

"And the wounded and ill?" Those the mists attacked, but didn't kill, would be sick and cramped for several days, perhaps longer. If the usual percentages held, then nearly a thousand of the townsfolk would fall into that category.

"When we leave tomorrow, we'll have the koloss carry them. If we can get to the canal, then we can probably fit most of them on the barges."

Vin didn't like feeling exposed. She'd spent her childhood hiding in corners, her adolescence playing the silent nighttime assassin. So it was incredibly difficult *not* to feel exposed while traveling with five thousand tired townsfolk along one of the Southern Dominance's most obvious routes.

She walked a short distance away from the townspeople—she never rode—and tried to find something to distract herself from thinking about the deaths the evening before. Unfortunately, Elend was riding with Fatren and the other town leaders, busy trying to smooth relations. That left her by herself.

Except for her single koloss.

The massive beast lumbered beside her. She kept it close partially out of convenience; she knew it would make the townsfolk keep their distance from her. As willing as she was to be distracted, she didn't want to deal with those betrayed, frightened eyes. Not right now.

Vin could feel her koloss tugging at her, trying to break free. It didn't like being controlled—it wanted to attack her. It could not, fortunately; she would continue to control it unless someone else managed to steal the beast from her.

Even linked as they were, there was so much Vin didn't understand about the creatures. During the thousand years of the Lord Ruler's reign, he had kept the koloss separated from humankind, letting very little be known about them beyond their brutal prowess in battle and their simple bestial nature.

She looked up, and found the koloss staring at her with its bloodred eyes. Its skin was stretched tight across its face, the nose pulled completely flat. The skin was torn near the right eye, and a jagged rip ran down to the corner of its mouth, letting a flap of blue skin hang free, exposing the red muscles and bloodied teeth below.

"Don't look at me," the creature said, speaking in a sluggish voice. Its words were slurred, partially from the way its lips were pulled.

"What?" Vin asked.

"You don't think I'm human," the koloss said. It spoke slowly and deliberately, like the others she had heard. It was as if they had to think hard between each word.

"You *aren't* human," Vin said. "You're something else."

"I will be human," the koloss said. "We will kill you. Take your cities. Then we will be human."

Vin shivered. It was a common theme among koloss. She'd heard others make similar remarks. There was something very chilling about the flat, emotionless way the koloss spoke of slaughtering people.

They were created by the Lord Ruler, she thought. *Of course they're twisted. As twisted as he was.*

"What is your name?" she asked the koloss.

It continued to lumber beside her. Finally it answered. "Human."

"I know you want to be human," Vin said. "What is your name?"

"That is my name. Human. You call me Human."

Vin frowned as they walked. *That almost seemed . . . clever.* She'd never taken the opportunity to talk to koloss before. She'd always assumed that they were of a homogeneous mentality—the same stupid beast repeated over and over.

"All right, Human," she said, curious. "How long have you been alive?"

He walked for a while, so long that Vin thought he had forgotten the question. Then he spoke. "Don't you see my bigness?"

"Your bigness? Your size?"

Human just kept walking.

"So you all grow at the same rate?"

He didn't answer. Vin shook her head, suspecting that the question was too abstract for the beast.

"I'm bigger than some," Human said. "Smaller than some—but not many. That means I'm old."

Another sign of intelligence, she thought, raising an eyebrow. From what Vin had seen of other koloss, Human's logic was impressive.

"I hate you," Human said after a short time spent walking. "I want to kill you. But I can't kill you."

"No," Vin said. "I won't let you."

"You're big inside. Very big."

"Yes," Vin said. "Human, where are the koloss women?"

The creature walked several moments. "Women?"

"Like me," Vin said.

"We're not like you," he said. "We're big on the outside only."

"No," Vin said. "Not my size. My . . ." How did one describe gender? Short of stripping, she couldn't think of any methods. So she decided to try a different tactic. "Are there baby koloss?"

"Baby?"

"Small ones," Vin said.

The koloss pointed toward the marching koloss army. "Small ones," he said, referring to some of the five-foot-tall koloss.

"Smaller," Vin said.

"None smaller."

Koloss reproduction was a mystery that, to her knowledge, nobody had ever cracked. After a year spent fighting with the beasts, she'd never found out where new ones came from. Whenever Elend's koloss armies grew too small, she and he stole new ones from the Inquisitors.

Yet it was ridiculous to assume that the koloss didn't reproduce. She'd seen koloss camps that weren't controlled by an Allomancer, and the creatures killed each other with fearful regularity. At that rate, they would have killed themselves off after a few years. Yet they had lasted for ten centuries.

That implied a rapid rise from child to adult, or so Sazed and Elend thought. They hadn't been able to confirm their theories, and she knew their ignorance frustrated Elend greatly—especially since his duties as emperor left little time for the studies he'd once enjoyed so much.

"If there are none smaller," Vin asked, "then where do new koloss come from?"

"New koloss come from us," Human finally said.

"From you?" Vin asked, frowning as she walked. "That doesn't tell me much."

Human didn't say anything further. His talkative mood had apparently passed.

From us, Vin thought. *They bud off of each other, perhaps?* She'd heard of some creatures that, if you cut them the right way, each half would grow into a new animal. But that couldn't be the case with koloss—she had seen battlefields filled with their dead, and no pieces rose to form new koloss. But she'd also never seen a female koloss. Though most of the beasts wore crude loincloths, they were—as far as she knew—all male.

Further speculation was cut off as she noticed the line ahead bunching up; the crowd was slowing. Curious, she dropped a coin and left Human behind, shooting herself over the people. The mists had retreated hours ago, and though night was once more approaching, for the moment it was both light and mistless.

Therefore, as she shot through the falling ash, she easily picked out the canal up ahead. It cut unnaturally through the ground, far straighter than any river. Elend speculated that the constant ashfall would soon put an end to most of the canal systems. Without skaa laborers to dredge them on a regular basis, they would fill up with ashen sediment, eventually clogging to uselessness.

Vin soared through the air, completing her arc, heading toward a large mass of tents stationed beside the canal. Thousands of fires spat smoke into the afternoon air, and men milled about, training, working, or preparing. Nearly fifty thousand soldiers bivouacked here, using the canal route as a supply line back to Luthadel.

Vin dropped another coin, bounding through the air again. She quickly caught up to the small group of horses that had broken off from Elend's line of tired, marching skaa. She landed—dropping a coin and Pushing against it slightly to slow her descent, tossing up a spray of ash as she hit.

Elend reined in his horse, smiling as he surveyed the camp. The expression was rare enough on his lips these days that Vin found herself smiling as well. Ahead, a group of men

waited for them—their scouts would have long since noticed the townspeople's approach.

"Lord Elend!" said a man sitting at the head of the army
contingent. "You're ahead of schedule!"

"I assume you're ready anyway, General," Elend said,
dismounting.

"Well, you know me," Demoux said, smiling as he approached. The general wore well-used armor of leather and
steel, his face bearing a scar on one cheek, the left side of
his scalp missing a large patch of hair where a koloss blade
had nearly taken his head. Ever formal, the weathered soldier bowed to Elend, who slapped him on the shoulder
affectionately.

Vin's smile lingered. *I remember when that man was little more than a fresh recruit standing frightened in a tunnel.* Demoux wasn't that much older than she was, although
his tanned face and callused hands gave that impression.

"We've held position, my lord," Demoux said as Fatren
and his brother dismounted and joined the group. "Not that
there was much to hold it against. Still, it was good for my
men to practice fortifying a camp."

Indeed, the army's camp beside the canal was surrounded by heaped earth and spikes—quite the feat, considering the army's size.

"You did well, Demoux," Elend said, turning back to
look over the townspeople. "Our mission was a success."

"I can see that, my lord," Demoux said, smiling. "That's
a fair pack of koloss you picked up. I hope the Inquisitor
leading them wasn't *too* sad to see them go."

"Couldn't have bothered him too much," Elend said.
"Since he was dead at the time. We found the storage cavern as well."

"Praise the Survivor!" Demoux said.

Vin frowned. Hanging outside his clothing, Demoux
wore a necklace that bore a small silver spear: the increasingly popular symbol of the Church of the Survivor. It
seemed odd to her that the weapon that had killed Kelsier
would become the symbol of his followers.

Of course, she didn't like to think about the other possibility—that the spear might not represent the one that had killed Kelsier. It might very well represent the one that she had used to kill the Lord Ruler. She'd never asked Demoux which it was. Despite two and a half years of growing Church power, Vin had never become comfortable with her own part in its doctrine.

"Praise the Survivor indeed," Elend said, looking over the army's supply barges. "How did your project go?"

"Dredging the southern bend?" Demoux asked. "It went well—there was blessed little else to do while we waited. You should be able to get barges through there now."

"Good," Elend said. "Form two task forces of five hundred men. Send one with barges back to Vetitan for the supplies we had to leave down in that cavern. They will transfer the supplies to the barges and send them up to Luthadel."

"Yes, my lord," Demoux said.

"Send the second group of soldiers north to Luthadel with these refugees," Elend said, nodding toward Fatren. "This is Lord Fatren. He's in command of the townspeople. Have your men respect his wishes, as long as they are reasonable, and introduce him to Lord Penrod."

Once—not long ago—Fatren would probably have complained about being handed off. However, his time with Elend had transformed him surprisingly quickly. The dirty leader nodded gratefully at the escort. "You . . . aren't coming with us then, my lord?"

Elend shook his head. "I have other work to do, and your people need to get to Luthadel, where they can begin farming. Though if any of your men wish to join my army, they are welcome. I'm always in need of good troops, and against the odds, you succeeded in training a useful force."

"My lord . . . why not just compel them? Pardon me, but that's what you've done so far."

"I compelled your people to safety, Fatren," Elend said. "Sometimes a drowning man will fight the one who tries to save him and must be compelled. My army is a different matter. Men who don't want to fight are men you can't depend on in battle, and I won't have any of those in my army. You need to go to Luthadel—your people need you—but please let your soldiers know that I will gladly accept any of them into our ranks."

"All right," Fatren said. "And . . . thank you, my lord."

"You are welcome. Now, General Demoux, have Sazed and Breeze returned yet?"

"They should arrive sometime this evening, my lord," Demoux said. "One of their men rode ahead to let us know."

"Good," Elend said. "I assume my tent is ready?"

"Yes, my lord," Demoux said.

Elend nodded, suddenly looking very tired to Vin.

"My lord?" Demoux asked eagerly. "Did you find the . . . other item? The location of the final cache?"

"Yes. It's in Fadrex."

"Cett's city?" Demoux asked, laughing. "Well, he'll be happy to hear that. He's been complaining for a year that we haven't gotten around to conquering it back for him."

Elend smiled wanly. "I've been half convinced that if we did, Cett would decide that he—and his soldiers—didn't need us anymore."

"He'll stay, my lord," Demoux said. "After the scare Lady Vin gave him last year . . . "

Demoux glanced at Vin, trying to smile, but she saw it in his eyes. Respect, far too much of it. He didn't joke with her the way he did with Elend. She still couldn't believe that Elend had joined that silly religion of theirs. Elend's intentions had been political—by joining the skaa faith, Elend had forged a link with the common people. Still, the move made her uncomfortable.

A year of marriage had taught her, however, that there were some things one simply had to ignore. She could love Elend for his desire to do the right thing, including when she thought he'd done the opposite.

"Call a meeting this evening, Demoux," Elend said. "We have much to discuss—and let me know when Sazed arrives."

"Should I inform Lord Hammond and the others of the meeting's agenda, my lord?"

Elend glanced toward the ashen sky. "Conquering the world, Demoux," he said. "Or at least what's left of it."

Allomancy was indeed born with the mists. Or at least Allomancy began at the same time as the mists' first appearances. When Rashek took the power at the Well of Ascension, he became aware of certain things. Some were whispered to him by Ruin; others were granted to him as an instinctive part of the power.

One of these was an understanding of the Three Metallic Arts. He knew, for instance, that the nuggets of metal in the Chamber of Ascension would make those who ingested them into Mistborn. These were, after all, fractions of the very power in the Well.

9

TENSOON HAD VISITED THE TRUSTWARREN before; he was of the Third Generation. He had been born seven centuries ago, when the kandra were still new—though by that time the First Generation had already given over the raising of new kandra to the Second Generation.

The Seconds hadn't done well with TenSoon's generation—or at least that was how the Seconds felt. They'd wanted to form a society of individuals who followed strict rules of respect and seniority. A "perfect" people who lived to serve their Contracts—and, of course, the members of the Second Generation.

Up until his return, TenSoon had generally been considered one of the least troublesome of the Thirds. He'd been known as a kandra who cared little for Homeland politics, one who served out his Contracts faithfully, content to keep as far away from the Seconds and their machinations as possible. No one could have predicted that TenSoon would end up on trial for the most heinous of kandra crimes.

His guards marched him into the center of the Trustwarren—right onto the platform itself. TenSoon wasn't certain whether to be honored or ashamed. Even as a member of the Third Generation, he hadn't often been allowed so near the Trust.

The room was large and circular, with metal walls. The platform was a massive steel disc set into the rock floor. It wasn't very high—perhaps a foot tall—but it was ten feet in diameter. TenSoon's feet felt chilly hitting its surface, and he was reminded once more of his nudity. They didn't bind his hands; that would have been too much of an insult even for him. Kandra obeyed the Contract. He would not run, and he would not strike down one of his own. He was better than that.

The room was lit by lamps rather than glowstone, each lamp enclosed in blue glass. Oil was difficult to get—the Second Generation, for good reason, didn't want to rely on supplies from the world of men. The people above, including most of the Father's servants, didn't know there was a centralized kandra government. It was much better that way.

In the blue light, TenSoon could easily see the members of the Second Generation—all twenty of them, standing behind their lecterns, arranged in tiers on the far side of the room. They were close enough to see and speak to—yet far enough away that TenSoon felt isolated, standing alone in the center of the platform with cold feet. He looked down, and noticed the small hole in the floor near his toes, cut into the steel disc of the platform.

The Trust, he thought. It was directly underneath him.

"TenSoon of the Third Generation," a voice said.

TenSoon looked up. It was KanPaar, of course. He was a tall kandra—or rather he preferred to use a tall True Body. Like all of the Seconds, his bones were constructed of the purest crystal—his with a deep red tint. It was an impractical body in many ways. Those bones wouldn't stand up to much punishment. Yet for the life of an administrator in the Homeland, the weakness of the bones was apparently an acceptable trade-off for their sparkling beauty.

"I am here," TenSoon said.

"You insist on forcing this trial?" KanPaar said, keeping his voice lofty, bolstering his thick accent. By staying away from humans for so long, his language hadn't been corrupted by their dialects. The Seconds' accents were similar to that of the Father, supposedly.

"Yes," TenSoon said.

KanPaar's sigh was audible from where he stood behind his fine stone lectern. Finally, he angled his head toward the upper reaches of the room, from which the First Generation watched, sitting in their individual alcoves running around the perimeter, shadowed to the point where they were little more than humanoid lumps. They did not speak. That was for the Seconds.

The doors behind TenSoon opened, bringing the sound of hushed voices and rustling feet. He turned, smiling to himself as he watched them enter. Kandra of various sizes and ages. The youngest ones wouldn't be allowed to attend an event this important, but those of the adult generations— everyone up through the Ninth Generation—could not be denied. This was his victory, perhaps the only one he would have in the entire trial.

If he was to be condemned to endless imprisonment, then he wanted his people to know the truth. More important, he wanted them to hear this trial, to hear what he had to say. He would not convince the Second Generation, and who knew what the Firsts would silently think, sitting in their shadowed alcoves? The younger kandra, however . . . perhaps they would listen. Perhaps they would do something, once TenSoon was gone. He watched them file in, filling the stone benches. There were hundreds of kandra now. The elder generations—Firsts, Seconds, Thirds— were small in number, since many had been killed in the early days, when humans had feared them. Later generations were well populated—the Tenth Generation had over a hundred individuals in it. The Trustwarren's benches had been constructed to hold the entire kandra population, but they were now filled merely by those who happened to be free from both duty and Contract.

He had hoped that MeLaan wouldn't be in that group. Yet she was virtually the first in the doors. For a moment, he worried that she'd rush across the chamber—stepping on the platform, where only the most blessed or cursed were allowed. Instead, she halted right inside the doorway, forcing others to push around her in annoyance as they found seats.

He shouldn't have recognized her. She had a new True Body, an eccentric one with bones made of wood. They were thin and willowy in an exaggerated, unnatural way: her wooden skull long with a pointed triangular chin, her eyes too large, twisted bits of cloth sticking from her head like hair. The younger generations were pushing the boundaries of propriety, annoying the Seconds. Once, TenSoon would probably have agreed with them—and he was still something of a traditionalist. Yet this day, her rebellious body simply made him smile.

That seemed to give her comfort, and she found a seat near the front, with a group of other Seventh Generationers. They all had deformed True Bodies—one much too blocky, another actually sporting four arms.

"TenSoon of the Third Generation," KanPaar said formally, stilling the crowd of watching kandra. "You have obstinately demanded judgment before the First Generation. By the First Contract, we cannot condemn you without allowing you the opportunity to plead before the Firsts. Should they see fit to stay your punishment, you will be freed. Otherwise, you must accept the fate the Council of Seconds assigns you."

"I understand," TenSoon said.

"Then," KanPaar said, leaning forward on his lectern. "Let us begin."

He's not worried at all, TenSoon realized. *He actually sounds like he's going to enjoy this.*

And why not? After centuries of preaching that the Third Generation is filled with miscreants? They've tried all this time to overcome their mistakes with us—mistakes such as giving us too much freedom, letting us think that we were as good as they were. By proving that I—the most temperate of the Thirds—am a danger, KanPaar will win a struggle he's been fighting for most of his life.

TenSoon had always found it strange how threatened the Seconds felt by the Thirds. It had taken them but a single generation to understand their mistakes—the Fourths were nearly as loyal as the Fifths, with only a few deviant members.

And yet, with some of the younger generations— MeLaan and her friends providing an example—acting as they did . . . well, perhaps the Seconds had a right to feel threatened. And TenSoon was to be their sacrifice. Their way of restoring order and orthodoxy.

They were certainly in for a surprise.

Nuggets of pure Allomancy, the power of Preservation itself. Why Rashek left one of those nuggets at the Well of Ascension, I do not know. Perhaps he didn't see it, or perhaps he intended to save it to bestow upon a fortunate underling.

Perhaps he feared that someday he would lose his powers, and would need that nugget to grant him Allomancy once more. In any case, I bless Rashek's oversight, for without that nugget, Elend would have died that day at the Well.

10

LARSTAISM WAS A DIFFICULT ONE for Sazed to evaluate. The religion seemed innocent enough. They knew much about it; a Keeper during the fourth century had managed to uncover an entire trove of prayer materials, scriptures, notes, and writings that had once belonged to a high-ranking member of the religion.

Yet the religion itself didn't seem very . . . well, religious. It had focused on art, not the sacred in the usual sense, and had centered around donating money to support monks so that they could compose poetry and paint and sculpt works of art. That blocked Sazed's attempts to dismiss it, as he couldn't find any contradictions in its doctrines. It didn't have enough of those for them to conflict with one another.

He held the paper in front of him, shaking his head, reading over the sheet again. It was strapped to the front of the portfolio to keep it from being caught in the wind, and a parasol strapped to his saddle kept most of the ash from smearing the page. He had heard Vin complain that she didn't know how people could possibly read while riding a horse, but this method made it rather easy.

He didn't have to turn pages. He simply read the same words over and over, turning them in his mind, playing with them. Trying to decide. Did this one have the truth? It was the one that Mare, Kelsier's wife, had believed. She'd been one of the few people Sazed had ever met who had chosen to believe in an old religion he had preached.

> The Larsta believed that life was about seeking the divine. They taught that art draws us closer to understanding divinity. Since not all men can spend their time in art, it is to the benefit of society as a whole to support a group of dedicated artists to create great works, which then elevate those who experience them.

That was all well and good, in Sazed's estimation, but what about questions of life and death? What about the spirit? What *was* the divine, and how could such terrible things happen to the world if divinity did exist?

"You know," Breeze said from the saddle of his horse, "there's something amazing about all of this."

The comment broke Sazed's concentration. He sighed, looking up from his research. The horse continued to clop along beneath him. "Amazing about what, Lord Breeze?"

"The ash," Breeze said. "Covering everything, making the land all black. It's simply astounding how dreary the landscape has become. During the Lord Ruler's reign, everything was brown, and most plants grown outdoors looked as if they were on the very edge of sickly death. I thought *that* was depressing. But ash falling every day, burying the entire land . . ." The Soother shook his head, smiling. "I wouldn't have thought it possible for things to be worse without the Lord Ruler. But, well, we've certainly made a mess! Destroying the world. That's no mean feat, if you think about it. I wonder if we should be impressed with ourselves."

Sazed frowned. Occasional flakes drifted from the sky, the upper atmosphere darkened by its usual haze. The ashfall was light, if persistent, falling steadily for nearly two months now. Their horses trudged through a good half foot of the stuff as they moved northward, accompanied by a hundred of Elend's soldiers. How long would it be before the ash grew so deep that travel was impossible? It already drifted several feet high in some places.

Everything was black—the hills, the road, the entire countryside. Trees drooped with the weight of ash on their leaves and branches. Most of the ground foliage was likely dead—bringing two horses with them on the trip to Lekal City had been difficult, for there was nothing for them to graze on. The soldiers had been forced to carry feed.

"I do have to say, however," Breeze continued, chatting along in his normal way, protected from the ash by a parasol attached to the back of his saddle, "the ash *is* a tad unimaginative."

"Unimaginative?"

"Why yes," Breeze said. "While I do happen to like black as a color for suits, I otherwise find it to be a somewhat uninspired hue."

"What else would the ash be?"

Breeze shrugged. "Well, Vin says that there's something behind all this, right? Some evil force of doom or whatever? If *I* were said force of doom, then I certainly wouldn't have used my powers to turn the land black. It lacks flair. Red. Now *that* would be an interesting color. Think of the possibilities—if the ash were red, the rivers would run like blood. Black is so monotonous that you can forget about it, but red—you'd always be thinking, 'Why, look at that. That hill is red. That evil force of doom trying to destroy me certainly has style.'"

"I'm not convinced there is any 'evil force of doom,' Breeze," Sazed said.

"Oh?"

"The Ashmounts have *always* spewed out ash. Is it really that much of a stretch to assume that they have become more active than before? Perhaps this is all the result of natural processes."

"And the mists?"

"Weather patterns change, Lord Breeze," Sazed said. "Perhaps it was simply too warm during the day for them to come out before. Now that the Ashmounts are emitting more ash, it would make sense that the days are growing colder, so the mists stay longer."

"Oh? And if that were the case, my dear man, then why haven't the mists stayed out during the day in the winters? It was colder then than the summer, but the mists always left when day arrived."

Sazed grew silent. Breeze made a good point. Yet as Sazed checked each new religion off his list, he wondered more and more if they were simply *creating* an enemy in this force Vin had felt. He didn't know anymore. He didn't believe for a moment that she would have fabricated her stories. But if there were no truth in the religions, was it too much of a stretch to infer that the world was ending merely because it was time?

"Green," Breeze finally said.

Sazed turned.

"Now that would be a color with style," Breeze said. "Different. You can't see green and forget about it—not as you can with black or brown. Wasn't Kelsier always talking about plants being green once? Before the Ascension of the Lord Ruler, before the first time the Deepness came upon the land?"

"That's what the histories claim."

Breeze nodded thoughtfully. "Style indeed," he said. "It would be pretty, I think."

"Oh?" Sazed asked, genuinely surprised. "Most people with whom I have spoken seem to find the concept of green plants rather odd."

"I thought that once, but now, after seeing black all day,

every day . . . Well, I think a little variety would be nice. Fields of green . . . little specks of color . . . what did Kelsier call those?"

"Flowers," Sazed said. The Larsta had written poems about them.

"Yes," Breeze said. "It will be nice when those return."

"Return?"

Breeze shrugged. "The Church of the Survivor teaches that Vin will someday cleanse the sky of ash and the air of mists. I figure while she's at it, she might as well bring back the plants and the flowers. Seems like a suitably feminine thing to do, for some reason."

Sazed sighed, shaking his head. "Lord Breeze," he said, "I realize that you are simply trying to encourage me. However, I have serious trouble believing that *you* accept the teachings of the Church of the Survivor."

Breeze hesitated. Then he smiled. "So I overdid it a bit, did I?"

"A tad."

"It's difficult to tell with you, my dear man. You're so aware of my touch on your emotions that I can't use much Allomancy, and you've been so . . . well, different lately." Breeze's voice grew wistful. "Still, it would be nice to see those green plants our Kelsier always spoke of. After six months of ash . . . well, it makes a man at least *want* to believe. Perhaps that's enough for an old hypocrite like me."

The sense of despair inside Sazed wanted to snap that simply *believing* wasn't enough. Wishing and believing had gotten him nowhere. It wouldn't change the fact that the plants were dying and the world was ending.

It wasn't worth fighting, because nothing meant anything.

Sazed forced himself to stop that line of thought, but it was difficult. He sometimes worried about his melancholy. Unfortunately, much of the time he had trouble summoning the effort even to care about his own pessimistic bent.

The Larsta, he told himself. *Focus on that religion. You need to make a decision.*

Breeze's comments had set Sazed thinking. The Larsta focused so much on beauty and art as being "divine." Well, if divinity was related to art, then a god *couldn't* in any way be involved in what was happening to the world. The ash, the dismal, depressing landscape . . . it was more than just "unimaginative," as Breeze had put it. It was completely insipid. Dull. Monotonous.

Religion not true, Sazed wrote at the bottom of the paper. *Teachings are directly contradicted by observed events.*

He undid the straps on his portfolio and slipped the sheet in, one step closer to having gone through all of them. Sazed could see Breeze watching out of the corner of his eye; the Soother loved secrets. Sazed doubted the man would be all that impressed if he discovered what the work was really about. In any case, Sazed wished that Breeze would leave him alone when it came to these studies.

I shouldn't be curt with him, Sazed thought. He knew the Soother was, in his own way, merely trying to help. Breeze had changed since they'd first met. Early on—despite glimmers of compassion—Breeze really had been the self-ish, callous manipulator that he now only pretended to be. Sazed suspected that Breeze had joined Kelsier's team not out of a desire to help the skaa, but because of the challenge the scheme had presented, not to mention the rich reward Kelsier had promised.

That reward—the Lord Ruler's atium cache—had proven to be a myth. Breeze had found other rewards instead.

Up ahead, Sazed noticed someone moving through the ash. The figure wore black, but against the field of ash it was easy to pick out a hint of flesh tone. It appeared to be one of their scouts. Captain Goradel called the line to a halt, then sent a man forward to meet the scout. Sazed and Breeze waited patiently.

"Scout report, Lord Ambassador," Captain Goradel said, walking up to Sazed's horse a short time later. "The emperor's army is a few hills away—less than an hour."

"Good," Sazed said, relishing the thought of seeing something other than the dreary hills of black.

"They've apparently seen us, Lord Ambassador," Goradel said. "Riders are approaching. In fact, they are—"

"Here," Sazed said, nodding into the near distance, where he saw a rider crest the hill. This one was very easy to pick out against the black. Not only was it moving quickly—actually galloping its poor horse along the road—but it was also pink.

"Oh dear," Breeze said, sighing.

The bobbing figure resolved into a young woman with golden hair, wearing a bright pink dress—one that made her look younger than her twenty years. Allrianne had a fondness for lace and frills, and she tended to wear colors that made her stand out. Sazed might have expected someone like her to be a poor equestrian. Allrianne, however, rode with easy mastery, something one would need in order to remain astride a galloping horse while wearing such a frivolous dress.

The young woman brought her horse to a halt in front of Sazed's soldiers, spinning the animal in a flurry of ruffled fabric and golden hair. About to dismount, she hesitated, eyeing the half-foot-deep layer of ash on the ground.

"Allrianne?" Breeze said after a moment of silence.

"Hush," she said. "I'm trying to decide if it's worth getting my dress dirty to scamper over and hug you."

"We could wait until we get to the camp . . ."

"I couldn't embarrass you in front of your soldiers that way," she said.

"Technically, my dear," Breeze said, "they're not *my* soldiers at all, but Sazed's."

Reminded of Sazed's presence, Allrianne looked up. She smiled prettily toward Sazed, then bent herself in a horseback version of a curtsy. "Lord Ambassador," she said, and Sazed felt a sudden—and unnatural—fondness for the young lady. She was Rioting him. If there was anyone more brazen with their Allomantic powers than Breeze, it was Allrianne.

"Princess," Sazed said, nodding his head to her.

Finally, Allrianne made her decision and slipped off the

horse. She didn't quite scamper—instead she held up her dress in a rather unladylike fashion. It would have been immodest if she hadn't been wearing several layers of lace petticoats underneath.

Eventually, Captain Goradel came over and helped her up onto Breeze's horse so that she was sitting in the saddle in front of him. The two had never been officially married—perhaps partially because Breeze felt embarrassed to be in a relationship with a woman so much younger than him. When pressed on the issue, Breeze had explained that he didn't want to leave her as a widow when he died—something he seemed to assume would happen immediately, though he was in his mid-forties.

We'll all die soon, the way things are going, Sazed thought. *Our ages do not matter.*

Perhaps that was part of why Breeze had finally accepted having a relationship with Allrianne. In any case, it was obvious from the way he looked at her—from the way he held her with a delicate, almost reverent touch—that he loved her very much.

Our social structure is breaking down, Sazed thought as the column began to march again. *Once, the official stamp of a marriage would have been essential, especially in a relationship involving a young woman of her rank.*

And yet, who was there to be official for now? The obligators were all but extinct. Elend and Vin's government was a thing of wartime necessity—a utilitarian, martially organized alliance of cities. And looming over it all was the growing awareness that something was seriously wrong with the world.

Why bother to get married if you expected the world to end before the year was out?

Sazed shook his head. This was a time when people needed structure—needed *faith*—to keep them going. He should have been the one to give it to them. The Church of the Survivor tried, but it was too new, and its adherents were too inexperienced with religion. Already there were arguments about doctrine and methodology, and each city of the New Empire was developing its own variant of the religion.

In the past, Sazed had taught religions while claiming to believe in each one, but not trying to live them. He'd accepted each as being special in its own way, and offered them up as a waiter might serve an appetizer he himself didn't plan to eat.

Doing so now seemed hypocritical to Sazed. If this people needed faith, then he should not be the one to give it to them. He would not teach lies, not anymore.

Sazed splashed his face with the basin's cold water, enjoying the pleasurable shock. The water dribbled down his cheeks and chin, carrying with it stains of ash. He dried his face with a clean towel, then took out his razor and mirror so that he could shave his head properly.

"Why do you keep doing that?" asked an unexpected voice.

Sazed spun. His tent in the camp had been empty moments before. Now someone stood behind him. Sazed smiled. "Lady Vin."

She folded her arms, raising an eyebrow. She had always moved stealthily, but she was getting so good that it amazed him. She'd not even rustled the tent flap with her entrance. Her standard shirt and trousers after male fashion doubtless contributed to her stealth, though over the last three years she had grown her raven hair to a feminine shoulder length. There had been a time when Vin had seemed to crouch wherever she went, always trying to hide, rarely meeting the eys of others. That had changed. She was still easy to miss, with her quiet ways, thin figure, and small stature. But she now always looked people in the eye.

And that made a big difference.

"General Demoux said that you were resting, Lady Vin," Sazed noted.

"Demoux knows better than to let me sleep through your arrival."

Sazed smiled to himself, then gestured toward a chair.

"You can keep shaving," she said. "It's all right."

"Please," he said, gesturing again.

Vin sighed, taking the seat. "You never answered my question, Saze," she said. "Why do you keep wearing those steward's robes? Why do you keep your head shaved like a Terris servant? Why worry about showing disrespect while I'm here? You're not a servant anymore."

He sighed, carefully sitting in the chair across from Vin. "I'm not sure *what* I am anymore, Lady Vin."

The tent walls flapped in the gentle breeze, a bit of ash blowing in through the doorway, which Vin hadn't tied closed behind her. She frowned at his comment. "You're Sazed."

"Emperor Venture's chief ambassador."

"No," Vin said. "That might be what you *do,* but that's not what you *are.*"

"And what am I, then?"

"Sazed," she repeated. "Keeper of Terris."

"A Keeper who no longer wears his coppperminds?"

Vin glanced toward the corner and the trunk where he kept them. The knowledge of peoples long dead sat there waiting to be taught, waiting to be added to. "I fear that I have become a very selfish man, Lady Vin," Sazed said quietly.

"That's silly," Vin said. "You've spent your entire life serving others. I know of nobody more selfless than you."

"I do appreciate that sentiment," he said. "But I fear that I must disagree. Lady Vin, we are not new to sorrow. You know better than anyone here, I think, the hardships of life in the Final Empire. We have all lost people dear to us. And yet, I seem to be the only one unable to get over my loss. I feel childish. Yes, Tindwyl is dead. In all honesty, I did not have much time with her before she passed. I have no reason to feel as I do.

"Still, I cannot wake up in the morning and not see darkness ahead of me. When I place the metalminds upon my arms, my skin feels cold, and I remember time spent with her. Life lacks all hope. I should be able to move on, but I cannot. I am weak of will, I think."

"That just isn't true, Sazed," Vin said.

"I must disagree."

"Oh?" Vin asked. "And if you really were weak of will, would you be able to disagree with me?"

Sazed smiled. "When did you get so good at logic?"

"Living with Elend," Vin said with a sigh. "If you prefer irrational arguments, don't marry a scholar."

I almost did. The thought came to Sazed unbidden, but it quieted his smile nonetheless. Vin must have noticed, for she winced slightly.

"Sorry," she said, looking away.

"It is all right, Lady Vin," Sazed said. "I simply . . . I feel so weak. I cannot be the man my people wish me to be. I am perhaps the very last of the Keepers. It has been a year since the Inquisitors attacked my homeland, killing even the child Feruchemists, and we have seen no evidence that others of my sect survived. Some were out of the city, certainly and inevitably, but either Inquisitors found them or other tragedy did. There has been enough of that lately, I think."

Vin sat with her hands in her lap, looking uncharacteristically weak in the dim light. Sazed frowned at the pained expression on her face. "Lady Vin?"

"I'm sorry," she said. "It's just that . . . you've always been the one who gives advice, Sazed. But now what I need advice about is you."

"There is no advice to give, I fear."

They sat in silence for a few moments.

"We found the stockpile," Vin said. "The next-to-last cavern. I made a copy for you of the words we found, etched in a thin sheet of steel so they'll be safe."

"Thank you."

Vin sat, appearing uncertain. "You're not going to look at it, are you?"

Sazed hesitated, then shook his head. "I do not know."

"I can't do this alone, Sazed," Vin whispered. "I can't fight it by myself. I *need* you."

The tent grew quiet. "I . . . am doing what I can, Lady Vin," Sazed finally said. "In my own way. I must find answers for myself before I can provide them to anyone else. Still, have the etching delivered to my tent. I promise that I will at least look at it."

She nodded, then stood. "Elend's having a meeting tonight. To plan our next moves. He wants you there." She trailed a faint perfume as she moved to leave. She lingered beside his chair. "There was a time," she said, "after I'd taken the power at the Well of Ascension, when I thought Elend would die."

"But he did not," Sazed said. "He lives still."

"It doesn't matter," Vin said. "I thought him dead. I knew he was dying—I held that power, Sazed, power you *can't imagine*. Power you'll never be *able* to imagine. The power to destroy worlds and remake them anew. The power to see and to understand. I saw him, and I knew he would die. And knew I had the power to save him."

Sazed looked up.

"But I didn't," Vin said. "I let him bleed, and released the power instead. I consigned him to death."

"How?" Sazed asked. "How could you do such a thing?"

"Because I looked into his eyes," Vin said, "and knew it was what he wanted me to do. You gave me that, Sazed. You taught me to love him enough to let him die."

She left him alone in the tent. A few moments later, he returned to his shaving and found something sitting beside his basin. A small, folded piece of paper.

It contained an aged, fading drawing of a strange plant. A flower. The picture had once belonged to Mare. It had gone from her to Kelsier, and from him to Vin.

Sazed picked it up, wondering what Vin intended to say by leaving him the picture. Eventually he folded it up and slipped it into his sleeve, then returned to his shaving.

*The First Contract, oft spoken of by the kandra, was origi-
nally a series of promises made by the First Generation to the
Lord Ruler. They wrote these promises down, and in doing so
codified the first kandra laws. They were worried about gov-
erning themselves independently of the Lord Ruler and his empire. So they took what they had written to him, asking for his
approval.*

*He commanded it cast into steel, then personally scratched a
signature into the bottom. This code was the first thing that a kandra learned upon awakening from his or her life as a mistwraith.
It contained commands to revere earlier generations, simple legal
rights granted to each kandra, provisions for creating new kandra,
and a demand for ultimate dedication to the Lord Ruler.*

*Most disturbingly, the First Contract contained a provision
which, if invoked, would require the mass suicide of the entire
kandra people.*

11

KANPAAR LEANED FORWARD ON HIS lectern, red crystalline bones sparkling in the lamplight. "Very well then,
TenSoon, traitor to the kandra people. You have demanded
this judgment. Make your plea."

TenSoon took a deep breath—it felt so good to be able to
do that again—and opened his mouth to speak.

"Tell them," KanPaar continued, sneering, "explain, if you
can, why you killed one of our own. A fellow kandra."

TenSoon froze. The Trustwarren was quiet—the generations of kandra were far too well behaved to rustle and make noise like a crowd of humans. They sat with their bones of rock, wood, or metal, waiting for TenSoon's answer.

KanPaar's question wasn't the one TenSoon had expected.

"Yes, I killed a kandra," TenSoon said, standing cold and naked on the platform. "That is not forbidden."

"Need it be forbidden?" KanPaar accused, pointing. "Humans kill each other. Koloss kill each other. But they are both of Ruin. *We* are of Preservation, the chosen of the Father. We don't kill one another!"

TenSoon frowned. This was a strange line of questioning. *Why ask this?* he thought. *My betrayal of all our people is surely a greater sin than the murder of one.*

"I was compelled by my Contract," TenSoon said frankly. "You must know, KanPaar. *You* are the one who assigned me to the man Straff Venture. We all know what kind of person he was."

"No different from any other *man*," spat one of the Seconds.

Once, TenSoon would have agreed. But he now knew that there were at least some humans who *were* different. He had betrayed Vin, yet she hadn't hated him for it. She had understood, and had felt mercy. Even if they hadn't already become friends, even if he hadn't grown to respect her greatly, that one moment would have earned her his devoted loyalty.

She was counting on him, whether or not she knew it. He stood a little straighter, looking KanPaar in the eyes. "I was assigned to the man Straff Venture by paid Contract," TenSoon said. "He gave me over to the whims of his twisted son, Zane. It was Zane who commanded that I kill the kandra OreSeur and take his place, so that I could spy on the woman Vin."

There were a few hushed whispers at her name. *Yes, you've heard of her. The one who slew the Father.*

"And so you did what this Zane commanded?" KanPaar asked loudly. "You killed another kandra. You murdered a *member of your own generation!*"

"You think I enjoyed it?" TenSoon demanded. "OreSeur was my generation brother, a kandra I had known for seven hundred years! But the Contract—"

"Forbids killing," KanPaar said.

"It forbids the killing of men."

"And is not a kandra life worth more than that of a man?"

"The words are specific, KanPaar," TenSoon snapped. "I know them well—I helped write them! We were both there when these service Contracts were created using the First Contract as a model! They forbid us from killing humans, but not each other."

KanPaar leaned forward again. "Did you argue with this Zane? Suggest perhaps that he should perform the murder? Did you *try* to get out of killing one of our people?"

"I do not argue with my masters," TenSoon said. "And I certainly didn't want to tell the man Zane how to kill a kandra. His instability was well known."

"So you didn't argue," KanPaar said. "You simply killed OreSeur. And then you took his place, pretending to be him."

"That is what we do," TenSoon said with frustration. "We take the place of others, acting as spies. That is the entire *point* of the Contract!"

"We do these things to *humans,*" snapped another Second. "This is the first case where a kandra has been used to imitate another kandra. It is a disturbing precedent you set."

It was brilliant, TenSoon thought. *I hate Zane for making me do it, but I can still see the genius in it. Vin never once suspected me. Who would?*

"You should have refused to do this act," KanPaar said. "You should have pled the need for clarification of your Contract. If others were to begin using us in this way, to kill one another, then we could be wiped out in a matter of years!"

"You betrayed us all with your rashness," said another.

Ah, TenSoon thought. *So that is their plan. They establish me as a traitor first, so that what I say later lacks credibility.* He smiled. He was of the Third Generation; it was time he started acting like it.

"I betrayed us with my rashness?" TenSoon asked. "What of you, glorious Seconds? Who was it who allowed a Contract to be assigned to Kelsier? You gave a kandra servant *to the very man who was planning to kill the Father*!"

KanPaar stiffened as if he'd been slapped, translucent face angry in the blue lamplight. "It is not your place to make accusations, Third!"

"I have no place anymore, it seems," TenSoon said. "None of us do, now that the Father is dead. We have no right to complain, for we helped it happen."

"How were we to know this man would succeed when others hadn't," a Second sputtered. "He paid so well that—"

KanPaar cut the other off with a sharp wave of the hand. It wasn't good for those of the Second Generation to defend themselves. But HunFoor—the kandra who had spoken—hadn't ever really fit in with the others of his generation. He was a little more . . . dense.

"You shall speak no more of this, Third," KanPaar said, pointing at TenSoon.

"How can I defend myself if I cannot—"

"You aren't *here* to defend yourself," KanPaar said. "This is not a trial—you have already admitted your guilt. This is a judgment. Explain your actions, then let the First Generation pronounce your fate!"

TenSoon fell silent. It was not time to push. Not yet.

"Now," KanPaar said, "this thing you did in taking the place of one of your own brothers is bad enough. Need we speak on, or would you accept judgment now?"

"We both know that OreSeur's death has little to do with why I am here," TenSoon said.

"Very well," said KanPaar. "Let us move on then. Why don't you tell the First Generation why—if you are such a

Contract-abiding kandra—you *broke* Contract with your master, disobeying his interests and helping his enemy instead?"

KanPaar's accusation echoed in the room. TenSoon closed his eyes, thinking back to that day over a year ago. He remembered sitting silently on the floor of Keep Venture, watching as Zane and Vin fought.

No. It hadn't been a fight. Zane had been burning atium, which had made him all but invincible. Zane had played with Vin, toying with and mocking her.

Vin hadn't been TenSoon's master—TenSoon had killed her kandra and taken his place, spying on Vin at Zane's order. Zane. *He* had been TenSoon's master. *He* had held TenSoon's Contract.

But against all of his training, TenSoon had helped Vin. And in doing so, he had revealed to her the great secret of the kandra. Their weakness: that an Allomancer could use their powers to take complete control of a kandra's body. The kandra served their Contracts to keep this secret hidden—they became servants, lest they end up as slaves. TenSoon opened his eyes to the quiet chamber. This was the moment he had been planning for.

"I didn't break my Contract," he announced.

KanPaar snorted. "You said otherwise when you came to us a year ago, Third."

"I told you what happened," TenSoon said, standing tall. "What I said was not a lie. I helped Vin instead of Zane. Partially because of my actions, my master ended up dead at Vin's feet. But I did not break my Contract."

"You imply that Zane *wanted* you to help his enemy?" KanPaar said.

"No," TenSoon said. "I did not break my Contract because I decided to serve a greater Contract. The First Contract!"

"The Father is dead!" one of the Seconds snapped. "How could you serve our Contract with him?"

"He is dead," TenSoon said. "That is true. But the First

Contract did not die with him! Vin, the Heir of the Survivor, was the one who killed the Lord Ruler. *She* is our Mother now. Our First Contract is with her!"

He had expected outcries of blasphemy and condemnation. Instead he got shocked silence. KanPaar stood stupefied behind his stone lectern. The members of the First Generation were silent, as usual, in their shadowed alcoves.

Well, TenSoon thought, *I suppose that means I should continue.* "I *had* to help the woman Vin," he said. "I could not let Zane kill her, for I had a duty to her—a duty that began the moment she took the Father's place."

KanPaar finally found his voice. "*She?* Our Mother? She killed the Lord Ruler!"

"And took his place," TenSoon said. "She is one of us, in a way."

"Nonsense!" KanPaar said. "I had expected rationalizations, TenSoon—perhaps even lies. But these fantasies? These blasphemies?"

"Have you been outside recently, KanPaar?" TenSoon asked. "Have you left the Homeland in the last century at all? Do you understand what is happening? The Father is *dead*. The land is in upheaval. While returning to the Homeland a year ago, I saw the changes in the mists. They no longer behave as they always did. We cannot continue as we have. The Second Generation may not yet realize it, but Ruin has come! Life will end. The time that the World-bringers spoke of—perhaps the time for the Resolution—is here!"

"You are delusional, TenSoon. You've been among the humans too—"

"Tell them what this is all really about, KanPaar," Ten-Soon interrupted, voice rising. "Don't you want my *real* sin known? Don't you want the others to hear?"

"Don't force this, TenSoon," KanPaar said, pointing again. "What you've done is bad enough. Don't make it—"

"I told her," TenSoon said, cutting him off once more. "I told her our *secret*. At the end, she used me. Like the Allomancers of old. She took control of my body, using the

Flaw, and she made me fight against Zane! *This* is what I've done. I've betrayed us all. She knows—and I'm certain that she has told others. Soon they'll all know how to control us. And do you know *why* I did it? Is it not the point of this judgment for me to speak of my purposes?"

He kept talking, despite the fact that KanPaar tried to speak over him. "I did it because she has the *right* to know our secret," TenSoon shouted. "She is the Mother! She inherited everything the Lord Ruler had. Without her, we have nothing. We cannot create new Blessings, or new kandra, on our own! The Trust is hers now! We should go to her. If this truly is the end of all things, then the Resolution will soon come. She will—"

"Enough!" KanPaar bellowed.

The chamber fell silent again.

TenSoon stood, breathing deeply. For a year, trapped in his pit, he'd planned how to proclaim that information. His people had spent a thousand years, ten generations, following the teachings of the First Contract. They deserved to hear what had happened to him.

Yet it felt so . . . inadequate to scream it out like some raving human. Would any of his people really believe? Would he change anything at all?

"You have, by your own admission, betrayed us," KanPaar said. "You've broken Contract, you've murdered one of your own generation, and you've told a human how to dominate us. You demanded judgment. Let it come."

TenSoon turned and looked up toward the alcoves where the members of the First Generation watched.

Perhaps . . . perhaps they'll see that what I say is true. Perhaps my words will shock them, and they'll realize that we need to offer service to Vin rather than sit in these caves and wait while the world ends around us.

But nothing happened. No motion, no sound. At times TenSoon wondered if anyone still lived up there. He hadn't spoken with a member of the First Generation for centuries—they limited their communications strictly to the Seconds.

If they did still live, none of them took the opportunity to offer TenSoon clemency. KanPaar smiled. "The First Generation has ignored your plea, Third," he said. "Therefore, as their servants, we of the Second Generation will offer judgment on their behalf. Your sentencing will occur in one month's time."

TenSoon frowned. *A month? Why wait?*

In any case, it was over. He bowed his head, sighing. He'd had his say. The kandra now knew that their secret was out—the Seconds could no longer hide that fact. Perhaps his words would inspire his people to action.

TenSoon would probably never know.

Rashek moved the Well of Ascension, obviously.

It was clever of him—perhaps the cleverest thing he did. He knew that the power would one day return to the Well, for power such as this—the fundamental power by which the world was formed—does not simply run out. It can be used, and therefore diffused, but it will always be renewed.

So, knowing that rumors and tales would persist, Rashek changed the very landscape of the world. He put mountains in what became the North, and named that location Terris. Then he flattened his true homeland, and built his capital there.

He constructed his palace around that room at its heart, the room where he would meditate, the room that was a replica of his old hovel in Terris. A refuge created during the last moments before his power ran out.

12

"I'M WORRIED ABOUT HIM, ELEND," Vin said, sitting on their bedroll.

"Who?" Elend asked, looking away from the mirror. "Sazed?"

Vin nodded. When Elend awoke from their nap, she was already up, bathed, and dressed. He worried about *her* sometimes, working herself as hard as she did. He worried more now that he too was Mistborn, and understood the limitations of pewter. The metal strengthened the body, letting one postpone fatigue—but at a price. When the pewter ran out or was turned off, the fatigue returned, crashing down on you like a collapsing wall.

Yet Vin kept going. Elend was burning pewter too, pushing himself, but she seemed to sleep half as much as he did. She was harder than he was—strong in ways he would never know.

"Sazed will face his own problems," Elend said, returning to his dressing. "He must have lost people before."

"This is different," Vin said. He could see her in the reflection, sitting cross-legged behind him in her simple clothing. Elend's stark white uniform was the opposite. It shone with its gold-painted wooden buttons, intentionally crafted with too little metal in them to be affected by Allomancy. The clothing had been made with a special cloth that was easier to scrub clean of ash. Sometimes he felt guilty at all the work it took to make him look regal. Yet it was necessary. Not for his vanity, but for his image. The image for which his men marched to war. In a land of black, Elend wore white—and became a symbol.

"Different?" Elend asked, doing up the buttons on his jacket sleeves. "What is different about Tindwyl's death? She wasn't the only one to fall during the assault on Luthadel. So did Clubs and Dockson. You killed my own father in it, and I beheaded my best friend shortly before then. We've all lost people."

"He said something like that himself," Vin said. "But it's more than a death to him. I think he sees a kind of betrayal in Tindwyl's passing—he always was the only one of us who had faith. Somehow, he lost that when she died."

"The only one of us who had faith?" Elend asked, plucking a wooden, silver-painted pin off his desk and affixing it to his jacket. "What about this?"

"You belong to the Church of the Survivor, Elend," Vin said. "But you don't have faith. Not as Sazed did. It was like . . . he *knew* everything would turn out all right. He trusted that something was watching over the world."

"He'll deal with it."

"It's not just him, Elend," Vin said. "Breeze tries too hard."

"What does that mean?" Elend asked with amusement.

"He Pushes on everyone's emotions," Vin said. "He Pushes too hard, trying to make others happy, and he laughs too hard. He's afraid, worried. He shows it by overcompensating."

Elend smiled. "You're getting as bad as he is, reading everybody's emotions and telling them how they're feeling."

"They're my friends, Elend," Vin said. "I *know* them. And I'm telling you—they're giving up. One by one, they're beginning to think we can't win this one."

Elend fastened the final button, then looked at himself in the mirror. Sometimes he still wondered if he fit the ornate suit, with its crisp whiteness and implied regality. Past the short beard, warrior's body, and scarred skin, he stared into his own eyes, searching for the king behind them. As always, he wasn't completely impressed with what he saw.

He carried on anyway, for he was the best they had. Tindwyl had taught him that. "Very well," he said. "I trust that you're right about the others—I'll do something to fix it."

After all, that was his job. The title of emperor carried with it only a single duty.

To make everything better.

"All right," Elend said, pointing to a map of the empire hanging on the wall of the conference tent. "We timed the arrival and disappearance of the mists each day, then Noorden and his scribes analyzed them. They've given us these perimeters as a guide."

The group leaned in, studying the map. Vin sat at the rear of the tent, as was still her preference. Closer to the shadows. Closer to the exit. She'd grown more confident, true—but that didn't make her careless. She liked to be able to keep an eye on everyone in the room, even if she trusted them.

And she did. Except maybe Cett. The obstinate man sat at the front of the group, his quiet teenage son at his side as always. Cett—or *King* Cett, one of the monarchs who had sworn allegiance to Elend—had an unfashionable beard, a more unfashionable mouth, and two legs that didn't work. That hadn't kept him from nearly conquering Luthadel over a year before.

"Hell," Cett said. "You expect us to be able to read that thing?"

Elend tapped the map with his finger. It was a rough sketch of the empire, similar to the one they'd found in the cavern, but more up to date. It had several large concentric circles inscribed on it.

"The outermost circle is the place where the mists have completely taken the land, and no longer leave at all during the daylight." Elend moved his finger inward to another circle. "This circle passes through the town we just visited, where we found the cache. This marks four hours of daylight. Everything inside the circle gets more than four hours. Everything outside it gets less."

"And the final circle?" Breeze asked. He sat with Allrianne as far away from Cett as the tent would allow. Cett still had a habit of throwing things at Breeze: insults for the most part, and occasionally knives.

Elend eyed the map. "Assuming the mists keep creeping toward Luthadel at the same rate, that circle represents the area that the scribes feel will get enough sunlight this summer to support crops."

The room fell silent.

Hope is for the foolish, Reen's voice seemed to whisper in the back of Vin's mind. She shook her head. Her brother, Reen, had trained her in the ways of the street and the underground, teaching her to be mistrustful and paranoid. In doing so, he'd also taught her to survive. It had taken Kelsier to show her that it was possible to both trust and survive—and it had been a hard lesson. Even so, she still often heard Reen's phantom voice in her head—more a memory than anything else—whispering her insecurities, bringing up the brutal things he had taught her.

"That's a fairly small circle, El," Ham said, still studying the map. The large-muscled man sat with General Demoux between Cett and Breeze. Sazed sat quietly to the side. Vin glanced at him, trying to judge if their previous conversation had lifted his depression any, but she couldn't tell.

They were a small group: only nine, counting Cett's son, Gneorndin. But it included pretty much all that was left of Kelsier's crew, except for Spook, who was doing reconnaissance in the North. Everyone was focused on the map. The final circle was indeed very small—not even as large as the Central Dominance, with its imperial capital of Luthadel. Over ninety percent of the empire wouldn't be able to support crops this summer.

"And this small bubble will be gone by next winter," Elend said.

Vin watched the others contemplate, and realize—if they hadn't already—the horror of what was upon them. *It's like Alendi's logbook said,* she thought. *They couldn't fight the Deepness with armies. It destroyed cities, bringing a slow, terrible death. They were helpless.*

The Deepness. That was what they'd called the mists—or at least that was what the surviving records called them. Perhaps the thing they fought, the primal force Vin had released, was behind the obfuscation.

"All right, people," Elend said, folding his arms. "We need options. Kelsier recruited you because you could do the impossible. Well, our predicament is pretty impossible."

"He didn't recruit me," Cett pointed out. "I got pulled by my balls into this little fiasco."

"I wish I cared enough to apologize," Elend said, staring at them. "Come on. I know you have thoughts."

"Well, my dear man," Breeze said, "the most obvious option appears to be the Well of Ascension. It seems the power there was built to fight the mists."

"Or to free the thing hiding in them," Cett said.

"That doesn't matter," Vin said, causing heads to turn. "There's no power at the Well. It's gone. Used up. If it ever returns, I suspect it will be in another thousand years."

"That's a little long to stretch the supplies in those storage caches," Elend said.

"What if we grew plants that need very little light?" Ham asked. As always, the Thug wore simple trousers and a vest. The pewter he burned made him resistant to heat and cold, so he'd cheerfully walk around sleeveless on a day that would send most men running for shelter.

Well, maybe not cheerfully. Ham hadn't changed overnight, as Sazed had. But he had lost some of his joviality. He tended to sit around a lot with a look of consternation on his face, as if considering things very, very carefully—and not much liking the answers he came up with.

"There are plants that don't need light?" Allrianne asked, cocking her head.

"Mushrooms and the like," Ham said.

"I doubt we could feed an entire empire on mushrooms," Elend said. "Though it's a good thought."

"There have to be other plants too," Ham said. "Even if the mists come all day, there will be some light that gets through. Some plants have to be able to live on that."

"Most likely plants that we can't eat, my dear man," Breeze pointed out.

"Yes, but maybe animals can," Ham said.

Elend nodded thoughtfully.

"Blasted little time left for horticulture," Cett noted. "We should have been working on this sort of thing years ago."

"We didn't know most of this until a few months ago," Ham said.

"True," Elend said. "But the Lord Ruler had a thousand years to prepare. That's why he made the storage caverns—and we still don't know what the last one contains."

"I don't like relying on the Lord Ruler, Elend," Breeze said, shaking his head. "He must have prepared those caches knowing that he'd be dead if anyone ever had to use them."

Cett nodded. "The idiot Soother has a point. If I were

the Lord Ruler, I'd have stuffed those caches with poisoned food and pissed-in water. If I had to die, then everyone else ought to as well."

"Fortunately, Cett," Elend said, raising an eyebrow, "the Lord Ruler has proven more altruistic than we might have expected."

"Not something I ever thought I'd hear," Ham noted.

"He was emperor," Elend said. "We may not have liked his rule, but I can understand him somewhat. He wasn't spiteful—nor was he evil, exactly. He simply . . . got carried away. Besides, he resisted this thing that we're fighting."

"This thing?" Cett asked. "The mists?"

"No," Elend said. "The thing that was trapped in the Well of Ascension."

It is called Ruin, Vin thought. *It will destroy everything.*

"This is why I've decided we need to secure that last cache," Elend said. "The Lord Ruler lived through this once—he knew how to prepare. Perhaps we'll find plants that can grow without sunlight. Each of the caches so far has had repeats—food stores, water—but each one has held something new as well. In Vetitan, we found large stores of the first eight Allomantic metals. The thing in that last cache might be what we need in order to survive."

"That's it then!" Cett said, smiling broadly through his beard. "We *are* marching on Fadrex, aren't we?"

Elend nodded curtly. "Yes. The main force of the army will march for the Western Dominance once we break camp here."

"Ha!" Cett said. "Penrod and Janarle can suck on *that* for a few days."

Vin smiled faintly. Penrod and Janarle were the two other most important kings under Elend's imperial rule. Penrod governed Luthadel, which was why he wasn't with them currently, and Janarle ruled the Northern Dominance—the kingdom that included House Venture's hereditary lands.

The largest city in the north, however, had been seized in a revolt while Janarle—with Elend's father, Straff Venture— had been away laying siege to Luthadel. So far, Elend hadn't been able to spare the troops necessary to retake Urteau from its dissidents, so Janarle ruled in exile, his smaller force of troops used to maintain order in the cities he *did* control.

Both Janarle and Penrod had made a habit of finding reasons to keep the main army from marching on Cett's homeland.

"Those bastards won't be at all happy when they hear about this," Cett said.

Elend shook his head. "Does everything you say have to contain one vulgarity or another?"

Cett shrugged. "What's the point of speaking if you can't say something interesting?"

"Swearing isn't interesting," Elend said.

"That's your own damned opinion," Cett said, smiling. "And you really shouldn't be complaining, Emperor. If you think the things *I* say are vulgar, you've been living in Luthadel far too long. Where I come from, people are embarrassed to use pretty words like 'damn.' "

Elend sighed. "Anyway, I—"

He was cut off as the ground began to shake. Vin was on her feet in seconds, looking for danger as the others cursed and reached for stability. She threw open the tent flap, peering through the mists. Yet the shaking subsided quickly, and it caused very little chaos in the camp, all things considered. Patrols moved about, checking for problems—officers and Allomancers under Elend's command. Most of the soldiers simply remained in their tents.

Vin turned back toward the tent's interior. Some of the travel furniture had fallen over, but that was the only disturbance. The others slowly returned to their seats. "Sure have been a lot of those lately," Ham said. Vin met Elend's eyes, and could see concern in them.

We can fight armies, we can capture cities, but what of ash, mists, and earthquakes? What about the world falling apart around us?

"Anyway," Elend said, voice firm despite the concerns Vin knew he must feel, "Fadrex has to be our next goal. We can't risk missing the cache and the things it might contain."

Like the atium, Reen whispered in Vin's head as she reclaimed her seat. "Atium," she said out loud.

Cett perked up. "You think it'll be there?"

"There are theories," Elend said, eyeing Vin. "But we have no proof."

"It will be there," she said. *It has to be. I don't know why, but we have to have it.*

"I hope it isn't," Cett said. "I marched halfway across the blasted empire to steal that atium. If it turns out I left it beneath my own city . . ."

"I think we're missing something important, El," Ham said. "Are you talking about *conquering* Fadrex City?"

The room fell still. Up until this point, Elend's armies had been used defensively, attacking koloss garrisons or the camps of small warlords and bandits. They had bullied a few cities into joining with him, but they had never actually assaulted a city and taken it by force.

Elend turned, looking toward the map again. From the side, Vin could see his eyes—the eyes of a man hardened by a year and a half of near-perpetual war.

"Our primary goal will be to take the city by diplomacy," Elend said.

"Diplomacy?" Cett said. "Fadrex is *mine*. That damn obligator stole it from me! There's no need to worry your conscience about attacking him, Elend."

"No need?" Elend asked, turning. "Cett, those are your people—your soldiers—we'd have to kill to get into that city."

"People die in war," Cett said. "Feeling bad about it doesn't remove the blood from your hands, so why bother? Those soldiers turned against me; they deserve what they'll get."

"It's not that simple," Ham said. "If there was no way for the soldiers to fight this usurper, then why expect them to give up their lives?"

"Especially for a man who was himself a usurper," Elend said.

"In any case," Ham said, "reports describe that city as being very well defended. It will be a tough stone to break, El."

Elend stood quietly for a moment, then eyed Cett, who still looked inordinately pleased with himself. The two appeared to share something—an understanding. Elend was a master of theory, and had probably read as much on war as anyone. Cett seemed to have a sixth sense for warfare and tactics, and had replaced Clubs as the empire's prime military strategist.

"Siege," Cett said.

Elend nodded. "If King Yomen won't respond to diplomacy, then the only way we'll get in that city—short of killing half our men breaking in—is by besieging it and making him desperate."

"Do we have time for that?" Ham asked, frowning.

"Other than Urteau," Elend said, "Fadrex City and the surrounding areas are the sole major section of the Inner Dominances that maintains a strong enough force to be threatening. That, plus the cache, means we can't afford to leave them alone."

"Time is on our side, in a way," Cett said, scratching his beard. "You don't just attack a city like Fadrex, Ham. It has fortifications, one of the few cities apart from Luthadel that could repel an army. But since it's outside the Central Dominance, it's probably already hurting for food."

Elend nodded. "While we have all of the supplies we found in the storage caches. If we block off the highway, then hold the canal, they'll *have* to surrender the city eventually. Even if they've found the cache—which I doubt—we will be able to outlast them."

Ham frowned. "I guess. . . ."

"Besides," Elend added, "if things get tough, we do have about twenty thousand koloss we can draw upon."

Ham raised an eyebrow, though said nothing. The implication was clear. *You'd turn koloss against other people?*

"There is another element to this," Sazed said softly. "Something we have as of yet not discussed." Several people turned, as if they'd forgotten he was there.

"The mists," Sazed said. "Fadrex City lies well beyond the mist perimeter, Emperor Venture. Will you subject your army to more than fifteen percent casualties before you arrive at the city?"

Elend fell silent. So far he'd managed to keep most of his soldiers out of the mists. It seemed wrong to Vin that their army had been protected from the sickness, while the townsfolk had been forced to go out in the mists. Yet where they camped, there was still a significant amount of mistless daylight, and they also had enough tents to hold all the soldiers, something they'd lacked when moving the townsfolk.

Mists rarely went into structures, even cloth ones. There had been no reason to risk killing some of the soldiers, since they'd been able to avoid it. It seemed hypocritical to Vin, but so far it still made sense.

Elend met Sazed's eyes. "You make a good point," he said. "We can't protect the soldiers from this forever. I forced the people of Vetitan to immunize themselves; I suspect that I will have to make the army do the same, for the same reasons."

Vin sat back quietly. She often wished for the days when she'd had nothing to do with such decisions—or better yet when Elend hadn't been forced to make them.

"We march for Fadrex," Elend said again, turning from the group. He pointed at the map. "If we're going to pull through this—and by 'we' I mean all the people of the New Empire—we're going to need to band together and concentrate our populations near the Central Dominance. Because it's the one place that can grow food this summer, we'll need every bit of manpower we can muster to clear ash and prepare the fields. That means bringing the people of Fadrex under our protection.

"It also means," he said, pointing toward the northeastern section of the map, "that we'll need to suppress the rebellion in Urteau. Not only does the city there contain a storage cache—with grain we desperately need for a second planting down in the Central Dominance—but the city's new rulers are gathering strength and an army. Urteau is well within staging distance of Luthadel, as we discovered when my father marched on us. I will *not* have a repeat of that event."

"We don't have enough troops to march on both fronts at once, El," Ham said.

Elend nodded. "I know. In fact, I'd rather avoid marching on Urteau. That was my father's seat—the people there had good reason to rebel against him. Demoux, report?"

Demoux stood. "We had a steel-inscribed message from Spook while Your Majesty was away," he said. "The lad says that the faction controlling Urteau is made up of skaa rebels."

"That sounds promising," Breeze noted. "Our kind of people."

"They're . . . quite harsh with noblemen, Lord Breeze," Demoux said. "And they include anyone with noble parents in that group."

"A little extreme, I'd think," Ham said.

"A lot of people thought Kelsier was extreme too," Breeze said. "I'm certain we can talk reason into these rebels."

"Good," Elend said, "because I'm counting on you and Sazed to bring Urteau under our control without the use of force. There are only five of these caches, and we can't afford to lose one. Who knows what we'll eventually discover in Fadrex—it might require us to return to the other caches to find something we missed." He turned, looking at Breeze, then Sazed.

"We can't just sneak the food out of Urteau," he said. "If the rebellion in that city spreads, it could cause the entire empire to fracture into splinters. We *have* to bring the men there to our side."

The members of the room nodded, as did Vin. They knew from personal experience how much power a small rebellion could exert on an empire.

"The Fadrex siege could take some time," Elend said. "Long before summer arrives, I want you to have secured that northern cache and subdued the rebellion. Send the seed stock down to the Central Dominance for planting."

"Don't worry," Breeze said. "I've seen the kinds of governments skaa set up—by the time we get there, the city will probably be on the edge of collapse anyway. Why, they'll likely be relieved to get an offer to join the New Empire!"

"Be wary," Elend said. "Spook's reports have been sparse, but it sounds as if tensions in the city are acute. We'll send a few hundred soldiers with you as protection." He looked back at the map, eyes narrowing slightly. "Five caches, five cities. Urteau is part of all this, somehow. We can't afford to let it slip away."

"Your Majesty," Sazed said. "Is my presence required on that trip?"

Elend frowned, glancing at Sazed. "You have something else you need to be doing, Sazed?"

"I have research I would do," the Keeper said.

"I respect your wishes, as always," Elend said. "If you think this research is important . . ."

"It's of a personal nature, Your Majesty," Sazed said.

"Could you do it while helping in Urteau?" Elend asked. "You're a Terrisman, which lends you a credibility none of us can claim. Beyond that, people respect and trust you, Sazed—with good reason. Breeze, on the other hand, has something of a . . . reputation."

"I worked hard for it, you know," Breeze said.

"I'd really prefer to have you lead that team, Sazed," Elend said. "I can't think of a better ambassador than the Holy First Witness himself."

Sazed's expression was unreadable. "Very well," he finally said. "I shall do my best."

"Good," Elend said, turning to regard the rest of the group. "Then there's one last thing I need to ask of you all."

"And what is that?" Cett asked.

Elend stood for a few moments, looking over their heads, appearing thoughtful. "I want you to tell me about the Survivor," he said.

"He was lord of the mists," Demoux said immediately.

"Not the rhetoric," Elend said. "Someone tell me about the man, Kelsier. I never met him, you know. I saw him once, right before he died, but I never knew him."

"What's the point?" Cett asked. "We've all heard the stories. He's practically a god, if you listen to the skaa."

"Please," Elend said.

The tent was still for a few moments before Ham spoke. "Kell was . . . grand. He wasn't just a man, he was bigger than that. Everything he did was large—his dreams, the way he talked, the way he thought. . . ."

"And it wasn't false," Breeze added. "I can tell when a man is being a fake. That's why I started my first job with Kelsier, in fact. Amid all the pretenders and posturers, he was genuine. Everyone wanted to be the best. Kelsier really was."

"He was a man," Vin said quietly. "Only a man. Yet you always knew he'd succeed. He made you be what he wanted you to be."

"So he could use you," Breeze said.

"But you were better when he was done with you," Ham added.

Elend nodded slowly. "I wish I could have known him. Early in my career, I always compared myself to him. By the time I heard of Kelsier, he was already becoming a legend. It was unfair to force myself to try to be him, but I worried regardless. Anyway, those of you who knew him, maybe you can answer another question for me. What do you think he'd say, if he saw us now?"

"He'd be proud," Ham said immediately. "I mean, we defeated the Lord Ruler, and we built a skaa government."

"What if he saw us at this conference?" Elend said.

The tent fell still again. When someone spoke what they were all thinking, it came from a source Vin hadn't expected.

"He'd tell us to laugh more," Sazed whispered.

Breeze chuckled. "He was completely insane, you know. The worse things got, the more he'd joke. I remember how chipper he was at the very first meeting after one of our worst defeats, when we lost most of our skaa army to that fool Yeden. Kell walked in, a spring in his step, making one of his inane jokes."

"Sounds insensitive," Allrianne said.

"No," Ham said. "He was merely determined. He always said that laughter was something the Lord Ruler couldn't take from him. He planned and executed the overthrow of a thousand-year empire—and he did it as a kind of penance for letting his wife die thinking that he hated her. But he did it all with a smirk on his lips. Like every joke was his way of slapping fate in the face."

"We need what he had," Elend said.

The room's eyes turned back toward him.

"We can't keep doing this," Elend said. "We bicker among ourselves. We mope about, watching the ash fall, convinced that we're doomed."

Breeze chuckled. "I don't know if you noticed the earthquake a few minutes ago, my dear man, but the world appears to be ending. That is an indisputably depressing event."

"We can survive this," Elend said, determination in his voice. "But the only way that will happen is if our people don't give up. They need leaders who laugh, leaders who feel that this fight *can* be won. So, this is what I ask of you. I don't care if you're an optimist or a pessimist—I don't care if secretly you think we'll all be dead before the month ends. On the outside I want to see you smiling. Do it in defiance if you have to. If the end does come, I want this group to meet that end smiling. As the Survivor taught us."

Slowly, the members of the former crew nodded—including Sazed, though his face seemed troubled.

Cett just shook his head. "You people are all insane. How I ended up with you, I'll never know."

Breeze laughed. "Now that's a lie, Cett. You know *exactly* how you ended up joining us. We threatened to kill you if you didn't!"

Elend was looking at Vin. She met his eyes and nodded once. It had been a good speech. She wasn't certain if his words would change anything—the crew could never again be the way it had been at the beginning, laughing freely around Clubs's table in the evening hours. But maybe, if they kept Kelsier's smile in mind, they'd be less likely to forget exactly why it was they kept struggling on.

"All right, people," Elend finally said. "Let's start preparations. Breeze, Sazed, Allrianne—I'll need you to talk with the scribes about supply estimates for your trip. Ham, send word to Luthadel and tell Penrod to have our scholars work on culturing plants that can grow in very little sunlight. Demoux, pass the word to the men. We march tomorrow."

Hemalurgy is so named because of the connection to blood. It is no coincidence, I believe, that death is always involved in the transfer of powers via Hemalurgy. Marsh once described it as a "messy" process. Not the adjective I would have chosen. It's not disturbing enough.

13

I'M MISSING SOMETHING, MARSH THOUGHT.

He sat in the koloss camp. Just sitting. He hadn't moved in hours. Ash dusted him like a statue. Ruin's attention had been focused elsewhere lately, and Marsh had been left with more and more time to himself.

He still didn't struggle. Struggle only brought Ruin's attention.

Isn't that what I want? he thought. *To be controlled?* When Ruin forced him to see things its way, the dying world seemed wonderful. That bliss was far superior to the dread he felt while sitting on the stump, slowly being buried in ash.

No. No, that's not what I want! It was bliss, true, but it was false. As he had once struggled against Ruin, he now struggled against his own sense of inevitability.

What am I missing? he thought again, distracting himself. The koloss army—three hundred thousand strong—hadn't moved in weeks. Its members were slowly yet relentlessly killing each other.

It seemed a waste of resources to let the army stagnate. For now, the creatures were eating the dead plants beneath the ash. *They can't possibly live on that for long, can they?* Marsh didn't know much about the koloss, despite spending the better part of a year with them. They appeared to be able to eat almost anything to survive, as if merely filling their stomachs were more important than actual nutrition.

What was Ruin waiting for? Why not bring his army in and attack? Marsh was familiar enough with Final Empire geography to recognize that he was stationed in the North, near Terris. Why not move down and strike Luthadel?

There were no other Inquisitors in the camp. Ruin had called them to other tasks, leaving Marsh alone. Of all the Inquisitors, Marsh had been given the largest number of new spikes—he had ten new ones planted at various places in his body. That ostensibly made him the most powerful of the Inquisitors. Why leave him behind?

Yet . . . what does it matter? he wondered. *The end has come. There is no way to beat Ruin. The world will end.*

He felt guilty for the thought. If he could have turned his eyes downward in shame, he would have. There had been a time when he'd run the entire skaa rebellion. Thousands had looked to him for leadership. And then . . . Kelsier had been captured. As had Mare, the woman both Kelsier and Marsh had loved.

When Kelsier and Mare had been cast into the Pits of Hathsin, Marsh had left the rebellion. His rationale had been simple. If the Lord Ruler could catch Kelsier—the most brilliant thief of his time—then he would catch Marsh eventually too. It hadn't been fear that had driven Marsh's retirement, but plain realism. Marsh had always been practical. Fighting had proven useless. So why do it?

And then Kelsier had returned and done what a thousand years of rebellious skaa hadn't been able to: He'd overthrown the empire, facilitating the death of the Lord Ruler.

That should have been me, Marsh thought. *I served the rebellion all my life, then gave up just before they finally won.*

It was a tragedy, and it was made worse by the fact that Marsh was doing it again. He was giving up.

Damn you, Kelsier! he thought with frustration. *Can't you leave me be even in death?*

Yet one harrowing, undeniable fact remained. Mare had been right. She had chosen Kelsier over Marsh. And then, when both men had been forced to deal with her death, only one had given up.

The other had made her dreams come true.

Marsh knew why Kelsier had decided to overthrow the Final Empire. It hadn't been for the money, the fame, or even—as most suspected—for revenge. Kelsier knew Mare's heart. He'd known that she dreamed of days when plants flourished and the sky was not red. She'd always carried with her that little picture of a flower, a copy of a copy of a copy—a depiction of something that had been lost to the Final Empire long ago.

But, Marsh thought bitterly, *you didn't actually make her dreams a reality, Kelsier. You failed. You killed the Lord Ruler, but that didn't fix anything. It made things worse!*

The ash continued to fall, blowing around Marsh in a lazy breeze. Koloss grunted, and in the near distance one screamed as his companion killed him.

Kelsier was dead now. But he had died for her dream. Mare had made the correct choice, but she was dead too. Marsh wasn't. Not yet. *I can fight still,* he told himself. *But how?* Moving a single finger would draw Ruin's attention.

Although during the last few weeks, he hadn't struggled

at all. Perhaps that was why Ruin decided it could leave Marsh alone for so long. The creature—or the force, or whatever it was—wasn't omnipotent. But Marsh suspected it could move about freely, watching the world and seeing what was happening in various parts of it. No walls could block its view—it seemed to be able to watch anything.

Except a man's mind.

Perhaps . . . perhaps if I stop struggling long enough, I'll be able to surprise it when I finally decide to strike.

It seemed as good a plan as any. And Marsh knew exactly what he would do, when the time came. He'd remove Ruin's most useful tool. He'd pull the spike from his back and kill himself. Not out of frustration, and not out of despair. He knew that he had some important part to play in Ruin's plans. If he removed himself at the right time, it could give the others the chance they needed.

It was all he could give. Yet it seemed fitting, and his new confidence made him wish he could stand and face the world with pride. Kelsier had killed himself to secure freedom for the skaa. Marsh would do the same—and in doing so, hope to help save the world from destruction.

THE END OF PART ONE

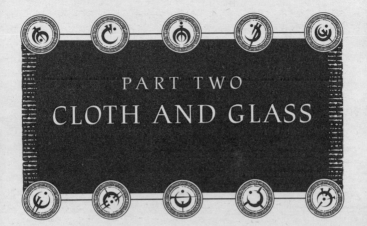

PART TWO
CLOTH AND GLASS

Ruin's consciousness was trapped by the Well of Ascension, kept mostly impotent. That night, when we discovered the Well for the first time, we found something we didn't understand. A black smoke clogging one of the rooms.

Though we discussed it after the fact, we couldn't decide what it was. How could we possibly have known?

It was part of the body of a god—or rather the power of a god, since the two are really the same thing. Ruin and Preservation inhabited power and energy in the same way a person inhabits flesh and blood.

14

SPOOK FLARED TIN.

He let it burn within him—burn brightly, burn powerfully. He never turned it off anymore. He just left it on, letting it roar, a fire within him. Tin was one of the slowest-burning of metals, and it wasn't difficult to obtain in the amounts necessary for Allomancy.

He moved down the silent street. Few people went out after dark, regardless of Kelsier's now-famous proclamations that the skaa need not fear the mists. Deep and mysterious, dark and omnipresent, the nightly mists were one of the great constants of the Final Empire. Thicker than a simple fog, they swirled in definite patterns—almost as if the different banks, streams, and fronts of mist were living things. Almost playful, yet enigmatic.

To Spook, they were barely an inconvenience anymore. He'd always been told not to flare his tin too much; he'd been warned not to become dependent upon it. It would do dangerous things to his body, people said. And the truth was, they were right. He had flared his tin nonstop for a year straight—never letting up, keeping his body in a constant state of super-heightened senses—and it *had* changed him. He worried that the changes would indeed be dangerous.

But he needed them, for the people of Urteau needed him.

Stars blazed in the sky above him, a million tiny suns shining through the mists that had—over the past year—become diaphanous and weak. At first Spook had thought the world was changing. Then he had realized that it was merely his perception. Tin helped an Allomancer pierce the mists, but by flaring tin for so long he had somehow permanently enhanced his senses to a point far beyond what others could attain.

He'd almost stopped. The flared tin had begun as a reaction to Clubs's death. He still felt terrible about the way he'd escaped Luthadel, leaving his uncle to die. During those first few weeks, Spook had flared his metals as almost a penance—he'd wanted to feel everything around him, take it all in, even though it was painful. Perhaps *because* it was painful.

Then he'd started to change, and that had worried him. But the crew always talked about how hard Vin pushed herself. She rarely slept, using pewter to keep herself awake and alert. Spook didn't know how that worked—he was no Mistborn, and could only burn one metal—but he figured that if burning his single metal could give him an advantage, he'd better take it. Because they were going to need every advantage they could get.

The starlight was like daylight to him. During daytime, he now had to wear a cloth tied across his eyes to protect them, and even then going outside was sometimes blinding. His skin had become so sensitive that each pebble in the ground—each crack, each flake of stone—felt like a knife jabbing him through the soles of his shoes. The chill spring air seemed freezing, and he wore a thick cloak.

He had concluded that these nuisances were small prices to pay for the opportunity to become . . . whatever it was he had become. As he moved down the street, he could hear people shuffling and turning in their beds, even through their walls. He could sense a footstep from many yards away. He could see on a dark night as no other human ever had.

Perhaps he'd find a way to become useful to the others. Always before, he'd been the least important member of the crew. The dismissible boy who ran errands or kept watch while the others made plans. He didn't resent them for that—they'd been right to give him such simple duties. Because of his street dialect, he'd been difficult to understand, and while all the other members of the crew had been handpicked by Kelsier, Spook had joined by default since he was Clubs's nephew.

Spook sighed, shoving his hands in his trouser pockets as he walked down the too-bright street. He could feel each and every thread in the fabric.

Dangerous things were happening, he knew: the way the mists lingered during the day, the way the ground shook periodically as if it were a sleeping man suffering a terrible dream. Spook worried he wouldn't be of much help in the critical days to come. He had fled from Luthadel the previous year out of fear—leaving his uncle to die—but also out of a knowledge of his own impotence. He wouldn't have been able to help during the siege.

He didn't want to be in that position again. He wanted to be able to help. He wouldn't run into the woods, hiding while the world ended around him. Elend and Vin had sent him to Urteau to gather as much information as he could about the Citizen and his government there, so Spook intended to do his best. If that meant pushing his body beyond what was safe, so be it.

He approached a large intersection and looked both ways down the crossed streets—the view clear as day to his eyes. *I may not be Mistborn, and I may not be emperor,* he thought. *But I'm something. Something new. Something Kelsier would be proud of.*

Maybe this time I can help.

He saw no motion in either direction, so he slipped onto the street and moved to the north. It felt strange sometimes, slinking quietly along a street that seemed brightly lit. Yet he knew that to others it would be dark, with only diffuse starlight to see by, the mists blocking and obscuring as ever. He brushed through them, barely noticing their presence.

He heard the patrol long before he saw it. How could someone *not* hear that clanking of armor, not feel that clatter of feet on the cobblestones? He froze, standing with his back to the earthen wall bordering the street, watching for the patrol.

They bore a torch—to Spook's enhanced eyes, it was a blazing beacon of near-blinding brilliance. The torch marked them as fools. Its light wouldn't help; just the reverse. The glow reflected off the mists, enveloping the guards in a glowing bubble that ruined their night vision.

Spook stayed where he was, motionless. The patrol clanked forward, moving down the street. They passed within a few feet of him, but didn't notice him standing there. There was something . . . invigorating about being able to watch, feeling at once completely exposed and perfectly unseen. It made him wonder why the new Urteau government even bothered with patrols. Of course, the government's skaa officials would have very little experience with the mists.

As the guard patrol disappeared around a corner— their glaring light receding with them—Spook returned to his task. The Citizen would be meeting with his aides this night, if his schedule held. Spook intended to listen in on that conversation. He moved carefully down the street.

No city could compare with Luthadel in sheer size, but Urteau made a respectable effort. As the hereditary home of the Venture line, it had once been a much more important—and well-maintained—city than it was now.

That decline had begun before the death of the Lord Ruler. The most obvious sign of that was the roadway Spook now walked on. Once, the city had been crisscrossed with canals that had functioned as watery streets. Those canals had gone dry some time ago, leaving the city riddled with deep, dusty troughs that grew muddy when it rained. Rather than filling them in, the people had simply begun to use the empty bottoms as roads.

The street Spook now used had once been a wide waterway capable of accommodating large barges. Ten-foot-high walls rose on either side of the sunken street, and buildings loomed above, built up against the rim of the canal. Nobody had been able to give Spook a definite or consistent answer as to why the canals had emptied—some blamed earthquakes, others blamed droughts. The fact remained, however, that in the hundred years since the canals had lost their water, nobody had found an economical way to refill them.

Spook continued down the street, feeling like he was walking in a deep ravine. Numerous ladders—and the occasional ramp or flight of stairs—led up to the sidewalks and buildings above, but few people ever walked up there. The streetslots—as the city's residents called them—had become normal.

Spook caught the scent of smoke as he walked. He glanced up, and noted a gap in the horizon of buildings. A building on this street had been burned to the ground. The house of a nobleman. Since Spook's sense of smell was as acute as his other senses, it was possible he was smelling smoke from long ago, when buildings had burned during the initial rampages following Straff Venture's death. Yet the scent seemed too strong for that. Too recent.

Spook hurried on. Urteau was dying slowly, decaying, and a lot of the blame could be placed on its ruler, the Citizen. Long ago, Elend had given a speech to the people of Luthadel. It had been the night when the Lord Ruler had died, the night of Kelsier's rebellion. Spook remembered Elend's words well, for he'd warned that if the people founded their new government on hatred and bloodshed, it would consume itself with fear, jealousy, and chaos.

Spook had been in that audience, listening. He now saw that Elend was right. The skaa of Urteau had overthrown their noble rulers, and in a way Spook was proud of them for doing so. He felt a growing fondness for the city, partially because of how devoutly they tried to follow what the Survivor had taught. Yet their rebellion hadn't ceased with the ousting of the nobility. As Elend had predicted, the city had become a place of fear and death.

The question was not *why* it had happened, but how to stop it.

For now, that wasn't Spook's job. He was only supposed to gather information. Only familiarity—gained during weeks spent investigating the city—let him know when he was getting close, for it was frustratingly difficult to keep track of where one was down in the streetslots. At first he had tried to stay out of them, slipping through smaller alleyways above. Unfortunately, the slots networked the entire city, and he'd wasted so much time going up and down that he'd eventually realized that the slots really were the sole viable way of getting around.

Unless one were Mistborn, of course. But Spook couldn't hop from building to building on lines of Allomantic power. He was stuck in the slots. He made the best of it.

He picked a ladder and swung onto it, climbing up. Though he wore leather gloves, he could feel the grain of the wood. Up top, there was a small sidewalk running along the streetslot. An alleyway extended ahead of him, leading into a cluster of houses. A building at the end of the small street was his goal, but he did not move toward it. Instead he waited quietly, searching for the signs he knew were there. Sure enough, he caught a rustling motion in a window a few buildings down. His ears detected the sound of footsteps in another building. The street ahead of him was being watched.

Spook turned away. While the sentries were very careful to watch the alleyway, they unintentionally left another avenue open: their own buildings. Spook crept to the right, moving on feet that could feel each pebble beneath them, listening with ears that could hear someone's increased breathing when they spotted something unusual. He rounded a building, turning away from the watchful eyes, and entered a dead-end alleyway on the other side. There, he lay a hand against the wall of the building.

There were vibrations in the room; it was occupied, so he moved on. The next room alerted him immediately, as he heard whispered voices within. The third room, however, gave him nothing. No vibrations of motion. No whispers. Not even the muted thudding of a heartbeat—which he could sometimes hear if the air was still enough. Taking a deep breath, Spook quietly worked open the window lock and slipped in.

It was a sleeping chamber, empty as he'd anticipated. He'd never come through this particular room before. His heart thumped as he closed the shutters, then slipped across the floor. Despite the near-total darkness, he had no trouble seeing in the room. It barely seemed dim to him.

Outside the room, he found a more familiar hallway. He easily snuck past two rooms where guards watched the street. There was a thrill in doing these infiltrations. Spook was in one of the Citizen's own guardhouses, steps away from large numbers of armed soldiers. They should have taken care to secure their own building better.

He crept up the stairs, making his way to a small, rarely used room on the third floor. He checked for vibrations, then slipped in. The austere chamber was piled with a mound of extra bedrolls and a dusty stack of uniforms. Spook smiled as he moved across the floor, stepping carefully and quietly, his highly sensitive toes able to feel loose, squeaky, or warped boards. He sat down on the windowsill, confident that nobody outside would be able to see well enough to spot him.

The Citizen's house lay a few yards away. Quellion decried ostentation, and had chosen for his headquarters a structure of modest size. It had probably once been a minor nobleman's home, and had only a small yard, which Spook could easily see into from his vantage. The building glowed, light streaking from every crack and window, as if it were filled with some awesome power and on the verge of bursting.

But then, that was merely the way that Spook's overflared tin made him see any building that had lights on inside.

Spook leaned his back against the window's frame, his legs up on the windowsill. The window contained neither glass nor shutters, but there were nail holes in the wood, indicating that there had once been something there. The reason the shutters had been removed didn't matter to Spook—their lack meant that this room was unlikely to be entered at night. Mists had already claimed the room, though they were so faint to Spook's eyes that he had had trouble seeing them.

For a while, nothing happened. The building and grounds below remained silent and still in the night air. Eventually, however, *she* appeared.

Spook perked up, watching the young woman leave the house and enter the garden. She had on a light brown skaa's dress—a garment she somehow wore with striking elegance. Her hair was darker than the dress, but not by much. Spook had seen very few people with her shade of deep auburn hair—at least, few people who had been able to keep it clean of ash and soot.

Everyone in the city knew of Beldre, the Citizen's sister. She was said to be beautiful—and in this case the rumors were true. But nobody had mentioned her sadness. With his tin flared so high, Spook felt like he was standing next to her. He could see her sorrowful eyes, reflecting light from the shining building behind her.

There was a bench in the yard, by a small shrub. It was the lone plant left in the garden; the rest had been torn up and plowed under, leaving behind blackish-brown earth. From what Spook had heard, the Citizen had declared that ornamental gardens were of the nobility. He claimed that such places had only been possible through the sweat of skaa slaves—one more way the nobility had achieved high levels of luxury by creating equally high levels of work for their servants. When the people of Urteau had whitewashed the city's murals and shattered its stained-glass windows, they had also torn up all the ornamental gardens.

Beldre sat down on her bench, hands held motionless in her lap, looking down at the sad shrub. Spook tried to convince himself that she wasn't the reason why he made certain to always sneak in and listen to the Citizen's evening conferences, and he was mostly successful. These were some of the best spying opportunities Spook got. Being able to see Beldre was merely a bonus. Not that he cared *that* much, of course. He didn't even know her.

He thought that as he sat there staring down at her, wishing he had some way to talk to her.

But this wasn't the time for that. Beldre's exile to the garden meant that her brother's meeting was about to start. He always kept her near, but apparently didn't want her hearing state secrets. Unfortunately for him, his window opened toward Spook's vantage point. No normal man—nor an ordinary Tineye or Mistborn—could have heard what was being said inside. But Spook wasn't, by any stretched definition of the word, normal.

I won't be useless anymore, he thought with determination as he listened for words spoken in confidence. They passed through the shutters, crossed the short space, and arrived at his ears.

"All right, Olid. What news?" The voice was familiar to Spook by now: Quellion, the Citizen of Urteau.

"Elend Venture has conquered another city," said a second voice—Olid, the foreign minister.

"Where?" Quellion demanded. "What city?"

"An unimportant one," Olid said. "To the south. Barely five thousand people."

"It makes no sense," said a third voice. "He immediately abandoned the city, taking its populace with him."

"But he got another koloss army somehow," Olid added.

Good, Spook thought. The fourth storage cavern was theirs. Luthadel wouldn't starve for a while yet. That left only two to secure—the one here in Urteau, and the last one, wherever that turned out to be.

"A tyrant needs no real reason for what he does," Quellion said. He was a young man, but not foolish. At times he sounded like other men Spook had known—wise men. The difference was one of extremity.

Or perhaps timing?

"A tyrant conquers for the thrill of control," Quellion continued. "Venture isn't satisfied with the lands he's taken—he never will be. He'll just keep on conquering. Until he comes for us."

The room fell silent.

"He's reportedly sending an ambassador to Urteau," the third voice said. "A member of the Survivor's own crew."

Spook perked up.

Quellion snorted. "One of the liars? Coming here?"

"To offer us a treaty, the rumors say," Olid said.

"So?" Quellion asked. "Why do you mention this, Olid? Do you think we should make a pact with the tyrant?"

"We can't fight him, Quellion," Olid said.

"The Survivor couldn't fight the Lord Ruler," Quellion said. "But he did anyway. He died, but still won, giving the skaa courage to rebel and overthrow the nobility."

"Until that bastard Venture took control," the third voice said.

The room fell silent again.

"We can't give in to Venture," Quellion eventually said. "I will not hand this city to a nobleman, not after what the Survivor did for us. Of all the Final Empire, only Urteau achieved Kelsier's goal of a skaa-ruled nation. Only we burned the homes of the nobility. Only we cleansed our town of them and their society. Only we obeyed. The Survivor will watch over us."

Spook shivered quietly. It felt strange to be hearing men he didn't know speak of Kelsier in such tones. Spook had walked with Kelsier, learned from him. What right did these men have to speak as if they had known the man who had become their Survivor?

The conversation turned to matters more mundane. They discussed new laws that would forbid certain kinds of clothing once favored by the nobility, and then made a decision to give more funding to the genealogical survey committee. They needed to root out any in the city who were hiding noble parentage. Spook took notes so he could pass them on to the others. However, he had trouble keeping his eyes from trailing back down to the young woman in the garden.

What brings her such sorrow? he wondered. A part of him wanted to ask—to be brash, as the Survivor would have been, and hop down to demand of this solemn, solitary woman why she stared at that plant with such melancholy. In fact, he nearly stood up before he caught himself.

He might be unique, he might be powerful, but—as he had to remind himself again—he was no Mistborn. His was the way of silence and stealth.

So he settled back. Content for the moment to watch her, feeling that somehow—despite their distance, despite his ignorance—he understood that feeling in her eyes.

The ash.

I don't think the people really understood how fortunate they were. During the thousand years before the Collapse, they pushed the ash into rivers, piled it up outside cities, and generally let it be. They never understood that without the microbes and plants Rashek had developed to break down the ash particles, the land would quickly have been buried.

Though of course that did eventually happen anyway.

15

THE MISTS BURNED. BRIGHT, FLARING, lit by the red sunlight, they seemed a fire that enveloped her.

Mist during the day was unnatural. But even the night-mists didn't seem to be Vin's anymore. Once, they had shadowed and protected her. Now she found them increasingly alien. When she used Allomancy it seemed that the mists pulled away from her slightly, like a wild beast shying from a bright light.

She stood alone before the camp, which was silent despite the fact that the sun had risen hours ago. Elend had not yet ordered his soldiers inoculated against the mists, so they remained in their tents. Ham argued that exposing them wasn't necessary, but Vin's instinct said that Elend would stick to his plan. They needed to be immune.

Why? Vin thought, looking up through the sunlit mists. *Why have you changed? What is different?* The mists danced around her, moving in their usual, strange pattern of shifting streams and swirls. Then it seemed to Vin that they began to move more rapidly. Quivering. Vibrating.

The sun's heat grew, and the mists finally retreated, vanishing like water evaporating from a warming pan. The sunlight hit her in a wave, and Vin turned, watching the mists go, their death an echoing scream.

They're not natural, Vin thought as guards called the all clear. The camp immediately began to shift and move, men striding from tents, going about the morning's activity with urgency. Vin stood at the head of the camp, dirt road beneath her feet, motionless canal to her right. Both seemed more real now that the mists were gone.

She had asked Sazed and Elend their opinions of the mists—whether they were natural or . . . something else. And both men, like the scholars they were, had quoted theories to support *both* sides of the argument. Sazed at least had eventually made a decision—he'd come down on the side of the mists being natural.

Even the way that the mists choke some people, leaving others alive, could be explained, Lady Vin, he had said. *After all, insect stings kill some people while barely bothering others.*

Vin wasn't that interested in theories and arguments. She had spent most of her life thinking of the mists like any other weather pattern. Reen and the other thieves had mostly scoffed at tales that made the mists out to be supernatural. Yet as Vin had become an Allomancer, she had grown to know the mists. She *felt* them, a sense that seemed to have grown more potent on the day she'd touched the power of the Well of Ascension.

They disappeared too quickly. When they burned away in the sunlight, they withdrew like a person fleeing for safety. Like a man who used all of his strength fighting, then finally gave up to retreat. And the way they didn't appear indoors—it was as if they understood that they were excluded, unwelcome.

Vin glanced back toward the sun, a scarlet ember glowing behind the dark haze of the upper atmosphere. She wished TenSoon were there, so she could talk to him about her worries. She missed the kandra a great deal, more than she'd ever assumed that she would. His frankness had been a good match to her own. She still didn't know what had happened to him after he'd returned to his people; she'd tried to find another kandra to deliver a message for her, but the creatures had become scarce lately.

She sighed and turned, walking quietly back into camp.

It was impressive how quickly the men managed to get the army moving. The mornings sequestered in their tents were spent caring for armor and weapons, the cooks preparing what they could. By the time Vin had crossed a short distance, cooking fires had burst alight, and tents began to collapse, soldiers working quickly to prepare for departure.

As she passed, some of the men saluted. Others bowed their heads in reverence. Still others glanced away, looking uncertain. Vin didn't blame them. Even *she* wasn't sure what her place was in the army. As Elend's wife, she was technically their empress, though she wore no royal garb. To many she was a religious figure, the Heir of the Survivor. She didn't really want that title either.

She found Elend and Ham conversing outside the imperial tent, which was in an early stage of disassembly. Though they stood out in the open, their mannerisms completely nonchalant, Vin was immediately struck by how far the two men were standing from the workers, as if Elend and Ham didn't want the men to hear. Burning tin, she could make out what they were saying long before she reached them.

"Ham," Elend said quietly, "you know I'm right. We can't keep doing this. The farther we penetrate into the Western Dominance, the more daylight we'll lose to the mists."

Ham shook his head. "You'd really stand by and watch your own soldiers die, El?"

Elend's face grew hard, and he met Vin's eyes as she joined them. "We can't afford to wait out the mists every morning."

"Even if it saves lives?" Ham asked.

"Slowing down *costs* lives," Elend said. "Each hour brings the mists closer to the Central Dominance. We're planning to be at siege for some time, Ham—meaning we need to get to Fadrex as soon as possible."

Ham glanced at Vin, looking for support. She shook her head. "I'm sorry, Ham. Elend is right. We can't have our entire army dependent upon the whims of the mists. We'd be exposed—if someone attacked us in the morning, our men would have to either respond and get struck down by the mists, or hide in their tents and wait."

Ham frowned, then excused himself, tromping through the fallen ash to help a group of soldiers pack away their tents. Vin stepped up beside Elend, watching the large soldier go.

"Kelsier was wrong about him," she said.

"Who?" Elend asked. "Ham?"

"After Kelsier died," Vin said, "we found a last note from him. He said that he'd chosen the members of the crew as leaders in his new government. Breeze to be an ambassador, Dockson to be a bureaucrat, and Ham to be a general. The other two fit their roles perfectly, but Ham . . ."

"He gets too involved," Elend said. "He has to know each man he commands personally or it makes him uncomfortable. And when he knows them all that well, he grows attached."

Vin nodded, watching Ham begin to laugh and work with the soldiers.

"Listen to us," Elend said, "callously talking about the lives of those who follow us. Perhaps it would be better to grow attached, like Ham. Maybe then I wouldn't be so quick to order people to their deaths."

Vin glanced at Elend, concerned at the bitterness in his voice. He smiled, trying to cover it up, then glanced away. "You need to do something with that koloss of yours. He's been poking around the camp, scaring the men."

She frowned. As soon as she thought of the creature, she became aware of where it was—near the edge of the camp.

It was always under her command, but she could only take direct, full control of it when she concentrated. Otherwise it would follow her general orders—staying in the area, not killing anything.

"I should go make sure the barges are ready to move," Elend said. He glanced at her, and when she didn't indicate that she'd go with him, he gave her a quick kiss, then departed.

Vin moved through the camp once more. Most of the tents were down and stowed, and the soldiers were making quick work of their food. She passed out of the perimeter, and found Human sitting quietly, ash starting to drift against him. He watched the camp with red eyes, his face broken by the ripped skin that hung from his right eye down to the corner of his mouth.

"Human," she said, folding her arms.

He looked over at her, then stood, ash falling from his eleven-foot, overly muscled blue frame. Even with the number of creatures she'd killed, even knowing she controlled this one completely, Vin had a moment of reflexive fear as she stood before the massive beast with its tightly stretched skin and bleeding rips.

"Why did you come to camp?" she said, shaking off her panic.

"I am human," he said with his slow, deliberate tone.

"You're koloss," she said. "You know that."

"I should have a house," Human said. "Like those."

"Those are tents, not houses," Vin said. "You can't come to camp this way. You have to stay with the other koloss."

Human turned, glancing toward the south, where the koloss army waited, separate from the humans. They remained under Elend's control, twenty thousand in number, now that they'd picked up the ten thousand that had been waiting with the main bulk of the army. It made sense to leave them to Elend, due to his raw Allomantic power.

Human looked back at Vin. "Why?"

"Why do you have to stay with the others?" Vin asked. "Because you make the people in the camp uncomfortable."

"Then they should attack me," Human said.

"That's why you're not a human," Vin said. "We don't attack people merely because they make us uncomfortable."

"No," Human said. "You make *us* kill them instead."

Vin paused, cocking her head. Human looked away, staring at the human camp again. His beady red eyes made his face hard to read, but Vin almost sensed a . . . longing in his expression.

"You're one of us," Human said.

Vin looked up. "Me?"

"You're like us," he said. "Not like them."

"Why do you say that?" Vin asked.

Human looked down at her. "Mist," he said.

Vin felt a momentary chill, though she had no real idea why. "What do you mean?"

Human didn't respond.

"Human," she said, trying another tactic. "What do you think of the mists?"

"They come at night."

"Yes, but what do you think of them. Your people. Do they fear the mists? Does it ever kill them?"

"Swords kill," Human said. "Rain doesn't kill. Ash doesn't kill. Mist doesn't kill."

Fairly good logic, Vin thought. *A year ago I would have agreed with it.* She was about to give up on the line of reasoning, but Human continued.

"I hate it," he said.

Vin raised an eyebrow.

"I hate it because it hates me," Human said. "*You* feel it."

"Yes," Vin said, surprising herself. "I do."

Human regarded her, a line of blood trailing out of the ripped skin near his eye, running stark down his blue skin, mixing with flakes of ash. Finally he nodded, as if giving approval to her honest reply.

Vin shivered. *The mist isn't alive,* she thought. *It can't hate me. I'm imagining things.*

But . . . once, years ago, she had drawn upon the mists. When fighting the Lord Ruler, she had somehow gained a power over them. It had been like she'd used the mist itself to fuel her Allomancy instead of metals. It was only with that power that she'd been able to defeat the Lord Ruler.

That had been more than two years ago, and she'd never been able to replicate the event. She'd tried time and again, and after so many failures she was beginning to think she must have been mistaken. Certainly in more recent times, the mist was unfriendly. She kept telling herself there was nothing supernatural about it, but she knew that wasn't true. What of the mist spirit, the thing that had tried to kill Elend—and then had saved him by showing her how to make him into an Allomancer? It was real, of that she was certain, even if she hadn't seen it since.

What of the hesitance she felt toward the mists, and how they pulled away from her? The way they stayed out of buildings, the way they killed. It all pointed to what Human had said. The mists—the Deepness—hated her. Finally she acknowledged what she had been resisting for so long.

The mists were her enemy.

*They are called Allomantic savants. Men or women who flare
their metals so long, and so hard, that the constant influx of Allomantic power transforms their very physiology.*

*In most cases, with most metals, the effects of this are slight.
Seekers, for instance, often become bronze savants without
knowing it. Their range is simply expanded from burning the
metal so long. Becoming a pewter savant is dangerous, as it requires pushing the body so hard in a state where one cannot feel
exhaustion or pain. Most accidentally kill themselves before the
process is complete, and in my opinion the benefit isn't worth the
effort.*

*Tin savants, however . . . they are something special. En-
dowed with senses beyond what any normal Allomancer would
need or want, they become slaves to what they touch, hear, see,
smell, and taste. Yet the abnormal power of these senses gives
them a distinct and interesting advantage.*

*One could argue that, like an Inquisitor who has been trans-
formed by a Hemalurgic spike, the Allomantic savant is no longer human.*

16

SPOOK AWOKE TO DARKNESS.

That was happening less and less frequently lately. He
could feel the blindfold on his face, tied tightly across his
eyes and over his ears. It dug into his overly sensitive skin,
but it was far better than the alternative, with starlight as
bright as the sun and footsteps in the hallway as loud as

thunderclaps. Even with the thick cloth, his ears plugged with wax, and the shutters drawn tight and hung with a cloth, it was sometimes hard for him to sleep.

The muffling was dangerous. It left him vulnerable. Yet lack of sleep would be more dangerous. Perhaps what he'd done to his body by burning tin would kill him. But the more time he spent among the people of Urteau, the more he felt they were going to need his help to survive the dangers that were coming. He needed an edge. He worried that he'd made the wrong decision, but at least he'd made a decision. He would continue as he had, and hope that it was enough.

He groaned quietly, sitting up, taking off the cloth and pulling the wax from his ears. The room was dark, but the faint light creeping through the shutters—their gaps stuffed with cloth—was enough for him to see by.

Tin flared comfortably in his stomach. His reserve was nearly gone, burned away during the night. His body now used it as instinctively as it drew breath or blinked. He had heard that Thugs could burn pewter to heal themselves even while unconscious. The body understood what it needed.

He reached into a pail beside his bed, pulling out a small handful of tin dust. He'd brought a lot with him from Luthadel, and augmented this by buying more through the underground. Fortunately, tin was relatively cheap. He dumped his handful into a mug on his nightstand, then moved to the door. The room was small and cramped, but he didn't have to share it with anyone. That made it lavish by skaa standards.

He squeezed his eyes shut, then pulled open the door. The intense luminosity of a sunlit hallway crashed against him, and he felt about on the ground, his teeth gritted. He found the jug of fresh water—drawn from the well for him by the inn's servants—and pulled it inside, then shut the door.

He blinked, walking across the room to fill his mug and wash down the tin. It would be enough for the entire day.

He took an extra handful and stuffed it into a pouch, just in case.

A few minutes later he was dressed and ready. He sat down on the bed and closed his eyes, preparing for the day. If the Citizen's spies were to be believed, other members of Elend's team were on their way to Urteau. They were probably under orders to secure the storage cache and quell the rebellion; Spook would need to learn as much as he could before they arrived.

He went over plans, thinking to himself. He could feel feet thumping in the rooms around him—the wooden structure seemed to shake and tremble like some enormous hive filled with bustling workers. Outside he could hear voices calling, yelling, speaking. Bells rang faintly. It was early yet, barely past noon, but the mists would be gone—Urteau got six or seven hours of mistless daylight, making it a place where crops could still grow and man could still thrive.

Normally Spook would have slept through the hours of daylight. But there were things he needed to do. He opened his eyes, then reached to his nightstand and picked up a pair of spectacles. They had been specially crafted at his request to hold lenses that made no corrections to his vision—they were filled with ordinary glass.

He put these on, then retied the cloth around his head, covering the front and sides of the lenses. Even with his heightened senses, he couldn't see through his own eyelids. But with the spectacles on, he could open his eyes and wear the cloth at the same time. He felt his way to the window, then pulled off the blanket and threw open the shutters.

Hot—nearly burning—sunlight bathed him. The cloth bit into the skin of his head. But he could see. The cloth blocked just enough light to keep him from being blinded, yet was translucent enough to allow vision. It was like the mists, in fact—the cloth was nearly invisible to him, for his eyes were enhanced beyond the point of reason. His mind filtered out the cloth's interference.

Spook nodded to himself, then picked up his dueling cane and made his way from the room.

"I know you're a quiet one," Durn said, rapping softly on the ground in front of him with a pair of sticks. "But you have to admit that this is better than living under the lords."

Spook sat in a streetslot, head slightly bowed, back to the stone wall that had sustained the canal, buildings looming like fortress walls above. Marketpit was the widest of the streetslots of Urteau. Once it had been a waterway so broad that three boats abreast could moor in its center while leaving room on both sides for the passage of others in either direction. Now it had become a central boulevard for the city, which also made it a prime location for tradesmen and beggars.

Beggars such as Spook and Durn. Few people passing paid any attention to the ragged men. Nobody paused to notice that one of them seemed to be watching the crowd carefully, despite the dark cloth over his eyes, while the other spoke far too articulately to have been educated in the gutter.

Spook didn't respond to Durn's question. In his youth, the way he talked—with a thick accent, language littered with slang—had marked him, made people dismiss him. Even now, he didn't have a glib tongue or charming manner like Kelsier's. So instead Spook tried to say as little as possible. Less chance of getting into trouble that way.

Oddly, instead of finding him easier to dismiss when he didn't talk, it seemed that people paid more attention to him. Durn continued to pound out his rhythm, a street performer with no audience. It was too soft against the earthen floor for anyone who wasn't Spook to hear.

Durn's rhythm was perfect. Any minstrel would have envied him.

"I mean, look at the market," Durn continued. "Under the Lord Ruler, most skaa could never engage openly in commerce. We have something beautiful here. Skaa ruling skaa. We're happy."

Spook could see the market. It seemed to him that if the people were truly happy, they'd wear smiles rather than walk with downcast eyes. They'd be shopping and browsing rather than quickly picking out what they wanted, then moving on. Plus, if the city were the utopia it was supposed to be, there wouldn't be a need for the dozens of soldiers who watched the crowd. Spook shook his head. Everybody wore nearly the same clothing—colors and styles dictated by the Citizen's orders. Even begging was heavily regulated. Men would soon arrive to count Spook's offerings, tally how much he had earned, then take the Citizen's cut.

"Look," Durn said, "do you see anyone being beaten or killed on the street? Surely that's worth a few strictures."

"The deaths happen in quiet alleys now," Spook said softly. "At least the Lord Ruler killed us openly."

Durn frowned, sitting back, thumping the ground with his sticks. It was a complex pattern. Spook could feel the vibrations through the ground, and found them soothing. Did the people know the talent they passed, quietly beating the ground they walked upon? Durn could have been a master musician. Unfortunately, under the Lord Ruler, skaa didn't play music. And under the Citizen . . . well, it generally wasn't good to draw attention to yourself, no matter the method.

"There it is," Durn said suddenly. "As promised."

Spook glanced up. Through the mutters, sounds, flashes of color, and powerful scents of refuse, people, and goods for sale, Spook saw a group of prisoners being escorted by soldiers in brown.

Sometimes the flood of sensation was almost overwhelming. As he'd once told Vin, burning tin wasn't about what one could sense, but about what one could ignore. He had learned very well to focus on the senses he needed, shunting aside that which would distract.

The marketgoers made way for the soldiers and their prisoners. The people bowed their heads, watching solemnly.

"You still want to follow?" Durn asked.

Spook stood.

Durn stood as well and grabbed Spook by the shoulder. He knew that Spook could really see, but they both maintained the act. It was common among beggars to adopt a guise of being afflicted in an attempt to elicit more coins. Durn walked with a masterful false limp, and had his hair pulled out in sickly-appearing patches. But Spook could smell soap on the man's skin and fine wine on his breath. He was a thief lord; there were few more powerful in the city. Yet he was clever enough with his disguises that he could walk about on the streets unnoticed.

They weren't the only ones following the soldiers and their prisoners. Skaa wearing the approved grey trailed the group like ghosts—a quiet, shuffling mass in the falling ash. The soldiers walked to a ramp leading out of the streetslots, guiding the people into a wealthier section of the town, where some of the canals had been filled in and cobbled.

Soon the dead spots began to appear. Charred scars—ruins that had once been homes. The smell of smoke was almost overpowering to Spook, and he had to start breathing through his mouth.

They didn't have to walk far before arriving at their destination. The Citizen was in attendance. He rode no horse—those had all been shipped to the farms, for only crass noblemen were too good to walk the ground on their own feet. He did, however, wear red.

"What's that he's wearing?" Spook whispered as Durn led him around the edge of the crowd. The Citizen and his retinue stood on the steps of a grand mansion, and the skaa were clustering around. Durn led Spook to a place where a group of toughs had muscled themselves an exclusive piece of the street with a good vantage of the Citizen. They nodded to Durn, letting him pass without comment.

"What do you mean?" Durn asked. "The Citizen is wearing what he always does—skaa trousers and a work shirt."

"They're red," Spook whispered. "That's not an approved color."

"As of this morning it is. Government officers can wear it. That way they stand out, and people in need can find them. Or at least that's the official explanation."

Spook frowned. Then something else caught his attention. She was there.

It was only natural—she accompanied her brother wherever he went. He worried for her safety, seldom letting her out of his sight. She wore the same look as always, eyes sorrowful within a frame of auburn hair.

"Sad group today," Durn said, and at first Spook thought he was referring to Beldre. But Durn was nodding toward the group of prisoners. They looked like the rest of the people in the city—grey clothing, ash-stained faces, subservient postures. The Citizen stepped forward to explain the differences.

"One of the first proclamations this government made," he announced, "was one of solidarity. We are a skaa people. The 'noblemen' chosen by the Lord Ruler oppressed us for ten centuries. Urteau, we decided, would become a place of freedom. A place like the Survivor prophesied would come."

"You've got the number?" Durn whispered to Spook.

Spook nodded. "Ten," he said, counting the prisoners. "The ones we expected. You're not earning your coin, Durn."

"Watch."

"These," the Citizen said, bald scalp shining in the red sunlight as he pointed at the prisoners. "These didn't heed our warning. They knew, as do all of you, that any nobleman who stayed in this city would forfeit his life! This is our will—*all* of our will.

"Like all of their kind, these were too arrogant to listen. They tried to hide. But they think themselves above us; they always will. That exposes them."

He paused, then spoke again. "And that is why we do what we must."

He waved his soldiers forward. They shoved the prisoners up the steps. Spook could smell the oil on the air as the soldiers opened the house's door and pushed the people in. Then the soldiers barred the door from the outside and took up a perimeter. Each soldier lit a torch and threw it on the building. It didn't take superhuman senses to feel the heat that soon blazed to life, and the crowd shied away—revolted and frightened, but fascinated.

The windows had been boarded shut. Spook could see fingers trying to pry the wood free, could hear people screaming. He could hear them thumping against the locked door, trying to break their way out, crying in terror.

He longed to do something. Yet tin Allomancy gave him no power to fight an entire squad of soldiers on his own. Elend and Vin had sent him to gather information, not play their hand. Still he cringed, calling himself a coward as he turned from the burning building.

"This should not be," Spook whispered harshly.

"They were noblemen," Durn said.

"No they weren't! Their parents might have been, but these were skaa. Normal people, Durn."

"They have noble blood."

"So do we all, if you look back far enough," Spook said.

Durn shook his head. "It's the way it must be. This is the Survivor—"

"Do *not* speak his name in association with this barbarity," Spook hissed.

Durn was quiet for a moment, the only sounds those of the flames and the people they burned to death. Finally he spoke. "I know it's hard to see, and perhaps the Citizen is too eager. But . . . I heard *him* speak once. The Survivor. This is the sort of thing he taught. Death to the noblemen; rule by the skaa. If you'd heard him, you'd understand. Sometimes you have to destroy in order to build something better."

Spook closed his eyes. Heat from the fire seemed to be searing his skin. He *had* heard Kelsier speak to crowds of skaa. And Kelsier had said the things that Durn now referred to. At that time, the Survivor had been a voice of hope, of spirit. His same words repeated now, however, became tools of hatred and destruction. Spook felt sick.

"Again, Durn," he said, looking up, feeling particularly harsh, "I don't pay you to spout Citizen propaganda at me. Tell me why I'm here, or you'll get no further coin from me."

The large beggar turned, meeting Spook's eyes behind the cloth. "Count the skulls," he said quietly. With that, Durn took his hand off Spook's shoulder and retreated into the crowd.

Spook didn't follow. The scents of smoke and burning flesh were growing too powerful for him. He turned, pushing his way through the crowd, seeking fresh air. He stumbled up against a building and breathed deeply, his ribs brushing the rough grain of its wood. It seemed that the falling flakes of ash were a part of the pyre behind, bits of death cast upon the wind.

He heard voices. Spook turned, noting that the Citizen and his guards had moved away from the fire. Quellion was addressing the crowd, encouraging them to be vigilant. Spook watched for a time, and finally the crowd began to leave, trailing the Citizen toward Marketpit.

He's punished them. Now he needs to bless them. Often, especially after executions, the Citizen visited the people personally, moving between stalls in the market, shaking hands and giving encouragement.

Spook took off down a side street. He soon passed out of the wealthier section of town, arriving at a place where the street fell away before him—the retaining wall had collapsed, forming a slope into the dry canal. He hopped down, skidding his way to the bottom. He pulled up the hood of his cloak, obscuring his covered eyes, and made his way through the busy thoroughfare with the dexterity of one who had grown up a street urchin.

Despite taking a roundabout route, he arrived at Marketpit before the Citizen and his retinue. Spook watched through the shower of ash as the man moved down a broad ramp of earth, trailed by a following that numbered in the hundreds.

You want to be him, Spook thought, crouching beside a merchant's stall. *Kelsier died to bring this people hope, and now you think to steal his legacy.*

This man was no Kelsier. This man was not worthy to utter the Survivor's name.

The Citizen moved about, maintaining a paternal air, speaking to the people of the market. He touched them on the shoulders, shook hands, and smiled benevolently. "The Survivor would be proud of you." Spook could hear his voice over the noise of the crowd. "The ash that falls is a sign from him—it represents the fall of the empire, the ashes of tyranny. From those ashes we will make a new nation! One ruled by skaa."

Spook edged forward, pulling down his hood and feeling before him with his hands, as if he were blind. He carried his dueling cane across his back, in a strap obscured by the folds of his baggy grey shirt.

He was more than capable when it came to moving through crowds. While Vin had always worked hard to remain obscure and unseen, Spook had managed to achieve both things without ever trying. In fact, he'd often tried the opposite. He'd dreamed of being a man like Kelsier—for even before he'd met the Survivor, Spook had heard stories of him. The greatest skaa thief of their time, bold enough to try to rob the Lord Ruler.

But try as he might, Spook had never been able to distinguish himself. It was too easy to ignore yet another ash-faced boy, especially if you couldn't understand his thick Eastern slang. It had taken actually meeting Kelsier—seeing how he could move people with his words—to convince Spook to abandon his dialect. That was when Spook had begun to understand that there was a power in words.

Spook subtly moved his way toward the front of the crowd watching the Citizen. He was jostled and shoved, but nobody cried out against him. A blind man who had gotten caught up in the press of people was easy to ignore—and what was ignored could get where it wasn't supposed to. With some careful positioning, Spook soon placed himself at the front of the group, barely an arm's length from the Citizen.

The man smelled of smoke.

"I understand, good woman," the Citizen was saying as he held an elderly woman's hands. "But your grandson is needed where he is, in the fields. Without him and his kind, we would not be able to eat! A nation ruled by skaa also has to be one *worked* by skaa."

"But . . . can't he come back, even for a bit?" the woman asked.

"In time, good woman," the Citizen said. "In time." His crimson uniform made him the only splash of color on the street, and Spook found himself staring. He tore his eyes away and continued to maneuver, for the Citizen was not his goal.

Beldre stood to the side, as usual. Always watching, but never interacting. The Citizen was so dynamic that his sister was easily forgotten. Spook understood that feeling well. He let a soldier jostle him, pushing him out of the Citizen's way. That jostle placed Spook right next to Beldre. She smelled faintly of perfume.

I thought that was supposed to be forbidden.

What would Kelsier have done? He'd have attacked, perhaps killing the Citizen. Or he'd have countered the man in another way. Kelsier wouldn't have let such terrible things happen—he'd have acted.

Perhaps he would have tried to make an ally out of someone trusted by the Citizen?

Spook felt his heart—always so much louder to him now—beat faster. The crowd began to move once more, and he let himself get shoved up against Beldre. The guards weren't watching—they were focused on the Citizen, keeping him safe with so many random elements around.

"Your brother," Spook whispered in her ear, "you approve of his murders?"

She spun, and he noticed for the first time that her eyes

were green. He let the crowd shove him away as she searched, trying to figure out who had spoken. The crowd, following her brother, carried her from Spook.

Spook waited, being jostled in the sea of elbows for a short time. Then he began to maneuver, pushing through the people with subtle care until he was back beside Beldre.

"You think this is any different from what the Lord Ruler did?" he whispered. "I once saw him gather up random people and execute them in the Luthadel city square."

She spun again, finally identifying Spook among the moving crowd. He stood still, meeting her eyes despite the blindfold. People flowed between them, and she was carried away.

Her mouth moved. Only someone with the enhanced senses of tin could have seen with enough detail to make out the words on her lips.

"Who are you?"

He pushed his way through the crowd one more time. The Citizen was apparently planning to make a big speech ahead, capitalizing on the increasingly large crowd. People were bunching up around the podium that stood in the middle of the market; it was getting more difficult to pass through them.

Spook reached her, but felt the crowd pulling him away. So he stretched between a pair of bodies and grabbed her hand, tugging her wrist as he moved with the surges of the crowd's motion. She spun, but she didn't cry out. The people thronged around them, and she turned to meet his blindfolded eyes.

"Who are you?" Beldre repeated. Though he was close enough to have heard her had she spoken, no sound escaped her lips. She just mouthed the words. Behind her, on the podium, her brother began to preach.

"I'm the man who will kill your brother," Spook said softly.

He had expected a reaction from her—a shout perhaps. An accusation. His actions here had been impulsive, born from his frustration at not being able to help the people who were executed. If she *did* cry out, he realized, it could bring his death.

Yet she remained silent, flakes of ash falling between them.

"Others have said that same thing," she mouthed.

"Others were not me."

"And who are you?" she asked a third time.

"The companion of a god. A man who can see whispers and feel screams."

"A man who thinks he knows better for this people than their own chosen ruler?" she mouthed. "There will always be dissenters who balk at what must be done."

He still had her hand. He gripped it tightly, pulling her close. The crowd thronged the podium, leaving her and Spook at their rear, shells left on a beach by the retreating waves.

"I *knew* the Survivor, Beldre," he whispered harshly. "He named me, called me friend. What you've done in this city would horrify him—and I'm *not* going to let your brother continue to pervert Kelsier's legacy. Bring him warning, if you must. Tell Quellion that I'm coming for him."

The Citizen had stopped speaking. Spook glanced toward the lectern. Quellion stood upon it, looking out over his crowd of followers. Right at Spook and Beldre, standing together at the rear of the crowd. Spook hadn't realized how exposed they had become.

"You there!" the Citizen cried. "What are you doing with my sister!"

Damn! Spook thought, releasing the woman and dashing away. But the streetslots' high, steep walls meant there were few ways out of the market, and those were all being watched by members of Quellion's security forces. At the Citizen's shouted command, soldiers began to dash forward from their posts, wearing leather and carrying steel.

Fine, Spook thought, charging the nearest group of soldiers. If he could get through them, he could reach a ramp upward, perhaps disappear into the alleys between buildings above.

Swords scraped from scabbards. Behind Spook, people cried out in shock. He reached into the ragged folds of his cloak and whipped forth his dueling cane.

And then he was among them.

Spook wasn't a warrior, not really. He'd trained with Ham; Clubs had insisted that his nephew know how to defend himself. But the crew's true warriors had always been their Mistborn, Vin and Kelsier, with Ham—as a Pewterarm—providing brute force if necessary.

Yet Spook had spent a lot of time training lately, and had discovered something interesting. He had something Vin and Kelsier could never have had: a blurring array of sensory knowledge that his body could instinctively use. He could feel disturbances in the air and tremors in the floor, could know where people were simply by how close their heartbeats sounded.

He was no Mistborn, but he was still very dangerous. He felt a soft wind, and knew a sword was swinging for him. He ducked. He felt a footstep on the ground, and knew someone was attacking from the side. He stepped away. It was almost like having atium.

Sweat flew from his brow as he spun, and he cracked his dueling cane into the crown of one soldier's head. The man fell; Spook's weapon was crafted of the finest hardwood. To be certain, he swung the butt of the cane down on the man's temple, knocking him out of the battle for good.

He heard someone grunt next to him—soft, yet telling. Spook whipped his weapon to the side and smacked it against the attacking soldier's forearm. The bones broke, and the soldier cried out, dropping his weapon. Spook rapped him on the head. Then Spook spun, lifting his cane to block the third soldier's strike.

Steel met wood, and the steel won, Spook's weapon breaking. But it stopped the sword strike long enough for Spook to duck away and grab a fallen warrior's sword. It was different from the swords he'd practiced with; the men of Urteau preferred long, thin blades. Still, Spook only had one soldier left. If he could cut the man down, he'd be free.

Spook's opponent seemed to realize that he had the advantage. If Spook ran, it would expose his back. But if Spook stayed, he'd soon be overwhelmed. The soldier circled warily, trying to stall for time.

So Spook attacked. He raised his blade, trusting in his enhanced senses to compensate for the difference in training. The soldier raised his weapon to parry as Spook swung.

Spook's sword froze in the air.

He stumbled, trying to force the weapon forward, but it was strangely held in place—as if he were trying to push it through something solid rather than air. It was as if . . .

Someone was Pushing against it. Allomancy. Spook glanced desperately around him, and immediately found the source of the power. The person Pushing had to be directly opposite Spook, for Allomancers could only Push away from themselves.

Quellion, the Citizen, had joined his sister. The Citizen met Spook's gaze, and Spook could see effort in the man's eyes as he clutched his sister, using her weight for support as he Pushed Spook's sword, interfering in the battle as Kelsier once had long ago, when visiting the caverns where his army trained.

Spook dropped the weapon, letting it fly backward out of his hands, then threw himself down. He felt the draft of an enemy sword swinging overhead, narrowly missing him. His own weapon clanged to the ground a short distance from him, its ringing loud in his ears.

He didn't have time to gather his breath; he could only push himself up to dodge the soldier's follow-up blow. Fortunately, Spook wasn't wearing any metal that Quellion could Push against to influence the fight any further. That was a habit that Spook was glad he'd never lost.

The only choice was to run. He couldn't fight, not with an Allomancer interfering. He turned while the soldier prepared another swing. Then Spook threw himself forward, getting within the soldier's guard. He ducked under the man's arm and dashed to the side, hoping to run past and leave the soldier confused.

Something caught his foot.

Spook spun. At first he assumed Quellion was Pulling on him somehow. Then he saw that the soldier on the ground—the first one he'd felled—had grabbed his foot.

I hit that man in the head twice! Spook thought with frustration. *There's no way he's still conscious!*

The hand squeezed his foot, yanking Spook with an inhuman strength. The man had to be a Thug like Ham.

Spook was in serious trouble.

He kicked, managing to break free, then stumbled to his feet. But a Thug could use the power of pewter to run faster and farther than Spook.

Two Allomancers, counting the Citizen himself, Spook thought. *Somebody isn't as disdainful of noble blood as he claims!*

The two soldiers advanced on him. Yelling in frustration—hearing his own heart thump like a pounding drum—Spook threw himself at the Thug and grappled the man, taking him by surprise. In that moment of confusion, Spook spun him around, using the Thug's body as a shield to protect himself from the third soldier.

He hadn't counted on the Citizen's brutal training. Quellion always spoke of sacrifice and necessity. Apparently this philosophy extended to his soldiers, for the man with the sword rammed his weapon straight through his friend's back, piercing his heart and driving the weapon directly into Spook's chest. It was a move only a man with the strength and precision of a Thug could have performed.

Three Allomancers, Spook thought, dazed, as the soldier tried to pull his sword free from two bodies. The body of the dead man was a weight that snapped the blade.

How did I survive this long? They must have been trying

*not to reveal their powers. Trying to remain hidden from
the population . . .*

Spook stumbled backward, blood on his chest. Oddly, he
didn't feel pain. His heightened senses should have made
the pain so powerful that—

It hit. Everything went black.

*The subtlety displayed in the ash-eating microbes and enhanced
plants shows that Rashek got better and better at using the power.
It burned out in a matter of minutes—but to a god, minutes can
pass like hours. During that time, Rashek began as an ignorant
child who shoved a planet too close to the sun, grew into an adult
who could create Ashmounts to cool the air, then finally became
a mature artisan who could develop plants and creatures for specific purposes.*

*It also shows his mindset during his time with Preservation's
power. Under its influence he was clearly in a protective mode.
Instead of leveling the Ashmounts and trying to push the planet
back into place, he was reactive, working furiously to fix problems that he himself had caused.*

17

ELEND RODE AT THE FRONT of his men, astride a brilliant white stallion that had been scrubbed clean of ash. He
turned his mount, surveying the ranks of nervous soldiers.
They waited in the evening light, and Elend could see their
terror. They had heard rumors, then had those rumors

confirmed by Elend the day before. Today, his army would become immunized to the mists.

Elend rode through their ranks, General Demoux astride a roan stallion next to him. Both horses were big destriers, brought on the trip more to impress than for usefulness. Elend and the other officers would spend most of the trip in canal boats rather than on horseback.

He didn't worry about the morality of his decision to expose his forces to the mists—or at least he didn't worry about it at that moment. Elend had learned something very important about himself: He was honest. Perhaps too honest. If he was uncertain, it would show in his face. The soldiers would sense his hesitation. So he'd learned to confine his worries and concerns to when he was alone with those closest to him. That meant Vin saw too much of his brooding, but it left him free at other times to project confidence.

He moved quickly, letting his horse's hooves beat a thunder for the men to hear. Occasionally he heard captains call out for their men to be firm. Even so, Elend saw the anxiety in his soldiers' eyes. And could he blame them? This day, the men would face an enemy that they could not fight, could not resist. Within the hour, seven hundred of them would lie dead. About one in fifty. Not bad odds, on a grand scale—but that meant little to a man feeling the mist creep around him.

The men stood their ground. Elend was proud of them. He had given those who wished it the opportunity to return to Luthadel instead of facing the mists; he still needed troops in the capital. Almost none had left. The vast majority had instead lined up in ranks without having to be ordered, wearing full battle gear, armor polished and oiled, uniforms as clean as possible in the ash-stained wilderness. It felt right to Elend for them to be in their armor. It made them seem they were going to battle—and in a way they were.

They trusted him. They knew that the mists were advancing toward Luthadel, and understood the importance of capturing the cities with storage caverns. They believed in Elend's ability to do something to save their families.

Their trust made him more determined. He reined in his horse, turning the massive beast beside a rank of soldiers. He flared pewter, giving his body more strength and his lungs more power, then Rioted the emotions of the men to make them braver.

"Be strong!" he shouted

Heads turned toward him, and the clanking of armor hushed. His own voice was so loud in his ears that he had to dampen his tin. "These mists will strike some of us down. Most of us will be untouched—and most who fall will recover! Then none of us need fear the mists again. And we need not risk a morning attack from Fadrex City as we hide in our tents, the mists spilling in and a sixth of our men shaking on the ground!"

He turned his horse, Demoux following behind, and moved along the ranks. "I do not know why the mists kill. But I trust in the Survivor! He named himself Lord of the Mists. If some of us die, then it is his will. Keep the faith!"

His reminders seemed to have some effect. The soldiers stood a little straighter, facing west toward where the sun would soon set. Elend reined in again, sitting tall and letting himself be seen.

"They look strong, my lord," Demoux said quietly, moving his horse up beside Elend's. "It was a good speech."

Elend nodded.

"My lord . . ." Demoux said, "did you mean what you said about the Survivor?"

"Of course I did."

"I'm sorry, my lord," Demoux said. "I didn't mean to question your faith, it's just that . . . well, you don't have to keep up the charade of belief, if you don't want to."

"I gave my word, Demoux," Elend said, frowning and glancing at the scarred general. "I do what I say."

"I believe you, my lord," Demoux said. "You are an honorable man."

"But?"

"But . . . if you don't really believe in the Survivor, I don't think he would want you speaking in his name."

Elend opened his mouth to reprimand Demoux for his lack of respect, but stopped himself. The man spoke with honesty, from his heart. That wasn't the kind of thing to punish.

Besides, he might have had a point. "I don't know what I believe, Demoux," Elend said, looking back at the field of soldiers. "Certainly not in the Lord Ruler. Sazed's religions have been dead for centuries, and even he has stopped talking about them. It seems to me that leaves the Church of the Survivor as the only real option."

"With all due respect, my lord," Demoux said. "That's not a very strong profession of faith."

"I'm having trouble with faith lately, Demoux," Elend said, looking up, watching flakes of ash drift through the air. "My last god was killed by the woman I eventually married—who you claim as a religious figure, but who spurns your devotion."

Demoux nodded quietly.

"I don't reject your god, Demoux," Elend said. "I meant what I said—I think having faith in Kelsier is better than the alternatives. And considering what's going to be coming at us in the next few months, I'd rather believe that something—anything—is out there helping us."

They were quiet for a few moments.

"I know that the Lady Heir objects to our worship of the Survivor, my lord," Demoux finally said. "She knew him, as did I. What she doesn't understand is that the Survivor has become so much more than just the man Kelsier."

Elend frowned. "That sounds like you calculatedly made him a god, Demoux—that you believe in him as a symbol only."

Demoux shook his head. "I'm saying that Kelsier was a man, but a man who gained something—a mantle, a portion of something eternal and immortal. When he died, he wasn't merely Kelsier the crewleader. Don't you think it odd that he was never Mistborn before he went to the Pits?"

"That's the way Allomancy works, Demoux," Elend said. "You don't gain your powers until you Snap—until you face something traumatic, something that nearly kills you."

"And you don't think that Kelsier experienced those kinds of events before the Pits?" Demoux asked. "My lord, he was a thief who robbed from obligators and noblemen. He lived a very dangerous life. You think he could have avoided beatings, near-deaths, and emotional anguish?"

Elend hesitated.

"He gained his powers at the Pits," Elend said quietly, "because something else came upon him. People who knew him speak of how he was a changed man when he came back. He had purpose—he was driven to accomplish something the rest of the world thought impossible."

Demoux shook his head. "No, my lord. Kelsier the man died in those Pits, and Kelsier the Survivor was born. He was granted great power, and great wisdom, by a force that is beyond us all. *That* is why he accomplished what he did. *That* is why we worship him. He still had the follies of a man, but he had the hopes of a divinity."

Elend turned away. The rational, scholarly side of him understood exactly what was happening. Kelsier was gradually being deified, his life made more and more mystical by those who followed him. Kelsier had to be invested with heavenly power, for the Church couldn't continue to revere a mere man.

Another part of Elend was glad for the rationalization, if only because it made the story that much more believable. After all, Demoux was right. How *did* a man living on the streets last so long before Snapping?

Someone screamed.

Elend looked up, scanning the ranks. Men began to shuffle as the mists appeared, sprouting in the air like growing plants. He couldn't see the soldier who had fallen. Soon the point was moot, for others began to scream.

The sun began to be obscured, blazing red as it approached

the horizon. Elend's horse shuffled nervously. The captains ordered the men to remain steady, but Elend could still see motion. In the group before him, pockets opened in the ranks as men randomly collapsed, marionettes whose strings had been cut. They shook on the ground, other soldiers backing away in horror, mist moving all around.

They need me, Elend thought, grabbing his reins, Pulling on the emotions of those around him. "Demoux, let's ride."

He turned his horse. Demoux did not follow.

Elend spun. "Demoux? What—"

He choked off immediately. Demoux sat in the mists, shaking horribly. Even as Elend watched, the balding soldier slipped from his saddle, collapsing to the ankle-deep ash below.

"Demoux!" Elend yelled, hopping down, feeling like a fool. He'd never thought to wonder if Demoux was susceptible—he'd assumed that he, like Vin and the others, was already immune. Elend knelt beside Demoux, his legs in the ash, listening to soldiers scream and captains yell for order. His friend shook and twisted, gasping in pain.

And the ash continued to fall.

Rashek didn't solve all the world's problems. In fact, with each thing he did fix, he created new issues. However, he was clever enough that every subsequent problem was smaller than the ones before it. So instead of plants that died from the distorted sun and ashy ground, we got plants that didn't provide quite enough nutrition.

He did save the world. True, the near-destruction was his fault in the first place—but he did an admirable job, all things considered. At least he didn't release Ruin to the land as we did.

18

SAZED SLAPPED HIS HORSE ON the rump, sending it galloping away. The beast's hooves kicked up chunks of packed ash as it ran. Its coat had once been a keen white; now it was a rough grey. Its ribs were beginning to show—it was malnourished to the point that it was no longer reasonable to expect it to carry a rider, and they could no longer afford to spare food for it.

"Now that's a sad sight," Breeze noted, standing beside Sazed on the ash-covered road. Their guard of two hundred soldiers waited quietly, watching the beast run. Sazed couldn't help feeling that the release of their final horse was a symbol.

"You think it will survive?" Breeze asked.

"I suspect that it will still be able to poke beneath the ash and find nourishment for a time," Sazed said. "It will be difficult, however."

Breeze grunted. "Living's difficult work for all of us,

these days. Well, I wish the creature the best of luck. Are you going to join Allrianne and me in the carriage?"

Sazed glanced over his shoulder toward the vehicle, which had been lightened, then rigged to be pulled by soldiers. They had removed the doors and hung curtains instead, and had removed sections of the back as well. With the decreased weight and two hundred men to take turns, the vehicle wouldn't be too much of a burden. Still, Sazed knew he would feel guilty being pulled by others. His old servant's instincts were too strong.

"No," Sazed said. "I shall walk for a bit. Thank you."

Breeze nodded, moving to the carriage to sit with Allrianne, a soldier holding a parasol over his head until he was inside. Now exposed to the ash, Sazed put up the hood of his travel robe, hefted his portfolio in his arm, and then strode across the black ground to the front of the line.

"Captain Goradel," he said. "You may continue your march."

They did so. It was a rough hike—the ash was growing thick, and it was slick and tiring to walk on. It moved and shifted beneath their feet, almost as difficult as walking on sand. As hard as the hike was, it wasn't enough to distract Sazed from his troubled feelings. He had hoped that visiting the army—meeting with Elend and Vin—would give him a respite. The two were dear friends, and their affection for one another tended to bolster him. He had, after all, been the one to perform their marriage.

Yet this meeting had left him even more troubled. *Vin allowed Elend to die,* he thought. *And she did it because of things I taught her.*

He carried the picture of a flower in his sleeve pocket, trying to make sense of his conversation with Vin. How had Sazed become the one that people came to with their problems? Couldn't they sense that he was a hypocrite, capable of formulating answers that sounded good, yet incapable of following his own advice? He felt lost. He felt a weight squeezing him, telling him to give up.

How easily Elend spoke of hope and humor, as if being happy were simply a decision one made. Some people assumed that it was. Once, Sazed might have agreed with them. Now his stomach twisted, and he felt sick at the thought of taking essentially any action. His thoughts were constantly invaded by doubts.

This is what religion is for, Sazed thought as he tromped through the ash at the head of the column, carrying his pack on his shoulders. *It helps people through times like these.*

He looked down at his portfolio. Then he opened it and leafed through the pages as he walked. Hundreds finished, and not a single one of the religions had provided the answers he sought. Perhaps he knew them too well. Most of the crew had trouble worshipping Kelsier as the other skaa did, for they knew of his faults and his quirks. They knew him as a man first, as a god second. Perhaps the religions were the same to Sazed. He knew them so well that he could see their flaws too easily.

He did not disparage the people who had followed the religions, but Sazed—so far—had found only contradiction and hypocrisy in each one he studied. Divinity was supposed to be perfect. Divinity didn't let its followers get slaughtered, and certainly didn't allow the world to be destroyed by good men who were trying to save it.

One of the remaining ones would provide an answer. There *had* to be truth he could discover. As his feelings of dark suffocation threatened to overwhelm him, he fell to his studies, taking out the next sheet in line and strapping it to the outside of the portfolio. He would analyze it as he walked, carrying the portfolio with the sheet on the bottom when he wasn't reading, thereby keeping the ash off it.

He'd find the answers. He dared not think what he would do if there weren't any.

They eventually passed into the Central Dominance, entering lands where men could still struggle for food and life. Breeze and Allrianne stayed in the carriage, but Sazed was glad to walk, even if it made it difficult to study his religions.

He wasn't certain what to make of the cultivated fields. They passed scores of them—Elend had packed as many people as possible into the Central Dominance, then had ordered all of them to grow food for the next winter. Even those skaa who had lived in the cities were well accustomed to hard work, and they quickly did as Elend ordered. Sazed wasn't certain if the people understood quite how dire their situation was, or if they were simply happy to have someone tell them what to do.

The roadside was heaped with tall piles of ash. Each day, the skaa workers had to clear away the ash that had fallen during the night. This unending task—along with the need to carry water to most of the new, unirrigated fields—created a very labor-intensive system of agriculture.

The crops did grow, however. Sazed's troop passed field after field, each one budding with brown plants. The sight should have brought him hope. Yet it was difficult to gaze upon the sprouting stalks and not feel a greater despair. They looked so weak and small next to the massive piles of ash. Leaving aside the mists, how was Elend going to feed an empire in these conditions? How long would it be before there was simply too much ash to move?

Skaa worked the fields, their postures much as they had been during the days of the Lord Ruler. What had really changed for them?

"Look at them," a voice said. Sazed turned to see Captain Goradel walking up beside him. Bald and rugged, the man had a good-natured disposition—a trait common in the soldiers whom Ham promoted.

"I know," Sazed said quietly.

"Even with the ash and the mist, seeing them gives me hope."

Sazed raised his eyes sharply. "Really?"

"Sure," Goradel said. "My family were farmers, Master Terrisman. We lived in Luthadel, but worked the outer fields."

"But you were a soldier," Sazed said. "Weren't you the

one who led Lady Vin into the palace the night she killed the Lord Ruler?"

Goradel nodded. "Actually, I led Lord Elend into the palace to rescue Lady Vin, though she turned out to not need much help from us. Anyway, you're right. I was a soldier in the Lord Ruler's palace—my parents disowned me when I joined up. But I just couldn't face working in the fields my whole life."

"It is arduous work."

"No, it wasn't that," Goradel said. "It wasn't the labor, it was the . . . hopelessness. I couldn't stand to work all day to grow something I knew would belong to someone else. That's why I left the fields to become a soldier, and that's why seeing these farms gives me hope."

Goradel nodded toward a passing field. Some of the skaa looked up, then waved as they saw Elend's banner. "These people," Goradel said, "they work because they want to."

"They work because if they don't, they will starve."

"Sure," Goradel said. "I guess that's so. But they're not working because someone will beat them if they don't— they're working so that their families and their friends will live. There's a difference in that, to a farmer. You can see it in the way they stand."

Sazed frowned as they walked, but said nothing further.

"Anyway, Master Terrisman," Goradel said, "I came to suggest that we make a stop at Luthadel for supplies."

"I suspected that we would do so," Sazed said. "I, however, will need to leave you for a few days as you go to Luthadel. Lord Breeze can take command. I shall meet up with you on the northern highway."

Goradel nodded, going to make the arrangements. He didn't ask why Sazed wanted to leave the group, or what his destination was.

Several days later, Sazed arrived—alone—at the Pits of Hathsin. There was little to distinguish the area, now that the ash covered everything. Sazed's feet kicked up clumps of it as he moved to the top of a hill. He looked down on the valley that contained the Pits—the place where Kelsier's wife had been murdered. The place where the Survivor had been born.

It was now the home of the Terris people.

There were few of them remaining. They had never been a very large population, and the coming of the mists and the difficult trek down to the Central Dominance had claimed many lives. There were perhaps forty thousand of them left. And a good many of the men were eunuchs like Sazed.

Sazed started downward. The valley had been a natural place to settle the Terris people. During the days of the Lord Ruler, hundreds of slaves had worked here, watched over by hundreds of soldiers. That had ended when Kelsier had returned to the Pits and destroyed their ability to produce atium. However, the buildings and infrastructure that had supported the Pits still existed. There was plenty of fresh water and some shelter. The Terris people had improved on this, building other structures across the valley, making what was once the most terrifying of prison camps into a group of pastoral villages.

As Sazed walked down the hillside, he could see people brushing away the ash from the ground, letting the natural plant life poke through to provide grazing for the animals. The scrub that formed the dominant foliage in the Central Dominance was a resilient, hardy group of plants adapted to ash and didn't need as much water as farm crops. That meant the Terris people now had relatively easy lives. They were herdsmen, as they had been during the centuries before the Lord Ruler's Ascension. A hardy, short-legged breed of sheep mulled about on the hills, chewing down the uncovered stalks of scrub.

The Terris people, Sazed thought, *living lives easier than most. What a strange world it has become.*

His approach soon attracted attention. Children ran for their parents, and heads poked from shacks. Sheep began to gather around Sazed as he walked, perhaps hoping that he had come bearing treats.

Several aged men rushed up the hillside, moving as quickly as their gnarled limbs would allow. They—like Sazed—still wore their steward's robes. Also like Sazed, they kept them clean of ash, showing the colorful V-shaped patterns that ran down the fronts. Those patterns had once indicated the noble house that the steward served.

"Lord Sazed!" one of the men said eagerly.

"Your Majesty!" said another.

Your Majesty. "Please," Sazed said, raising his hands. "Do not call me that."

The two aged stewards glanced at each other. "Please, Master Keeper. Let us get you something warm to eat."

Yes, the ash was black. No, it should not have been. Most common ash has a dark component, but is as much grey or white as it is black.

Ash from the Ashmounts . . . it was different. Like the mists, the ash covering our land was not natural. Perhaps it was the influence of Ruin's power—as black as Preservation was white. Or perhaps it was the nature of the Ashmounts, which were designed and created specifically to blast ash and smoke into the sky.

19

"GET UP!"

Everything was dark.

"Get up!"

Spook opened his eyes. Everything seemed so dull, so

muted. He could barely see. The world was a dark blur. And he felt . . . numb. Dead. Why couldn't he feel?

"Spook, you need to get up!"

The voice was clear. Yet everything else felt muddy. He couldn't quite manage to think. He blinked, groaning. What was wrong with him? His spectacles and cloth were gone. That should have left him free to see, but everything was so dark.

He was out of tin.

There was nothing burning in his stomach. The familiar flame, a comforting candle within, was no longer there. It had been his companion for over a year, always there. He'd feared what he was doing, but had never let it die. And now it was gone.

That was why everything seemed so dull. Was this really how other people lived? How he used to live? He could barely see—the sharp, rich detail he'd grown accustomed to was gone. The vibrant colors and crisp lines. Instead, everything was bland and vague.

His ears felt clogged. His nose . . . he couldn't smell the boards beneath him, couldn't tell what tree the wood came from by its scent. He couldn't smell the bodies that had passed. He couldn't feel the thumpings of people moving about in other rooms.

And . . . he *was* in a room. Pressing his right hand to his forehead, he sat up, trying to think. Immediately, a pain by his shoulder made him gasp. The wound had not been cared for. He remembered the sword piercing him in the chest near his shoulder. That was not a wound one recovered from easily. Indeed, his left arm didn't seem to work right—one of the reasons he was having so much trouble rising.

"You've lost a lot of blood," the voice said. "You'll die soon, even if the flames don't take you. Don't bother to look for the pouch of tin at your belt—they took that."

"Flames?" Spook croaked, blinking. How did people survive in a world that was this dark?

"Can't you feel them, Spook? They're near."

There *was* a light nearby, down a hallway. Spook shook his head, trying to clear his mind. *I'm in a house,* he thought. *A nice one. A nobleman's house.*

And they're burning it down.

This finally gave him motivation to stand, though he immediately dropped again, his body too weak—his mind too fuzzy—to keep him on his feet.

"Don't walk," the voice said. Where had he heard that voice before? He trusted it. "Crawl," it said.

Spook did as commanded, crawling forward.

"No, not *toward* the flames! You have to get out, so you can punish those who did this to you. Think, Spook!"

"Window," Spook croaked, turning and crawling toward one of them.

"Boarded shut," the voice said. "You saw this before, from the outside. There's only one way to survive. You have to listen to me."

Spook nodded dully.

"Go out the room's other door. Crawl toward the stairs leading to the second floor."

Spook did so, forcing himself to keep moving. His arms were so numb they felt like weights tied to his shoulders. He'd been flaring tin so long that normal senses didn't seem to work for him anymore. He found the stairs, though by the time he got there he was coughing. That would be because of the smoke, a part of his mind told him. It was probably a good thing he was crawling.

He could feel the heat as he climbed. The flames seemed to be chasing him, claiming the room behind him as he moved up the stairs, still dizzy. He reached the top, then slipped on his own blood and slumped against the wall, groaning.

"Get up!" the voice said.

Where have I heard that voice before? he thought. *Why do I want to do what it says?* It was so close. He'd have it, if his mind weren't so muddled. Yet he obeyed, forcing himself to his hands and knees again.

"Second room on the left," the voice commanded.

Spook crawled without thinking. Flames crept up the stairs, licking at the walls. Though his nose was weak, he suspected the house had been soaked with oil. It made for a faster, more dramatic burn that way.

"Stop. This is the room."

Spook turned left and crawled through a doorway. The room was a study, well furnished. The thieves in the city complained that ransacking places like this one wasn't worth the effort. The Citizen forbade ostentation, so expensive furniture couldn't be sold, even on the black market. Nobody wanted to be caught owning luxuries, lest they end up burning to death in one of the Citizen's executions.

"Spook!"

Spook had heard of the executions. He'd never seen one. He'd paid Durn to keep an eye out for the next one. Spook's coin would get him advance warning, as well as a good position to watch the building burn down. Plus, Durn promised he had another tidbit, something Spook would be interested in. Something worth the coin he'd paid.

Count the skulls.

"Spook!"

Spook opened his eyes. He'd fallen to the floor and begun to drift off. Flames were already burning the ceiling. The building was dying. There was no way Spook would get out, not in his current condition.

"Go to the desk," the voice commanded.

"I'm dead," Spook whispered.

"No you're not. Go to the desk."

Spook turned his head, looking at the flames. A figure stood in them, a dark silhouette. The walls dripped, bubbled, and hissed, their plaster and paints blackening. Yet this shadow of a person didn't seem to mind the fire. That figure seemed familiar. Tall. Commanding.

"You . . . ?" Spook whispered.

"Go to the desk!"

Spook rolled to his knees. He crawled, dragging his useless arm, moving to the desk.

"Right drawer."

Spook pulled it open, then slumped against it. Something was inside.

Vials?

He reached for them eagerly. They were the kinds of vials used by Allomancers to store metal shavings. With hands trembling, Spook picked one up, but it slipped free of his numb fingers. It shattered. He stared at the liquid from the vial—an alcohol solution that would keep the metal flakes from corroding, as well as help the Allomancer drink them down.

"Spook!" the voice said.

Dully, Spook took another vial. He worked off the stopper with his teeth, feeling the heat of the blaze around him. The far wall was nearly gone. The fires crept toward him.

He drank the contents of the vial, then searched within himself, seeking tin. But there was none. Spook cried out in despair, dropping the vial. It had contained no tin. How would that have saved him anyway? It would have made him feel the flames and his wound more acutely.

"Spook!" the voice commanded. "Burn it!"

"There is no tin!" Spook yelled.

"Not tin! The man who owned this house was no Tineye!"

Not tin. Spook blinked. Then—reaching within himself—he found something completely unexpected. Something he'd never thought to see, something that shouldn't have existed.

A new metal reserve. He burned it.

His body flared with strength. His trembling arms became steady. His weakness seemed to flee, cast aside like darkness before the rising sun. He felt tension and power, and his muscles grew taut with anticipation.

"Stand!"

His head snapped up. He leaped to his feet, and this time the dizziness was gone. His mind still felt numb, but one thing was clear to him. Only a single metal could have changed his body, making it strong enough to work despite his terrible wound and blood loss.

Spook was burning pewter.

The figure stood in the flames, dark, hard to make out. "I've given you the blessing of pewter, Spook," the voice said. "Use it to escape this place. You can break through the boards on the far end of that hallway, escape onto the roof of the building nearby. The soldiers won't be watching for you—they're too busy controlling the fire so it doesn't spread."

Spook nodded. The heat didn't bother him anymore. "Thank you."

The figure stepped forward, becoming more than a silhouette. Flames played against the man's firm face, and Spook's suspicions were confirmed. There was a reason he'd trusted that voice, a reason he had done what it had said.

He would do anything this man commanded.

"I didn't give you pewter just so you could live, Spook," Kelsier said, pointing. "I gave it to you so you could get revenge. Now, go!"

More than one person reported feeling a sapient hatred in the mists. This is not necessarily related to the mists killing people. For most—even those it struck down—the mists seemed merely a weather phenomenon, no more sapient or vengeful than a terrible disease.

For some few, however, there was more. Those it favored, it swirled around. Those it was hostile to, it pulled away from. Some felt peace within it, others hatred. It all came down to Ruin's subtle touch, and how much one responded to his promptings.

20

TENSOON SAT IN HIS CAGE.

The cage's very existence was an insult. Kandra were not like humans—even if he were not imprisoned, TenSoon would not have run or tried to escape. He had come willingly to his fate.

Yet they locked him up. He wasn't sure where they had gotten the cage—it certainly wasn't something kandra normally would need. Still, the Seconds had found it and erected it in one of the main caverns of the Homeland. It was made of iron plates and hard steel bars, with a strong wire mesh stretched across all four faces to keep him from reducing his body to base muscles and wriggling through. Another insult.

TenSoon sat in the cage, naked on the cold iron floor. Had he accomplished anything other than his own condemnation? Had his words in the Trustwarren been of any value at all?

Outside the bars, the caverns glowed with the light of cultivated mosses, and kandra went about their duties. Many paused to study him. This was the purpose of the long delay between his judgment and sentencing. The Second Generationers didn't need weeks to ponder what they were going to do to him. But since he had forced them to let him speak his mind, the Seconds wanted to make certain he was properly punished. They put him on display, like some human in the stocks. In all the history of the kandra people, no other had ever been treated in such a way. His name would be a byword of shame for centuries.

But we won't last centuries, he thought angrily. *That was what my speech was all about.*

He hadn't given it very well. How could he explain to the people what he felt? That their traditions were coming to a focus, that their lives—which had been stable for so long— were in drastic need of change?

What happened above? Did Vin go to the Well of Ascension? What of Ruin and Preservation? The gods of the kandra people were at war again, and the only ones who knew of them were pretending that nothing was happening.

As he sat, the kandra lived their lives. Some trained the members of the newer generations—he could see Elevenths moving along, little more than blobs with some glistening bones. The transformation from mistwraith to kandra was a difficult one. Once given a Blessing, the mistwraith would lose most of its instincts as it gained sapience, and would have to relearn how to form muscles and bodies. It was a process that took many, many years.

Other adult kandra went about food preparation. They would stew a mixture of algae and fungi in stone pits not unlike the one in which TenSoon would spend eternity. Despite his former hatred of humankind, he had always found the opportunity to enjoy outside food—particularly aged meat—a very tempting consolation for going out on a Contract. Now, he barely had enough to drink, let alone to eat.

He sighed, staring through the bars at the vast cavern. The caves of the Homeland were enormous, far too large for the kandra to fill. But that was what many of his people liked about them. After spending years in a Contract— serving a master's whims, often for decades at a time—a place that offered the option of solitude was precious.

Solitude, TenSoon thought. *I'll have plenty of that soon enough.* Contemplating an eternity in prison made him a little less annoyed with those who came to gawk at him. They would be the last of his people he ever saw. He recognized many of them. The Fourths and Fifths came to spit at the ground before him, showing their devotion to the Seconds. The Sixths and the Sevenths—who made up the bulk of the Contract fillers—came to pity him and shake their heads at a friend fallen. The Eighths and Ninths came out of curiosity, amazed that one so aged could have fallen so far.

And then he saw a familiar face amid the watching groups. TenSoon turned away, ashamed, as MeLaan approached, pain showing in those overly large eyes of hers.

"TenSoon?" her whisper soon came.

"Go away, MeLaan," he said quietly, his back to the bars, which only let him look out at another group of kandra watching him from across the room.

"TenSoon . . ." she repeated.

"You need not see me like this, MeLaan. Please go."

"They shouldn't be able to do this to you," she said, and he could hear the anger in her voice. "You're nearly as old as they, and far more wise."

"They are the Second Generation," TenSoon said. "They are chosen by those of the First. They lead us."

"They don't *have* to lead us."

"MeLaan!" he said, finally turning toward her. Most of the gawkers stayed at a distance, as if TenSoon's crime were a disease they could catch. MeLaan crouched alone next to his cage, her True Body of spindly wooden bones making her look unnaturally slim.

"You could challenge them," MeLaan said quietly.

"What do you think we are?" TenSoon asked. "Humans, with their rebellions and upheavals? We are kandra. We are of Preservation. We follow order."

"You still bow before them?" MeLaan hissed, pressing her thin face against the bars. "After what you said—with what is happening above?"

TenSoon paused. "Above?"

"You were right, TenSoon," she said. "Ash cloaks the land in a mantle of black. The mists come during the day, killing both crops and humans. Men march to war. Ruin has returned."

TenSoon closed his eyes. "They will do something," he said. "The First Generation."

"They are old," MeLaan said. "Old, forgetful, impotent."

TenSoon opened his eyes. "You have changed much."

She smiled. "They should never have given children of a new generation to be raised by the Thirds. There are many of us, the younger ones, who would fight. The Seconds can't rule forever. What can we do, TenSoon? How can we help you?"

Oh, child, he thought. *You think they don't know about you?*

Those of the Second Generation were not fools. They might be lazy, but they were old and crafty—TenSoon understood this, for he knew each of them quite well. They would have kandra listening, waiting to see what was said at his cage. A kandra of the Fourth or Fifth Generation who had the Blessing of Awareness could stand a distance away and still hear every word.

TenSoon was kandra. He had returned to receive his punishment because that was what was right. It was more than honor, more than Contract. It was who he was.

Yet if the things MeLaan had said were true . . .

Ruin has returned.

"How can you just sit here?" MeLaan said. "You're stronger than they are, TenSoon."

TenSoon shook his head. "I broke Contract, MeLaan."

"For a higher good."

At least I convinced her.

"Is it true, TenSoon?" she asked very quietly.

"What?"

"OreSeur. He had the Blessing of Potency. You must have inherited it, when you killed him. But they didn't find it on your body when they took you. So what did you do with it? Can I fetch it for you? Bring it, so that you can fight?"

"I will not fight my own people, MeLaan," TenSoon said.

"Someone must lead us!" she hissed.

That statement was true. But it wasn't TenSoon's right. Nor was it really the right of the Second Generation—or even the First Generation. It was the right of the one who had created them. That one was dead. But another had taken his place.

MeLaan was silent for a time, still kneeling by his cage. Perhaps she waited for him to offer encouragement, or to become the leader she sought. He didn't speak.

"So, you came to die," she finally said.

"To explain what I've discovered. What I've felt."

"And then what? You come, proclaim dread news, then leave us to solve the problems on our own?"

"That's not fair, MeLaan," he said. "I came to be the best kandra I know how to be."

"Then fight!"

He shook his head.

"It's true then," she said. "The others of my generation, they said that you were broken by that last master of yours. The man Zane."

"He did not break me," TenSoon said.

"Oh?" MeLaan said. "And why did you return to the Homeland in that . . . body you were using?"

"The dog's bones?" TenSoon said. "Those weren't given to me by Zane, but by Vin."

"So *she* broke you."

TenSoon exhaled quietly. How could he explain? On one hand, it seemed ironic to him that MeLaan—who intentionally wore a True Body that was inhuman—would find his use of a dog's body so distasteful. Yet he could understand. It had taken him quite some time to appreciate the advantages of those bones.

He hesitated.

But no. He had not come to bring revolution. He had come to explain, to serve the interests of his people. He would do that by accepting his punishment, as a kandra should.

And yet . . .

There was a chance. A slim one. He wasn't certain whether he wanted to escape, but if there was an opportunity . . .

"Those bones I wore," TenSoon found himself saying. "You know where they are?"

MeLaan frowned. "No. Why would you want them?"

TenSoon shook his head again. "I don't," he said, choosing his words carefully. "They were disgraceful! I was made to wear them for months, forced into the humiliating role of a dog. I would have discarded them, but I had no corpse to ingest and take, so I had to return here wearing that horrid body."

"You're avoiding the real issue, TenSoon."

"There is no real issue, MeLaan," he said, turning away from her. Whether or not his plan worked, he didn't want the Seconds punishing her for associating with him. "I will not rebel against my people. Please, if you truly wish to help me, then let me be."

MeLaan hissed quietly, and he heard her stand. "You were once the greatest of us."

TenSoon sighed as she left. *No, MeLaan. I was never great. Until recently, I was the most orthodox of my generation, a conservative distinguished solely by my hatred of humans. Now I've become the greatest criminal in the history of our people, but I did so mostly by accident.*

That isn't greatness. That's just foolishness.

It should be no surprise that Elend became such a powerful Al-lomancer. It is a well-documented fact—though that documen-tation wasn't available to most—that Allomancers were much stronger during the early days of the Final Empire.

In those days, an Allomancer didn't need duralumin to take control of a kandra or koloss. A simple Push or Pull on the emo-tions was enough. In fact, this ability was one of the main reasons that the kandra devised their Contracts with the humans—for at that time not only Mistborn, but Soothers and Rioters could take control of them at the merest of whims.

21

DEMOUX SURVIVED.

He was among the vast majority of the sixth of the sol-diers who got sick—those who did not die. Vin sat atop the cabin of her narrowboat, arm resting on a wooden ledge, idly fingering her mother's earring—which she wore in her left ear as always. Koloss brutes trudged along the towpath, dragging the barges and boats down the canal. Many of the barges carried supplies—tents, foodstuffs, pure water. But several had now been emptied, their contents hauled in the packs of the surviving soldiers, to make room for the ill.

Vin turned her gaze away from the barges and toward the front of the narrowboat. Elend stood at the prow as usual, staring westward. He did not brood. He looked like a king, standing straight-backed, staring determinedly toward his goal. He appeared so different now from the man he had once been, with his full beard, his longer hair, his uniforms that had been scrubbed white. They were growing worn. Not ragged; they were still clean and sharp, as white as things could get in the current state of the world. But they were no longer new. They were the uniforms of a man who had been at war for a year and a half straight.

Vin knew him enough to sense that all was not well. She also knew him enough to sense that he didn't want to talk about it at the moment.

She stood and stepped down, burning pewter unconsciously to heighten her balance. She slid a book off a bench at the boat's edge, and settled down softly. Elend would talk to her eventually—he always did. For the moment, she had something else to engage her. She opened the book to the marked page and reread a particular paragraph.

The Deepness must be destroyed. I have seen it, and I have felt it. This name we give it is too weak a word, I think. Yes, it is deep and unfathomable, but it is also terrible. Many do not realize that it is sapient, but I have sensed its mind, such as it is, the few times I have confronted it directly.

She eyed the page for a moment, sitting back on her bench. Beside her, the passing canal waters were covered with a froth of floating ash.

The book was Alendi's logbook, written a thousand years before by a man who thought himself the Hero of Ages. Alendi hadn't completed his quest; he had been killed by one of his packmen, Rashek, who had then taken the power at the Well of Ascension and become the Lord Ruler.

Alendi's story was frighteningly close to Vin's own. She had also assumed herself to be the Hero of Ages. She had traveled to the Well, and had been betrayed. Not by a companion—but instead by the force imprisoned within the Well. The force that, she believed, was behind the prophecies about the Hero of Ages in the first place.

Why do I keep returning to this paragraph? she thought, eyeing it again. Perhaps it was because of what Human had said to her—that the mists hated her. She had felt that hatred, and it appeared that Alendi had felt the same thing.

But could she trust the logbook's words? The force she had released, the thing they called Ruin, had proven that it could change things in the world. Small things, yet important ones. Like the text of a book, which was why Elend's officers were now instructed to send all messages via memorized words or letters etched into metal.

Regardless, if there had been any clues to be gained by reading the logbook, Ruin would have removed them long ago. Vin felt that she'd been led by the nose for the last three years, pulled by invisible strings. She had thought she was having revelations and making great discoveries, but all she'd really been doing was following Ruin's bidding.

Yet Ruin is not omnipotent, Vin thought. *If it were, there would have been no fight. It wouldn't have needed to trick me into releasing it.*

It cannot know my thoughts. . . .

Even that knowledge was frustrating. What good were her thoughts? Always before, she'd had Sazed, Elend, or TenSoon to talk with about problems like this. This wasn't a task for Vin; she was no scholar. Yet Sazed had turned his back on his studies, TenSoon had returned to his people, and Elend was far too busy lately to worry about anything but his army and its politics. That left Vin. And she still found reading and scholarship to be stuffy and boring.

But she was also becoming more and more comfortable with the idea of doing what was necessary, no matter how distasteful. She was no longer solely her own person. She belonged to the New Empire. She had been its knife—now it was time to try a different role.

I have to do it, she thought, sitting in the red sunlight. *There is a puzzle here—something to be solved. What was it Kelsier liked to say?*

There's always another secret.

She remembered Kelsier standing boldly before a small

group of thieves, proclaiming that they would overthrow the Lord Ruler and free the empire. *We're thieves,* he'd said. *And we're extraordinarily good ones. We can rob the unrobbable and fool the unfoolable. We know how to take an incredibly large task and break it down to manageable pieces, then deal with each of those pieces.*

When he'd written up the team's goals and plans on a small board, Vin had been amazed by how possible he had made an impossible task seem. That day, a small part of her had begun to believe that Kelsier could overthrow the Final Empire.

All right, Vin thought. *I'll begin like Kelsier did, by listing the things that I know for certain.*

There *had* been a power at the Well of Ascension, so that much about the stories was true. There had also been something alive, imprisoned in or near the Well. It had tricked Vin into using the power to destroy its bonds. Maybe she could have used that power to destroy Ruin instead, but she'd given it up.

She sat thoughtfully, tapping her finger against the logbook. She could remember wisps of how it had felt to hold that power. It had awed her, yet at the same time felt natural and right. In fact, as she held it, *everything* had felt natural. The workings of the world, the ways of men . . . it was as if the power had been more than mere capability. It had been understanding as well.

That was a tangent. She needed to focus on what she knew before she could philosophize on what she needed to do. The power was real, and Ruin was real. Ruin had retained some ability to change the world while confined— Sazed had confirmed that his texts had been altered to suit Ruin's purpose. Now Ruin was free, and Vin assumed that it was behind the violent mist killings and the falling ash.

Though, she reminded herself, *I don't know either of those things for certain.* What did she know about Ruin? She had touched it, felt it, in that moment when she had released it. It had a need to destroy, yet it was not a force of simple chaos. It didn't act randomly. It planned and thought.

And it didn't seem able to just do anything it wanted. Almost as if it followed specific rules . . .

She hesitated. "Elend?" she called.

The emperor turned from his place at the prow.

"What is the first rule of Allomancy?" Vin asked. "The first thing I taught you?"

"Consequence," Elend said. "Every action has consequences. When you Push on something heavy, it will push you back. If you Push on something light, it will fly away."

It was the first lesson Kelsier had taught Vin, and she assumed it was also the first lesson his master had taught him.

"It's a good rule," Elend said, returning to his contemplation of the horizon. "It works for all things in life. If you throw something into the air, it will come back down. If you bring an army into a man's kingdom, he will react accordingly."

Consequence, she thought, frowning. *As with things falling when thrown. That's what Ruin's actions feel like to me. Consequences.* Perhaps it was a remnant of touching the power, or perhaps merely a rationalization her unconscious mind was giving her. Yet she felt a logic to Ruin. She didn't understand that logic, but she could recognize its presence.

Elend turned back toward her. "That's what I like about Allomancy, in fact. Or at least the theory of it. The skaa whisper about it, call it mystical, but it's really quite rational. You can tell what an Allomantic Push is going to do as certainly as you can tell what will happen when you drop a rock over the side of this boat. For every Push, there is a Pull. There are no exceptions. It makes simple, logical sense—unlike the ways of men, which are filled with flaws, irregularities, and double meanings. Allomancy is a thing of nature."

A thing of nature.

For every Push, there is a Pull. A consequence.

"That's important," Vin whispered.

"What?"

A consequence.

The thing she had felt at the Well of Ascension had been a thing of destruction, as Alendi described in his logbook. But it hadn't been a creature, and not a person. It had been a force—a thinking one, but a force nonetheless. And forces had rules. Allomancy, weather, even the pull of the ground. The world was a place that made sense. A place of logic. Every Push had a Pull. Every force had a consequence.

She had to discover the laws relating to the thing she was fighting. That would tell her how to beat it.

"Vin?" Elend asked, studying her face.

Vin looked away. "It's nothing, Elend. Nothing I can speak of at least."

He watched her for a moment. *He thinks that you're plotting against him,* Reen whispered from the back of her mind. Fortunately, the days when she had listened to Reen's words were long past. Indeed, as she watched Elend, she saw him nod slowly and accept her explanation. He returned to his own contemplations.

She rose, walking forward, laying a hand on his arm. He sighed, raising his arm and wrapping it around her shoulders, pulling her close. That arm, once the weak limb of a scholar, was now muscular and firm.

"What are you thinking about?" she asked.

"You know."

Vin nodded.

Elend sighed. "But it's more than how I feel about the soldiers' deaths, Vin. I fear I'm becoming like *him*."

"Who?"

"The Lord Ruler."

Vin snorted quietly, pulling closer to him.

"This is something he would have done," Elend said. "Sacrificing his own men for a tactical advantage."

"You explained this to Ham," Vin said. "We can't afford to waste time."

"It's still ruthless," Elend said. "The problem isn't that those men died, it's that I was so willing to make it happen. I feel . . . *brutal,* Vin. How far will I go to see my goals achieved? I'm marching on another man's kingdom to take it from him."

"For the greater good."

"Which has been the excuse of tyrants throughout all time. I know that. Yet I press on. *This* is why I didn't want to be emperor. This is why I let Penrod take my throne from me during the siege. I didn't want to be the kind of leader who had to do things like this. I want to protect, not besiege and kill! But is there any other way? Everything I do feels like it *must* be done. Such as exposing my own men in the mists. Such as marching on Fadrex City. We have to get to that storage cache—it's the only lead we have that could give us a clue as to what we're supposed to do! It all makes such sense. Ruthless, brutal sense."

Ruthlessness is the most practical of emotions, Reen's voice whispered. She ignored it. "You've been listening to Cett too much."

"Perhaps," Elend said. "Yet his is a logic I find difficult to ignore. I grew up as an idealist, Vin—we both know that's true. Cett provides a balance. The things he says are much like what Tindwyl used to say."

He paused, shaking his head. "A short time ago, I was talking with Cett about Snapping. The noble houses were always desperate to ensure that they found the Allomancers among their children."

"So they had them beaten," Vin whispered.

Elend nodded. "One of the great dirty secrets of so-called noble life. I haven't talked much about the details, but children often didn't survive the beatings, which had to be brutal in order to bring out any latent Allomantic abilities. The process was different for each house, but they generally specified an age before adolescence. Every boy and girl who reached that age was taken and beaten near to death."

Vin shivered.

"I vividly remember mine," Elend said. "Father didn't beat me himself, but he did watch. The saddest thing about the beatings was that most of them were pointless. Only a handful of children, even among the Great Houses, Snapped and became Allomancers. I didn't. I was beaten for nothing."

"You stopped the beatings, Elend," Vin said. He had drafted a bill soon after becoming king. It was now an individual's personal choice whether to undergo a supervised beating, and only after coming of age.

"And I was wrong," Elend said softly.

Vin looked up.

"Allomancers are our most powerful resource, Vin," Elend said, gazing out over the marching soldiers. "Cett lost his kingdom, nearly his life, because he couldn't marshal enough Allomancers to protect him. And I made it illegal to search out Allomancers in my population."

"Elend, you stopped the *beating of children*."

"And if those beatings could save lives?" Elend asked. "Like exposing my soldiers could save lives? What about Kelsier? He gained his powers as a Mistborn only *after* he was trapped in the Pits of Hathsin. What would have happened if he'd been beaten properly as a child? He would always have been Mistborn. He could have saved his wife."

"And then he wouldn't have had the courage or motivation to overthrow the Final Empire."

"And is what we have any better?" Elend asked. "The longer I've held this throne, Vin, the more I've come to realize that some of the things the Lord Ruler did weren't evil, but simply effective. Right or wrong, he maintained order in his kingdom."

Vin breathed out slowly. "I don't like this hardness in you, Elend."

He looked out over the blackened canal waters. "It doesn't control me, Vin. I don't agree with most of the things the Lord Ruler did. I'm just coming to understand him—and that understanding worries me." She saw questions in his eyes, but also strength. He looked down and met her gaze. "I can hold this throne only because I know that at one point, I was willing to give it up in the name of what was right. If I ever lose that, Vin, you need to tell me. Can you?"

Vin nodded.

His eyes sought the horizon again. *What is it he hopes to see?* she wondered.

"There has to be a balance, Vin," he said. "Somehow we'll find it. The balance between who we wish to be and who we need to be." He sighed. "But for now," he said, looking to the canal, "we have to be satisfied with who we are."

Vin glanced over to see a small courier skiff from another narrowboat pulling up alongside theirs. A man in simple brown robes stood upon it. He wore large spectacles, as if attempting to obscure the intricate Ministry tattoos around his eyes, and he was smiling happily.

Vin smiled as well. Once, she had thought that a happy obligator was *always* a bad sign. That was before she'd known Noorden. During the days of the Lord Ruler, the contented scholar had probably lived most of his life in his own little world. He provided a strange proof that even among what had once been—in her opinion—the most evil organization in the empire, one could find good men.

"Your Excellency," Noorden said, stepping off the skiff and bowing. A couple of assistant scribes joined him on deck, lugging books and ledgers.

"Noorden," Elend said, joining the man on the foredeck. Vin followed. "You have done the counts I asked?"

"Yes, Your Excellency," Noorden said as an aide opened up a ledger on a pile of boxes. "I must say, this was a difficult task, what with the army moving about and the like."

"I'm certain you were thorough as always, Noorden," Elend said. He glanced at the ledger, which seemed to make sense to him, though all Vin saw was a bunch of random numbers.

"What's it say?" she asked.

"It lists the number of sick and dead," Elend said. "Of our thirty-eight thousand, nearly six thousand were taken by the sickness. We lost a bit over five hundred and fifty."

"Including one of my own scribes," Noorden said, shaking his head.

Vin frowned. Not at the death, but at something else, something itching at her mind . . .

"Fewer dead than expected," Elend said, pulling thoughtfully at his beard.

"Yes, Your Excellency," Noorden said. "I guess these soldier types are more rugged than the average skaa population. The sickness, whatever it is, didn't strike them as hard."

"How do you know?" Vin asked, looking up. "How do you know how many *should* have died?"

"Previous experience, my lady," Noorden said in his chatty way. "We've been tracking these deaths with some interest. Since the disease is new, we're trying to determine precisely what causes it. Perhaps that will lead us to a way to treat it. I've had my scribes reading what we can, trying to find clues of other diseases like this. It seems a bit similar to the shakewelts, though that's usually brought on by—"

"Noorden," Vin said, frowning. "You have figures? Specific numbers?"

"That's what His Excellency asked for, my lady."

"How many fell sick to the disease?" Vin asked. "Exactly?"

"Well, let me see . . ." Noorden said, shooing his scribe away and checking the ledger. "Five thousand two hundred and forty-three."

"What percentage of the soldiers is that?" Vin asked.

Noorden waved over a scribe and did some calculations. "About thirteen and a half percent, my lady," he said, adjusting his spectacles.

Vin frowned. "Did you include the men who died in your calculations?"

"Actually, no," Noorden said.

"And which total did you use?" Vin asked. "The total number of men in the army, or the total number who hadn't been in the mists before?"

"The first."

"Do you have a count for the second number?" Vin asked.

"Yes, my lady," Noorden said. "The emperor wanted an accurate count of which soldiers would be affected."

"Use that number instead," Vin said, glancing at Elend. He seemed interested.

"What is this about, Vin?" he asked as Noorden and his men worked.

"I'm . . . not sure," Vin said.

"Numbers are important for generalizations," Elend said. "But I don't see how . . ." He trailed off as Noorden looked up from his calculations, then cocked his head, saying something softly to himself.

"What?" Vin asked.

"I'm sorry, my lady," Noorden said. "I was a bit surprised. The calculation came out to be exact—precisely sixteen percent of the soldiers fell sick. To the man."

"A coincidence, Noorden," Elend said. "It isn't *that* remarkable for calculations to come out exact."

Ash blew across the deck. "No," Noorden said, "no, you are right, Your Excellency. A simple coincidence."

"Check your ledgers," Vin said. "Find percentages based on other groups of people who have caught this disease."

"Vin," Elend said, "I'm no statistician, but I have worked with numbers in my research. Sometimes natural phenomena produce seemingly odd results, but the chaos of statistics actually results in normalization. It might appear strange that the numbers in this case broke down to an exact percentage, but that's just the way statistics works."

"Sixteen," Noorden said. He looked up. "Another exact percentage."

Elend frowned, stepping over to the ledger.

"This third one here isn't a whole number," Noorden said, "but that's only because the base number isn't a multiple of twenty-five. A fraction of a person can't really become sick, after all. Yet the sickness in this population here is within a single person of being sixteen percent on the nose."

Elend knelt down, heedless of the ash that had dusted the deck since it had last been swept. Vin looked over his shoulder, scanning the numbers.

"It doesn't matter how old the average member of the population is," Noorden said, scribbling. "Nor does it matter where they live. Each one shows the *identical* percentage of people falling sick."

"How could we have not noticed this before?" Elend asked.

"Well, we did, after a fashion," Noorden said. "We knew that *about* four in twenty-five caught the sickness. However, I hadn't realized how exact the numbers were. This is indeed odd, Your Excellency. I know of no other disease that works this way. Look, here's an entry where a hundred scouts were sent into the mists, and *precisely* sixteen of them fell sick!"

Elend looked troubled.

"What?" Vin asked.

"This is wrong, Vin," Elend said. "Very wrong."

"It's as if the chaos of normal random statistics has broken down," Noorden said. "A population should never react with this precision—there should be a curve of probability, with smaller populations reflecting the expected percentages less accurately."

"At the very least," Elend said, "the sickness should affect the elderly in different ratios from the healthy."

"In a way, it does," Noorden said as one of his assistants handed him a paper with further calculations. "The *deaths* respond that way, as we would expect. But the total number who fall sick is always sixteen percent! We've been paying so much attention to how many died, we didn't notice how unnatural the percentages were for those stricken."

Elend stood. "Check on this, Noorden," he said, gesturing toward the ledger. "Do interviews, make certain the data hasn't been changed by Ruin, and find out if this trend holds. We can't jump to conclusions with only four or five examples. It could still all be a large coincidence."

"Yes, Your Excellency," Noorden said, looking a bit

shaken. "But . . . what if it's not a coincidence? What does it mean?"

"I don't know," Elend said.

It means consequence, Vin thought. *It means that there are laws, even if we don't understand them.*

Sixteen. Why sixteen percent?

The beads of metal found at the Well—beads that made men into Mistborn—were the reason Allomancers used to be more powerful. Those first Mistborn were as Elend Venture became— possessing a primal power, which was then passed down through the lines of the nobility, weakening a bit with each generation.

The Lord Ruler was one of these ancient Allomancers, his power pure and unadulterated by time and breeding. That is part of why he was so mighty compared to other Mistborn—though admittedly his ability to mix Feruchemy and Allomancy was what produced many of his most spectacular abilities. Still, it is interesting to me that one of his "divine" powers—his essential Allomantic strength—was something every one of the original nine Allomancers possessed.

22

SAZED SAT IN ONE OF the nicer buildings at the Pits of Hathsin—a former guardhouse—holding a mug of hot tea. The Terris elders sat in chairs before him, a small stove providing warmth. On the next day, Sazed would have to leave to catch up with Goradel and Breeze, who would be well on their way to Urteau by now.

The sunlight was dimming. The mists had already come, and they hung right outside the glass window. Sazed could barely make out depressions in the dark ground outside—cracks in the earth. There were dozens of the cracks; the Terris people had built fences to mark them. Only a few years ago, before Kelsier had destroyed the atium crystals, men had been forced to crawl down into those cracks, seeking small geodes that had beads of atium at their centers.

Each slave who hadn't been able to find at least one geode a week had been executed. There were likely still hundreds, perhaps thousands of corpses pinned beneath the ground, lost in deep caverns, dead without anyone knowing or caring.

What a terrible place this was, Sazed thought, turning away from the window as a young Terriswoman closed the shutters. Before him on the table were several ledgers that showed the resources, expenditures, and needs of the Terris people.

"I believe I suggested keeping these figures in metal," Sazed said.

"Yes, Master Keeper," said one of the elderly stewards. "We copy the important figures into a sheet of metal each evening, then check them weekly against the ledgers to make certain nothing has changed."

"That is well," Sazed said, picking through one of the ledgers, sitting in his lap. "And sanitation? Have you addressed those issues since my last visit?"

"Yes, Master Keeper," said another man. "We have prepared many more latrines, as you commanded—though we do not need them."

"There may be refugees," Sazed said. "I wish for you to be able to care for a larger population, should it become necessary. But please. These are merely suggestions, not commands. I claim no authority over you."

The group of stewards shared glances. Sazed had been busy during his time with them, which had kept him from dwelling on his melancholy thoughts. He'd made sure they had enough supplies, that they kept a good communication with Penrod in Luthadel, and that they had a system in place for settling disputes among themselves.

"Master Keeper," one of the elders finally said, "how long will you be staying?"

"I must leave in the morning, I fear," Sazed said. "I came simply to check on your needs. This is a difficult time to live in, and you could be easily forgotten by those in Luthadel, I think."

"We are well, Master Keeper," said one of the others. He was the youngest of the elders, and he was only a few years younger than Sazed. Most of the men here were far older—and wiser—than he. That they should look to him seemed wrong.

"Will you not reconsider your place with us, Master Keeper?" asked another. "We want not for food or land. Yet what we do lack is a leader."

"The Terris people were oppressed long enough, I think," Sazed said. "You have no need for another tyrant king."

"Not a tyrant," one said. "One of our own."

"The Lord Ruler was one of our own," Sazed said quietly.

The group of men looked down. That the Lord Ruler had proven to be Terris was a shame to their entire people.

"We need someone to guide us," one of the men said. "Even during the days of the Lord Ruler, he was not our leader. We looked to the Keeper Synod."

The clandestine leaders of Sazed's sect had led the Terris people for centuries, secretly working to make certain that Feruchemy endured, despite the Lord Ruler's attempts to breed the power out of the people. Their sudden eradication at the hands of the Inquisitors was a severe blow.

"Master Keeper," said Master Vedlew, senior of the elders.

"Yes, Master Vedlew?"

"You do not wear your copperminds."

Sazed looked down. He hadn't realized it was noticeable that, beneath his robes, he wasn't wearing the metal bracers. "They are in my pack."

"It seems odd to me," Vedlew said, "that you should work

so hard during the Lord Ruler's time, always wearing your metalminds in secret, despite the danger. Yet now that you are free to do as you wish, you carry them in your pack."

Sazed shook his head. "I cannot be the man you wish me to be. Not now."

"You are a Keeper."

"I was the lowest of them," Sazed said. "A rebel and a reject. They cast me from their presence. The last time I left Tathingdwen, I did so in disgrace. The common people cursed me in the quiet of their homes."

"Now they bless you, Master Sazed," said one of the men.

"I do not deserve those blessings."

"Deserve them or not, you are all we have left."

"Then we are a sorrier people than we may appear."

The room fell silent.

"There was another reason I came here, Master Vedlew," Sazed said, looking up. "Tell me, have any of your people died recently in . . . odd circumstances?"

"Of what do you speak?" the aged Terrisman asked.

"Mist deaths," Sazed said. "Men who are killed by simply going out into the mists during the day."

"That is a tale of the skaa," one of the other men scoffed. "The mists are not dangerous."

"Indeed," Sazed said carefully. "Do you send your people out to work in them during the daylight hours, when the mists have not yet retreated for the day?"

"Of course we do," said the younger Terrisman. "Why, it would be foolish to let those hours of work pass."

Sazed found it difficult not to let his curiosity focus on that fact. Terrismen weren't killed by the daymists.

What was the connection?

He tried to summon the mental energy to think on the issue, but he felt traitorously apathetic. He just wanted to hide somewhere where nobody would expect anything of him. Where he wouldn't have to solve the problems of the world, or even deal with his own religious crisis.

Yet a little part of him—a spark from before—refused to simply give up. He would at least continue his research, and would do what Elend and Vin asked of him. It wasn't *all* he could do, and it wouldn't satisfy the Terrismen who sat here, looking at him with needful expressions.

But for the moment, it was all Sazed could offer. To stay at the Pits would be a surrender, he knew. He needed to keep moving, keep working.

"I'm sorry," he said to the men, setting aside the ledger. "But this is how it must be."

During the early days of Kelsier's original plan, I remember how much he confused us all with his mysterious "Eleventh Metal." He claimed that there were legends of a mystical metal that would let one slay the Lord Ruler—and that Kelsier had located that metal through intense research.

Nobody really knew what he did in the years between his escape from the Pits of Hathsin and his return to Luthadel. When pressed, he simply said that he had been in "the West." Somehow in his wanderings he discovered stories that no Keeper had ever heard. Most of the crew didn't know what to make of the legends he spoke of. This might have been the first seed that made even his oldest friends begin to question his leadership.

23

IN THE EASTERN LANDS, NEAR the wastelands of grit and sand, a young boy fell to the ground inside a skaa shack. It was many years before the Collapse, and the Lord Ruler still lived. Not that the boy knew of such things. He was a dirty, ragged thing—like most other skaa children in the Final Empire. Too

young to be put to work in the mines, he spent his days ducking away from his mother's care and running about with the
packs of children who foraged in the dry, dusty streets.

Spook hadn't been that boy for some ten years. In a way,
he was aware that he was delusional—that the fever of his
wounds was causing him to come in and out of consciousness, dreams of the past filling his mind. He let them run.
Staying focused required too much energy.

And so, he remembered what it felt like as he hit the
ground. A large man—all men were large compared with
Spook—stood over him, skin dirtied with the dust and
grime of a miner. The man spat on the dirty floor beside
Spook, then turned to the other skaa in the room. There
were many. One was crying, the tears leaving clean lines on
her cheeks, washing away the dust.

"All right," the large man said. "We have him. Now what?"

The people glanced at each other. One quietly closed the
shack's door, shutting out the red sunlight.

"There's only one thing to be done," another man said.
"We turn him in."

Spook looked up. He met the eyes of the crying woman.
She glanced away. "Wasing the where of what?" Spook demanded.

The large man spat again, setting a boot on Spook's neck,
pushing him down on the rough wood. "You shouldn't have
let him run around with those street gangs, Margel. Damn
boy is barely coherent now."

"What happens if we give him up?" asked one of the
other men. "I mean, what if they decide we're like him?
They could have *us* executed! I've seen it before. You turn
someone in, and those . . . things come searching for everyone who knew him."

"Problems like his run in the family, they do," another
man said.

The room grew quiet. They all knew about Spook's family.

"They'll kill us," said the frightened man. "You know
they will! I've seen them, seen them with those spikes in
their eyes. Spirits of death, they are."

"We can't just let him run about," another man said. "They'll discover what he is."

"There's only one thing to be done," the large man said, pressing down on Spook's neck even harder.

The room's occupants—the ones Spook could see—nodded solemnly. They couldn't turn him in. They couldn't let him go. But nobody would miss a skaa urchin. No Inquisitor or obligator would ask twice about a dead child found in the streets. Skaa died all the time.

That was the way of the Final Empire.

"Father," Spook whispered.

The heel came down harder. "You're not my son! My son went into the mists and never came out. You must be a mistwraith."

Spook tried to object, but his neck was pressed down too tight. He couldn't breathe, let alone speak. The room started to grow black. Yet his ears—supernaturally sensitive, enhanced by powers he barely understood—heard something.

Coins.

The pressure on his neck grew weaker. He was able to gasp for breath, his vision returning. And there, spilled on the ground before him, was a scattering of beautiful copper coins. Skaa weren't paid for their work—the miners were given goods instead, barely enough to survive on. Yet Spook had seen coins occasionally, passing between noble hands. He'd once known a boy who had found a coin, lost in the dusty grime of the street.

A larger boy had killed him for it. Then a nobleman had killed that boy when he'd tried to spend it. It seemed to Spook that no skaa would want coins—they were far too valuable, far too dangerous. Yet every eye in the room stared at that spilled bag of wealth.

"The bag in exchange for the boy," a voice said. Bodies parted to where a man sat at a table at the back of the room. He wasn't looking at Spook. He just sat, quietly spooning gruel into his mouth. His face was gnarled and twisted, like leather that had been sitting in the sun for far too long. "Well?" the gnarled man said between bites.

"Where did you get this kind of money?" Spook's father demanded.

"None of your business."

"We can't let the boy go," one of the skaa said. "He'll betray us! Once they catch him, he'll tell them that we knew!"

"They won't catch him," the gnarled man said, taking another bite of food. "He'll be with me, in Luthadel. Besides, if you *don't* let him go, I'll go ahead and tell the obligators about you all." He paused, lowering his spoon, glancing at the crowd with a crusty look. "Unless you're going to kill me too."

Spook's father finally took his heel off Spook's neck as he stepped toward the gnarled stranger. But Spook's mother grabbed her husband's arm. "Don't, Jedal," she said softly—but not too softly for Spook's enhanced ears. "He'll kill you."

"He's a traitor," Spook's father spat. "Servant in the Lord Ruler's army."

"He brought us coins. Surely taking his money is better than simply killing the boy."

Spook's father looked down at the woman. "*You* did this! You sent for your brother. You knew he'd want to take the boy!"

Spook's mother turned away.

The gnarled man set down his spoon, then stood. People pulled away from his chair in apprehension. He walked with a pronounced limp as he crossed the room.

"Come on, boy," he said, not looking at Spook as he opened the door.

Spook rose slowly, tentatively. He glanced at his mother and father as he backed away. Jedal stooped down, gathering up the coins. Margel met Spook's eyes, then turned away. *This is all I can give you,* her posture seemed to say.

Spook turned, rubbing his neck, and rushed into the hot red sunlight after the stranger. The older man hobbled along, walking with a cane. He glanced at Spook as he walked.

"You have a name, boy?"

Spook opened his mouth, then stopped. His old name

didn't seem like it would do anymore. "Lestibournes," he said.

The old man didn't bat an eye. Later, Kelsier would decide that "Lestibournes" was too difficult to say, and would name him "Spook" instead. Spook never did figure out whether or not Clubs knew how to speak Eastern street slang. Even if he did, Spook doubted that he'd understood the reference.

Lestibournes. Lefting I'm born.

Street slang for "I've been abandoned."

I now believe that Kelsier's stories, legends, and prophecies about the "Eleventh Metal" were fabricated by Ruin. Kelsier was looking for a way to kill the Lord Ruler, and Ruin—ever subtle— provided a way.

That secret was indeed crucial. Kelsier's Eleventh Metal provided the clue we needed to defeat the Lord Ruler. However, even in this we were manipulated. The Lord Ruler knew Ruin's goals, and would never have released him from the Well of Ascension. So Ruin needed other pawns—and for that to happen, the Lord Ruler needed to die. Our greatest victory was shaped by Ruin's subtle fingers.

24

DAYS LATER, MELAAN'S WORDS STILL pricked Ten-Soon's conscience.

You come, proclaim dread news, then leave us to solve the problems on our own? During his year of imprisonment, it had seemed simple. He would make his accusations, deliver his information, then accept the punishment he deserved.

But now, strangely, that felt like the easy way out. If he let himself be taken in such a manner, how was he better than the First Generation? He would be avoiding the issues, content to be locked away, knowing that the outside world was no longer his problem.

Fool, he thought. *You'll be imprisoned for eternity— or at least until the kandra are destroyed and you die of starvation. That's not the easy way out! By accepting your punishment, you're doing the honorable, orderly thing.*

And by so doing, he would leave MeLaan and the others to be destroyed as their leaders refused to take action. And he would leave Vin without the information she needed. Even from within the Homeland, he could feel the occasional rumbles in the rock. The earthquakes were still remote, and the others likely ignored them. But TenSoon worried.

The end could be nearing. If it was, then Vin needed to know the truths about the kandra. Their origins, their beliefs. Perhaps she could use the Trust. Yet if he told Vin anything more, it would mean an even greater betrayal of his people. Perhaps a human would have found it ridiculous that he would hesitate now. However, so far his true sins had been impulsive, and he'd only later rationalized what he'd done. If he fought his way free of prison, it would be different. Willful and deliberate.

He closed his eyes, feeling the chill of his cage, alone in the large cavern—the place was mostly abandoned during the sleeping hours. What was the point? Even with the Blessing of Presence—which let TenSoon focus despite his uncomfortable confines—he could think of no way to escape the meshed cage and its Fifth Generation guards, who all bore the Blessing of Potency. And if he did get out of the cage, TenSoon would have to pass through dozens of small caverns. With his body mass as low as it was, he didn't have the muscles to fight, and he couldn't outrun kandra who had the Blessing of Potency. He was trapped.

In a way, this was comforting. Escape was not something he preferred to contemplate—it simply wasn't the kandra way. He had broken Contract, and deserved punishment. There was honor in facing the consequences of one's actions.

Wasn't there?

He shifted positions in his cell. Unlike that of a real human, the skin of his naked body did not become sore or chapped from the extended exposure, for he could re-form his flesh to remove wounds. However, there was little to do about the cramped feeling he got from being forced to sit in the small cage for so long.

Motion caught his attention. TenSoon turned, surprised to see VarSell and several other large Fifths approaching his cage, their quartzite stone True Bodies ominous in size and coloring.

Time already? TenSoon thought. With the Blessing of Presence, he was able to mentally recount the days of his imprisonment. It was nowhere near time. He frowned, noting that one of the Fifths carried a large sack. For a moment, TenSoon had a flash of panic as he pictured them towing him away inside the sack.

It looked filled already, however.

Dared he hope? Days had passed since his conversation with MeLaan, and while she had returned several times to look at him, they had not spoken. He'd almost forgotten his words to her, said in the hope that they would be overheard by the minions of the Second Generation. VarSell opened the cage and tossed the sack in. It rattled with a familiar sound. Bones.

"You are to wear those to the trial," VarSell said, leaning down and putting a translucent face up next to TenSoon's bars. "Orders of the Second Generation."

"What is wrong with the bones I now wear?" TenSoon asked carefully, pulling over the sack, uncertain whether to be excited or ashamed.

"They intend to break your bones as part of your punishment," VarSell said, smiling. "Something like a public execution—but where the prisoner lives through the process. It's a simple thing, I know—but the display ought to leave . . . an impression on some of the younger generations."

TenSoon's stomach twisted. Kandra could re-form their bodies, true, but they felt pain as acutely as any human. It would take quite a severe beating to break his bones, and with the Blessing of Presence, there would be no release of unconsciousness for him.

"I still don't see the need for another body," TenSoon said, pulling out one of the bones.

"No need to waste a perfectly good set of human bones, Third," VarSell said, slamming the cage door closed. "I'll be back for your current bones in a few hours."

The leg bone he pulled out was not that of a human, but a dog. A large wolfhound. They were the very bones TenSoon had been wearing when he'd returned to the Homeland over a year before. He closed his eyes, holding the smooth bone in his fingers.

A week ago, he'd spoken of how much he detested these bones, hoping that the Second Generation's spies would carry the news to their masters. The Second Generation was far more traditional than MeLaan, and even she had found the thought of wearing a dog's body distasteful. To the Seconds, forcing TenSoon to wear an animal's body would be supremely degrading.

That was exactly what TenSoon had been counting on.

"You'll look good, wearing that," VarSell said, turning to leave. "When your punishment comes, everyone will be able to see you for what you really are. No *kandra* would break his Contract."

TenSoon rubbed the thighbone with a reverent finger, listening to VarSell's laughter. The Fifth had no way of knowing that he'd just given TenSoon the means he needed to escape.

The Balance. Is it real?

We've almost forgotten this small piece of lore. Skaa used to talk about it, before the Collapse. Philosophers discussed it a great deal in the third and fourth centuries, but by Kelsier's time it was mostly a forgotten topic.

But it was real. There was a physiological difference between skaa and nobility. When the Lord Ruler altered humankind to make them more capable of dealing with ash, he changed other things as well. Some groups of people—the noblemen—were created to be less fertile, but taller, stronger, and more intelligent. Others—the skaa—were made to be shorter, hardier, and to have many children.

The changes were slight, however, and after a thousand years of interbreeding, the differences had largely been erased.

25

"FADREX CITY," ELEND SAID, STANDING in his customary place near the narrowboat's prow. Ahead, the broad Conway Canal—the primary canal route to the west—continued into the distance, turning to the northwest. To Elend's left, the ground rose in a broken incline, forming a set of steep rock formations. He could see them rising much higher in the distance.

Closer to the canal, a broad city was nestled in the center of a large group of rock formations. The dark red and orange rocks were the type left behind when wind and rain wore away weaker sections of stone, and many of them reached high, as spires. Others formed jagged hedgelike barriers with the appearance of stacks of enormous blocks that had been fused together, reaching some thirty and forty feet into the air.

Elend could barely see the tips of the city's buildings over the stone formations. Fadrex had no formal city wall, of course—only Luthadel had been allowed one of those—but the rising rocks around the city formed a set of terrace-like natural fortifications.

Elend had been to the city before. His father had made certain to introduce him in all of the Final Empire's main cultural centers. Fadrex hadn't been one, but it had been on the way to Tremredare, once known as the capital of the West. In forging his new kingdom, however, Cett had ignored Tremredare, instead establishing his capital in Fadrex. A clever move, in Elend's estimation—Fadrex was smaller, more defensible, and had been a major supply station for numerous canal routes.

"The city looks different from the last time I was here," Elend said.

"Trees," Ham said, standing next to him. "Fadrex used to have trees growing on the rocky shelves and plateaus." Ham glanced at him. "They're ready for us. They cut down the trees to provide a better killing field and to keep us from sneaking up close."

Elend nodded. "Look down there."

Ham squinted, though it obviously took him a moment to pick out what Elend's tin-enhanced eyes had noticed. On the northern side of the city—the one closest to the main canal route—the rock terraces and shelves fell down into a natural canyon. Perhaps forty feet across, it was the only way into the city, and was half taken up by the canal side branch that served Fadrex. The defenders had cut several troughs into the rocky floor of the canyon, then flooded them by connecting to the canal. They were bridged at the moment, but getting through that narrow entryway, with moats in front of the army and archers presumably loosing arrows from the rocky shelves above, with a gate at the end . . .

"Not bad," Ham said. "I'm only half glad they decided not to drain the canal on us."

As they'd moved west, the land had risen—requiring the convoy to pass through several massive lock mechanisms. The last four had been jammed intentionally, requiring hours of effort to get them working.

"They rely on it too much," Elend said. "If they survive our siege, they'll need to ship in supplies. Assuming any can be had."

Ham fell silent. Finally he turned, looking back along the dark canal behind them. "El," he said. "I don't think that many more will be traveling this canal. The boats barely made it this far—there's too much ash clogging it. If we go home, we'll do so on foot."

" 'If' we go home?"

Ham shrugged. Despite the colder western weather, he still wore no coat atop his vest. Now that Elend was an Allomancer, he could at last understand the habit. While burning pewter, Elend barely felt the chill, though several of the soldiers had complained about it in the mornings.

"I don't know, El," Ham said. "It seems portentous to me. Our canal closing behind us as we travel. Kind of like fate is trying to strand us here."

"Ham," Elend said, "*everything* seems portentous to you. We'll be fine."

Ham shrugged.

"Organize our forces," Elend said, pointing. "Dock us in that inlet over there, and set up camp on the mesa."

Ham nodded. However, he still looked backward. Toward Luthadel, toward what they had left behind.

They don't fear the mists, Elend thought, staring up through the darkness at the rocky formations that marked the entrance into Fadrex City. Bonfires blazed up there, lighting the night. Often such lights were futile—signifying man's fear of the mists. These fires were different somehow. They seemed a warning, a bold declaration of confidence. They burned brightly, high, as if floating in the sky.

Elend turned, walking into his illuminated commander's tent, where a small group of people sat waiting for him. Ham, Cett, and Vin. Demoux was absent, still recovering from mistsickness.

We're spread thin, Elend thought. *Spook and Breeze in the North, Penrod at Luthadel, Felt watching the storage cache in the East . . .*

"All right," Elend said, letting the tent flaps close behind him. "Looks like they're holed up in there pretty well."

"Initial scout reports are in, El," Ham said. "We're guessing about twenty-five thousand defenders."

"Not as many as I expected," Elend said.

"That bastard Yomen has to keep control of the rest of my kingdom," Cett said. "If he pulled all of his troops into the capital, the other cities would overthrow him."

"What?" Vin asked, sounding amused. "You think they'd rebel and switch back to your side?"

"No," Cett said, "they'd rebel and try to take over the kingdom themselves! That's the way this works. Now that the Lord Ruler is gone, every little lord or petty obligator with half a taste of power thinks he can run a kingdom. Hell, I tried it—so did you."

"We were successful," Ham pointed out.

"And so was Lord Yomen," Elend said, folding his arms. "He's held this kingdom since Cett marched on Luthadel."

"He all but forced me out," Cett admitted. "He had half the nobility turning on me before I even struck toward Luthadel. I said I was leaving him in charge, but we both knew the truth. He's a clever one—clever enough to know he can hold that city against a larger force, letting him spread his troops out to maintain the kingdom, and to endure a longer siege without running out of supplies."

"Unfortunately, Cett's probably right," Ham said. "Our initial reports placed Yomen's forces at somewhere around eighty thousand men. He'd be a fool to not have a few units within striking distance of our camp. We'll have to be wary of raids."

"Double the guards and triple scout patrols," Elend said, "particularly during the early morning hours, when the daymist is out to obscure, but the sun is up to provide light."

Ham nodded.

"Also," Elend said thoughtfully, "order the men to stay in their tents during the mists—but tell them to be ready for a raid. If Yomen thinks that we're afraid to come out, perhaps we can bait one of his 'surprise' attacks against us."

"Clever," Ham said.

"That won't get us past those natural walls though," Elend said, folding his arms. "Cett, what do you say?"

"Hold the canal," Cett said. "Post sentries up around those upper rock formations to make certain that Yomen doesn't resupply the city via secret means. Then move on."

"What?" Ham asked with surprise.

Elend eyed Cett, trying to decide what the man meant. "Attack surrounding cities? Leave a force here that's large enough to stymie a siege-break, then capture other parts of his territory?"

Cett nodded. "Most of the cities around here aren't fortified at all. They'd cave in without a fight."

"A good suggestion," Elend said. "But we won't do it."

"Why not?" Cett asked.

"This isn't just about reconquering your homeland, Cett," Elend said. "Our primary reason for coming here is to secure that storage cache—and I hope to do that without resorting to pillaging the countryside."

Cett snorted. "What do you expect to find in there? Some magical way to stop the ash? Even atium wouldn't do that."

"Something's in there," Elend said. "It's the only hope we have."

Cett shook his head. "You've been chasing a puzzle left by the Lord Ruler for the better part of a year, Elend. Hasn't it ever occurred to you that the man was a sadist? There's no secret. No magical way out of this. If we're going to survive the next few years, we're going to have to do it on our own—and that means securing the Western Dominance. The plateaus in this area represent some of the most elevated farmland in the empire—and higher altitude means closer to the sun. If you're going to find plants that survive despite the daymists, you'll have to grow them here."

They were good arguments. *But I can't give up,* Elend thought. *Not yet.* Elend had read the reports of supplies back in Luthadel, and had seen the projections. Ash was killing crops as much as or more than the mists were. More land wouldn't save his people—they needed something else. Something that, he hoped, the Lord Ruler left for them.

The Lord Ruler didn't hate his people, and he wouldn't want them to die out, even if he were defeated. He left food, water, supplies. And if he knew secrets, he would have hidden them in the caches. There will be something here.

There has to be.

"The cache remains our primary target," Elend said. To the side, he could see Vin smiling.

"Fine," Cett said, sighing. "Then you know what we have to do. This siege could take a while."

Elend nodded. "Ham, send our engineers in under cover of mist. See if they can find a way for our troops to cross those troughs. Have the scouts search out streams that might run into the city—Cett, presumably you can help us locate some of these. And once we get spies into the city, have them search out food stores that we can ruin."

"A good start," Cett said. "Of course, there's one easy way to sow chaos in that city, to perhaps make them surrender without a fight . . ."

"We're not going to assassinate King Yomen," Elend said.

"Why not?" Cett demanded. "We've got *two* Mistborn. We'll have no difficulty killing off the Fadrex leadership."

"We don't work that way," Ham said, face growing dark.

"Oh?" Cett asked. "That didn't stop Vin from tearing a hole through my army and attacking *me* before we teamed up."

"That was different," Ham said.

"No," Elend said, interrupting. "It wasn't. The reason we're not going to assassinate Yomen, Cett, is because I want to try diplomacy first."

"Diplomacy?" Cett asked. "Didn't we just march an army of forty thousand soldiers on his city? That's not a diplomatic move."

"True," Elend said. "But we haven't attacked, not yet. Now that I'm here in person, I might as well try talking before sending out knives in the night. We might be able to persuade Lord Yomen that an alliance will benefit him more than a war."

"If we make an alliance," Cett said, leaning forward in his chair, "I don't get my city back."

"I know," Elend said.

Cett frowned.

"You seem to be forgetting yourself, Cett," Elend said. "You did not 'team up' with me. You knelt before me, offering up oaths of service in exchange for not getting executed. Now, I appreciate your allegiance, and I *will* see you rewarded with a kingdom to rule under me. However, you don't get to choose where that kingdom is, nor when I will grant it."

Cett paused, sitting in his chair, one arm resting on his useless, paralyzed legs. Finally he smiled. "Damn, boy. You've changed a lot in the year I've known you."

"So everyone is fond of telling me," Elend said. "Vin. You think you can get into the city?"

She raised an eyebrow. "I hope that was meant to be rhetorical."

"It was meant to be polite," Elend said. "I need you to do some scouting. We know next to nothing about what's been going on in this dominance lately—we've focused all of our efforts on Urteau and the South."

Vin shrugged. "I can go poke around a bit. I don't know what you expect me to find."

"Cett," Elend said, turning, "I need names. Informants, or perhaps some noblemen that might still be loyal to you."

"Noblemen?" Cett asked, amused. "Loyal?"

Elend rolled his eyes. "How about some that could be bribed to pass on a little information."

"Sure," Cett said. "I'll write up some names and locations. Assuming they still live in the city. Hell, assuming they're even still alive. Can't count on much these days."

Elend nodded. "We won't take any further action until we have more information. Ham, make certain the soldiers dig in well—use the field fortifications that Demoux taught them. Cett, see that those guard patrols get set up, and make certain our Tineyes remain alert and on watch. Vin will scout and see if she can sneak into the cache as she did in Urteau. If we know what's in there, then we can better judge whether to gamble on trying to conquer the city or not."

The various members of the group nodded, understanding that the meeting was over. As they left, Elend stepped out into the mists, looking up at the distant bonfires burning on the rocky heights.

Quiet as a sigh, Vin stepped up to his side, following his gaze. She stood for a few moments. Then she glanced back toward where a pair of soldiers were entering the tent to carry Cett away. Her eyes narrowed in displeasure.

"I know," Elend said quietly. He could tell that she was thinking of Cett again and his influence over Elend.

"You didn't deny that you might turn to assassination," Vin said softly.

"Hopefully it won't come to that."

"And if it does?"

"Then I'll make the decision that is best for the empire."

Vin was silent for a moment. Then she glanced at the fires above.

"I could come with you," Elend offered.

She smiled, then kissed him. "Sorry," she said. "But you're noisy."

"Come now. I'm not *that* bad."

"Yes you are," Vin said. "Plus you smell."

"Oh?" he asked, amused. "What do I smell like?"

"An emperor. A Tineye would pick you out in seconds."

Elend raised his eyebrows. "I see. And don't you possess an imperial scent as well?"

"Of course I do," Vin said, wrinkling her nose. "But I know how to get rid of it. In any case, you're not good enough to go with me, Elend. I'm sorry."

Elend smiled. *Dear, blunt Vin.*

Behind him, the soldiers left the tent, carrying Cett. An aide walked up, delivering to Elend a short list of informants and noblemen who might be willing to talk. Elend passed it to Vin. "Have fun," he said.

She dropped a coin between them, kissed him again, then shot up into the night.

I am only beginning to understand the brilliance of the Lord Ruler's cultural synthesis. One of the benefits afforded him by being both immortal and—for all relevant purposes—omnipotent was a direct and effective influence on the evolution of the Final Empire.

He was able to take elements from a dozen different cultures and apply them to his new "perfect" society. For instance, the architectural brilliance of the Khlenni builders is manifest in the keeps that the high nobility construct. Khlenni fashion sense— suits for gentlemen, gowns for ladies—is another thing the Lord Ruler decided to appropriate.

I suspect that despite his hatred of the Khlenni people—of whom Alendi was one—Rashek had a deep-seated envy of them as well. The Terris of the time were pastoral herdsmen, the Khlenni cultured cosmopolitans. However ironic, it is logical that Rashek's new empire would mimic the high culture of the people he hated.

26

SPOOK STOOD IN HIS SMALL one-room lair, a room that was illegal. The Citizen forbade such places where a man could live unaccounted for, unwatched. Fortunately, forbidding such places didn't eliminate them.

It only made them more expensive.

Spook was lucky. He barely remembered leaping from the burning building, clutching six Allomantic vials, coughing and bleeding. He didn't at all remember making it back to his lair. He should probably be dead. Even surviving the fires, he should have been sold out—if the proprietor of his little illegal inn had realized who Spook was and what he'd escaped, the promise of a reward would undoubtedly have been irresistible.

But Spook was free. Perhaps the other thieves in the lair thought he had been on the wrong side of a robbery. Or perhaps they simply didn't care. Either way, he was able to stand in front of the room's small mirror, shirt off, looking in wonder at his wound.

I'm alive, he thought. *And . . . I feel pretty good.*

He stretched, rolling his arm in its socket. The wound hurt far less than it should have. In the very dim light, he was able to see the cut, scabbed over and healing. Pewter burned in his stomach—a beautiful complement to the familiar flame of tin.

He was something that shouldn't exist. In Allomancy, people either had only one of the eight basic powers, or they had all fourteen powers. One or all. Never two. Yet Spook had tried to burn other metals without success. Somehow he had been given pewter alone to complement his tin. Amazing as that was, it was overshadowed by a greater wonder.

He had seen Kelsier's spirit. The Survivor had returned and had shown himself to Spook.

Spook had no idea how to react to that. He wasn't particularly religious, but . . . well, a dead man—who some called a god—had appeared to him and saved his life. He worried that it had been a hallucination. But if that were so, how had he gained the power of pewter?

He shook his head, reaching for his bandages, but paused as something twinkled in the mirror's reflection. He stepped closer, relying—as always—upon starlight from outside to provide illumination. With his tin, it was easy to see the bit of metal sticking from the skin next to his shoulder, though it protruded only a tiny fraction of an inch.

The tip of that man's sword, Spook realized, *the one that stabbed me. It broke—the end must have gotten embedded in my skin.* He gritted his teeth, reaching to pull it free.

"No," Kelsier said. "Leave it. It, like the wound you bear, is a sign of your survival."

Spook started. He glanced about, but there was no apparition this time. Just the voice. Yet he was certain he'd heard it.

"Kelsier?" he hesitantly asked.

There was no response.

Am I going mad? Spook wondered. *Or . . . is it as the Church of the Survivor teaches?* Could it be that Kelsier had become something greater, something that watched over his followers? And if so, did Kelsier *always* watch him? That felt a little . . . unsettling. But if it brought him the power of pewter, then who was he to complain?

Spook turned and put his shirt on, stretching his arm again. He needed more information. How long had he been delirious? What was Quellion doing? Had the others from the crew arrived yet?

Taking his mind off his strange visions for the moment, he slipped out of his room and onto the dark street. As lairs went, his wasn't all that impressive—a room behind a hidden door in a slum alleyway wall. Still, it was better than living in one of the crowded shanties he passed as he made his way through the dark, mist-covered city.

The Citizen liked to pretend that everything was perfect in his little utopia, but Spook had not been surprised to find that it had slums, the same as every other city he'd ever visited. There were many people in Urteau who, for one reason or another, weren't fond of living in the parts of town where the Citizen could keep watch on them. These had aggregated in a place known as the Harrows, a cramped canal far from the main trenches.

The Harrows was clogged with a disorderly mash of wood and cloth and bodies. Shacks leaned on shacks, buildings leaned precariously against earth and rock, and the entire mess piled on top of itself, creeping up the canal walls toward the dark sky above. Here and there, people slept under only a dirty sheet stretched between two bits of urban flotsam—their millennium-old fear of the mists giving way before simple necessity.

Spook shuffled down the crowded canal. Some of the piles of half-buildings reached so high and wide that the sky narrowed to a mere crack far above, shining down its midnight light, too dim to be of use to any eyes but Spook's.

Perhaps the chaos was why the Citizen chose not to visit the Harrows. Or perhaps he was waiting to clean them out until he had a better grip on his kingdom. Either way, his strict society, mixed with the poverty it was creating, made for a curiously open nighttime culture. The Lord Ruler had patrolled the streets. The Citizen, however, preached that the mists were of Kelsier—so he could hardly forbid people to go out in them. Urteau was the first place in Spook's experience where a person could walk down a street at midnight and find a small tavern open and serving drinks. He moved inside, cloak pulled tight. There was no proper bar, just a group of dirty men sitting around a dug-out firepit in the ground. Others sat on stools or boxes in the corners. Spook found an empty box and sat down.

Then he closed his eyes and listened, filtering through the conversations. He could hear them all, of course—even with his earplugs in. So much of being a Tineye wasn't about what you could hear, but what you could ignore.

Footsteps thumped near him, and he opened his eyes. A man wearing trousers sewn with a dozen different buckles and chains stopped in front of Spook, then thumped a bottle on the ground. "Everyone drinks," the man said. "I have to pay to keep this place warm. Nobody sits for free."

"What have you got?" Spook asked.

The bartender kicked the bottle. "House Venture special vintage. Aged fifty years. Used to go for six hundred boxings a bottle."

Spook smiled, fishing out a pek—a coin minted by the Citizen to be worth a fraction of a copper clip. A combination of economic collapse and the Citizen's disapproval of luxury meant that a bottle of wine that had once been worth hundreds of boxings was now practically worthless.

"Three for the bottle," the bartender said, holding out his hand.

Spook brought out two more coins. The bartender left the bottle on the floor, so Spook picked it up. He had been offered no corkscrew or cup—both likely cost extra—though this vintage of wine had a cork that stuck up half an inch above the bottle's lip. Spook eyed it.

I wonder. . . .

He had his pewter on a low burn—not flared as his tin was. Just there enough to help with the fatigue and the pain. In fact, it did its job so well that he'd nearly forgotten about his wound during the walk to the bar. He stoked the pewter a bit, and the rest of the wound's pain vanished. Then Spook grabbed the cork, pulling it with a quick jerk. It came free of the bottle with barely a hint of resistance.

Spook tossed the cork aside. *I think I'm going to like this,* he thought with a smile.

He took a drink of the wine straight from the bottle, listening for interesting conversations. He had been sent to Urteau to gather information, and he wouldn't be much use to Elend or the others if he stayed lying in bed. Dozens of muffled conversations echoed in the room, most of them harsh. This wasn't the kind of place where one found men loyal to the local government—which was precisely why Spook had made his way to the Harrows in the first place.

"They say he's going to get rid of coins," a man whispered at the firepit. "He's making plans to gather them all up, keep them in his treasury."

"That's foolish," another voice replied. "He minted his own coins—why take them now?"

"It's true," the first voice said. "I seen him speak on it myself. He says that men shouldn't have to rely on coins—that we should have everything together, not having to buy and sell."

"The Lord Ruler never let skaa have coins either," another voice grumbled. "Seems that the longer old Quellion is in charge, the more he looks like that rat the Survivor killed."

Spook raised an eyebrow, taking another chug of wine. Vin, not Kelsier, was the one who had killed the Lord Ruler. But Urteau was a significant distance from Luthadel. They probably hadn't known about the Lord Ruler's fall until weeks after it happened.

He moved on to another conversation, searching for those who spoke in furtive whispers. He found exactly what he was listening for in a couple of men sharing a bottle of fine wine as they sat on the floor in the corner.

"Most everyone is catalogued now," the man whispered. "But he's not done yet. He has those scribes of his, the genealogists. They're asking questions, interrogating neighbors and friends, trying to trace everyone back five generations, looking for noble blood."

"But he only kills those who have noblemen back two generations."

"There's going to be a division," the other voice whispered. "Every man who is pure five generations back will be allowed to serve in the government. Everyone else will be forbidden. It's a time when a man could make a great deal of coin if he could help people hide certain events in their past."

Hum, Spook thought, taking a swig of wine. Oddly, the alcohol didn't seem to be affecting him much. *The pewter,* he realized. *It strengthens the body, makes it more resistant to pains and wounds. And perhaps helps it avoid intoxication?*

He smiled. The ability to drink and not grow drunk was an advantage of pewter that nobody had told him about. There had to be a way to use such a skill.

Spook turned his attention to other bar patrons, searching for useful tidbits. Another conversation was about work in the mines, and he felt a chill and a flicker of remembrance. The men spoke of a coal mine, not a gold mine, but the grumbles were the same. Cave-ins. Dangerous gas. Stuffy air and uncaring taskmasters.

That would have been my life, Spook thought. *If Clubs hadn't come for me.*

To this day, he still didn't understand. Why had Clubs traveled so far—visiting the distant eastern reaches of the

Final Empire—to rescue a nephew he'd never met? Surely there had been young Allomancers in Luthadel who had been equally deserving of his protection.

Clubs had spent a fortune traveling a long distance in an empire where skaa were forbidden to leave their home cities, and had risked betrayal by Spook's father. For that, Clubs had earned the loyalty of a wild street boy who— before that time—had run from any authority figure who tried to control him.

What would it be like? Spook thought. *If Clubs hadn't come for me, I would never have been in Kelsier's crew. I might have hidden my Allomancy and refused to use it. I might have simply gone to the mines, living the same life as any other skaa.*

The men commiserated about the deaths of several who had fallen to a cave-in. It seemed that for them, little had changed since the days of the Lord Ruler. Spook's life would have been like theirs, he suspected. He'd be out in those Eastern wastes, living in sweltering dust when outside, working in cramped confines the rest of the time.

Most of his life, it seemed that he had been a flake of ash, pushed around by whatever strong wind came his way. He'd gone where people told him to go, done what they'd wanted him to. Even as an Allomancer, Spook had lived his life as a nobody. The others had been great men. Kelsier had organized an impossible revolution. Vin had struck down the Lord Ruler. Clubs had led the revolutionary armies, becoming Elend's foremost general. Sazed was a Keeper, and had carried the knowledge of centuries. Breeze had moved waves of people with his clever tongue and skillful Soothing, and Ham was a powerful soldier. But Spook, he had merely watched, not really doing anything.

Until the day he ran away, leaving Clubs to die.

Spook sighed, looking up. "I just want to be able to help," he whispered.

"You can," Kelsier's voice said. "You can be great. Like I was."

Spook started, glancing about. But nobody else appeared to have heard the voice. Spook settled back uncomfortably. But the words made sense. Why did he always berate himself so much? True, Kelsier hadn't picked him to be on the crew, but now the Survivor had appeared to Spook and granted him the power of pewter.

I could help the people of this city, he thought. *As Kelsier helped those of Luthadel. I could do something important: bring Urteau into Elend's empire, deliver the storage cache as well as the loyalty of the citizens.*

I ran away once. I don't ever have to do that again. I won't ever *do that again!*

Smells of wine, bodies, ash, and mold hung in the air. Spook could feel the very grain in the stool beneath him despite his clothing, the movements of people throughout the building vibrating the ground beneath his feet. And with all of this, pewter burned within him. He flared it, made it strong alongside his tin. The bottle cracked in his hand, his fingers pressing too hard, though he released it quickly enough to keep it from shattering. It fell toward the floor, and he snatched it from the air with his other hand, the arm moving with blurring quickness.

Spook blinked, awed at the speed of his own motions. Then he smiled. *I'm going to need more pewter,* he thought.

"That's him."

Spook froze. Several of the conversations in the room had stopped, and to his ears—accustomed to a cacophony—the growing silence was eerie. He glanced to the side. The men who had been speaking of the mines were looking at Spook, speaking softly enough that they probably assumed he couldn't hear them.

"I'm telling you I saw him get *run through* by the guards. Everyone thought he was dead even before they burned him."

Not good, Spook thought. He hadn't thought himself memorable enough for people to notice. But . . . then again, he had attacked a group of soldiers in the middle of the city's busiest market.

"Durn's been talking about him," the voice continued. "Said he was of the Survivor's own crew . . ."

Durn, Spook thought. *So he* does *know who I really am. Why has he been telling people my secrets? I thought he was more careful than that.*

Spook stood up as nonchalantly as he could, then fled into the night.

Yes, Rashek made good use of his enemy's culture in developing the Final Empire. Yet other elements of imperial culture were a complete contrast to Khlennium and its society. The lives of the skaa were modeled after the slave peoples of the Cazzi. The Terris stewards resembled the servant class of Urtan, which Rashek conquered relatively late in his first century as Lord Ruler.

The imperial religion, with its obligators, appears to have arisen from the bureaucratic mercantile system of the Hallant, a people who were very focused on weights, measures, and permissions. The fact that the Lord Ruler would base his Church on a financial institution shows—in my opinion—that he worried less about true faith in his followers, and more about stability, loyalty, and quantifiable measures of devotion.

27

VIN SHOT THROUGH THE DARK night air. Mist swirled about her, a spinning, seething storm of white upon black. It darted near her body, as if snapping at her, but never came closer than a few inches away—as if blown back by some current of air. She remembered a time when the mist had skimmed close to her skin, rather than being repelled. The transition had been gradual; it had taken months before she had realized the change.

She wore no mistcloak. It felt odd to be leaping about in the mists without one of the garments, but in truth she was quieter this way. Once, the mistcloak had been useful in making guards or thieves turn away at her approach. However, like the era of friendly mists, that time had passed. So instead she wore only a black shirt and trousers, both closely fitted to her body to keep the sounds of flapping fabric to a minimum. As always, she wore no metal save for the coins in her pouch and an extra vial of metals in her sash. She pulled out a coin now—its familiar weight wrapped in a layer of cloth—and threw it beneath her. A Push against the metal sent it slamming into the rocks below, but the cloth dampened the sound of its striking. She used the Push to slow her descent.

She landed carefully on a rock ledge, then Pulled the coin back into her hand. She crept across the rocky shelf, fluffy ash beneath her toes. Not far away, a small group of guards sat in the darkness, whispering and watching Elend's army camp—which appeared as little more than a haze of firelight in the mists. The guards spoke of the spring chill, commenting that it seemed colder this year than it had in previous ones. Though Vin was barefoot, she rarely noticed the cold. A gift of pewter.

Vin burned bronze, and heard no pulses. None of the men were burning metals. One of the reasons Cett had come to Luthadel in the first place was because he'd been unable to raise enough Allomancers to protect him from Mistborn assassins. No doubt Lord Yomen had experienced similar trouble recruiting Allomancers, and he probably wouldn't have sent those he did have out into the cold to watch an enemy camp.

Vin crept past the guard post. She didn't need Allomancy to keep quiet—she and her brother, Reen, had sometimes been burglars, sneaking into homes. She had a lifetime of training that Elend would never know or understand. He could practice with pewter all he liked—and he really was getting better—but he'd never be able to replicate instincts honed by a childhood spent sneaking to stay alive.

As soon as she was past the guards, she jumped into the mists again, using her sound-deadened coins as anchors. She gave the fires at the front of the city a wide berth, instead rounding to the other side of Fadrex. Most of the patrols would be at the front of the city, for the rear was protected by the steep walls of the rising rock formations. That barely inconvenienced Vin, and she soon found herself dropping several hundred feet through the air along a rock wall before landing in an alley at the very back of the city.

She took to the roofs and did a quick survey, jumping from street to street in wide Allomantic leaps. She was quickly impressed with Fadrex's size. Elend had called the city "provincial," and Vin had imagined a town barely larger than a village. Once they'd arrived, she'd instead begun to imagine a barricaded, austere city—more like a fort. Fadrex was neither.

She should have realized that Elend—who had been raised in the sprawling metropolis of Luthadel—would have a skewed concept of what constituted a large city. Fadrex was plenty big. Vin counted several skaa slums, a smattering of noble mansions, and even two Luthadel-style keeps. The grand stone structures sported the typical arrangement of stained-glass windows and soaring, buttressed walls. These were undoubtedly the homes of the most important nobles in the city.

She landed on a rooftop near one of the keeps. Most of the buildings in the city were only a single story or two, which was quite a change from the high tenements of Luthadel. They were spaced out a bit more, and tended to be flat and squat rather than tall and peaked. That made the massive keep seem so much larger by comparison. The building was rectangular, with a row of three peaked towers rising from each end. Ornamented white stonework ran around the entire perimeter at the top.

And the walls, of course, were lined with beautiful stained-glass windows lit from within. Vin crouched on a low rooftop, looking at the colored beauty of the swirling mists. For a moment she was taken back to a time three years before, when she had attended balls in keeps like this one in Luthadel as part of Kelsier's plan to overthrow the Final Empire. She had been an uncertain, nervous thing then, worried that her newfound world of a trustworthy crew and beautiful parties would collapse around her. And in a way, it had—for that world was gone. She had helped to destroy it.

Yet during those months, she had been content. Perhaps more content than any other time in her life. She loved Elend, and was glad life had progressed to the point where she could call him husband, but there had been a delicious innocence about her early days with the crew. Dances spent with Elend reading at her table, pretending to ignore her. Nights spent learning the secrets of Allomancy. Evenings spent sitting around the table at Clubs's shop, sharing laughter with the crew. They'd faced the challenge of planning something as large as the fall of an empire, yet felt no burden of leadership or weight of responsibility for the future.

Somehow, among the fall of kings and collapse of worlds, she had grown into a woman. Once she had been terrified of change. Then she had been terrified of losing Elend. Now her fears were more nebulous—worries of what would come after she was gone, worries of what would happen to the people of the empire if she failed to divine the secrets she sought.

She turned from her contemplation of the large castle-like keep, Pushing herself off a chimney brace and into the night. Attending those balls in Luthadel had changed her dramatically, leaving a residual effect that she'd never been able to shake. Something within her had responded instantly to the dancing and the parties. For the longest time, she'd struggled to understand how that part of her fit into the rest of her life. She still wasn't certain she knew the answer. Was Valette Renoux—the girl she had pretended to be at the balls—really a part of Vin, or no more than a fabrication devised to serve Kelsier's plot?

Vin bounded across the city, making cursory notes of fortifications and troop placements. Ham and Demoux would probably find a way to get true military spies into the city eventually, but they'd want to hear preliminary information from Vin. She also paid attention to living conditions. Elend had hoped that the city would be struggling, a factor that his siege would exacerbate, making Lord Yomen more likely to capitulate.

She found no obvious signs of mass starvation or disrepair—though it was difficult to tell much at night. The city streets were kept swept of ash, and a remarkable number of the noble homes appeared occupied. She would have expected the noble population to be the first to bolt at news of an approaching army.

Frowning to herself, Vin completed her loop of the city, landing in a particular square that Cett had suggested. The mansions here were separated from each other by large grounds and cultivated trees; she walked along the street, counting them off. At the fourth mansion, she leaped up and over the gate, then moved up the hill to the house.

She wasn't certain what she expected to find—Cett had been absent from the city for a year and a half, after all. Yet he'd indicated that this informant was the most likely to be of help. True to Cett's instructions, the rear balcony of the mansion was lit. Vin waited in the darkness, suspicious, the mist cold and unfriendly, yet providing cover. She didn't trust Cett—she worried that he still bore her a grudge for her attack on his keep in Luthadel a year before. Wary, she dropped a coin and launched herself into the air.

A lone figure sat on the balcony, fitting the description in Cett's instructions. Those same instructions gave this informant the nickname Slowswift. The old man appeared to be reading by the light of a lamp. Vin frowned, but as instructed, she landed on the balcony railing, crouching by a ladder that would have allowed a more mundane visitor to approach.

The old man did not glance up from his book. He puffed quietly on a pipe, a thick woolen blanket across his knees. Vin wasn't certain whether he noticed her. She cleared her throat.

"Yes, yes," the old man said calmly. "I shall be with you in a moment."

Vin cocked her head, looking at the strange man with his bushy eyebrows and frosty white hair. He was dressed in a nobleman's suit, with a scarf and an overcoat that bore an oversized fur collar. He appeared to be completely unconcerned by the Mistborn crouching on his railing.

Eventually the elderly man closed his book, then turned toward her. "Do you enjoy stories, young lady?"

"What kind of stories?"

"The best kind, of course," Slowswift said, tapping his book. "The kind about monsters and myths. Longtales, some call them—stories told by skaa around the fires, whispering of mistwraiths, shades, spren, and brollins and such."

"I don't have much time for stories," Vin said.

"Seems that fewer and fewer people do, these days." A canopy kept off the ash, but he seemed unconcerned about the mists. "It makes me wonder what is so alluring about the real world that gives them all such a fetish for it. It's not a very nice place these days."

Vin did a quick check with bronze, but the man burned nothing. What was his game? "I was told that you could give me information," she said carefully.

"That I can certainly do," the man said. Then he smiled, glancing at her. "I have a wealth of information—though I suspect that you might find most of it useless."

"I'll listen to a story, if that's what it will cost."

The man chuckled. "There's no surer way to kill a story than to make it a 'cost,' young lady. What is your name, and who sent you?"

"Vin Venture," Vin said. "Cett gave me your name."

"Ah," the man said. "That scoundrel still alive?"

"Yes."

"Well, I suppose I could chat with someone sent by an old writing friend. Come down off that railing—you're giving me vertigo."

Vin climbed down, wary. "Writing friend?"

"Cett is one of the finest poets I know, child," said Slowswift, waving her toward a chair. "We shared our work with one another for a good decade or so before politics stole him away. He didn't care for stories either. To him, everything had to be gritty and 'real,' even his poetry. Seems like an attitude with which you'd agree."

Vin shrugged, sitting in the indicated chair. "I suppose."

"I find that ironic in a way you shall never understand," the old man said, smiling. "Now, what is it you wish of me?"

"I need to know about Yomen, the obligator king."

"He's a good man."

Vin frowned.

"Oh," Slowswift said. "You didn't expect that? Everyone who is your enemy must also be an evil person?"

"No," Vin said, thinking back to the days before the fall of the Final Empire. "I ended up marrying someone my friends would have named an enemy."

"Ah. Well then, Yomen is a fine man, and a decent king. A fair bit better a king than Cett ever was, I'd say. My old friend tries too hard, and that makes him brutal. He doesn't have the subtle touch that a leader needs."

"Then what has Yomen done that is so good?" Vin asked.

"He kept the city from falling apart," Slowswift said, puffing on his pipe. The smoke mixed with the swirling mists. "Plus he gave both nobility and skaa what they wanted."

"Which was?"

"Stability, child. For a time the world was in turmoil—neither skaa nor nobleman knew his place. Society was collapsing, and people were starving. Cett did little to stop that—he fought constantly to keep what he'd killed to obtain. Then Yomen stepped in. He represented continuity with the Lord Ruler and his Ministry, and the people were ready to accept an obligator as a leader. Yomen immediately took control of the plantations and brought food to his people, then he returned the factories to operation, started work in the Fadrex mines again, and gave the nobility a semblance of normalcy."

Vin sat quietly. Before, it would have seemed incredible to her that—after a thousand years of oppression—the people would willingly return to slavery. Yet something similar had happened in Luthadel. They had ousted Elend, who had granted them great freedoms, and had put Penrod in charge—all because he promised them a return to what they had lost.

"Yomen is an obligator," she said.

"People like what is familiar, child."

"They're oppressed."

"Someone must lead," the old man said. "And someone must follow. That is the way of things. Yomen has given the people something they've been crying for since the Collapse—identity. The skaa may work, they may be beaten, they may be enslaved, but they know their place. The nobility may spend their time going to balls, but there is an order to life again."

"Balls?" Vin asked. "The world is ending, and Yomen is throwing *balls*?"

"Of course," Slowswift said, taking a long, slow puff on his pipe. "Yomen rules by maintaining the familiar. He gives the people what they had before—and balls were a large part of life before the Collapse, even in a smaller city such as Fadrex. Why, there is one happening tonight, at Keep Orielle."

"On the very day an army arrived to besiege the city?"

"You just pointed out that the world itself seems close to disaster," the old man said, pointing at her with his pipe. "In the face of that, an army doesn't mean much. Plus, Yomen understands something even the Lord Ruler didn't—Yomen always personally attends the balls thrown by his subjects. In doing so, he comforts and reassures them. That makes a day like this, when an army arrived, a perfect day for a ball."

Vin sat back, uncertain what to think. Of all the things she had expected to find in the city, courtly balls were decidedly low on the list. "So," she said, "what's Yomen's weakness? Is there something in his past that we can use? What quirks of personality make him vulnerable? Where should we strike?"

Slowswift puffed softly on his pipe, a breeze blowing mist and ash across his elderly figure.

"Well?" Vin asked.

The old man let out a breath of mist and smoke. "I told you that I like the man, child. What would possess me to give you information to use against him?"

"You're an informant," Vin said. "That's what you do— sell information."

"I'm a storyteller," Slowswift corrected. "And not every story is meant for every set of ears. Why should I talk to those who would attack my city and overthrow my liege?"

"We'd give you a powerful position in the city once it is ours."

Slowswift snorted. "If you think such things would interest me, then Cett clearly told you little regarding my temperament."

"We could pay you well."

"I sell information, child. Not my soul."

"You're not being very helpful," Vin noted.

"And tell me, dear child," he said, smiling slightly. "Why exactly should I care?"

Vin frowned. *This is,* she thought, *undoubtedly the strangest informant meeting I've ever been to.*

Slowswift puffed on his pipe. He didn't appear to be waiting for her to say anything. In fact, he seemed to think the conversation was over.

He's a nobleman, Vin thought. *He likes the way that the world used to be. It was comfortable. Even skaa fear change.*

Vin stood. "I'll tell you why you should care, old man. Because the ash is falling, and soon it will cover up your pretty little city. The mists kill. Earthquakes shake the landscape, and the Ashmounts burn hotter and hotter. Change is looming. Eventually no one, including Yomen, will be able to ignore it. You hate change. I hate it too. But things can't stay the same—and that's well, for when nothing changes in your life, it's as good as being dead." She turned to leave.

"They say you'll stop the ash," the old man said quietly from behind. "Turn the sun yellow again. They call you Heir of the Survivor. Hero of Ages."

Vin turned her head to look through the traitorous mist toward the man with his pipe and closed book. "Yes," she said.

"Seems like quite the destiny to live up to."

"It's either that or give up."

Slowswift sat silently for a moment. "Sit down, child," the old man finally said, gesturing toward the seat once more.

Vin reseated herself.

"Yomen is a good man," Slowswift said, "but only a middling leader. He's a bureaucrat, a member of the Canton of Resource. He can make things happen—get supplies to the right places, organize construction projects. Ordinarily, that would have made him a good enough ruler. However . . ."

"Not when the world is ending," Vin said softly.

"Precisely. If what I've heard is true, then your husband is a man of vision and action. If our little city is going to survive, we'll need to be part of what you are offering."

"What do we do then?"

"Yomen has few weaknesses," Slowswift said. "He's a calm man, and an honorable one. However, he has an unfailing belief in the Lord Ruler and his organization."

"Even now?" Vin asked. "The Lord Ruler died!"

"Yes, so?" Slowswift asked, amused. "And your Survivor? Last I checked, he was somewhat dead as well. Didn't seem to hinder his revolution much, now did it?"

"Good point."

"Yomen is a believer," Slowswift said. "That may be a weakness; it may be a strength. Believers are often willing to attempt the seemingly impossible, then count on providence to see them through." He paused, glancing at Vin. "That sort of behavior can be a weakness *if* the belief is misplaced."

Vin said nothing. Belief in the Lord Ruler *was* misplaced. If he'd been a god, then she wouldn't have been able to kill him. In her mind, it was a simple matter.

"If Yomen has another weakness," Slowswift said, "it is his wealth."

"Hardly a weakness."

"It is if you can't account for its source. He got money somewhere—a suspiciously vast amount of it, far more than local Ministry coffers should have been able to provide. Nobody knows where it came from."

The cache, Vin thought, perking up. *He really does have the atium!*

"You reacted a little too strongly to that one," Slowswift said, taking a puff on his pipe. "You should try to give less away when speaking with an informant."

Vin flushed.

"Anyway," the old man said, turning back to his book, "if that is all, I should like to return to my reading. Give my regards to Ashweather."

Vin nodded, rising and moving over toward the banister. As she did, however, Slowswift cleared his throat. "Usually," he noted, "there is compensation for acts such as mine."

Vin raised an eyebrow. "I thought you said that stories shouldn't cost."

"Actually," Slowswift noted, "I said that a story itself shouldn't be a cost. That is very different from the story costing something. And while some will argue, I believe that a story without cost is one considered worthless."

"I'm sure that's the only reason," Vin said, smiling slightly as she tossed her bag of coins—minus a few cloth-covered ones to use for jumping—to the old man. "Gold imperials. Still good here, I assume?"

"Good enough," the old man said, tucking them away. "Good enough."

Vin jumped out into the night, leaping a few houses away, burning bronze to see if she felt any Allomantic pulses from behind. She knew that her nature made her irrationally suspicious of people who appeared weak. For the longest time, she'd been convinced that Cett was Mistborn simply because he was paraplegic. Still, she checked on Slowswift. This was one old habit that she didn't feel much need to extinguish.

No pulses came from behind. Soon she moved on, pulling out Cett's instructions, searching out a second informant. She trusted Slowswift's words well enough, but she would like confirmation. She picked an informant on the other end of the spectrum—a beggar named Hoid whom Cett claimed could be found in a particular square late at night.

A few quick jumps brought her to the location. She landed atop a roof and looked down, scanning the area. The ash had been allowed to drift here, piling in corners, making a general mess of things. A group of lumps huddled in an alley beside the square. Beggars without home or job. Vin had lived that way at times, sleeping in alleys, coughing up ash, hoping it wouldn't rain. She soon located a figure that wasn't sleeping like the others, but sitting quietly in the light ashfall. Her ears picked out a faint sound. The man was humming to himself, as the instructions said that he might be doing.

Vin hesitated.

She couldn't decide what it was, but something bothered her about the situation. It wasn't right. She didn't stop to think; she simply turned and jumped away. That was one of the big differences between her and Elend—she didn't always need a reason. A feeling was enough. He always wanted to tease things out and find a *why,* and she loved him for his logic. However, he would have been frustrated about her decision to turn from the square as she had.

Perhaps nothing bad would have happened if she'd gone into the square. Perhaps something terrible would have occurred. She would never know, nor did she need to know. As she had countless other times in her life, Vin simply accepted her instincts and moved on.

Her flight took her along a street that Cett had noted in his instructions. Curious, Vin didn't search out another informant, but instead followed the road, bounding from anchor to anchor in the pervasive mists. She landed on a cobbled street a short distance from a building with lit windows.

Blocky and utilitarian, the building was nonetheless daunting—if only because of its size. Cett had written that the Canton of Resource was the largest of the Steel Ministry buildings in the city. Fadrex had acted as a kind of way station between Luthadel and more important cities to the west. Near several main canal routes and well fortified against banditry, the city was the perfect place for a Canton of Resource regional headquarters. Yet Fadrex hadn't been important enough to attract the Cantons of Orthodoxy or Inquisition—traditionally the most powerful of the Ministry departments.

That meant that Yomen, as head obligator at the Resource building, had been the area's top religious authority. From what Slowswift said, Vin assumed that Yomen was pretty much a standard Resource obligator: dry and boring, but terribly efficient. So of course he'd chosen to make his old Canton building into his palace. It was what Cett had suspected, and Vin could easily see that it was true. The building bustled with activity despite the late hour, and was guarded by platoons of soldiers. Yomen had probably chosen the building in order to remind everyone where his authority originated.

Unfortunately, it was also where the Lord Ruler's supply cache would be located. Vin sighed, turning from her contemplation of the building. Part of her wanted to sneak in and try to find her way down to the cavern beneath. Instead she dropped a coin and shot herself into the air. Even Kelsier wouldn't have tried breaking in on his first night of scouting. She'd gotten into the one in Urteau, but it had been unguarded. She had to confer with Elend and study the city for a few days before she did something as bold as sneak into a fortified palace.

Using starlight and tin, Vin read off the name of the third and final informant. It was another nobleman, which wasn't surprising, considering Cett's own station. She began moving in the direction indicated—and noticed something.

She was being followed.

She only caught hints of him behind her, obscured by the patterns of swirling mist. Tentatively, Vin burned bronze, and was rewarded with a very faint thumping from behind. An obscured Allomantic pulse. Usually when an Allomancer burned copper—as the one behind her was doing—it made him invisible to the Allomantic bronze sense. Yet for some reason Vin had never been able to explain, she could see through this obfuscation. The Lord Ruler had been able to do likewise, as had his Inquisitors.

Vin continued to move. The Allomancer following her obviously believed himself—or herself—invisible to Vin's senses. He moved with quick, easy bounds, following at a safe distance. He was good without being excellent, and he was clearly Mistborn, for only a Mistborn could have burned both copper and steel at the same time.

Vin wasn't surprised. She'd assumed that if there were any Mistborn in the city, her leaping would draw their attention. Just in case, she hadn't bothered burning any copper, leaving her pulses open to be heard by anyone—Mistborn or Seeker—who was listening. Better an enemy drawn out than one hiding in the shadows.

She increased her pace, though not suspiciously so, and the person following had to move quickly to keep up. Vin kept going toward the front of the city, as if planning to leave. As she got closer, her Allomantic senses produced twin blue lines pointing at the massive iron brackets holding the city gates to the rock at their sides. The brackets were large, substantial sources of metal, and the lines they gave off were bright and thick.

Which meant they would make excellent anchors. Flaring her pewter to keep from being crushed, Vin *Pushed* on the brackets, throwing herself backward.

Immediately, the Allomantic pulses behind her disappeared.

Vin shot through ash and mist, even her tight clothing flapping slightly from the wind. She quickly Pulled herself down to a rooftop and crouched, tense. The other Allomancer must have stopped burning his metals. But why would he do that? Did he know that she could pierce copperclouds? If he did, then why had he followed her so recklessly?

Vin felt a chill. There was something else that gave off Allomantic pulses in the night. The mist spirit. She hadn't seen it in over a year. In fact, during her last encounter with it, it had nearly killed Elend—only to then restore him by making him Mistborn.

She still didn't know how the spirit fit into all of this. It wasn't Ruin—she had felt Ruin's presence when she'd freed him at the Well of Ascension. They were different.

I don't know if this was *the spirit tonight,* Vin told herself. Yet the one tailing her had vanished so abruptly. . . .

Confused and chilled, she Pushed herself out of the city and quickly made her way back to Elend's camp.

One final aspect of the Lord Ruler's cultural manipulation is quite interesting: that of technology.

I have already mentioned that Rashek chose to use Khlenni architecture, which allowed him to construct large structures and gave him the civil engineering necessary to build a city as large as Luthadel. In other areas, however, he suppressed technological advancements. Gunpowder, for instance, was so frowned upon by Rashek that knowledge of its use disappeared almost as quickly as knowledge of the Terris religion.

Apparently, Rashek found it alarming that, armed with gunpowder weapons, the most common of men could be nearly as effective as archers with years of training. So he favored archers. The more training-dependent military technology was, the less likely it was that the peasant population would be able to rise up and resist him. Indeed, skaa revolts always failed in part for this very reason.

28

"ARE YOU SURE IT WAS the mist spirit?" Elend asked, a half-finished letter—scribed into a steel foil sheet—sitting on his desk before him. He'd decided to sleep in his cabin aboard the narrowboat, instead of in a tent. Not only was it more comfortable, he felt more secure with walls around him, as opposed to canvas.

Vin sighed, sitting down on their bed, pulling her legs up and setting her chin on her knees. "I don't know. I kind of got spooked, so I fled."

"Good thing," Elend said, shivering as he remembered what the mist spirit had done to him.

"Sazed was convinced that the mist spirit wasn't evil," Vin said.

"So was I," Elend said. "I'm the one who walked up to it, telling you that I felt it was friendly. That was right about the time it stabbed me."

Vin shook her head. "It was trying to keep me from releasing Ruin. It thought that if you were dying, I would take the power for myself and heal you, rather than giving it up."

"You don't know its intentions for certain, Vin. You could be connecting coincidences in your mind."

"Perhaps. But it did lead Sazed to discover that Ruin was altering text."

That much was true—if Sazed's account of the matter could be trusted. The Terrisman had been a little . . . inconsistent since Tindwyl had died. *No,* Elend told himself, feeling an instant stab of guilt. *No, Sazed is trustworthy. He might be struggling with his faith, but he is still twice as reliable as the rest of us.*

"Oh, Elend," Vin said softly. "There's so much we don't know. Lately, I feel like my life is a book written in a language I can't read. The mist spirit is related to all this, but I can't begin to fathom how."

"It's probably on our side," Elend said, though it was hard not to keep flashing back to memories of how it had felt to be stabbed, to feel his life fading away. To die, knowing what it would do to Vin.

He forced himself to focus on the conversation at hand. "You think the mist spirit tried to keep you from releasing Ruin, and Sazed says it gave him important information. That makes it the enemy of our enemy."

"For the moment," Vin said. "But the mist spirit is much weaker than Ruin. I've felt them both. Ruin was . . . vast. Powerful. It can hear whatever we say—can see all places at once. The mist spirit is far fainter. More of a memory than a real force or power."

"Do you still think it hates you?"

Vin shrugged. "I haven't seen it in over a year. Yet I'm pretty sure that it isn't the sort of thing that changes, and I always felt hatred and animosity from it." She paused, frowning. "That was the beginning. The night I first saw the mist spirit was when I began to sense that the mists were no longer my home."

"Are you sure the spirit isn't what kills people and makes them sick?"

"Yes, I'm sure." Vin was adamant about this, though Elend felt she was a bit quick to judge. Something ghostly, moving about in the mists? It seemed like exactly the kind of thing that would be related to people dying suddenly in those same mists.

Of course, the people who fell to the mists didn't die of stabbings, but of a shaking disease. Elend sighed, rubbing his eyes. His incomplete letter to Lord Yomen sat on his desk—he'd have to finish it in the morning.

"Elend," Vin said. "Tonight I told someone that I'd stop the ash from falling and turn the sun yellow."

Elend raised an eyebrow. "That informant you spoke of?"

Vin nodded. The two sat in silence.

"I never expected you to admit something like that," he finally said.

"I'm the Hero of Ages, aren't I? Sazed said so, before he started having issues. It's my destiny."

"The same destiny that said you would take up the power of the Well of Ascension, then release it for the greater good of mankind?"

Vin nodded.

"Vin," Elend said, smiling, "I really don't think destiny is the sort of thing we need to worry about at the moment. I mean, we have proof that the prophecies were twisted by Ruin in order to trick people into freeing him."

"Someone has to worry about the ash," Vin said.

There wasn't much he could say to that. The logical side

of him wanted to argue, to claim they should focus on the things they could do—making a stable government, uncovering the secrets left by the Lord Ruler, securing the supplies in the caches. Yet the constant ashfall seemed to be growing denser. If that continued, it wouldn't be long before the sky was nothing more than a solid black storm of ash.

It was just so difficult to think that Vin—his wife— could do anything about the color of the sun or the falling ash. *Demoux is right,* he thought, tapping his fingers across the metallic letter to Lord Yomen. *I'm really not a very good member of the Church of the Survivor.*

He looked across the cabin at her, sitting on the bed, expression distant as she thought about things that shouldn't have to be her burden. Even after leaping about all night, even after their days spent traveling, even with her face dirtied by ash, she was beautiful.

At that moment, Elend realized something. Vin didn't need another person worshipping her. She didn't need another faithful believer like Demoux, especially not in Elend. He didn't need to be a good member of the Church of the Survivor. He needed to be a good husband.

"Well then," he said, "let's do it."

"What?" Vin asked.

"Save the world," Elend said. "Stop the ash."

Vin snorted quietly. "You make it sound like a joke."

"No, I'm serious," he said, standing. "If this is what you feel you must do—what you feel that you are—then let's do it. I'll help however I can."

"What about what you said before?" Vin said. "In the last storage cavern—that you had no way to affect the larger issues, so you would just deal with the armies."

"I was wrong."

Vin smiled, and suddenly Elend felt as if the world had been put back together a tiny amount.

"So," Elend said, sitting on the bed beside her. "What have you got? Any thoughts?"

Vin paused. "Yes," she said. "But I can't tell you."

Elend frowned.

"It's not that I don't trust you," Vin said. "It's Ruin. In the last storage cavern, I found a second inscription on the plaque, down near the bottom. It warned me that anything I speak—or that I write—will be known by our enemy. So if we talk too much, *he* will know our plans."

"That makes it a bit difficult to work on the problem together."

Vin took his hands. "Elend, do you know why I finally agreed to marry you?"

Elend shook his head.

"Because I realized that you trusted me," Vin said. "Trusted me as nobody ever has before. On that night when I fought Zane, I decided I had to give my trust to you. This force that's destroying the world, we have something it can never understand. I don't necessarily need your help; I need your trust. Your hope. It's something I've never had of myself, and I rely on yours."

Elend nodded slowly. "You have it."

"Thank you."

"You know," Elend added, "during those days when you refused to marry me, I constantly thought about how strange you were."

She raised an eyebrow. "Well, that's romantic."

Elend smiled. "Oh, come on. You have to admit that you're unusual, Vin. You're some strange mixture of a noblewoman, a street urchin, and a cat. Plus you've managed—in our short three years together—to kill not only my god, but my father, my brother, *and* my fiancée. That's kind of like a homicidal hat trick. It's a strange foundation for a relationship, wouldn't you say?"

Vin rolled her eyes.

"I'm glad I don't have any other close relatives," Elend said. Then he eyed her. "Except for you, of course."

"I'm not about to drown myself, if that's what you're getting at."

"No," Elend said. "I'm sorry. I . . . well, you know. Anyway, I was explaining something. In the end, I stopped worrying about how strange you seemed. I realized that it didn't really *matter* if I understood you, because I trusted you. Does that make sense? In any case, I guess I'm saying that I agree. I don't really know what you're doing, and I don't have any clue how you're going to achieve it. But, well, I trust that you'll do it."

Vin pulled close to him.

"I do wish there were something I could do to help," Elend said.

"Then take the whole numbers part," Vin said, frowning distastefully. Though she'd been the one to think something was odd about the percentages of those who fell to the mists, Elend knew that she found numbers troublesome. She didn't have the training, or the practice, to deal with them.

"You're sure that's related?" Elend asked.

"You were the one who thought that the percentages were so strange."

"Good point. All right, I'll work on it."

"But don't tell me what you discover," Vin said.

"Well, how is *that* going to help anything?"

"Trust," Vin said. "You can tell me what to do, only don't tell me why. Maybe we can stay ahead of this thing."

Stay ahead of it? Elend thought. *It has the power to bury the entire empire in ash, and can apparently hear every single word we say. How do we "stay ahead" of something like that?* But he had just promised to trust Vin, so he did so.

Vin pointed at the table. "Is that your letter to Yomen?"

Elend nodded. "I'm hoping that he'll talk to me, now that I'm here."

"Slowswift does seem to think that Yomen is a good man. Maybe he'll listen."

"Somehow I doubt it," Elend said. He sat quietly for a moment, then made a fist, gritting his teeth in frustration. "I told the others I want to try diplomacy, but I *know* Yomen is going to reject my message. That's why I brought my army in the first place. I could have sent you to sneak in like you did in Urteau, but sneaking in didn't help us much there. We still have to secure the city if we want the supplies.

"We *need* this city. Even if you hadn't felt so driven to discover what was in the cache, I would have come here. The threat Yomen poses to our kingdom is too strong, and the possibility that the Lord Ruler left important information in that cache can't be ignored. Yomen has grain in that storage, but the land here won't get enough sunlight to grow it. So he'll probably feed it to the people—a waste, when we don't have enough to plant and fill the Central Dominance. We have to take this city, or at least make an ally out of it.

"But what do I do if Yomen won't talk? Send armies to attack nearby villages? Poison the city's supplies? Since he's found the cache, that means he'll have more food than we hoped. Unless we destroy that, he might outlast our siege. But if I do destroy it, his people will starve." Elend shook his head. "Do you remember when I executed Jastes?"

"That was well within your right," Vin said quickly.

"I believe it was," Elend said. "But I killed him because he led a group of koloss to my city, then let them ravage my people. I've nearly done the same thing here. There are twenty thousand of the beasts outside."

"You can control them."

"Jastes thought he could control them too," Elend said. "I don't want to turn those creatures loose, Vin. But what if the siege fails, and I have to try to break Yomen's fortifications? I won't be able to do that without the koloss." He shook his head. "If only I could *talk* to Yomen. Perhaps I could make him see reason, or at least convince myself he needs to fall."

"There . . . might be a way."

Elend glanced over, catching Vin's eyes.

"They're still staging balls inside the city," she said. "And King Yomen attends every one."

Elend blinked. At first he assumed that he must have misunderstood her. But the look in her eyes—that wild determination—persuaded him otherwise. Sometimes he saw a touch of the Survivor in her, or at least of the man the stories claimed Kelsier had been. Bold to the point of recklessness. Brave and brash. He'd rubbed off on Vin more than she cared to admit.

"Vin," he said flatly, "did you just suggest that we attend a *ball* being held in the middle of a city we're besieging?"

Vin shrugged. "Sure. Why not? We're both Mistborn—we can get into that city without much trouble at all."

"Yes, but . . ." He trailed off.

I'd have a room filled with the very nobility I'm hoping to intimidate—not to mention have access to the man who refuses to meet with me, in a situation where he'd have trouble running away without coming off as a coward.

"You think it's a good idea," Vin said, smiling impishly.

"It's a *crazy* idea," Elend said. "I'm emperor—I shouldn't be sneaking into the enemy city so I can go to a party."

Vin narrowed her eyes, staring at him.

"I will admit, however," Elend said, "that the concept *does* have considerable charm."

"Yomen won't come meet us," Vin said, "so we go in and crash his party."

"It's been a while since I've been to a ball," Elend said speculatively. "I'll have to dig up some good reading material for old time's sake."

Suddenly, Vin grew pale. Something was wrong, Elend sensed. Not with what he'd said, but something else. *What is it? Assassins? Mist spirits? Koloss?*

"I realized something," Vin said, looking at him with those intense eyes of hers. "I can't go to a ball—I didn't bring a gown!"

The Lord Ruler didn't only forbid certain technologies; he suppressed technological advancement completely. It seems odd now that during the entirety of his thousand-year reign, little progress was made. Farming techniques, architectural methods— even fashion remained remarkably stable during the Lord Ruler's reign.

He constructed his perfect empire, then tried to make it stay that way. For the most part, he was successful. Pocket watches— another Khlenni appropriation—that were made in the tenth century of the empire were nearly identical to those made during the first. Everything stayed the same.

Until it all collapsed.

29

LIKE MOST CITIES IN THE Final Empire, Urteau had been forbidden a city wall. In the early days of Sazed's life, before he'd rebelled, the fact that cities couldn't build fortifications had always seemed a subtle indication to him of the Lord Ruler's vulnerability. After all, if the Lord Ruler was worried about rebellions and cities that could stand up to him, then perhaps he knew something that nobody else did: that he *could* be defeated.

Such thoughts had led Sazed to Mare, then to Kelsier. And now they led him to Urteau—a city that at long last *had* rebelled against noble leadership. Unfortunately, it lumped Elend Venture in with all the other nobles.

"I don't like this, Master Keeper," Captain Goradel said, walking beside Sazed, who—for the sake of his image— now rode in the carriage with Breeze and Allrianne. After leaving the Terris people behind, Sazed had managed to catch up with Breeze and the others only two days before, and they were finally entering the city that was their destination.

"Things are supposed to be brutal in there," Goradel continued. "I doubt you'll be safe."

"I expect it's not as bad as you think," Sazed said.

"What if they take you captive?" Goradel asked.

"My dear man," Breeze said, leaning forward to look out at Goradel. "That's why kings *send* ambassadors. This way, if someone gets captured, the king is still safe. We, my friend, are something Elend can never be: expendable."

Goradel frowned at that. "I don't *feel* very expendable."

Sazed peered out at the large city through the falling ash. It was one of the oldest cities in the empire. He noted with interest that as they approached, the road sloped downward, entering a canal trough.

"What's this?" Allrianne asked, sticking her blonde head out of the other side of the carriage. "Why'd they build their roads in ditches?"

"Canals, my dear," Breeze said. "The city used to be filled with them. Now they're empty—an earthquake or something diverted a river."

"It's creepy," she said, bringing her head back in. "It makes the buildings look twice as tall."

As they went farther into the city—their two hundred soldiers marching around them in formation—they were met by a delegation of Urteau soldiers in brown uniforms. Sazed had sent word ahead of their coming, and the king— the Citizen, they called him—had given Sazed leave to bring his small contingent of troops into the city.

"They say that their king asks to meet with you immediately, Master Terrisman," Goradel said, returning to the carriage.

"The man doesn't waste time, does he?" Breeze asked.

"We'll go then," Sazed said, nodding to Goradel.

"You aren't wanted here."

Quellion, the Citizen, was a short-haired man with rough skin and an almost military bearing. Sazed wondered where the man—apparently a simple farmer before the Collapse—had gained such leadership skills.

"I realize that you have no desire to see foreign soldiers in your city," Sazed said carefully. "However, you must have realized that we do not come to conquer. Two hundred men is hardly an invading force."

Quellion stood at his desk, arms clasped behind him. He wore what appeared to be ordinary skaa trousers and shirt, though both had been dyed a deep red verging on maroon. His "audience chamber" was a large conference room in what had once been a nobleman's house. The walls had been whitewashed and the chandelier removed. Stripped of its furniture and finery, the room felt like a box.

Sazed, Breeze, and Allrianne sat on hard wooden stools, the only comfort the Citizen had offered them. Goradel stood at the rear with ten of his soldiers as a guard.

"It isn't about the soldiers, Terrisman," Quellion said. "It's about the man who sent you."

"Emperor Venture is a good and reasonable monarch," Sazed said.

Quellion snorted, turning to make a remark to one of his companions. He had many of these—perhaps twenty—and Sazed assumed they were members of his government. Most wore red like Quellion, though their clothing hadn't been dyed as deeply.

"Elend Venture," Quellion said, raising a finger, turning back to Sazed, "is a liar and a tyrant."

"That isn't true."

"Oh?" Quellion asked. "And how did he gain his throne? By defeating Straff Venture and Ashweather Cett in war?"

"War was—"

"War is often the excuse of tyrants, Terrisman," Quellion said. "My reports said that his Mistborn wife forced the kings to kneel before him that day—forced them to swear their loyalty to him or be slaughtered by his koloss brutes. Does that sound like the actions of a 'good and reasonable' man?"

Sazed didn't respond.

Quellion stepped forward, laying both hands palm-down on the top of his desk. "Do you know what we've done to the noblemen in this city, Terrisman?"

"You've killed them," Sazed said quietly.

"As the Survivor ordered," Quellion said. "You claim to have been his companion before the fall. Yet you serve one of the very noble houses he sought to overthrow. Doesn't that strike you as inconsistent, Terrisman?"

"Lord Kelsier accomplished his purpose in the death of the Lord Ruler," Sazed said. "Once that was achieved, peace—"

"Peace?" Quellion asked. "Tell me, Terrisman. Did you ever hear the Survivor speak of peace?"

Sazed hesitated. "No," he admitted.

Quellion snorted. "At least you're honest. The only reason I'm talking to you is because Venture was clever enough to send a Terrisman. If he'd sent a nobleman, I would have killed the cur and sent his blackened skull as an answer."

The room fell silent. Tense. After a few moments of waiting, Quellion turned from Sazed, facing his companions. "You sense that?" he asked his men. "Can you feel yourselves begin to feel ashamed? Examine your emotions—do you suddenly feel a fellowship with these servants of a liar?"

He glanced back, at Breeze. "I've warned you all of Allomancy, the black tool of the nobility. Well, now you get to feel it. That man—sitting beside our *distinguished* Terrisman—is known as Breeze. He's one of the world's most vile men. A Soother of no small skill."

Quellion turned to address him. "Tell me, Soother. How

many friends have your magics made for you? How many enemies have you forced to kill themselves? That pretty girl next to you—did you use your arts to hex her into your bed?"

Breeze smiled, raising his cup of wine. "My dear man, you have plainly found me out. However, instead of congratulating yourself for noticing my touch, perhaps you should ask yourself why I manipulated you into saying what you just did."

Quellion paused—though of course Breeze was bluffing. Sazed sighed. An indignant reaction would have been far more appropriate—but that wasn't Breeze's way. Now the Citizen would spend the rest of the meeting wondering if his words were being guided by Breeze.

"Master Quellion," Sazed said, "these are dangerous times. Surely you have noticed that."

"We can protect ourselves well enough," Quellion said.

"I'm not speaking of armies or bandits, Citizen. I'm speaking of mists and ash. Have you noticed that the mists are lingering longer and longer during the daylight hours? Have you noticed them doing strange things to your people, causing the deaths of some who go out?"

Quellion did not contradict him or call his words foolish. That told Sazed enough. People had died in this city.

"The ash falls perpetually, Citizen," Sazed said. "The mists are deadly, and the koloss run free. This would be a good time to have powerful alliances. In the Central Dominance we can grow better crops, for we get more sunlight. Emperor Venture has discovered a method of controlling the koloss. Whatever is to come in the next few years, it would be very advantageous to be Emperor Venture's friend."

Quellion shook his head as if in resignation. He turned to his companions once more. "You see—just as I told you. First he tells us he comes in peace, then he moves on to threats. Venture controls the koloss. Venture controls the food. Next he'll be saying that Venture controls the mists!" Quellion turned back to Sazed. "We don't have any use for threats here, Terrisman. We aren't worried about our future."

Sazed raised an eyebrow. "And why is that?"

"Because *we* follow the Survivor," Quellion said. "Be gone from my sight."

Sazed stood. "I would like to stay in the city and perhaps meet with you again."

"That meeting will not happen."

"Regardless," Sazed said. "I would prefer to stay. You have my promise that my men will not cause trouble. Might I have your leave?" He bowed his head in deference.

Quellion muttered something under his breath before waving a hand at him. "If I forbid you, then you'll simply sneak in. Stay if you must, Terrisman, but I warn you— follow our laws and do not make trouble."

Sazed bowed farther, then retreated with his people.

"Well," Breeze said, settling into the carriage, "murderous revolutionaries, everybody wearing the same grey clothing, ditchlike streets where every tenth building has been burned to the ground. This is a lovely place Elend chose for us to visit. Remind me to thank him upon our return."

Sazed smiled, though he felt little humor.

"Oh, don't look so grim, old man," Breeze said, waving with his cane as the carriage began to roll, their soldiers surrounding it. "Something tells me that Quellion there isn't half as threatening as his bearing implies. We'll convince him eventually."

"I'm not certain, Lord Breeze. This place . . . it's different from the other cities we've visited. The leaders aren't as desperate, and the people are more subservient. We won't have an easy time of it here, I think."

Allrianne poked Breeze's arm. "Breezy, do you see that over there?"

Breeze squinted against the afternoon light, and Sazed leaned forward, glancing outward. A group of people had created a bonfire in the courtyard. The massive blaze sent a twisting line of smoke into the air. Sazed's mind reflexively reached for a tinmind to draw upon and enhance his vision. He shoved the impulse aside, instead squinting.

"It looks like . . ."

"Tapestries," said one of their soldiers, marching next to the carriage. "And furniture—rich things that are signs of the nobility, according to the Citizen. That was staged for your benefit. Quellion probably keeps storehouses of the stuff so that he can order them burned at dramatically appropriate times."

Sazed froze. The soldier was remarkably well informed. Sazed looked closely, suspicious. Like all their men, this one wore his cloak hood up to ward off the falling ash. As the man turned his head, Sazed could see that—oddly— he wore a thick bandage tied across his eyes, as if he were blind. Despite that, Sazed recognized his face.

"Spook, my dear boy!" Breeze exclaimed. "I knew you'd turn up eventually. Why the blindfold?"

Spook didn't answer the question. Instead he turned, glancing at the burning flames of the bonfire. There seemed a . . . tension to his posture.

The cloth must be thin enough to see through, Sazed thought. That was the only explanation for the way Spook moved with ease and grace, despite the cloth. Though it certainly seemed thick enough to be obscuring.

Spook turned back to Sazed. "You're going to need a base of operations in the city. Have you chosen one yet?"

"Not yet," Breeze said. "We were thinking of using an inn."

"There aren't any true inns in the city," Spook said. "Quellion says that citizens should care for one another, letting visitors stay in each other's homes."

"Hmm," Breeze said. "Perhaps we'll need to camp outside."

Spook shook his head. "No. Follow me."

"The Ministry Canton of Inquisition?" Sazed asked, frowning as he climbed out of the carriage.

Spook stood ahead of them, on the steps leading into the grand building. He turned, nodding his strangely cloth-wrapped head. "Quellion hasn't touched any of the Ministry buildings. He ordered them boarded up, but he didn't ransack or burn them. I think he's afraid of Inquisitors."

"A healthy and rational fear, my boy," Breeze said from within the carriage.

Spook snorted. "The Inquisitors aren't going to bother us, Breeze. They're far too busy trying to kill Vin. Come on."

He walked up the steps, and Sazed followed. Behind, he heard Breeze sigh with an exaggerated sound, then call for one of the soldiers to bring a parasol against the ash.

The building was broad and imposing, as were most Ministry offices. During the days of the Lord Ruler, they had stood as reminders of imperial might in every city across the Final Empire. The priests who had filled them had mostly been bureaucrats and clerks—but that had been the real power of the empire: its control of resources and its management of people.

Spook stood beside the building's wide, boarded-up doors. Like most structures in Urteau, it was built of wood rather than stone. He stared up, as if watching the falling ash, as he waited for Sazed and Breeze. He had always been a quiet one, more so since his uncle's death during the assault on Luthadel. As Sazed arrived, Spook began to rip boards free from the front of the building. "I'm glad you're here, Sazed," he said.

Sazed moved to help pull off boards. He heaved, trying to get the nails undone—yet he must have chosen one of the more stubborn boards, for though the ones Spook grabbed came free with ease, Sazed's refused to budge. "And why is it you're glad I am here, Lord Spook?"

Spook snorted. "I'm no lord, Saze. Never did get Elend to give me a title."

Sazed smiled. "He said that you only wanted one to impress women."

"Of course I did," Spook said, smiling as he ripped free another board. "What other reason would there be to have a title? Anyway, please just call me Spook. It's a good name."

"Very well."

Spook reached over and used a single casual hand to pull off the board Sazed had tried to budge. *What?* Sazed thought with shock. Sazed was by no means muscular—but he hadn't thought Spook was either. The lad must have been practicing with weights.

"Anyway," Spook said, turning, "I'm glad you're here, because I have things to discuss with you. Things that others might not understand."

Sazed frowned. "Things of what nature?"

Spook smiled, then threw his shoulder against the door, opening it into a dark, cavernous chamber. "Things of gods and men, Sazed. Come on."

The boy disappeared into the darkness. Sazed waited outside, but Spook never lit a lantern. He could hear the young man moving around inside.

"Spook?" he finally called out. "I can't see in there. Do you have a lantern?"

There was a pause. "Oh," Spook's voice said. "Right." A moment later a light sparked, and a lantern began to glow.

Breeze sauntered up behind Sazed. "Tell me, Sazed," he said quietly, "is it me, or has that boy changed since we last saw him?"

"He seems far more self-confident," Sazed said, nodding to himself. "More capable as well. But what do you suppose is the purpose of that blindfold?"

Breeze shrugged, taking Allrianne's arm. "He always was an odd one. Perhaps he thinks it will disguise him and help keep him from being recognized as a member of Kelsier's crew. Considering the improvement in the boy's disposition—and diction—I'm willing to deal with a quirk or two."

Breeze and Allrianne entered the building, and Sazed waved to Captain Goradel, indicating that he should form a perimeter outside. The man nodded, sending a squad of soldiers up to follow Sazed and the others. Finally, Sazed went in.

He wasn't certain what he had been expecting. The building had been part of the Canton of Inquisition—the most infamous of the Ministry's arms. It wasn't a place Sazed relished entering. The last Inquisition building he'd entered had been the Conventical of Seran, and it had been decidedly eerie. This building, however, proved to be nothing like the Conventical—it was simply another bureaucratic office. It was furnished a little more austerely than most Ministry buildings, true, but it still had tapestries on the wooden walls and broad red rugs on the floor. The trim was of metal, and there were hearths in every room.

As Sazed followed Breeze and Spook through the building, he was able to imagine how the building would have been during the days of the Lord Ruler. There would have been no dust then, but instead an air of crisp efficiency. Administrators would have sat at those desks, collecting and filing information about noble houses, skaa rebels, and even other Ministry Cantons—there had been a longstanding feud between the Canton of Orthodoxy, which had administered the Lord Ruler's empire, and the Canton of Inquisition, which had policed it.

This was not a place of fear at all, but of ledgers and files. The Inquisitors had probably visited this building rarely. Spook led them through several cluttered rooms toward a smaller storage chamber at the rear. Sazed could see that the dust on the floor there had been disturbed.

"You've been here before?" he asked, entering the room after Spook, Breeze, and Allrianne.

Spook nodded. "As has Vin. Don't you remember the report?" With that, he felt about on the floor, eventually finding a hidden latch and opening a trapdoor. Sazed peered down into the dark cavern below.

"What's he talking about?" Allrianne whispered to Breeze. "Vin's been here?"

"She did reconnaissance in this city, dear," Breeze said. "To find . . ."

"The cache," Sazed said as Spook began to climb down a ladder into the darkness. He left the lantern behind. "The supply cache put here by the Lord Ruler. All of them are underneath Ministry buildings."

"Well, that's what we're here to recover, isn't it?" Allrianne asked. "So, we've got it. Why bother with that Citizen fellow and his crazy peasants?"

"There's no way we could get these supplies out of the city with the Citizen in control." Spook's voice drifted up, echoing slightly. "There's too much down here."

"Besides, my dear," Breeze said, "Elend didn't send us merely to get these supplies—he sent us to quell a rebellion. We can't have one of our major cities in revolt, and we *particularly* can't afford to let the rebellion spread. I must say though, it does feel odd to be on this side of the problem—stopping a rebellion rather than starting one."

"We may have to organize a rebellion *against* the rebellion, Breeze," Spook's voice echoed from below. "If that makes you feel more comfortable. Anyway, are you three coming down or not?"

Sazed and Breeze shared a look, then Breeze gestured toward the dark pit. "After you."

Sazed picked up the lantern and climbed down the ladder. At the bottom, he found a small stone chamber, one wall of which had been pulled back to reveal a cavern. He stepped inside, Breeze reaching the ground behind him, then helping Allrianne down.

Sazed raised the lantern, staring quietly.

"Lord Ruler!" Breeze said, stepping up next to him. "It's enormous!"

"The Lord Ruler prepared these caches in case of a disaster," Spook said, standing ahead of them in the cavern. "They were meant to help the empire through what we're now facing. They wouldn't be much good if they weren't created on a grand scale."

"Grand" was correct. They stood on a ledge near the ceiling of the cavern, and a vast chamber extended below. Sazed could see row upon row of shelves lining the cavern floor.

"I think we should set up our base here, Sazed," Spook said, moving toward stairs that led down to the cavern floor. "It's the sole defensible place in the city. If we move our troops into the building above, we can use this cavern for supplies—and can fall back in here in an emergency. We could defend this even against a determined assault."

Sazed turned, regarding the stone doorway into the chamber. It was small enough that only one man could pass through at a time—which meant that it would be very easy to guard. And there was probably a way to shut it.

"Suddenly I feel a whole lot safer in this city," Breeze noted.

Sazed nodded. He turned, regarding the cavern once more. In the distance, he could hear something. "Is that water?"

Spook was moving down steps. Again, his voice echoed hauntingly in the chamber. "Each cache has a specialty— something it contains more of than all the others."

Sazed started down the stairs as Goradel's soldiers entered the chamber behind Breeze. Though the soldiers had brought more lanterns, Breeze and Allrianne stuck close to Sazed as they descended.

Soon Sazed realized he could see something sparkling. He held the lantern high, pausing on the steps as he saw that some of the darkness in the distance was too flat to be part of the cavern floor.

Breeze whistled quietly as they studied the enormous underground lake. "Well," he noted, "I guess now we know where all the water from those canals went."

*Originally, men assumed that Rashek's persecution of the Terris
religion came from hatred. Yet now that we know Rashek was himself a Terrisman, his destruction of that religion seems odd. I suspect it had something to do with the prophecies about the Hero
of Ages. Rashek knew that Preservation's power would eventually
return to the Well of Ascension. If the Terris religion had been allowed to survive, perhaps someday a person would find their way
to the Well and take up the power, then use it to defeat Rashek
and overthrow his empire. So he obscured knowledge of the Hero
and what he was supposed to do, hoping to keep the secret of the
Well to himself.*

30

"YOU'RE NOT GOING TO TRY to talk me out of this?" Elend
asked, amused.

Ham and Cett shared a look.

"Why would we do that, El?" Ham asked, standing at
the front of the boat. In the distance the sun was setting,
and the mists had already begun to gather. The boat rocked
quietly, and soldiers milled about on the shore, preparing
for night. One week had passed since Vin's initial scouting
of Fadrex, and she still hadn't managed to sneak into the
storage cache.

The night of the next ball had arrived, and Elend and Vin
were planning to attend.

"Well, I can think of a few reasons why you might object," Elend said, counting them off on his fingers. "First,

it isn't wise to expose me to potential capture. Second, by revealing myself at the party I'll show that I'm Mistborn, confirming rumors that Yomen may not believe. Third, I'll be putting both of our Mistborn in the same place, where they can be easily attacked—that can't be a good idea. Finally, there's the fact that going to a ball in the middle of a war is just *plain crazy*."

Ham shrugged, leaning with one elbow on the deck railing. "This isn't so different from when you entered your father's camp during the siege of Luthadel. Except you weren't Mistborn then, and you weren't in such a position of political power. Yomen would be crazy to make a move against you—he has to know that if you're in the same room with him, he's in mortal danger."

"He'll run," Cett said from his seat. "This party will end the moment you arrive."

"No," Elend said, "I don't think it will." He glanced toward their cabin. Vin was still getting ready—she'd had the camp tailors modify one of the cooking girls' dresses. Elend was worried. No matter how good the dress turned out to be, it would look out of place compared to the lavish ball gowns.

He turned back to Cett and Ham. "I don't think Yomen will run. He has to know that if Vin wanted to kill him, she'd attack his palace in secret. He's trying very hard to pretend that nothing has changed since the Lord Ruler disappeared. When we show up at the ball, it will make him think that we're willing to pretend with him. He'll stay and see if he can gain some advantage by meeting us on his terms."

"The man's a fool," Cett said. "I can't believe he'd want to return to the way things were."

"At least he's trying to give his subjects what they want. That's where you went wrong, Cett. You lost your kingdom the moment you left because you didn't care to try pleasing anyone."

"A king doesn't have to please anyone," Cett snapped. "He's the one with the army—that means other people have to please *him*."

"Actually," Ham said, rubbing his chin, "that theory can't be true. A king has to please somebody—after all, even if he intended to *force* everyone to do what he said, he'd still have to please his army. But then, I guess if the army is pleased merely by being allowed to push people around, you might have an argument. . . ."

Ham trailed off, looking thoughtful. Cett scowled. "Does everything have to be some damn logic puzzle to you?" he demanded. Ham continued to rub his chin.

Elend smiled, glancing at the cabin again. It was good to hear Ham acting like himself. Cett protested against Ham's comments almost as much as Breeze did. In fact . . . *Maybe that's why Ham hasn't been quite so prone to his little logic puzzles lately,* Elend thought. *There hasn't been anyone around to complain about them.*

"So, Elend . . ." Cett said. "If you die, I'm in charge, right?"

"Vin will take command if something happens to me," Elend said. "You know that."

"Right," Cett said. "And if both of you die?"

"Sazed is next in the imperial succession after Vin, Cett. We've discussed that."

"Yes, but what about this army?" Cett said. "Sazed is off in Urteau. Who leads these men until we meet up with him?"

Elend sighed. "If Yomen manages to kill both Vin and me, then I suggest that you run—because yes, you'd be in charge here, and the Mistborn who killed us is likely to come for you next."

Cett smiled in satisfaction, though Ham frowned at this.

"You've never wanted titles, Ham," Elend pointed out. "And you've chafed at every leadership position I've given you."

"I know," he said. "But what about Demoux?"

"Cett has more experience," Elend said. "He's a better man than he pretends, Ham. I trust him. That will have to be enough for you. Cett, if things turn bad, I charge you with returning to Luthadel and searching out Sazed to tell him that he's emperor. Now, I think that—"

Elend paused as the door to his cabin opened. He turned, putting on his best consoling smile, then froze.

Vin stood in the doorway wearing a stunning black gown with silver trim, cut after a modern fashion. It managed to look sleek despite the bell-shaped skirt, which fanned out with petticoats. Her pure black hair, which she often wore pulled back in a tail, was down, and it now reached to her collarbone, neatly trimmed and curling just slightly. The only jewelry she wore was her simple earring, the one she'd gotten from her mother when she was a child.

He always thought she was beautiful. And yet . . . how long had it been since he'd seen her in a gown, with her hair and makeup done? He tried to say something, give her a compliment, but his voice caught in his throat.

She walked over on light feet, kissing him briefly. "I'll take that as an indication that I managed to put this thing on right. I'd forgotten what a *pain* gowns could be. And the makeup! Honestly, Elend, you're never allowed to complain about those suits of yours again."

Beside them, Ham was chuckling. Vin turned. "What?"

"Ah, Vin," Ham said, leaning back and folding his muscular arms, "when did you go and grow up on me? It seems like only last week you were scrambling about, hiding in corners, wearing the haircut of a boy and the attitude of a mouse."

Vin smiled fondly. "Do you remember when we first met? You thought I was a twixt."

Ham nodded. "Breeze nearly fainted dead away when he found we'd been talking with a Mistborn all that time! Honestly, Vin. Sometimes I can't believe that you were that same frightened girl Kelsier brought into the crew."

"It's going on four years now, Ham. I'm nearly twenty."

"I know," Ham said, sighing. "You're like my own children, grown up before I had time to know them as kids. In fact, I probably know you and El better than I know either of them."

"You'll be with them again, Ham," Vin said, reaching

over and laying a hand on his shoulder. "Once this is all over."

"Oh, I know that," he said, smiling, ever the optimist. "But you can never have back what you've missed. I hope all of this turns out to be worth it."

Elend shook his head, finally finding his voice. "I have only one thing to say. If that dress is what the cooking girls are wearing, I'm paying them *far* too much."

Vin laughed.

"Seriously, Vin," Elend said. "The army's tailors are good, but there's no way that dress came from materials we had in camp. Where did you get it?"

"It's a mystery," Vin said, narrowing her eyes and smiling. "We Mistborn are incredibly mysterious."

Elend cocked his head. "Um . . . I'm Mistborn too, Vin. That doesn't make any sense."

"We Mistborn need not make sense," Vin said. "It's beneath us. Come on—the sun's already down. We need to get moving."

"Have fun dancing with our enemies," Ham said as Vin hopped from the boat, then Pushed herself up through the mists. Elend waved farewell, Pushing himself into the air as well. As he shot away, his tin-enhanced ears heard Ham's voice talking to Cett.

"So . . . you can't go anywhere unless someone carries you, right?" the Thug asked.

Cett grunted.

"Well then," Ham said, sounding very pleased, "I've got a good number of philosophical puzzles you might enjoy."

Allomantic jumping was *not* easy when one was wearing a ball gown. Every time Vin started to descend, the bottom of the dress flared up around her, ruffling and flapping like a flock of startled birds.

Vin wasn't particularly worried about showing off what was under the dress. Not only was it too dark for most people to see, but she wore leggings beneath the petticoats. Unfortunately, flapping dresses—and the drag they created in the air—made steering a jump much more difficult. They also made a lot of noise. She wondered what the guards thought as she passed over the rocky shelves that were the natural city walls. To her ear, she sounded like a dozen waving flags beating against themselves in the middle of a windstorm.

She slowed, aiming for a rooftop that had been cleared of ash. She hit lightly, bouncing up and spinning, dress flaring, before landing and waiting for Elend. He followed, landing less smoothly with a hard thump and a grunt. It wasn't that he was bad at Pushing and Pulling—he simply hadn't had as much practice as Vin. She'd probably been much the same way during her first years as an Allomancer.

Well . . . maybe not me, she thought fondly as Elend dusted himself off. *But I'm sure a lot of other Allomancers were about at Elend's level after only a year of practice.*

"That was quite the series of jumps, Vin," Elend said, puffing slightly as he glanced back toward the clifflike rock formations, their fires burning high in the night. Elend wore his standard white military uniform, one of those that Tindwyl had designed for him. He'd had this one scrubbed free of ash, and he'd gotten his beard trimmed.

"I couldn't land often," Vin explained. "These white petticoats will stain with ash easily. Come on—we need to get inside."

Elend turned, smiling in the darkness. He actually looked excited. "The dress. You paid a dressmaker in the city to make it for you?"

"Actually, I paid a friend in the city to have it made for me, and to get me the makeup." She jumped away, heading toward Keep Orielle—which according to Slowswift was the site of the evening's ball. She kept to the air, never landing. Elend followed behind, using the same anchors.

Soon they approached a burst of color in the mists, like an aurora from one of Sazed's stories. The bubble of light turned into the massive keep she had seen during her previous infiltration, its stained-glass windows shining from within. Vin angled herself downward, streaking through the mists. She briefly considered dropping to the ground out in the courtyard—away from watchful eyes—so that she and Elend could approach the doors subtly. Then she decided against it.

This wasn't an evening for subtlety.

Instead she dropped directly down onto the carpeted steps leading up to the main entrance of the castle-like building. Her landing blew away flakes of ash, cleaning a patch of carpet. Elend landed by her a second later, then stood up straight, his brilliant white cape flapping around him. At the top of the steps, a pair of uniformed servants had been greeting guests and ushering them into the building. Both men froze, stunned expressions on their faces.

Elend held out his arm to Vin. "Shall we?"

Vin took the arm. "Yes," she said. "Preferably before those men can get the guards."

They strode up the steps, sounds of surprise coming from behind, where a small group of noblemen had been exiting their carriage. Ahead, one of the servants moved forward and cut off Vin and Elend. Elend carefully placed a hand on the man's chest, then shoved him aside with a pewter-fueled push. The man stumbled backward into the wall. The other one went running for the guards.

In the antechamber, waiting nobility began to whisper and question. Vin heard them asking if anyone recognized these strange newcomers, one in black, the other in white. Elend strode forward firmly, Vin at his side, causing people to stumble over themselves and move out of the way. Elend and Vin passed quickly through the small room, and Elend handed a name card to a servant who waited to announce arrivals into the ballroom proper.

They waited on the servant, and Vin realized that she'd begun holding her breath. It seemed as if she were reliving a dream—or was it a fond memory? For a moment she was that same young girl of three years before, arriving at Keep Venture for her very first ball, nervous and worried that she wouldn't be able to play her part.

Yet she felt none of that same insecurity. She didn't worry if she'd find acceptance or belief. She'd slain the Lord Ruler. She'd married Elend Venture. And, more remarkable than either accomplishment, somehow among the chaos and mess she'd discovered who she was. Not a girl of the streets, though that was where she'd been raised. Not a woman of the court, though she appreciated the beauty and grace of the balls. Someone else.

Someone she liked.

The servant reread Elend's card, growing pale. He looked up. Elend met the man's eyes, then gave a small nod as if to say, "Yes, I'm afraid that it's true."

The servant cleared his throat, and Elend led Vin into the ballroom.

"High Emperor, Lord Elend Venture," the servant announced in a clear voice. "And the Empress Vin Venture, Heir of the Survivor, Hero of Ages."

The entire ballroom grew suddenly and unnaturally quiet. Vin and Elend paused at the front of the room, giving the gathered nobility a chance to see them. It appeared that Keep Orielle's grand main hall, like Keep Venture's, was also its ballroom. However, instead of being tall with a broad, arched roof, this room had a relatively low ceiling and small, intricate designs in the stonework. It was as if the architect had tried for beauty on a delicate scale rather than an imposing one.

The entire chamber was crafted from white marble of various shades. While it was large enough to hold hundreds of people—plus a dance floor and tables—it still felt intimate. The room was divided by rows of ornamental marble pillars, and it was further partitioned with large stained-glass panels that ran from floor to ceiling. Vin was impressed—most keeps in Luthadel left their stained glass to the perimeter walls, so they could be lit from without. While this keep did have some of those, she quickly realized that the true masterpieces had been placed here, freestanding in the ballroom, where they could be admired from both sides.

"By the Lord Ruler," Elend whispered, scanning the gathered people. "They really *do* think they can ignore the rest of the world, don't they?"

Gold, silver, bronze, and brass sparkled upon figures in brilliant ball gowns and sharp gentlemen's suits. The men generally wore dark clothing, and the women generally wore colors. A group of musicians played strings in a far corner, their music unimpeded by the shocked atmosphere. Servants waited, uncertain, bearing drinks and foods.

"Yes," Vin whispered. "We should move out of the doorway. When the guards come, we'll want to be mingled in the crowd to make the soldiers hesitant to attack."

Elend smiled, and she knew he was remarking to himself about her tendency to keep her back from being exposed. However, she also knew that he realized she was right. They walked down the short set of marble steps, joining the party.

Skaa might have shied away from such a dangerous couple, but Vin and Elend wore the costume of noble propriety. The aristocracy of the Final Empire were adept at playing pretend—and when they were uncertain how to behave, they fell back on the old standard: proper manners.

Lords and ladies bowed and curtsied, acting as if the emperor and empress's attendance had been completely expected. Vin let Elend take the lead, as he had far more experience than she with matters of court. He nodded to those they passed, displaying just the right amount of self-assurance. Behind, guards finally arrived at the doors. They came no farther, plainly wary of disturbing the party.

"There," Vin said, turning her head to their left. Through a stained-glass partition, she could make out a figure sitting at an elevated table.

"I see him," Elend said, leading her around the glass, and giving Vin her first sight of Aradan Yomen, king of the Western Dominance.

He was younger than she'd expected—perhaps as young as Elend. Roundfaced with serious eyes, Yomen had his head shaved bald, after the manner of obligators. His dark grey robes were a mark of his station, as were the complicated patterns of tattoos around his eyes, which proclaimed him a very high-ranking member of the Canton of Resource.

Yomen stood up as Vin and Elend approached. He looked utterly dumbfounded. Behind, the soldiers had begun to carefully work their way into the room. Elend paused a distance from the high table, with its white cloth and pure crystal place settings. He met Yomen's gaze, the other guests so quiet that Vin guessed most were holding their breaths.

Vin checked her metal reserves, turning slightly, keeping an eye on the guards. Then, from the corner of her eye she saw Yomen raise his hand and subtly wave the guards back.

Chatter began in the room almost immediately. Yomen sat down, looking troubled, and did not return to his meal.

Vin looked up at Elend. "Well," she whispered, "we're in. What now?"

"I need to talk to Yomen," Elend said. "But I'd like to wait a bit first; give him a chance to get used to our presence."

"Then we should mingle."

"Split up? We can cover more nobility that way."

Vin hesitated.

"I can protect myself, Vin," Elend said, smiling. "I promise."

"All right." Vin nodded, though that wasn't the only reason she'd hesitated.

"Talk to as many people as you can," Elend said. "We're here to shatter this people's image of safety. After all, we just proved that Yomen can't keep us out of Fadrex—and we're showing that we're so unthreatened by him that we'll waltz into a ball he's attending. Once we've made a bit of a stir, I'll talk to their king, and they'll all be certain to listen in."

Vin nodded. "When you mingle, watch for people who look like they might be willing to support us against the current government. Slowswift implied that there are some in the city who aren't pleased with the way their king is handling things."

Elend kissed her cheek, and then she was alone. Vin

stood in her beautiful gown, feeling a moment of shock. Over the last two years, she'd explicitly worked to keep herself out of situations where she would dress up and mingle with nobility. She'd determinedly worn trousers and shirts, making it her self-appointed duty to sow discomfort in those she found too full of themselves.

Yet she had been the one to suggest this infiltration to Elend. Why? Why put herself in this position again? She wasn't displeased with who she was—she didn't need to prove anything by putting on another silly gown and making courtly conversation with a bunch of nobility she didn't know.

Did she?

No use fidgeting about it now, Vin thought, scanning the crowd. Noble balls in Luthadel—and she could only assume here—were very polite affairs designed to encourage mingling, and therefore facilitate political give and take.

The party was made up of small groups—some mixed couples, but many clusters of solely women or men. A pair was not expected to stay together the entire time. There were side rooms where gentlemen could retire and drink with their allies, leaving the women to converse in the ballroom.

Vin walked forward, slipping a cup of wine off the tray of a passing servant. By splitting up, Elend and she had indicated they were open to conversation with others. Unfortunately, it had been so long since Vin was last alone at a party like this that she felt awkward, uncertain whether to approach one of the groups or wait to see if anyone came to her.

That first night in Keep Venture she'd played a part, hiding in her role as Valette Renoux. She couldn't do that anymore. Everyone knew who she really was. That would have bothered her once, but it didn't anymore. Still, she couldn't just do what she'd done then—stand around and wait for others to come to her. The entire room seemed to be staring at her.

She strode through the beautiful white room, aware of how much her black dress stood out against the women in their colors. She moved around the sheets of colored glass that hung from the ceiling like crystalline curtains. She'd learned from her earlier balls that there was one thing she could always count on: Whenever noblewomen gathered, one always set herself up as the most important.

Vin found her with ease. The woman had dark hair and tan skin, and she sat at a table surrounded by sycophants. Vin recognized that arrogant look, that way the woman's voice was just loud enough to be imperious, but just soft enough to make everyone hang on her words.

Vin approached with determination. Years ago, she'd been forced to start at the bottom. She didn't have time for that. She didn't know the subtle political intricacies of the city—the alliances and rivalries. However, there was one thing of which she was fairly confident.

Whichever side this woman was on, Vin wanted to be on the opposite one.

Several of the sycophants glanced up as Vin approached, and they grew pale. Their leader had the poise to remain aloof. *She'll try to ignore me,* Vin thought. *I can't leave her that option.* Vin sat at the table directly across from the woman. Then Vin turned and addressed several of the younger sycophants.

"She's planning to betray you," Vin said.

The women glanced at each other.

"She has plans to get out of the city," Vin said. "When the army attacks, she won't be here. And she's going to leave you all to die. Make an ally of me, however, and I will see that you are protected."

"Excuse me?" the lead woman said, her voice indignant. "Did I invite you to sit here?"

Vin smiled. *That was easy.* A thieving crewleader's basis of power was money—take that away, and he'd fall. For a woman such as this, her power was in the people who listened to her. To make her react, one merely had to threaten to take her minions.

Vin turned to confront the woman. "No, you didn't invite

me. I invited myself. Someone needs to warn the women here."

The woman sniffed. "You spread lies. You know nothing of my supposed plans."

"Don't I? You're not the type to let a man like Yomen determine your future, and if the others here think about it, they'll realize that there's no way you would let yourself get caught in Fadrex City without plans to escape. I'm surprised you're even still here."

"Your threats do not frighten me," the lady said.

"I haven't threatened you yet," Vin noted, sipping her wine. She gave a careful Push on the emotions of the women at the table, making them more worried. "We could get to that, if you wish—though technically I have your entire city under threat already."

The woman narrowed her eyes at Vin. "Don't listen to her, ladies."

"Yes, Lady Patresen," one of the women said, speaking a little too quickly.

Patresen, Vin thought, relieved that someone had finally mentioned the woman's name. *Do I know that name?* "House Patresen," Vin said idly. "Isn't that a cousin family of House Elariel?"

Lady Patresen remained silent.

"I killed an Elariel once," Vin said. "It was a good fight. Shan was a clever woman, and a skilled Mistborn." She leaned in. "You may think that the stories about me are exaggerations. You may assume that I didn't really kill the Lord Ruler, and that the talk is simply propaganda crafted to help stabilize my husband's rule.

"Think as you wish, Lady Patresen. But there is one thing you *must* understand. You are not my adversary. I don't have *time* for people like you. You're a petty woman in an insignificant city, part of a doomed culture of nobility. I'm not talking to you because I want to be part of your schemes; you can't even understand how unimportant they are to me. I'm merely here to voice a warning. We're going to take this city—and when we do, there will be little room for people who were against us."

Patresen paled slightly. But her voice was calm when she spoke. "I doubt that's true. If you could take the city as easily as you claim, then you would have already."

"My husband is a man of honor," Vin said, "and decided that he wished to speak with Yomen before attacking. I, however, am not so temperate."

"Well, *I* think that—"

"You don't understand, do you?" Vin asked. "It doesn't matter what you think. Look, I know you're the type with powerful connections. Those connections will have told you by now the numbers we bring. Forty thousand men, twenty thousand koloss, and a full contingent of Allomancers. Plus two Mistborn. My husband and I did not come to this conference to make allies, or even enemies. We came to give warning. I suggest you take it."

She punctuated her last comment with a powerful Soothing. She wanted it to be obvious to the women, to let them know that they were indeed under her power. Then she stood, trailing away from the table.

What she had said to Patresen wasn't really that important—the important thing was that Vin had been seen confronting the woman. Hopefully that would put Vin on a side in the local politics, making her less threatening to some factions in the room. That in turn would make her more accessible, and—

The sound of chairs scooting back from the table came from behind her. Vin turned, suspicious, and saw most of Lady Patresen's clique approaching in a hurry, leaving their leader sitting virtually alone at her table, a scowl on her face.

Vin tensed.

"Lady Venture," one of the women said. "Perhaps you would let some of us . . . introduce you at the party?"

Vin frowned.

"Please," the woman said quietly.

Vin blinked in surprise. She'd expected the women to resent her, not *listen* to her. She glanced about. Most of the women looked so intimidated that Vin thought they might wilt away like leaves in the sun. Feeling a little bemused, Vin nodded her head and let herself be led into the party for introductions.

Rashek wore both black and white. I think he wanted to show that he was a duality, Preservation and Ruin.

This was a lie. After all, he had touched only one of the powers— and in a very small way at that.

31

"LORD BREEZE GUESSED CORRECTLY," SAZED said, standing at the front of their small group. "As far as I can tell, the diversion of waters into this underground reservoir was intentional. The project must have taken decades. It required widening natural passageways so that the water— which once fed the river and canals above—instead flowed into this cavern."

"Yes, but what's the point?" Breeze asked. "Why waste so much effort to move a river?"

Three days in Urteau had allowed them to do as Spook had suggested, moving their troops into the Ministry building, ostensibly taking up residence. The Citizen couldn't know about the cache, otherwise he would have ransacked it. That meant Sazed and his team held a distinct advantage should events in the city turn ugly.

They had pulled some of the furniture from the building

above and arranged it—with sheets and tapestries to create rooms—amid the shelves in the cavern. Logic dictated that the cavern was the best place to spend their time, for should someone attack the Ministry building, the cavern was where they wanted to be. True, they'd be trapped—but with the supplies they had, they'd be able to survive indefinitely and work out a plan of escape.

Sazed, Breeze, Spook, and Allrianne sat in one of these partitioned-off areas among the shelves of food. "The reason the Lord Ruler made this lake is simple, I think." Sazed turned, glancing over his shoulder at it. "That water comes via an underground river, filtered—in all probability—through layers of rock. It is pure water, the likes of which you rarely see in the Final Empire. No ash, no sediment. The purpose of that water is to sustain a population should a disaster occur. If it were still flowing into the canals above, it would quickly get soiled and polluted by the population living in the city."

"The Lord Ruler was looking to the future," Spook said, still wearing his strange eye bandage. He'd turned aside all questions and promptings regarding why he wore it, though Sazed was beginning to suspect it had to do with burning tin.

Sazed nodded at the young man's comment. "The Lord Ruler wasn't worried about causing financial ruin in Urteau—he merely wanted to make certain this cavern had access to a constant, flowing source of fresh water."

"Isn't all of this beside the point?" Allrianne asked. "So we have water. What about that maniac running the city?"

The others turned to look to Sazed. *I am, unfortunately, in charge.* "Well," he said, "we should speak of this. Emperor Venture has asked us to secure the city. As the Citizen has proven unwilling to meet with us further, we shall have to discuss other options."

"That man needs to go," Spook said. "We need assassins."

"I fear that wouldn't work well, my dear boy," Breeze said.

"Why not?" Spook asked. "We killed the Lord Ruler, and that worked pretty well."

"Ah," Breeze said, raising a finger, "but the Lord Ruler was irreplaceable. He was a god, so killing him created a psychological impact on his populace."

Allrianne nodded. "This Citizen's not a force of nature, but a man—and men can be replaced. If we assassinate Quellion, one of his lackeys will simply take over in his stead."

"And we will be branded as murderers," Breeze added.

"What then?" Spook asked. "We leave him alone?"

"Of course not," Breeze said. "If we want to take this city, we need to undermine him, *then* remove him. We prove that his entire system is faulty—that his government is, in essence, silly. If we manage that, we won't stop just him, we'll stop everyone who has worked with him and supported him. That is the only way we're going to take Urteau short of marching an army in here and seizing it by force."

"And since His Majesty kindly left us *without* any troops to speak of . . ." Allrianne said.

"I am not convinced that such rash action is required," Sazed said. "Perhaps, given more time, we'll be able to work with this man."

"Work with *him*?" Spook asked. "You've been here three days—isn't that enough for you to see what Quellion is like?"

"I have seen," Sazed said. "And to be perfectly honest, I do not know that I can fault the Citizen's views."

The cavern fell silent.

"Perhaps you should explain yourself, my dear man," Breeze said, sipping at a cup of wine.

"The things that the Citizen says are not false," Sazed said. "We cannot blame him for teaching the very same things that Kelsier did. The Survivor spoke of killing the nobility—goodness knows, we all saw him engaging in *that* activity often enough. He spoke of revolution and of skaa ruling themselves."

"He spoke of extreme actions during extreme times," Breeze said. "That's what you do when you need to motivate people. Even Kelsier wouldn't have taken it this far."

"Perhaps," Sazed said. "But can we really be surprised that people who heard Kelsier speak have created this society? And what right have we to take it from them? In a way, they've been truer to Kelsier than we have. Can you really say that you think he'd be pleased to find out that we put a nobleman on the throne not one day after he died?"

Breeze and Spook glanced at each other, and neither contradicted him.

"It's just wrong," Spook finally said. "These people claim to know Kelsier, but they don't. He didn't want people to be grim and bullied—he wanted them to be free and happy."

"Indeed," Breeze said. "Besides, we *did* choose to follow Elend Venture—and he's given us an order. Our empire needs these supplies, and we can't afford to let an organized rebellion seize and control one of the most important cities in the empire. We need to secure this cache and protect the people of Urteau. It's for the greater good, and all that!"

Allrianne nodded her agreement—and as always, Sazed felt her touch on his emotions.

For the greater good . . . Sazed thought. He knew that Spook was right. Kelsier wouldn't want this warped society being perpetuated in his name. Something needed to be done. "Very well," he said. "What should our course of action be?"

"Nothing, for now," Breeze said. "We need time to feel out the city's climate. How close are the people to rebelling against dear Quellion? How active is the local criminal element? How corruptible are the men who serve the new government? Give me some time to discover answers to these questions, and then we can decide what to do."

"I still say we do it as Kelsier did," Spook said. "Why can't we topple the Citizen like he did the Lord Ruler?"

"There's another reason that won't work," Breeze said, sipping his wine.

"What's that?" Spook asked.

"It's very simple, my dear boy," Breeze said. "We don't have Kelsier anymore."

Sazed nodded. That much was true—though he did wonder if they would ever be rid of the Survivor's legacy. In a way, the battle in this town had been inevitable. If Kelsier had possessed one flaw, it was his overwhelming hatred of the nobility. It was a passion that had driven him, had helped him accomplish the impossible. However, Sazed feared it would destroy those whom it had infected.

"Take the time you need, Breeze," Sazed said. "Let me know when you think we are ready to take the next step."

Breeze nodded, and the meeting broke up. Sazed stood, sighing quietly. As he did, he met Breeze's eyes, and the man winked at him with a smile that seemed to say, "This won't be half as difficult as you think." Sazed smiled back, and he felt Breeze's touch on his emotions, trying to encourage him.

Yet the Soother's hand was too light. Breeze couldn't have known the conflict that still twisted within Sazed. A conflict about much more than Kelsier and the problems in Urteau. He was glad for the time spent waiting in the city, for he still had much work to do with the religions listed in his portfolio.

Even that labor was difficult for him to get to recently. He did his best to give the others leadership, as Elend had asked. But the pernicious darkness Sazed felt inside him refused to be shaken away. It was more dangerous to him, he knew, than anything else he had faced while serving with the crew, because it made him feel he didn't care.

I must keep working, he decided, walking away from the meeting place, carefully sliding his portfolio off a nearby shelf. *I have to keep searching. I must not give up.*

It was far more difficult than that. In the past, logic and thought had always been his refuge. However, his emotions didn't respond to logic. No amount of thinking about what he *should* be doing would be of use.

He ground his teeth, walking, hoping that the motion would help him work out the knots within himself. A part of him wanted to go among the people and study the new form of the Church of the Survivor that had sprung up here in Urteau. But that seemed a waste of time. The world was ending; why study one more religion? He already knew this one was false; he'd dismissed the Church of the Survivor early in his studies. It was filled with more contradictions than almost any in his portfolio.

More filled with passion as well.

All the religions in his collection were alike in one respect; they had failed. The people who'd followed them had died, been conquered, their religions stamped out. Was that not proof enough for him? He'd tried preaching them, but he'd only rarely had any success.

It was all meaningless. Everything was ending anyway.

No! Sazed thought. *I will find the answers. The religions didn't disappear completely—the Keepers preserved them. There must be answers in one of them. Somewhere.*

Eventually he found his way to the cavern wall that held the steel plaque inscribed by the Lord Ruler. They already had a record of what it said, but Sazed wanted to see it and read it for himself. He looked up at the metal, which reflected the light of a nearby lantern, and read the words of the very man who had destroyed so many religions.

The plan is simple. When the power returns to the Well, I will take it and make certain the thing remains trapped.

And still I worry. It has proven far more clever than I had assumed, infecting my thoughts, making me see and feel things I do not wish to. It is so subtle, so careful. I cannot see how it could cause my death, but still I worry.

If I am dead, these caches will provide some measure of protection for my people. I fear what is coming. What might be. If you read this now, and I am gone, then I fear for you. Still, I will try to leave what help I can.

There are metals of Allomancy which I have shared

with none. If you are a priest of mine, working this cavern and reading these words, know that you will incur my wrath if you share this knowledge. However, if it is true that the force has returned and I am unable to deal with it, then perhaps knowledge of electrum will give you some aid. My researchers have discovered that mixing an alloy of forty-five percent gold and fifty-five percent silver creates a new Allomantic metal. Burning it will not give you the power of atium, but will provide some help against those who themselves burn it.

And that was it. Next to the words was a map indicating the location of the next cache—the one in the small southern mining town that Vin and Elend had secured a short time ago. Sazed read over the words again, but they served only to enhance his despair. Even the Lord Ruler appeared to feel helpless in the face of their current predicament. He'd planned to be alive, he'd planned for none of this to happen. But he'd known that his plans might not work.

Sazed turned, leaving the plaque behind, walking to the bank of the underground lake. The water lay like black glass, undisturbed by wind or ash, though it did ripple slightly from the current. A pair of lanterns sat by the edge of the water, burning quietly, marking the bank. Behind him, a short distance away, some of the soldiers had made camp—though a good two-thirds of them kept to the upstairs to make certain the building had the look of being lived in. Others searched the cavern walls in hopes of finding a secret exit. They would all be a lot more comfortable within the cavern if they knew they had a means of escaping it, should they get attacked.

"Sazed."

Sazed turned, then nodded to Spook as the young man walked up to join him on the bank of the black still water. They stood together placidly, contemplative.

This one has troubles of his own, Sazed thought, noting the way Spook watched the waters. Then, surprisingly,

Spook reached up and untied the cloth from his eyes. He pulled it free, revealing a pair of spectacles underneath, perhaps used to keep the cloth from pressing his eyes closed. Spook removed the spectacles and blinked, squinting. His eyes began to water, then he reached down and put out one of the two lanterns, leaving Sazed standing in very dim light. Spook sighed, standing and wiping his eyes.

So it is his tin. As Sazed considered the thought, he realized that he had often seen the young man wearing gloves—as if to protect his skin. Sazed suspected that if he watched closely, he'd see the boy put in earplugs as well. *Curious.*

"Sazed," Spook said, "I wanted to talk to you about something."

"Please, speak as you wish."

"I . . ." Spook trailed off, then glanced at Sazed. "I think Kelsier is still with us."

Sazed frowned.

"Not alive, of course," Spook said quickly. "But I think he's watching over us. Protecting us . . . that sort of thing."

"That's a pleasant sentiment, I think," Sazed said. *Though completely false.*

"It's not just a sentiment," Spook replied. "He's here. I was wondering if there was anything in any of those religions you studied that talked about things like that."

"Of course," Sazed said. "Many of them spoke of the dead remaining as spirits to help or curse the living."

They fell silent, Spook clearly waiting for something.

"Well?" Spook asked. "Aren't you going to preach a religion to me?"

"I don't do that anymore," Sazed said quietly.

"Oh," Spook said. "Um, why not?"

Sazed shook his head. "I find it hard to preach to others that which has offered me no solace, Spook. I am looking through them, trying to discover which—if any of them—are right and true. Once I have that knowledge, I will be happy to share with you any that seem most likely to contain truth. For now, however, I believe none of them, and therefore will preach none of them."

Surprisingly, Spook didn't argue with him. Sazed had found it frustrating that his friends—people who for the most part were determined atheists—would grow so offended when he threatened to join them in their lack of belief. Yet Spook didn't offer any arguments.

"It makes sense," the young man eventually said. "Those religions *aren't* true. After all, Kelsier is the one who watches over us, not those other gods."

Sazed closed his eyes. "How can you say that, Spook? You lived with him—you knew him. We both know that Kelsier was no god."

"The people of this city think he is."

"And where has it gotten them? Their belief has brought oppression and violence. What is the good of faith if *this* is the result? A city full of people misinterpreting their god's commands? A world of ash and pain and death and sorrow?" Sazed shook his head. "That is why I no longer wear my metalminds. Religions that cannot offer more than this do not deserve to be taught."

"Oh," Spook said. He knelt down, dipping a hand in the water, then shivered. "That makes sense too, I guess—though I'd have guessed it was because of *her*."

"What do you mean?"

"Your woman," Spook said. "The other Keeper—Tindwyl. I heard her talk about religion. She didn't think much of it. I'd have thought that maybe you wouldn't talk about religion anymore because that might be what she'd have wanted."

Sazed felt a chill.

"Anyway," Spook said, standing and wiping off his hand, "the people of this city know more than you think they do. Kelsier *is* watching over us."

With that, the boy wandered off. Sazed paid him little mind. He stood, staring at the ebony waters.

Because that might be what she'd have wanted . . .

Tindwyl had thought religion to be foolish. She had said that people who looked toward ancient prophecies or unseen forces were seeking excuses. During her last few weeks with Sazed, this had often been a topic of conversation—even slight contention—between the two of them, for their research had dealt with the prophecies regarding the Hero of Ages.

That research had turned out to be useless. At best, the prophecies were the vain hopes of men who wished for a better world. At worst, they had been cleverly placed to further the goals of a malignant force. Either way, he had believed strongly in his work at that time. And Tindwyl had helped him. They had searched their metalminds, sifting through centuries of information, history, and mythology, seeking references to the Deepness, the Hero of Ages, and the Well of Ascension. She had worked with him, claiming that her interest was academic, not religious. Sazed suspected that she'd had a different motivation.

She'd wanted to be with him. She had suppressed her distaste for religion out of a desire to be involved with what he found important. And now that she was dead, Sazed found himself doing what *she'd* found important. Tindwyl had studied politics and leadership. She'd loved to read the biographies of great statesmen and generals. Had he unconsciously agreed to become Elend's ambassador so that he could involve himself in Tindwyl's studies, just as she—before her death—had given herself over to his?

He wasn't certain. In truth, he thought his problems were deeper than that. However, the fact that *Spook* had been the one to make such an astute observation gave Sazed pause. It was quite a clever way of looking at things. Instead of contradicting him, Spook had offered a possible explanation.

Sazed was impressed. He looked across the waters for a time, contemplating what Spook had said. Then he pulled out the next religion in his portfolio and began to consider it. The sooner he got through them, the sooner he could—hopefully—find the truth.

Allomancy is clearly of Preservation. The rational mind will see this. For in the case of Allomancy, net power is gained. It is provided by an external source—Preservation's own body.

32

"ELEND, IS THAT REALLY YOU?"

Elend turned with shock. He'd been mingling at the ball, talking with a group of men who had turned out to be distant cousins of his. The voice from behind, however, was far more familiar. "Telden?" Elend asked. "What are you doing here!"

"I live here, El," Telden said, clasping hands with him. To the side, Elend's cousins made a graceful withdrawal.

Elend was dumbfounded. He hadn't seen Telden since his house had escaped Luthadel in the days of chaos following the death of the Lord Ruler. Once, this man had been one of Elend's best friends. "I thought you were in BasMardin, Tell," Elend said.

"No," Telden said. "That's where my house settled, but I thought that the area was too dangerous, what with the koloss rampages. I moved inward to Fadrex once Lord Yomen came to power—he quickly gained a reputation for being able to provide stability."

Elend smiled. The years had changed his friend. Telden had once been the model of a debonair ladies' man, his hair and expensive suits intended to draw attention. It wasn't that the older Telden had grown sloppy, but he obviously didn't take as much care to appear stylish. He'd always been a large man—tall and rectangular—and the extra weight he'd gained made him look far more . . . ordinary than he once had.

"Elend," Telden said, shaking his head. "You know, for the longest time I refused to believe that you'd really managed to seize power in Luthadel."

"You were there at my coronation!"

"I thought they had picked you as a puppet, El," Telden said, rubbing his wide chin. "I thought . . . well, I'm sorry. I guess I didn't have much faith in you."

Elend laughed. "You were right not to, my friend. I turned out to be a terrible king."

Telden plainly wasn't sure how to reply to that.

"I did get better at the job," Elend said. "I just had to stumble through a few messes first."

Partygoers shuffled around in the divided ballroom. Though those watching did their best to appear uninterested and aloof, Elend could tell that they were doing the noble equivalent of gawking. He glanced toward where Vin stood in her gorgeous black dress, surrounded by a group of women. She seemed to be doing well—she took to the courtly scene far better than she let herself think or admit. She was graceful, poised, and the center of attention.

She was also alert—Elend could tell by the way she managed to keep her back to a wall or glass partition. She'd be burning iron or steel, watching for sudden movements of metal that might indicate an attacking Coinshot. Elend began burning iron as well, and he made certain to keep burning brass to Soothe the emotions of those in the room, keeping them from feeling too angry or threatened by his intrusion. Other Allomancers—Breeze or even Vin—would have had trouble Soothing an entire room at once. For Elend, with his inordinate power, it took barely any attention.

Telden looked troubled as he stood. Elend tried to say something to restart their conversation, but he struggled to come up with anything that wouldn't sound awkward. It had been two and a half years since Telden had left Luthadel. Before that, he had been one of the friends with whom Elend had discussed political theory, planning with the idealism of youth for the day when they would lead their houses. Yet the days of youth—and their idealistic theories—were gone.

"So . . ." Telden said. "This is where we end up, is it?"

Elend nodded.

"You're not . . . really going to attack the city, are you?" Telden asked. "Tell me you're only here to intimidate Yomen."

"No," Elend said softly. "I will conquer the city if I have to, Telden."

Telden flushed. "What happened to you, Elend? Where is the man who talked about rights and legality?"

"The world caught up with me, Telden," Elend said. "I can't be the man I was."

"So you become the Lord Ruler instead?"

Elend hesitated. It felt odd to have another confront him with his own questions and arguments. Part of him felt a stab of fear—if Telden asked these things, then Elend had been correct to worry about them. Perhaps they were true.

Yet a stronger impulse flared within him. An impulse nurtured by Tindwyl, then refined by a year of struggling to bring order to the shattered remains of the Final Empire.

An impulse to trust himself.

"No, Telden," Elend said firmly. "I'm not the Lord Ruler. A parliamentary council rules in Luthadel, and there are others like it in every city I've brought into my empire. This is the first time that I've marched on a city with my armies out of a need to conquer rather than to protect—and that is only because Yomen took this city from an ally of mine."

Telden snorted. "You set yourself up as emperor."

"Because that's what the people *need*, Telden," Elend said. "They don't want to return to the days of the Lord Ruler—but they would rather do that than live in chaos. Yomen's success here proves that much. The people want to know that someone is watching over them. They had a god-emperor for a thousand years—now is not the time to leave them without a leader."

"You mean to tell me you're no more than a figurehead?" Telden said, folding his arms.

"Hardly," Elend said. "But eventually I hope to be. We both know I'm a scholar and not a king."

Telden frowned. He didn't believe Elend. Yet Elend found that fact didn't bother him. Something about saying those words, about confronting the skepticism, made him recognize the validity of his own confidence. Telden didn't understand—he hadn't lived through what Elend had. The young Elend wouldn't have agreed with what he was now doing. A part of that youth still had a voice within Elend's soul—and he would never quiet it. But it was time to stop letting it undermine him.

Elend put a hand on his friend's shoulder. "It's all right, Tell. It took me years to convince you that the Lord Ruler was a terrible emperor. I fully expect it to take the same amount of time to convince you that I'll be a good one."

Telden smiled wanly.

"Going to tell me that I've changed?" Elend asked. "Seems all the rage lately."

Telden laughed. "I thought that was obvious. No need to point it out."

"What then?" Elend asked.

"Well . . ." Telden said. "I was going to chide you for not inviting me to your wedding! I'm hurt, El. Truly. I spent the better part of my youth giving you relationship advice, then when you finally pick a girl, you don't let me know about the marriage!"

Elend laughed, turning to follow Telden's gaze toward Vin. Confident and powerful, yet somehow delicate and graceful. Elend smiled with pride. Even during the glory days of the Luthadel ball scene, he couldn't remember a woman commanding as much attention as Vin now did. And unlike Elend, she'd stepped into this ball without knowing a single person.

"This must be how a proud parent feels," Telden said, laying a hand on Elend's shoulder. "There were days I was convinced that you were hopeless, El! I figured you'd someday wander into a library and disappear completely. We'd find you twenty years later covered with dust, picking through some philosophy text for the seven hundredth time. Yet here you are, married—and to a woman like that!"

"Sometimes I don't understand either," Elend said. "I can't ever come up with any logical reason why she would want to be with me. I just . . . have to trust her judgment."

"In any case, you did well."

Elend raised an eyebrow. "I seem to remember that *you* once tried to talk me out of spending time with her."

Telden flushed. "You have to admit, she *was* acting very suspiciously when she came to those parties."

"Yes," Elend said. "She seemed too much like a real person to be a noblewoman." He looked over at Telden, smiling. "However, if you'll excuse me, I have something I need to do."

"Of course, El," Telden said, bowing slightly as Elend withdrew. The move felt a little odd coming from Telden. They didn't really know each other anymore. But they did have memories of friendship.

I didn't tell him that I killed Jastes, Elend thought as he made his way through the room, its members parting easily for him. *I wonder if he knows.*

Elend's enhanced hearing picked out a general rise in excitement among the whispered conversations as people realized what he was doing. He'd given Yomen long enough to deal with his surprise; it was time to confront the man. Though part of Elend's purpose in visiting the ball was to intimidate the local nobility, the main reason was still to speak with their king.

Yomen watched Elend approach the high table—and to his credit, the obligator did not appear frightened at the prospect of a meeting. His meal still remained uneaten, however. Elend didn't wait for permission to come to the table, but he did pause and wait as Yomen waved for servants to clear space and set Elend a place directly across the high table from him.

Elend sat, trusting in Vin—mixed with his own burning

steel and tin—to warn him of attacks from behind. He was the only one on this side of the table, and Yomen's dining companions all withdrew as Elend seated himself, leaving the two rulers alone. In another situation, the image might have looked ridiculous: two men seated across from each other with empty table wings extending a great distance to either direction. The white tablecloth and crystalline dinnerware were pristine, as would have been the case during the Lord Ruler's day.

Elend had sold all such finery he owned, struggling to feed his people during the last two winters.

Yomen laced his fingers on the table in front of him—his meal taken away by silent servants—and studied Elend, his cautious eyes framed by intricate tattoos. Yomen wore no crown, but he *did* wear a single bead of metal tied so that it hung in the center of his forehead.

Atium.

"There is a saying in the Steel Ministry," Yomen eventually said. " 'Sit down to dine with evil, and you will consume it with your meal.' "

"Then it's a good thing we're not eating," Elend said, smiling slightly.

Yomen did not return the smile.

"Yomen," Elend said, growing more serious. "I come to you now, not as an emperor seeking for new lands to control, but as a desperate king seeking allies. The world has become a dangerous place—the land itself seems to be fighting us, or at least falling apart beneath us. Accept my hand of friendship, and let us be done with wars."

Yomen didn't reply. He simply sat, fingers laced, studying Elend.

"You doubt my sincerity," Elend said. "I can't say that I blame you, since I marched my army up to your doorstep. Is there a way that I can persuade you? Would you be willing to enter into talks or parley?"

Again, no answer. So this time Elend waited. The room around them felt still.

At last, Yomen spoke. "You are a flagrant and garish man, Elend Venture."

Elend bristled. Perhaps it was the ball setting, perhaps it was the way Yomen so flippantly ignored his offer. But Elend found himself responding to the comment in a way he might have years before, when he hadn't been a king at war. "It's a bad habit I've always had. I'm afraid that the years of rule—and of being trained in propriety—haven't changed one fact: I'm a terribly rude man. Bad breeding would be my guess."

"You find this a game," the obligator said, his eyes hard. "You come to my city to slaughter my people, then you dance into my ball hoping to frighten the nobility to the point of hysteria."

"No," Elend said. "No, Yomen, this is no game. The world seems near to ending, and I'm merely doing my best to help as many people survive as possible."

"And doing your best includes conquering my city?"

Elend shook his head. "I'm not good at lying, Yomen. So I'll be truthful with you. I don't want to kill anyone—as I said, I'd rather we simply made a truce and were done with it. Give me the information I seek, pool your resources with mine, and I will not force you to give up your city. Deny me, and things will grow more difficult."

Yomen sat quietly for a moment, music still being played softly in the background, vibrating over the hum of a hundred polite conversations.

"Do you know why I detest men such as you, Venture?" Yomen asked.

"My insufferable charm and wit? I doubt it's my good looks—but compared to that of an obligator, I suppose even my face could be enviable."

Yomen's expression darkened. "How did a man like you ever end up at a table of negotiation?"

"I was trained by a surly Mistborn, a sarcastic Terrisman, and a group of disrespectful thieves," Elend said, sighing. "Plus on top of that, I was a fairly insufferable person to begin with. But kindly continue with your insult—I didn't mean to interrupt."

"I detest you," Yomen continued, "because you have the gall to believe that you *deserve* to take this city."

"I do," Elend said. "It belonged to Cett; half the soldiers I brought with me on this march once served him, and this is their homeland. We've come to liberate, not conquer."

"Do these people look to you as if they need liberation?" Yomen said, nodding to the dancing couples.

"Yes, actually," Elend said. "Yomen, you're the upstart here—not me. You have no right to this city, and you know it."

"I have the right given me by the Lord Ruler."

"We don't accept the Lord Ruler's right to rule," Elend said. "That's why we killed him. Instead we look to the *people's* right to rule."

"Is that so?" Yomen said, hands still laced before him. "Because as I recall, the people of *your* city chose Ferson Penrod to be their king."

Good point, Elend had to admit.

Yomen leaned forward. "This is the reason I detest you, Venture. You're a hypocrite of the worst kind. You pretended to let the people be in charge—but when they ousted you and picked another, you had your Mistborn conquer the city back for you. You rule by force, not by common consent, so don't talk to me about *rights*."

"There were . . . circumstances in Luthadel, Yomen. Penrod was working with our enemies, and he bought himself the throne through manipulating the assembly."

"That sounds like a flaw in the system," Yomen said. "A system that *you* set up—a system replacing the one of order that existed before it. A people depend on stability in their government; they need someone to look to. A leader that they can trust, a leader with true authority. Only a man chosen by the Lord Ruler has that claim on authority."

Elend studied the obligator. The frustrating thing was, he almost agreed with the man. Yomen said things that Elend himself had said, though twisted a bit by his perspective as an obligator.

"Only a man chosen by the Lord Ruler has that claim on authority . . ." Elend said, frowning. The phrase sounded familiar. "That's from Durton, isn't it? *Calling of Trust*?"

Yomen hesitated. "Yes."

"I prefer Gallingskaw, when it comes to divine right."

Yomen made a curt gesture. "Gallingskaw was a heretic."

"That makes his theories invalid?" Elend asked.

"No," Yomen said. "It shows that he lacked the ability to reason soundly—otherwise he wouldn't have gotten himself executed. *That* affects the validity of his theories. Besides, there is no divine mandate in the common man as he proposed."

"The Lord Ruler was a common man before he took his throne," Elend said.

"Yes," Yomen said, "but the Lord Ruler touched divinity at the Well of Ascension. That imprinted the Sliver of Infinity upon him, and gave him the Right of Inference."

"Vin, my wife, touched that same divinity."

"I don't accept that story," Yomen said. "As it has been said, the Sliver of Infinity was unique, unplanned, uncreated."

"Don't bring Urdree into this," Elend said, raising a finger. "We both know he was more a poet than a real philosopher—he ignored convention, and never gave proper attributions. At least give me the benefit of the doubt and quote Hardren. He'd give you a much better foundation."

Yomen opened his mouth, then stopped, frowning. "This is pointless," he said. "Arguing philosophy will not remove the fact that you have an army camped outside my city, nor change the fact that I find you a hypocrite, Elend Venture."

Elend sighed. For a moment, he'd thought that they might be able to respect one another as scholars. There was one problem, however. He saw true loathing in Yomen's eyes. And he suspected that there was a deeper reason for it than his alleged hypocrisy. After all, Elend *had* married the woman who had killed Yomen's god.

"Yomen," Elend said, leaning in. "I realize we have differences. But one thing seems clear—we both care about the people of this empire. We both took the time to study political theory, and we both apparently focused on the texts that held forth the good of the people as the prime reason for rule. We should be able to make this work.

"I want to offer you a deal. Accept kingship under me— you'd be able to stay in control, with few changes to your government. I will need access to the city and its resources, and we will need to discuss setting up a parliamentary council. Other than that, you may continue as you wish— you can even keep throwing your parties and teaching about the Lord Ruler. I will trust your judgment."

Yomen did not scoff at the offer, but Elend could tell that he also didn't give it much weight. He had likely already known what Elend would say.

"You mistake one thing, Elend Venture," Yomen said.

"And that is?"

"That I can be intimidated, bribed, or influenced."

"You're no fool, Yomen," Elend said. "Sometimes fighting isn't worth its cost. We both know that you can't beat me."

"That is debatable," Yomen said. "Regardless, I do not respond well to threats. Perhaps if you didn't have an army camped on my doorstep, I could see my way to an alliance."

"We both know that without an army on your doorstep, you wouldn't have listened to me," Elend said. "You refused every messenger I sent before I marched here."

Yomen shook his head. "You seem more reasonable than I would have thought, Elend Venture, but that doesn't change the facts. You already have a large empire of your own. In coming here, you betray your arrogance. Why did you need my dominance? Wasn't what you already had enough?"

"Firstly," Elend said, raising a finger, "I must remind you again that you seized this kingdom from an ally of mine. I had to come here eventually, if only to make good on promises I gave Cett. However, there's something much larger at play here." Elend hesitated, then made a gamble. "I need to know what is in your storage cavern."

Elend was rewarded with a slight look of surprise on Yomen's face, and that was all the confirmation Elend needed. Yomen did know about the cavern. Vin was right. And considering the atium displayed so prominently on his forehead, perhaps she was also right about what was contained in the cavern.

"Look, Yomen," Elend said, speaking quickly. "I don't care about the atium—it's barely of any value anymore. I need to know what instructions the Lord Ruler left in that cavern. What information is there for us? What supplies did he find necessary for our survival?"

"I don't know what you are talking about," Yomen said flatly. He wasn't a particularly good liar.

"You asked me why I came here," Elend said. "Yomen, it's not about conquering or taking this land from you. I realize you may find that hard to believe, but it's the truth. The Final Empire is dying. Surely you've seen that. Mankind needs to band together, pool its resources—and you have vital clues we need. Don't force me to break down your gates to get them. Work with me."

Yomen shook his head. "Once more you err, Venture. You see, I don't care if you attack me." He met Elend's eyes. "It would be better for my people to fight and to *die* than to be ruled by the man who overthrew our god and destroyed our religion."

Elend held those eyes, and saw determination in them.

"That's how it has to be?" Elend said.

"It is," Yomen said. "I can expect an attack in the morning then?"

"Of course not," Elend said, standing. "Your soldiers aren't starved yet. I'll get back to you in a few months." *Maybe then you'll be more willing to deal.*

He turned to go, then glanced back at Yomen. "Nice party, by the way," he said. "Regardless of what I believe, I do think that your god would be pleased with what you've done here. I think you should reconsider your prejudices.

The Lord Ruler probably isn't fond of Vin and me, but I'd say that he'd rather your people live than get themselves killed."

Elend nodded in respect, then left the high table, feeling more frustrated than he showed. Yomen and he had been so close, yet at the same time an alliance seemed impossible. Not while the obligator had such hatred of him and Vin.

He forced himself to relax, walking. There was little he could do about the situation at the moment—it would take the siege to make Yomen rethink his position. *I'm at a ball,* Elend thought, wandering. *I should enjoy what I can of it— let myself be seen by the nobility here, intimidating them and making them think about helping us instead of Yomen.*

A thought occurred to him. He glanced at Vin, then waved a servant over to him.

"My lord?" the man asked.

"I need you to fetch something for me," Elend said.

Vin was the center of attention. Women pandered to her, hung on her words, and looked to her as a model. They wanted to know news from Luthadel, to hear about fashion, politics, and events from the great city. They didn't reject her, or even seem to resent her.

The instant acceptance was the strangest thing Vin had ever experienced. She stood amid the women in their gowns and finery, and was foremost among them. She knew that it was only because of her power—yet the women of this city seemed almost desperate to have someone to look to. An empress.

And Vin found herself enjoying it. There was a part of her that had craved this acceptance since the first day she'd attended a ball. She'd spent those months being mistreated by most of the women of court—some had let her join with their company, but she'd always been an inconsequential country noblewoman with no connections or significance. It was a shallow thing, this acceptance, but sometimes even shallow things felt important. Plus there was something else about it. As she smiled toward a newcomer—a young niece that one of the women wanted to have meet her—Vin realized what it was.

This is part of me, she thought. *I didn't want it to be—perhaps because I didn't believe that I deserved it. I found this life too different, too full of beauty and confidence. Yet I am a noblewoman. I do fit in here.*

I was born to the streets through one parent, but I was born to this through the other.

She'd spent the first year of Elend's reign trying so hard to protect him. She'd forced herself to focus on her street side, the side that had been trained to be ruthless, for that would give her the power to defend what she loved. Yet Kelsier had shown her another way to be powerful. And that power was connected with the nobility—with their intrigue, their beauty, and their clever schemes. Vin had taken almost immediately to life at court, and that had frightened her.

That's it, she thought, smiling at another curtsying young woman. *That's why I always felt this was wrong. I didn't have to work for it, so I couldn't believe that I deserved it.*

She'd spent sixteen years on the streets—she'd earned that side of her. Yet it had taken her barely a month to adapt to noble life. It had seemed impossible to her that something that came so easily could be as important a part of her as the years spent on the streets.

But it was.

I had to confront this, she realized. *Tindwyl tried to make me do it over a year ago, but I wasn't ready.*

She needed to prove to herself not only that she could move among the nobility, but that she belonged with them. Because that proved something much more important: that the love she'd earned from Elend during those early months wasn't based on a falsehood.

It's . . . true, Vin thought. *I can be both. Why did it take me so long to figure it out?*

"Excuse me, ladies," a voice said.

Vin smiled, turning as the women parted to make way for Elend. Several of the younger ones got dreamy expressions on their faces as they regarded Elend with his warrior's body, his rugged beard, and his white imperial uniform. Vin suppressed a huff of annoyance. *She'd* loved him long before he'd become dreamy.

"Ladies," Elend said to the women, "as Lady Vin will be quick to tell you, I'm rather ill-mannered. That in itself would be a small sin. Unfortunately, I'm also quite unconcerned about my own disregard for propriety. So therefore, I'm going to steal my wife away from you all and selfishly monopolize her time. I'd apologize, but that's not the sort of thing we barbarians do."

With a smile, he held out his elbow to her. Vin smiled in return, taking his arm and allowing him to lead her away from the pack of women.

"Thought you might want some room to breathe," Elend said. "I can only imagine how it must make you feel to be surrounded by a virtual army of puffballs."

"I appreciate the rescue," Vin said, though it wasn't true. How was Elend to know that she'd suddenly discovered she fit in with those puffballs? Besides, just because they wore frills and makeup didn't mean they weren't dangerous, as she'd easily learned during her first months. The thought distracted her such that she didn't notice where Elend was leading her until they were almost there.

When she did realize it, she stopped immediately, jerking Elend back. "The dance floor?" she asked.

"Indeed," he said.

"But I haven't danced in almost three years!"

"Neither have I," Elend said. He stepped closer. "But it would be terrible to miss the opportunity. After all, we never did get to dance."

It was true. Luthadel had gone into revolt before they'd gotten an opportunity to dance together, and after that there hadn't been time for balls or frivolity. She knew Elend understood how much she regretted not having had the chance. He'd asked her to dance on the first night when they'd met, and she'd turned him down. She still felt she'd given up some unique opportunity that first evening.

So she let him lead her up onto the slightly raised dance floor. Couples whispered, and as the song ended, everyone else furtively departed the dance floor, leaving Vin and Elend alone—a figure in lines of white, and another in curves of black. Elend put an arm at her waist, turning her toward him, and Vin found herself traitorously nervous.

This is it, she thought, flaring pewter to keep from shaking. *It's finally happening. I finally get to dance with him!*

At that moment—as the music began—Elend reached into his pocket and pulled out a book. He raised it with one hand, the other on her waist, and began to read.

Vin's jaw dropped, then she whacked him on the arm. "What do you think you're doing?" she demanded as he shuffled through the dance steps, still holding his book. "Elend! I'm trying to have a special moment here!"

He turned toward her, smiling with a terribly mischievous grin. "Well, I want to make that special moment as authentic as possible. I mean, you are dancing with *me,* after all."

"For the first time!"

"All the more important to be certain that I make the right impression, Miss Valette!"

"Oh, for . . . Will you please just put the book away?"

Elend smiled more broadly, but slid the book back into his pocket, taking her hand and dancing with her in a more proper manner. Vin flushed as she saw the confused crowd standing around the dance floor. They clearly had no idea what to make of Elend's behavior.

"You *are* a barbarian," Vin told him.

"A barbarian because I read books?" Elend said lightly. "That's one that Ham will have a great time with."

"Honestly," Vin said, "where did you even get a book here?"

"I had one of Yomen's servants fetch it for me," Elend said. "From the keep library. I knew they'd have it—*Trials of Monument* is a rather famous work."

Vin frowned. "Do I recognize that title?"

"It was the book that I was reading that night on the Venture balcony," Elend said. "The time we first met."

"Why, Elend! That's almost romantic—in a twisted 'I'm going to make my wife want to kill me' sort of way."

"I thought you'd appreciate it," he said, turning lightly.

"You're in rare form tonight. I haven't seen you like this for quite some time."

"I know," he said, sighing. "To be honest, Vin, I feel a bit guilty. I'm worried that I was too informal during my conversation with Yomen. He's so stiff that my old instincts—the ones that always made me respond to people such as him with mockery—came out."

Vin let him lead the dance. "You're just acting like yourself. That's a good thing."

"My old self didn't make a good king," Elend said.

"The things you learned about kingship didn't have to do with your personality, Elend," Vin said. "They had to do with other things—about confidence and decisiveness. You can have those things and still be yourself."

Elend shook his head. "I'm not sure I can. Certainly, tonight I should have been more formal. I allowed the setting to make me lax."

"No," Vin said firmly. "No, I'm *right* about this, Elend. You've been doing the exact thing I have. You've been so determined to be a good king that you've let it quash who you really are. Our responsibilities shouldn't have to destroy us."

"They haven't destroyed you," he said, smiling behind his short beard.

"They nearly did," Vin said. "Elend, I had to realize that I could be both people—the Mistborn of the streets and the woman of the court. I had to acknowledge that the new person I'm becoming is a valid extension of who I am. But for you, it's the opposite! You have to realize that who you were is still a valid part of you. That person makes silly comments, and does things merely to provoke a reaction. But he's also lovable and kindhearted. You can't lose those things simply because you're emperor."

He got that expression on his face, the thoughtful one, the one that meant he was going to argue. Then he hesitated.

"Coming to this place," he said, looking at the beautiful windows and watching the nobility, "has reminded me of what I spent most of my life doing. Before I had to be a king. Even then, I was trying to do things my way—like going off and reading during balls. But I didn't do it in the library; I did it in the ballroom. I didn't want to hide. I wanted to express discontent with my father, and reading was my way."

"You were a good man, Elend," Vin said. "Not an idiot, as you now seem to think that you were. You were a little undirected, but still a good leader. You took control of Luthadel and stopped the skaa from committing a slaughter in their rebellion."

"But then, the whole Penrod fiasco . . ."

"You had things to learn," Vin said. "As I did. But please don't become someone else, Elend. You can be both Elend the emperor and Elend the man."

He smiled widely and pulled her close, pausing their dance. "Thank you," he said, then kissed her. She could tell that he hadn't made his decision yet—he still thought that he needed to be more of a hard warrior than a kind scholar. But he *was* thinking. That was enough at the moment.

Vin looked up into his eyes, and they returned to the dance. Neither spoke; they simply let the wonder of the moment hold them. It was a surreal experience for Vin. Their army was outside, the ash was falling perpetually, and the mists were killing people. Yet within this room of white marble and sparkling colors, she danced with the man she loved for the first time.

They both spun with the grace of Allomancy, stepping as if on the wind, moving as if made of mist. The room grew hushed, the nobility a theater audience watching some grand performance, not two people who hadn't danced in years. Yet Vin knew it was wonderful, something that had rarely been seen. Most noble Mistborn couldn't afford to appear too graceful, lest they give away their secret powers.

Vin and Elend had no such inhibitions. They danced to make up for the three years lost, to throw their joy in the face of an apocalyptic world and a hostile city. The song began to wind down. Elend pulled her against him, and her tin let her feel his heartbeat so close. It was beating far more swiftly than a simple dance could account for.

"I'm glad we did this," he said.

"There's another ball soon," she said. "In a week or so."

"I know," he said. "As I understand it, that ball is going to be held at the Canton of Resource."

Vin nodded. "Thrown by Yomen himself."

"And if the supply cache is hidden anywhere in the city, it will most likely be beneath that building."

"We'd have an excuse—and a precedent—to get in."

"Yomen has some atium," Elend said. "He's wearing a bead of it on his forehead. Though just because he has one bead doesn't mean he has a wealth of it."

Vin nodded. "I wonder if he's found the storage cavern."

"He has," Elend said, "I'm sure of it. I got a reaction out of him when I mentioned it."

"That still shouldn't stop us," Vin said, smiling. "We go to his ball, sneak into the cavern, find out what the Lord Ruler left there, then decide what to do about the siege—and the city—based on that?"

"Seems like a good plan," Elend said. "Assuming I can't get him to listen to reason. I was *close,* Vin. I can't help but think there might be a chance to bring him to our side."

She nodded again.

"All right then," he said. "Ready to make a grand exit?"

Vin smiled. As the music ended, Elend spun and threw her to the side, and she Pushed off the metal rim of the dance floor. She shot out over the crowd, guiding herself toward the exit, her dress flapping.

Behind, Elend addressed the crowd. "Thank you so much for letting us join you. Anyone who wants to escape the city will be allowed passage through my army."

Vin landed and saw the crowd turn as Elend jumped

over their heads, fortunately managing to guide himself through the relatively low room without crashing into any windows or hitting the ceiling. He joined her at the doors, and they escaped through the antechamber and into the night.

Hemalurgy is of Ruin. It destroys. By taking abilities from one person and giving them to another, in reduced amounts, some power is lost. In line with Ruin's own appointed purpose, breaking down the universe into smaller and smaller pieces, Hemalurgy gives great gifts—but at a high cost.

33

HUMANS MIGHT HAVE SCORNED TENSOON, perhaps throwing things at him or yelling curses as he passed. Kandra were too orderly for that kind of display, but TenSoon could feel their disdain. They watched as he was taken from his cage, then led to the Trustwarren for judgment. Hundreds of eyes regarded him, set in bodies with bones of steel, glass, rock, and wood. The younger kandra were more extreme in form, the older more orthodox.

All were accusatory.

Before, at the trial, the crowd had been curious—perhaps horrified. That had changed; TenSoon's time spent in the display cage had worked as intended. The Second Generation had been able to promote his infamy, and kandra who might once have been sympathetic to him now watched with disgust. In a thousand years of history, the kandra had never had a criminal such as TenSoon.

He bore the stares and the scorn with a raised head, padding through the corridor in a dog's body. It was strange to him, how natural the bones felt. He'd spent mere months wearing them, but putting them on again—discarding the scrawny, naked human body—felt more like coming home than returning to the Homeland had a year before.

And so, what was supposed to be a humiliation for him became instead a triumph. It had been a wild hope, but he'd manipulated the Second Generation into giving him back the dog's body. The sack had even contained the body's hair and nails—likely they had collected the entire mess after forcing TenSoon to abandon it and enter his prison a year ago.

The comfortable bones lent him strength. This was the body that Vin had given him. She was the Hero of Ages. He had to believe that.

Otherwise he was about to make a very large mistake.

His guards led him into the Trustwarren. This time there were too many observers to fit into the room, so the Seconds declared that those younger than the Seventh Generation had to wait outside. Still, kandra filled the rows of stone seats. They sat silently as TenSoon was led to the slightly raised metallic disc set into the center of the stone floor. The broad doors were left open, and younger kandra crowded there, listening.

TenSoon looked upward as he stepped onto his platform. The lumplike shadows of the First Generation waited above, each one in his separate alcove, backlit faintly in blue.

KanPaar approached his lectern. TenSoon could see the satisfaction in the way KanPaar slid across the floor. The Second felt that his triumph was complete—what happened to those who ignored the directives of the Second Generation would not soon be forgotten. TenSoon settled on his haunches, guarded by two kandra with the Blessing of Potency twinkling in each shoulder. They carried large mallets.

"TenSoon of the Third Generation," KanPaar said loudly. "Are you ready to bear the sentence of your judgment?"

"There will be no judgment," TenSoon said. His words slurred, coming from the dog's mouth, but they were clear enough to understand.

"No judgment?" KanPaar asked, amused. "You now seek to back out of what you yourself demanded?"

"I came to give information, not to be judged."

"I—"

"I'm not speaking to you, KanPaar," TenSoon said, turning from the Second to look up. "I'm talking to them."

"They heard your words, Third," KanPaar snapped. "Control yourself! I will not let you turn this judgment into a circus, as you did before."

Only a kandra would consider a mild argument to be a circus. TenSoon smiled, and didn't turn away from the First Generation's alcoves.

"Now," KanPaar said. "We—"

"You!" TenSoon bellowed, causing KanPaar to sputter again. "First Generation! How long will you sit in your comfortable home, pretending that the world above doesn't exist? You think that if you ignore the problems, they won't affect you? Or is it that you've stopped believing in your own teachings?

"The days of mist have come! The endless ash now falls! The earth shakes and trembles. You can condemn me, but you must not ignore me! The world will soon die! If you want people—in all of their forms—to survive, you must act! You must be ready! For you may soon need to command our people to accept the Resolution!"

The room fell silent. Several of the shadows above shuffled, as if discomforted—though kandra generally didn't react in such a way. It was too disorderly.

Then a voice—soft, scratchy, and very tired—spoke from above. "Proceed, KanPaar."

The comment was so unexpected that several members of the audience gasped. The First Generation never spoke in the presence of lessers. TenSoon wasn't awed—he'd seen them, and talked with them, before they'd grown too superior to deal with anyone but the Seconds. No, he wasn't awed. He was just disappointed.

"My faith in you was misplaced," he said, mostly to himself. "I should not have returned."

"TenSoon of the Third Generation!" KanPaar said, standing up straight, crystalline True Body sparkling as he pointed. "You have been sentenced to the ritual imprisonment of ChanGaar! You will be beaten to the point of fracture, then bricked into a pit with a single hole for your daily slop. You will remain there for ten generations! Only afterward will you be executed by starvation! Know that your greatest sin was that of rebellion. If you had not strayed from the advice and wisdom of this council, you would never have thought it right to break the First Contract. Because of you, the Trust has been endangered, as has each kandra of every generation!"

KanPaar let the pronouncement ring in the chamber. TenSoon sat quietly on his haunches. KanPaar had obviously expected some kind of response from him, but TenSoon gave none. Finally, KanPaar gestured to the guards beside TenSoon, who hefted their fearsome hammers.

"You know, KanPaar," TenSoon said, "I learned a few important things while wearing these bones a year ago."

KanPaar gestured again. The guards raised their weapons.

"It's something I had never paused to consider," TenSoon said. "Humans, if you think about it, simply aren't built for speed. Dogs, however, *are*."

The hammers fell.

TenSoon leaped forward.

His powerful dog's haunches launched him into motion. He was a member of the Third Generation; no one had been eating and emulating bodies longer than he had, and he knew how to pack muscles into a body. In addition, while wearing the bones of a wolfhound, he had been forced to try to keep up with his Mistborn master. He had effectively undergone months of training by one of the most talented Allomancers the world had ever known.

On top of that, a body mass that had been transformed from a scrawny human made quite a substantial wolfhound. This, combined with his skill in crafting bodies, meant that when TenSoon jumped, he *jumped*. His guards cried out in shock as TenSoon sprang away, his leap taking him at least ten feet across the room. He hit the ground running, but didn't head for the door. They'd be expecting that.

Instead he sprang directly toward KanPaar. The foremost of the Seconds cried out, raising ineffectual hands as a hundred pounds of wolfhound crashed into him, throwing him to the stone floor. TenSoon heard sharp cracks as KanPaar's delicate bones shattered, and KanPaar screamed in a very un-kandralike way.

That seems appropriate, TenSoon thought, shoving his way through the ranks of the Seconds, shattering bones. *Honestly, what kind of vain fool wears a True Body made of crystal?*

Many of the kandra didn't know how to react. Others— especially the younger ones—had spent a lot of time around humans on Contracts, and they were more accustomed to chaos. These scattered, leaving their elder companions sitting on the benches in shock. TenSoon darted between bodies, heading toward the doors. The guards near the podium—the ones who would have shattered his bones— rushed to KanPaar, their filial sense of duty overriding their desire to prevent TenSoon's escape. Besides, they must have seen the crowd clogging the doorway, and assumed that he would be slowed.

As soon as he reached the crowd, TenSoon jumped once more. Vin had required him to be able to leap incredible heights, and he'd practiced with many different muscle structures. This jump wouldn't have impressed Vin—TenSoon no longer had the Blessing of Potency he'd stolen from OreSeur—but it was more than enough to let him clear the watching kandra. Some cried out, and he landed in a pocket of open space, then leaped again toward the open cavern beyond.

"No!" he heard echoing from the Trustwarren. "Go after him!"

TenSoon took off in a loping dash down one of the corridors. He ran quickly—far more quickly than anything bipedal could have managed. With his canine body, he hoped he'd be able to outrun even kandra bearing the Blessing of Potency.

Farewell, my home, TenSoon thought, leaving the main cavern behind. *And farewell to what little honor I had left.*

THE END OF PART TWO

PART THREE

THE BROKEN SKIES

Feruchemy, it should be noted, is the power of balance. Of the three powers, solely it was known to men before the conflict between Preservation and Ruin came to a head. In Feruchemy, power is stored up, then later drawn upon. There is no loss or gain of energy—merely a changing of the time and rate of its use.

34

MARSH STRODE INTO THE SMALL town. Workers atop the makeshift gate—flimsy enough that a determined knock would send it toppling—froze in place. Ash sweepers reacted to his passing with shock, then horror. It was odd, how they watched, too terrified to flee. Or at least too terrified to be the first one to flee.

Marsh ignored them. The earth trembled beneath him in a beautiful song—quakes were common, here, in the shadow of Mount Tyrian, the Ashmount closest to Luthadel. Marsh walked through Elend Venture's own territory. But the emperor had abandoned it. That seemed an invitation to Marsh, and to the one who controlled him. They were really the same. Marsh smiled as he walked.

A small piece of him was still free. But he let it sleep. Ruin needed to think he had given up. That was the point. So Marsh held back only a tiny bit, and he did not fight. He let the ashen sky become a thing of bespeckled beauty, and treated the death of the world as a blessed event.

Biding his time. Waiting.

The village was an inspiring sight. The people were
starving here, even though they were within the Central
Dominance, Elend Venture's "protected" area. They had
the wonderful haunted expressions of those who were close
to giving up hope. The streets were barely maintained, the
homes—which had once been the dwellings of noblemen,
but were now filled with hungry skaa—covered in ash, their
gardens stripped and their structures cannibalized to feed
fires during the winter.

The gorgeous sight made Marsh smile with satisfaction.
Behind him, people started to move at last, fleeing, doors
slamming. There were probably some six or seven thousand living in the town. They were not Marsh's concern. Not
at the moment.

He was interested only in a single specific building. It
looked little different from the others, a mansion in a fine
row. The town had once been a stopping place for travelers,
and had grown to be a favored location for nobility to construct second homes. A few noble families had lived here
permanently, overseeing the many skaa who had worked
the plantations and fields on the plains outside.

The building Marsh chose was slightly better maintained
than those around it. The garden was still more weeds than
cultivation, and the outer mansion walls hadn't seen a good
scrubbing in years. But fewer sections of it looked to have
been broken apart for firewood, and a guard stood watch at
the front gate.

Marsh killed him with one of the razor-sharp metal triangles that had once been used in the Lord Ruler's ceremo-
nies. Marsh Pushed it through the guard's chest even as the
man opened his mouth in challenge. The air was oddly still
and quiet as the guard's voice cut off, and he toppled to the
side in the road. The skaa who watched from nearby homes
knew better than to react, and didn't stir.

Marsh hummed to himself as he strolled up the front
walk to the mansion, startling a small flock of ravens who
had come to roost. Once this path would have been a calm-
ing stroll through gardens, the way marked by flagstones.

Now it was simply a hike through a weed-filled field. The man who owned the place clearly couldn't afford more than the lone gate guard, and nobody raised an alarm at Marsh's approach. He was able to walk right up to the front doors. Smiling to himself, he knocked.

A maidservant opened the doors. She froze when she saw Marsh, taking in his spiked eyes, his unnaturally tall figure, his dark robes. Then she began to tremble.

Marsh held out a hand, palm up, with another of the triangles. Then he Pushed it straight into her face. It snapped out the back of her skull, and the woman toppled. He stepped over her body and entered the house.

It was far nicer inside than the exterior had led him to expect. Rich furnishings, freshly painted walls, intricate ceramics. Marsh raised an eyebrow and scanned the room with his spiked eyes. The way his sight worked, it was hard for him to distinguish colors, but he was familiar enough with it now that he could pick them out if he wanted. The Allomantic lines from the metals inside most things were quite expressive.

To Marsh, the mansion was a place of pristine whiteness and bright blobs of expensive color. He searched through it, burning pewter to enhance his physical abilities, allowing him to walk more lightly than would otherwise have been possible. He killed two more servants in the course of his exploration, and eventually moved up to the second floor.

He found the man he wanted sitting at a desk in a top-floor room. Balding, wearing a rich suit. He had a petite mustache set in a round face, and was slumped, eyes closed, a bottle of hard liquor empty at his feet. Marsh saw this with displeasure.

"I come all this way to get you," Marsh said. "And when I finally find you, I discover you intoxicated into a stupor?"

The man had never met Marsh, of course. That didn't stop Marsh from feeling annoyed that he wouldn't be able to see the look of terror and surprise in the man's eyes when he found an Inquisitor in his home. Marsh would miss out on the fear, the anticipation of death. Briefly, Marsh was tempted to wait until the man sobered up so that the killing could be performed properly.

But Ruin would have none of that. Marsh sighed at the injustice of it, then slammed the unconscious man down against the floor and drove a small bronze spike through his heart. It wasn't as large or thick as an Inquisitor spike, but it killed just as well. Marsh ripped it out of the man's heart, leaving the former nobleman dead, blood pooling on the floor.

Then Marsh walked out, leaving the building. The nobleman—Marsh didn't know his name—had used Allomancy recently. The man was a Smoker, a Misting who could create copperclouds, and the use of his ability had drawn Ruin's attention. Ruin had been wanting an Allomancer to drain.

So Marsh had come to harvest the man's power and draw it into the spike. It seemed something of a waste to him. Hemalurgy—particularly Allomantic imbuements—was much more potent when one could drive the spike through the victim's heart and directly into a waiting host. That way, very little of the Allomantic ability was lost. Doing it this way—killing the Allomancer to make a spike, then traveling somewhere else to place it—would grant the new host far less power.

But there was no getting around it in this case. Marsh shook his head as he stepped over the maidservant's body once more, moving out into the unkempt gardens. No one accosted or even looked at him as he made his way to the front gates. There, however, he was surprised to find a few skaa men kneeling on the ground.

"Please, Your Grace," one said as Marsh passed. "Please send the obligators back to us. We will serve better this time."

"You have lost that opportunity," Marsh said, staring at them with his spikeheads.

"We will believe in the Lord Ruler again," another said. "He fed us. Please. Our families have no food."

"Well," Marsh said. "You needn't worry about that for long."

The men knelt, confused, as Marsh left. He didn't kill

them, though part of him wished to. Unfortunately, Ruin wanted to claim that privilege for himself.

Marsh walked across the plain outside the town. After about an hour he stopped, turning to look back at the community and the towering Ashmount behind it.

At that moment, the top left half of the mountain exploded, spewing a deluge of dust, ash, and rock. The earth trembled, and a booming sound washed over Marsh. Then, flaming hot and red, a large gout of lava began to flow down the Ashmount toward the edge of the shallow lake and the town on its shore.

Marsh shook his head. Yes. Food was *hardly* this town's biggest problem. They really needed to get their priorities straight.

Hemalurgy is a power about which I wish I knew far less. To Ruin, power must have an inordinately high cost—using it must be attractive, yet must sow chaos and destruction in its very implementation.

In concept, it is quite a simple art. A parasitic one. Without other people to steal from, Hemalurgy would be useless.

35

"YOU'LL BE ALL RIGHT HERE?" Spook asked.

Breeze turned away from the brightened tavern, raising an eyebrow. Spook had brought him—along with several of Goradel's soldiers in street clothing—to one of the larger, more reputable locations. Voices rang within.

"Yes, this should be fine," Breeze said, eyeing the tavern. "Skaa out at night. Never thought I'd see that. Perhaps the world really *is* ending."

"I'm going to go to one of the poorer sections of town," Spook said quietly. "There are some things I want to check on."

"Poorer sections," Breeze said musingly. "Perhaps I should accompany you. I've found that the poorer people are, the more likely they are to let their tongues wag."

"No offense, Breeze, but I think you'd stand out."

"What?" Breeze asked, nodding toward his utilitarian brown worker's outfit—quite a change from his usual suit and vest. "I'm wearing these dreadful clothes, aren't I?"

"Clothing isn't everything, Breeze. You've got a bearing about you. Plus you don't have much ash on you."

"I was infiltrating the lower ranks before you were born, child," Breeze said, wagging a finger at him.

"All right," Spook said. He reached to the ground, scooping up a pile of ash. "Let's just rub this into your clothing and on your face."

Breeze balked. "I'll . . . meet you back at the lair."

Spook smiled, dropping the ash as he disappeared into the mists.

"I never did like him," Kelsier whispered.

Spook left the richer section of town, moving at a brisk pace. When he hit the streetslot he didn't stop, but simply leaped off the edge of the road and plummeted twenty feet.

His cloak flapped behind him as he fell. Landing easily, he continued his quick pace. Without pewter, he would certainly have broken some limbs. Now he moved with the same dexterity he'd once envied in Vin and Kelsier. He felt exhilarated. With pewter flaring within him, he never felt tired—never even felt fatigued. Simple acts like walking down the street made him feel full of grace and power.

He moved quickly to the Harrows, leaving behind the streets of better men, entering the cluttered, overpacked streetslot alley, knowing exactly where he'd find his quarry. Durn was one of the leading figures in the Urteau underworld. Part informant, part beggar lord, the unfulfilled musician had become a sort of mayor of the Harrows. Men like that had to be where people could find and pay them.

Spook still remembered that first night after waking from his fevers a few weeks ago, the night when he'd visited a tavern and heard men talking about him. Over the next few days, he'd visited several other taverns, and had heard others mention rumors of Spook. Sazed and Breeze's arrival had kept Spook from confronting Durn— the apparent source of the rumors—about what he'd been telling people. It was time to correct that oversight.

Spook picked up his pace, leaping mounds of discarded boards, dashing around piles of ash, until he reached the hole that Durn called home. It was a section of canal wall that had been hollowed out to form a cave. Though the wooden framing around the door looked as rotted and splintered as everything else in the Harrows, Spook knew it to be reinforced on the back with a thick oaken bar.

Two brutes sat watch outside. They eyed Spook as he stopped in front of the door, cloak whipping around him. It was the same one he'd been wearing when he'd been tossed into the fire, and it was still spotted with burn marks and holes.

"The boss isn't seeing anyone right now, kid," said one of the big men, not rising from his seat. "Come back later."

Spook kicked the door. It broke free, its hinges snapping, the bar shattering its mountings and tumbling backward.

He stood for a moment, shocked. He had too little experience with pewter to gauge its use accurately. If he was shocked, the two brutes were stunned. They sat staring at the broken door.

"You may need to kill them," Kelsier whispered.

No, Spook thought. *I just have to move quickly.* He dashed into the open hallway, needing no torch or lantern by which to see. He whipped spectacles and a cloth out of his pocket as he approached the door at the end of the hallway, fixing them in place as the guards called out behind him.

He threw his shoulder against the door with a bit more

care, slamming it open but not breaking it. He moved into a well-lit room where four men sat playing chips at a table. Durn was winning.

Spook pointed at the men as he skidded to a halt. "You three. Out. Durn and I have business."

Durn sat at the table, looking genuinely surprised. The brutes rushed up behind Spook, and he turned, falling to a crouch, reaching under his cloak for his dueling cane.

"It's all right," Durn said, standing. "Leave us."

The guards hesitated, angry. But they withdrew, Durn's gambling partners going with them. The door closed.

"That was quite the entrance," Durn noted, retaking his seat at the table.

"You've been talking about me, Durn," Spook said, turning. "I've heard people discussing me in taverns, mentioning your name. You've been spreading rumors about my death, telling people that I was on the Survivor's crew. How did you know who I was, and why have you been using my name?"

"Oh, come now," Durn said, scowling. "How anonymous did you think you were? You're the Survivor's friend, and you spend a good half of your time living in the emperor's own palace."

"Luthadel's a long way from here."

"Not so far that news doesn't travel," Durn said. "A Tineye comes to town, spying about, flaunting seemingly endless funds? It wasn't really that hard to figure out who you were. Besides, there's your eyes."

"What about them?" Spook asked.

The ugly man shrugged. "Everyone knows that strange things happen around the Survivor's crew."

Spook wasn't certain what to make of that. He walked forward, looking over the cards on the table. He picked one up, feeling its paper. His heightened senses let him feel the bumps on the back.

"Marked cards?" he asked.

"Of course," Durn said. "Practice game, to see if my men could read the patterns right."

Spook tossed the card onto the table. "You still haven't told me why you've been spreading rumors about me."

"No offense, kid," Durn said. "But . . . well, you're supposed to be dead."

"If you believed that, then why bother talking about me?"

"Why do you think?" Durn said. "The people love the Survivor—and anything related to him. That's why Quellion uses his name so often. But if I could show that Quellion killed one of Kelsier's own crew . . . well, there are a lot of people in this city who wouldn't like that."

"So, you're just trying to help," Spook said flatly. "Out of the goodness of your heart."

"You're not the only one who thinks Quellion is killing this city. If you're really of the Survivor's crew, you'll know that sometimes people fight."

"I find it difficult to think of you as an altruist, Durn. You're a thief."

"So are you."

"We didn't know what we were getting into," Spook said. "Kelsier promised us riches. How do *you* gain from all this?"

Durn snorted. "The Citizen is very bad for business. Venture red wine being sold for a fraction of a clip? Our smuggling has been choked to a trickle because everyone fears buying our goods. Things were *never* this bad under the Lord Ruler." He leaned in. "If your friends staying in the old Ministry building think they can do something about that lunatic running this city, then tell them they'll have my support. There isn't a large underground left in this city, but Quellion will be surprised at the damage it can do if manipulated the right way."

Spook stood quietly for a moment. "There's a man milking for information in the tavern on Westbrook Lane. Send someone to contact him. He's a Soother—the best one you'll ever meet—but he stands out a bit. Make your offer to him."

Durn nodded.

Spook turned to go, then glanced back at Durn. "Don't mention my name to him, or what happened to me."

With that, he left through the hallway, passing the guards and the displaced crooks from the card game. Spook pulled off his blindfold as he stepped into the daylike brightness of the starlit night.

He strolled through the Harrows, trying to decide what he thought of the meeting. Durn hadn't revealed anything all *that* important. Yet Spook felt as if something were happening around him, something he hadn't planned on and couldn't quite decipher. He was becoming more comfortable with Kelsier's voice, and with his own pewter, but he was still worried he wouldn't be able to live up to the position he'd fallen into.

"If you don't get to Quellion soon," Kelsier said, "he's going to find your friends. He's already preparing assassins."

"He won't send them," Spook said quietly. "Especially if he's heard Durn's rumors about me. Everyone knows that Sazed and Breeze were on your crew. Quellion won't take them out unless they prove to be such a threat that he has no other choice."

"Quellion is an unstable man," Kelsier said. "Don't wait too long. You don't want to find out how irrational he can be."

Spook fell silent. Then he heard footsteps, approaching quickly. He felt the vibrations in the ground. He spun and loosened his cloak, reaching for his weapon.

"You're not in danger," Kelsier said softly.

Spook relaxed as someone rushed around the alley corner. It was one of the men from Durn's chips game. The man was puffing, his face flushed with exhaustion. "My lord!" he said.

"I'm no lord," Spook said. "What happened? Is Durn in danger?"

"No, sir," the man said. "I just . . . I . . ."

Spook raised an eyebrow.

"I need your help," the man said between breaths. "When we realized who you were, you were already gone. I just . . ."

"Help with what?" Spook said tersely.

"My sister, sir," the man said. "She got taken by the Citizen. Our . . . father was a nobleman. Durn hid me, but Mailey, she got sold by the woman I'd left her with. Sir, she's only seven. He's going to burn her in a few days!"

Spook frowned. *What does he expect me to do?* He opened his mouth to ask that very question, then stopped. He wasn't the same man anymore. He wasn't limited as the old Spook would have been. He could do something else.

What Kelsier would have done.

"Can you gather ten men?" Spook asked. "Friends of yours, willing to take part in some late-night work?"

"Sure. I guess. Does this have to do with saving Mailey?"

"No," Spook said. "It has to do with your payment for saving Mailey. Get me those workers, and I'll do what I can to help your sister."

The man nodded eagerly.

"Do it now," Spook said, pointing. "We start tonight."

In Hemalurgy, the type of metal used in a spike is important, as is the positioning of that spike on the body. For instance, steel spikes take physical Allomantic powers—the ability to burn pewter, tin, steel, or iron—and bestow them upon the person receiving the spike. Which of these four is granted depends on where the spike is placed.

Spikes made from certain other metals steal Feruchemical abilities. For example, all of the original Inquisitors were given a gold spike, which—after first being pounded through the body of a Feruchemist—gave the Inquisitor the ability to store up healing power. (Though they couldn't do so as quickly as a real Feruchemist, as per the law of Hemalurgic decay.) This is obviously where the Inquisitors got their infamous ability to recover from wounds quickly, and was also why they needed to rest so much.

36

"YOU SHOULDN'T HAVE GONE IN," Cett said flatly.

Elend raised an eyebrow, riding his stallion through the center of his camp. Tindwyl had taught him that it was good to be seen by one's people, especially in situations where he could control the way he was perceived. He happened to agree with this particular lesson, so he rode, wearing a black cloak to mask the ash's smudges, making certain his soldiers knew that he was among them. Cett rode with him, tied into his specially made saddle.

"You think I put myself in too much danger by entering the city?" Elend asked, nodding to a group of soldiers who had paused in their morning labors to salute him.

"No," Cett said, "we both know that I don't give a damn whether you live or die, boy. Besides, you're Mistborn. You could have gotten out if things turned dangerous."

"Why then?" Elend asked. "Why was it a mistake?"

"Because you met the people inside. You talked with them, danced among them. Hell, boy. Can't you see why that's such a problem? When the time comes to attack, you'll worry about the people you're going to hurt."

Elend rode in silence for a moment. The morning mists were a normal thing to him now. They obscured the camp, masking its size. Even to his tin-enhanced eyes, distant tents became silhouetted lumps. It was as if he rode through some mythical world, a place of muffled shadows and distant noises.

Had it been a mistake for him to enter the city? Perhaps. Elend knew the theories Cett spoke of—he understood how important it was for a general to view his enemies not as individuals, but as numbers. Obstacles.

"I'm happy with my choice," Elend said.

"I know," Cett said, scratching at his thick beard. "That's what frustrates me, to be honest. You're a compassionate man. That's a weakness, but it isn't the real problem. The *problem* is your inability to deal with your own compassion."

Elend pursed his lips.

"You should know better than to let yourself grow attached to your enemy, Elend," Cett said. "You should have known how you would react, and planned so that you could avoid this very situation! Hell, boy, every leader has weaknesses—the ones who win are the ones who learn how to smother those weaknesses, not give them fuel!"

When Elend didn't respond to that, Cett simply sighed. "All right then, let's talk about the siege. The engineers have blocked off several streams that lead into the city, but they don't think those were the primary sources of water."

"They weren't," Elend said. "Vin has located six main wells within the city."

"We should poison them," Cett said.

Elend fell silent. The two halves of him still warred. The man he had been simply wanted to protect as many people as possible. The man he was becoming was more realistic. That man knew that sometimes he had to kill—or at least cause discomfort—in order to save.

"Very well," Elend said. "I'll have Vin do it tonight—and I'll have her leave a message written on the wells saying what we've done."

"What good will that do?" Cett asked, frowning.

"I don't want to kill the people, Cett," Elend said, "I want to worry them. This way they'll go to Yomen for water. With the entire city making demands, he should go through the water supply in his storage cache pretty quickly."

Cett grunted. But he seemed pleased that Elend had taken his suggestion. "And the surrounding villages?"

"Feel free to bully them," Elend said. "Organize a force of ten thousand and send them out to harass—but not kill. I want Yomen's spies in the area to send him worried notes about his kingdom collapsing."

"You're trying to play this halfway, lad," Cett said. "Eventually you'll have to choose. If Yomen doesn't surrender, you'll have to attack."

Elend reined in his horse by the command tent. "I know," he said softly.

Cett snorted, but he fell silent as servants came out of the tent to unstrap him from the saddle. As they began, however, the earth started to tremble. Elend cursed, struggling to maintain control of his horse as it grew skittish. The shaking rattled tents, knocking poles free and collapsing a couple of them, and Elend heard the clang of metal as cups, swords, and other items were knocked to the ground. Eventually the rumbling subsided, and he glanced over at Cett. The man had managed to keep control of his mount, though one of his useless legs swung free from the saddle and he looked about to fall off. His son, Gneorndin, rushed to his side to help.

"Damn things are growing more and more frequent," Cett said.

Elend calmed his horse, which stood puffing in the mists. Throughout the camp, men cursed and yelled. The last earthquake had been only a few weeks before. Earthquakes weren't supposed to be common in the Final Empire— during his youth, he'd never heard of one happening in the inner dominances.

He sighed, climbing from his horse and handing the beast off to an aide, then followed Cett into the command tent. The servants sat Cett in a chair and retreated, leaving the two of them alone. Cett glanced up at Elend, looking troubled. "Did that fool Ham tell you about the news from Luthadel?"

"Or the lack of it?" Elend asked, sighing. "Yes." Not a peep had come from the capital city, let alone the supplies Elend had ordered brought down the canal.

"We don't have *that* much time, Elend," Cett said quietly. "A few months at most. Time enough to weaken Yomen's resolve, perhaps make his people so thirsty that they begin to look forward to invasion. But if we don't get resupplied, there's no way we'll be able to maintain this siege."

Elend glanced at the older man. Cett sat in his chair with an arrogant expression, meeting his eyes. So much of what the man did was about posturing; since he had lost the use of his legs to disease long ago, he couldn't intimidate people physically. So he found other ways to make himself threatening.

Cett knew how to hit where it hurt. He could pick at the exact faults that bothered people and exploit their virtues in ways that Elend had rarely seen even accomplished Soothers manage. And he did all this while concealing a heart that Elend suspected was far softer than Cett would ever admit.

He seemed particularly on edge this day, as if worried

about something. Something important to him—something he'd been forced to leave behind perhaps?

"She'll be all right, Cett," Elend said. "Nothing will happen to Allrianne while she's with Sazed and Breeze."

Cett snorted, waving an indifferent hand—though he did glance away. "I'm better off without the damn fool of a girl around. Let that Soother have her, I say! Anyway, we're not talking about me, we're talking about you and this siege!"

"Your points have been noted, Cett," Elend said. "We will attack if I deem it necessary." As he spoke, the tent flaps parted and Ham sauntered in, accompanied by a figure Elend hadn't seen in weeks—at least not out of bed.

"Demoux!" Elend said, approaching the general. "You're up and about!"

"Barely, Your Majesty," Demoux said. His face was still pale. "However, I have recovered enough strength to move around a bit."

"The others?" Elend asked.

"Mostly up and about as well," Ham said. "Demoux is among the last batch. A few more days, and the army will be at full strength."

Minus those who died, Elend thought.

Cett eyed Demoux. "Most of the men recovered weeks ago. A bit more frail in the constitution than one might expect, eh, Demoux? That's what I've been hearing at least."

Demoux blushed.

Elend frowned at this. "What?"

"It is nothing, Your Majesty," Demoux said.

"It's never 'nothing' in my camp, Demoux," Elend said. "What am I missing?"

Ham sighed, pulling over a chair. He sat on it reversed, resting his muscular arms across its back. "It's only a rumor moving through the camp, El."

"Soldiers," Cett said. "They're all the same—superstitious as housewives."

Ham nodded. "Some of them have gotten it into their heads that the men who got sick from the mists were being punished."

"Punished?" Elend asked. "For what?"

"Lack of faith, Your Majesty," Demoux said.

"Nonsense," Elend said. "We all know that the mists struck randomly."

The others shared looks, and Elend had to reconsider. *No. The strikes weren't random—at least the statistics surrounding them weren't.* "Regardless," he said, deciding to change the subject, "what are your daily reports?"

The three men took turns talking about their various duties in the bivouac. Ham saw to morale and training, Demoux to supplies and camp duties, Cett to tactics and patrols. Elend stood with hands clasped behind him, listening to the reports with half an ear. They weren't much different from the previous day, though it was good to see Demoux at his duties. He was far more efficient than his assistants.

As they talked, Elend's mind wandered. The siege was going fairly well, but a part of him—the part trained by Cett and Tindwyl—chafed at the waiting game. He might be able to take the city straight out. He had koloss, and all accounts said that his troops were far more experienced than those within Fadrex. The rock formations would provide cover for the defenders, but Elend wasn't in so bad a position that he couldn't win.

But doing so would cost many, many lives.

That was the step he balked at—the last step that would take him from defender to aggressor. From protector to conqueror. And he was frustrated at his own hesitance.

There was another reason Cett would call having gone into the city bad for Elend. It had been better for Elend to think of Yomen as an evil tyrant, a corrupt obligator loyal to the Lord Ruler. Now, unfortunately, he knew Yomen to be a reasonable man. And one with good arguments. In a way, Yomen's indictment of Elend was true. He spoke of democracy, yet he had taken his throne by force.

It was what the people had needed from him, he believed. However, it did make him a hypocrite. Still, by that same logic he knew he should send Vin to assassinate Yomen.

But could Elend order the death of a man who had done nothing wrong other than getting in his way?

Assassinating the obligator seemed as twisted an action as sending his koloss to attack the city. *Cett is right,* Elend thought. *I'm trying to play both sides on this one.* For a moment, while talking to Telden during the ball, he had felt so sure of himself. And in truth, he still believed what he'd claimed. Elend *wasn't* the Lord Ruler. He *did* give his people more freedom and more justice.

However, he realized that this siege could tip the balance between who he was and who he feared he would become. Could he really justify invading Fadrex, slaughtering its armies and pillaging its resources, ostensibly in the name of protecting the people of the empire? Could he dare do the opposite: retreat from Fadrex and leave the secrets in that cavern—the secrets that could potentially save the entire empire—to a man who still thought the Lord Ruler would return to save his people?

He wasn't ready to decide. For now, he was determined to exhaust every other option. Anything that would keep him from needing to invade the city. That included besieging the city to make Yomen more pliant. That also included sneaking Vin into the storage cavern. Her reports indicated that the building was heavily guarded. She wasn't certain if she could get into it on an ordinary night. During a ball, defenses might be more porous. It would be the perfect time to try to get a glimpse at what was hidden in that cavern.

Assuming Yomen hasn't simply removed the Lord Ruler's inscription, Elend thought. *Or that there was even something there in the first place.*

Yet there was a chance. The Lord Ruler's final message, the last bit of help he had left for his people. If Elend could find a way to get that help without breaking his way into the city, killing thousands, he would take it.

Eventually the men finished with their reports, and Elend dismissed them. Ham went quickly, wanting to get in a morning sparring session. Cett was gone a few moments later, carried back to his own tent. Demoux lingered. It was sometimes hard to remember quite how young he was—barely older than Elend. The balding scalp and numerous scars made the man appear much older, as did the still-visible effects of his extended illness.

Demoux was hesitant about something. Elend waited, and finally the man dropped his eyes, looking embarrassed. "Your Majesty," he said, "I feel that I must ask to be released from my post as general."

"And why do you say that?" Elend asked carefully.

"I don't think I'm worthy of the position anymore."

Elend frowned.

"Only a man trusted by the Survivor should command in this army, my lord," Demoux said.

"I'm sure that he does trust you, Demoux."

Demoux shook his head. "Then why did he give me the sickness? Why pick me, of all the men in the army?"

"I've told you it was random luck, Demoux."

"My lord," Demoux said, "I hate to disagree, but we both know that isn't true. After all, you were the one who pointed out that those who fell sick did so at Kelsier's will."

Elend hesitated. "I did?"

Demoux nodded. "That evening when we exposed our army to the mists, you shouted out for them to remember that Kelsier is the Lord of the Mists, and that the sickness must therefore be his will. I think you were right. The Survivor *is* Lord of the Mists. He proclaimed it so himself, during the nights before he died. He's behind the sickness, my lord. I know he is. He saw those who lacked faith, and he cursed them."

"That isn't what I meant, Demoux," Elend said. "I was implying that Kelsier wanted us to suffer this setback, but not that he was targeting specific individuals."

"Either way, my lord, you said the words."

Elend waved his hand dismissively.

"Then how do you explain the strange numbers, my lord?" Demoux asked.

"I'm not sure," Elend said. "I'll admit that the number of

people who fell sick does produce an odd statistic, but that doesn't say anything about you specifically, Demoux."

"I don't mean that number, my lord," Demoux said, still looking down. "I mean the number who remained sick while the others recovered."

Elend paused. "Wait. What is this?"

"Haven't you heard, my lord?" Demoux asked in the quiet tent. "The scribes have been talking about it, and it's gotten around to the army. I don't think that most of them understand the numbers and such, but they understand that *something* strange is happening."

"What numbers?" Elend asked.

"Six thousand people got taken by the sickness, my lord," Demoux said.

Exactly sixteen percent of the army, Elend thought.

"Of those, over five hundred died," Demoux said. "Of those remaining, almost everyone recovered in one day."

"But some didn't," Elend said. "Like you."

"Like me," Demoux said softly. "Three hundred and sixty-three of us remained sick when the others got better."

"So?" Elend asked.

"That's exactly one-sixteenth of those who fell to the sickness, my lord," Demoux said. "Thirty-six died, but the other three hundred and twenty-seven of us stayed sick *exactly* sixteen days. To the hour."

The tent flap softly rustled in the breeze. Elend fell quiet, and couldn't completely suppress a shiver. "Coincidence," he finally said. "Statisticians looking for connections can *always* find odd coincidences and statistical anomalies, if they try hard enough."

"This doesn't seem like a simple anomaly, my lord," Demoux said. "It's precise. The same number keeps showing up over and over. Sixteen."

Elend shook his head. "Even if it does, Demoux, it doesn't *mean* anything. It's only a number."

"It's the number of fortnights the Survivor spent in the Pits of Hathsin," Demoux said.

"Coincidence."

"It's how old Lady Vin was when she became Mistborn."

"Again, coincidence," Elend said.

"There seem to be an awful lot of coincidences related to this, my lord," Demoux said.

Elend frowned, folding his arms. Demoux had a point. *My denials are getting us nowhere. I need to know what people are thinking, not just contradict them.*

"All right, Demoux," Elend said. "Let's say that none of these things are coincidences. You seem to have a theory of what they mean."

"It's what I said earlier, my lord," Demoux said. "The mists are of the Survivor. They take certain people and kill them, others of us they make sick—leaving the number sixteen as a proof that he really was behind the event. So therefore, the people who grow the most sick are the ones who have displeased him the most."

"Well, except for the ones who *died* from the sickness," Elend noted.

"True," Demoux said, looking up. "So . . . maybe there's hope for me."

"That wasn't supposed to be a comforting comment, Demoux. I still don't accept all of this. There *are* oddities, but your interpretation is based on speculation. Why would the Survivor be displeased with you? You're one of his most faithful priests."

"I took the position for myself, my lord," Demoux said. "He didn't choose me. I just . . . started teaching what I'd seen, and people listened to me. That must be what I did to offend him. If he'd wanted that from me, he'd have chosen me when he was alive, don't you think?"

I don't think the Survivor cared much about this when he was alive, Elend thought. *He merely wanted to stir up enough anger in the skaa that they would rebel.*

"Demoux," Elend said, "you know that the Survivor didn't organize this religion when he was alive. Only men and women like you—those who looked toward his teachings *after* he died—have been able to build up a community of the faithful."

"True," Demoux said. "But he *did* appear to some people after his death. I wasn't one of those people."

"He didn't appear to anyone," Elend said. "That was OreSeur the kandra wearing his body. You know that, Demoux."

"Yes," Demoux said. "But that kandra acted at the Survivor's request. And I wasn't on the list to get visited."

Elend laid a hand on Demoux's shoulder, looking in the man's eyes. He had seen the general, worn and weathered beyond his age, determinedly stare down a savage koloss a full five feet taller than he was. Demoux was not a weak man, either in body or in faith.

"Demoux," Elend said, "I mean this in the kindest way, but your self-pity is interfering. If these mists took *you,* then we need to use that as proof that their effects have *nothing* to do with Kelsier's displeasure. We don't have time for you to question yourself right now—we both know you're twice as devoted as any other man in this army."

Demoux flushed.

"Think about it," Elend said, giving Demoux a little extra Allomantic shove in the emotions. "Rather than letting you mope, we need to move on and find the *real* reason the mists are behaving as they are."

Demoux stood for a moment, then finally nodded. "Perhaps you're right, my lord. Maybe I'm jumping to conclusions."

Elend smiled. Then he reconsidered his own words. *Obvious proof that a person's faithfulness has nothing to do with whether they're taken by the mists . . .*

It wasn't quite true. Demoux was one of the strongest believers in the camp. What of the others who had been sick as long as he? Had they perhaps been men of extreme faith as well? Elend opened his mouth to ask the question. That was when the shouting started.

Hemalurgic decay was less obvious in Inquisitors that had been created from Mistborn. Since they already had Allomantic powers, the addition of other abilities made them awesomely strong.

In most cases, however, Inquisitors were created from Mistings. It appears that Seekers like Marsh were the favored recruits. For when a Mistborn wasn't available, an Inquisitor with enhanced bronze abilities was a powerful tool for searching out skaa Mistings.

37

SCREAMS ROSE IN THE DISTANCE. Vin started upright in her cabin. She hadn't been sleeping, though she'd been close. Another night of scouting Fadrex City had left her tired.

All fatigue was forgotten as the sounds of battle clanged from the north. *Finally!* she thought, throwing off her blankets and dashing from the cabin. Still in her standard trousers and shirt, she downed one of her vials of metals as she scrambled across the deck of the narrowboat.

"Lady Vin!" one of the bargemen called. "The camp has been attacked!"

"And about time too," Vin said as she Pushed herself off the boat's cleats, hurling herself into the air. She shot through the morning mists, curls and wisps of white making her feel as a bird might flying through a cloud.

With tin, she soon found the battle. Several groups of men on horseback had ridden into the north section of camp, and were apparently trying to make their way toward the supply barges, which floated in a well-protected bend in the canal. A group of Elend's Allomancers had set up a perimeter at one side, Thugs in the front, Coinshots picking off the riders from behind. The regular soldiers held the middle, fighting well, since the horsemen were slowed by the camp's barricades and fortifications.

Elend was right, Vin thought with pride, descending through the air. *If we hadn't exposed our men to the mists, we'd be in trouble now.*

The king's planning had saved their supplies and lured out one of Yomen's harrying forces. The riders had probably expected to run easily through the camp—catching the soldiers unaware and trapped by mist—then set fire to the supply barges. Instead, Elend's scouts and patrols had provided enough warning, and the enemy cavalry was bogged down in a head-on fight.

Yomen's soldiers were punching through into the camp on the south. Though Elend's soldiers fought well, their enemies were mounted. Vin plunged down through the sky, flaring pewter to strengthen her body. She threw a coin, Pushing on it to slow herself, and hit the dark ground, tossing up a huge spray of ash. The southern bank of riders had penetrated as far as the third line of tents. Vin chose to land right in the middle of them.

No horseshoes, Vin thought as soldiers began to turn toward her. *And stone-tipped spears instead of swords. Yomen certainly is careful.*

It was almost a challenge. Vin smiled, the adrenaline feeling good after so many days spent waiting. Yomen's captains began to call out, turning their attack toward Vin. In seconds they had a force of some thirty riders galloping straight at her.

Vin stared them down. Then she jumped. She didn't need steel to get herself high—her pewter-enhanced muscles were enough for that. She crested the lead soldier's spear, feeling it pass through the air beneath her. Ash swirled in the morning mists as Vin's foot took the soldier in the face, launching him backward from the saddle. She landed by his rolling body, then dropped a coin and Pushed herself to the side, out of the way of galloping hooves. The unfortunate rider she'd unhorsed cried out as his friends inadvertently trampled him.

Vin's Push carried her through the open flaps of a large canvas sleeping tent. Rolling, she Pushed against the tent's metal stakes, ripping them from the ground.

The walls shook, and there was a snap of canvas as the tent shot upward into the air, spread taut as its stakes all went different directions. Ash blew outward, and soldiers on both sides of the conflict turned toward Vin. Standing, she waited until the tent had fallen in the air before her, then Pushed. The canvas caught the air, puffing out, and the stakes ripped free from the tent, shooting forward to spear horses and riders.

Men and beasts fell. The canvas fluttered to the ground. She smiled, then jumped over the discarded tangle as the riders tried to organize another assault. She didn't give them time. Elend's soldiers in the area had pulled back, shoring up the center of the defensive line, leaving Vin free to attack without fear of harming her own men.

She dashed between the horsemen, their massive mounts hindering them as they tried to keep track of her. Men and horses spun, and Vin Pulled, tearing tents out of the ground and using their metal stakes as darts. Dozens fell before her.

The sound of galloping came from behind, and Vin spun to see that one of the enemy officers had managed to organize another charge. Ten men came straight at her, some with spears leveled, others drawing bows.

Vin didn't like killing. But she loved Allomancy—loved the challenge of using her skills, the strength and thrill of the Pushes and Pulls, the energetic sense of power that came only from a body flared with pewter. When men such as these gave her an excuse to fight, she didn't restrain herself.

The arrows didn't stand a chance against her. Pewter gave her speed and balance as she spun out of the way, Pulling on a metal source behind her. She jumped into the air as a rippling tent passed beneath her, carried forward by her Pull a moment before. She landed, then Pushed on several of its stakes—a couple on each of two tent corners. The tent folded upon itself, looking a bit like a napkin with someone pulling tightly on opposite corners.

And this hit the legs of the horses like a tripwire. Vin burned duralumin and Pushed. The horses in front screamed, the improvised weapon scattering them to the ground. The canvas ripped, and the stakes pulled free, but the damage was done—those in front tripped those behind, and men tumbled beside their beasts.

Vin downed another vial to replenish her steel. Then she Pulled, whipping another tent toward her. As it drew close, she jumped, then spun and Pushed the tent toward another group of mounted men. The tent's stakes struck one of the soldiers in the chest, throwing him backward. He crashed through the other soldiers, causing chaos.

The man hit the ground, slumping lifeless into the ash. Still tied to him by the stakes in his chest, the canvas tent fluttered down, covering his body like a funeral shroud. Vin spun, seeking more enemies. But the riders were beginning to withdraw. She stepped forward, intending to chase them down, but halted. Someone was watching her—she could see his shadow in the mist. She burned bronze.

The figure thumped with the power of metals. Allomancer. Mistborn. He was far too short to be Elend, but she couldn't tell much more than that through the shadow of mist and ash. Vin didn't stop to think. She dropped a coin and shot herself toward the stranger.

He leaped backward, Pushing himself into the air as well. Vin followed, rapidly leaving the camp behind, bounding after the Allomancer. He quickly made his way to the city, and she followed, moving in vast leaps over an ashen landscape. Her quarry crested the rock formations at the front of the city, and Vin followed, landing a few feet from a surprised guard patrol, then launched herself over crags and windswept rocks into Fadrex proper.

The other Allomancer stayed ahead of her. There was no playfulness to his motions, as there had been with Zane. This man was really trying to escape. Vin followed, now leaping over rooftops and streets. She gritted her teeth, frustrated at her inability to catch up. She timed each jump perfectly, barely pausing as she chose new anchors and Pushed herself from arc to arc.

Yet he was good. He rounded the city, forcing her to push herself to keep up. *Fine!* she thought, then prepared her duralumin. She'd gotten close enough to the figure that he was no longer shadowed in mist, and she could see that he was real and corporeal, not some phantom spirit. She was increasingly certain that this was the man she'd sensed watching her when she'd first come into Fadrex. Yomen had a Mistborn.

To fight him, she'd first need to catch him. She waited for the moment when he was beginning to crest one of his arcing jumps, then extinguished her metals and burned duralumin. Then she Pushed.

A crash sounded behind her as her unnatural Push shattered the door she'd used as an anchor. She was thrown forward like an arrow released from a bow. She approached her opponent with terrible speed.

And found nothing. Vin cursed, reigniting her tin. She couldn't leave it on while burning duralumin—otherwise her tin would burn away in a single flash, leaving her blinded. But she'd effectively done the same thing by turning it off. She Pulled herself down from her duralumin Push to land maladroitly atop a nearby roof. She crouched as she scanned the misty air.

Where did you go? she thought, burning bronze, trusting in her innate—yet still unexplained—ability to pierce copperclouds to reveal her opponent. No Allomancer could hide from Vin unless he completely turned off his metals.

Which apparently this man had done. Again. This was the second time he'd eluded her.

It bespoke a disquieting possibility. Vin had tried hard to keep her ability to pierce copperclouds a secret, but it had been over three years since her discovery of it. Zane had known about it, and she couldn't know who else had guessed, based on things she could do. Her secret could very well be out.

Vin remained on that rooftop for a few moments, but knew she'd find nothing. A man clever enough to escape her at the exact moment when her tin was down would also be clever enough to remain hidden until she was gone. In fact, it made her wonder why he had let her see him in the first . . .

Vin stood bolt upright, then downed a metal vial and Pushed herself off the rooftop, jumping with a furious anxiety back toward the camp.

She found the soldiers cleaning up the wreckage and bodies at the camp's perimeter. Elend was moving among them calling out orders, congratulating the men, and generally letting himself be seen. Indeed, sight of his white-clothed form immediately brought Vin a sense of relief.

She landed next to him. "Elend, were you attacked?"

He glanced at her. "What? Me? No, I'm fine."

Then that's not what the Allomancer was sent to distract me from, she thought, frowning. It had seemed so obvious. It—

Elend pulled her aside, looking worried. "*I'm* fine, Vin, but there's something else—something's happened."

"What?" Vin asked.

Elend shook his head. "I think this was all a diversion—the entire attack on the camp."

"But if they weren't after you," Vin said, "and they weren't after our supplies, then what was there to divert us from?"

Elend met her eyes. "The koloss."

"How did we miss *this*?" Vin asked, sounding frustrated.

Elend stood with a troop of soldiers on a plateau, waiting as Vin and Ham inspected the burned siege equipment. Down below, he could see Fadrex City, and his own army camped outside it. The mists had retreated a short time ago. It was disturbing that from this distance he couldn't make out the canal—the falling ash had darkened its waters and covered the landscape to the point that everything looked black.

At the base of the plateau's cliffs lay the remnants of their koloss army. Twenty thousand had become ten thousand in a few brief moments as a well-laid trap had rained down destruction on the beasts while Elend's troops were distracted. The daymists had kept his men from seeing what was going on until it was too late. Elend had felt the deaths, but had misinterpreted them as koloss sensing the battle.

"Caves in the back of those cliffs," Ham said, poking at a bit of charred wood. "Yomen probably had the trebuchets stored in the caves before we arrived, though I'd guess they were originally being built for an assault on Luthadel. In any case, this plateau was a perfect staging area for a barrage. I'd say Yomen meant to use them to attack our army, but when we camped the koloss beneath the plateau . . ."

Elend could still hear the screams in his head—the koloss, full of bloodlust and frothing to fight, yet unable to attack their enemies, which were high atop the plateau. The falling rocks had done a lot of damage. And then the creatures had slipped away from him. Their aggravation had been too powerful, and for a time he hadn't been able to keep them from turning on each other. Most of the deaths had come as the koloss attacked each other. Roughly one of every two had died as they paired off and killed each other.

I lost control of them, he thought. It had only been for a short while, and it had only happened because they hadn't been able to get at their enemies. But it set a dangerous precedent.

Vin, frustrated, kicked a large chunk of burned wood, sending it tumbling down the side of the plateau.

"This was a *very* well-planned attack, El," Ham said, speaking in a soft voice. "Yomen must have seen us sending out extra patrols in the mornings, and correctly guessed that we were expecting an attack during those hours. So he gave us one—then hit us where we should have been the strongest."

"It cost him a lot though," Elend said. "He had to burn his own siege equipment to keep it away from us, and he has to have lost hundreds of soldiers—plus their mounts—in the attack on our camp."

"True," Ham said. "But would you trade a couple dozen siege weapons and five hundred men for ten thousand koloss? Plus, Yomen has to be worried about keeping that cavalry mobile—the Survivor only knows where he got enough grain to feed those horses as long as he did. Better for him to strike now and lose them in battle than to have them starve."

Elend nodded slowly. *This makes things more difficult. With ten thousand fewer koloss . . .* Suddenly the forces were much more evenly matched. Elend could maintain his siege, but storming the city would be far more risky.

He sighed. "We shouldn't have left the koloss so far outside the main camp. We'll have to move them in."

Ham didn't seem to like that.

"They're not dangerous," Elend said. "Vin and I can control them." *Mostly.*

Ham shrugged. He moved back through the smoking wreckage, preparing to send messengers. Elend walked forward, approaching Vin, who stood at the edge of the cliff. Being up so high still made him a bit uncomfortable, but she seemed not to notice the sheer drop.

"I should have been able to help you regain control of them," she said quietly, staring out into the distance. "Yomen distracted me."

"He distracted us all," Elend said. "I felt the koloss in my head, but I still couldn't figure out what was going on. I'd regained control of them once you got back, but by then it was too late."

"Yomen has a Mistborn," Vin said.

"You're sure?"

Vin nodded.

One more thing, he thought. He contained his irritation, however. His men needed to see him confident. "I'm giving a thousand of the koloss to you," he said. "We should have split them up earlier."

"You're stronger," Vin said.

"Not strong enough, apparently."

Vin sighed. "Let me go down below." They'd found that proximity helped with taking control of koloss.

"I'll pull off a section of a thousand or so, then let go. Be ready to grab them as soon as I do."

Vin nodded, then stepped off the edge of the plateau.

I should have realized I was getting caught up in the excitement of the battle, Vin thought as she fell through the air. It was so obvious to her now. And unfortunately, the results of the attack left her more pent-up and anxious than she had before.

She tossed a coin and landed. Even a drop of several hundred feet didn't bother her anymore. It was odd to think about. She remembered timidly standing atop the Luthadel city wall, afraid to use her Allomancy to jump off, despite Kelsier's coaxing. Now she could step off a cliff and muse thoughtfully to herself on the way down.

She walked across the powdery ground. The ash came up to the top of her calves and would have been difficult to walk in without pewter to give her strength. The ashfalls were growing increasingly dense.

Human approached her almost immediately. She couldn't tell if the koloss was simply reacting to their bond, or if he was actually aware and interested enough to pick her out. He had a new wound on his arm, a result of the fighting. He fell into step beside her as she moved up to the other koloss, his massive form plainly having no trouble with the deep ash.

As usual, there was little emotion to the koloss camp. A short time before, they had been screaming in bloodlust, attacking each other as stones crashed down from above. Now they simply sat in the ash, gathered in small groups, ignoring their wounds. They would have had fires going if there had been wood available. Some few dug, finding handfuls of dirt to chew on.

"Don't your people care, Human?" Vin asked.

The massive koloss looked down at her, ripped face bleeding slightly. "Care?"

"That so many of you died," Vin said. She could see corpses lying about, forgotten in the ash save for the ritual flaying that the koloss did instead of burial. Several koloss still worked, moving between bodies, ripping off the skin.

"We take care of them," Human said.

"Yes," Vin said. "You pull their skin off. Why do you do that?"

"They are dead," Human said, as if that were enough explanation.

To the side, a large group of koloss stood up, commanded by Elend's silent orders. They separated themselves from the main camp, trudging out into the ash. A moment later they began to look around, no longer moving as one.

Vin reacted quickly. She turned off her metals, burned duralumin, then flared zinc in a massive Pull, Rioting the koloss emotions. As expected, they snapped under her control, as Human was.

Controlling this many was more difficult, but still well within her abilities. Vin ordered them to be calm, and to not kill, then let them return to the camp. From now on, they would remain in the back of her mind, no longer requiring Allomancy to manipulate. They were easy to ignore unless their passions grew strong.

Human watched them. "We are . . . fewer," he said.

Vin started. "Yes," she said. "You can tell that?"

"I . . ." Human trailed off, beady little eyes watching his camp. "We fought. We died. We need more. We have too many swords." He pointed in the distance, to a large pile of metal. Wedge-shaped koloss swords that no longer had owners.

You can control a koloss population through the swords, Elend had once told her. *They fight to get bigger swords as they grow. Extra swords go to the younger, smaller koloss.*

But nobody knows where those come from.

"You need koloss to use those swords, Human," Vin said.

Human nodded.

"Well," she said. "You'll need to have more children then."

"Children?"

"More," Vin said. "More koloss."

"You need to give us more," Human said, looking at her.

"Me?"

"You fought," he said, pointing at her shirt. There was blood there, not her own.

"Yes, I did," Vin said.

"Give us more."

"I don't understand," Vin said. "Please, just show me."

"I can't," Human said, shaking his head as he spoke in his slow tone. "It's not right."

"Wait," Vin said. "Not right?" It was the first real statement of values she'd gotten from a koloss.

Human looked at her, and she could see consternation on his face. So, Vin gave him an Allomantic nudge. She didn't know exactly what to ask him to do, and that made her control of him weaker. Yet she Pushed him to do as he was thinking, trusting that his mind was fighting with his instincts for some reason.

He screamed.

Vin backed away, shocked, but Human didn't attack her. He ran into the koloss camp, a massive blue monster on two legs, kicking up ash. Others stepped away from him—not out of fear, for they wore their characteristic impassive faces. They simply appeared to have enough sense to stay out of the way of an enraged koloss of Human's size.

Vin followed carefully as Human approached one of the dead bodies of a koloss who still wore his skin. Human didn't rip the skin off, however, but flung the corpse over his shoulder and took off running toward Elend's camp.

Uh-oh, Vin thought, dropping a coin and taking to the air. She bounded after Human, careful not to outpace him. She considered ordering him back, but did not. He was acting unusually, true, but that was a good thing. Koloss generally didn't do *anything* unusual. They were predictable to a fault.

She landed at the camp's guard post and waved the soldiers away. Human continued on, barreling into the camp, startling the men. Vin stayed with him, keeping the soldiers at a distance.

Human paused in the middle of camp, a bit of his passion wearing off. Vin nudged him again. After looking about, Human took off toward the broken section of camp, where Yomen's soldiers had attacked.

Vin followed, growing more and more curious. Human hadn't taken out his sword. Indeed, he didn't seem angry at all, merely . . . intense. He arrived at a section where tents had fallen and men had died. The battle was still only a few hours old, and soldiers moved about, cleaning up. Triage tents had been set up beside the battlefield. Human headed for those.

Vin rushed ahead, cutting him off as he reached the tent with the wounded. "Human," she said warily. "What are you doing?"

He ignored her, slamming the dead koloss down on the ground. Now, finally, Human ripped the skin off the corpse. It came off easily—this was one of the smaller koloss, whose skin hung in folds, far too large for its body.

Human pulled the skin free, causing several of the watching guards to groan in disgust. Vin watched closely despite the stomach-wrenching sight. She felt like she was on the verge of understanding something very important.

Human reached down, and pulled something out of the koloss corpse.

"Wait," Vin said, stepping forward. "What was that?"

Human ignored her. He pulled out something else, and this time Vin caught a flash of bloodied metal. She followed his fingers as he moved, and saw the item before he pulled it free and hid it in his palm.

A spike. A small metal spike driven into the side of the dead koloss. There was a rip of blue skin by the spikehead, as if . . .

As if the spikes were holding the skin in place, Vin thought. *Like nails holding cloth to a wall.*

Spikes. Spikes like . . .

Human retrieved a third and fourth spike, then stepped forward into the tent. Surgeons and soldiers moved back in fear, crying out for Vin to do something as Human approached the bed of a wounded soldier. Human looked from one unconscious man to another, then reached for one of them.

Stop! Vin commanded in her mind.

Human froze in place. Only then did the complete horror of what was happening occur to her. "Lord Ruler," she whispered. "You were going to turn them into koloss, weren't you? That's where you come from. That's why there are no koloss children."

"I am *human,*" the large beast said quietly.

Hemalurgy can be used to steal Allomantic or Feruchemical powers and give them to another person. However, a Hemalurgic spike can also be created by killing a normal person, one who is neither an Allomancer nor a Feruchemist. In that case, the spike instead steals the power of Preservation existing within the soul of the person. (The power that gives all people sapience.)

A Hemalurgic spike can extract this power, then transfer it to another person, granting them residual abilities similar to those of Allomancy. After all, Preservation's body—a tiny trace of which is carried by every human being—is the very same essence that fuels Allomancy.

And so, a kandra granted the Blessing of Potency is actually acquiring a bit of innate strength similar to that of burning pewter. The Blessing of Presence grants mental capacity in a similar way, while the Blessing of Awareness is the ability to sense with greater acuity, and the rarely used Blessing of Stability grants emotional fortitude.

38

SOMETIMES SPOOK FORGOT THE MIST was there. It had become such a pale, translucent thing to him. Nearly invisible. Stars in the sky blazed like a million limelights shining down on him. It was a beauty only he could see.

He turned, looking across the burned remains of the building. Skaa workers carefully sifted through the mess. It was hard for Spook to remember that they couldn't see well in the night's darkness. He had to keep them packed closely together, working as much by touch as by sight.

The scent was terrible. Yet burning pewter seemed to help mitigate that. Perhaps the strength it gave him extended to his ability to avoid unintentional reactions such as retching or coughing. During his youth, he had wondered about the pairing of tin and pewter. Other Allomantic pairs were opposites—steel Pushed on metals, iron Pulled on them. Copper hid Allomancers, bronze revealed Allomancers. Zinc enflamed emotions, brass depressed them. Yet tin and pewter didn't seem opposites—one enhanced the body, the other the senses.

But they *were* opposites. Tin made his sense of touch so sharp that each step had once been uncomfortable. Pewter enhanced his body, making it resistant to pain—and so as he picked his way across the blackened ruin, his feet didn't hurt as much. In a similar way, where light had once blinded him, pewter let him endure far more before needing his blindfold.

The two complemented each other—just like the other pairs of Allomantic metals. He felt *right* having the one to go with the other. How had he survived without pewter? He had been a man with only one half of an ability. Now he was complete.

And yet, he did wonder what it would be like to have the other powers too. Kelsier had given him pewter. Could he perhaps bless Spook with iron and steel as well?

A man directed the line of working figures. His name was Franson; he was the one who had asked Spook to rescue his sister. The execution was a mere day away. Soon the child would be thrown into a burning building of her own, but Spook was working on ways to stop that. There wasn't much he could do at the moment, so in the meantime, Franson and his men dug.

It had been some time since Spook had gone to spy on the Citizen and his councillors. He'd shared the information he'd gleaned with Sazed and Breeze, and they'd seemed appreciative. However, with the increased security around the Citizen's home, they'd suggested that it was foolhardy to risk more spying until they'd figured out their plans for the city. Spook had accepted their guidance, though he felt himself growing anxious. He missed going to see Beldre, the quiet woman with the lonely eyes.

He didn't know her. He couldn't fool himself that he did. Yet when they'd met and spoken that once, she hadn't screamed or betrayed him. She'd seemed intrigued by him. That was a good sign, right?

Fool, he thought. *She's the Citizen's own sister! Talking to her nearly got you killed. Focus on the task at hand.*

Spook watched the work for a time longer. Eventually, Franson—dirty and exhausted in the starlight—approached him. "My lord," Franson said, "we've gone over this section four times now. The men in the basement pit have moved all the debris and ash to the sides, and have sifted through it twice. Whatever we were going to find, we've found it."

Spook nodded. Franson was probably right. Spook removed a small pouch from his pocket, handing it to Franson. It clinked, and the large skaa man raised an eyebrow.

"Payment," Spook said, "for the other men. They've worked here for three nights."

"They're friends, my lord," he said. "They just want to see my sister rescued."

"Pay them anyway," Spook said. "And tell them to spend the coins on food and supplies as soon as they can—before Quellion abolishes coinage in the city."

"Yes, my lord," Franson said. Then he glanced to the side, where a mostly burned banister still stood upright. This was where the workers had placed the objects they had located in the wreckage: nine human skulls. They cast eerie shadows in the starlight. Leering, burned, and blackened.

"My lord," Franson said. "May I ask the point of this?"

"I watched this building burn down," Spook said. "I was there when these poor people were herded into the mansion, then locked inside. I couldn't do anything."

"I'm . . . sorry, my lord," Franson said.

Spook shook his head. "It's past now. But there is something their deaths can teach us."

"My lord?"

Count the skulls, Durn had said.

Spook knew Durn would probably explain himself if pushed, but they both seemed to understand something important. Spook needed to see it for himself. He needed to know what the Citizen was doing.

And now he did. "Ten people were sent into this building to die, Franson," Spook said. "Ten people. Nine skulls."

The man frowned. "What does that tell us?"

"It tells us there's a way to get your sister out."

"I'm not certain what to make of this, Lord Breeze," Sazed said. They sat at a table in one of Urteau's skaa bars. The alcohol flowed freely, and workers packed the place, despite the darkness and the mists.

"What do you mean?" Breeze asked. They sat alone, though Goradel and three of his toughs sat wearing street clothing at the next table over.

"This is very strange to me," Sazed said. "Skaa having their own bars is odd enough. But skaa going out at night?"

Breeze shrugged. "Perhaps their fear of the night was more a product of the Lord Ruler's influence than of the mists. With his troops on the streets watching for thieves, there were reasons other than mist to stay inside at night."

Sazed shook his head. "I have studied these things, Lord Breeze. The skaa fear of the mists was an ingrained superstitious mindset—it was a part of their lives. And Quellion has broken it down in little over a year."

"Oh, I think the wine and beer probably did the breaking," Breeze said. "You'd be surprised at what men will go through in order to get themselves properly intoxicated."

Sazed eyed Breeze's own cup—the man had taken quite a liking to the skaa bars, despite the fact that he was forced to wear mundane clothing. Of course, the clothing probably wasn't necessary anymore. If the city had even a halfway decent rumor mill, people would have already connected Breeze to the visitors who had met with Quellion a few days before. And now that Sazed had come to the bar, any suspicions would have been confirmed. There was no way to hide Sazed's identity. His nationality was obvious. He was too tall, too bald, and he had the typical Terris long face with drooping features and earlobes stretched out by the application of numerous earrings.

The time for anonymity had passed, though Breeze had used it well. During the few days when people hadn't known who he was, he'd managed to build both goodwill and contacts in the local underground. Now he and Sazed could sit and enjoy a quiet drink without drawing much attention. Breeze would, of course, be Soothing the people to ensure that—but even so, Sazed was impressed. For one as fond of high society as Breeze, the man did a remarkable job of relating to ordinary skaa workers.

A group of men laughed at the next table, and Breeze smiled, then stood and made his way over to join them. Sazed remained where he was, a mug of untouched wine before him. In his opinion, there was a clear reason the skaa were no longer afraid to go out in the mists. Their superstitions had been overcome by something stronger: Kelsier. The one they were now calling the Lord of the Mists.

The Church of the Survivor had spread much farther than Sazed had expected. It wasn't organized the same way in Urteau as in Luthadel, and the focus seemed to be different, but the fact remained that men were worshipping Kelsier. The differences were part of what made the whole phenomenon fascinating.

What am I missing? Sazed thought. *What is the connection here?*

The mists killed. Yet these people went out in the mists. Why weren't the people terrified of them?

This is not my problem, Sazed told himself. *I need to remain focused. I've let my studies of the religions in my portfolio lapse.* He was getting close to being finished, and that worried him. So far, every single religion had proven full of inconsistencies, contradictions, and logical flaws. He was growing more and more worried that among the hundreds of religions in his metalminds, he would never be able to find the truth.

A wave from Breeze distracted him. So Sazed stood—forcing himself not to show the despair he felt—and moved over to their table. The men made room.

"Thank you," Sazed said, sitting.

"You forgot your cup, friend Terrisman," one of the men pointed out.

"I apologize," Sazed said. "I have never been one fond of intoxicants. Please do not take offense. Your thoughtful gift was nevertheless appreciated."

"Does he always talk like that?" one of the men asked, looking at Breeze.

"You've never known a Terrisman, have you?" asked another.

Sazed flushed, at which Breeze chuckled, laying a hand on Sazed's shoulder. "All right, gentlemen. I've brought you the Terrisman as requested. Go ahead, ask your questions."

There were six local men at the table—all mine workers, from what Sazed could tell. One of the men leaned forward, hands clasped in front of him, knuckles scarred by rock. "Breeze here says a lot of things," the man said in a low voice. "But people like him always make promises. Quellion said a lot of the same things a year ago, when he was taking control after Straff Venture left."

"Yes," Sazed said. "I can understand your skepticism."

"But," the man said, raising a hand. "Terrismen don't lie. They're good people. Everyone knows that—lords, skaa, thieves, and obligators."

"So we wanted to talk to you," another of the men said. "Maybe you're different; maybe you'll lie to us. But better to hear it from a Terrisman than a Soother."

Breeze blinked, revealing a faint hint of surprise. Apparently he hadn't realized they'd been aware of his abilities.

"Ask your questions," Sazed said.

"Why did you come to this city?" one of the men asked.

"To take control of it," Sazed said.

"Why do you care?" another asked. "Why does Venture's son want Urteau?"

"Two reasons," Sazed said. "First, because of the resources it offers. I cannot go into details, but suffice it to say that your city is very desirable for economic reasons. The second reason, however, is equally important. Lord Elend Venture is one of the best men I have ever known. He believes he can do better for this people than the current government."

"That wouldn't be hard," one of the men grumbled.

Another man shook his head. "What? You want to give the city back to the Ventures? One year, and you've forgotten the things that Straff used to do in this city?"

"Elend Venture is not his father," Sazed said. "He is a man worthy of being followed."

"And the Terris people?" one of the skaa asked. "Do they follow him?"

"In a way," Sazed said. "Once, my people tried to rule themselves, as your people now do. However, they realized the advantages of an alliance. My people have moved to the Central Dominance, and they accept the protection of Elend Venture." *Of course,* Sazed thought, *they'd rather follow me. If I would be their king.*

The table fell silent.

"I don't know," one of the men said. "What business do we have even talking about this? I mean, Quellion is in charge, and these strangers don't have an army to take his throne away from him. What's the point?"

"The Lord Ruler fell to us when we had no army," Breeze pointed out, "and Quellion himself seized the government from noble rule. Change can occur."

"We're not trying to form an army or rebellion," Sazed quickly added. "We merely want you to start . . . thinking. Talking with your friends. You are plainly influential men. Perhaps if Quellion hears of discontent among his people, he will begin to change his ways."

"Maybe," one of the men said.

"We don't need these outsiders," the other man repeated. "The Survivor of the Flames has come to deal with Quellion."

Sazed blinked. *Survivor of the Flames?* He caught a sly smile on Breeze's lips—the Soother had apparently heard the term before, and now he appeared to be watching Sazed for a reaction.

"The Survivor doesn't enter into this," one of the men said. "I can't believe we're even *thinking* of rebellion. Most of the world is in chaos, if you hear the reports! Shouldn't we just be happy with what we've got?"

"You're starting to twitch, Sazed," Breeze whispered. "You might as well ask. No harm in asking, right?"

No harm in asking.

"The . . . Survivor of the Flames?" Sazed asked. "Why do you call Kelsier that?"

"Not Kelsier," one of the men said. "The other Survivor. The new one."

"The Survivor of Hathsin came to overthrow the Lord Ruler," one of the men said. "So can't we assume the Survivor of the Flames has come to overthrow Quellion? Maybe we *should* listen to these men."

"If the Survivor is here to overthrow Quellion," another man said, "then he won't need the help of these types. They only want the city for themselves."

"Excuse me," Sazed said. "But . . . might we meet this new Survivor?"

The group of men shared looks.

"Please," Sazed said. "I was a friend to the Survivor of Hathsin. I should very much like to meet a man whom you have deemed worthy of comparison to him."

"Tomorrow," one of the men said. "Quellion tries to keep the dates quiet, but they get out. There will be executions near Marketpit. Be there."

Even now, I can barely grasp the scope of all this. The events surrounding the end of the world seem larger than the Final Empire and the people within it. I sense Shards of something from long ago, a fractured presence, something spanning the void.

I have delved and searched, and have only been able to come up with a single name: Adonalsium. Who or what it was, I do not yet know.

39

TENSOON SAT ON HIS HAUNCHES. Horrified.

Ash rained down like shards of a broken sky, floating, making the very air look pocked and sickly. Although he sat atop a windswept hill, a layer of ash around him smothered the plant life there. Some trees had branches broken by the weight of repeated ash pileups.

How could they not see? he thought. *How can they hide in their hole of a Homeland, content to let the land above die?*

Yet TenSoon had lived for hundreds of years, and a part of him understood the tired complacency of the First and Second Generations. At times he'd felt the same thing himself. A desire to simply wait. To spend years idly, content in the Homeland. He'd seen the outside world—seen more of it than any human or koloss would ever know. What need had he of experiencing more?

The Seconds had seen him as more orthodox and obedient than his brethren, all because he had continually wanted to leave the Homeland and serve Contracts. The Second Generation had misunderstood him. TenSoon hadn't served out of a desire to be obedient. He'd done it out of fear that he'd become as content and apathetic as the Seconds and begin to think that the outside world didn't matter to the kandra people.

He shook his head, then rose to all fours and loped down the hill, scattering ash into the air with each bound. As frightening as things had gotten, he was happy for one thing. The wolfhound's body felt good on him. There was such a power in it—a capacity for movement—that no human body could match. It was almost as if this were the form he *always* should have worn. What better body for a kandra with an incurable wanderlust? A kandra who had left his Homeland behind more often than any other, serving under the hated hands of human masters, all because of his fear of complacency?

He made his way through the thin forest cover, over hills, hoping that the blanket of ash wouldn't make it too difficult for him to navigate. The falling ash did affect the kandra people—it affected them greatly. They had legends about this exact event. What good was the First Contract, what good was the waiting, the protection of the Trust? To most of the kandra, apparently, these things had become a point unto themselves.

Yet these things *meant* something. They had an origin. TenSoon hadn't been alive then. However, he had known the First Generation and been raised by the Second. He grew up during days when the First Contract—the Trust, the Resolution—had been more than mere words. The First Contract was a set of instructions. Actions to take when the world began to fail. Not just ceremony, and not just metaphor. He knew that its contents frightened some of the kandra. For them, it was better for the First Contract to be a philosophical, abstract thing—for if it were still concrete, still relevant, it would require great sacrifices of them.

TenSoon stopped running; he was up to his wolfhound belly in deep black ash. The location looked vaguely familiar.

He turned south, moving through a small rocky hollow—
the stones now just dark lumps—looking for a place he
had been over a year before. A place he'd visited after he
had turned against Zane and left Luthadel to return to the
Homeland.

He scrambled up a few rocks, then rounded a stone out-
crop, knocking lumps of ash off with his passing. They
broke apart as they fell, throwing more flakes into the air.

And there it was. The hollow in the rock, the place where
he had stopped a year before. He remembered it, despite
how the ash had transformed the landscape. The Blessing
of Presence, serving him again. How would he get along
without it?

I would not be sapient without it, he thought, smiling
grimly. It was the bestowal of a Blessing on a mistwraith
that brought the creature to wakefulness and true life. Each
kandra got one of the four: Presence, Potency, Stability, or
Awareness. It didn't matter which one a kandra gained; any
of the four would give him or her sapience, changing the
mistwraith into a fully conscious kandra.

In addition to sapience, each Blessing gave something
else. A power. But there were stories of kandra who had
gained more than one by taking them from others.

TenSoon stuck a paw into the depression, digging out the
ash, working to uncover the things he had hidden a year before. He found them quickly, rolling one—then the other—
out onto the rock shelf in front of him. Two small, polished
iron spikes. It took two spikes to form a single Blessing.
TenSoon didn't know why this was. It was simply the way
of things.

TenSoon lay down, commanding the skin of his shoulder
to part, and absorbed the spikes into his body. He moved
them through muscles and ligaments—dissolving several
organs, then re-forming them with the spikes piercing them.

Immediately he felt power wash through him. His body
became stronger. It was more than the simple adding of
muscles—he could do that by re-forming his body. No, this
gave each muscle an extra innate strength, making them

work much better, much more powerfully, than they would have otherwise.

The Blessing of Potency. He'd retrieved the two spikes from OreSeur's body. Without this Blessing, TenSoon would never have been able to follow Vin as he had during their months together. It more than doubled the power and endurance of each muscle. He couldn't regulate or change the level of that added strength—this was not Feruchemy or Allomancy, but something different. Hemalurgy.

A person had died to create each spike. TenSoon tried not to think about that too much, just as he tried not to think about how he only had this Blessing because he had killed one of his own generation. The Lord Ruler had provided the spikes each century, giving the number requested, so that the kandra could craft a new generation.

He now had four spikes, two Blessings, and was one of the most powerful kandra alive. His muscles strengthened, TenSoon jumped confidently from the top of the rock formation, falling some twenty feet to land safely on the ash-covered ground below. He took off, running far more quickly now. The Blessing of Potency resembled the power of an Allomancer burning pewter, but it would not keep TenSoon moving indefinitely, nor could he flare it for an extra burst of power. On the other hand, it required no metals to fuel it.

He made his path eastward. The First Contract was explicit. When Ruin returned, the kandra were to seek out the Father to serve him. Unfortunately, the Father was dead. The First Contract didn't take that possibility into consideration. So—unable to go to the Father—TenSoon did the next best thing. He went looking for Vin.

Originally, we assumed that a koloss was a combination of two people into one. That was wrong. Koloss are not the melding of two people, but five, as evidenced by the four spikes needed to make them. Not five bodies, of course, but five souls.

Each pair of spikes grants what the kandra would call the Blessing of Potency. However, each spike also distorts the koloss body a little more, making it increasingly inhuman. Such is the cost of Hemalurgy.

40

"NOBODY KNOWS PRECISELY HOW INQUISITORS are made," Elend said from the front of the tent, addressing a small group that included Ham, Cett, the scribe Noorden, and the mostly recuperated Demoux. Vin sat at the back, still trying to sort through what she had discovered. Human . . . all koloss . . . they had once been people.

"There are lots of theories about it, however," Elend said. "Once the Lord Ruler fell, Sazed and I did some research and discovered a few interesting facts from the obligators we interviewed. For instance, Inquisitors are made from ordinary men—men who remember who they were, but gain new Allomantic abilities."

"Our experience with Marsh proves that as well," Ham said. "He was still Marsh, even with all those spikes driven through his body. And he gained the powers of a Mistborn."

"Excuse me," Cett said, "but will someone please explain what the hell this has to do with our siege of the city? There aren't any Inquisitors here."

Elend folded his arms. "This is important, Cett, because we're at war with more than just Yomen. Something we don't understand, something far greater than those soldiers in Fadrex."

Cett snorted. "You still believe in this talk of doom and gods and the like?"

"Noorden," Elend said, looking at the scribe. "Please tell Lord Cett what you told me earlier today."

The former obligator nodded. "Well, my lord, it's like this. Those numbers relating to the percentage of people who fall ill to the mists, they're simply *too* regular to be natural. Nature works in organized chaos—randomness on the small scale, with trends on the large scale. I cannot believe that anything natural could have produced such precise results."

"What do you mean?" Cett asked.

"Well, my lord," Noorden said. "Imagine that you hear a tapping sound somewhere outside your tent. If it repeats occasionally with no set pattern, then it might be the wind blowing a loose flap against a pole. However, if it repeats with exact regularity, you know that it must be a person striking something. You'd be able to make the distinction immediately, because you've learned that nature can be repetitive in a case like that, but not *exact*. These numbers are the same, my lord. They're too organized, too repetitive to be natural. They had to have been crafted by somebody."

"You're saying that a person made those soldiers sick?" Cett asked.

"A person? . . . No, not a person, I'd guess," Noorden said. "But *something* intelligent must have done it. That's the only conclusion I can draw. Something with an agenda, something that cares to be precise."

The room fell silent.

"And this relates to Inquisitors, my lord?" Demoux asked carefully.

"It does," Elend said. "At least it does if you think as I do—which I'll admit not many people do."

"For better or for worse . . ." Ham said, smiling.

"Noorden, what do you know of how Inquisitors are made?" Elend asked.

The scribe grew uncomfortable. "I was in the Canton of Orthodoxy, as you may know, not the Canton of Inquisition."

"Surely there were rumors," Elend asked.

"Well, of course," Noorden said. "More than rumors, in fact. The higher obligators were *always* trying to discover how the Inquisitors got their power. There was a rivalry between the Cantons, you see, and . . . well, I suppose you don't care about that. Regardless, we *did* have rumors."

"And?" Elend asked.

"They said . . ." Noorden began. "They said that an Inquisitor was a fusion of many different people. In order to make an Inquisitor, the Canton of Inquisition had to get a whole group of Allomancers, then combine their powers into one."

Again, silence in the room. Vin pulled her legs up, wrapping her arms around her knees. She didn't like talking about Inquisitors.

"Lord Ruler!" Ham swore quietly. "That's it! *That's* why the Inquisitors were so keen on hunting down skaa Mistings! Don't you see! It wasn't only because the Lord Ruler ordered half-breeds to be killed—it was so that the Inquisitors could perpetuate themselves! They needed Allomancers to kill so that they could make new Inquisitors!"

Elend nodded from his place at the front of the room. "Somehow those spikes in the Inquisitors' bodies transfer Allomantic ability. You kill eight Mistings, and you give all their powers to one other man, such as Marsh. Sazed once told me that Marsh was always hesitant to speak of the day he was made an Inquisitor, but he did say that it was . . . messy."

Ham nodded. "And when Kelsier and Vin found his room the day he was taken and made an Inquisitor, they found a corpse in there. One they initially assumed was Marsh!"

"Later, Marsh said that more than one person had been killed there," Vin said quietly. "There just hadn't been enough . . . left of them to tell."

"Again," Cett said, "does this all have a point?"

"Well, it seems to be doing a good job of annoying you," Ham said lightly. "Do we *need* any other point?"

Elend gave them both hard looks. "The point is, Cett, that Vin discovered something earlier this week."

The group turned toward her.

"Koloss," Vin said. "They're made from humans."

"What?" Cett asked, frowning. "That's absurd."

"No," Vin said, shaking her head. "I'm sure of it. I've checked living koloss. Hidden in those folds and rips of skin on their bodies, they are pierced by spikes. Smaller than the Inquisitor spikes, and made from different metals, but all of the koloss have them."

"Nobody has been able to figure out where new koloss come from," Elend said. "The Lord Ruler guarded the secret, and it's become one of the great mysteries of our time. Koloss kill each other with regularity when someone isn't actively controlling them. Yet there always seem to be more of the creatures. How?"

"Because they are constantly refilling their numbers," Ham said, nodding slowly. "From the villages they ransack."

"Did you ever wonder," Elend said, "back during the siege of Luthadel, why Jastes's koloss army attacked a random village before coming for us? The creatures needed to replenish their ranks."

"They always walk around," Vin said, "wearing clothing, talking about being human. Yet they can't quite remember what it was like. Their minds have been broken."

"The other day," Elend said, "Vin finally got one of them to show her how to make new koloss. From what he did, and from what he's said since, we believe that he was going to try to *combine* two men into one. That would make a creature with the strength of two men, but the mind of neither."

"A third art," Ham said, looking up. "A third way to use the metals. There is Allomancy, which draws power from the metals. There is Feruchemy, which uses metals to draw power from your own body, and there is . . ."

"Marsh called it Hemalurgy," Vin said quietly.

"Hemalurgy . . ." Ham said. "Which uses the metals to draw power from *someone else's* body."

"Great," Cett said. "Point?"

"The Lord Ruler created servants to help him," Elend said. "Using this art . . . this Hemalurgy . . . he made soldiers, the koloss. He made spies, the kandra. And he made priests, the Inquisitors. He built them all with weaknesses so that he could control them."

"I first learned how to take control of the koloss because of TenSoon," Vin said. "He inadvertently showed me the secret. He mentioned that the kandra and koloss were cousins, and I realized I could control one just as I had the other."

"I . . . still don't see where you're heading with this," Demoux said, glancing from Vin to Elend.

"The Inquisitors must have the same weakness, Demoux," Elend said. "This Hemalurgy leaves the mind . . . wounded. It allows an Allomancer to creep in and take control. The nobility always wondered what made the Inquisitors so fanatically devoted to the Lord Ruler. They weren't like ordinary obligators—they were far more obedient. Zealous to a fault."

"It happened to Marsh," Vin whispered. "The first time I met him after he'd been made an Inquisitor, he seemed different. But he grew odder during the year following the Collapse. Finally he turned on Sazed, tried to kill him."

"What we're suggesting," Elend said, "is that something is controlling the Inquisitors and the koloss. Something is exploiting the weakness the Lord Ruler built into the creatures and is using them as its pawns. The troubles we've been suffering, the chaos following the Collapse—it's *not* simply chaos. No more than the patterns of people who fall sick to the mists are chaotic. I know it seems obvious, but the important thing here is that we now know the method. We understand why they can be controlled and how they're being controlled."

Elend continued to pace, his feet marking the dirty tent floor. "The more I think about Vin's discovery, the more I come to believe that this is all connected. The koloss, the kandra, and the Inquisitors are not three separate oddities, but part of a single cohesive phenomenon. Now, on the surface, knowledge of this third art . . . this Hemalurgy . . . doesn't seem like much. We don't intend to use it to make more koloss, so what good is the knowledge?"

Cett nodded, a serious expression on his face. Elend, however, had drifted a bit, staring out the open tent flaps, losing himself in thought. It was something he'd once done frequently, back when he spent more time on scholarship. He wasn't addressing Cett's questions. He was speaking his own concerns, following his own logical path.

"This war we're fighting," Elend continued, "it isn't just about soldiers. It isn't just about koloss, or about taking Fadrex City. It's about the sequence of events we inadvertently started the moment we struck down the Lord Ruler. Hemalurgy—the origin of the koloss—is part of a pattern. The percentages that fall sick from the mists are also part of the pattern. The less we see chaos, and the more we see the *pattern*, the better we're going to be at understanding exactly what we fight—and how to defeat it."

Elend turned toward the group. "Noorden, I want you to change the focus of your research. Up until now, we've assumed that the movements of the koloss were random. I'm no longer convinced that is true. Research our old scout reports. Draw up lists and plot movements. Pay particular attention to bodies of koloss that we specifically know *weren't* under the control of an Inquisitor. I want to see if we can discover why they went where they did."

"Yes, my lord," Noorden said.

"The rest of you stay vigilant," Elend said. "I don't want another mistake like last week's. We can't afford to lose any more troops, even koloss."

They nodded, and Elend signaled the end of the meeting. Cett was carried away to his tent, Noorden bustled off to begin this new research, and Ham went in search of something to eat. Demoux, however, stayed. Vin stood and stepped up to Elend's side, taking his arm as he turned to address Demoux.

"My lord . . ." Demoux said, looking a bit embarrassed. "I assume General Hammond has spoken to you?"

What's this? Vin thought, perking up.

"Yes, Demoux," Elend said with a sigh. "But I really don't think it's something to worry about."

"What?" Vin asked.

"There is a certain level of . . . ostracism happening in the camp, my lady," Demoux said. "Those of us who fell sick for two weeks, rather than a day, are being regarded with a measure of suspicion."

"Suspicion that you no longer agree with, right, Demoux?" Elend punctuated this remark with a stern, kingly look.

Demoux nodded. "I trust your interpretation, my lord. It's just that . . . well, it is difficult to lead men who distrust you. And it's much harder for the others like me. They've taken to eating together, staying away from the others during their free time. It's reinforcing the division."

"What do you think?" Elend asked. "Should we try to force reintegration?"

"That depends, my lord," Demoux said.

"On?"

"On several factors," Demoux said. "If you're planning to attack soon, reintegrating would be a bad idea—I don't want men fighting alongside those they don't trust. However, if we're going to continue the siege for some time, then forcing them back together might make sense. The larger segment of the army would have time to learn to trust the mistfallen again."

Mistfallen, Vin thought. *Interesting name.*

Elend looked down at her, and she knew what he was thinking. The ball at the Canton of Resource was a mere few days away. If Elend's plan went well, then perhaps they wouldn't have to attack Fadrex.

Vin didn't have great hopes for that option. Plus, without resupply from Luthadel they couldn't count on much anymore. They could continue the siege as planned for months, or they might end up having to attack within a few weeks.

"Organize a new company," Elend said, turning to Demoux. "Fill it with these mistfallen. We'll worry about dealing with superstition after we hold Fadrex."

"Yes, my lord," Demoux said. "I think that . . ."

They continued talking, but Vin stopped paying attention as she heard voices approaching the command tent. It was probably nothing. Even so, she moved around so that she was between the approaching people and Elend, then checked her metal reserves. Within moments she could determine who was talking. One was Ham. She relaxed as the tent flap opened, revealing him in his standard vest and trousers, leading a wearied red-haired soldier. The exhausted man had ash-stained clothing and wore the leathers of a scout.

"Conrad?" Demoux asked with surprise.

"You know this man?" Elend asked.

"Yes, my lord," Demoux said. "He's one of the lieutenants I left back in Luthadel with King Penrod."

Conrad saluted. "My lord," the man said. "I bring news from the capital."

"Finally!" Elend said. "What word from Penrod? Where are those supply barges I sent for?"

"Supply barges, my lord?" Conrad asked. "My lord, King Penrod sent me to ask *you* for resupply. There are riots in the city, and some of the food stores have been pillaged. King Penrod sent me to ask you for a contingent of troops to help him restore order."

"Troops?" Elend asked. "What of the garrison I left with him? He should have plenty of men!"

"They're not enough, my lord," Conrad said. "I don't know why. I can only relay the message I was sent to deliver."

Elend cursed, slamming his fist against the command tent's table. "Can Penrod not do the *one* thing I asked of him? All he needed to do was hold lands we already have secure!"

The soldier jumped at the outburst, and Vin watched with concern. But Elend managed to control his temper. He took a deep breath, waving to the soldier. "Rest yourself, Lieutenant Conrad, and get some food. I will want to speak with you further about this later."

Vin found Elend later that night, standing on the perimeter of the camp, looking up at the Fadrex watch fires on the cliffs above. She laid a hand on his shoulder, and the fact that he didn't jump indicated that he'd heard her coming. It was still a little strange to her that Elend, who had always seemed slightly oblivious of the world around him, was now a capable Mistborn, with tin to enhance his ears that let him hear even the softest footsteps approaching.

"You talked to the messenger?" she asked as he put his arm around her. Ash fell around them. A couple of Elend's soldier Tineyes passed on patrol, carrying no lights, silently walking the perimeter of the camp. Vin had just returned from a similar patrol, though hers had been around the perimeter of Fadrex. She did a couple of rounds every night, watching the city for unusual activity.

"Yes," Elend said. "Once he'd had some rest, I spoke to him in depth."

"Bad news?"

"Much of what he said before. Penrod apparently never got my orders to send food and troops. Conrad was one of four messengers Penrod sent to us. We don't know what happened to the other three. Conrad was chased by a group of koloss, and he only got away by baiting them with his horse, sending it one direction and hiding as they chased it down and butchered it. He slipped away while they were feasting."

"Brave man," Vin said.

"Lucky as well," Elend said. "In any case, it seems unlikely that Penrod will be able to send us support. There are food stores in Luthadel, but if the news of riots is true, Penrod won't be able to spare the soldiers it would take to guard supplies on their way to us."

"So . . . where does that leave us?" Vin asked.

Elend looked at her, and she was surprised to see determination in his eyes, not frustration. "With knowledge."

"What?"

"Our enemy has exposed himself, Vin. Attacking our messengers directly with hidden groups of koloss? Trying to undermine our supply base in Luthadel?" Elend shook his head. "Our enemy *wants* this to appear random, but I see the pattern. It's too focused, too intelligent, to be happenstance. He's trying to make us pull away from Fadrex."

Vin felt a chill. Elend made to say more, but she reached up and laid a hand on his lips, quieting him. He seemed confused, but then apparently understood, for he nodded. *Whatever we say, Ruin can hear,* Vin thought. *We can't give away what we know.*

Still, something passed between them. A knowledge that they had to stay at Fadrex, that they *had* to find out what was in that storage cavern. For their enemy was working hard to keep them from doing so.

Vin nodded to Elend, indicating that she agreed with his determination. Still, she worried. Luthadel was to have been their rock in all of this—their secure position. If it was falling apart, what did they have?

More and more, she was beginning to understand that there would be no falling back. No retreat to develop alternative plans. The world was collapsing around them, and Elend had committed himself to Fadrex.

If they failed here, there would be nowhere else to go.

Eventually Elend squeezed her shoulder, then walked off into the mists to check on some of the guard posts. Vin remained alone, staring up at those bonfires, feeling a worrisome sense of foreboding. Her thoughts from before, in the fourth storage cavern, returned to her. Fighting wars, besieging cities, playing at politics—it wasn't enough. These things wouldn't save them if the land itself died.

But what else could they do? The only option they had was to take Fadrex and hope the Lord Ruler had left them some clue. She still felt an inexplicable desire to find the atium. Why was she so certain it would help?

She closed her eyes, not wanting to face the mists, which—as always—pulled away from her, leaving a half inch or so of empty air around her. She reached out to them, trying once more to draw upon them as she had when she'd fought the Lord Ruler. She called to them as she had so many times, pleaded with them in her mind, strove to access their power. And she felt she *should* be able to. There was a strength to the mists, trapped within them. But it wouldn't yield to her. It was as if something kept it back, some blockage perhaps? Or maybe a simple whim on the part of the mists.

"Why?" she whispered, eyes still closed. "Why help me that once, but never again? Am I mad, or did you really give me power when I demanded it?"

The night gave her no answers. Finally she sighed and turned away, seeking refuge in the tent.

Hemalurgic spikes change people physically, depending on which powers are granted, where the spike is placed, and how many spikes someone has. Inquisitors, for instance, are changed drastically from the humans they used to be. Their hearts are in different places from those of humans, and their brains rearrange to accommodate the lengths of metal jabbed through their eyes. Koloss are changed in even more drastic ways.

One might think that kandra are changed most of all. However, one must remember that new kandra are made from mistwraiths and not humans. The spikes worn by the kandra cause only a small transformation in their hosts—leaving their bodies mostly like that of a mistwraith, but allowing their minds to begin working. Ironically, while the spikes dehumanize the koloss, they give a measure of humanity to the kandra.

41

"DON'T YOU SEE, BREEZE?" SAZED said eagerly. "This is an example of what we call ostension—a legend being emulated in real life. The people believed in the Survivor of Hathsin, and so they have made for themselves *another* survivor to help them in their time of need."

Breeze raised an eyebrow. They stood near the back of a crowd gathering in the market district, waiting for the Citizen to arrive.

"It is fascinating," Sazed said. "This is an evolution of the Survivor legend that I never anticipated. I knew that they might deify him—in fact, that was almost inevitable. However, since Kelsier was once an ordinary person, those who worship him can imagine *other* people achieving the same status."

Breeze nodded distractedly. Allrianne stood beside him, looking quite petulant about having been required to wear drab skaa clothing.

Sazed ignored their lack of excitement. "I wonder what the future of this will be. Perhaps there will be a *succession* of Survivors for this people. This could be the foundation of a religion with true lasting potential, since it could re-invent itself to suit the needs of the populace. Of course, new Survivors mean new leaders—each one with different opinions. Rather than a line of priests who promote ortho-doxy, each new Survivor would seek to establish himself as distinct from those he succeeded. It could make for nu-merous factions and divisions in the body of worshippers."

"Sazed," Breeze said. "What ever happened to not col-lecting religions?"

"I'm . . . not really collecting this religion. I'm merely theorizing about its potential."

Breeze raised an eyebrow.

"Besides," Sazed said. "It might have to do with our cur-rent mission. If this new Survivor is indeed a real person, he may be able to help us overthrow Quellion."

"Or," Allrianne noted, "he might present a challenge to us for leadership of the city once Quellion falls."

"True," Sazed admitted. "Either way, I see no reason for you to complain, Breeze. Did you not *want* me to become interested in religions again?"

"That was before I realized you'd spend the entire eve-ning, then the next morning, chattering about it," Breeze said. "Where is Quellion anyway? If I miss lunch because of his executions, I'll be rather annoyed."

Executions. In his excitement, Sazed had nearly forgot-ten what it was they had come to see. His eagerness deflated, and he remembered why Breeze was acting so solemnly. The man spoke lightly, but the concern in his eyes indicated how disturbed he was by the thought of the Citizen burning innocent people to death.

"There," Allrianne said, pointing toward the other side of the market. Something was making a stir: the Citizen, wearing a bright blue costume. It was a new approved color—one he alone was allowed to wear. His councillors surrounded him in red.

"Finally," Breeze said, following the crowd as they bunched up around the Citizen.

Sazed followed, his steps growing reluctant. Now that he thought about it, he was tempted to use his troops to try to stop what was about to occur. But he knew that would be foolish. Playing his hand now to save a few would ruin their chances of saving the entire city. With a sigh, he followed Breeze and Allrianne, moving with the crowd. He also suspected that watching the murders would remind him of the pressing nature of his duties in Urteau. Theological studies would wait for another time.

"You will have to kill them," Kelsier said.

Spook crouched quietly atop a building in the wealthier section of Urteau. Below, the Citizen's procession was approaching; Spook watched it through cloth-wrapped eyes. It had taken many coins—nearly the last of what he'd brought with him from Luthadel—to learn the location of the executions sufficiently in advance so that he could get into position.

He could see the sorry individuals who Quellion had decided to murder. Many of them were like Franson's sister—people who had been discovered to have noble parentage. Several others, however, were only spouses of those with noble blood. Spook also knew of one man in this group who had spoken out too loudly against Quellion. His connection to the nobility was tenuous; he was a craftsman who had once catered to a noble clientele.

"I know you don't want to do it," Kelsier said. "But you can't lose your nerve now."

Spook felt powerful—pewter lent him an air of invincibility that he'd never before imagined. He had slept barely a few hours in the last six days, but he didn't feel tired. He had a sense of balance that any cat would have envied, and he had strength his muscles shouldn't have been able to produce.

Yet power wasn't everything. His palms were sweating beneath his cloak, and he felt beads of perspiration creeping down his brow. He was no Mistborn. He wasn't Kelsier or Vin. He was just Spook. What was he thinking?

"I can't do it," he whispered.

"You can," Kelsier said. "You've practiced with the cane—I've watched. Plus you stood up to those soldiers in the market. They nearly killed you, but you were fighting two Thugs. You did very well."

"I . . ."

"You need to save those people, Spook. Ask yourself: What would *I* do if I were there?"

"I'm not you."

"Not yet," Kelsier whispered.

Not yet.

Below, Quellion preached against the people about to be executed. Spook could see Beldre, the Citizen's sister, at his side. Spook leaned forward. Was that really a look of sympathy, even pain, in her eyes as she watched the unfortunate prisoners herded toward the building? Or was that merely what Spook wanted to see in her? He followed her gaze, watching the prisoners. One of them was a child, holding fearfully to a woman as the group was prodded into the building that would become their pyre.

Kelsier's right, Spook thought. *I can't let this happen. I may not succeed, but at least I have to try.* His hands continued to shake as he moved through the hatch atop his building and dashed down the steps, cloak whipping behind him. He rounded a corner, heading for the wine cellar.

Noblemen were strange creatures. During the days of the Lord Ruler, they had often feared for their lives as much as skaa thieves did, for court intrigue often led to imprisonment or assassination. Spook should have realized what he was missing from the beginning. No thieving crew would build a lair without a bolt-hole for emergency escapes.

Why would the nobility be any different?

He leaped, cloak flapping as he dropped the last few steps. He hit the dusty floor, and his enhanced ears heard Quellion begin to rant up above. The skaa crowds were murmuring. The flames had started. There, in the darkened basement of the building, Spook found a section of the wall already open, a secret passageway leading from the building next door. A group of soldiers stood in the passageway.

"Quickly," Spook heard one of them say, "before the fire gets here."

"Please!" another voice cried, her words echoing through the passageway. "At least take the child!"

People grunted. The soldiers moved on the opposite end of the passage from Spook, keeping the people in the other basement from escaping. They had been sent by Quellion to spare one of the prisoners. Out in the open, the Citizen made a show of denouncing anyone with noble blood. Allomancers, however, were too valuable to kill. So he chose his buildings carefully—only burning those with hidden exits through which he could extract the Allomancers.

It was the perfect way to show orthodoxy, yet maintain a grip on the city's most powerful resource. But it wasn't this hypocrisy that made Spook's hands stop shaking as he charged the soldiers.

It was the crying child.

"*Kill them!*" Kelsier screamed.

Spook whipped out one of his dueling canes. One of the soldiers finally noticed him, spinning in shock.

He fell first.

Spook hadn't realized how hard he could swing. The soldier's helmet flew through the hidden passageway, its metal crumpled. The other soldiers cried out as Spook leaped over their fallen companion in the close confines. They carried swords, but had trouble drawing them.

Spook, however, had brought daggers.

He pulled one free, wielding it with a swing powered by both pewter and fury, enhanced senses guiding his steps. He cut through two soldiers, elbowing their dying bodies aside, pressing his advantage. At the end of the passageway, four soldiers stood with a short skaa man.

Fear shone in their eyes.

Spook threw himself forward. The shocked soldiers at last overcame their surprise and threw open the secret door, stumbling over themselves as they entered the basement of the building on the other side.

The structure was already well on its way to burning down. Spook could smell the smoke. The rest of the condemned people were in the room—they had probably been trying to get through the doorway to follow their friend who had escaped. Now they were forced backward as the soldiers shoved their way in, finally drawing their swords.

Spook gutted the slowest of the four soldiers, then left his dagger in the body and pulled out a second dueling cane. The firm length of wood felt good in his hand as he spun between shocked civilians, attacking the soldiers.

"The soldiers can't be allowed to escape," Kelsier whispered. "Otherwise Quellion will know that the people were rescued. You have to leave him confused."

Firelight flickered in a hallway beyond the well-furnished basement room. Spook could feel the heat already. Grimly, the three backlit soldiers raised their swords. Smoke began to creep in along the ceiling, spreading like a black mist. The prisoners cringed, confused.

Spook dashed forward, spinning as he swung both of his canes at one of the soldiers. The man took the bait, side-stepping Spook's attack, then lunged forward. In an ordinary fight, Spook would have been skewered.

Pewter and tin saved him. Spook moved on feet made light, feeling the wind of the oncoming sword, knowing where it would pass. His heart thudded in his chest as the sword sliced through the fabric at his side, but missed his flesh. He brought a cane down, cracking the man's sword arm, then smacked the other into his skull.

The soldier fell, surprise visible in his dying eyes as Spook pushed past him.

The next soldier was already swinging. Spook brought up both of his canes, crossing them to block. The sword bit through one, spinning half of the cane into the air, but got caught in the second. Spook snapped his weapon to the side, pushing the blade away, then spun within the man's reach and took him down with an elbow to the stomach.

Spook punched the man's head as he fell. The sound of bone on bone cracked in the burning room. The soldier slumped at Spook's feet.

I can actually do this! Spook thought. *I'm like them. Vin and Kelsier. No more hiding in basements or fleeing from danger. I can fight!*

He spun, smiling.

And found the final soldier standing with Spook's own knife held to the neck of a young girl. The soldier stood with his back to the burning hallway, eyeing escape through the hidden passage. Behind the man, flames were curling around the wooden doorframe, licking the room.

"The rest of you, get out!" Spook said, not turning from the soldier. "Go out the rear door of the building you find at the end of this tunnel. You'll find men there. They'll hide you in the underground, then get you out of the city. Go!"

Some had already fled, and the others moved at his command. The soldier stood, watching, clearly trying to decide his course. He must have known he was facing an Allomancer—no ordinary man could have taken down so many soldiers so quickly. Fortunately, it appeared that Quellion hadn't sent his own Allomancers into the building. He likely kept them above, protecting him.

Spook stood still. He dropped the broken dueling cane, but held the other tightly to keep his hand from shaking. The girl whimpered.

What would Kelsier have done?

Behind him, the last of the prisoners was fleeing into the passage. "You!" Spook said without turning. "Bar that door from the outside. Quickly!"

"But—"

"Do it!" Spook yelled.

"No!" the soldier said, pressing the knife against the girl's neck. "I'll kill her!"

"Do and you die," Spook said. "You know that. Look at me. You're not getting past me. You're—"

The door thunked closed.

The soldier cried out, dropping the girl, and rushed toward the door, plainly trying to get to it before the bar fell on the other side. "That's the only way out! You'll get us—"

Spook broke the man's knees with a single crack of the dueling cane. The soldier screamed, falling to the ground. Flames burned on three of the walls now. The heat was already intense.

The door's bar thudded into place. Spook looked down at the soldier. Still alive.

"Leave him," Kelsier said. "Let him burn in the building."

Spook hesitated.

"He would have let all of those people die," Kelsier said. "Let him feel what he would have done to these—what he has already done several times, at Quellion's command."

Spook left the groaning man on the ground, moving over to the secret door. He threw his weight against it.

It held.

Spook cursed quietly, raising a boot and kicking the door. It remained solid.

"That door was built by noblemen who feared they would be pursued by assassins," Kelsier said. "They were familiar with Allomancy, and would make certain the door was strong enough to resist a Thug's kick."

The fire grew hotter. The girl huddled on the floor, whimpering. Spook whirled, staring down the flames, feeling their heat. He stepped forward, but his amplified senses were so keen that the heat seemed amazingly powerful to him.

He gritted his teeth, picking up the girl.

I have pewter now, he thought. *It can balance the power of my senses.*

That will have to be enough.

Smoke billowed out the windows of the condemned building. Sazed waited with Breeze and Allrianne, standing at the back of a solemn crowd. The people were oddly silent as they watched the flames claim their prize. Perhaps they sensed the truth.

That they could be taken and killed as easily as the poor wretches who died inside.

"How quickly we come around," Sazed whispered. "It wasn't long ago that men were forced to watch the Lord Ruler cut the heads from innocent people. Now we do it to ourselves."

Silence. Yells sounded from within the building. The screams of dying men.

"Kelsier was wrong," Breeze said.

Sazed frowned, turning.

"He blamed the noblemen," Breeze said. "He thought that if we got rid of them, things like this wouldn't happen."

Sazed nodded. The crowd began to grow restless, shuffling about, murmuring. And Sazed felt himself agreeing with them. Something needed to be done about this atrocity. Why did nobody fight? Quellion stood there, surrounded by his proud men in red. Sazed gritted his teeth, growing angry.

"Allrianne, dear," Breeze said, "this isn't the time."

Sazed started. He turned, glancing at the young woman. She was crying.

By the Forgotten Gods, Sazed thought, finally recognizing her touch on his emotions, Rioting them to make him angry at Quellion. *She's as good as Breeze is.*

"Why not?" she said. "He deserves it. I could make this crowd rip him apart."

"And his second-in-command would take control,"

Breeze said, "then execute these people. We haven't prepared enough."

"It seems that you're never done preparing, Breeze," she snapped.

"These things require—"

"Wait," Sazed said, raising a hand. He frowned, watching the building. One of the building's boarded windows—high in a peaked attic section on top of the roof—seemed to be shaking.

"Look!" Sazed said. "There!"

Breeze raised an eyebrow. "Perhaps our Flame God is about to make his appearance, eh?" He smiled at what he obviously found a ridiculous concept. "I wonder what we were supposed to learn during this revolting little experience. Personally, I think the men who sent us here didn't know what they—"

One of the planks suddenly flew off the window, spinning in the air, swirling smoke behind it. Then the window burst outward.

A figure in dark clothing leaped through the shattering mess of boards and smoke, landing on the rooftop. His long cloak appeared to be on fire in places, and he carried a small bundle in his arms. A child. The figure rushed along the top of the burning rooftop, then leaped off the front of the building, trailing smoke as he fell to the ground.

He landed with the grace of a man burning pewter, not stumbling despite the two-story fall, his burning cloak billowing out around him. People backed away, surprised, and Quellion spun in shock.

The man's hood fell to his shoulders as he stood upright. Only then did Sazed recognize him.

Spook stood tall, seeming in the sunlight to be older than he really was. Or perhaps Sazed had never seen him as anything but a child until that moment. Either way, the young man regarded Quellion proudly, eyes wrapped with a blindfold, his body smoking as he held the coughing child in his arms. He didn't seem the least bit intimidated by the troop of twenty soldiers that surrounded the building.

Breeze cursed. "Allrianne, we're going to need that Riot after all!"

Sazed suddenly felt a weight pressing against him. Breeze Soothed away his distracting emotions—his confusion, his concern—and left Sazed, along with the crowd, completely open to Allrianne's focused burst of enraged anger.

The crowd exploded with motion, people crying out in the name of the Survivor, rushing the guards. For a moment, Sazed feared that Spook wouldn't take the opportunity to run. Despite the strange bandage on Spook's eyes, Sazed could tell that the boy was staring straight at Quellion—as if in challenge.

Fortunately, Spook did turn away. The crowd distracted the advancing soldiers, and Spook ran on feet that seemed to move far too quickly. He ducked down an alleyway, carrying the girl he had rescued, his cloak trailing smoke. As soon as Spook had a safe head start, Breeze smothered the crowd's will to rebel, keeping them from getting themselves cut down by the soldiers. The people backed away, dispersing. The Citizen's soldiers stayed close around their leader. Sazed could hear frustration in the Citizen's voice as he called for the inevitable retreat. He couldn't spare more than a few men to chase down Spook, not with the potential of a riot. He had to get himself to safety.

As soldiers marched away, Breeze turned an eye toward Sazed. "Well," he noted, "*that* was unexpected."

I think that the koloss were more intelligent than we wanted to give them credit for being. For instance, originally they used only spikes the Lord Ruler gave them to make new members. He would provide the metal and the unfortunate skaa captives, and the koloss would create new "recruits."

At the Lord Ruler's death, the koloss should quickly have died out. This was how he had designed them. If they got free from his control, he expected them to kill themselves off and end their rampage. However, they somehow deduced that spikes in the bodies of fallen koloss could be harvested, then reused.

They then no longer required a fresh supply of spikes. I often wonder what effect the constant reuse of spikes had on their population. A spike can only hold so much of a Hemalurgic imbuement, so they could not create spikes that granted infinite strength, no matter how many people those spikes killed and drew power from. But did the repeated reuse of spikes perhaps bring more humanity to the koloss they made?

42

WHEN MARSH ENTERED LUTHADEL, HE was far more careful than he had been when he'd entered the nameless town at the western border of the dominance. An Inquisitor moving through the capital of Elend's empire would not go unreported, and might draw undue attention. The emperor was gone, and he had left his playground open to be used by others. No need to spoil that.

So Marsh moved at night, his cloak's hood up, burning steel and jumping about on coins. Even so, seeing the magnificent city—sprawling, dirty, yet still *home*—was hard for the watching, waiting part of Marsh. Once, he had run the skaa rebellion in this city. He felt responsible for its occupants, and the thought of Ruin doing to them what he'd done to the people of the other town, the one where the Ashmount had blown . . .

There was no Ashmount that close to Luthadel. Unfortunately, there were things Ruin could do to a city that didn't involve natural forces. On his way to Luthadel, Marsh had stopped at no fewer than four villages, where he had quietly killed the men guarding their food stores, then set fire to the buildings that contained them. He knew that the other Inquisitors went about the world, committing similar atrocities as they searched for the thing Ruin desired above all others. The thing Preservation had taken from him.

He had yet to find it.

Marsh leaped over a street, landing atop a peaked roof, running along its edge and toward the northeastern side of the city. Luthadel had changed during the year since he'd last seen it. The Lord Ruler's forced labor projects had brutalized the skaa, but had kept things clean of ash and given the oversized city a sense of order. There was none of that now. Growing food was obviously a priority—and keeping the city clean could wait for later, if there was a later.

There were far more trash heaps than before, and ash—which would have once been scraped into the river that ran through the city—was now piled in alleys and against buildings. Marsh felt himself begin to smile at the beauty of the disrepair, and his tiny rebellious part withdrew and hid.

He couldn't fight. Now was not the time.

He soon arrived at Keep Venture, seat of Elend's government. It had been invaded by koloss during the siege of Luthadel, its lower stained-glass windows shattered by the beasts. The windows had been replaced by boards. Marsh smiled, then Steelpush-leaped up to a balcony on the second floor. He was familiar with this building. Before he'd been taken by Ruin, he had spent several months living here, helping Emperor Venture keep control in his city.

Marsh found Penrod's rooms easily. They were the only ones occupied, the only ones guarded. Marsh crouched a few corridors down, watching with his inhuman eyes as he considered his next course of action.

Impaling an unwilling subject with a Hemalurgic spike was a very tricky prospect. The spike's size was, in this case, immaterial. Just as a pinch of metal dust could fuel Allomancy for a time, or a small ring could hold a small Feruchemical charge, a rather small bit of metal could work for Hemalurgy. Inquisitor spikes were made large to be intimidating, but in many instances a small pin could be as effective as a massive spike. It depended on how long the spike remained outside a person's body after being used to kill someone.

For Marsh's purposes this day, a small spike was preferable; he didn't want to give Penrod powers, just pierce him with metal. Marsh pulled out the spike he had made from the Allomancer in the doomed town a few days before. It was about five inches long—bigger than it needed to be, strictly speaking. However, Marsh would need to drive this spike forcefully into a man's body, which meant it needed to be at least large enough to hold its shape. There were some two or three hundred bind points across a human's body. Marsh didn't know them all; Ruin would guide his hand when the time came to strike, making sure the spike was delivered to the correct place. His master's direct attention was focused elsewhere at the moment, and he was giving Marsh general commands to get into position and prepare for the attack.

Hemalurgic spikes. The hidden part of himself shivered, remembering the day when he had unexpectedly been made into an Inquisitor. He'd thought that he had been discovered. He'd been working as a spy for Kelsier in the Steel Ministry. Little did he know that he hadn't been singled out as suspicious, but as extraordinary.

The Inquisitors had come for him at night, while he'd

waited nervously to meet with Kelsier and pass on what he assumed would be his final message to the rebellion. They'd burst through the door, moving more quickly than he could react. They gave him no option. They'd simply slammed him to the ground, then thrown a screaming woman on top of him.

Then the Inquisitors had pounded a spike right through her heart and into Marsh's eye.

The pain was too great for him to recall. That moment was a hole in his memory, filled with vague images of the Inquisitors repeating this process, killing other unfortunate Allomancers and pounding their powers—their very souls, it seemed—into Marsh's body. When it was finished, he lay groaning on the floor, a new flood of sensory information making it difficult for him to think. Around him, the other Inquisitors had danced about, cutting apart the other bodies with their axes, rejoicing in the addition of another member to their ranks.

In a way, that was the day of his birth. What a wonderful day. Penrod, however, would not have such joy. He wasn't to be made into an Inquisitor; he would get only one small spike. One that had been made days ago and been allowed to sit outside a body, leaking power all that time.

Marsh waited for Ruin to come to him in force. Not only would the spike have to be planted precisely, but Penrod would have to leave it in long enough for Ruin to begin influencing his thoughts and emotions. After the spike was pounded in, the skin could heal around the metal and it would still work. But to begin with it had to touch his blood.

How did one make a person forget about five inches of metal sprouting from their body? How did one make others ignore it? Ruin had tried to get a spike into Elend Venture on several occasions now, and had always failed. In fact, most attempts failed. The few people claimed with the process, however, were worth the effort.

Ruin came upon him, and he lost control of his body. He moved without knowing what he was going to do, following direct orders. *Down the corridor. Don't attack the guards. In through the door.*

Marsh shoved aside the two watching soldiers, kicking the door down and bursting into the antechamber.

Right. To the bedchamber.

He was through the room in a heartbeat, the two soldiers outside belatedly shouting for help. Penrod was an aging man with a dignified air. He had the presence of mind to leap from his bed at the sounds, grabbing a hardwood dueling cane from its place atop his nightstand.

Marsh smiled. A dueling cane? Against an Inquisitor? He pulled his obsidian hand axe from the sheath at his side.

Fight him, Ruin said, *but do not kill him. Make it a difficult battle, but allow him to feel that he's holding you off.*

It was an odd request, but Marsh's mind was so directly controlled that he couldn't pause to think about it. He simply leaped forward to attack.

It was harder than it seemed. He had to make sure to strike with the axe in ways that Penrod could block. Several times, he had to tap speed from one of his spikes—which doubled as a Feruchemical metalmind—to suddenly inch his axe in the right direction, lest he accidentally behead the king of Luthadel.

Yet Marsh did it. He cut Penrod a few times, fighting all the while with the small spike held hidden in his left palm, letting the king think he was doing well. Within moments, the guards had joined the fight, which allowed Marsh to keep up appearances even better. Three normal men against an Inquisitor was still no contest, but from their perspectives maybe it would seem like one.

It wasn't long before a troop of some dozen guards burst into the chamber outside the bedroom, coming to aid their king.

Now, Ruin said. *Act frightened, get ready to put the spike in, and prepare to flee out the window.*

Marsh tapped speed and moved. Ruin precisely guided his left hand as he slammed it into Penrod's chest, driving the spike directly into the man's heart. Marsh heard Penrod scream, smiled at the sound, and leaped out the window.

A short time later, Marsh hung outside that same window, unseen and unnoticed by the numerous guard patrols. He was far too skilled, far too careful, to be spotted listening with tin-enhanced ears, hanging underneath an outcropping of stone near the window. Inside, surgeons conferred.

"When we try to pull the spike out, the bleeding increases dramatically, my lord," one voice explained.

"The shard of metal got dangerously close to your heart," said another.

Dangerously close? Marsh smiled from his upside-down perch. Since Penrod was conscious, the surgeons would assume that the spike had come close, but somehow barely missed piercing the heart. Yet it had.

"We fear pulling it out," the first surgeon said. "How . . . do you feel?"

"Remarkably good, actually," said Penrod. "There is an ache, and some discomfort. But I feel strong."

"Then let us leave the shard for now," the first surgeon said, sounding concerned. But what else could he do? If he *did* pull the spike out, it *would* kill Penrod. A clever move by Ruin.

They would wait for Penrod to regain his strength, then try again to remove the spike. And again it would threaten Penrod's life. They'd have to leave it. And with Ruin now able to touch his mind—not control him, but just nudge things in certain directions—Penrod would soon forget about the spike. The discomfort would fade, and with the spike under his clothing, no one would find it irregular.

And then he would be Ruin's as surely as any Inquisitor. Marsh smiled, let go of the outcropping, and dropped to the dark streets below.

For all that it disgusts me, I cannot help but be impressed by Hemalurgy as an art.

In Allomancy and Feruchemy, skill and subtlety come through the application of one's powers. The best Allomancer might not be the most powerful, but instead the one who can most skillfully manipulate the Pushes and Pulls of metals. The best Feruchemist is the one who is most capable of sorting the information in his copperminds, or most able to manipulate his weight with iron.

The art that is unique to Hemalurgy is the knowledge of where to place the spikes.

43

VIN LANDED WITH A HUSHED rustle of cloth. She crouched in the night, holding up her dress to keep it from brushing the ashen rooftop, then peered into the mists.

Elend dropped beside her, then fell into a crouch, asking no questions. She smiled, noting that his instincts were getting better. He watched the mists too, though he plainly didn't know what he was looking for.

"He's following us," Vin whispered.

"Yomen's Mistborn?" Elend asked.

Vin nodded.

"Where?" he asked.

"Three houses back," Vin said.

Elend squinted, and she felt one of his Allomantic pulses suddenly increase in speed. He was flaring tin.

"That lump on the right side?" Elend asked.

"Close enough," Vin said.

"So . . ."

"So he knows I've spotted him," Vin said. "Otherwise I wouldn't have stopped. Right now we're studying one another."

Elend reached to his belt, slipping out an obsidian knife.

"He won't attack," Vin said.

"How do you know?"

"Because," Vin said. "When he intends to kill us, he'll try to do it when you and I aren't together—or when we're sleeping."

That seemed to make Elend more nervous. "Is that why you've been staying up all night lately?"

Vin nodded. Forcing Elend to sleep alone was a small price to pay for keeping him safe. *Is it you back there following us, Yomen?* she wondered. *On the night of your own party? That would be quite the feat.* It didn't seem likely, but still Vin was suspicious. She had a habit of suspecting *everyone* of being Mistborn. She thought it was healthy, even if she had often been wrong.

"Come on," she said, rising. "Once we get into the party, we shouldn't have to worry about him."

Elend nodded, and the two continued along their path to the Canton of Resource, which sat atop a small rise.

The plan is simple, Elend had said earlier. *I'll confront Yomen, and the nobility won't be able to help gathering around to gawk. At that point, you sneak away and see if you can find your way to the storage chamber.*

It really was a simple plan—the best ones usually were. If Elend confronted Yomen, it would keep the attention of the guards on him, hopefully letting Vin slip out. She'd need to move quickly and quietly, and would probably have to eliminate some guards—all without raising an alarm. Yet this appeared to be the sole entrance. Not only was Yomen's fortress of a building well lit and particularly well guarded, but his Mistborn was good. The man had detected her every other time she'd tried to sneak in—always remaining at a distance, his mere presence warning her that he could raise the alarm in a heartbeat.

Their best chance was the ball. Yomen's defenses, and his Mistborn, would be focused on their master, keeping him safe.

They landed in the courtyard, causing carriages to stop and guards to turn in shock. Vin glanced to Elend in the misty darkness. "Elend," she said quietly, "I need you to promise me something."

He frowned. "What?"

"Eventually I'm going to get spotted," Vin said. "I'll sneak as best I can, but I doubt we'll get through this without creating a disturbance. When it hits, I want you to get out."

"Vin, I can't do that. I have to—"

"No," Vin said sharply. "Elend, you don't have to help me. You *can't* help me. I love you, but you're not as good at this as I am. I can take care of myself, but I need to know that I won't have to take care of you too. If anything goes wrong—or if things go right, but the building goes on alert—I want you to get out. I'll meet you at the camp."

"And if you get into trouble?" Elend said.

Vin smiled. "Trust me."

He paused, then nodded. Trusting her was one thing he could do—something he'd always done.

The two strode forward. It felt very strange to be attending a ball at a Ministry building. Vin was accustomed to stained glass and ornamentation, but Canton offices were generally austere—and this one was no exception. It was only a single story tall, and it had sheer flat walls with very small windows on this side. No limelights illuminated the exterior, and while a couple of large tapestry banners fluttered against the stonework, the sole indication that this night was special was the cluster of carriages and nobility in the courtyard. The soldiers in the area had noted Vin and Elend, but made no move to engage or slow them.

Those watching—both nobility and soldiers—were interested, but few looked surprised. Vin and Elend were expected.

Vin's hunch about that was confirmed when she moved up the steps and nobody moved to intercept them. The guards at the door watched suspiciously, but let her and Elend pass.

Inside, she found a long entry hall lit by lamps. The flow of people turned left, so Vin and Elend followed, twisting through a few labyrinthine corridors until they approached a larger meeting hall.

"Not exactly the most impressive place for a ball, eh?" Elend said as they waited their turn to be announced.

Vin nodded. Most noble keeps had exterior entrances directly into their ballroom. The room ahead—from what she could see of it—had been adapted from a standard Ministry meeting room. Rivets covered the floor where benches had once been, and there was a stage on the far side of the room, where obligators had probably once stood to give instruction to their subordinates. That was where Yomen's table had been set up.

It was too small to be a truly practical ballroom. The people there weren't exactly cramped, but neither did they have the space the nobility preferred for forming small groups where they could gossip.

"There seem to be other party rooms," Elend said, nodding to several corridors leading from the main "ballroom." People were trailing in and out of them.

"Places for people to go if they feel too crowded," Vin said. "This building could be tough to escape, Elend. Don't let yourself get cornered. Looks like an exit over there to the left."

Elend followed her gaze as they walked into the main room. Flickering torchlight and trails of mist indicated a courtyard or atrium. "I'll stay close to it," he said. "And avoid going to any of the smaller side rooms."

"Good," Vin said. She also noted something else—twice during the trip through the corridors to the ballroom, she'd seen stairwells leading down. That implied a fairly large basement, something uncommon in Luthadel. *The Canton building goes down rather than up,* she decided. It made sense, assuming that there really was a storage cache below.

The door herald announced them without needing a card to read from, and the two entered the room. The party was nowhere near as lavish as the one at Keep Orielle had been. There were snacks, but no dinner—likely because there wasn't room for dining tables. There was music and dancing, but the room was not draped in finery. Yomen had elected to leave the simple, stark Ministry walls uncovered.

"I wonder why he bothers to hold balls," Vin whispered.

"He probably had to start them," Elend said. "To prompt the other nobility. Now he's part of the rotation. It's smart of him though. It gives a man some measure of power to be able to draw the nobility into his home and be their host."

Vin nodded, then eyed the dance floor. "One dance before we split up?"

Elend wavered. "To tell you the truth, I feel a bit too nervous."

Vin smiled, then kissed him lightly, completely breaking noble protocol. "Give me about an hour before the distraction. I want to get a feel for the party before I sneak away."

They parted, Elend heading directly for a group of men that she didn't recognize. Vin wandered—she didn't want to get bogged down by conversation, so she avoided the women she recognized from Keep Orielle. She knew that she should probably have worked to reinforce her contacts, but the truth was that she felt a bit of what Elend did. Not truly nervousness, but rather a desire to avoid typical ball activities. She wasn't here to mingle. She had more important tasks to be concerned with.

So she meandered through the ballroom, sipping a cup of wine and studying the guards. There were a lot of them, which was probably good. The more guards there were in the ballroom, the fewer there would be in the rest of the building. Theoretically.

Vin kept moving, nodding to people, but withdrawing anytime one of them tried to make conversation with her. If she had been Yomen, she would have assigned a few soldiers to keep watch on her, to make certain she didn't stray anywhere sensitive. Yet none of the men seemed to be all that focused on her. As the hour passed, she grew more and more frustrated. Was Yomen really so incompetent that he wouldn't keep watch on a known Mistborn who entered his home base?

Annoyed, Vin burned bronze. Perhaps there were Allomancers nearby. She nearly jumped in shock when she felt the pulses coming from right beside her.

There were two of them. Courtly puffs—women whose names she didn't know, but who looked distinctly dismissible. That was probably the idea. They stood chatting with a couple of other women a short distance from Vin. One was burning copper, the other was burning tin—Vin would never have picked them out if she hadn't had the ability to pierce copperclouds.

As Vin drifted through the room, the two followed, moving with an impressive level of skill as they slid in and out of conversations. They always stuck close enough to Vin to be within tin-enhanced hearing range, yet stayed far enough away in the relatively crowded room that Vin would never have picked them out without Allomantic help.

Interesting, she thought, moving toward the perimeter of the room. At least Yomen wasn't underestimating her. But now, how to give the women the slip? They wouldn't be distracted by Elend's disturbance, and they certainly wouldn't let Vin sneak away without raising an alarm.

As she wandered, working on the problem, she noted a familiar figure at the edge of the ballroom. Slowswift sat in his usual suit, smoking his pipe as he relaxed in one of the chairs set there for the elderly or the danced out. She trailed over toward him.

"I thought you didn't come to these things," she noted, smiling. Behind, her two shadows expertly worked their way into a conversation a short distance away.

"I only come when my king holds them," Slowswift said.

"Ah," Vin said, then she drifted away. Out of the corner of her eye, she noted Slowswift frowning. He'd obviously expected her to speak to him further, but she couldn't risk his saying anything incriminating. At least not yet. Her tails extricated themselves from their conversation, the speed of Vin's departure forcing them to do so awkwardly. After walking for a bit, Vin paused, giving the women the chance to get into yet another conversation.

Then she spun and walked quickly back to Slowswift, trying to look as if she'd just remembered something. Her tails, intent on appearing natural, had trouble following. They hesitated, and Vin gained a few seconds of freedom.

She leaned down to Slowswift as she passed. "I need two men," she said. "Ones you trust against Yomen. Have them meet me in an area of the party that is more secluded, a place where people can sit and chat."

"The patio," Slowswift said. "Down the left corridor, then outside."

"Good," Vin said. "Tell your men to go there, but then wait until I approach them. Also, please send a messenger to Elend. Tell him I need another half hour."

Slowswift nodded to the cryptic comment, and Vin smiled as her shadows drew closer. "I hope you feel better soon," she said, putting on a fond smile.

"Thank you, my dear," Slowswift said, coughing slightly.

Vin trailed away again. She slowly made her way in the direction Slowswift had indicated, the exit she'd picked out earlier. Sure enough, a few moments later she passed into mist, and she found herself standing on a lantern-lit garden patio. Though tables had been set up for people to relax, the patio was sparsely populated. Servants wouldn't go out in the mists, and most nobility—though they didn't like to admit it—found the mists disconcerting. Vin wandered over to an ornate metal railing, then leaned against it, looking up at the sky, feeling the mists around her and idly fingering her earring.

Soon her two shadows appeared, chatting quietly, and Vin's tin let her hear that they were talking about how stuffy the other room had been. Vin smiled, maintaining her posture as the two women took chairs a distance away, continuing to chat. After that, two young men wandered in and sat down at another table. They weren't as natural about the process as the women, but Vin hoped they weren't suspicious enough to draw attention.

Then she waited.

Life as a thief—a life spent preparing for jobs, watching in spy holes, and carefully choosing the right opportunity to pick a pocket—had taught her patience. It was one urchin attribute she had never lost. She stood staring at the sky, giving no indication at all that she intended to leave. Now she simply had to wait for the distraction.

You shouldn't have relied on him for the distraction, Reen whispered in her mind. *He'll fail. Never let your life depend on the competence of someone whose life isn't also on the line.*

It had been one of Reen's favorite sayings. She didn't think of him often anymore—or really anyone from her old life. That life had been one of pain and sorrow. A brother who beat her to keep her safe, a crazy mother who had inexplicably slaughtered Vin's baby sister.

Now, that life was a faint echo. She smiled to herself, amused at how far she had come. Reen might have called her a fool, but she trusted Elend—trusted him to succeed, trusted him with her life. That was something she could never have done during her early years.

After about ten minutes, someone came out from the party and wandered over to the pair of women. He spoke with them briefly, then returned to the party. Another man came twenty minutes after that, doing the same thing. Hopefully the women were passing on the information Vin wished: that Vin had apparently decided to spend an indeterminate amount of time outside, staring at the mists. Those inside wouldn't expect her to return anytime soon.

A few moments after the second messenger returned to the party, a man rushed out and approached one of the tables. "You have to come hear this!" he whispered to the people at the table—the only ones currently on the patio who had nothing to do with Vin. That group left. Vin smiled. Elend's distraction had come.

Vin jumped into the air, then Pushed against the railing beside her, launching herself across the patio.

The women had clearly grown bored, chatting idly to themselves. It took them a few moments to notice Vin's movement. In those moments, Vin shot across the now-empty patio, dress flapping as she flew. One of the women opened her mouth to yell.

Vin extinguished her metals, then burned duralumin and brass, *Pushing* on the emotions of both women.

She'd done this only once before, to Straff Venture. A duralumin-fueled Brasspush was a terrible thing; it flattened a person's emotions, making them feel empty, completely void of all feeling. Both women gasped, and the one who had been standing stumbled to the ground, falling silent.

Vin landed hard, her pewter still off lest she mix it with duralumin. She put her pewter back on immediately, however, rolling up to her feet. She took one of the women with an elbow to the stomach, then grabbed her face and slammed it down into the table, knocking her out. The other woman sat dazedly on the ground. Vin grimaced, then grabbed the woman by the throat, choking her.

It felt brutal, but Vin didn't let up until the woman fell unconscious—proven by the fact that she let her Allomantic coppercloud fall. Vin sighed, releasing the woman. The unconscious spy slumped to the floor.

Vin turned. Slowswift's young men stood by anxiously. Vin waved them over.

"Stash these two in the bushes," Vin said quickly, "then sit at the table. If anyone asks after them, say that you saw them follow me back into the party. Hopefully that will keep everyone confused."

The men flushed. "We—"

"Do as I say or flee," Vin snapped. "Don't argue with me. I left them both alive, and I can't afford to let them report that I've escaped their watch. If they stir, you'll have to knock them out again."

The men nodded reluctantly.

Vin reached up and unbuttoned her dress, letting the garment fall to the ground and revealing the sleek, dark clothing she wore underneath. She gave the dress to the men to hide as well, then moved into the building, away from the party. Inside the misty corridor, she found a stairwell and slipped down it. Elend's distraction would be in full progress by now. Hopefully it would last long enough.

"That's right," Elend said, arms folded, staring down Yomen. "A duel. Why make the armies fight for the city? You and I could settle this ourselves."

Yomen didn't laugh at the ridiculous idea. He simply sat at his table, his thoughtful eyes set in a bald, tattooed head, the single bead of atium tied to his forehead sparkling in the lantern light. The rest of the crowd was reacting as Elend had expected. Conversations had died, and people had rushed in, packing into the main ballroom to watch the confrontation between emperor and king.

"Why do you think that I would consent to such a thing?" Yomen finally asked.

"All accounts say that you are a man of honor."

"But you are not," Yomen said, pointing at Elend. "This very offer proves that. You are an Allomancer—there would be no contest between us. What honor would there be in that?"

Elend didn't really care. He just wanted Yomen occupied as long as possible. "Then choose a champion," he said. "I'll fight him instead."

"Only a Mistborn would be a match for you," Yomen said.

"Then send one against me."

"Alas, I have none. I won my kingdom through fairness, legality, and the Lord Ruler's grace—not through threat of assassination like you."

No Mistborn, you say? Elend thought, smiling. *So, your "fairness, legality, and grace" don't preclude lying?* "You would really let your people die?" Elend said loudly, sweeping his hand across the room. More and more people were gathering to watch. "All because of your pride?"

"Pride?" Yomen said, leaning forward. "You call it pride to defend your own rule? I call it pride to march your armies into another man's kingdom, seeking to intimidate him with barbaric monsters."

"Monsters your own Lord Ruler created and used to intimidate and conquer as well," Elend said.

Yomen paused. "Yes, the Lord Ruler created the koloss," he said. "It was his prerogative to determine how they were used. Besides, he kept them far away from civilized cities—yet you march them right up to our doorstep."

"Yes," Elend said, "and they haven't attacked. That's because I can control them as the Lord Ruler did. Wouldn't that suggest that I have inherited his right to rule?"

Yomen frowned, perhaps noticing that Elend's arguments kept changing—that he was saying whatever came to mind in order to keep the discussion going.

"You may be unwilling to save this city," Elend said, "but there are others in it who are wiser. You don't think I came here without allies, do you?"

Yomen hesitated again.

"Yes," Elend said, scanning the crowd. "You're not just fighting me, Yomen. You're fighting your own people. Which ones will betray you, when the time comes? How well can you trust them, exactly?"

Yomen snorted. "Idle threats, Venture. What is this really about?" However, Elend could tell that his words bothered Yomen. The man *didn't* trust the local nobility. He would have been a fool to do so.

Elend smiled, preparing his next argument. He could keep this discussion going for quite some time. For if there was one thing in particular that he had learned by growing up in his father's house, it was how to annoy people.

You have your distraction, Vin, Elend thought. *Let's hope you can end the fight for this city before it really begins.*

Each spike, positioned very carefully, can determine how the recipient's body is changed by Hemalurgy. A spike in one place creates a monstrous, near-mindless beast. In another place, a spike will create a crafty and homicidal Inquisitor.

Without the instinctive knowledge granted by taking the power at the Well of Ascension, Rashek would never have been able to use Hemalurgy. With his mind expanded, and with a little practice, he was able to intuit where to place spikes that would create the servants he wanted.

It is a little-known fact that the Inquisitors' torture chambers were actually Hemalurgic laboratories. The Lord Ruler was constantly trying to develop new breeds of servant. It is a testament to Hemalurgy's complexity that, despite a thousand years of trying, he never managed to create anything with it beyond the three kinds of creatures he developed during those few brief moments holding the power.

44

VIN CREPT DOWN THE STONE stairwell, small sounds echoing eerily from below. She had no torch or lantern, and the stairwell was not lit, but enough light reflected up from below to let her tin-enhanced eyes see.

The more she thought about it, the more the large basement made sense. This was the Canton of Resource—the arm of the Ministry that had been in charge of feeding the people, maintaining the canals, and supplying the other Cantons. Vin supposed that this basement had once been well stocked with supplies. If the cache really was here, it would be the first that she had discovered hidden beneath a Canton of Resource building. Vin expected great things from it. What better place to hide your atium and your most important resources than with an organization that was in charge of transportation and storage across the entire empire?

The stairwell was utilitarian and steep. Vin wrinkled her nose at the musty air, which seemed all the more stuffy to her tin-enhanced sense of smell. Still, she was grateful for tin's enhanced vision, not to mention the enhanced hearing, which let her pick out clinking armor below—an indication that she needed to move quite carefully.

So she did. She reached the bottom of the stairwell and peeked around the corner. Three narrow stone corridors split off from the stairwell landing, each heading in a different direction at ninety-degree angles. The sounds were coming from the right, and as Vin leaned out a bit more, she nearly jumped as she saw a pair of guards standing lazily against the wall a short distance away.

Guards standing in the corridors, Vin thought, ducking back into the stairwell. *Yomen definitely wants to protect something down here.*

Vin crouched down on the rough, cool stone. Pewter, steel, and iron were of relatively little use at the moment. She could take down both guards, but it would be risky, since she couldn't afford to make any noise. She didn't know where the cache was—and therefore couldn't afford to make a disturbance, not yet.

Vin closed her eyes, burning brass and zinc. She carefully—and slowly—Soothed the emotions of the two soldiers. She heard them settle back, leaning against the side of the corridor. Then she Rioted their sense of boredom, tugging on that single emotion. She peeked around the corner once more, keeping the pressure on, waiting.

One of the men yawned. A few seconds later, the other one did. Then they both yawned at once. And Vin scuttled straight across the landing and into the shadowed hallway beyond. She pressed herself against the wall, heart beating quickly, and waited. No cry came, though one of the guards did mumble something about being tired.

Vin smiled in excitement. It had been a long time since she'd had to truly sneak. She had spied and scouted, but had relied on the mists, the darkness, and her ability to move quickly to protect her. This was different. It reminded her of the days when she and Reen had burgled houses.

What would my brother say now? she wondered, padding down the corridor on unnaturally light, quiet feet. *He'd think I've gone crazy, sneaking into a building not for wealth, but for information.* To Reen, life had been about survival—the simple, harsh facts of survival. Trust nobody. Make yourself invaluable to your team, but don't be too threatening. Be ruthless. Stay alive.

She hadn't abandoned his lessons. They'd always be part of her—they were what had kept her alive and careful, even during her years with Kelsier's crew. She just no longer listened to them exclusively. She tempered them with trust and hope.

Your trust will get you killed someday, Reen seemed to whisper in the back of her mind. But of course Reen himself hadn't stuck to his code perfectly. He'd died protecting Vin, refusing to give her up to the Inquisitors, although doing so might have saved his life.

Vin continued forward. It soon became evident that the basement was an extensive grid of narrow corridors surrounding larger rooms. She peeked into one, creaking the door open, and found some supplies. They were basic kinds of things, flour and such—not the carefully canned, organized, and catalogued long-term supplies of a storage cache.

There must be a loading dock down one of these corridors, Vin guessed. *It probably slopes down toward the city's canal branch, at the bottom of the rise the building is on.*

Vin moved on, but she knew she wouldn't have time to

search each of the basement's many rooms. She approached another intersection of corridors and crouched down, frowning. Elend's diversion wouldn't last forever, and someone would eventually discover the women she'd knocked unconscious. She needed to get to the cache quickly.

She glanced around. The corridors were sparsely lit by the occasional lamp. Yet there seemed to be more light coming from the left. She moved down this corridor, and the lamps became more frequent. Soon she caught the sound of voices, and she moved more carefully, approaching another intersection. She peeked down it. To the left she noted a pair of soldiers standing in the distance. To her right there were four.

Right it is then, she thought. However, this was going to be a little more difficult.

She closed her eyes, listening carefully. She could hear both groups of soldiers, but there seemed to be something else. Other groups in the distance. Vin picked one of these and begin to Pull with a powerful Riot of emotions. Soothing and Rioting weren't blocked by stone or steel, so the intervening walls were no hindrance.

She waited. Nothing happened. She was trying to Riot the men's sense of anger and irritability, but she didn't know if she was Pulling in the right direction. In addition, Rioting and Soothing weren't as precise as Pushing steel. Breeze always explained that the emotional makeup of a person was a complex jumble of thoughts, instincts, and feelings. An Allomancer couldn't control minds or actions. She could only nudge.

Unless . . .

Taking a deep breath, Vin extinguished all of her metals. Then she burned duralumin and zinc, and *Pulled* in the direction of the distant guards, hitting them with a powerfully enhanced burst of emotional Allomancy.

Immediately, a curse echoed through the hallway. Vin cringed. Fortunately the noise wasn't directed at her. The guards in the corridor perked up, and the argument in the distance grew louder, more fervent. Vin didn't need to burn tin to hear when the scuffle broke out, men yelling at each other.

The guards to the left rushed away, moving to find out what the source of the disturbance was. The ones to her right left two men behind, so Vin drank a vial of metal, then Rioted their emotions, enhancing their senses of curiosity to the point of breaking.

The two men left, rushing after their companions, and Vin scurried down the corridor. She soon saw that her instincts had proven correct—the four men had been guarding a door into one of the storage rooms. Vin braced herself, then opened the door and ducked inside. The trapdoor there was closed, but she knew how to find it. She pulled it open, then jumped into the darkness beneath her.

She Pushed a coin below her as she fell, using the sound of its strike to let her know how far down the floor was. She landed on rough stonework, standing in complete darkness—pitch black beyond what tin would let her see in. She felt around, however, and found a lantern on the wall. She pulled out her flint and soon had light.

And there it was, the door in the wall leading into the storage cavern. The rock mountings had been torn apart, the door forced. The wall was still there, and the door was intact, but getting it open had obviously taken some great amount of work. The door was open slightly, barely wide enough for a person to get through. It had clearly taken Yomen a lot of effort to even get it that far.

He must have known it was here, Vin thought, standing up straight. *But . . . why break it open like this? He has a Mistborn who could have opened the door with an Ironpull.*

Heart fluttering in anticipation, Vin slipped through the opening and into the silent storage cache. She immediately jumped down to the cache floor and began searching for the plaque that would contain the Lord Ruler's information. She just had to—

Stone scraped against stone behind her.

Vin spun, feeling an instant of sharp and dreadful realization.

The stone door closed.

". . . and *that*," Elend said, "is why the Lord Ruler's system of government *had* to fall."

He was losing them. He could tell—more and more people were trailing away from the argument. The problem was, Yomen actually *was* interested.

"You make a mistake, young Venture," the obligator said, tapping the table idly with his fork. "The sixth-century stewardship program was not devised by the Lord Ruler. The newly formed Canton of Inquisition proposed it as a means of population control for the Terris, and the Lord Ruler agreed to it provisionally."

"That provision turned into a means of subjugating an entire race of people," Elend said.

"That subjugation started far earlier," Yomen said. "Everyone knows the history of this, Venture. The Terris were a people who absolutely refused to submit to imperial rule, and they had to be strictly reined in. However, can you honestly say that Terris stewards were treated poorly? They're the most honored servants in all of the empire!"

"I'd hardly call being made into a favored slave a fair return for losing one's manhood," Elend said, raising an eyebrow and folding his arms.

"There are at least a dozen sources I could quote you on that," Yomen said with a wave of his hand. "What about Trendalan? He claimed that being made a eunuch had left him free to pursue more potent thoughts of logic and of harmony, since he wasn't distracted by worldly lusts."

"He didn't have a choice in the matter," Elend said.

"Few of us have choice in our stations," Yomen replied.

"I prefer people to have that choice," Elend said. "You'll notice that I have given the skaa freedom in my lands, and given the nobility a parliamentary council by which they have a hand in ruling the city in which they live."

"High ideals," Yomen said, "and I recognize Trendalan's own words in what you claim to have done. However, even he said that it would be unlikely for such a system to continue in stability for long."

Elend smiled. It had been a long time since he'd had such a good argument. Ham never delved deeply into topics—he enjoyed philosophical questions, but not scholarly debates—and Sazed didn't like to argue.

I wish I could have met Yomen when I was younger, Elend thought. *When I had time to simply worry about philosophy. Oh, the discussions we could have had . . .*

Of course, those discussions probably would have ended up with Elend in the hands of the Steel Inquisitors for being a revolutionary. Still, he had to admit that Yomen was no fool. He knew his history and his politics—he merely happened to have completely erroneous beliefs. Another day, Elend would have been happy to persuade him of that fact.

Unfortunately, this particular argument was growing increasingly tense for Elend. He couldn't maintain both Yomen's attention and that of the crowd. Each time he tried to do something to get the crowd back, Yomen seemed to get suspicious—and each time Elend tried to engage the king, the crowd grew bored with the philosophical debate.

So it was that Elend was actually relieved when the yells of surprise finally came. Seconds later, a pair of soldiers rushed into the room carrying a dazed and bloodied young woman in a ball gown.

Lord Ruler, Vin! Elend thought. *Was that really necessary?*

Elend glanced back at Yomen, and the two shared a look. Then Yomen stood. "Where is the Empress Venture!" he demanded.

Time to go, Elend thought, remembering his promise to Vin. However, something occurred to him. *I'll probably never have another chance to get this close to Yomen,* Elend thought. *And there's one sure way to prove whether or not he's an Allomancer.*

Try to kill him.

It was bold, perhaps foolish, but he was growing certain he'd never convince Yomen to surrender his city. He'd claimed that he wasn't Mistborn, and it was vital to see if he was lying or not. So, trusting his instincts in this matter, Elend dropped a coin and Pushed himself up onto the stage. Ballgoers began to cry out, their idyllic world shattering as Elend whipped out a pair of glass daggers. Yomen paled and backed away. Two guards who had been pretending to be Yomen's dinner partners stood up from their seats, pulling staves from beneath the table.

"You liar," Yomen spat as Elend landed on the dining table. "Thief, butcher, *tyrant!*"

Elend shrugged, then shot coins at the two guards, easily dropping them both. He jumped for Yomen, grabbing the man around the neck, yanking him backward. Gasps and screams came from the crowd.

Elend squeezed, choking Yomen. No strength flooded the man's limbs. No Allomantic Pull or Push tried to shake him from Elend's grasp. The obligator barely struggled.

Either he's no Allomancer, Elend thought, *or he's one hell of an actor.*

He let Yomen go, pushing the king toward his dining table. Elend shook his head—that was one mystery that was—

Yomen jumped forward, pulling out a glass knife, slashing. Elend started, ducking backward, but the knife hit, slicing a gash in his forearm. The cut blazed with pain, enhanced by Elend's tin, and he cursed, stumbling away.

Yomen struck again, and Elend *should* have been able to dodge. He had pewter, and Yomen was still moving with the clumsiness of an unenhanced man. Yet the attack moved with Elend, somehow managing to take him in the side. Elend grunted, blood hot on his skin, and he looked into Yomen's eyes. The king pulled the knife free, easily dodging Elend's counterstrike. It was almost like . . .

Elend burned electrum, giving himself a bubble of false atium images. Yomen hesitated immediately, confusion on his face.

He's burning atium, Elend thought with shock. *That means he* is *Mistborn!*

Part of Elend wanted to stay and fight, but the cut in his side was bad—bad enough that he knew he needed to get it taken care of soon. Cursing his own stupidity, he Pushed himself into the air, dropping blood on the terrified nobility clustered below. He should have listened to Vin—he was going to get a serious lecture when he returned to camp.

He landed, and noted that Yomen had chosen not to follow. The obligator king stood behind his table, holding a knife red with Elend's blood, watching with anger.

Elend turned, tossing a handful of coins and Pushing them into the air above the heads of the ballgoers—careful not to hit any of them. They cowered in fear, throwing themselves to the ground. Once the coins landed, Elend Pushed off them to send himself in a short, low jump through the room and toward the exit Vin had indicated. Soon he entered an outdoor patio cloaked with mist.

He glanced back at the building, feeling frustrated, though he didn't know why. He had done his part—he'd kept Yomen and his guests distracted for a good half hour. True, he'd gotten himself wounded, but he *had* discovered that Yomen was an Allomancer. That was worth knowing.

He dropped a coin and shot himself into the air.

Three hours later, Elend sat in the command tent with Ham, waiting quietly.

He got his side and arm patched. Vin didn't arrive.

He told the others about what had happened. Vin didn't arrive.

Ham forced him to get something to eat. Elend paced for an hour after that, and still Vin did not return.

"I'm going back," Elend said, standing.

Ham looked up. "El, you lost *a lot* of blood. I'd guess that only pewter is keeping you on your feet."

It was true. Elend could feel the edges of fatigue beneath his veil of pewter. "I can handle it."

"You'll kill yourself that way," Ham said.

"I don't care. I—" Elend cut off as his tin-enhanced ears heard someone approaching the tent. He pulled aside the flaps before the man arrived, startling him.

"My lord!" the man said. "Message from the city."

Elend snatched the letter, ripping it open.

Pretender Venture,

I have her, as you have probably guessed. There's one thing I've always noted about Mistborn. To a man, they are overconfident. Thank you for the stimulating conversation. I'm glad I was able to keep you distracted for so long.

King Yomen

Vin sat quietly in the dark cavern, her back resting against the stone block that was the door to her prison. Beside her on the rock floor sat the dwindling lantern she'd brought into the massive room.

She'd Pushed and she'd Pulled, trying to force her way out. However, she'd soon realized that the broken stones she'd seen on the outside—the work project she'd assumed had been used to open the door—had actually served a different purpose. Yomen had apparently removed the metal plates inside the door, the ones that an Allomancer could Push or Pull on to open it. That left the door as simply a stone block. With duralumin-enhanced pewter, she still should have been able to push that open. Unfortunately, she found it difficult to get leverage on the floor, which sloped down away from the block. In addition, they must have done something to the hinges—or perhaps piled up more rock against the other side—for she couldn't get the door to budge.

She ground her teeth in frustration, sitting with her back to the stone door. Yomen had set an intentional trap for her. Had she and Elend been that predictable? Regardless, it was

a brilliant move. Yomen knew he couldn't fight them. Instead he'd simply captured Vin. It had the same effect, but
without any of the risks. And she'd fallen right into the trap.

She'd searched the entire room, trying to find a way out,
but had come up with nothing. Worse, she'd located no
hidden stock of atium. It was hard to tell with all the cans
of food and other sources of metal, but her initial search
hadn't been promising.

"Of course it won't be in here," she muttered to herself. "Yomen wouldn't have had time to pull out all of these
cans, but if he were planning to trap me, he certainly would
have removed the atium. I'm such an *idiot!*"

She leaned back, annoyed, frustrated, exhausted.

I hope Elend did what I said, Vin thought. If he had gotten captured too . . .

Vin knocked her head against the obstinate stones, frustrated.

Something sounded in the darkness.

Vin froze, then quickly scrambled up into a crouch. She
checked her metal reserves—she had plenty, for the moment.

I'm probably just—

It came again. A soft footfall. Vin shivered, realizing
that she had only cursorily checked the chamber, and then
she'd been searching for atium and other ways out. Could
someone have been hiding inside the entire time?

She burned bronze, and felt him. An Allomancer. Mistborn. The one she had felt before; the man she had chased.

So that's it! she thought. *Yomen* did *want his Mistborn
to fight us—but he knew he had to separate us first!* She
smiled, standing. It wasn't a perfect situation, but it was
better than thinking about the immobile door. A Mistborn
she could beat, then hold hostage until they released her.

She waited until the man was close—she could tell by
the beating of the Allomantic pulses that she hoped he
didn't know she could feel—then spun, kicking her lantern
toward him. She jumped forward, guiding herself toward
her enemy, who stood outlined by the lantern's last flickers.

He looked up at her as she soared through the air, her daggers out.

And she recognized his face.

Reen.

THE END OF PART THREE

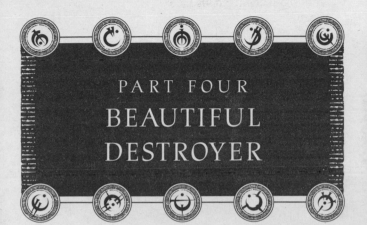

PART FOUR
BEAUTIFUL
DESTROYER

A man with a given power—such as an Allomantic ability—who then gained a Hemalurgic spike granting that same power would be nearly twice as strong as a natural unenhanced Allomancer.

An Inquisitor who was a Seeker before his transformation would therefore have an enhanced ability to use bronze. This simple fact explains how many Inquisitors were able to pierce copperclouds.

45

VIN LANDED, ABORTING HER ATTACK, but still tense, eyes narrow with suspicion. Reen was backlit by the fitful lantern light, looking much as she remembered. The four years had changed him, of course—he was taller, broader of build—but he had the same hard face unrelieved by humor. His posture was familiar to her; during her childhood, he had often stood as he did now, arms folded in disapproval.

It all returned to her. Things she thought she'd banished into the dark, quarantined parts of her mind: blows from Reen's hand, harsh criticism from his tongue, furtive moves from city to city.

And yet, tempering these memories was an insight. She was no longer the young girl who had borne her beatings in confused silence. Looking back, she could see the fear Reen had shown in the things he had done. He'd been terrified that his half-breed Allomancer of a sister would be discovered and slaughtered by the Steel Inquisitors. He'd beaten her when she made herself stand out. He'd yelled at her when she was too competent. He'd moved her when he'd feared that the Canton of Inquisition had caught their trail.

Reen had died protecting her. He had taught her paranoia and distrust out of a twisted sense of duty, for he'd believed that was the only way she would survive on the streets of the Final Empire. And she'd stayed with him, enduring the treatment. Inside—not buried all that deeply—she'd known something very important. Reen had loved her.

She met the eyes of the man standing in the cavern. Then she slowly shook her head. *No,* she thought. *It looks like him, but those eyes are* not *his.*

"Who are you?" she demanded.

"I'm your brother," the creature said, frowning. "It's only been a few years, Vin. You've grown brash—I thought I'd taught you better than that."

He certainly has the mannerisms down, Vin thought, walking forward warily. *How did he learn them? Nobody thought Reen was of any importance during his life. They wouldn't have known to study him.*

"Where did you get his bones?" Vin asked, circling the creature. The cavern floor was rough and lined with packed shelves. Darkness extended in all directions. "And how did you get the face so perfect? I thought kandra had to digest a body to make a good copy."

He had to be a kandra, after all. How else would someone manage such a perfect imitation? The creature turned, regarding her with a confused expression. "What is this nonsense? Vin, I realize that we're not the type to reunite with a fond embrace, but I *did* expect you to recognize me."

Vin ignored the complaints. Reen, then Breeze, had taught her too well. She'd know Reen if she saw him. "I need information," she said. "About one of your kind. He is called TenSoon, and he returned to your Homeland a year ago. He said he was going to be put on trial. Do you know what happened to him? I would like to contact him, if possible."

"Vin," the false Reen said firmly, "I am *not* a kandra."

We'll see about that, Vin thought, reaching out with zinc and hitting the impostor with a duralumin-fueled blast of emotional Allomancy.

He didn't so much as stumble. Such an attack would have put a kandra under Vin's control, just as it did with koloss. Vin wavered. It was growing difficult to see the impostor in the waning lantern light, even with tin enhancing her eyes.

The failed emotional Allomancy meant that he wasn't a kandra. But he wasn't Reen either. There seemed only one logical course to follow.

She attacked.

Whoever the impostor was, he knew her well enough to anticipate this move. Though he exclaimed in mock surprise, he immediately jumped back, getting out of her reach. He moved on light feet—light enough that Vin was reasonably certain he was burning pewter. In fact, she could still feel the Allomantic pulses coming from him, though for some reason it was hard for her to pin down exactly which metals he was burning.

In any case, the Allomancy was an additional confirmation of her suspicions. Reen had not been an Allomancer. True, he could have Snapped during their time apart, but she didn't think he had any noble blood to impart him an Allomantic heritage. Vin had gained her powers from her father, the parent she and Reen had not shared.

She attacked experimentally, testing this impostor's skill. He stayed out of her reach, watching carefully as she alternately prowled and attacked. She tried to corner him against the shelves, but he was too careful to be caught.

"This is pointless," the impostor said, jumping away once more.

No coins, Vin thought. *He doesn't use coins to jump.*

"You'd have to expose yourself too much to hit me, Vin," the impostor said, "and I'm obviously good enough to stay out of your reach. Can't we stop this and get on to more important matters? Aren't you even a bit curious as to what I've been doing these last four years?"

Vin backed into a crouch, like a cat preparing to pounce, and smiled.

"What?" the impostor asked.

At that moment, her stalling paid off. Behind them, the overturned lantern finally flickered out, plunging the cavern into darkness. But Vin, with her ability to pierce copper-clouds, could still sense her enemy. She'd dropped her coin pouch when she'd first sensed someone in the room—she bore no metal to give him warning of her approach.

She launched herself forward, intending to grab her enemy around the neck and pull him into a pin. The Alloman-tic pulses didn't let her see him, but they did tell her exactly where he was. That would be enough of an edge.

She was wrong. He dodged her as easily as he had before.

Vin fell still. *Tin,* she thought. *He can hear me coming.*

So she kicked over a storage shelf, then attacked again as the crash of the falling shelf echoed loudly in the chamber, cans spilling across the floor.

The impostor evaded her again. Vin froze. Something was very wrong. Somehow he always sensed her. The cavern fell silent. Neither sound nor light bounced off its walls. Vin crouched, the fingers of one hand resting lightly on the cool stone before her. She could feel the thumping, his Allomantic power washing across her in waves. She focused on it, trying to differentiate the metals that had produced it. Yet the pulses felt opaque. Muddled.

There's something familiar about them, she realized. *When I first sensed this impostor, I thought . . . I thought he was the mist spirit.*

There was a reason the pulses felt familiar. Without the light to distract her, making her connect the figure with Reen, she could see what she'd been missing.

Her heart began to beat quickly, and for the first time this evening—imprisonment included—she began to feel afraid. The pulses felt exactly like the ones she'd felt a year ago. The pulses that had led her to the Well of Ascension.

"Why have you come here?" she whispered to the blackness.

Laughter. It rang in the empty cavern, loud, free. The thumpings approached, though no footsteps marked the thing's movement. The pulses suddenly grew enormous and overpowering. They washed across Vin, unbounded by the cavern's echoes, an unreal sound that passed through things both living and dead. She stepped backward in the darkness, and nearly tripped over the shelves she'd knocked down.

I should have known you wouldn't be fooled, a kindly voice said in her head. The thing's voice. She'd heard it only once before, a year ago, when she'd released it from its imprisonment in the Well of Ascension.

"What do you want?" she whispered.

You know what I want. You've always known.

And she did. She had sensed it in the moment when she had touched the thing. Ruin. It had very simple desires. To see the world come to its end.

"I will stop you," she said. Yet it was hard to not feel foolish speaking the words to a force she did not understand, a thing that existed beyond men and beyond worlds.

It laughed again, though this time the sound was only inside her head. She could still feel Ruin pulsing—though not from any specific place. It surrounded her. She forced herself to stand up straight.

Ah, Vin, Ruin said, its voice almost fatherly in tone. *You act as if I were your enemy.*

"You are my enemy. You seek to end the things I love."

And is an ending always bad? it asked. *Must not all things, even worlds, someday end?*

"There is no need to hasten that end," Vin said. "No reason to force it."

All things are subject to their own nature, Vin, Ruin said, seeming to flow around her. She could feel its touch upon her—wet and delicate, like mist. *You cannot blame me for being what I am. Without me, nothing would end. Nothing* could *end. And therefore nothing could grow. I am life. Would you fight life itself?*

Vin fell silent.

Do not mourn because the time of this world's end has arrived, Ruin said. *That end was ordained from the very moment of the world's conception. There is a beauty in death—the beauty of finality, the beauty of completion.*

For nothing is truly complete until the day it is at last destroyed.

"Enough," Vin snapped, feeling alone and smothered in the chill darkness. "Stop taunting me. Why have you come here?"

Come here? it asked. *Why do you ask that?*

"What is your purpose in appearing now?" Vin said. "Have you simply come to gloat over my imprisonment?"

I have not just appeared, Vin, Ruin said. *Why, I have never left. I've always been with you. A part of you.*

"Nonsense," Vin said. "You only just revealed yourself."

I revealed myself to your eyes, yes, Ruin said. *But I see that you do not understand. I've always been with you, even when you could not see me.*

It paused, and there was silence both outside and inside her head.

When you're alone, no one can betray you, a voice whispered in the back of her mind. Reen's voice. The voice she heard sometimes, almost real, like a conscience. She'd taken it for granted that the voice was merely part of her psyche—something left over from Reen's teachings. An instinct.

Anyone will betray you, Vin, the voice said, repeating a bit of advice it commonly gave. As it spoke, it slowly slid from Reen's voice into that of Ruin. *Anyone.*

I've always been with you. You've heard me in your mind since your first years of life.

Ruin's escape deserves some explanation. This is a thing that even I had a problem understanding.

Ruin could not have used the power at the Well of Ascension. It was of Preservation, Ruin's fundamental opposite. Indeed, a direct confrontation of these two forces would have caused the destruction of both.

However, Ruin's prison was fabricated of that power. Therefore it was attuned to the power of Preservation—the very power of the Well. When that power was released and dispersed rather than utilized, it acted as a key. The subsequent "unlocking" is what freed Ruin.

46

"ALL RIGHT," BREEZE SAID, "SO does somebody want to speculate on how our team's spy ended up becoming a pseudo-religious vigilante freedom fighter?"

Sazed shook his head. They sat in their cavern lair beneath the Canton of Inquisition. Breeze, declaring that he was tired of travel rations, had ordered several of the soldiers to break open some of the cavern's supplies to prepare a more suitable meal. Sazed might have complained, but the truth was that the cavern was so well stocked that even a determinedly eating Breeze wouldn't be able to make a dent in it.

They had waited all day for Spook to return to the lair. Tensions in the city were high, and most of their contacts had gone to ground, weathering the Citizen's paranoia regarding a rebellion. Soldiers walked the streets, and a sizable contingent had set up camp right outside the Ministry building. Sazed was worried that the Citizen had associated Breeze and Sazed with Spook's appearance at the executions. It seemed that their days of moving about freely in the city were at an end.

"Why hasn't he come back?" Allrianne asked. She and Breeze sat at a fine table pilfered from an empty nobleman's mansion. They had changed into their fine clothing—a suit on Breeze, a peach dress on Allrianne. They always changed as soon as possible, perhaps eager to reaffirm to themselves who they really were.

Sazed did not dine with them; he didn't have much of an appetite. Captain Goradel leaned against a bookcase a short distance away, determined to keep a close eye on his charges. Though the good-natured man wore his usual smile, Sazed could tell from the orders he'd given his soldiers that he was worried about the possibility of an assault. He made certain that Breeze, Allrianne, and Sazed stayed within the protective confines of the cavern. Better to be trapped than dead.

"I'm sure the boy is fine, my dear," Breeze said, answering Allrianne's question. "It's likely he hasn't returned because he fears implicating us in what he did today."

"Either that," Sazed said, "or he can't get past the soldiers watching outside."

"He sneaked into a burning building while we were watching, my dear man," Breeze said, "I doubt he'd have trouble with a bunch of toughs, especially now that it's dark out."

Allrianne shook her head. "It would have been better if he'd managed to sneak *out* of that building as well, rather than jumping off the roof in front of everyone."

"Perhaps," Breeze said. "But part of being a vigilante rebel is letting your enemies know what you are about. The psychological effect produced by leaping from a burning building carrying a child is compelling indeed. And to do that right in front of the tyrant who tried to execute said child? I wasn't aware that dear little Spook had such a flair for drama!"

"He's not so little anymore, I think," Sazed said quietly. "We have a habit of ignoring Spook too much."

"Habits come from reinforcement, my dear man," Breeze said, wagging a fork at Sazed. "We paid little attention to the lad because he rarely had an important role to play. It isn't his fault—he was simply young."

"Vin was young as well," Sazed noted.

"Vin, you must admit, is something of a special case."

Sazed couldn't argue with that.

"In any case," Breeze said, "when we examine the facts, what happened isn't all that surprising. Spook has had months to become known to Urteau's underground population, and he is of the Survivor's own crew. It is logical that they would begin to look to him to save them, much as Kelsier saved Luthadel."

"We're forgetting one thing, Lord Breeze," Sazed said. "He jumped from a rooftop ledge two stories up and landed on a cobbled street. Men do not survive falls such as that without broken bones."

Breeze hesitated. "Staged, you think? Perhaps he worked out some kind of landing platform to soften the fall?"

Sazed shook his head. "I believe it a stretch to assume that Spook could plan, and execute, a staged rescue like that. He would have needed the aid of the underground, which would have ruined the effect. If they knew that his survival was a trick, then we wouldn't have heard the rumors we did about him."

"What then?" Breeze asked, shooting a glance at Allrianne. "You're not truly suggesting that Spook has been *Mistborn* all this time, are you?"

"I do not know," Sazed said softly.

Breeze shook his head, chuckling. "I doubt he could have hidden that from us, my dear man. Why, he would have had to go through that entire mess of overthrowing the Lord Ruler, then the fall of Luthadel, without ever revealing that he was anything more than a Tineye! I refuse to accept that."

Or, Sazed thought, *you refuse to accept that you wouldn't have detected the truth.* Still, Breeze had a point. Sazed had known Spook as a youth. The boy had been awkward and shy, but he hadn't been deceitful. It was truly a stretch to imagine him having been a Mistborn from the beginning.

Yet Sazed had seen that fall. He had seen the grace of the jump, the distinctive poise and natural dexterity of one burning pewter. Sazed found himself wishing for his copperminds so that he could search for references about people spontaneously manifesting Allomantic powers. Could a man be a Misting early in life, then transform into a full Mistborn later?

It was a simple thing, related to his duties as an ambassador. Perhaps he could spend a little time going through his stored memories, seeking examples. . . .

He quashed that line of thought. *Don't be silly,* he thought. *You're just looking for excuses. You* know *that it's impossible for an Allomancer to gain new powers. You won't find any examples because there aren't any.*

He didn't need to go through his metalminds. He had set those aside for a very good reason—he could not be a Keeper, could not share the knowledge he'd collected, until he could sort the truth from the lies.

I've let myself get distracted lately, he thought with determination, rising from his place and leaving the others. He walked over to his room in the cache, with the sheets hung there cutting off his view of the others. Sitting on the table was his portfolio. In the corner, next to a shelf full of cans, sat his sack full of metalminds.

No, Sazed thought. *I made a promise to myself. I will keep it. I will not allow myself to become a hypocrite merely because some new religion appears and waves at me. I will be strong.*

He sat down at the table, opening his portfolio, and took out the next sheet in the line. It listed the tenets of the Nelazan people, who had worshipped the god Trell. Sazed had always been partial to this religion because of its focus on learning and the study of mathematics and the heavens.

He'd saved it for near the end, but had done so more out of worry than anything else. He'd wanted to put off what he'd known would happen.

Sure enough, as he read about the religion, he saw the holes in its doctrines. True, the Nelazans had known a great deal about astronomy, but their teachings on the afterlife were sketchy—almost whimsical. Their doctrine was purposefully vague. They'd taught, then allowed all men to discover truth for themselves. Reading this, however, left Sazed frustrated. What good was a religion without answers? Why believe in something if the response to half of his questions was "Ask Trell, and he will answer"?

He didn't dismiss the religion immediately. He forced himself to put it aside, acknowledging that he wasn't in the right mood for studying. He wasn't in the mood for much of anything at all.

What if Spook really has become Mistborn? he wondered, his mind drawn back to the previous conversation. It seemed impossible. Yet a lot of things they thought they'd known about Allomancy—such as the existence of only ten metals—had turned out to be falsehoods taught by the Lord Ruler in order to hide powerful secrets.

Perhaps it *was* possible for an Allomancer to spontaneously manifest new powers. Or perhaps there was a more mundane reason Spook had managed such a high fall. It could be related to the thing that made Spook's eyes so sensitive. Drugs perhaps?

Either way, Sazed's worry about what was happening kept him from being able to focus on studying the Nelazan religion as he should. He kept getting the feeling that something very important was occurring. And Spook was at the center of it.

Where was that boy?

"I know why you're so sad," Spook said.

Beldre turned, the surprise clear on her face. She didn't

see him at first. He must have been too deep in the misty shadows. It was growing hard for him to tell.

He stepped forward, moving across the plot of land that had once been a garden outside the Citizen's home. "I figured it out," Spook said. "At first, I thought that sadness had to do with this garden. It must have been beautiful once. You would have seen it in its glory, before your brother ordered all ornamental gardens plowed under. You were related to nobility, and probably lived in their society."

Her eyes widened further at this.

"Yes, I know," Spook said. "Your brother is an Allomancer. He's a Coinshot; I felt his Pushes. That day at Marketpit."

She remained silent—more beautiful than the garden could ever have been—though she did take a step backward as her gaze finally found him in the mists.

"Eventually," Spook continued, "I decided that I must be wrong. Nobody mourns so much for a simple garden, no matter how lovely. After that, I thought the sadness in your eyes must come from being forbidden to take part in your brother's councils. He always sends you out into the garden when he meets with his most important officials. I know what it's like to feel useless and excluded among important people."

He took another step forward. The rough earth lay torn beneath his feet, covered by an inch of ash, the dreary remnants of what had once been fertile ground. To his right stood the lone shrub that Beldre often came to gaze at. He didn't look toward it; he kept his eyes on her.

"I was wrong," he said. "Being forbidden your brother's conferences would lead to frustration, but not such pain. Not such regret. I know that sorrow now. I killed for the first time this afternoon. I helped overthrow empires, then helped build them anew. And I'd never killed a man. Not until today."

He stopped, then looked into her eyes. "Yes, I know that sorrow. What I'm trying figure out is why *you* feel it."

She turned away. "You shouldn't be here," she said. "There are guards watching—"

"No," Spook said. "Not anymore. Quellion sent too many men into the city—he's afraid that he'll suffer a revolution like the one in Luthadel. Like the one he inspired here when he seized power. He's right to be afraid, but he was wrong to leave his own palace so poorly guarded."

"Kill him," Kelsier whispered. "Quellion is inside; this is the perfect chance. He deserves it, you know he does."

No, Spook thought. *Not today. Not in front of her.*

Beldre glanced back at him, her eyes growing hard. "Why have you come? To taunt me?"

"To tell you that I understand," Spook said.

"How can you say that?" she said. "You don't understand me—you don't know me."

"I think I do," Spook said. "I saw your eyes today, when you watched those people being marched to their deaths. You feel guilty. Guilty for your brother's murders. You sorrow because you feel you should be able to stop him." He took a step forward. "You can't, Beldre. He's been corrupted by his power. He might once have been a good man, but no longer. Do you realize what he's doing? Your brother is murdering people to get Allomancers. He captures them, then threatens to kill their families unless they do as he asks. Are those the actions of a good man?"

"You are a simplistic fool," Beldre whispered, though she wouldn't meet his eyes.

"I know," Spook said. "What are a few deaths when it comes to securing the stability of a kingdom?" He shook his head. "He's killing children, Beldre. And he's doing it merely to cover up the fact that he's gathering Allomancers."

Beldre was silent for a moment. "Go," she finally said.

"I want you to come with me."

She looked up.

"I'm going to overthrow your brother," Spook said. "I am a member of the Survivor's own crew. We took down the Lord Ruler—Quellion will hardly provide us with a challenge. You don't have to be here when he falls."

Beldre snorted quietly in derision.

"It's not just about your safety," Spook said. "If you join with us, it will be a strong blow to your brother. Perhaps it will convince him that he is wrong. There could be a more peaceful way of making this happen."

"I'm going to start screaming in three heartbeats," Beldre said.

"I don't fear your guards," Spook said.

"I don't doubt that," Beldre said. "But if they come, you'll have to kill again."

Spook wavered. But he stayed where he was, calling her bluff.

So she started screaming.

"Go kill him!" Kelsier said over her screams. "Now, before it's too late! Those guards you killed—they were only following orders. *Quellion,* he's the true monster."

Spook ground his teeth in frustration, then finally ran, fleeing from Beldre and her screams, leaving Quellion alive.

For the moment.

The group of rings, clasps, ear loops, bracelets, and other bits of metal gleamed on the table like a treasure hoard of legend. Of course, most of the metals were rather mundane. Iron, steel, tin, copper. Little gold, and no atium.

Yet to a Feruchemist, the metals were worth far more than their economic value. They were batteries, stores that could be filled, then drawn upon. One made of pewter, for instance, could be filled with strength. Filling it would drain the Feruchemist of strength for a time—making him weak enough that simple tasks grew difficult—but the price was worthwhile. For when necessary, he could draw that strength forth.

Many of these metalminds spread out on the table in front of Sazed, save for the rings, were empty at the moment. Sazed had last used them during the horrific battle that had ended with the fall—then rescue—of Luthadel over a year before. That battle had left him drained in more ways than one.

At the center of the collection were the most important metalminds of all. Four bracers—meant to clasp onto the upper or lower arms—sat gleaming and polished, made of the purest copper. They were the largest of his metalminds, for they held the most. Images, thoughts, or sounds that were stored away in copperminds wouldn't decay or change, as memories could while held in the mind.

When Sazed had been a young man, an older Feruchemist had read out the entire contents of his copperminds. Sazed had stored the knowledge in his own; they contained the sum total of Keeper knowledge. The Lord Ruler had worked hard to smother people's memories of the past. But the Keepers had gathered them—stories of how the world had been before the ash came and the sun had turned red. The Keepers had memorized the names of places and kingdoms, the wisdom of those who were lost.

And they had memorized the religions that had been forbidden by the Lord Ruler. These he had worked the most diligently to destroy, so the Keepers had worked with equal diligence to rescue and secure them so that someday they could be taught again. Above all, the Keepers had searched for one thing: knowledge of their own religion, the beliefs of the Terris people, forgotten during the destructive chaos following the Lord Ruler's ascension. However, despite centuries of work, the Keepers had never recovered this knowledge most precious of all.

I wonder what would have happened if we had *found it,* Sazed thought, picking up a steelmind and quietly polishing it. *Probably nothing.* He'd given up on his work with the religions in his portfolio for the moment, feeling too discouraged to study.

There were fifty religions left in his portfolio. Why was he deluding himself, hoping to find any more truth in them than he had in the previous two hundred and fifty? None of the religions had managed to survive the years. Shouldn't he simply let them be? Looking through them seemed part of the great fallacy in the work of the Keepers. They'd struggled to remember the beliefs of men, but those beliefs had already proven they lacked the resilience to survive. Why bring them back to life? That seemed as pointless as reviving a sickly animal so it could fall to predators again.

As Sazed polished, out of the corner of his eye he saw Breeze watching. The Soother had come to Sazed's "room," complaining that he couldn't sleep, not with Spook still outside somewhere. Sazed had nodded, but continued his task. He didn't wish to get into a conversation; he wanted to be alone.

Breeze, unfortunately, stood and came over. "Sometimes I don't understand you, Sazed," Breeze said.

"I do not endeavor to be mysterious, Lord Breeze," Sazed said, moving on to a small bronze ring.

"Why take such good care of them?" Breeze asked. "You never wear them anymore. In fact, you seem to spurn them."

"I do not spurn the metalminds, Lord Breeze. In a way, they are the only sacred thing I have left in my life."

"But you don't wear them either."

"No. I do not."

"But why?" Breeze asked. "You think that she would have wanted this? She was a Keeper too—do you honestly think she'd want you to give up your metalminds?"

"This particular habit of mine is *not* about Tindwyl."

"Oh?" Breeze asked, sighing as he seated himself at the table. "What do you mean? Because honestly, Sazed, you're confusing me. I understand people. It bothers me that I can't understand you."

"After the Lord Ruler's death," Sazed said, putting down the ring, "do you know what I spent my time doing?"

"Teaching," Breeze said. "You left to go and restore the lost knowledge to the people of the Final Empire."

"And did I ever tell you how that teaching went?"

Breeze shook his head.

"Poorly," Sazed said, picking up another ring. "The people didn't really care. They weren't interested in the religions of the past. And why should they have been? Why worship something that people *used* to believe in?"

"People are always interested in the past, Sazed."

"Interested, perhaps," Sazed said, "but interest is not faith. These metalminds, they are a thing of museums and old libraries. They are of little use to modern people. During the years of the Lord Ruler's reign, we Keepers pretended that we were doing vital work. We *believed* that we were doing vital work. Yet in the end, nothing we did had any real value. Vin didn't need this knowledge to kill the Lord Ruler.

"The thoughts in these metalminds will die with me. And at times I can't make myself regret that fact. This is not an era for scholars and philosophers. Scholars and philosophers do not help feed starving children."

"So you don't wear them anymore?" Breeze said. "Because you think they're useless?"

"More than that," Sazed said. "To wear these metalminds would be to pretend. I would be pretending that I find the things in them to be of use, and I have not yet decided whether that is true. To wear them now would seem a betrayal. I set them aside, for I can do them no justice. I'm not ready to believe, as we did before, that gathering knowledge and religions is more important than taking action. Perhaps if the Keepers had fought, rather than simply memorized, the Lord Ruler would have fallen centuries ago."

"But *you* resisted, Sazed," Breeze said. "You fought."

"I don't represent myself any longer, Lord Breeze," Sazed said softly. "I represent all Keepers, since I am apparently the last. And I, as the last, do not believe in the things I once taught. I cannot with good conscience imply that I am the Keeper I once was."

Breeze sighed, shaking his head. "You don't make sense."

"It makes sense to me."

"No, I think you're just confused. This may not seem to you like a world for scholars, my dear friend, but I think you'll be proven wrong. It seems to me that now—suffering in the darkness that might be the end of everything—is when we need knowledge the most."

"Why?" Sazed said. "So I can teach a dying man a religion that I don't believe? To speak of a god, when I know there is no such being?"

Breeze leaned forward. "Do you really believe that? That nothing is watching over us?"

Sazed sat quietly, slowing in his polishing. "I have yet to decide for certain," he finally said. "At times I have hoped to find some truth. However, today that hope seems very distant to me. There is a darkness upon this land, Breeze, and I am not sure that we can fight it. I am not sure that I want to fight it."

Breeze looked troubled. He opened his mouth, but before he could respond, a rumble rolled through the cavern. The rings and bracers on the table quivered and clinked together as the entire room shook, and there was a clatter as some foodstuffs fell—though not too many, for Captain Goradel's men had done good work in moving most of the stockpile off the shelves and to the ground, in order to deal with the quakes.

Eventually the shaking subsided. Breeze sat with a white face, looking up at the ceiling of the cavern. "I tell you, Sazed," he said. "Every time one of those quakes comes, I wonder at the wisdom of hiding in a cave. Not the safest place during an earthquake, I should think."

"We have no other option at the moment," Sazed said.

"True, I suppose. Do . . . does it seem to you like those quakes are coming more frequently?"

"Yes," Sazed said, picking up a few fallen bracelets. "Yes, they are."

"Maybe . . . this region is more prone to them," Breeze said, not sounding convinced. He turned, glancing to the side as Captain Goradel rounded a shelf and approached them in a rush.

"Ah, come to check on us, I see," Breeze said. "We survived the quake quite handily. No need for urgency, my dear captain."

"It's not that," Goradel said, puffing slightly. "It's Lord Spook. He's returned."

Sazed and Breeze shared a look, then rose from their chairs, following Goradel to the front of the cavern. They found Spook walking down the steps. His eyes were uncovered, and Sazed saw a new hardness in the young man's expression.

We really haven't *been paying enough attention to the lad*.

The soldiers backed away. There was blood on Spook's clothing, though he didn't appear wounded. His cloak was burned in places, and the bottom ended in a charred rip.

"Good," Spook said, noticing Breeze and Sazed, "you're here. Did that quake cause any damage?"

"Spook?" Breeze asked. "No, we're all fine here. No damage. But—"

"We have little time for chatter, Breeze," Spook said, walking past them. "Emperor Venture wants Urteau, and we're going to deliver it to him. I need you to start spreading rumors in the city. It should be easy—some of the more important elements in the underworld already know the truth."

"What truth?" Breeze asked, joining Sazed as they followed Spook through the cavern.

"That Quellion is using Allomancers," Spook said, his voice echoing in the cavern. "I've now confirmed what I suspected before—Quellion recruits Mistings from the people he arrests. He rescues them from his own fires, then holds their families hostage. He relies on the very thing he's preaching against. The entire foundation for his rule, therefore, is a lie. Exposing that lie should cause the entire system to collapse."

"That's capital, we can certainly do that . . ." Breeze said, glancing at Sazed again. Spook kept going, and Sazed followed, trailing Spook as he walked through the cavern. Breeze turned away, probably to fetch Allrianne.

Spook stopped beside the water's edge. He stood there for a moment, then turned toward Sazed. "You said that you have been studying the construction that brought the water down here, diverting it from the canals."

"Yes," Sazed said.

"Is there a way to reverse the process?" Spook asked. "Make the water flood the streets again?"

"Perhaps," Sazed said. "I am not certain that I have the engineering expertise to accomplish the feat, however."

"Is there knowledge in your metalminds that would help you?" Spook asked.

"Well . . . yes."

"Then use them," Spook said.

Sazed paused, appearing uncomfortable.

"Sazed," Spook said. "We don't have much time—we have to take this city before Quellion decides to attack and destroy us. Breeze is going to spread the rumors, then I am going to find a way to expose Quellion as a liar before his people. He's an Allomancer."

"Will that be enough?"

"It will if we give them someone else to follow," Spook said, turning back to look across the waters. "Someone who can survive fires; someone who can restore water to the city streets. We'll give them miracles and a hero, then expose their leader as a hypocrite and a tyrant. Confronted with that, what would *you* do?"

Sazed didn't respond immediately. Spook made good points, even about Sazed's metalminds still being useful. Yet Sazed wasn't certain what he thought of the changes in the young man. Spook seemed to have grown far more competent, but . . .

"Spook," Sazed said, stepping in closer, speaking quietly enough that the soldiers standing behind couldn't hear. "What is it you aren't sharing with us? How did you survive the leap from that building? Why do you cover your eyes with cloth?"

"I . . ." Spook faltered, showing a hint of the insecure boy he had once been. For some reason, seeing that made Sazed more comfortable. "I don't know if I can explain, Saze," Spook said, some of his pretension evaporating.

"I'm still trying to figure it out myself. I'll explain eventually. For now, can you just trust me?"

The lad had always been a sincere one. Sazed searched those eyes, so eager.

And found something important. Spook cared. He cared about this city, about overthrowing the Citizen. He'd saved those people earlier, when Sazed and Breeze had done nothing but stand outside watching.

Spook cared, and Sazed did not. Sazed tried—he grew frustrated with himself because of his depression, which had been worse this evening than it usually was.

His emotions had been so traitorous lately. He had trouble studying, had trouble leading, had trouble being of any use whatsoever. But looking into Spook's eager eyes, he was almost able to forget his troubles for a moment.

If the lad wanted to take the lead, then who was Sazed to argue?

He glanced toward his room, where the metalminds lay. He had gone so long without them. They tempted him with their knowledge.

As long as I don't preach the religions they contain, he thought, *I'm not a hypocrite. Using the specific knowledge Spook requests will at least bring some small meaning to the suffering of those who worked to gather knowledge of engineering.*

It seemed a weak excuse. But in the face of Spook taking the lead and offering a good reason to use the metalminds, it was enough.

"Very well," Sazed said. "I shall do as you request."

Ruin's prison was not like those that hold men. He wasn't bound by bars. In fact, he could move about freely.

His prison, rather, was one of impotence. In the terms of forces and gods, this meant balance. If Ruin were to push, the prison would push back, essentially rendering Ruin powerless. And because much of his power was stripped away and hidden, he was unable to affect the world in any but the most subtle of ways.

I should stop here and clarify something. We speak of Ruin being "freed" from his prison. But that is misleading. Releasing the power at the Well tipped the aforementioned balance in Ruin's direction, but he was still too weak to destroy the world in the blink of an eye as he yearned to do. This weakness was caused by part of Ruin's power—his very body—having been taken and hidden from him.

Which was why Ruin became so obsessed with finding the hidden part of his self.

47

ELEND STOOD IN THE MISTS.

Once he had found them disconcerting. They had been the unknown—something mysterious and uninviting, that belonged to Allomancers and not to ordinary men.

Yet now he was an Allomancer. He stared up at the shifting, swirling, spinning banks of vapor. Rivers in the sky. He almost felt as if he should get pulled along in some phantom current. When he'd first displayed Allomantic powers, Vin had explained Kelsier's now-infamous motto. *The mists are our friend. They hide us. Protect us. Give us power.*

Elend continued to stare upward. It had been three days since Vin's capture.

I shouldn't have let her go, he thought again, his heart twisting within him. *I shouldn't have agreed to such a risky plan.*

Vin had always been the one to protect him. What did they do now, when she was in danger? Elend felt so inadequate. Had their situations been reversed, Vin would have found a way to get into the city and rescue him. She'd have assassinated Yomen, would have done *something.*

But Elend didn't have her flair of brash determination. He was too much of a planner and was too well acquainted with politics. He *couldn't* risk himself to save her. He'd already put himself into danger once, and in so doing had risked the fate of his entire army. He couldn't do that again, particularly not by going into Fadrex, where Yomen had already proven himself a skilled manipulator.

No further word had come from Yomen. Elend expected ransom demands, and was terrified of what he might have to do if they came. Could he trade the fate of the world for Vin's life? No. Vin had faced a similar decision at the Well of Ascension, and had chosen correctly. Elend had to follow her example, had to be strong.

Yet the thought of her captured came close to paralyzing him with dread. Only the spinning mists seemed to comfort him.

She'll be all right, he told himself, not for the first time. *She's Vin. She'll figure a way out of it. She'll be all right. . . .*

It felt that after a lifetime of finding the mists unsettling, he would now find them so comforting. Vin didn't see them that way, not anymore. Elend could sense it in the way she acted, in the words she spoke. She distrusted the mists. Even hated them. And Elend couldn't blame her. After all, they had changed—bringing destruction and death.

Yet Elend found it hard to distrust the mists. They just

felt right. How could they be his enemy? They spun, swirling around him slightly as he burned metals, like leaves spinning in a playful wind. As he stood there, they seemed to soothe away his concerns about Vin's captivity, giving him confidence that she would find a way out.

He sighed, shaking his head. Who was he to trust his own instincts about the mists over Vin's? Her instincts had been born of a lifetime of struggling to survive. What did Elend have? Instincts born of a lifetime of partygoing and dancing?

Sound came from behind him. People walking. Elend turned, eyeing a pair of servants carrying Cett in his chair.

"That damn Thug isn't around here, is he?" Cett asked as the servants set him down.

Elend shook his head as Cett waved the servants away. "No," Elend said. "He's investigating some kind of disturbance in the ranks."

"What happened this time?" Cett asked.

"Fistfight," Elend said, turning away, looking back toward Fadrex City's watch fires.

"The men are restless," Cett said. "They're a little like koloss, you know. Leave them too long, and they'll get into trouble."

Koloss are like them, *actually,* Elend thought. *We should have seen it earlier. They are men—except reduced to their most base emotions.*

Cett sat quietly in the mists for a time, and Elend continued his contemplations.

Eventually Cett spoke, his voice uncharacteristically soft. "She's as good as dead, son. You know that."

"No, I don't," Elend said.

"She's not invincible," Cett said. "She's a damn good Allomancer, true. But take her metals away . . ."

She'll surprise you, Cett.

"You don't even look worried," Cett said.

"Of course I'm worried," Elend said, growing more certain. "I just . . . well, I trust her. If anyone can get out, Vin will."

"You're in denial," Cett said.

"Perhaps."

"Are we going to attack?" Cett asked. "Try and get her back?"

"This is a siege, Cett," Elend said. "The point is to *not* attack."

"And our supplies?" Cett asked. "Demoux had to put the soldiers on half rations today. We'll be lucky not to starve ourselves before we can get Yomen to surrender."

"We have time yet," Elend said.

"Not much. Not with Luthadel in revolt." Cett was silent for a moment, then continued. "Another of my raiding parties returned today. They had the same things to report."

The same news as all the others. Elend had authorized Cett to send soldiers into nearby villages, to scare the people, perhaps pillage some supplies. Yet each of the raiding groups had returned empty-handed, bearing the same story.

The people in Yomen's kingdom were starving. Villages barely survived. The soldiers hadn't the heart to hurt them any further, and there wasn't anything to take anyway.

Elend turned toward Cett. "You think me a bad leader, don't you?"

Cett looked up, then scratched at his beard. "Yes," he admitted. "But, well . . . Elend, you've got one thing going for you as a king that I never did."

"And that is?"

He shrugged. "The people like you. Your soldiers trust you, and they know you have too kind a heart for your own good. You have a strange effect on them. Lads such as those, they should have been eager to rob villages, no matter how impoverished. Especially considering how on-edge our men are and how many fights there have been in camp. Yet they didn't. Hell, one of the groups felt so sorry for the villagers that they stayed for a few days and helped water the fields and do repairs to some of the homes!"

Cett sighed, shaking his head. "A few years ago, I would have laughed at anyone who chose loyalty as a basis for rule. But . . . with the world falling apart as it is, I think even *I* would rather have someone to trust than someone to fear. I guess that's why the soldiers act as they do."

Elend nodded.

"I thought a siege was a good idea," Cett said. "But I don't think it will work anymore, son. The ash is falling too hard now, and we don't have supplies. This whole thing is becoming a damn mess. We need to strike and take what we can from Fadrex, then retreat to Luthadel and try to hold it through the summer while our people grow crops."

Elend fell silent, then turned as he heard something else in the mists. Shouting and cursing. It was faint—Cett probably couldn't hear it. Elend left, hurrying toward the sound, leaving Cett behind.

Another fight, Elend realized as he approached one of the cooking fires. He heard yells, blustering, and the sounds of men brawling. *Cett's right. Goodhearted or not, our men are getting too restless. I need—*

"Stop this immediately!" a new voice called. Ahead, through the dark mists, Elend could see figures moving about the firelight. He recognized the voice; General Demoux had arrived on the scene.

Elend slowed. Better to let the general deal with the disturbance. There was a big difference between being disciplined by one's military commander and one's emperor. The men would be better off if Demoux was the one to punish them.

However, they kept fighting.

"Stop this!" Demoux yelled again, moving into the conflict. A few of the brawlers listened to him, pulling back. The rest paid him no heed. Demoux pushed himself into the melee, reaching to pull apart two of the combatants.

And one of them punched him. Square in the face, throwing Demoux to the ground.

Elend cursed, dropping a coin and Pushing himself forward. He fell directly into the middle of the firelight, Pushing out with a Soothing to dampen the emotions of those fighting.

"Stop!" he bellowed.

They did, freezing up, one of the soldiers standing over the fallen General Demoux.

"What is going on here?" Elend demanded, furious. The soldiers looked down. "Well?" Elend said, turning toward the man who had punched Demoux.

"I'm sorry, my lord," the man grumbled. "We just . . ."

"Speak, soldier," Elend said, pointing, Soothing the man's emotions, leaving him compliant and docile.

"Well, my lord," the man said. "They're cursed, you know. They're the reason Lady Vin got taken. They were speaking of the Survivor and his blessings, and that just smacked me as hypocrisy, you know? Then *of course* their leader would show, demanding that we stop. I just . . . well, I'm tired of listening to them, is all."

Elend frowned in anger. As he did so, a group of the army's Mistings—Ham at their head—shoved through the crowd. Ham met Elend's eyes, and Elend nodded toward the men who had been fighting. Ham made quick work of them, gathering them up for reprimand. Elend walked over, pulling Demoux to his feet. The battle-scarred general looked more shocked than anything.

"I'm sorry, my lord," Demoux said quietly. "I should have seen that coming . . . I should have been ready for it."

Elend merely shook his head. The two of them watched quietly until Ham joined them, his Mistings pushing the troublemakers away. The rest of the crowd dispersed, returning to their duties. The solitary bonfire burned alone in the night, as if shunned as a new symbol of bad luck.

"I recognized a number of those men," Ham said, joining Elend and Demoux as the troublemakers were led away. "Mistfallen."

"This is *ridiculous*," Elend said. "So they remained sick a while longer. That doesn't make them cursed!"

"You don't understand superstition, my lord," Demoux said, rubbing his chin. "The men look for someone to blame for their ill luck. And . . . well, it's easy to see why they'd be feeling their luck was bad lately. They've been hard on *anyone* who was sickened by the mists, but they're hardest on us who were out the longest."

"I refuse to accept such idiocy in my army," Elend said. "Ham, did you see one of those men strike Demoux?"

"They *hit* him?" Ham asked with surprise. "Their general?"

Elend nodded. "The big man I was talking to. Bilg is his name, I think. You know what will have to be done."

Ham cursed, turning away.

Demoux looked uncomfortable. "Maybe we could just . . . throw him in solitary confinement or something."

"No," Elend said through his teeth. "No, we hold to the law. If he'd struck his captain, maybe we could let him off. But deliberately striking one of my generals? The man will have to be executed. Discipline is falling apart as it is."

Ham wouldn't look at him. "The other fight I had to break up was also between a group of regular soldiers and some mistfallen."

Elend ground his teeth in frustration. Demoux did meet his eyes. *You know what needs to be done,* he seemed to say.

Being a king isn't always about doing what you want, Tindwyl had often said. *It's about doing what needs to be done.*

"Demoux," Elend said. "I think the problems in Luthadel are even more serious than our difficulties with discipline. Penrod looked toward us for support. I want you to gather a group of men and take them back along the canal with the messenger, Conrad. Lend aid to Penrod and bring the city back under control."

"Yes, my lord," Demoux said. "How many soldiers should I take?"

Elend met his eyes. "About three hundred should suffice." The number who were mistfallen. Demoux nodded and withdrew into the night.

"It's the right thing to do, El," Ham said softly.

"No it's not," Elend said. "Just like it's not right to have to execute a soldier because of a single lapse in judgment. But we need to keep this army together."

"I guess," Ham said.

Elend turned, glancing up through the mists. Toward Fadrex City. "Cett is correct," he finally said. "We can't simply continue to sit out here, not while the world is dying."

"So what do we do about it?" Ham asked.

Elend wavered. What to do about it indeed? Retreat and leave Vin—and probably the entire empire—to its doom? Attack, causing the deaths of thousands, becoming the conqueror he feared? Was there no other way to take the city?

Elend turned and struck out into the night. He found his way to Noorden's tent, Ham following curiously. The former obligator was awake—he kept odd hours. As Elend entered the tent, he stood hurriedly and bowed in respect.

On the table, Elend found what he wanted. The thing he had ordered Noorden to work on. Maps. Troop movements. The locations of koloss bands.

Yomen refuses to be intimidated by my forces, Elend thought. *Well, let's see if I can turn the odds against him.*

*Once "freed," Ruin was able to affect the world more directly.
The most obvious way he did this was by making the Ashmounts
emit more ash and the earth begin to break apart. As a matter of
fact, I believe that much of Ruin's energy during those last days
was dedicated to these tasks.*

*He was also able to affect and control far more people than
before. Where he had once influenced only a few select individuals, he could now direct entire koloss armies.*

48

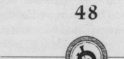

AS DAYS PASSED IN THE cavern, Vin regretted knocking over the lantern. She tried to salvage it, searching with
blind fingers. But the oil had spilled. She was locked in
darkness.

With a thing that wanted to destroy the world.

Sometimes she could sense it pulsing near her, watching
silently—like some fascinated patron at a carnival show.
Other times it vanished. Walls meant nothing to it. The first
time it disappeared, she felt a sense of relief. However, moments later she heard Reen's voice in her mind. *I haven't
left you,* it said. *I'm always here.*

The words chilled her, and she thought—just briefly—
that it had read her mind. But she decided that her thoughts
would have been easy to guess. Looking back through her
life, she realized that Ruin couldn't have spoken each and
every time she heard Reen's voice in her head. A lot of the
time she heard Reen, it was in response to what she'd been

thinking rather than what she'd been doing or saying. Since Ruin couldn't read minds, those comments couldn't have come from it.

But Ruin had been speaking to her for so long, it was difficult to separate her own memories from its influence. Yet she had to trust in the Lord Ruler's promise that Ruin couldn't read her mind. The alternative was to abandon hope. And she wouldn't do that. Each time Ruin spoke to her, it gave her clues about its nature. Those clues might give her the means to defeat it.

Defeat it? Vin thought, leaning against a rough stone wall of the cavern. *It's a force of nature, not a man. How could I even think to defeat something like that?*

Time was difficult to gauge in the perpetual blackness, but she figured from her sleep patterns that it had been around three or four days since her imprisonment.

Everyone called the Lord Ruler a god, Vin reminded herself. *I killed him.*

Ruin had been imprisoned once. That meant that it *could* be defeated, or at least bottled up. But what did it mean to imprison an abstraction—a force—such as Ruin? It had been able to speak to her while imprisoned. But its words had felt less forceful then. Less . . . directed. Ruin had acted more as an influence on her childhood, giving her impressions that manifested through memories of Reen. Almost like it had influenced her emotions. Did that mean it used Allomancy? It did indeed pulse with Allomantic power.

Zane heard voices, Vin realized. *Right before he died, he seemed to be talking to something.* She felt a chill as she rested her head against the wall.

Zane had been mad. Perhaps there was no connection between the voices he heard and Ruin. Yet it seemed too much of a coincidence. Zane had tried to get her to go with him, to seek out the source of the pulses—the ones that had eventually led her to free Ruin.

So, Vin thought, *Ruin can influence me regardless of distance or containment. And now that it has been freed, it can manifest directly. That brings up another question. Why hasn't it already destroyed us all? Why play games with armies?*

The answer to that seemed obvious. She sensed Ruin's boundless will to destroy. She felt that she knew its mind. One drive. One impulse: to ruin. So if it hadn't accomplished its goal yet, that meant it couldn't. It was hindered. Limited to indirect, gradual means of destruction—like the falling ash and the light-stealing mists.

Still, those methods *would* eventually be effective. Unless Ruin was stopped. But how?

It was imprisoned before . . . but what did the imprisoning? She'd once thought that the Lord Ruler had been the one behind Ruin's imprisonment. But that was wrong. Ruin had *already* been imprisoned when Rashek had traveled to the Well of Ascension and slain Alendi to stop the presumed Hero of Ages from doing what Vin had eventually done: accidentally releasing Ruin.

Ironically, it had been *better* that a selfish man such as Rashek had taken the power. For he had kept the power for himself, rather than giving it up and freeing the enemy they now faced.

Ruin's prior imprisonment meant that the Deepness—the mists—wasn't related to Ruin. Or at least the connection wasn't as simple as she'd assumed. Letting Ruin go hadn't been what had prompted the mists to start coming during the day and killing people. In fact, the daymists had started to appear as much as a year *before* she'd released Ruin, and the mists had started killing people in Luthadel some hours before Vin had found her way to the Well.

So . . . what do I know? Ruin was imprisoned long ago. Perhaps by something that I can find and use again?

She stood up. Too much sitting and thinking had made her restless, and she began to walk, feeling her way along the wall.

During her first day of imprisonment she'd begun, by

touch, to scout the cavern. It was huge like the other caches, and the process had taken her several days. But she'd had nothing else to do. Unlike the cache in Urteau, this one had no pool or water source. And as Vin investigated, she discovered that Yomen had removed all of the water barrels from what she assumed was their place in the far right corner. He'd left the canned food and other supplies— the cavern was so enormous that he would have had trouble finding time to remove everything, let alone finding a place to store it somewhere else—but not the water.

That left Vin with a problem. She felt her way along the wall, locating a shelf where she'd set an open can of stew. Even with pewter and a rock, it had taken her a frightfully long time to get into the can. Yomen had been clever enough to remove the tools she could have used for opening the food stores, and Vin only had one vial's worth of pewter remaining. She'd opened some ten cans of food on her first day, burning away what pewter she'd had inside her. That food was already dwindling, and she was feeling the need for water—the stew did little to quench her thirst.

She picked up the can of stew, carefully eating only a mouthful. It was almost gone. The taste reminded her of the hunger that was a growing complement to her thirst. She pushed the feeling away. She'd dealt with hunger for her entire childhood. It was nothing new, although it had been years since she'd last felt it.

She moved on, trailing fingers on the wall to keep her bearings. It seemed such a clever way to kill a Mistborn. Yomen couldn't defeat her, so he trapped her instead. Now he could merely wait for her to die of dehydration. Simple, effective.

Perhaps Ruin is speaking to Yomen too, she thought. *My imprisonment could all be part of Ruin's plan.*

Whatever that is.

Why had Ruin chosen her? Why not lead someone else to the Well of Ascension? Someone easier to control? She could understand why Ruin had chosen Alendi all those years before. During Alendi's time, the Well had been sequestered high in the mountains. It would have been a difficult trek, and Ruin would have needed the right person to plan, then survive, the expedition.

However, during Vin's day the Well had somehow been moved to Luthadel. Or perhaps Luthadel had been built on top of the Well. Either way it was there, right beneath the Lord Ruler's palace. Why had Ruin waited so long to free itself? And of all the people it could have chosen as its pawn, why Vin?

She shook her head as she arrived at her destination— the only other thing of interest in the vast cavern. A metal plaque on the wall. She reached up, brushing her fingers across the slick steel. She'd never been an excellent reader, and the last year—spent in war and travel—hadn't afforded her much time to improve her abilities. So it had taken her some time, feeling her way across each groove carved into the metal, to figure out what was written on the plaque.

There was no map. Or at least not like the ones in the previous storage caverns. Instead there was a simple circle with a dot at the center. Vin wasn't certain what it was supposed to mean. The text was equally frustrating. Vin ran her fingers across the grooves, though she had long since memorized what the words said.

I have failed you.

I have planned these caverns, knowing a calamity is coming, hoping that I might find some secret that would be of use should I fall to the thing's scheming. Yet I have nothing. I do not know how to defeat it. The only thing I can think of is to keep it at bay by taking the power at the Well for myself when it returns.

However, if you are reading this, I have failed. That means I am dead. As I write this, I find that prospect to be less tragic than I might previously have assumed.

I would rather not deal with the thing. It has been my constant companion, the voice that whispers to me always, telling me to destroy, begging me to give it freedom.

I fear that it has corrupted my thoughts. Though it cannot sense what I think, it can speak inside my head. Eight hundred years of this has made it difficult to trust my own mind. Sometimes I hear the voices and simply assume that I am mad.

That would certainly be preferable.

I do know that these words must be written in steel to be preserved. I have written them in a steel sheet, then ordered them scribed into a plaque, knowing that in doing so I reveal my weakness to my own priests. The thing has whispered to me that I am a fool to expose myself by writing this and letting others see it.

That is primarily why I decided to go through with the creation of this plaque. Doing so seemed to make the thing angry. That is reason enough, I think. It is good that some few of my loyal priests know of my weakness, if only for the good of the empire, should I somehow fall.

I have tried to be a good ruler. At first I was too young, too angry. I made mistakes. Yet I have tried so hard. I nearly destroyed the world with my arrogance, and I fear I have nearly destroyed it again through my rule. I can do better. I will do better. I will create a land of order.

The thoughts in my mind, however, make me wonder how much of what I do has been twisted from my original intentions. At times my empire seems a place of peace and justice. Yet if that is so, why can I not stop the rebellions? They cannot defeat me, and I must order them slaughtered each time they rise up. Can they not see the perfection of my system?

Regardless, this is not the place for justification. I need no justification, for I am—after a form—God.

Yet I know there is something greater than I. If I can be destroyed, it will be the cause of that destruction.

I have no advice to give. It is more powerful than I am. It is more powerful than this world. In fact, it claims to have created this world. It will destroy us all eventually.

Perhaps these storages will let mankind survive a little longer. Perhaps not. I am dead. I doubt that I should care.

Still, I do. For you are my people. I am the Hero of Ages. That is what it must mean: Hero of Ages, a hero that lives through the ages, as I do.

Know that the thing's power is not complete. Fortunately, I have hidden its body well.

And that was the end. Vin tapped the plaque with frustration. Everything about the words on it seemed contrived to frustrate her. The Lord Ruler had led them on this grand chase, then at the end he offered no hope? Elend was betting so much on what this plaque would contain, yet it was virtually worthless. At least the other ones had contained some relevant information about a new metal or the like.

I have failed you. It was infuriating—almost crushingly so—to come all this way, then find that the Lord Ruler had been as stumped as they were. And if he'd known more—as his words implied that he did—why hadn't he *shared* it on the plaque? Yet she could sense his instability through these words—his wavering back and forth from contrition to arrogance. Perhaps that was Ruin's influence on him. Or perhaps it was simply the way he had always been. Either way, Vin suspected that the Lord Ruler couldn't have told her much more that would have been of use. He'd done what he could, holding Ruin at bay for a thousand years. It had corrupted him, perhaps driven him mad.

That didn't stop her from feeling a sharp sense of disappointment at what the plaque contained. The Lord Ruler had been given a thousand years to worry about what would

happen to the land if he were killed before the power returned to the Well, and even he hadn't been able to come up
with a way out of the problem.

She looked up toward the plaque, invisible in the darkness.

There has to be a way! she thought, refusing to accept
the Lord Ruler's implication that they were doomed. *What
was it you wrote at the bottom? "I have hidden its body
well."*

That part seemed important. However, she hadn't been—

A sound rang through the darkness.

Vin turned immediately, growing tense, feeling for her
last metal vial. Proximity to Ruin had made her jumpy, and
she found her heart beating with anxiety as she listened to
the echoing sounds—stone grinding against stone.

The door to the cavern was opening.

One might ask why Ruin couldn't have used Inquisitors to release him from his prison. The answer to this is simple enough, if one understands the workings of power.

Before the Lord Ruler's death, he maintained too tight a grip on the Inquisitors to let Ruin control them directly. Even after the Lord Ruler's death, however, such a servant of Ruin could never have rescued him. The power in the Well was of Preservation, and an Inquisitor could only have taken it by first removing his Hemalurgic spikes. That, of course, would have killed him.

Thus, Ruin needed a much more indirect way to achieve his purpose. He needed someone he hadn't tainted too much, but someone he could lead by the nose, carefully manipulating.

49

SAZED MADE A SMALL NOTATION on his diagram, comparing measurements of the waterway. From what he could tell, the Lord Ruler hadn't needed to do much to create the underground lake. A small amount of water had already been flowing into the cavern. The Lord Ruler's engineers had simply widened the passageways, bringing in a steadier, surer flow that outpaced the natural drainage.

The result was an aquifer of good size. Some machinery in a side cave proved to be a mechanism for plugging the outlets at the bottom—presumably so that one could keep the water reserve from escaping, should something happen to the incoming supply. Unfortunately, there was no existing way to block off the inlets.

Before the Lord Ruler's creation of the reservoir, most of the water had flowed instead into the canals that were now the streetslots. Sazed assumed that if he could stop the water from entering the cavern, it would refill the canals.

I'll need to know more about water pressure, Sazed thought, *so I can provide enough weight to plug those inlets.* He thought he'd seen a book on the subject within his metalmind.

He leaned back in his chair, tapping his metalmind. Memory blossomed in his head as he withdrew a section of text: an index he'd made listing the titles of books he had in his storage. As soon as he pulled the text out, the words became as clear to him as if he'd just read and memorized them. He scanned through the list quickly, seeking the title he needed. When he found it, he scribbled it on a piece of paper. Then he placed the list inside his coppermind again.

The experience was odd. After replacing the list, he could recollect having drawn the material out—but he had no memory whatsoever of what the index had contained. There was a blank in his mind. Only the words scribbled on the paper explained things that he'd known mere seconds before. With that title, he could draw the appropriate book into his mind in its entirety. He selected the chapters he wanted, then returned the rest to the coppermind lest they decay.

And with those chapters, his knowledge of engineering was as fresh as if he'd just read and studied the book. He easily figured out the proper weights and balances he'd need to craft barriers that should return water to the streets above.

He worked alone, sitting at a fine salvaged desk, a lantern lighting the cavern around him. Even with the knowledge provided by his copperminds it was difficult work, with many calculations—not exactly the kind of research he was accustomed to. Fortunately, a Keeper's copperminds were not limited to his or her own interests. Each Keeper kept all of the knowledge. Sazed could vaguely remember the years he'd spent listening and memorizing. He'd only needed to know the information well enough to remember it for a short time, then he could dump it into a coppermind. In that way, he was one of both the smartest and the most ignorant men who had ever lived—he had memorized so much, but had intentionally forgotten it all.

Regardless, he had access to texts on engineering as well as religion. Knowing such things did not make him a brilliant mathematician or architect, but it did give him enough competence to make him a good deal better than a layman.

As he worked, he was finding it more and more difficult to deny that scholarship was something at which he excelled. He was not a leader. He was not a diplomat. Even while he served as Elend's chief ambassador, he'd spent much of his time looking through his religions. Now, when he should be heading the team in Urteau, more and more he found himself letting Spook take the lead.

Sazed was a man of research and letters. He found contentment in his studies. Although engineering wasn't an area he particularly enjoyed, the truth was he'd much rather study—no matter what the topic—than do anything else. *Is it such a shameful thing,* he thought, *to be the man who likes to provide information for others, rather than the one who has to use that information?*

The tapping of a cane on the ground announced Breeze's arrival. The Soother didn't need a cane to walk, but he preferred to carry one to look more gentlemanly. Of all the skaa thieves Sazed had known, Breeze did by far the best job of acting as a nobleman.

Sazed quickly jotted down a few more notations, then returned the chapters on water pressure to his coppermind. No need to let them decay while speaking to Breeze. For of course Breeze would want to talk. Sure enough, as soon as he sat at Sazed's table, he scanned the diagrams, then raised an eyebrow. "That's coming along nicely, my dear man. You may have missed your calling."

Sazed smiled. "You are kind, Lord Breeze, though I fear an engineer would find this plan unsightly. Still, I think it will be sufficient."

"You can really do it?" Breeze asked. "Make the waters flow as the lad asked? Is it even possible?"

"Oh, it is quite possible," Sazed said. "My expertise— not the plausibility of the task—is the item in question. The waters once filled those canals, and they can do so again. In fact, I believe that their return will be far more spectacular than the original flow. Before, much of the water was already diverted into these caverns. I should be able to block most of that and return the waters above in force. Of course, if Lord Spook wishes to keep the canals flowing, then we will have to let some of the water escape down here once more. Canal works generally don't have much of a current, especially in an area where there are many locks."

Breeze raised an eyebrow.

"Actually," Sazed continued, "canals are far more fascinating than you might expect. Take, for instance, the methods of transforming a natural river into a canal—making it what is called a navigation—or perhaps look at the methods of dredging used to remove silt and ash from the depths. I have one particular book by the infamous Lord Fedre, who—despite his reputation—was an absolute genius when it came to canal architecture. Why, I've had to . . ." Sazed trailed off, then smiled wanly. "I apologize. You're not interested in this, are you?"

"No," Breeze said, "but it's enough that *you* are, Sazed. It's good to see you excited about your studies again. I don't know what it was you were working on before, but it always bothered me that you wouldn't share it with anyone. Seemed like you were almost ashamed of what you were doing. Now, however—this is the Sazed I remember!"

Sazed looked down at his scribbled notes and diagrams. It was true. The last time that he had been so excited about a line of study was . . .

When he'd been with her. Working on their collection of myths and references regarding the Hero of Ages.

"In truth, Lord Breeze," Sazed said, "I do feel somewhat guilty."

Breeze rolled his eyes. "Sazed. Do you *always* have to be

feeling guilty about something? Back in the original crew, you felt you weren't doing enough to help us overthrow the Lord Ruler. Then once we killed him, you were distraught because you weren't doing what the other Keepers told you to. Exactly how you go about feeling guilty for *studying,* of all things?"

"I enjoy it."

"That's wonderful, my dear man," Breeze said. "Why be ashamed of that enjoyment? It's not as if you enjoy killing puppies or something like that. True, I think you're a bit crazy, but if you want to enjoy something so esoteric, then you should feel free. It leaves more room for those of us who prefer more common delights—such as getting drunk on Straff Venture's finest wines."

Sazed smiled. He knew that Breeze was Pushing on his emotions, making him feel better, but he did not rebel against the emotions. The truth was, he *did* feel good. Better than he had in some time.

Though still . . .

"It is not so straightforward, Lord Breeze," Sazed said, setting down his pen. "I feel happy being able to simply sit and read, without having to be in charge. That is why I feel guilty."

"Not everybody is meant to be a leader, Sazed."

"No," Sazed said, "but Lord Elend did put me in charge of securing this city. I should be planning our overthrow of the Citizen, not letting Lord Spook do it."

"My dear man!" Breeze said. "Have I taught you nothing? Being in charge isn't about *doing* anything—it's about making certain that other people do what they're supposed to! Delegation, my friend. Without it, we would have to bake our own bread and dig our own latrines!" Then Breeze leaned in. "And trust me. You don't want to taste anything I've had a hand in baking. Ever. Particularly after I've cleaned a latrine."

Sazed shook his head. "This isn't what Tindwyl would have wanted of me. She respected leaders and politicians."

"Correct me if you must," Breeze said, "but didn't she fall in love with *you,* not some king or prince?"

"Well, 'love' is perhaps too—"

"Come now, Sazed," Breeze said. "You were mooning about as surely as any teenage boy with a new fancy. And while she was a bit more reserved, she did love you. One didn't have to be a Soother to see that much."

Sazed sighed, looking down.

"Is this what she'd want of you, Sazed?" Breeze said. "To deny who you are? To become yet another stuffy politician?"

"I do not know, Lord Breeze," Sazed said softly. "I . . . I don't have her anymore. And so perhaps I can remember her by being involved in what she loved."

"Sazed," Breeze said frankly, "how is it you can be so wise in so many areas, yet be so completely *stupid* about this?"

"I . . ."

"A man *is* what he has passion about," Breeze said. "I've found that if you give up what you want most for what you *think* you should want more, you'll just end up miserable."

"And if what I want isn't what society needs?" Sazed said. "Sometimes we are required to do what we don't enjoy. That is a simple fact of life, I think."

Breeze shrugged. "I don't worry about that. I only do what I'm good at. In my case, that's making other people do things that I don't want to. It all fits together in the end."

Sazed shook his head. It wasn't that simple, and his depression lately hadn't *only* been tied to Tindwyl and her death. He had put off his study of the religions, but he knew he would be driven to return to them. The work with the canals was a welcome distraction, but even so, Sazed could feel his earlier conclusions and work looming.

He didn't *want* to discover that the last religions in the group held no answers. That was part of why it was so relaxing for him to study something else, for engineering didn't threaten his worldview. However, he could not distract himself forever. He would find the answers, or their lack, eventually. His portfolio sat beneath the desk, resting against the sack of metalminds.

For now, he allowed himself a reprieve. But even with his concern over the religions abated for the moment, there were issues that needed addressing. He nodded his head in the direction of the lake. Spook, barely visible, stood at the edge, speaking with Goradel and some of the soldiers.

"And what of him, Lord Breeze?" Sazed asked in a whisper, low enough that even Spook shouldn't be able to hear. "As I said, Emperor Venture placed me in charge of this matter. What if I let Spook take control, and then he fails? I worry that the young man is not . . . seasoned enough for this task."

Breeze shrugged. "He seems to be doing well so far. Remember how young Vin was when she killed the Lord Ruler."

"Yes," Sazed whispered, "but this situation is different. Spook seems odd lately. He is certainly hiding things from us. Why is he so determined to take this city?"

"I think it's good for the boy to show a little determination," Breeze said, sitting back in his chair. "That lad has been far too passive for most of his life."

"Do you not worry about his plan? This could easily collapse around us."

"Sazed," Breeze said. "Do you remember our meeting a few weeks back? Spook asked me why we couldn't just topple Quellion like we did the Lord Ruler."

"I remember," Sazed said. "You told him the reason we couldn't was because we didn't have Kelsier anymore."

Breeze nodded. "Well," he said softly, pointing his cane toward Spook, "my opinion has been revised. We don't have Kelsier, but it's looking more and more like we have something similar."

Sazed frowned.

"I'm not saying the lad has Kelsier's force of personality. His . . . presence. However, you've heard the reputation the boy is gaining among the people. Kelsier succeeded not because of who he was, but because of who people *thought* he was. That's something I didn't believe we could replicate. I'm starting to think I was wrong."

Sazed wasn't as easily convinced. Yet he kept his reservations to himself as he returned to his research. Spook must have noticed them looking over at him, for a few minutes later he made his way to Sazed's table. The boy blinked against the lantern light, soft though it was, and pulled up a chair. The fine furniture looked odd to Sazed, contrasted with the rows of dusty, utilitarian shelves.

Spook looked fatigued. *How long has it been since he slept?* Sazed thought. *He's still up whenever I bed down, and awake before I rise.*

"Something doesn't feel right here," Spook said.

"Oh?" Breeze asked. "Other than the fact that we're chatting beside an underground lake in a storehouse built by the Lord Ruler beneath an Inquisitor fortress?"

Spook gave the Soother a flat look, then glanced at Sazed. "I feel like we should have been attacked by now."

"What makes you say that?" Sazed asked.

"I know Quellion, Saze. The man's a bully after the classical style. He came to power through force, and he keeps control by giving the people plenty of alcohol and tiny freedoms, like letting them go to bars at night. At the same time though, he keeps everyone on the edge of fear."

"How *did* he take charge anyway?" Breeze asked. "How did he get control before some nobleman with a good set of house guards could do it?"

"Mists," Spook said. "He went out in them, and declared that anyone faithful to the Survivor would be safe in them. Then the mists started killing, and gave a handy confirmation of what he'd said. He made a big deal about the mists killing those who had evil in their hearts. The people were so worried about what was happening that they listened to him. He managed to make a law that required everyone to go out in the mists, so that they could see who died and who didn't. The ones who survived were—he declared—pure. He told them they could set up a nice little utopia. After that, they started killing nobility."

"Ah," Breeze said. "Clever."

"Yeah," Spook said. "He completely glossed over the fact that the nobility never got taken by the mists."

"Wait," Sazed said. "*What?*"

Spook shrugged. "Hard to confirm now, but that's what the stories say. The nobility seemed immune to the mistsickness. Not skaa who had noble blood, but actual nobility."

"How odd," Breeze noted.

More than odd, Sazed thought. *Downright strange. Does Elend know about this connection?* As Sazed considered it, it seemed unlikely that Elend knew. Their army and allies were all made up of skaa. The only nobility they knew were those back in Luthadel, and they had all chosen to stay inside at night rather than risk the mists.

"In any case," Spook said, "Quellion's a bully. And bullies don't like anyone in their turf who can challenge them. We should have had some kind of attempt on our lives by now."

"The lad has a point," Breeze said. "Quellion's type doesn't kill only in fancy executions. I'd bet that for every person he throws into one of those buildings, there are three dead in an alley somewhere, slowly being buried in ash."

"I've told Goradel and his men to be particularly careful," Spook said, "and I've prowled our perimeter. However, I haven't caught any assassins so much as spying on us. Quellion's troops sit out there watching us, but they're not doing anything."

Breeze rubbed his chin. "Perhaps Quellion is more afraid of us than you assume."

"Perhaps," Spook said, sighing. He rubbed his forehead.

"Lord Spook," Sazed said carefully, "you should sleep."

"I'm fine," Spook said.

If I didn't know better, I'd say he was burning pewter to stay awake, Sazed thought. *Or am I just looking for signs to confirm what I worried about before?*

We never questioned when Vin or Kelsier manifested powers beyond what normal Allomancers were capable of. Why should I be so suspicious of Spook? Is it simply be-

cause I know him too well? Do I focus on my memories of the boy when he has obviously become a man?

"Anyway," Spook said, "how goes the research?"

"Rather well, in fact," Sazed said, turning around several of his diagrams so that Spook could see them. "I am about ready to begin work on the actual construction."

"How long will it take, do you think?"

"A few weeks perhaps," Sazed said. "A short time, all things considered. Fortunately, the people who drained the canals left behind a large amount of rubble that I can use. In addition, the Lord Ruler stocked this storehouse quite well. There is timber as well as basic carpentry supplies, and even some pulley networks."

"What was that creature preparing for?" Breeze said. "Food and water I can understand. But blankets? Timber? *Pulleys?*"

"Disaster, Lord Breeze," Sazed said. "He included everything that the people would need in the event that the city was destroyed. There are bedrolls and infirmary supplies. Perhaps he feared koloss rampages."

"No," Spook said. "He prepared for exactly what is happening. Now, you'll be building something to plug the water? I kind of thought you'd just collapse the tunnels."

"Oh, goodness no," Sazed said. "We don't have the manpower or equipment to cause a cave-in. Also, I wouldn't want to do anything that would risk bringing the cavern down upon us. My plans are to build a wooden blocking mechanism that can be lowered into the current. Enough weight, along with the proper framework, should provide reinforcement to stop the flow. It's rather like the mechanisms used in the locks of canals."

"Which," Breeze added, "he'll be happy to tell you about. At length."

Sazed smiled. "I do think that—"

He was cut off, however, as Captain Goradel arrived, looking a fair bit more solemn than usual.

"Lord Spook," Goradel said. "Someone is waiting for you above."

"Who?" Spook asked, pulling his spectacles and bandage from a pocket. "Durn?"

"No, my lord. She says she's the Citizen's sister."

"I'm not here to join you," the woman—Beldre—said.

They sat in an austere audience chamber in the Inquisition building above their cavern. The room's chairs lacked any sort of cushioning, and steel plates hung on the wooden walls as decoration—to Sazed, they were uncomfortable reminders of what he had seen when he had visited the Conventical of Seran.

Beldre was a young woman with auburn hair. She wore a simple, Citizen-approved dress, dyed red. She sat with her hands in her lap, and while she met the eyes of those in the room, there was a nervous apprehension to her that weakened her position considerably.

"Why *are* you here then, my dear?" Breeze asked carefully. He sat in a chair across from Beldre. Allrianne sat at his side, watching the woman with an air of disapproval. Spook paced in the background, occasionally turning toward the window.

He thinks this is a feint, Sazed realized. *That the woman is a distraction to throw us off before we get attacked.* The boy wore his dueling canes strapped to his waist like swords. How well did he know how to fight?

"I'm here . . ." Beldre said, looking down. "I'm here because you're going to kill my brother."

"Now, where did you get an idea like that!" Breeze said. "We're in the city to forge a treaty with your brother, not assassinate him! Do we look like the types who would be good at that sort of thing?"

Beldre shot a glance at Spook.

"Him excluded," Breeze said. "Spook is harmless. Really, you shouldn't—"

"Breeze," Spook interrupted, glancing over with his strange, bandaged eyes. "That's enough. You're making us both seem like idiots. Beldre knows why we're here—everyone in the city knows."

The room fell silent.

He . . . looks a bit like an Inquisitor, wearing those spectacles beneath the bandages, Sazed thought, shivering.

"Beldre," Spook said. "You honestly expect us to think that you came here simply to plead for your brother's life?"

She glanced at Spook, defiantly meeting his eyes—or rather his bandages. "You can try to sound harsh, but I know you won't hurt me. You're of the Survivor's crew."

Spook folded his arms.

"Please," Beldre said. "Quellion is a good man like you. You have to give him more time. Don't kill him."

"You just said that you thought we would never harm you," Sazed said. "Why is your brother different?"

Beldre glanced down. "You're the ones who killed the Lord Ruler. You overthrew the entire empire. My brother doesn't believe it—he thinks that you rode the Survivor's popularity, claiming to be his friends after he'd sacrificed himself."

Spook snorted. "I wonder where your brother got an idea like that. Perhaps he knows someone else who's claimed to have the Survivor's blessing, *killing* people in his name . . ."

Beldre blushed.

"Your brother doesn't trust us," Sazed said. "Why do you?"

Beldre shrugged. "I don't know," she said quietly. "I guess . . . men who lie don't save children from burning buildings."

Sazed glanced at Spook, but couldn't read anything in the young man's hard expression. Finally Spook spoke. "Breeze, Sazed, Allrianne, outside with me. Goradel, watch her."

Spook pushed his way out into the hallway, and Sazed followed with the others. Once the door was closed, Spook turned to regard the rest of them. "Well?"

"I don't like her," Allrianne said, folding her arms.

"Of course you don't, dear," Breeze said. "You never like competition."

"Competition?" Allrianne huffed. "From a timid little thing like that? Honestly."

"What do you think, Breeze?" Spook asked.

"About the girl, or about you insulting me in there?"

"The first," Spook said. "Your pride isn't important right now."

"My dear fellow," Breeze said, "my pride is *always* important. As for the girl, I'll tell you this—she's terrified. Despite what she says, she's very, very frightened—which means that she hasn't done this sort of thing often. My guess is that she's noble."

Allrianne nodded. "Definitely. Look at her hands—when they're not shaking from fright, you can see that they're clean and soft. She grew up being pampered."

"She's obviously a bit naive," Sazed said. "Otherwise she wouldn't have come here expecting we'd listen to her, then let her go."

Spook nodded. He cocked his head, as if listening to something. Then he walked forward, pushing open the door to the room.

"Well?" Beldre asked, maintaining her false air of forcefulness. "Have you decided to listen to me?"

"In a way," Spook said. "I'm going to give you more time to explain your point. Plenty of time, actually."

"I . . . don't have long," Beldre said. "I need to get back to my brother. I didn't tell him I was leaving, and . . ." She trailed off, apparently seeing something in Spook's expression. "You're going to take me captive, aren't you?"

"Breeze," Spook said, turning. "How do you think the people would respond if I started spreading the rumor that the Citizen's own sister has turned against him, fleeing to our embassy for protection?"

Breeze smiled. "Well now. That's clever! Almost makes up for how you treated me. Have I mentioned yet how rude that was?"

"You can't!" Beldre said, standing, facing Spook. "Nobody will believe that I've deserted!"

"Oh?" Spook asked. "Did you speak to the soldiers outside before you came in here?"

"Of course not," Beldre said. "They'd have tried to stop me. I ran up the steps before they could."

"So they can confirm that you entered the building of your own will," Spook said. "Sneaking around a guard post."

"Doesn't look good," Breeze agreed.

Beldre wilted slightly, sitting down in her chair. *By the Forgotten Gods,* Sazed thought. *She really is naive. The Citizen must have expended a great deal of effort in sheltering her so.*

Of course, from what Sazed had heard, Quellion rarely let her out of his sight. She was always with him, being watched over. *How will he react?* Sazed thought with a chill. *What will he do when he learns we have her? Attack?*

Perhaps that was the plan. If Spook could force an outright attack from the Citizen, it would look bad. Especially bad when Quellion was turned back by a few soldiers—he couldn't know how well fortified their position was.

When did Spook get so clever?

Beldre looked up from her seat, a few tears of frustration gleaming in her eyes. "You can't do this. This is deceitful! What would the Survivor say if he knew what you were planning?"

"The Survivor?" Spook asked, chuckling. "I have a feeling he'd approve. If he were here, I think he'd suggest that we do this very thing."

One can see Ruin's craftiness in the meticulousness of his planning. He managed to orchestrate the downfall of the Lord Ruler only a short time before Preservation's power returned to the Well of Ascension. And then, less than two years later, he had freed himself.

On the scale of gods and their power, this tricky timing was as precise as an expert incision performed by the most talented of surgeons.

50

THE DOOR TO THE CAVERN opened.

Vin immediately downed her last vial of metals.

She jumped, tossing a coin behind her, leaping up onto the top of one of the freestanding shelves. The cavern echoed with the sound of stone grinding on stone as its door opened. Vin threw herself forward—Pushing off the coin—to shoot toward the front of the room. A crack of light outlined the door.

She gritted her teeth against the light, blinking as she landed. She pressed herself to the wall beside the door, clutching her knives, flaring pewter to help her deal with the sudden pain of the light after so long in the dark. Tears crept down her cheeks.

The door stopped moving. A solitary man stepped into the cavern, bearing a raised lantern. He wore a fine black suit and gentleman's hat.

Vin ignored him.

She slipped around the man and ducked through the door, entering the small chamber beyond. A group of startled workers shied back, dropping ropes that were connected to the door's opening mechanisms. Vin ignored these men as well, other than to shove her way through them. Dropping a coin, she Pushed herself upward. The wooden ladder's rungs became a blur beside her as she soared up and slammed into the trapdoor in the ceiling.

And bounced off it with a grunt of pain.

She desperately caught rungs of the ladder as she began to fall, ignoring the sudden sting in her shoulder from hitting so hard. She flared pewter and pushed down on a rung with her legs, then slammed her back up against the trapdoor, trying to force it open.

She strained. Then the rung broke beneath her feet, sending her toppling down once more. She cursed, Pushing off her coin to slow her fall, and hit the floor in a crouch.

The workers had retreated into a huddle—perhaps reluctant to remain in the small room with a Mistborn, but also loath to venture into the dark cavern. The suited nobleman had turned. He held his lantern high, illuminating Vin. A bit of broken ladder rung fell free and cracked to the stone floor beside her.

"The trapdoor is well secured with quite a large rock on top of it, Lady Venture," the nobleman said. Vin vaguely recognized him. He was a bit overweight, but was kempt, with very short hair and a thoughtful face.

"Tell the men up above to remove the stone," Vin said softly, raising a dagger.

"That is not going to happen, I'm afraid."

"I can make it happen," Vin said, stepping forward. The workers pulled away even farther.

The nobleman smiled. "Lady Venture, let me assure you of several things. The first is that you are the only Allomancer among us, so I have no doubt you could slaughter us with the barest effort. The second is that the stone above is not moving anytime soon, so we might as well sit down and have a pleasant chat, as opposed to brandishing weapons and threatening each other."

There was something . . . disarming about the man. Vin checked with bronze, but he wasn't burning any metals. Just to be certain, she Pulled a bit on his emotions, making him more trusting and friendly, then tried to Soothe away any sense of guile he might have felt.

"I see that you're at least considering my offer," the nobleman said, waving to one of the workers. The worker hastily opened his pack, pulling out two folding chairs, then arranged them on the ground before the open stone door. The nobleman placed the lantern to the side and sat down.

Vin crept a little closer. "Why do I recognize you?"

"I'm a friend of your husband," the nobleman said.

"Telden," Vin said, placing him. "Telden Hasting."

Telden nodded. She had seen him at the first ball they had attended here. But she'd known him from someplace earlier than that. He'd been one of Elend's friends in Luthadel, before the Collapse.

Warily, Vin took the offered seat, trying to figure out Yomen's game. Did he think she wouldn't kill Telden simply because he'd been Elend's friend?

Telden lounged in his chair, somewhat less proper than the average nobleman. He waved a worker forward, and the man presented two bottles. "Wine," Telden said. "One is pure, and the other contains a powerful sedative."

Vin raised an eyebrow. "This is to be some sort of guessing game?"

"Hardly," Telden said, opening one of the bottles. "I'm far too thirsty—and from what I hear, you're not the type who possesses an excessive amount of patience for games."

Vin cocked her head as Telden accepted two cups from a servant, then poured some of the ruby wine into each. As she watched, she realized why he was so disarming. He reminded her of Elend—the old, carefree Elend. From what she could tell, this Telden was genuinely still that way.

I have to grant Yomen that much, she thought. *His city may not be perfect, but he has created a place where men like Telden can retain some of their innocence.*

Telden took a drink of his wine, proffering the other cup

to Vin. She slid one of her knives into her sheath, then took the cup. She didn't drink—and had no intention of doing so.

"This is the wine without the sedative," Telden said. "Good vintage too. Yomen is a true gentleman—if he's going to send one of his friends down into a pit to die, he'll at least provide them with expensive wine to soften the blow."

"I'm supposed to believe that you're here to be imprisoned too?" Vin asked flatly.

"Of course not," Telden said. "Though many consider my mission to be hopeless."

"And that mission is?"

"To get you to drink some of the drugged wine, so that you can be safely transported up above."

Vin snorted.

"I see that you agree with my detractors," Telden said.

"You just gave yourself away," Vin said. "You said that I'm supposed to drink the wine and fall unconscious. That means you have a way to signal to those above that I've been dealt with, so they can remove the stone and let you out. You have the power to free us. And I have the power to make you do as I wish."

"Emotional Allomancy cannot control me to that extent," Telden said. "I'm no Allomancer, but I do know something of it. I suspect that you're manipulating my emotions right now—which really isn't necessary, since I'm being completely frank with you."

"I don't need Allomancy to make you talk," Vin said, glancing down at the knife she still had in her other hand.

Telden laughed. "You think that King Yomen—yes, he's up above—won't be able to tell if I'm speaking under duress? I have no doubt that you'd be able to break me, but mere threats won't make me betray my word, so you'd have to cut off a few fingers or something before I'd do as you ask. I'm pretty certain that Yomen and the others would hear me screaming."

"I could kill the servants," Vin said. "One at a time, until you agree to tell Yomen that I'm unconscious and have him open the door."

Telden smiled. "You think that I'd care if you kill them?"

"You're one of Elend's friends," Vin said. "You were one of those who talked philosophy with him."

"Philosophy," Telden said, "and politics. But Elend was the only one of us interested in the skaa. I assure you, the rest of us really didn't understand where he got such a fascination with them." He shrugged. "However, I'm not a heartless man. If you kill enough of them, perhaps I *would* break down and do as you ask. Might as well get started then."

Vin glanced at the servants. They seemed terrified of her, and Telden's words didn't help. After a few moments of silence, Telden chuckled.

"You are Elend's wife," he noted. "Yomen is aware of this, you see. He was mostly convinced you wouldn't kill any of us, despite your rather fearsome reputation. From what we hear, you have a habit of killing kings and gods, perhaps the occasional soldier. Skaa servants however . . ."

Vin looked away from the servants, but didn't meet Telden's eyes with her own, fearing that he'd see confirmation in them. He was wrong about her—she would kill those servants if she thought it would get her out. But she was uncertain. If screams would keep Yomen from opening the trapdoor, Vin would have slaughtered innocents for no reason.

"So," Telden said, finishing off his wine. "We are at a stalemate. We assume that you're running low on food down here, unless you've found a way to open those cans. And if you have, there's nothing you can do down here to help up above. My guess is that unless you take the wine, we'll all end up starving to death in this cavern."

Vin sat back in her chair. *There has to be a way out—a chance to exploit this.*

It was incredibly unlikely that she'd be able to break through that door above. She could *maybe* use duralumin and steel to Push her way through. But her steel and pewter would be gone, and she was out of metal vials.

Telden's words, unfortunately, held a great deal of truth. Even if Vin could survive in the cavern, she'd be stagnant and useless. The siege would continue above—she had no idea how that was going—and the world would continue to die from Ruin's machinations.

She needed to get out of the cavern. Even if that meant being put into Yomen's hands. She eyed the bottle of drugged wine.

Damn, she thought. *That obligator is far cleverer than we expected.* The wine would certainly have been prepared with enough strength to knock out an Allomancer.

However . . .

Pewter made the body resistant to all kinds of drugs. If she flared pewter with duralumin after drinking the wine, would it perhaps burn away the poison and leave her awake? She could pretend to be unconscious, then escape above.

It seemed a stretch. But what was she to do? Her food was almost gone, and her chances for escaping were slim. She didn't know what Yomen wanted—and Telden would be unlikely to tell her—but he must not want her dead. If that had been the case, he'd simply have left her to starve.

She had a choice. Either wait longer in the cavern, or gamble on a better chance to escape above. She thought for only a moment, then made up her mind. She reached for the bottle. Even if her trick with pewter didn't work, she'd rather gamble on getting into a better situation above.

Telden chuckled. "They did say that you were a decisive one. That's rather refreshing—I've spent far too long with stuffy noblemen who take years to come to any firm decisions."

Vin ignored him. She easily popped the cork off the bottle, then raised it and took a swig. The drugs began to take effect almost immediately. She settled back in her chair, letting her eyes droop, trying to give the impression that she was falling asleep. Indeed, it was very difficult to remain awake. Her mind was clouding despite flared pewter.

She slumped, feeling herself drift away. *Here goes,* she thought, then burned duralumin. Her body flared with hyperenhanced pewter. Immediately the feeling of tiredness went away. She almost bolted upright from the sudden burst of energy. Telden was chuckling. "I'll be," he said to one of the servants. "She actually went for it."

"You'd be dead if she hadn't, my lord," the servant said. "We'd all be dead."

And then the duralumin ran out. Her pewter disappeared with a puff, and with it went her immunity to the drug, which hadn't burned away. It had been a long shot anyway.

She barely heard her weapon click as it slipped from her fingers and hit the floor. Then she fell unconscious.

Once Ruin was free from his prison, he was able to influence people more strongly—but impaling someone with a Hemalurgic spike was difficult no matter the circumstances.

To achieve such things, he apparently began with people who already had a tenuous grip on reality. Their insanity made them more open to his touch, and he could use them to spike more stable people. In any case, it's impressive how many important people Ruin managed to spike. King Penrod, ruling Luthadel at the time, is a good example of this.

51

ELEND FLEW THROUGH THE MISTS. He'd never quite been able to manage Vin's horseshoe trick. Somehow she could keep herself in the air, bounding from Push to Push, then Pulling each horseshoe back up behind her after she used it. To Elend, the process looked like a cyclone of potentially lethal chunks of metal with Vin at the center.

He dropped a coin, then Pushed himself in a powerful leap. He'd given up on the horseshoe method after four or five failed attempts. Vin had seemed puzzled that he couldn't get it down—she'd apparently figured it out on her own, needing less than an hour's practice to perfect it.

But, well, that was Vin.

Elend made do with coins, of which he carried a rather large bag. Copper clips, the smallest of the old imperial coins, worked perfectly for his purposes—particularly since he was apparently much more powerful than other Mistborn. Each of his Pushes carried him farther than they should have, and he really didn't use that many coins, even when traveling a long distance.

It felt good to be away. He felt free as he plunged from his leap, dropping through the shifting darkness, then flared pewter and landed with a muffled thump. The ground in this valley was relatively free of ash—it had drifted, leaving a small corridor where it only came up to his mid-calf. So he ran for a few minutes, for a change.

A mistcloak fluttered behind him. He wore dark clothing rather than one of his white uniforms. It seemed appropriate; besides, he'd never really had a chance to be a true Mistborn. Since discovering his powers, he'd spent his life at war. There wasn't much need for him to go scuttling about in the darkness, especially not with Vin around to do it better.

I can see why Vin would find this intoxicating, he thought, dropping another coin and bounding between two hilltops. Even with the stress of Vin's capture and the threat to the empire, there was an exhilarating freedom about cruising through the mists. It almost allowed him to forget the wars, the destruction, and the responsibility.

Then he landed, ash coming up to nearly his waist. He stood for a few moments, looking down at the soft black powder. He couldn't escape it. Vin was in danger, the empire was collapsing, and his people were starving. It was his job to fix these things—that was the burden he'd taken upon himself when he'd become emperor.

He Pushed himself into the air, leaving a trail of ash fluttering in the mists behind him.

I certainly hope Sazed and Breeze are having better luck in Urteau, he thought. He was worried about his chances with Fadrex, and the Central Dominance would need the grain in the Urteau cache if they were going to plant enough food for the coming winter.

He couldn't worry about that now. He just had to count on his friends to be effective. Elend's job was to do something to help Vin. He couldn't sit and wait in the camp, letting Yomen pull the strings. Yet he didn't dare try to assassinate Yomen—not after the man had tricked both of them so cleverly.

So Elend pressed forward to the northeast, toward the last known location of a koloss army. The time for subtlety and diplomacy was over. Elend needed a threat—something he could hold over Yomen's head and, if necessary, use to batter him. And nothing was better at battering a city than koloss. Perhaps he was a fool for seeking out the brutes on his own. Perhaps it was wrong to give up on diplomacy. Yet he had made his decision. He had failed in so many things lately—protecting Vin, keeping Luthadel safe, defending his people—that he simply *needed* to act.

Ahead, he saw a light in the mists. He landed, running through a field of knee-deep ash. Only flared pewter gave him the strength to manage it. When he got closer, he saw a village. He heard screams. He saw shadows scrambling about in fright.

He leaped, dropping a coin, flaring his metals. He passed through curling mist, looming over the village and its frightened occupants, his mistcloak splaying out. Several of the homes were burning. And by that light he could see the dark, hulking forms of koloss moving through the streets. Elend picked a beast who was raising its weapon to strike, then Pulled. Below, he heard the koloss grunt, but it managed to hang onto its weapon. However, the koloss wasn't that much heavier than Elend, so it was Pulled up into the air by one arm as Elend was yanked downward.

Elend Pulled against a door hinge as he fell, edging himself to one side of the confused flying koloss. He sprayed it with coins as he passed.

Beast and weapon spun in the air. Elend landed in the street before a huddled group of skaa. The flying koloss's weapon hit the ashen earth point-first next to him. The koloss itself dropped dead on the other side of the street.

A large group of koloss turned, bloodred eyes shining in the firelight, frenzy making them excited about the prospect of a challenge. He would have to frighten them before he'd be able to take control. He was looking forward to that this time.

How could they possibly have once been people? Elend wondered, dashing forward and yanking the fallen koloss sword from the ground as he passed it, throwing out a spray of black soil. The Lord Ruler had created the creatures. Was this what had happened to those who had opposed him? Had they become koloss to make his army? The creatures had great strength and fortitude, and could subsist on the barest of sustenance. Yet making men—even your enemies—into monsters such as this?

Elend ducked forward, dropping one beast by shearing its legs at the knees. Then he jumped, lopping off the arm of another. He spun, slamming his crude sword through the chest of a third. He felt no remorse at killing what had once been innocents. Those people were dead. The creatures that remained would propagate themselves by using other humans unless they were stopped.

Or unless they were controlled.

Elend cried out, spinning through the group of koloss, wielding a sword that should have been too heavy for him. More and more creatures took notice, turning to tromp down streets lit by burning buildings. This was a very large group, by scout reports—some thirty thousand in number. That many would quickly overrun such a small village, annihilating it like a drift of ash before storm winds.

Elend would not let that happen. He fought, killing beast after beast. He'd come to gain a new army, but as the time passed he found himself fighting for another reason. How many villages such as this one had been destroyed without anyone in Luthadel pausing to give so much as a passing thought? How many subjects—claimed by Elend, even if they didn't know it—had he lost to the koloss? How many had he failed to protect already?

Elend sheared a koloss head free, then spun, Pushing two smaller beasts away by their swords. A massive twelve-footer was stomping forward, weapon raised. Elend gritted his teeth, then lifted his own sword, flaring pewter.

Weapon met weapon in the blazing village, metal ringing like an anvil under the hammer. And Elend stood his ground, matching strength with a monster twice his height.

The koloss halted, dumbfounded.

Stronger than I should be, Elend thought, twisting and cutting the surprised creature's arm free. *Why can't that strength protect the people I rule?*

He cried out, slicing the koloss clean through at the waist—if only to show that he could. The beast fell in two gory pieces.

Why? Elend thought with rage. *What strength must I possess, what must I do, to protect them?*

Vin's words, spoken months ago in the city of Vetitan, returned to him. She'd called everything he did short-term. But what more could he do? He was no slayer of gods, no divine hero of prophecy. He was no more than a man.

And it seemed that these days, ordinary men—even Allomancers—weren't worth much. He bellowed as he killed, ripping through another pack of koloss. But like his efforts at Fadrex, it just didn't seem to be enough.

Around him the village still burned. As he fought, he could hear women crying, children screaming, men dying. Even the efforts of a Mistborn were negligible. He could kill and kill, but that would not save the people of the village. He shouted, Pushing out with a Soothing, yet the koloss resisted him. He didn't bring a single one under his control. Did that mean that an Inquisitor controlled them? Or were they simply not frightened enough?

He fought on. And as he did, the prevalence of death

around him seemed a metaphor for all he had done over the last three years. He should have been able to protect the people—he'd tried *so hard* to protect the people. He'd stopped armies, overthrown tyrants, reworked laws, and scavenged supplies. Yet all of that was a tiny drop of salvation in a vast ocean of death, chaos, and pain. He couldn't save the empire by protecting a corner of it, the same way he couldn't save this village by killing a small fraction of the koloss.

What good was killing another monster if it was only replaced by two more? What good was food to feed his people if the ash smothered everything anyway? What good was he, an emperor who couldn't defend the people of a single village?

Elend had never lusted for power. He'd been a theorist and a scholar—ruling an empire had mostly been an academic exercise for him. Yet as he fought on that dark night in the burning mists and falling ash, he began to understand. As people died around him despite his most frenzied efforts, he could see what would drive men for more and more power.

Power to protect. At that moment, he would have accepted the powers of godhood, if it would mean having the strength to save the people around him.

He dropped another koloss, then spun as he heard a scream. A young woman was being pulled from a nearby house, despite an older man holding onto her arm, both yelling for help. Elend reached to his sash, pulling free his bag of coins. He tossed it into the air, then simultaneously Pushed on some of the coins inside and Pulled on others. The sack exploded with twinkling bits of metal, and Elend shot some forward into the body of the koloss yanking on the woman.

It grunted, but did not stop. Coins rarely worked against koloss—you had to hit them just right to kill them. Vin could do it.

Elend wasn't in a mood for such subtlety, even had he possessed it. He yelled in defiance, snapping more coins at the beast. He flipped them off the ground toward himself, then flung them forward, shooting missile after glittering missile into the creature's blue body. Its back became a glistening mass of too-red blood, and finally it slumped over.

Elend spun, turning from the relieved father and daughter to face down another koloss. It raised its weapon to strike, but Elend only shouted at it in anger.

I should be able to protect them! he thought. He needed to take control of the entire group, not waste time fighting them one at a time. But they resisted his Allomancy as he Pushed on their emotions again. Where was the Inquisitor guardian?

As the koloss swung its weapon, Elend flared pewter and flung himself to the side, then sheared the creature's hand free at the wrist. As the beast screamed in pain, Elend threw himself back into the fight. The villagers began to rally around him. They obviously had no training for war—they were likely under Yomen's protection and didn't need to worry about bandits or roving armies. Yet despite their lack of skill, they clearly knew to stay close to the Mistborn. Their desperate, pleading eyes prodded Elend on, drove him to cut down koloss after koloss.

For the moment, he didn't have to worry about the right or wrong of the situation. He could simply *fight*. The desire for battle burned within him like metal—even the desire to kill. So he fought on—fought for the surprise in the eyes of the townspeople, for the hope each of his blows seemed to inspire. They had given their lives up for lost, and then a man had dropped from the sky to defend them.

Over a year before, during the siege of Luthadel, Vin had attacked Cett's fortification and slaughtered three hundred of his soldiers. Elend had trusted that she had good reasons for the attack, but he'd never understood how she could do such a thing. At least not until this night, fighting in an unnamed village, too much ash in the dark sky, the mists on fire, koloss dying in ranks before him.

The Inquisitor didn't appear. Frustrated, Elend spun

away from a group of koloss, leaving one dying in his wake, then extinguished his metals. The creatures surrounded him, and he burned duralumin, then zinc, and *Pulled*.

The village fell silent.

Elend paused, stumbling slightly as he finished his spin. He looked through the falling ash, turning toward the remaining koloss—thousands and thousands of them—who now stood motionless and patient around him, under his control at last.

There's no way I took them all at once, he thought warily. What had happened to the Inquisitor? There was usually one with a mob of koloss this big. Had it fled? That would explain why Elend had suddenly been able to control the koloss.

Worried, yet uncertain what else to do, he turned to scan the village. Some people had gathered to stare at him. They seemed to be in shock—instead of doing something about the burning buildings, they simply stood in the mists, watching him.

He should have felt triumphant. Yet his victory was spoiled by the Inquisitor's absence. And by this point, very few structures remained in the village that weren't aflame. Elend hadn't saved the village. He'd found his koloss army as he'd planned, but he felt he'd failed in some greater way. He sighed, dropping his sword from tired, bloody fingers, then walked toward the villagers. As he moved, he was disturbed by the number of koloss bodies he passed. Had he really slain so many?

Another part of him—quiescent now, but still aflame—was sorry that the time for killing had ended. He stopped before a silent group of villagers.

"You're him, aren't you?" an elderly man asked.

"Who?" Elend asked.

"The Lord Ruler," the man whispered.

Elend looked down at his black uniform, encased in a mistcloak, both of which were slick with blood.

"Close enough," he said, turning to the east—toward where his human army camped many miles away, waiting for him to return with a new koloss force to aid them. There was only one reason for him to do that. Finally he acknowledged what he'd unconsciously decided the moment he'd set out to find more of the creatures.

The time for killing hasn't ended at all, he thought. *It has just begun.*

Near the end, the ash began to pile up in frightening amounts. I've spoken of the microbes the Lord Ruler devised to help the world deal with the ashfalls. They did not really feed on ash. Rather, they broke it down as an aspect of their metabolic functions. Volcanic ash is good for soil, depending on what one wishes to grow.

Too much of anything, however, is deadly. Water is necessary for survival, yet too much will drown. During the history of the Final Empire, the land balanced on the very knife-edge of disaster via the ash. The microbes broke it down about as rapidly as it fell, but when there was so much of it that it oversaturated the soil, it became more difficult for plants to survive.

In the end, the entire system fell apart. Ash fell so steadily that it smothered and killed, and the world's plant life died off. The microbes had no chance of keeping up, for they needed time and nutrients to reproduce.

52

DURING THE DAYS OF THE Lord Ruler, Luthadel had been the most crowded city in the world. Filled with three- and four-story tenements, it had been packed with the skaa who'd worked its numerous furnaces and forges, with the noble merchants who'd sold its goods, and with the high nobility who'd wanted to be near the imperial court. TenSoon had assumed that now, with the Lord Ruler dead and the imperial government shattered, Luthadel would become far less densely populated.

He had apparently been wrong.

Still wearing the wolfhound's body, he trotted along in amazement as he explored the streets. It seemed that every nook—every alleyway, every street corner, each and every tenement—had become home to a skaa family. The city smelled terrible, and refuse clogged the streets, buried in ash.

What is going on? he wondered. The skaa lived in filth, many of them looking sick, coughing piteously in their ash-filled gutters. TenSoon made his way toward Keep Venture. If there were answers to be found, he hoped to locate them there. Occasionally he had to growl at skaa who stared at him hungrily, and twice he had to run from gangs that ignored his growls.

Surely Vin and Elend would not have let this city fall so far, he thought as he hid in an alley. It was a foreboding sign. He'd left Luthadel without knowing whether or not his friends would survive the city's siege. Elend's banner—the spear and the scroll—flew at the front of the city, but could someone else have taken Elend's sign as their own? And what of the koloss army that had threatened to destroy Luthadel a year ago?

I should never have left her, TenSoon thought, feeling a stab of anxiety. *My foolish kandra sense of duty. I should have stayed here, and told her what I know, little though it is.*

The world could end because of my foolish honor.

He poked his head out of the alleyway, looking at Keep Venture. TenSoon's heart sank to see that its beautiful stained-glass windows had been shattered. Crude boards blocked the broken holes. There were guards at the front gates, however, which seemed a better sign.

TenSoon crept forward, trying to seem like a mangy stray. He kept to the shadows, edging his way up to the gate.

Then he lay down in some refuse to watch the soldiers. He expanded his eardrums, craning to hear what the men were saying.

It turned out to be nothing. The two guards stood quietly, looking bored and not a little disconsolate as they leaned against their obsidian-tipped spears. TenSoon waited, wishing that Vin were there to Pull on the emotions of the guards and make them more talkative.

Of course, if Vin were here I wouldn't have to be poking about for information, TenSoon thought with frustration. So he waited. Waited as the ash fell, waited until the sky darkened and the mists came out. Their appearance finally sparked some life into the guards. "I hate night duty," one of them muttered.

"Nothing wrong with night," the other one said. "Not for us. Mists didn't kill us. We're safe from them."

What? TenSoon thought, frowning.

"Are we safe from the king?" the first guard said quietly.

His companion shot him a glance. "Don't say such things."

The first guard shrugged. "I just hope the emperor gets back soon."

"King Penrod has all of the emperor's authority," the second guard said sternly.

Ah, TenSoon thought. *So Penrod managed to keep the throne. But . . . what's this about an emperor?* TenSoon feared that the emperor was Straff Venture. That terrible man had been the one poised to take Luthadel when Ten-Soon had left.

But what of Vin? TenSoon couldn't bring himself to believe that she had been defeated. He had watched her kill Zane Venture, a man who had been burning atium when Vin had none. By TenSoon's count, she'd done the impossible three times. She'd slain the Lord Ruler. She'd defeated Zane.

And she'd befriended a kandra who had been determined to hate her.

The guards fell silent again. *This is foolish,* TenSoon thought. *I don't have time to hide in corners and eaves-*

drop. The world is ending! He rose, shaking the ash from his body—which caused the guards to start, raising their spears anxiously as they searched the darkening night for the source of the sound.

TenSoon hesitated, their nervousness giving him an idea. He turned and loped off into the night. He'd grown to know the city quite well during his year serving with Vin—she had liked to patrol, particularly the areas around Keep Venture. However, it took TenSoon some time to find his way to where he was going. He had never visited the location, but he had heard it described.

Described by someone whom TenSoon had been killing at the time.

OreSeur, his generation brother, had helped overthrow the Father. At Kelsier's command, he had pretended to be a nobleman named Lord Renoux so that Kelsier would have an apparent nobleman to use as a front. But there had been a more important part for OreSeur to play in Kelsier's plot. A secret part that not even the other members of the crew had known until after Kelsier's death.

TenSoon arrived at the old warehouse. It stood where OreSeur had said it would. TenSoon shuddered, remembering OreSeur's screams. The kandra had died beneath TenSoon's torture, torture which had been necessary, for TenSoon had needed to learn all that he could. Every secret. All that he would need in order to convincingly imitate his brother.

That day, TenSoon's hatred of humans—and of himself for serving them—had burned more deeply than ever before. How Vin had overcome that, he still didn't know.

The warehouse before TenSoon was now a holy place, ornamented and maintained by the Church of the Survivor. A plaque hung out front, displaying the sign of the spear—the weapon by which both Kelsier and the Lord Ruler had died—and giving a written explanation of why the warehouse was important.

TenSoon knew the story already. This was the place where the crew had found a stockpile of weapons, left by the Survivor to arm the skaa people for their revolution. It had been discovered the same day that Kelsier had died, and rumors whispered that the spirit of the Survivor had appeared in this place, giving guidance to his followers. Those rumors were true, after a fashion. TenSoon rounded the building, following instructions OreSeur had given as he died. The Blessing of Presence let TenSoon recall the precise words, and despite the ash, he found the spot—a place where the cobbles were disturbed. Then he began to dig.

Kelsier, the Survivor of Hathsin, had indeed appeared to his followers that night years ago. Or at least his body had, with OreSeur wearing it to appear to the faithful skaa and give them encouragement. The legends of the Survivor, the whole religion that had sprung up around him, had been started by a kandra.

And TenSoon had eventually killed that kandra. But not before learning his secrets. Secrets such as where OreSeur had buried the bones of the Survivor, and how the man had looked.

TenSoon smiled as he unearthed the first bone. They were years old now, and he hated using old bones. Plus there would be no hair, so the body he created would be bald. Still, the opportunity was too valuable to pass up. He'd only seen the Survivor once, but with his expertise in imitation . . .

At least it was worth a try.

Wellen leaned against his spear, watching those mists. Rittle—his companion guard—said they weren't dangerous. But Rittle hadn't seen what they could do. What they could reveal. Wellen figured that he had survived because he respected them. That, and because he didn't think too hard about the things he had seen.

"You think Skiff and Jaston will be late to relieve us again?" Wellen asked, trying once more to start a conversation.

Rittle grunted. "Dunno, Wells." He never did care for small talk.

"I think maybe one of us should go see," Wellen said, eyeing the mist. "You know, ask if they've come in yet. . . ." He trailed off.

Something was out there.

Lord Ruler! he thought, cringing. *Not again!*

But no attack came from the mists. Instead, a dark figure strode forward. Rittle perked up, lowering his spear. "Halt!"

A man walked from the mists, wearing a black cloak, arms at his sides, hood up. His face, however, was visible. Wellen peered at it. That face looked familiar. . . .

Rittle gasped, then fell to his knees, clutching something at his neck—the pendant of a silver spear that he always wore. Wellen frowned. Then he noticed the scars on this newcomer's arms.

Lord Ruler! Wellen thought in shock, realizing where he'd seen this man's face. It had been in a painting, one of many available in the city, that depicted the Survivor of Hathsin.

"Rise," the stranger said, speaking in a benevolent voice.

Rittle stood on shaking feet. Wellen backed away, uncertain whether to be awed or terrified, and feeling a little of both.

"I have come to commend your faith," the Survivor said.

"My lord . . ." Rittle said, his head still bowed.

"Also," Kelsier said, raising a finger. "I have come to tell you I do not approve of how this city is being run. My people are sick, they starve, and they die."

"My lord," Rittle said, "there is not enough food, and there have been riots seizing that which was stockpiled. My lord, and the mists kill! Please, why have you sent them to kill us!"

"I did no such thing," Kelsier said. "I know that food is scarce, but you must share what you have and have hope. Tell me of the man who rules this city."

"King Penrod?" Rittle asked. "He rules for Emperor Elend Venture, who is away at war."

"Lord *Elend* Venture? And he approves of how this city is being treated?" Kelsier looked angry. Wellen cringed.

"No, my lord!" Rittle said, shaking. "I . . ."

"Lord Penrod is mad," Wellen found himself saying.

The Survivor turned toward him.

"Wells, you shouldn't . . ." Rittle said, but then trailed off, the Survivor shooting him a stern look.

"Speak," the Survivor said to Wellen.

"He speaks to the air, my lord," Wellen said, averting his eyes. "Talks to himself—claims that he can see the Lord Ruler standing beside him. Penrod . . . he's given lots of strange orders lately. Forcing the skaa to fight each other for food, claiming that only the strong should survive. He kills those who disagree with him. That kind of thing."

"I see," the Survivor said.

Surely he knows this already, Wellen thought. *Why bother asking?*

"Where is my Heir?" the Survivor asked. "The Hero of Ages, Vin."

"The Lady Empress?" Wellen asked. "She's with the emperor."

"Where?"

"Nobody knows for certain, my lord," Rittle said, still shaking. "She hasn't returned in a long time. My sergeant says that she and the emperor are in the South, fighting koloss. But I've heard other men say the army went west."

"That's not very helpful," Kelsier said.

Wellen perked up, remembering something.

"What?" the Survivor asked, apparently noticing Wellen's change in posture.

"An army troop stopped by the city a month ago," Wellen said, feeling proud. "They kept it quiet, but I was in the group that helped them resupply. Lord Breeze was with them, and he spoke of meeting up with others of your crew."

"Where?" Kelsier asked. "Where were they going?"

"North," Wellen said. "To Urteau. That must be where

the emperor is, my lord. The Northern Dominance is in rebellion. He must have taken his armies to quell it."

The Survivor nodded. "Very well," he said. He turned
as if to go, then looked back. "Pass what news you can,"
he said. "There isn't much time left. Tell the people that
when the mists leave, they should immediately find shelter.
A place underground, if possible."

Wellen hesitated, then nodded. "The caverns," he said.
"Where you trained your army?"

"That will do," Kelsier said. "Farewell."

The Survivor disappeared into the mists.

TenSoon left the gates of Keep Venture behind, running off
into the mists. He could perhaps have gotten into the building. However, he wasn't certain how well his imitation of
the Survivor would hold up under closer scrutiny.

He didn't know how reliable the two guards' information
was. But he had no better leads. Other people he had talked
to in the night hadn't been able to provide any information
about the army's movements. Evidently, Vin and Elend had
been gone from Luthadel for quite some time.

He rushed back to the patch of earth behind the warehouse
where he'd found Kelsier's body. He knelt in the darkness,
uncovering the sack he'd stuffed with bones. He needed to
get the dog's body and head north. Hopefully he would—

"You there!" a voice said.

TenSoon looked up reflexively. A man stood in the doorway of the warehouse, staring through the mists at Ten-
Soon. A lantern flared to life behind him, revealing a group
of people who had apparently taken up residence within the
holy place.

Uh-oh . . . TenSoon thought as those at the front adopted
shocked expressions.

"My lord!" the man in front said, quickly kneeling in his
sleeping robe. "You've returned!"

TenSoon stood, stepping carefully to hide the sack of
bones behind him. "I have," he said.

"We knew that you would," the man said as others began to whisper and cry out behind him. Many fell to their knees. "We stayed in this place, praying for you to come give us counsel. The king is mad, my lord! What do we do?"

TenSoon was tempted to expose himself as a kandra, but looking into their hopeful eyes, he found that he could not. Besides, perhaps he could do some good. "Penrod has been corrupted by Ruin," he said. "The thing that seeks to destroy the world. You must gather the faithful and escape this city before Penrod kills you all."

"My lord, where should we go?"

TenSoon hesitated. Where? "There is a pair of guards at the front of Keep Venture. They know of a place. Listen to them. You *must* get to somewhere underground. Do you understand?"

"Yes, lord," the man said. Behind, more and more people were edging forward, straining to catch a glimpse of TenSoon. He bore their scrutiny with some nervousness. Finally he bade them be careful, then fled into the night.

He found an empty building and quickly changed back to the dog's bones before anyone else could see him. When he was done, he eyed the Survivor's bones, feeling a strange . . . reverence.

Don't be silly, he told himself. *They're just bones, like hundreds of other sets you've used.* Still, it seemed foolish to leave such a potentially powerful tool behind. He carefully packed them into the sack he'd pilfered, then—using paws he'd created to have more dexterity than those of a real wolfhound—he tied the sack on his back.

After that, TenSoon left the city by the northern gate, running at full wolfhound speed. He would go to Urteau and hope that he was on the right path.

The pact between Preservation and Ruin is a thing of gods, and difficult to explain in human terms. Indeed, initially there was a stalemate between them. On one hand, each knew that only by working together could they create. On the other hand, both knew that they would never have complete satisfaction in what they created. Preservation would not be able to keep things perfect and unchanging, and Ruin would not be able to destroy completely.

Of course, Ruin eventually acquired the ability to end the world and gain the satisfaction he wanted. But then, that wasn't originally part of the bargain.

53

SPOOK FOUND HER SITTING ON the rocky lakeshore, looking out across the deep black waters, so still in the cavern's windless air. In the near distance, Spook could hear Sazed—with a large contingent of Goradel's men—working on their project to stanch the flow of water into the cavern.

Spook approached Beldre quietly, carrying a mug of warmed tea. It almost seemed to burn his flesh, which meant that it would be just right for normal people. He let his own food and drinks sit out until they cooled to room temperature.

He didn't wear his eye bandage. With pewter, he'd found that he could withstand a little lantern light. She didn't turn as he approached, so he cleared his throat. She jumped slightly. It was no wonder that Quellion worked so hard to shelter her—one could not fake Beldre's level of innocence. She wouldn't survive three heartbeats in the underground. Even Allrianne, who did her best to look like a puff, had an edge to her that bespoke an ability to be as hard as necessary in order to survive. Beldre though . . .

She's normal, Spook thought. *This is how people would be, if they didn't have to deal with Inquisitors, armies, and assassins.* For that, he actually envied her. It was a strange feeling, after so many years spent wishing that he were someone more important.

She turned back toward the waters, and he approached and sat beside her. "Here," he said, handing her the mug. "I know it gets a bit chilly down here, with the lake and the water."

She hesitated, then took the mug. "Thank you," she whispered. Spook let her roam free in the cavern—there was little she could sabotage, though he had warned Goradel's men to keep an eye on her. In any case, there was no way she was going to get out. Spook kept two dozen men guarding the exit, and had ordered the ladder to the trapdoor above raised, to be lowered only with proper authorization.

"Hard to believe this place was beneath your city all along, isn't it?" Spook said, trying to work into a conversation. Oddly, it had seemed easier to speak to her when he was confronting her in her gardens, surrounded by danger.

Beldre nodded. "My brother would have loved to find this place. He worries about food supplies. Fewer and fewer fish are being caught in the northern lakes. And crops . . . well, they're not doing so well, I hear."

"The mists," Spook said. "They don't let enough sunlight through for most plants."

Beldre looked down at her mug. She hadn't taken a sip yet.

"Beldre," Spook said, "I'm sorry. I considered kidnapping you from those gardens, but decided against it. However, with you showing up here alone . . ."

"It was too good an opportunity," she said bitterly. "I understand. It's my own fault. My brother always says I'm too trusting."

"There are times that would be an advantage."

Beldre sniffed quietly. "I've never known such times as that. It seems my entire life, I've only trusted and been hurt. This is no different."

Spook sat, frustrated with himself. *Kelsier, tell me what to say!* he thought. Yet God remained silent. The Survivor didn't seem to have much advice about things that didn't relate to securing the city.

It had all seemed so simple when Spook had given the order to capture her. Why was he now sitting here with this empty pit in his stomach?

"I believed in him, you know," Beldre said.

"Your brother?"

"No," she said. "The Lord Ruler. I was a good little noblewoman. I always gave my payments to the obligators—even paying extra and calling them in to witness the smallest things. I also paid them to tutor me in the history of the empire. I thought everything was perfect. So neat; so peaceful. And then they tried to kill me. Turns out I'm half skaa. My father wanted a child so desperately, and my mother was barren. He had two children with one of the maidservants—and my mother approved."

She shook her head. "Why would someone do that?" she continued. "I mean, why not pick a noblewoman? No. My father chose the servant woman. I guess he fancied her or something. . . ." She looked down.

"For me, it was my grandfather," Spook said. "I never knew him. Grew up on the streets."

"Sometimes I wish *I* had," Beldre said. "Then maybe this would all make sense. What do you do when the priests you've been paying to tutor you since you were a child—men you trusted more than your own parents—come to take you away for execution? I would have died too. I just went with them. Then . . ."

"Then what?" Spook asked.

"You saved me," she whispered. "The Survivor's crew. You overthrew the Lord Ruler, and in the chaos everybody forgot about people like me. The obligators were too busy trying to please Straff."

"And then your brother took over."

She nodded. "I thought he'd be a good ruler. He really is a good man! He only wants everything to be stable and secure. Peace for everyone. Yet sometimes the things he *does* to people . . . the things he *asks* of people . . ."

"I'm sorry," Spook said.

"And then you came. You rescued that child right in front of Quellion and me. You came to my gardens, and you didn't threaten me. I thought . . . maybe he really is as the stories say. Maybe he'll help. And like the idiot I always am, I came here."

"I wish things were simple, Beldre," Spook said. "I wish I could let you go. But this is for the greater good."

"That's exactly what Quellion always says, you know," she said.

Spook hesitated.

"You're a lot alike, you two," she said. "Forceful. Commanding."

Spook chuckled. "You really don't know me very well, do you?"

She flushed. "You're the Survivor of the Flames. Don't think I haven't heard the rumors—my brother can't keep me out of *all* his conferences."

"Rumors," Spook said, "are rarely reliable."

"You're a member of the Survivor's crew."

Spook shrugged. "True. Though I became a member by accident."

She frowned, glancing at him.

"Kelsier handpicked the others," Spook said. "Ham, Breeze, Sazed—and Vin. He chose my uncle too. And by doing so, he got me as a bonus. I . . . I was never really part of it all, Beldre. I was more like an observer. They posted me on watch and things like that. I sat in on the planning sessions, but everyone just treated me as an errand boy. I must have refilled Breeze's cup a hundred times during that first year!"

A hint of amusement showed on her face. "You make it sound like you were a servant."

"Pretty much," Spook said, smiling. "I couldn't talk very well—I'd grown used to speaking in an Eastern street slang, and everything I said came out garbled. I've still got an accent, they tell me. So I stayed quiet most of the time, embarrassed. The crew was nice to me, but I knew I was pretty much ignored."

"And now you're in charge of them all."

Spook laughed. "No. Sazed's the one really in charge of us here. Breeze ranks me too, but he lets me give orders because he's too lazy to do so. He likes to make people do things without them knowing it. Half the time, I figure the things I'm saying are ideas he somehow got into my head."

Beldre shook her head. "The Terrisman is in charge? But he looks to you!"

"He just lets me do what he doesn't want to," Spook said. "Sazed's a great man—one of the best I've known. But, well, he's a scholar. He's better off studying a project and writing notes than he is giving commands. So that only leaves me. I'm just doing the job that everyone else is too busy to do."

Beldre sat quietly for a moment, then finally took a sip of her tea. "Ah," she said. "It's good!"

"The Lord Ruler's own brew, for all we know," Spook said. "We found it down here, with the rest of this stuff."

"This is why you came, isn't it?" Beldre asked, nodding to the cavern. "I wondered why your emperor cared about Urteau. We haven't really been an important force in the world since the Venture line moved its center of power to Luthadel."

Spook nodded. "This is part of it, though Elend is also worried about the rebellion up here. It's dangerous, having a foe who is slaughtering noblemen controlling one of the major cities only a short distance north of Luthadel. That's all I can really tell you though. Most of the time, I feel like

I'm *still* just a bystander in all this. Vin and Elend, they're the ones who really know what's going on. To them, I'm the guy they could spare to spend months spying in Urteau while they did important work in the South."

"They are wrong to treat you so," Beldre said.

"No, it's all right," Spook said. "I've enjoyed being up here. It feels like I've finally been able to do something."

She nodded. After a short time, she set down her cup, wrapping her arms around her knees. "What are they like?" she asked. "I've heard so many stories. They say that Emperor Venture always wears white, and that the ash refuses to stick to him! He can quell an army just by looking at them. And his wife, the Survivor's heir. Mistborn . . ."

Spook smiled. "Elend is a forgetful scholar—twice as bad as Sazed ever was. He gets lost in his books and forgets about meetings he called. He only dresses with any sense of fashion because a Terriswoman bought him a new wardrobe. War has changed him some, but on the inside he's still a dreamer caught in a world with too much violence.

"And Vin . . . well, she really *is* different. I've never been sure what to make of her. Sometimes she seems as frail as a child. And then she kills an Inquisitor. She can be fascinating and frightening at the same time. I tried to court her once."

"Really?" Beldre said, perking up.

Spook smiled. "I gave her a handkerchief. I heard that's how you do it in noble society."

"Only if you're a romantic," Beldre said, smiling wistfully.

"Well, I gave her one," Spook said. "But I don't think she knew what I meant by it. And of course, once she *did* figure it out, she turned me down. I'm not sure what I was thinking, trying to court her. I mean, I'm just Spook. Quiet, incomprehensible, forgettable Spook."

He closed his eyes. *What am I saying?* Women didn't want to hear men talk about how insignificant they were. He'd heard that much. *I shouldn't have come to talk to her. I should have gone about giving orders. Looking like I was in charge.*

The damage had been done. She knew the truth about him. He sighed, opening his eyes.

"I don't think you're forgettable," Beldre said. "Of course, I'd be *more* likely to think fondly of you if you were to let me go."

Spook smiled. "Eventually. I promise."

"Are you going to use me against him?" Beldre asked. "Threaten to kill me if he doesn't give in?"

"Threats like that are hollow if you know you'll never do what you say," Spook said. "Honestly, Beldre, I'm not going to hurt you. In fact, I've got a feeling you'll be safer here than in your brother's palace."

"Please don't kill him, Spook," Beldre said. "Maybe . . . maybe you can help him somehow, help him see that he's being too extreme."

Spook nodded. "I'll . . . try."

"Do you promise?" she said.

"All right," Spook said. "I promise to at least try to save your brother. If I can."

"And the city too."

"And the city," Spook said. "Trust me. We've done this before—the transition will go smoothly."

Beldre nodded, and she actually seemed to believe him. *What kind of woman is still able to trust people after everything she's been through?* If she'd been Vin, she would have stabbed him in the back at the first opportunity, and that would have probably been the right thing to do. Yet this woman continued to trust. It was like finding a beautiful plant growing alone in a field of burnt ash.

"Once we're done, maybe you could introduce me to the emperor and empress," Beldre said. "They sound like interesting people."

"I'll never argue with that statement," Spook said. "Elend and Vin . . . well, they're certainly *interesting*. Interesting people with heavy burdens. Sometimes I wish I were powerful enough to do important works like them."

Beldre laid a hand on his arm, and he glanced down, a bit surprised. *What?*

"Power can be a terrible thing, Spook," she said quietly. "I'm . . . not pleased with what it's done to my brother. Don't wish so hard for it."

Spook met her eyes, then nodded and rose. "If you need anything, ask Sazed. He'll see to your comforts."

She looked up. "Where are you going?"

"To be seen."

"I want primary trade contracts on all the canals," Durn said. "And a title from the emperor."

"You?" Spook said. "A title? You think a 'lord' in front of your name is going to make that face any less ugly?"

Durn raised an eyebrow.

Spook chuckled. "Both are yours. I cleared it with Sazed and Breeze—they'll even draft you a contract, if you want."

Durn nodded appreciatively. "I do. Lords pay attention to things like that." They sat in one of his many backroom chambers—not in his private home, but in a place attached to a particular inn. An old set of drums hung on the wall.

Spook had had little trouble sneaking out past Quellion's soldiers standing watch at the front of the Ministry building. Before he'd gained enhanced abilities with tin, and long before he'd been able to burn pewter, he'd learned to sneak about in the night and spy. A group of soldiers had barely posed an obstacle for him. He couldn't remain cooped up in the cavern like the others. He had too much work to do.

"I want the Harrows dammed off," Spook said. "We'll flood the canals during the evening, when the markets are empty. Nobody lives in the streetslots except for those of you here in the slums. If you want to keep this place from flooding, you'll need a good *watertight* blockade in place."

"Already taken care of," Durn said. "When the Harrows were new, we pulled off the lock system from its mouth, but I know where it is. It'll fit back in place well enough to keep the water out, assuming we can install it correctly."

"You'd better," Spook said. "I don't want the deaths of half of the city's poorest people on my conscience. I'll warn you the day we intend to pull this off. See if you can get some of the goods out of the market, as well as keep people out of the streetslots. That, plus what you're doing for my reputation, will guarantee you the title you want."

Durn nodded, rising. "Well, let's go work on that reputation then." He led the way out into the commons of the bar. As always, Spook wore his burned cloak—it had become something of a symbol for him. He'd never worn a mistcloak, but this felt even better.

The people rose when he entered. He smiled, motioning for Durn's men to bring out wineskins—taken from the storage cavern and carried by Spook as he snuck out several nights in a row. "Tonight," he said, "you don't have to pay for Quellion's stolen liquor. That's his way of keeping you happy and content."

And that was the only speech he gave. He wasn't Kelsier, able to impress people with his words. Instead—at Breeze's suggestion—he stayed mostly quiet. He visited tables, trying to not be aloof, but also speaking little. He adoped a thoughtful expression and asked the people about their problems. He listened to stories of loss and hardship, and drank with them to the memory of those Quellion had murdered. And with his pewter, he never got drunk. He already had a reputation for that—the people regarded it mystically, as they did his ability to survive fire.

After that bar they visited another, and another after that. Durn was careful to keep him to the safest—yet most populated—of the locations. Some were in the Harrows, others were above. Through it all, Spook felt an amazing thing: his confidence growing. He really *was* a little like Kelsier. Vin might have been the one trained by the Survivor, but Spook was the one who was doing what he'd done—encouraging the people, leading them to rise up for their own sakes.

As the evening passed, the various bars became a blur. Spook breathed curses against Quellion, speaking of the murders and of the Allomancers the Citizen retained.

Spook didn't spread the rumors that Quellion was an Allo-mancer—he let Breeze do that more carefully. That way it wouldn't look like Spook was too eager to set the man up.

"To the Survivor!"

Spook looked up, holding his mug of wine, smiling as the bar patrons cheered.

"To the Survivor!" another said, pointing at Spook. "Survivor of the Flames!"

"To the death of the Citizen!" Durn said, raising his own mug—though he rarely drank from it. "Down with the man who said he'd let us rule, then took it all for himself!"

Spook smiled, taking a drink. He hadn't realized how exhausting it could be to simply sit around and speak to people. His flared pewter kept his body's weariness at bay, but it couldn't prevent the mental fatigue.

I wonder what Beldre would think if she saw this, he thought. *The men cheering me. She'd be impressed, wouldn't she? She'd forget how I droned on about how useless I was.*

Perhaps the visits to the bars had been fatiguing merely because he had something else he wished he could be doing. It was silly—she was his captive. He'd betrayed her trust. She was obviously just warming up to him in an effort to get him to let her go. Yet he couldn't help thinking back to their conversation, going over it again and again in his mind. Despite the stupid things he'd said, she'd laid her hand on his arm. That meant something, didn't it?

"You all right?" Durn asked, leaning in. "That's your tenth mug tonight."

"I'm fine," Spook said.

"You were looking a little distant there."

"I have a lot on my mind," Spook said.

Durn leaned back, frowning, but didn't say anything more.

Some things about his conversation with Beldre bothered Spook more than his own stupid comments. She seemed to truly be worried by the things that her brother had done. When Spook was in power, would she see him as she did Quellion? Would that be a bad thing or a good thing? She already said they were similar.

Power can be a terrible thing. . . .

He looked up, glancing at the people of the bar as they cheered him again, as the men had in the other bars. Kelsier had been able to handle adulation like this. If Spook wanted to be like Kelsier, then he'd have to deal with it as well, right?

Wasn't it a good thing to be liked? To have people willing to follow him? He could finally break away from the old Spook. He could stop being that boy, the one so insignificant and easily forgotten. He could leave that child behind, and become a man who was respected. And why shouldn't he be respected? He *wasn't* that boy anymore. He wore his bandages across his eyes, heightening his mystical reputation as a man who did not need light to see. Some even said that anywhere that fire burned, Spook could see.

"They love you," Kelsier whispered. "You deserve it."

Spook smiled. That was all the confirmation he needed. He stood, raising his arms before the crowd. They cheered in response.

It had been a long time coming. And it felt all the sweeter for the wait.

Preservation's desire to create sapient life was what eventually broke the stalemate. In order to give humankind awareness and independent thought, Preservation knew that he would have to give up part of himself—his own soul—to dwell within humankind. This would leave him a tiny bit weaker than his opposite, Ruin.

That tiny bit seemed inconsequential, compared with their total vast sums of power. However, over eons, this tiny flaw would allow Ruin to overcome Preservation, thereby bringing an end to the world.

This, then, was their bargain. Preservation got humankind, the only creations that had more Preservation than Ruin in them, rather than a balance. Independent life that could think and feel. In exchange, Ruin was given a promise—and proof—that he could bring an end to all they had created together. It was the pact.

And Preservation eventually broke it.

54

WHEN VIN AWOKE, SHE WAS not surprised to find herself bound. She *was* surprised to feel that she was wearing metal manacles.

The first thing she did—even before she opened her eyes—was reach inside for her metals. With steel and iron, perhaps she could use the manacles as weapons. With pewter . . .

Her metals were gone.

She kept her eyes closed, trying not to display the panic she felt, thinking through what had happened. She'd been in the cavern, trapped with Ruin. Elend's friend had come in, given her the wine, and she'd taken it. Gambled.

How long had it been since she'd fallen unconscious?

"Your breathing has changed," a voice reported. "You are obviously awake."

Vin cursed herself quietly. There was a very easy method for taking away an Allomancer's powers—easier than making them burn aluminum. You merely had to keep them drugged long enough for them to pass the metals through their body. As she thought about it, her mind shrugging off the effects of extended sleep, she realized this was what must have happened to her.

The silence continued. Finally, Vin opened her eyes. She expected to see cell bars. Instead she saw a sparsely furnished, utilitarian room—in a corner of the building, judging by the windows. She lay on a bench, head cushioned by a hard pillow. Her manacles were connected to a chain several feet long, which was in turn locked to the base of the bench. She tugged on the chain carefully, and determined that it was very well affixed.

The motion drew the attention of a pair of guards who stood beside the bench. They jumped slightly, raising staffs and eyeing her warily. Vin smiled to herself; part of her was proud that she could evoke such a response when chained and metalless.

"You, Lady Venture, present something of a problem." The voice came from the side. Vin raised herself up on one arm, looking over the bench's armrest. On the other end of the room—perhaps fifteen feet away—a bald figure in robes stood with his back to her. He stared out a large window facing west, the setting sun a violent crimson blaze around his silhouette.

"What do I do?" Yomen asked, still not turning toward her. "A single flake of steel, and you could slaughter my guards with their own buttons. A taste of pewter, and you could lift that bench and smash your way out of the room.

The logical thing to do would be to gag you, keep you drugged at all times, or kill you."

Vin opened her mouth to reply, but all that came out was a cough. She immediately tried to burn pewter to strengthen her body. The lack of metal was like missing a limb. As she sat up, coughing further and growing dizzy, she found herself craving the metal more than she'd imagined that she ever would. Allomancy wasn't supposed to be addictive, not like certain herbs or poisons. However, at that moment she could have sworn that all the scientists and philosophers were flat-out wrong.

Yomen made a sharp gesture with one arm, not turning from the sunset. A servant approached, bearing a cup for Vin. She eyed it uncertainly.

"If I wanted to poison you, Lady Venture," Yomen said, "I could do it without guile."

Good point, Vin thought wryly, accepting the cup and drinking the water it contained.

"Water," Yomen said. "Collected from rain, then strained and purified. You will find no trace metals in it to burn. I specifically ordered it kept in wooden containers only."

Clever, Vin thought.

The water quenched her thirst and stilled her cough. "So," she finally said, "if you're worried about me eating metals, why leave me ungagged?"

Yomen stood quietly for a moment. Then he turned, and she could see the tattoos across his eyes and face, his skin reflecting the vivid colors of the setting sun. On his forehead, he wore his single silvery bead of atium.

"Various reasons," said the obligator king.

Vin studied him, then raised the cup to take another drink. The motion jangled her manacles, which she eyed in annoyance as they again restricted her movement.

"They're made of silver," Yomen said. "A particularly frustrating metal for Mistborn, or so I am told."

Silver. Useless, unburnable silver. Like lead, it was one of the metals that provided no Allomantic powers at all.

"An unpopular metal indeed . . ." Yomen said, nodding to the side. A servant approached Vin, bearing something on a small platter. Her mother's earring. It was a dull thing, Allomantically, made of bronze with some silver plating. Much of the silver had worn off years ago, and the brownish bronze showed through, making the earring look to be the cheap bauble it was.

"Which is why," Yomen continued, "I am so curious as to why you would bother with an ornament such as this. I have had it tested. Silver on the outside, bronze on the inside. Why those metals? One useless to Allomancers, the other granting what is considered the weakest of Allomantic powers. Would not an earring of steel or of pewter make more sense?"

Vin eyed the earring. Her fingers itched to grab it, if only to feel metal between her fingers. If she'd had steel, she could have Pushed on the earring, using it as a weapon. Kelsier had once told her to keep wearing it for that simple reason. Yet it had been given to her by her mother. A woman Vin had never known. A woman who had tried to kill her.

Vin put the cup down and snatched the earring. Yomen watched curiously as she stuck it in her ear. He seemed . . . wary. Waiting for something.

If I really did have some trick planned, she thought, *he'd be dead in an instant. How can he stand there so calmly? Why give me my earring? Even if it isn't made of useful metals, I might find a way to use it against him.*

Her instincts told her he was trying an old street ploy— like throwing your enemy a dagger to make him attack. Yomen wanted to spring any traps she was planning. It seemed a silly move. How could he possibly hope to best a Mistborn?

Unless he himself is a Mistborn, Vin thought. *He feels he can beat me.*

He has atium, and is ready to burn it when I try something.

Vin did nothing, made no attack. She wasn't certain her

instincts about Yomen were right, but that didn't really matter. She couldn't attack, for the earring had no hidden secret. The truth was, she simply wanted it because it felt comfortable in her ear. She was accustomed to wearing it.

"Interesting," Yomen said. "Regardless, you are about to discover one of the reasons I have left you without a gag . . ." With that, he raised a hand toward the door. He clasped his hands behind his back as a servant opened the door, showing in an unarmed soldier in the white and brown of Elend's livery.

You should kill him, Ruin whispered in her mind. *All of them.*

"Lady Venture," Yomen said without looking at her. "I must ask you not to speak to this man except when I indicate, and answer only as I request. Otherwise he will have to be executed, and a fresh messenger sent for from your army."

The soldier paled. Vin frowned, eyeing the obligator king. Yomen was obviously a calm man, and he wanted to appear harsh. How much of it was an act?

"You can see that she is alive, as promised," Yomen said to the soldier.

"How do we know this is not a kandra in disguise?" the soldier asked.

"You can ask your question," Yomen said.

"Lady Venture," the soldier said, "what did you have for dinner the night before you went to the party inside the city?"

It was a good question to ask. A kandra would have interrogated her about important moments—such as her first meeting with Elend. Something like a meal, however, was so random that no kandra would have thought to ask about it. Now, if Vin could remember . . .

She looked at Yomen. He nodded—she could answer. "Eggs," she said. "Fresh eggs that I bought in the city, during one of my spying trips."

The man nodded.

"You have your answer, soldier," Yomen said. "Report to your king that his wife is still alive."

The soldier withdrew and the servants closed the door. Vin sat on the bench, waiting for a gag.

Yomen remained where he was, looking at her.

Vin looked back. Finally she spoke. "How long do you think that you can keep Elend placated? If you know anything of him at all, then you will realize he is a king first and a man second. He will do what he needs to do, even if it means my death."

"Eventually, perhaps," Yomen said. "However, for now the stall is effective. They say that you are a blunt woman, and appreciate brevity. Therefore I will be straightforward with you. My purpose in capturing you was not to use you as leverage against your husband."

"Is that so," she said flatly. "Why *did* you capture me then?"

"It is simple, Lady Venture," Yomen said. "I captured you so that I could execute you."

If he expected surprise from her, she didn't give it. She only shrugged. "Sounds like an unnecessarily formal term. Why not just cut my throat while I was drugged?"

"This city is a place of law," Yomen said. "We do not kill indiscriminately."

"This is war," Vin said. "If you wait for discrimination before you kill, you'll have a lot of unhappy soldiers."

"Your crime is not one of war, Lady Venture."

"Oh? And am I to know this crime, then?"

"It is the most simple crime of all. Murder."

Vin raised an eyebrow. Had she killed someone close to this man? Perhaps one of the noble soldiers in Cett's retinue, back a year ago when she'd assaulted Keep Hasting?

Yomen met her eyes, and she saw something in them. A loathing that he kept hidden behind the calm front. No, she hadn't killed one of his friends or relatives. She'd killed someone far more important to him.

"The Lord Ruler," she said.

Yomen turned away again.

"You can't honestly intend to try me for *that*," Vin said. "It's ridiculous."

"There will be no trial," Yomen said. "I am the authority in this city, and need no ceremony to give me direction or permission."

Vin snorted. "I thought you said this was a place of law."

"And I am that law," Yomen said calmly. "I believe in letting a person speak for themselves before I make my decision. I will give you time to prepare your thoughts— however, the men who will be guarding you have orders to kill you if it ever looks like you are putting something unapproved into your mouth."

Yomen glanced back at her. "I'd be very careful while I eat or drink, if I were you. Your guards have been told to err on the side of safety, and they know that I will not punish them if they accidentally kill you."

Kill him, Ruin's voice whispered. *You could do it. Take a weapon from one of those soldiers, then use it on Yomen.*

Vin frowned. Ruin still used Reen's voice—it was familiar, something that had always seemed a part of her. Discovering that it belonged to that *thing* . . . it was like finding out that her reflection really belonged to someone else, and that she'd never truly seen herself.

She ignored the voice. She wasn't sure why Ruin would want her to try killing Yomen. After all, Yomen had captured her—the obligator king was working on Ruin's side. Plus, Vin doubted her ability to cause the man any harm. Chained, lacking offensive metals . . . she'd be a fool to attack.

She also didn't trust Yomen's comments about keeping her alive so that she could speak in her defense. He was up to something. Yet she couldn't fathom what it might be. Why leave her alive? He was too clever a man to lack a reason.

Giving no hint of his motivations, Yomen turned again, looking out his window. "Take her away."

By sacrificing most of his consciousness, Preservation created Ruin's prison, breaking their deal and trying to keep Ruin from destroying what they had created. This event left their powers again nearly balanced—Ruin imprisoned, only a trace of himself capable of leaking out. Preservation reduced to a mere wisp of what he once was, barely capable of thought and action.

These two minds were independent of the raw force of their powers. Actually, I am uncertain how thoughts and personalities came to be attached to the powers in the first place—but I believe they were not there originally. For both powers could be detached from the minds that harnessed them.

55

IT TOOK ELEND MUCH LONGER to get back from the village than it had taken to get there. For one thing, he had left a lot of his coins with the villagers. He wasn't certain how much good money would do them in the coming weeks, but he'd felt that he had to do something. They were going to have a rough time of it the next few months. Their food stores nearly depleted, their homes burned by koloss, their water sources contaminated by ash, their capital—and king—besieged by Elend . . .

I have to stay focused, he told himself, walking through the falling ash. *I can't help every village. I have to worry about the larger picture.*

A picture that included using a force of koloss to destroy another man's city. Elend gritted his teeth, continuing to walk. The sun was creeping toward the horizon, and the mists had already started to appear, lit by the blazing fire of red sunlight. Behind him tromped some thirty thousand koloss. His new army.

That was another reason it took him a bit longer to return. He wanted to walk with the koloss army rather than jumping ahead of them, in case their Inquisitor appeared to steal them back. He still couldn't believe that such a large group hadn't been under any kind of direction.

I attacked a koloss army on my own, he thought as he slogged through a patch of thigh-deep ash. *I did it without Vin's help, intent on defeating their Inquisitor by myself.*

How had he thought to fight an Inquisitor on his own? Kelsier himself had barely been able to defeat one of the things.

Vin has killed three now, he thought. *We took them on together, but she was the one who killed each one.*

He didn't begrudge her the abilities she had, but he did feel occasional glimmers of envy. That amused him. It had never bothered him when he'd been an ordinary man, but now that he was Mistborn too, he found himself coveting her skill.

And despite her skill, she had been captured.

Elend tromped along, feeling a weight he couldn't shake. Everything seemed *wrong* to him. Vin imprisoned, while he was free. Mist and ash suffocating the land. Elend, despite all his powers, was unable to do anything to protect the people—and the woman—he loved.

And that was the third reason that he walked ploddingly with his koloss rather than returning immediately to his camp. He needed some time to think. Some time alone. Perhaps that was what had driven him to leave in the first place.

He'd known that their work was dangerous, but he'd never *really* thought that he might lose her. She was Vin. She always got out. She survived.

But what if this time she didn't?

He'd always been the vulnerable one—the common person in a world of Mistborn and koloss. The scholar who couldn't fight, who had to depend on Vin for protection. Even during the last year of fighting, she'd stayed close to him. If she'd been in danger, so had he; there hadn't been time to think about what would happen if he survived and she didn't.

He shook his head, pushing through the ash. He could have used koloss to flatten a trail for him. For the moment, however, he wanted to be by himself. So he walked ahead, a lone figure in black on a field of solid ash, backlit by a setting red sun.

The ashfalls were getting far worse. Before he'd left the village, he'd spent a day having his koloss clear the streets and rebuild some of the homes. Yet with the rate at which the ash was falling, the mist and even the possibility of other wandering koloss were becoming secondary problems. The ash alone would kill them. Already it buried trees and hills. It was up to his waist in places.

Perhaps if I'd stayed in Luthadel, he thought, *working with my scholars, we could have discovered a way to stop this. . . .*

No, that was foolish. What would they do? Plug the Ashmounts? Find a way to wash all the ash out into the sea? In the distance ahead of him through the evening mists, he could see a red glow in the sky, though the sun set on the opposite horizon. He could only assume that the light to the east came from fire and lava rising out of the Ashmounts.

What did he do about a dying sky, ash so thick he could barely move through it, and erupting volcanoes? So far, his way of dealing with these things had been to ignore them.

Or rather, to let Vin worry about them.

That's what really has me worried, he thought. *Losing the woman I love is bad enough. But losing the one I trusted to fix all this . . . that's truly frightening.*

It was an odd realization. The deep truth was, he really *did* trust Vin as more than a person. She was more like a force. Almost a god? It seemed silly, thinking about that directly. She was his wife. Even though he was a member of the

Church of the Survivor, it felt wrong to worship her, to think her divine.

And he didn't, not really. But he did trust her. Vin was a person of instinct, while Elend was one of logic and thought. Sometimes it seemed she could do the impossible simply because she didn't stop to *think* about how impossible it really was. If Elend came to a cliff, he paused, gauging the distance to the other side. Vin went ahead and jumped.

What would happen on the day she didn't reach the other side? What if the events they were tied up in were bigger than two people could hope to solve, even if one of those people was Vin? Considering it now, the possibility of discovering helpful information in the cache at Fadrex had been a slim hope.

We need help, Elend thought with frustration. He stopped in the ash, the darkness closing around him as night finally fell. The mists swirled.

Help. What did that mean? Help from some mysterious god like the ones who Sazed had preached about? Elend had never known a god other than the Lord Ruler. And he'd never really had faith in that creature—though meeting Yomen had changed his perspective on how some people worshipped the Lord Ruler.

Elend stood, looking up at the sky, watching the flakes of ash fall. Continuing their silent, yet ceaseless barrage against the land. Like the raven feathers of a soft pillow used to suffocate a sleeping victim.

We are doomed, he thought. Behind him, the koloss stopped their march, waiting upon his wordless order. *That's it. It's all going to end.*

The realization wasn't crushing. It was gentle, like the final tendril of smoke from a dying candle. He suddenly knew that they couldn't fight—that everything they'd done over the last year had been pointless.

Elend slumped to his knees. The ash came up to his chest. Perhaps this was one last reason why he'd wanted to walk home alone. When others were around, he felt as if he had to be optimistic. But alone he could face the truth.

And there, in the ash, he finally just gave up.

Someone knelt down beside him.

Elend jumped backward, scrambling to his feet and scattering ash. He flared pewter belatedly, giving himself the tense strength of a Mistborn about to attack. But there was nobody near him. He froze, wondering if he'd been imagining things. And then, burning tin and squinting in the darkness of the ashen night, he finally saw it. A creature of mist.

It wasn't really *composed* of mist. Rather, it was outlined in mist. The random shiftings suggested its figure, which was roughly that of a man. Elend had seen this creature twice before. The first time, it had appeared to him in the wilderness of the Northern Dominance.

The second time, it had stabbed him in the gut, leaving him to bleed to death.

Yet that had been an attempt to get Vin to take the power at the Well of Ascension and use it to heal Elend. The thing's intentions had been good, although it had nearly killed him. Plus, Vin said that this creature had led her to the bit of metal that had turned Elend into an Allomancer.

The mist spirit watched him, its figure barely distinguishable in the patterns of flowing mists.

"What?" Elend asked. "What do you want of me?"

The mist spirit raised its arm and pointed to the southeast.

That's all it did the first time it met me. It only pointed, as if trying to get me to go somewhere. I didn't understand what it meant then *either.*

"Look," Elend said, suddenly feeling exhausted. "If you want to say something, why not just say it?"

The mist spirit stood quietly in the mists.

"At least write it," Elend said. "The pointing isn't working." He knew that the creature—whatever it was—had some corporeality. After all, it had managed to stab Elend handily enough.

He expected the creature to continue standing there. But to Elend's surprise it followed the command, kneeling down. It reached out with a misty hand and began to scratch in the ash. Elend took a step forward, cocking his head to see what the thing was writing.

I will kill you, the words said. *Death, death, death.*

"Well . . . that's pleasant," Elend said, feeling an eerie chill.

The mist spirit seemed to slump. It knelt in the ash, making no impression in the ground.

Such odd words to write, Elend thought, *when it seemed to be trying to get me to trust it . . .* "It can change your words, can't it?" Elend asked. "The other force. It can rewrite pieces of text on paper, so why not things scratched in ash?"

The mist spirit looked up.

"That's why you ripped the corners off Sazed's papers," Elend said. "You couldn't write him a note, because the words would just get changed. So you had to do other things. More blunt things—like pointing."

The creature stood.

"So write more slowly," Elend said. "Use exaggerated motions. I'll watch the movements of your arm, and form the letters in my mind."

The mist spirit began immediately, waving its arms about. Elend cocked his head, watching its motions. He couldn't make any sense of them, let alone form letters out of them.

"Wait," he said, holding up a hand. "That isn't working. Either it's changing things, or you don't know your letters."

Silence.

Wait. Elend glanced at the text on the ground. *If the text changed . . .*

"It's here, isn't it," he said, feeling a sudden and icy chill. "It's here with us now."

The mist spirit remained still.

"Bounce around for a yes," Elend said.

The mist spirit began to wave its arms as it had before.

"Close enough," Elend said, shivering. He glanced around, but could see nothing else in the mists. If the thing Vin had released was there, then it made no impression.

Yet Elend thought he *could* feel something different. A slight increase in wind, a touch of ice in the air, the mists moving about more agitatedly. Perhaps he was just imagining things.

He focused his attention back on the mist spirit. "You're . . . not as solid as you were before."

The creature remained still.

"Is that a no?" Elend said, frustrated. The creature remained still.

Elend closed his eyes. Forcing himself to focus, thinking back to the logic puzzles of his youth. *I need to approach this more directly. Use questions that can be answered with a simple yes or no.* Why would the mist spirit be harder to see now than before? Elend opened his eyes.

"Are you weaker than you were before?" he asked.

The thing waved its arms.

Yes, Elend thought.

"Is it because the world is ending?"

More waving.

"Are you weaker than the other thing? The thing Vin set free?"

Waving.

"*A lot* weaker?"

It waved, though it seemed a bit disconsolate this time.

Great, Elend thought. Of course, he could have guessed that. Whatever the mist spirit was, it wasn't a magical answer to their problems. If it were, it would have saved them by now.

What we lack most is information, Elend thought. *I need to learn what I can from this thing.*

"Are you related to the ash?" he asked.

No motion.

"Are you causing the ashfalls?"

No motion.

"Is the other thing causing the ashfalls?"

This time it waved.

Okay. "Is it causing the mists to come in the day too?"

No motion.

"Are *you* causing the mists to come in the day?"

It seemed to pause in thought at this one, then it waved about less vigorously than before.

Is that a "maybe"? Elend wondered. *Or a "partially"?*

The creature fell still. It was getting harder and harder to see it in the mists. Elend flared his tin, but that didn't make the creature any more distinct. It seemed to be . . . fading.

"Where was it you wanted me to go?" Elend asked, more for himself than expecting an answer. "You pointed . . . southeast? Did you want me to go back to Luthadel?"

It waved with half enthusiasm again.

"Do you want me to attack Fadrex City?"

It stood still.

"Do you *not* want me to attack Fadrex City?"

It waved vigorously.

Interesting, he thought.

"The mists," Elend said. "They're connected to all this, aren't they?"

Waving.

"They're killing my men," Elend said.

It stepped forward, then stood still, somehow looking urgent.

Elend frowned. "You reacted to that. You mean to say they *aren't* killing my men?"

It waved.

"That's ridiculous. I've *seen* the men fall dead."

It stepped forward, pointing at Elend. He glanced down at his sash. "The coins?" he asked, looking up.

It pointed again. Elend reached into his sash. All that was there were his metal vials. He pulled one out. "Metals?"

It waved vigorously. It just continued to wave and wave. Elend looked down at the vial. "I don't understand."

The creature fell still. It was getting more and more vague, as if it were evaporating.

"Wait!" Elend said, stepping forward. "I have another question. One more before you go!"

It stared him in the eyes.

"Can we beat it?" Elend asked softly. "Can we survive?"

Stillness. Then the creature gave a brief wave. Not a vigorous one, but hesitant. Uncertain. It evaporated, maintaining that same wave, the mists becoming indistinct and leaving no sign that the creature had been there.

Elend stood in the darkness. He turned and glanced at his koloss army, who waited like the trunks of dark trees in the distance. Then he turned back, scanning for any further signs of the mist spirit. Finally he turned and began to tromp his way back to Fadrex. The koloss followed.

He felt . . . stronger. It was silly—the mist spirit hadn't really given him any useful information. It had been almost like a child. The things it had told him were mostly confirmations of what he'd already suspected.

Yet as he walked, he moved with more determination. If only because he knew there were things in the world he didn't understand—and that meant that perhaps there were possibilities he didn't see. Possibilities for survival.

Possibilities to land safely on the other side of the chasm, even when logic told him not to jump.

I don't know why Preservation decided to use his last bit of life appearing to Elend during his trek back to Fadrex. From what I understand, Elend didn't learn much from the meeting. By then, Preservation was but a shadow of himself—and that shadow was under immense destructive pressure from Ruin.

Perhaps Preservation—or the remnants of what he had been—wanted to get Elend alone. Or perhaps he saw Elend kneeling in that field, and knew that the emperor of men was very close to lying down in the ash, never to rise again. Either way, Preservation did appear, and in so doing exposed himself to Ruin's attacks. Gone were the days when Preservation could turn away an Inquisitor with a bare gesture; gone were the days when he could strike a man down to bleed and die.

By the time Elend saw the "mist spirit," Preservation must have been barely coherent. I wonder what Elend would have done, had he known that he was in the presence of a dying god—that on that night, he had been the last witness of Preservation's passing. If Elend had waited a few more minutes on that ashen field, he would have seen a body—short of stature, black hair, prominent nose—fall from the mists and slump dead onto the ground.

As it was, the corpse was left alone to be buried in ash. The world was dying. Its gods had to die with it.

56

SPOOK STOOD IN THE DARK cavern, looking at his board and paper. He had it propped up like an artist's canvas, though he wasn't sketching images but ideas. Kelsier had always outlined his plans for the crew on a charcoal board. It seemed a good idea, although Spook wasn't explaining plans to a crew, but rather trying to work them out for himself.

The trick was going to be getting Quellion to expose himself as an Allomancer before the people. Durn had told them what to look for, and the crowds would be ready, waiting for confirmation of what they had been told. However, for Spook's plan to work, he'd have to catch the Citizen in a public place, then get the man to use his powers in a way that was obvious to those watching.

I can't let him merely Push on a distant metal then, he thought, scratching a charcoal note to himself on the board. *I'll need him to shoot into the air, or perhaps blast some coins. Something visible, something we can tell everyone to watch for.*

That would be tough, but Spook was confident. He had several ideas written on the board, ranging from attacking Quellion at a rally to tricking him into using his powers when he thought nobody was looking. Slowly, the thoughts were gelling into a cohesive plan.

I really can *do this,* Spook thought, smiling. *I always felt such awe for Kelsier's leadership abilities. But it's not as hard as I thought.*

Or at least that was what he told himself. He tried not to think about the consequences of a failure. Tried not to think about the fact that he still held Beldre hostage. Tried not to worry about the fact that when he awoke some mornings— his tin having burned away during the night—his body felt completely numb, unable to feel anything until he got more metal as fuel. Tried not to focus on the riots and incidents his appearances, speeches, and work among the people were causing.

Kelsier kept telling him not to worry. That should be enough for him. Shouldn't it?

After a few minutes he heard someone approaching, footsteps quiet—but not too quiet for him—on the stone. The rustle of a dress, yet without perfume, let him know exactly who it was.

"Spook?"

He lowered the charcoal and turned. Beldre stood at the far side of his "room." He'd made himself an alcove between several of the storage shelves, partitioned off with sheets—his own personal office.

The Citizen's sister wore a beautiful noble gown of green and white. Spook smiled. "You like the dresses?"

She looked down, flushing slightly. "I . . . haven't worn anything like this in years."

"Nobody in this city has," Spook said, setting down the charcoal and wiping his fingers on a rag. "But then, that makes it pretty easy to get them, if you know which buildings to loot. It looks like I matched your size pretty well, eh?"

"Yes," she said quietly, drifting forward. The gown really did look good on her, and Spook found it a little difficult to focus as she drew closer. She eyed his charcoal board, then frowned. "Is . . . that supposed to make any sense?"

Spook shook himself free of his trance. The charcoal board was a mess of scratches and notations. That in itself would have made it difficult enough to read. However, there was something else that made it more incomprehensible.

"It's mostly written in Eastern street slang," Spook said.

"The dialect you grew up speaking?" she said, fingering the board's edge, careful not to touch the writing lest she smudge it.

Spook nodded.

"The words are different," she said. "Wasing?"

"It kind of means 'was doing,'" Spook explained. "You start sentences with it. 'Wasing the run of there' would mean 'I was running to that place.'"

"Wasing the where of how of the finds," Beldre said, smiling slightly to herself as she read from the board. "It sounds like gibberish!"

"Wasing the how of wanting the doing," Spook said, smiling, falling into a full accent. Then he flushed, turning away.

"What?" she asked.

Why do I always act so foolish around her? he thought. *The others always made fun of my slang—even Kelsier thought it was silly. Now I start speaking it in front of her?*

He'd been feeling confident and sure as he studied his plans before she arrived. Why was it that she could always make him fall out of his leadership role and return to being the old Spook? The Spook who had never been important.

"You shouldn't be ashamed of the accent," Beldre said. "I think it's charming."

"You just said it was gibberish," Spook said, turning back to her.

"But that's the best part!" Beldre said. "It's gibberish on *purpose,* right?"

Spook remembered with fondness how his parents had responded to his adoption of the slang. It had been a type of power, being able to say things that only his friends could understand. Of course, he'd started speaking in it so much that it had been hard to switch back.

"So," Beldre said, eyeing the board. "What does it say?"

Spook hesitated. "Just random thoughts," he said. She was his enemy—he had to remember that.

"Oh," she said. Something unreadable crossed her face, then she turned away from the board.

Her brother always banished her from his conferences, Spook thought. *Never told her anything important. Left her feeling like she was useless . . .*

"I need to get your brother to use his Allomancy in front of the people," Spook found himself saying. "To let them see that he's a hypocrite."

Beldre looked back.

"The board is filled with my ideas," Spook said. "Most of them aren't very good. I'm leaning toward simply attacking him, making him defend himself."

"That won't work," Beldre said.

"Why not?"

"He won't use Allomancy against you. He wouldn't expose himself like that."

"If I threaten him strongly enough he will."

Beldre shook her head. "You promised not to hurt him. Remember?"

"No," Spook said, raising a finger. "I promised to *try* to find another way. And I don't intend to kill him. I just need to make him *think* that I'd kill him."

Beldre fell silent again. His heart lurched.

"I won't do it, Beldre," Spook said. "I won't kill him."

"You promise that?"

Spook nodded.

She looked up at him, then smiled. "I want to write him a letter. Perhaps I can talk him into listening to you; we could avoid the need for this in the first place."

"All right . . ." Spook said. "But you realize I'll have to read the letter to make certain you're not revealing anything that could hurt my position."

Beldre nodded.

Of course, he'd do more than read it. He'd rewrite it on another sheet of paper, changing the line order, and then add a few unimportant words. He'd worked on too many thieving crews to be unaware of ciphers. But assuming that Beldre was being honest with him, a letter from her to Quellion was a good idea. It couldn't help but strengthen Spook's position.

He opened his mouth to ask whether or not her sleeping accommodations were acceptable, but cut off as he heard someone approaching. Harder footsteps this time. Captain Goradel, he guessed.

Sure enough, the soldier appeared around the corner to Spook's room a short time later.

"My lord," the soldier said. "You should see this."

The soldiers were gone.

Sazed looked through the window with the others, inspecting the empty plot of ground where Quellion's troops had been camped for the last few weeks, watching the Ministry building.

"When did they leave?" Breeze asked, rubbing his chin thoughtfully.

"Just now," Goradel explained.

The move felt ominous to Sazed. He stood beside Spook, Breeze, and Goradel—though the others seemed to take the soldiers' retreat as a good sign.

"Well, it will make sneaking out easier," Goradel noted.

"More than that," Spook said. "It means I can incorporate our own soldiers in the plan against Quellion. We'd never have gotten them out of the building secretly with half an army on our doorstep, but now . . ."

"Yes," Goradel said. "But where did they go? Do you think Quellion is suspicious of us?"

Breeze snorted. "That, my dear man, sounds like a question for your scouts. Why not have them search out where that army went?"

Goradel nodded. But then, to Sazed's slight surprise, the soldier looked toward Spook for a confirmation. Spook gave a nod himself, and the captain moved off to give the orders.

He looks to the boy over Breeze and me, Sazed thought. He shouldn't have been surprised. He had agreed to let Spook take the lead, and to Goradel, all three of them— Sazed, Breeze, Spook—were probably equal. All were in Elend's inner circle, and of the three, Spook was the best warrior. It made sense for Goradel to look to him as a source of authority.

It felt strange to see Spook giving orders to the soldiers. Spook had always been so quiet during the days of the original crew. Yet Sazed was beginning to respect the boy too. Spook knew how to give orders in a way that Sazed could not, and he had shown remarkable foresight in his preparations in Urteau, as well as in his plans to overthrow Quellion. He had a flair for the dramatic that Breeze kept saying was remarkable.

But there was that bandage on the boy's eyes, and the other things he hadn't explained. Sazed knew that he should have pushed harder for answers, but the truth was that he trusted Spook. Sazed had known Spook since he'd barely been capable of communicating with others.

As Goradel moved off, Spook looked to Sazed and Breeze. "Well?"

"Quellion is planning something," Breeze said. "Seems too early to jump to conclusions though."

"I agree," Spook said. "For now, we go forward with the plan."

With that they split up. Sazed turned and made his way back down and over to the far side of the cavern, where a large group of soldiers worked in an area well lit with lanterns. On his arms, he wore the familiar weight of his copperminds—two on his forearms, two on his upper arms. In them sat the knowledge of engineering he needed to complete the task Spook had assigned him.

Lately, Sazed didn't know what to think. Each time he climbed the ladder and looked out over the city, he saw worse signs. The ashfalls were heavier. The earthquakes were growing more and more frequent, more and more violent. The mists were lingering later and later in the day. The sky grew dark, the red sun more like a vast bleeding scar than a source of light and life. The Ashmounts made the horizon red during the night.

It seemed to him that the end of the world should be a time when men *found* faith, not a time when they lost it. Yet the little time that he'd devoted to studying the religions in his portfolio had not been encouraging. Twenty more religions eliminated, leaving a mere thirty potential candidates.

He shook his head to himself, moving among the toiling soldiers. Several groups worked on wooden contraptions filled with rocks—weight systems that would fall to block off the water running into the cavern. Others worked on the system of pulleys that would lower the mechanism. After a half hour or so, Sazed determined that they were all doing their tasks well, and went to return to his calculations. However, as he walked to his table, Spook approached.

"Riots," Spook said, falling into step beside Sazed.

"Excuse me, Lord Spook?"

"That's where the soldiers went. Some people started a fire, and the soldiers guarding us were needed to put it out before the whole city went up. There's a lot more wood here than there is in Central Dominance cities."

Sazed frowned. "Our actions here are becoming dangerous, I fear."

Spook shrugged. "Seems like a good thing to me. This city is on the edge of snapping, Saze. Just like Luthadel was when we took control."

"Only the presence of Elend Venture kept that city from destroying itself," Sazed said quietly. "Kelsier's revolution could easily have turned into a disaster."

"It will be all right," Spook said.

Sazed eyed the young man as the two of them walked through the cavern. Spook seemed to be trying hard to project an air of confidence. Perhaps Sazed was growing cynical, but he found it difficult to be as optimistic as Spook.

"You don't believe me," Spook said.

"I'm sorry, Lord Spook," Sazed said. "It's not that . . . it's simply that it seems difficult to have faith in anything lately."

"Oh."

They walked silently for a while, eventually finding themselves at the edge of the glassy underground lake. Sazed paused by the waters, his worries gnawing at his insides. He stood for a long moment, feeling frustrated, but not really having an outlet.

"Don't you worry, Spook?" Sazed finally asked. "Worry that we'll fail?"

"I don't know," Spook said, shuffling.

"And it's so much more than *this*," Sazed said, waving at the work crews. "The very sky seems to be our enemy. The land is dying. Don't you wonder what good any of this is? Why we even struggle? We're all doomed anyway!"

Spook flushed. Then he looked down. "I don't know," he repeated. "I . . . I understand what you're doing, Sazed. You're trying to find out if I doubt myself. I guess you can see through me."

Sazed frowned, but Spook wasn't looking.

"You're right," the young man said then, wiping his brow, "I *do* wonder if I'll fail. I guess Tindwyl would be annoyed at me, wouldn't she? She didn't think that leaders should doubt themselves."

That gave Sazed pause. *What am I doing?* he thought, horrified at his outburst. *Is this what I've really become? During most of my life, I resisted the Synod, rebelling against my own people. Yet I was at peace, confident that I was doing the right thing.*

Now I come here, where people need me most, and I sit around and snap at my friends, telling them we're all going to die?

"But," Spook said, looking up, "though I doubt myself, I still think we'll be all right."

Sazed was surprised at the hope he saw in the boy's eyes. *That's what I've lost.*

"How can you say that?" Sazed asked.

"I don't know, really," Spook said. "I just . . . Well, do you remember that question you asked me when you first got here? We were standing by the lake, right over there. You asked me about faith. You asked what good it was, if it just led people to hurt each other, like Quellion's faith in the Survivor has done."

Sazed looked out over the lake. "Yes," he said softly. "I remember."

"I've been thinking about that ever since," Spook said. "And . . . I think I might have an answer."

"Please."

"Faith," Spook said, "means that it doesn't matter what happens. You can trust that somebody is watching. Trust that somebody will make it all right."

Sazed frowned.

"It means that there will always be a way," Spook whispered, staring forward, eyes glazed, as if seeing things that Sazed could not.

Yes, Sazed thought. *That is what I have lost. And it's what I need to get back.*

I have come to see that each power has three aspects: a physical one, which can be seen in the creations made by Ruin and Preservation; a spiritual one in the unseen energy that permeates the whole world; and a cognitive one in the minds who controlled that energy.

There is more to this. Much more that even I do not yet comprehend.

57

YOU SHOULD KILL THEM.

Vin looked up as she heard a pair of guards pass the door to her cell. There was one good thing about Ruin's voice—it tended to warn her when people were nearby, even if it did always tell her to kill them.

A part of her wondered if she had in fact gone mad. After all, she saw and heard things that nobody else could. However, if she were mad, there would be no reliable way for her to realize it. So she decided to simply accept what she heard and move on.

In truth, she was glad for Ruin's voice on occasion. Other than Ruin, she was alone in the cell. All was still. The soldiers did not speak—likely at Yomen's orders. Plus, each time Ruin spoke she felt she learned something. For instance, she had learned that Ruin could either manifest in person or affect her from a distance. When its actual presence was not with her in the cell, Ruin's words were far more basic and vague.

Take Ruin's order that she kill the guards. She couldn't follow that suggestion, not from within the cell. It wasn't so much a specific order as it was an attempt to change her inclinations. Again that reminded her of the way Allomancy could exert a general influence over a person's emotions.

General influence . . .

Something occurred to her. She reached out with her mind, and—sure enough—she could still feel the thousand koloss that Elend had given her. They were under her control still, distant, obeying the general orders she'd given them before.

Could she use them somehow? Deliver a message to Elend perhaps? Get them to attack the city and free her? As she considered them, both plans seemed flawed. Sending them to Fadrex would only get them killed, as well as risk upsetting whatever plans Elend had for a potential attack. She could send them to find Elend, but that would probably get them killed by the camp guards, who would be afraid they were bloodlusting. Plus, what would she have them do if they did get to him? She could order them to take actions, like attack or pick someone up, but she'd never tried something as delicate as ordering one to speak certain words.

She tried forming those words in her head and getting them to the koloss, but all she sensed back was confusion. She'd have to work on that some more. Thinking about it, she wondered if getting a message to Elend would really be the best way to use them. It would let Ruin know about a potential tool she had that he perhaps hadn't noticed.

"I see he found a cell for you," a voice said.

Vin looked up, and there it was. Still wearing Reen's form, Ruin stood in the small cell with her. It maintained a straight-backed posture, standing almost benevolently over her. Vin sat up on her cot. She'd never thought that of all her metals, she would miss bronze so much. When Ruin returned to visit in "person," burning bronze had let her feel it via bronzepulses and gave her warning that it had arrived, even if it didn't appear to her.

"I'll admit that I'm disappointed in you, Vin," Ruin said.

It used Reen's voice, but imbued it with a sense of . . . age. Of quiet wisdom. The fatherly nature of that voice, mixed with Reen's face and her own knowledge of the thing's desire to destroy, was disturbing.

"The last time you were captured and locked away without metals," Ruin continued, "not a night passed before you'd killed the Lord Ruler and overthrown the empire. Now you've been soundly imprisoned for what . . . a week now?"

Vin didn't respond. *Why come taunt me? Does it expect to learn something?*

Ruin shook its head. "I would have thought at the very least that you'd have killed Yomen."

"Why are you so concerned with his death?" Vin asked. "It seems to me that he's on your side."

Ruin shook its head, standing with hands clasped behind its back. "You still don't understand, I see. You're *all* on my side, Vin. I created you. You're my tools—each and every one of you. Zane, Yomen, you, your dear Emperor Venture . . ."

"No. Zane was yours, and Yomen is obviously misguided. But Elend . . . he'll fight against you."

"But he can't," Ruin said. "That's what you refuse to understand, child. You *cannot* fight me, for by the mere act of fighting you advance my goals."

"Perhaps evil men help you," Vin said. "But not Elend. He's a good person, and not even you can deny that."

"Vin, Vin. *Why* can't you see? This isn't about good or evil. Morality doesn't enter into it. Good men will kill as quickly for what they want as evil men—only the things they want are different."

Vin fell silent.

Ruin shook its head again. "I keep trying to explain. This process we are engaged in, the end of all things—it's not a *fight,* but a simple culmination of inevitability. Can any man make a pocket watch that won't eventually wind down? Can you imagine a lantern that won't eventually burn out? All things end. Think of me as a caretaker—the one who watches the shop and makes certain that the lights are turned out, that everything is cleaned up, once closing time arrives."

For a moment, he made her question. There was some truth in his words, and seeing the changes in the land these last few years—changes that started before Ruin was released—did make her wonder.

Yet something about the conversation bothered her. If what Ruin said was completely true, then why did he care about her? Why return and speak to her?

"I guess you've won then," she said quietly.

"Won?" Ruin asked. "Don't you understand? There was nothing for me to win, child. Things happen as they must."

"I see," Vin said.

"Yes, perhaps you do," Ruin said. "I think that *you* just might be able to." It turned and began to walk quietly from one side of the cell toward the other. "You are a piece of me, you know. Beautiful destroyer. Blunt and effective. Of all those I've claimed over this brief thousand years, you are the only one I suspect might be capable of understanding me."

Why, Vin thought, *it's gloating! That's why Ruin is here— because it wants to make certain someone understands what it has accomplished!* There was a feeling of pride and victory in Ruin's eyes. They were human emotions—which Vin could understand.

At that moment, Ruin stopped being an *it* in her mind, and instead became a *he.*

Vin began to think—for the first time—that she could find a way to beat Ruin. He was powerful, perhaps even incomprehensible. But she had seen humanity in him, and that humanity could be deceived, manipulated, and broken. Perhaps it was this same conclusion that Kelsier had drawn, after looking into the Lord Ruler's eyes that fateful night when he had been captured. She finally felt as if she understood him, and what it must have felt like to undertake something so bold as the defeat of the Lord Ruler.

But Kelsier had years to plan, Vin thought. *I . . . I have no idea how long I have. Not long, I would guess.* As she thought, another earthquake began. The walls trembled, and Vin heard guards cursing in the hallway as something fell and broke. And Ruin . . . he seemed to be in a state of bliss, his eyes closed, mouth open slightly as the building and city rumbled.

Eventually, all fell still. Ruin opened his eyes, staring her down. "This work I do, it's about *passion,* Vin. It's about dynamic events; it's about change! That is why you and your Elend are so important to me. People with passion are people who will destroy—for a man's passion is not *true* until he proves how much he's willing to sacrifice for it. Will he kill? Will he go to war? Will he break and discard that which he has, all in the name of what he *needs*?"

It's not merely that Ruin feels that he's accomplished something, Vin thought. *He feels that he's overcome. Despite what he claims, he feels that he's won—that he's defeated something . . . but who or what? Us? We would be no adversary for a force like Ruin.*

A voice from the past seemed to whisper to her from long ago. *First, there's something you have to understand about Allomancy.*

Consequence. Action and reaction. If Ruin had power to destroy, then there was something that opposed him. There had to be. Ruin had an opposite, an opponent. Or he once had.

"What did you do to him?" Vin asked.

Ruin hesitated, frowning as he turned toward her.

"Your opposite," Vin said. "The one who once stopped you from destroying the world."

Ruin was silent for a long moment. Then he smiled, and Vin saw something chilling in that smile. A knowledge that he was right. Vin *was* part of him. She understood him.

"Preservation is dead," Ruin said.

"You killed him?"

Ruin shrugged. "Yes, but no. He gave of himself to craft

a cage. Though his throes of agony have lasted several thousand years, now at last he is gone. And the bargain has come to its fruition."

Preservation, Vin thought, a piece of a gigantic whole clicking into place. *The opposite of Ruin. A force like that couldn't have* destroyed *his enemy, because he would represent the opposite of destruction. But imprisonment, that would be within his powers.*

Imprisonment that ended when I gave up the power at the Well.

"And thus you see the inevitability," Ruin said softly.

"You couldn't create it yourself, could you?" Vin asked. "The world, life. You can't create, you can only destroy."

"He couldn't create either," Ruin said. "He could only preserve. Preservation is not creation."

"And so you worked together," Vin said.

"Both with a promise," Ruin said. "My promise was to work with him to create you—life that thinks, life that loves."

"And his promise?" Vin asked, fearing that she knew the answer.

"That I could destroy you eventually," Ruin said softly. "And I have come to claim what was promised me. The sole point in creating something is to watch it die. Like a story that must come to a climax, what I have done will not be fulfilled until the end has arrived."

It can't be true, Vin thought. *Preservation. If he represents a power in the universe, then he couldn't truly have been destroyed, could he?*

"I know what you are thinking," Ruin said. "You cannot enlist Preservation's power. He is dead. He couldn't kill me, you see. He could only imprison me."

Yes. I figured that last part out already. You really can't read my mind, can you.

Ruin continued. "It was a villainous act, I must say. Preservation tried to escape our bargain. Would you not call that an evil deed? It is as I said before—good and evil have little to do with ruin or preservation. An evil man will protect that which he desires as surely as a good man."

But something is keeping Ruin from destroying the world now, she thought. *For all his words about stories and endings, he is not a force that would wait for an "appropriate" moment. There is more to this, more that I'm not understanding.*

What is holding him back?

"I've come to you," Ruin said, "because I want you at least to watch and see. To know. For it has come."

Vin perked up. "What? The end?"

Ruin nodded.

"How long?" Vin asked.

"Days," Ruin said. "But not weeks."

Vin felt a chill, realizing something. He had come to her, finally revealing himself, because she was captured. He thought that there was no further chance for humankind. He assumed that he had won.

Which means that there is a way to beat him, she thought with determination. *And it involves me. But I can't do it here, or he wouldn't have come to gloat.*

And that meant she had to get free. Quickly.

Once you begin to understand these things, you can see how Ruin was trapped even though Preservation's mind was gone, expended to create the prison. Though Preservation's consciousness was mostly wiped out, his spirit and body were still in force. And as an opposite force of Ruin, these could still prevent Ruin from destroying.

Or at least keep him from destroying things too quickly. Once his mind was freed from its prison, the destruction accelerated rapidly.

58

"THROW YOUR WEIGHT HERE," SAZED said, pointing at a wooden lever. "The counterweights will fall, swinging down all four floodgates and stemming the flow into the cavern. I warn you, however—the explosion of water above will be rather spectacular. We should be able to fill the city's canals in a matter of hours, and I suspect that a portion of the northern end of the city will be flooded."

"To dangerous levels?" Spook asked.

"I do not think so," Sazed said. "The water will burst out through the conduits in the interchange building beside us. I've inspected the equipment there, and it appears sound. The water *should* flow directly into the canals, and from there exit the city. In any case, I would not want to be in those streetslots when this water comes. The current will be quite swift."

"I've taken care of that," Spook said. "Durn is going

to make certain the people know to be clear of the water-ways."

Sazed nodded. Spook couldn't help but be impressed. The complicated construct of wood, gears, and wire looked like it should have taken months to build, not weeks. Large nets of rocks weighed down the four gates that hung ready to block off the river.

"This is amazing, Saze," Spook said. "With a sign as spectacular as the reappearance of the canal waters, the people will be *certain* to listen to us instead of the Citizen." Breeze and Durn's men had been working hard over the last few weeks, whispering to the people to watch for a miracle from the Survivor of the Flames. Something extraordinary, something to prove—once and for all—who was the right-ful master of the city.

"It is the best I could do," Sazed said, with a modest bow of the head. "The seals won't be perfectly tight, of course. However, that should matter little."

"Men?" Spook said, turning to four of Goradel's soldiers. "You understand what you are to do?"

"Yes, sir," the lead soldier said. "We wait for a messen-ger, then throw the lever there."

"If no messenger comes," Spook said, "throw the switch at nightfall."

"And," Sazed said, raising a finger, "don't forget to twist the sealing mechanism in the other room, plugging the water flow *out* of this chamber. Otherwise the lake will eventually empty. Better that we keep this reservoir full, just in case."

"Yes, sir," the soldier said, giving a nod.

Spook turned and looked over the cavern. Soldiers bus-tled about, preparing. He was going to need most of them for the night's activities. They seemed eager—they'd spent too long holed up in the cavern and the building above. To one side, Beldre regarded Sazed's contraption with interest. Spook broke away from the soldiers, approaching her with a quick step.

"You're really going to do it?" she said. "Return the water to the canals?"

Spook nodded.

"I sometimes imagined what it would be like to have the waters back," she said. "The city wouldn't feel as barren—it would become important, like it was during the early days of the Final Empire. All those beautiful waterways. No more ugly gashes in the ground."

"It will be a wonderful sight," Spook said, smiling.

Beldre shook her head. "It amazes me that you can be such different people at the same time. How can the man who would do such a beautiful thing for my city also plan such destruction?"

"Beldre, I'm not planning to destroy your city."

"Just its government."

"I do what needs to be done."

"Men say that so easily," Beldre said. "Yet everybody seems to have a different opinion of what 'needs' to be done."

"Your brother had his chance," Spook said.

Beldre looked down. She still carried with her the letter they'd received earlier in the day—a response from Quellion. Beldre's plea had been heartfelt, but the Citizen had responded with insults, implying that she had been forced to write the words because she was being held prisoner.

I do not fear a usurper, the letter read. *I am protected by the Survivor himself. You will not have this city, tyrant.*

Beldre looked up. "Don't do it," she whispered. "Give him more time. Please."

Spook hesitated.

"There is no more time," Kelsier whispered. "Do what must be done."

"I'm sorry," Spook said, turning from her. "Stay with the soldiers—I'm leaving four men to guard you. Not to keep you from fleeing, though they will do that. I want you in this cavern. I can't promise that the streets will be safe."

He heard her sniffle quietly behind him. He left her standing there, then walked toward the gathering group of soldiers. One man brought Spook his dueling canes and singed cloak. Goradel stood at the front of his soldiers, looking proud. "We're ready, my lord."

Breeze walked up beside him, shaking his head, his dueling cane tapping the ground. He sighed. "Well, here we go again. . . ."

The evening's occasion was a speech Quellion had been publicizing for some time. He had stopped the executions recently, as if finally realizing that the deaths were contributing to the instability of his rule. He apparently intended to swing back toward benevolence, holding rallies, emphasizing the wonderful things he was doing for the city.

Spook walked alone, a little ahead of Breeze, Allrianne, and Sazed, who chatted behind. Some of Goradel's soldiers followed as well, wearing common Urteau garb. Spook had split their force, sending it by different paths. It wasn't dark yet—to Spook the falling sun was bright, forcing him to wear his blindfold and spectacles. Quellion liked to give his speeches in the evening, so that the mists arrived during them. He liked the implied connection to the Survivor.

A figure hobbled out of a side streetslot next to Spook. Durn walked with a stooped posture, a cloak obscuring his figure. Spook respected the twisted man's insistence on leaving the security of the Harrows, going out to run jobs himself. Perhaps that was why he'd ended up as leader of the city's underground.

"People are gathering, as expected," Durn said, coughing quietly. "Some of your soldiers are already there."

Spook nodded.

"Things are unsettled in the city," Durn said. "It worries me. Factions I can't control have already started looting some of the off-limits noble mansions. My men are all busy trying to get people out of the streetslots."

"It will be all right," Spook said. "Most of the populace will be at the speech."

Durn was silent for a moment. "Word is that Quellion is

going to use his speech to denounce you, then finally order an attack on the Ministry building where you're staying."

"Then it's a good thing we won't be there," Spook said. "He shouldn't have withdrawn his soldiers, no matter how much he needed them to keep order in the city."

Durn nodded.

"What?" Spook said.

"I just hope you can handle this, lad. Once this night is through, the city will be yours. Treat it better than Quellion did."

"I will," Spook said.

"My men will create a disturbance for you at the meeting. Farewell." Durn took the next left, disappearing down another streetslot alleyway.

Ahead, the crowds were already gathering. Spook put up the hood of his cloak, keeping his eyes obscured as he wove his way through the crowd. He quickly left Sazed and the others behind, pushing his way up a ramp to the old city square—the place Quellion had chosen for his speech. His men had erected a wooden stage from which the Citizen could face the crowd. The speech was already in progress. Spook stopped not far from a guard patrol. Many of Quellion's soldiers surrounded the stage, eyeing the crowd.

Minutes passed, and Spook spent them listening to Quellion's voice ring, yet paying no attention to the words. Ash fell around him, dusting the crowd. Mists began to twist in the air.

He listened, listened with ears no other man had. He used Allomancy's strange ability to filter and ignore—hearing through the chatter and whispers and shuffles and coughs, the same way he somehow saw through the obscuring mists. He heard the city. Yells in the distance.

It was beginning.

"Too fast!" a voice whispered, a beggar moving up to Spook's side. "Durn sends word. Riots in the streets, ones he didn't start! Durn cannot control them. My lord, the city is beginning to burn!"

"It was a night not unlike this one," another voice whispered. Kelsier's voice. "A glorious night. When I took the city of Luthadel, and made it mine."

A disturbance began at the rear of the crowd; Durn's men were causing their distraction. Some of Quellion's guards pulled away to quash this nearby riot. The Citizen continued to shout his accusations. Spook heard his own name in Quellion's words, but the context was simply noise.

Spook tilted his head, looking up at the sky. Ash fell toward him, as if he were sailing through it into the air. Like a Mistborn.

His hood fell back. Men around him whispered in surprise.

A clock rang in the distance. Goradel's soldiers rushed the stage. Around him, Spook could feel a glow rising. The fires of rebellion burning in the city. Just like the night he had overthrown the Lord Ruler. The torches of revolution. Then the people had put Elend on the throne.

This time it would be Spook they elevated.

Weak no more, he thought. *Never weak again!*

The last of Quellion's soldiers rushed from the stage, moving into combat with Goradel's men. The crowd shied away from the battle, but nobody ran. They had been prepared well for the night's events. Many would be waiting, watching for the signs Spook and Durn had promised—signs revealed a few hours before, to minimize the risk of Quellion's spies learning Spook's plan. A miracle in the canals, and proof that Quellion was an Allomancer.

If the Citizen—or any of his guards on the stage—shot coins or used Allomancy to leap into the air, the people would see. They would know that they had been deceived. And that would be the end. The crowd surged away from the cursing soldiers, and their withdrawal left Spook standing alone. Quellion's voice finally trailed off. Some of his soldiers were running up to get him off the stage.

Quellion's eyes found Spook. Only then did they show fear.

Spook leaped. He couldn't Steelpush, but his legs were fueled by the power of flared pewter. He soared up, easily cresting the edge of the stage, and landed in a crouch. He pulled out a dueling cane, then rushed the Citizen.

Behind him, people began to cry out. Spook heard his name, Survivor of the Flames. Survivor. He wouldn't merely kill Quellion, but destroy him. Undermining his rule as Breeze had suggested. At that moment, the Soother and Allrianne would be manipulating the crowd, keeping them from running away in a panic. Holding them there.

So they could watch the show Spook was about to give.

The guards at Quellion's side saw Spook too late. He dropped the first one easily, crushing the man's skull inside his helmet. Quellion screamed for more help.

Spook swung at another man, who moved out of the way, supernaturally quick. Spook pulled to the side in time to dodge a blow, the weapon grazing his cheek. The man was an Allomancer—a pewter burner. The large brute carried no sword, but instead an obsidian-edged cudgel.

Pewter isn't spectacular enough, Spook thought. *The people won't know how to tell if a man is swinging too quickly or enduring too much. I have to make Quellion shoot coins.*

The Thug backed away, plainly noting Spook's own increased speed. He kept his weapon raised warily, but did not attack. He only had to stall so his companion had time to pull Quellion away. The Thug would be no easy fight—he would be more skilled than Spook, and even stronger.

"Your family is free," Spook lied quietly. "We saved them earlier. Help us capture Quellion—he no longer has any hold on you."

The Thug paused, lowering his weapon.

"Kill him!" Kelsier snapped.

That hadn't been Spook's plan, but he responded to the prompting. He dodged inside the Thug's reach. The man turned in shock, and as he did, Spook delivered a backhanded blow to his skull. Spook's dueling cane shattered. The Thug stumbled to the ground, and Spook snatched up the man's fallen weapon, the obsidian-lined cudgel.

Quellion was at the edge of the stage. Spook jumped,

sailing across the wooden platform. It was all right for him to use Allomancy; he hadn't preached against it. Only Quellion the hypocrite needed to fear using his powers.

Spook cut down the remaining guard as he landed—the jagged shards of obsidian ripping through flesh. The soldier fell, and Quellion spun.

"I don't fear you!" Quellion said, voice shaking. "I'm protected!"

"Kill him," Kelsier ordered, appearing visibly on the stage a short distance away. Usually the Survivor only spoke in his mind; he hadn't shown himself since that day in the burning building. It meant important things were happening.

Spook grabbed the Citizen by the front of his shirt, yanking him forward. Spook raised the length of wood, blood dripping from the obsidian shards onto his hand.

"*No!*"

Spook froze at that voice, then glanced to the side. *She* was there, shoving her way through the crowd, approaching the open space before the stage.

"*Beldre?*" Spook asked. "How did you get out of the cavern?"

But of course she couldn't hear him. Only Spook's supernatural hearing had allowed him to pick her voice out of the sounds of fear and battle. He met her eyes across the distance, and saw her whispered words more than he heard them.

Please. You promised.

"Kill him!"

Quellion chose that moment to try to pull away. Spook turned and yanked him again—harder this time, nearly ripping Quellion's shirt free as he threw the man down to the wooden platform. The Citizen cried out in pain, and Spook raised his brutal weapon with both hands.

Something sparked in the firelight. Spook barely felt the impact, though it shook him. He stumbled, looking down, seeing blood. Something had pierced the flesh of his left arm and shoulder. Not an arrow, though it had moved like one. His arm drooped, and though he couldn't feel the pain, it seemed that his muscles weren't working properly.

Something hit me. A . . . coin.

He turned. Beldre stood at the front of the crowd, crying, her hand raised toward him.

She was there that day I was captured, Spook thought numbly, *at her brother's side. He always keeps her near. To protect her, we thought.*

Or the other way around?

Spook stood up straighter, Quellion whimpering in front of him. Spook's arm dripped a trail of blood from where Beldre's coin had hit, but he ignored it, staring at her.

"You were always the Allomancer," he whispered. "Not your brother."

And then the crowd began to shout—likely prompted by Breeze. "The Citizen's sister is a Coinshot!"

"Hypocrite!"

"Liar!"

"He killed my uncle, yet left his own sister alive!"

Beldre cried out as the people, carefully prepared and planted, saw the proof that Spook had promised them. It didn't have the target he had intended, but the machine he had set in motion could not be halted now. The people gathered around Beldre, yelling in anger, shoving her among themselves.

Spook stepped toward her, raising his wounded arm. Then a shadow fell on him.

"She was always planning to betray you, Spook," Kelsier said.

Spook turned, looking at the Survivor. He stood tall and proud, like on the day he'd faced the Lord Ruler.

"You kept waiting for an assassin," Kelsier said. "You didn't realize that Quellion had already sent one. His sister. Didn't it strike you as strange that he'd let her get away from him and enter the enemy's own base? She was sent there to kill you. You, Sazed, and Breeze. The problem is, she was raised a pampered rich girl. She's not used to killing. She never was. You were never really in danger from her."

The crowd surged and Spook spun, worried about Beldre. However, he calmed a bit as he realized that the people were simply pulling her toward the stage. "Survivor!" people were chanting. "Survivor of the Flames!"

"King!"

They cast Beldre before him, pushing her up onto the platform. Her scarlet clothing was ripped, her figure battered, her auburn hair a mess. To the side, Quellion groaned, his arm apparently broken. Spook hadn't realized he'd done that.

Spook moved to help Beldre. She was bleeding from several small cuts, but she was alive. And she was crying.

"She's his bodyguard," Kelsier said, stepping toward Beldre. "That's why she was always with him. Quellion isn't an Allomancer. He never was."

Spook knelt beside her, cringing at her bruised form.

"Now, you must kill her," Kelsier said.

Spook looked up, blood seeping from the cut on his face, where the Thug had grazed him. It dripped from his chin. "*What?*"

"You want power, Spook?" Kelsier said, stepping forward. "You want to be a better Allomancer? Well, power must come from somewhere. It is never free. This woman is a Coinshot. Kill her, and you can have her ability. I will give it to you."

Spook looked down at the weeping woman. He felt surreal, as if he were not quite there. His breathing was labored, each breath coming as a gasp, his body shaking despite his pewter. People chanted his name. Quellion was mumbling something. Beldre continued to cry.

Spook reached up with his bloodied hand and ripped off his blindfold, his spectacles tumbling free. He stumbled to his feet and gazed out over the city.

And saw it burning.

The sounds of rioting echoed through the streets. Flames burned in a dozen different spots, lighting the mists, casting a hellish haze over the city. Not the fires of rebellion at all. The fires of destruction.

"This is wrong . . ." Spook whispered.

"You will take the city, Spook," Kelsier said. "You will have what you always wanted! You'll be like Elend, like Vin. Better than either! You'll have Elend's titles and Vin's power! You'll be like a god!"

Spook turned away from the burning city as something caught his attention. Quellion was reaching out with his good arm toward . . .

Toward Kelsier.

"Please," Quellion whispered. It seemed he could *see* the Survivor, though nobody else around them could. "My lord Kelsier, why have you forsaken me?"

"I gave you pewter, Spook," Kelsier said angrily, not looking at Quellion. "Will you deny me now? You must pull free a steel spike that supports this stage. Then you must take the girl and press her to your chest. Kill her with the spike, and drive it into your own body. That is the only way!"

Kill her with the spike . . . Spook thought, feeling numb. *This all began that day when I nearly died. I was fighting a Thug in the market; I used him as a shield. But . . . the other soldier struck anyway, stabbing through his companion and into me.*

Spook stumbled away from Beldre, kneeling beside Quellion. The man cried out as Spook forced him down against the wooden planks.

"That's right," Kelsier said. "Kill him first."

But Spook wasn't listening. He ripped Quellion's shirt, looking at the shoulder and chest. There was nothing odd about either. But the Citizen's upper arm had a length of metal piercing it. It appeared to be bronze. Hand shaking, Spook pulled the metal free. Quellion screamed.

But so did Kelsier.

Spook turned, bloodied bronze spike in his hand. Kelsier was enraged, his hands like claws as he stepped forward.

"What *are* you?" Spook asked.

The thing screamed, but Spook ignored it and looked down at his own chest. He ripped open his shirt, exposing the mostly healed wound next to his shoulder. A glimmer of metal still shone there, the tip of the sword. The sword that had passed through an Allomancer—killing the man—and then entered Spook's own body. Kelsier had told him to leave the broken shard there as a symbol of what Spook had gone through.

The point of the shard protruded from his skin. How had he forgotten about it? How had he ignored such a sizable piece of metal inside his body? Spook reached for it.

"No!" Kelsier said. "Spook, do you want to go back to being normal? Do you want to be useless again? You'll lose your pewter and return to being weak like you were when you let your uncle die!"

Spook wavered.

No, Spook thought. *Something is wrong. I was supposed to expose Quellion, get him to use his Allomancy, but I attacked instead. I wanted to kill. I forgot about our plans and preparation. I brought destruction to this city.*

This is not right!

He pulled the glass dagger from his boot. Kelsier screamed terribly in his ears, but Spook reached up anyway, slicing the flesh of his chest. He reached in with pewter-enhanced fingers and grabbed the steel shard that was embedded inside.

Then he ripped the bit of metal free and cast it across the stage, crying out at the shock of pain. Kelsier vanished immediately. And so did Spook's ability to burn pewter.

It hit him all at once—the fatigue of pushing himself so hard during his time in Urteau. The wounds he'd been ignoring. The sudden explosion of light, sound, smell, and sensation that pewter had let him resist. It overcame him like a physical force, crushing him down. He collapsed to the platform.

He groaned, unable to think anymore. He could simply let the blackness take him. . . .

Her city is burning.

Blackness . . .

Thousands will die in the flames.

The mists tickled his cheeks. In the cacophony, Spook had let his tin dim, relieving him of sensation, leaving him blissfully numb. It was better that way.

You want to be like Kelsier? Really like Kelsier? Then fight when you are beaten!

"Lord Spook!" The voice was faint.

Survive!

With a scream of pain, Spook flared tin. As the metal always did, it brought a wave of sensations—thousands of them, shocking him at once. Pain. Feeling. Hearing. Sounds, smells, lights.

And lucidity.

Spook forced himself to his knees, coughing. Blood still streamed down his arm. He looked up. Sazed was running toward the platform.

"Lord Spook!" Sazed said, puffing as he arrived. "Lord Breeze is trying to dampen the rioters, but we pushed this city too far, I think! The people will destroy it in their rage."

"The flames," Spook croaked. "We have to put out the fires. The city is too dry; it has too much wood. It will burn, with everyone in it."

Sazed looked grave. "There is no way. We must get out! This riot will destroy us."

Spook glanced to the side. Beldre was kneeling by her brother. She'd bound his wound, then made a make-shift sling for his arm. Quellion glanced at Spook, looking dazed. As if he'd just awoken from a dream.

Spook stumbled to his feet. "We won't abandon the city, Sazed."

"But—"

"*No!*" Spook said. "I ran from Luthadel and left Clubs to die. I will not run again! We can stop the flames. We just need water."

Sazed paused.

"Water," Beldre said, standing.

"The canals will fill soon," Spook said. "We can organize fire brigades—use the flood to stop the flames."

Beldre glanced down. "There will be no flood, Spook. The guards you left . . . I attacked them with coins."

Spook felt a chill. "Dead?"

She shook her head, her hair disheveled, her face scratched. "I don't know," she said quietly. "I didn't look."

"The waters have not come yet," Sazed said. "They . . . should have been released by now."

"Then we will bring them!" Spook snapped. He spun at Quellion, then stumbled, feeling dizzy. "You!" he said, pointing at the Citizen. "You would be king of this city? Well, lead this people then. Get control of them and prepare them to put out the fires."

"I can't," Quellion said. "They'll kill me for what I've done."

Spook wobbled, light-headed. He steadied himself against a beam, holding his head. Beldre took a step toward him.

Spook looked up and met Quellion's eyes. The fires of the city were so bright that his flared tin made it difficult to see. Yet he dared not release the metal—only the power of noise, heat, and pain was keeping him conscious.

"You *will* go to them," Spook said. "I don't give a damn if they rip you apart, Quellion. You're going to try to save this city. If you don't, I'll kill you myself. *Do you understand?*"

The Citizen stiffened, then nodded.

"Sazed," Spook said, "take him to Breeze and Allrianne. I'm going to the cache. I'll bring the floodwaters to the canals, one way or another. Have Breeze and the others form fire brigades to douse the flames as soon as there is water."

"It is a good plan," Sazed said. "But Goradel will lead the Citizen. I am coming with you."

Spook nodded wearily. Then, as Sazed moved off to get the guard captain—who had apparently established a defensive perimeter around the square—Spook climbed from the stage and forced himself to begin moving toward the cache.

Soon he noticed someone catch up to him. Then after a few moments, that person passed him and ran on. Part of his mind knew it was a good thing that Sazed had decided to move on—the Terrisman had created the mechanism that would flood the city. He would throw the lever. Spook wasn't needed.

Keep moving.

He did, walking on, each step in atonement for what he had done to the city. After a short time, he realized that someone was at his side, tying a bandage on his arm.

He blinked. "Beldre?"

"I betrayed you," she said, looking down. "But I didn't have a choice. I couldn't let you kill him. I . . ."

"You did the right thing," Spook said. "Something . . . something was interfering, Beldre. It had your brother. It almost had me. But now, we have to keep walking. The lair is close. Just up the ramp."

She supported him as they walked. Spook smelled the smoke before he got there. He saw the light, and felt the heat. He and Beldre climbed up to the top of the ramp, practically crawling, for she was nearly as battered as he was. However, Spook knew what he would find.

The Ministry building, like so much of the town, was burning. Sazed stood in front of it, hand raised before his eyes. To Spook's overenhanced senses, the brilliance of the flames was so great that he had to look away. The heat made him feel as if he were standing inches from the sun.

Sazed tried to get closer to the building, but was forced back. He turned toward Spook, shielding his face. "It's too hot!" he said. "We need to find some water, or perhaps some sand. Put out the fire before we can get below."

"Too late . . ." Spook whispered. "It will take too long."

Beldre turned, looking over her city. To Spook's eyes, smoke seemed to twist and rise everywhere in the bright sky, reaching up to meet the falling ash.

He set his jaw, then stumbled toward the fire.

"Spook!" she cried out. But she needn't have worried. The flames were too hot. The pain was so strong that he

had to pull back before he'd crossed half the distance. He
stumbled away, joining Beldre and Sazed, gasping quietly,
blinking tears. His heightened senses made it even more
difficult for him to approach the flames.

"There is nothing we can do now," Sazed said. "We must
gather crews and try again."

"I've failed," Spook whispered.

"No more than any of us," Sazed said. "This is my fault.
The emperor put me in command."

"We were supposed to bring security to the city," Spook
said. "Not destruction. I should be able to stop those fires.
But it hurts too much."

Sazed shook his head. "Ah, Lord Spook. You are no god,
to command fire at your whim. You are a man like the rest
of us. We're all just . . . men."

Spook allowed them to pull him away. Sazed was right,
of course. He was just a man. Just Spook.

Kelsier had chosen his crew with care. He'd left a note for
them, when he died. It had listed the others—Vin, Breeze,
Dockson, Clubs, and Ham. He'd spoken of them, of why
he'd picked them.

But not Spook. The only one who didn't fit in.

I named you, Spook. You were my friend.

Isn't that enough?

Spook froze, forcing the others to stop. Sazed and Beldre
looked at him. Spook stared into the night. A night that was
far too bright. The fires burned. The smoke was pungent.

"No," Spook whispered, feeling fully lucid for the first
time since the evening's violence had started. He pulled
free of Sazed's grip and ran back toward the burning building.

"Spook!" Two voices yelled in the night.

Spook approached the flames. His breathing grew forced,
and his skin grew hot. The fire was bright—consuming. He
dashed straight for it. Then, at the moment the pain became
too great, he extinguished his tin.

And became numb.

It happened just as it had before, when he had been
trapped in the building without any metals. Flaring tin for so

long had expanded his senses, but now that he wasn't burning it at all, those same senses became dull. His entire body grew deadened, lacking feeling or sensation.

He burst through the doorway into the building, flames raining around him.

His body burned. But he couldn't feel the flames, and the pain could not drive him away. The fire was bright enough that his weakened eyes could still see. He dashed forward, ignoring the fire, heat, and smoke.

Survivor of the Flames.

He knew the fires were killing him. Yet he forced himself onward, continuing to move long after the pain should have rendered him unconscious. He reached the room at the rear and skidded down the broken ladder.

The cavern was dark. He stumbled through it, pushing past shelves and furniture, making his way along the wall, moving with a desperation that warned him that his time was short. His body wasn't working right anymore—he had pushed it too far, and pewter could no longer make up the difference.

He was glad for the darkness. As he finally stumbled against Sazed's machine, he knew that he would have been horrified to see what the flames had done to his arms.

Groaning quietly, he groped in the dark with numb hands and found what he hoped was the lever. His fingers no longer worked enough to grasp it. But he threw his weight against it, moving the gears as required.

Then he slid down to the ground, alone with the cold and blackness.

THE END OF PART FOUR

PART FIVE
TRUST

I do not know what went on in the minds of the koloss—what memories they retained, what human emotions they truly still knew. I do know that our discovery of the one creature, who named himself Human, was tremendously fortunate. Without his struggle to become human again, we might never have understood how the koloss, the Inquisitors, and Hemalurgy were linked.

Of course, there was another part for him to play. Granted, not a large one, but still important, all things considered.

59

URTEAU HAD SEEN BETTER DAYS.

Vin certainly did her work here well, TenSoon thought as he padded through the city, shocked at the destruction. About two years earlier—before being sent to spy on Vin—he had been Straff Venture's kandra, and had often visited Urteau. While it had never matched Luthadel's noble majesty or sprawling poverty, it had been a fine city, worthy of being the seat of a Great House.

Now, a good third of the city was a burned ruin. Those buildings that hadn't burned down were either abandoned or overcrowded—an odd mixture, in TenSoon's opinion. Apparently noble homes were avoided, while skaa buildings were overpacked.

More remarkable, however, were the canals. They had been refilled somehow. TenSoon sat on his haunches, watching the occasional makeshift boat push its way through a canal, displacing the patina of ash that covered the water. Here and there, debris and refuse clogged the waterways, but they were passable in most places.

He rose, shaking his canine head, and continued on his way. He'd stowed the bag with Kelsier's bones outside, not wanting to look odd carrying a pack on his back.

What had been the purpose of burning the city, then restoring its canals? He would likely have to wait to find the answer. He'd seen no army camped nearby; if Vin had been here, she'd already moved on to another location. His goal now was to find what passed for leadership in the remains of the city, then continue on his way, hunting down the Hero of Ages.

As he walked, he heard the people talking—speaking of how they'd managed to survive the fires that had claimed much of the city. They actually seemed cheerful. There was despair too, but there seemed an inordinate amount of happiness. This was not a city whose people had been conquered.

They feel they defeated the fire, TenSoon thought, making his way along a more crowded street. *They don't see losing a third of the city as a disaster—they see saving two-thirds of it as a miracle.*

He followed the flow of traffic toward the center of town, where he finally found the soldiers he'd expected. They were definitely Elend's, bearing the spear and the scroll on the arms of their uniforms. However, they defended an unlikely location: a Ministry building.

TenSoon stopped and regarded it, cocking his head. The building was obviously a center of operations. People bustled about under the eyes of the watchful soldiers, moving in and out. If he wanted answers, he'd need to get inside. He briefly considered going to fetch Kelsier's bones. But he discarded that thought; he wasn't certain he wanted to deal with the ramifications of making the Survivor appear here. There was another way to get in—perhaps equally shocking, but far less theologically disturbing.

He padded over to the front of the building and walked

up the steps, drawing a few startled looks. As he approached the front doors, one of the guards shouted at him, waving the butt of a spear in his direction.

"Here now!" the man said. "This is no place for dogs. Whose hound is this?"

TenSoon sat back on his haunches. "I belong to no man," he said.

The guard jumped, and TenSoon got a twisted sense of pleasure. He immediately chided himself. The world was ending, and he went about startling random soldiers. Still, it *was* an advantage of wearing a dog's body that he'd never considered. . . .

"Wha . . ." the soldier said, looking around to see if he were the victim of some joke.

"I said," TenSoon repeated, "that I belong to no man. I am my own master."

It was a strange concept—the weight of which, undoubtedly, the guard could never grasp. TenSoon, a kandra, was outside the Homeland without a Contract. As far as he knew, he was the first of his people to do such a thing in seven hundred years. It felt oddly . . . satisfying.

Several people were staring at him now. Other guards had approached, looking to their comrade for an explanation.

TenSoon gambled. "I've come from Emperor Venture," he said. "I bear a message for your leaders here."

To TenSoon's satisfaction, several of the other guards jumped. The first one, however—now an old hand when it came to talking dogs—raised a hesitant finger, pointing into the building. "In there."

"Thank you," TenSoon said, rising and walking through a now-quiet crowd as he made his way into the Ministry offices. He heard comments about "trick" and "well-trained" behind him, and several guards ran past him, their expressions urgent. He wound his way through groups and lines of people, all ignorant of the odd occurrence at the entrance to the building. At the end of the lines, TenSoon found . . .

Breeze. The Soother sat in a thronelike chair, holding a cup of wine, appearing very pleased with himself as he made proclamations and settled disputes. He looked much as he had when TenSoon had served as Vin's servant. One of the guards stood whispering to Breeze. Both eyed TenSoon as he padded up to the front of the line. The guard paled slightly, but Breeze leaned forward, smiling.

"So," he said, tapping his cane lightly against the marble floor. "Were you always a kandra, or did you eat the bones of Vin's hound recently?"

TenSoon sat. "I was always a kandra."

Breeze nodded. "I knew there was something odd about you—far too well behaved for a wolfhound." He smiled, sipping his wine. "Lord Renoux, I presume? It's been a while."

"I'm a different kandra," TenSoon said. "It's . . . complicated."

That gave Breeze pause. He eyed TenSoon, who felt a moment of panic. Breeze was a Soother—and like all Soothers, he held the power to take control of TenSoon's body. The secret.

No, TenSoon told himself forcefully. *Mistings today are too weak to take control of one of us.*

"Drinking on the job, Breeze?" TenSoon asked, raising a canine brow.

"Of course," Breeze said, raising the cup. "What good is being in charge if you can't set your own working conditions?"

TenSoon snorted. He hadn't ever really liked Breeze—though perhaps that came from his bias against Soothers. Or perhaps his bias against all humans. Regardless, he wasn't inclined toward small talk. "Where is Vin?" he asked.

Breeze frowned. "I thought you brought a message from her?"

"I lied to the guards," TenSoon said. "I've actually come searching for her. I bring news she needs to hear—news regarding the mists and ash."

"Well then, my dear man . . . um . . . I suppose I mean my dear *doggie.* Anyway, let us retire, and you can talk to

Sazed. He's far more useful than I am regarding these sorts of things."

". . . and, with Spook barely having survived the ordeal," said the Terrisman, "I thought it best to let Lord Breeze take command. We set up shop in a different Ministry building—it appeared equipped to be a bureaucratic center— and had Breeze start listening to petitions. He is better at dealing with people than I am, I think, and seems to enjoy taking care of the day-to-day concerns of the citizenry."

The Terrisman sat on a chair, a portfolio open on the desk before him, a pile of notes beside it. Sazed looked different to TenSoon, for a reason that he couldn't pin down. The Keeper wore the same robes and had the same Feruchemical bracers on his arms. But there was something missing.

However, that was the least of TenSoon's problems.

"*Fadrex City?*" TenSoon asked, sitting on his own chair. They were in one of the Ministry building's smaller rooms, which had once been an obligator's sleeping quarters. Now it held only a desk and chairs, the walls and floor as austere as one might expect for Ministry furnishings.

Sazed nodded. "She and the emperor hoped to find another of these storage caverns there."

TenSoon slumped. Fadrex was halfway across the empire. Even with the Blessing of Potency, it would take weeks for him to get there. He had a very, very long run ahead of him.

"Might I ask what business you have with Lady Vin, kandra?" Sazed asked.

TenSoon hesitated. It felt odd, in a way, to speak so openly with Breeze, and now Sazed. These were men that TenSoon had watched for months while he acted like a dog. They'd never known him, yet he knew them.

He knew, for instance, that Sazed was dangerous. The Terrisman was a Keeper—a group that TenSoon and his brethren had been trained to avoid. Keepers were always prying for rumors, legends, and tales. The kandra had many secrets; if the Keepers were ever to discover the richness of kandra culture, it could be disastrous. They'd want to study, ask questions, and record what they found.

TenSoon opened his mouth to say "Nothing." But didn't he *want* someone to help with kandra culture? Someone who focused on religions, and who perhaps knew much of theology? Someone who knew about the legends of the Hero of Ages? Of all the members of the crew other than Vin, TenSoon had held Sazed in the highest regard.

"It has to do with the Hero of Ages," TenSoon said carefully. "And the advent of the world's end."

"Ah," Sazed said, rising. "Very well then. I shall give you whatever provisions you need. Will you be starting out immediately? Or will you be staying here to rest for a time?"

What? TenSoon thought. Sazed hadn't even twitched at the mention of religious matters. It didn't seem like him at all.

Yet Sazed continued speaking, as if TenSoon hadn't just hinted at one of the greatest religious secrets of their age.

I'll never understand humans, he thought, shaking his head.

The prison Preservation created for Ruin was not created out of Preservation's power, though it was of Preservation. Rather, Preservation sacrificed his consciousness—one could say his mind—to fabricate that prison. He left a shadow of himself, but Ruin, once escaped, began to suffocate and isolate this small vestige of his rival. I wonder if Ruin ever thought it strange that Preservation had cut himself off from his own power, relinquishing it and leaving it in the world, to be gathered and used by humankind.

In Preservation's gambit, I see nobility, cleverness, and desperation. He knew that he could not defeat Ruin. He had given too much of himself, and beyond that he was the embodiment of stasis and stability. He could not destroy, not even to protect. It was against his nature. Hence the prison.

Humankind, however, had been created by both Ruin and Preservation—with a hint of Preservation's own soul to give them sapience and honor. In order for the world to survive, Preservation knew he had to depend upon his creations. To give them his trust.

I wonder what he thought when those creations repeatedly failed him.

60

THE BEST WAY TO FOOL someone, in Vin's estimation, was to give them what they wanted. Or at least what they expected. As long as they assumed that they were one step ahead, they wouldn't look back to see if there were any steps that they'd completely missed.

Yomen had designed her prison well. Any metal used in the construction of her cot or facilities was Allomantically useless. Silver, while expensive, seemed the metal of choice—and there was very little of that. Only a few screws in the cot that Vin managed to work free with her fingernails.

Her meals—a greasy, flavorless gruel—were served in wooden bowls with wooden spoons. The guards were hazekillers trained to fight Allomancers, carrying staves and wearing no metal on their bodies. Her room was a simple stone construction with a solid wooden door, its hinges and bolts made of silver.

She knew from her guards' behavior that they expected something from her. Yomen had prepared them well, and so when they slid her food through the slot, she could see the tension in their bodies and in the speed of their retreat. It was like they were feeding a viper.

So the next time they came to take her to Yomen, she attacked.

She moved as soon as the door opened, wielding a wooden leg she'd pulled off her cot. She dropped the first guard with a club to the arm, then another strike on the back of his head. Her blows felt weak without pewter, but it was the best she could manage. She scrambled past the second guard in line, then slammed her shoulder into the stomach of the third. She didn't weigh much, but it was enough to get him to drop his staff—which she immediately grabbed.

Ham had spent a long time training her with the staff, and he'd often made her fight without Allomancy. Despite all their preparation, the guards were clearly surprised to see a metalless Allomancer make so much trouble, and she dropped two more of them.

Unfortunately, Yomen was no fool. He had sent so many guards to bring her that dropping four of them made little difference. There had to be at least twenty men in the hallway outside her cell, clogging her exit if nothing else.

Her goal was to give them what they expected, but not get herself killed. So as soon as she confirmed that her "escape attempt" really was doomed, she let one of the soldiers hit her on the shoulder and she dropped the staff with a grunt. Disarmed, she raised her hands and backed away. The soldiers, of course, swept her feet out from beneath her and piled on top, holding her down while one manacled her arms.

Vin suffered the treatment, shoulder pulsing with pain. How long would she have to go without metal before she'd stop instinctively trying to burn pewter? She hoped she'd never find out.

Eventually, the soldiers pulled her to her feet and pushed her down the hallway. The three she'd knocked down—not to mention the one that she'd disarmed—grumbled a bit, rubbing their wounds. All twenty men regarded her even more warily, if that was possible.

She didn't give them any trouble until they got her into Yomen's audience chamber. When they moved to chain her manacles to the bench, she squirmed a bit, earning herself a knee in the stomach. She gasped, then slumped to the floor by the bench. There, groaning, she rubbed her hands and wrists with the gruel grease that she'd soaked into her undershirt. It was smelly and grimy, but it was very slick—and the guards, distracted by her escape attempt, had completely forgotten to search her.

"Surely you didn't think to escape without any metals to burn," Yomen asked.

Vin lifted her head. He stood with his back to her once more, though this time the window he looked out was dark. Vin found it odd to see the mists curling up against the window glass. Most skaa couldn't afford glass, and most noblemen chose the colored kind. The darkness outside Yomen's window seemed a waiting beast, the mists its fur brushing the glass as it shifted.

"I would think that you'd be flattered," Yomen continued. "I didn't know if you were really as dangerous as reported, but I decided to assume that you were. You see, I—"

Vin didn't give him any more time. There were only two ways she could escape from the city: the first would be to find some metals, the second would be to take Yomen captive. She planned to try both.

She yanked her greased hands free from the manacles, which had been fastened to her arms when they were squirming and flexed. She ignored the pain and blood as the manacles scraped her hands, then she leaped to her feet, reaching into a fold in her shirt and pulling out the silver screws that she'd taken from her cot. These she tossed at the soldiers.

The men yelled in surprise and threw themselves to the ground, ducking her presumed Steelpush; their own preparation and worry worked against them. The screws bounced off the wall ineffectually, and the guards lay confused by her feint. She was halfway to Yomen before the first one thought to scramble to his feet.

Yomen turned. As always, he wore the little bead of atium at his forehead. Vin lunged for it.

Yomen stepped casually out of the way. Vin lunged again, feinting, then trying to elbow him in the stomach. Her attack didn't land, however, as Yomen—hands still clasped behind his back—sidestepped her again.

She knew that look on his face—of complete control, of power. Yomen clearly had little battle training, but he dodged her anyway.

He was burning atium.

Vin stumbled to a halt. *No wonder he wears that bit on his forehead,* she thought. *It's for emergencies.* She could see in his smile that he really *had* anticipated her. He'd known that she would try something, and he'd baited her, letting her get close. But he'd never really been in danger.

The guards finally caught up with her, but Yomen raised a hand, waving them back. Then he gestured toward the bench. Quietly, Vin returned and sat down. She had to think, and she certainly wasn't going to get anywhere with Yomen burning atium.

As she sat, Ruin appeared next to her—materializing as if from dark smoke, wearing Reen's body. None of the others reacted; they plainly couldn't see him.

"Too bad," Ruin said. "In a way, you almost had him. But then, in a way you were never really close either."

She ignored Ruin, looking up at Yomen. "You're Mistborn."

"No," he said, shaking his head. However, he didn't turn back toward his window. He stood facing her, wary. He'd probably extinguished his atium—it was far too valuable to leave burning—but he would have it in reserve, careful to watch her for signs of another attack.

"No?" Vin said, raising a skeptical eyebrow. "You were burning atium, Yomen. I saw that much."

"Believe as you wish," Yomen said. "But know this, woman: I do not lie. I've never needed lies, and I find that particularly true now, when the entire world is in chaos. People need truth from those they follow."

Vin frowned.

"Regardless, it is time," Yomen said.

"Time?" Vin asked.

Yomen nodded. "Yes. I apologize for leaving you for so long in your cell. I have been . . . distracted."

Elend, Vin thought. *What has he been doing? I feel so blind!*

She glanced at Ruin, who stood on the other side of the bench, shaking his head as if he understood far more than he was telling her. She turned back to Yomen. "I still don't understand," she said. "Time for what?"

Yomen met her eyes. "Time for me to make a decision about your execution, Lady Venture."

Oh, she thought. *Right.* Between her dealings with Ruin and her plans to escape, she'd nearly forgotten Yomen's declaration that he intended to let her defend herself before he executed her.

Ruin walked across the room, circling Yomen in a leisurely stroll. The obligator king stood, still meeting Vin's eyes. If he could see Ruin, he didn't show it. Instead he waved to a guard, who opened a side door, leading in several obligators in grey robes. They seated themselves on a bench across the room from Vin.

"Tell me, Lady Venture," Yomen said, turning back to her, "why did you come to Fadrex City?"

Vin cocked her head. "I thought this wasn't to be a trial. You said that you didn't need that sort of thing."

"I would think," Yomen replied, "that you would be pleased with any delay in the process."

A delay meant more time to think—more time to possibly escape. "Why did we come?" Vin asked. "We knew you had one of the Lord Ruler's supply caches beneath your city."

Yomen raised an eyebrow. "How did you know about it?"

"We found another one," Vin said. "It had directions to Fadrex."

Yomen nodded to himself. She could tell that he believed her, but there was something else. He seemed to be making connections that she didn't understand, and probably didn't have the information to understand. "And the danger my kingdom posed to yours?" Yomen asked. "That didn't have anything at all to do with your invasion of my lands?"

"I wouldn't say that," Vin said. "Cett had been pushing Elend to move into this dominance for some time."

The obligators conferred quietly at this comment, though Yomen stood aloof, arms folded as he regarded her. Vin found the experience unnerving. It had been years—from her days in Camon's crew—since she had felt so much in another's power. Even when she'd faced the Lord Ruler, she'd felt differently. Yomen seemed to see her as a tool.

But a tool to do what? And how could she manipulate his needs so that he kept her alive long enough for her to escape?

Make yourself indispensable, Reen had always taught. *Then a crewleader can't get rid of you without losing power.* The voice of her brother still seemed to whisper the words in her mind. Were they memories, interpretations of his wisdom, or effects of Ruin's influence? Regardless, it was good advice at the moment.

"So you came with the express purpose of invasion?" Yomen asked.

"Elend intended to try diplomacy first," Vin said carefully. "However, we both knew that it's a bit hard to play the diplomat when you camp an army outside someone's city."

"You admit to being conquerors then," Yomen said. "You *are* more honest than your husband."

"Elend is more sincere than either of us, Yomen," Vin snapped. "Just because he interprets things differently from you or me does not mean he's being dishonest when he expresses his view."

Yomen raised an eyebrow, perhaps at the quickness of her response. "A valid point."

Vin leaned back on the bench, wrapping her cut hands with a bit of clean cloth from her shirt. It felt quite odd to be speaking to Yomen. On one hand, she and he seemed very different. He was a bureaucrat obligator whose lack of muscle or warrior's grace proved that he'd spent his life concerned with forms and records. She was a child of the streets and an adult practiced in war and assassination.

Yet his mannerisms, his way of speaking, seemed to resemble her own. *Is this what I might have been more like*, she wondered, *had I not been born a skaa? A blunt bureaucrat rather than a terse warrior?*

As Yomen contemplated her, Ruin walked in a slow circle around the obligator king. "This one is a disappointment," Ruin said.

Vin glanced at Ruin briefly. He shook his head. "Such destruction this one could have caused, had he struck out rather than staying huddled in his little city, praying to his dead god. Men would have followed him. I could never get through to him in the long run, unfortunately. Not every ploy can be successful, particularly when the will of fools such as he must be accounted for."

"So," Yomen said, drawing her attention back to him, "you came to take my city because you heard of my stockpile, and because you feared a return of the Lord Ruler's power."

"I didn't say that," Vin said, frowning.

"Yet you feared me."

"As a foreign power," Vin said, "with a proven ability to undermine a government and take it over."

"I didn't take over," Yomen said. "I returned this city and the dominance to their rightful rule. But that is beside the point. I want you to tell me of this religion your people preach."

"The Church of the Survivor?"

"Yes," Yomen said. "You are one of its heads, correct?"

"No," Vin said. "They revere me. But I've never felt that I properly fit as part of the religion. Mostly it's focused around Kelsier."

"The Survivor of Hathsin," Yomen said. "He died. How is it that people worship him?"

Vin shrugged. "It used to be common to worship gods that one couldn't see."

"Perhaps," Yomen said. "I have . . . read of such things, though I find them difficult to understand. Faith in an unseen god—what sense does that make? Why reject the god that they lived with for so long—the one that they could see, and feel—in favor of one that died? One that the Lord Ruler struck down?"

"You do it," Vin said. "You're still worshipping the Lord Ruler."

"He's not gone," Yomen said.

Vin frowned.

"No," Yomen said, apparently noting her confusion. "I haven't seen or heard of him since his disappearance. However, neither do I put any credence in reports of his death."

"He was rather dead," Vin said. "Trust me."

"I don't trust you, I'm afraid," Yomen said. "Tell me of that evening. Tell me precisely what happened."

So Vin did. She told him of her imprisonment, and of her escape with Sazed. She told him of her decision to fight the Lord Ruler, and of her reliance on the Eleventh Metal. She left out her strange ability to draw upon the power of the mists, but she explained pretty much everything else—including Sazed's theory that the Lord Ruler had been immortal through the clever manipulation of his Feruchemy and Allomancy in combination.

And Yomen actually listened. Her respect for the man increased as she spoke, and as he didn't interrupt her. He wanted to hear her story, even if he didn't believe it. He was a man who accepted information for what it was—a tool to be used, yet to be trusted no more than any other tool.

"And so," Vin finished, "he is dead. I stabbed him through the heart myself. Your faith in him is admirable, but it can't change what happened."

Yomen stood silently. The older obligators, sitting on their benches, had grown white in the face. She knew that her testimony might have damned her, but for some reason she felt that honesty—plain, blunt honesty—would serve her better than guile. That was how she usually felt.

An odd conviction for one who grew up in thieving crews, she thought. Ruin had apparently grown bored during her account, and had walked over to look out a window.

"What I need to find out," Yomen finally said, "is why the Lord Ruler thought it necessary for you to *think* that you had killed him."

"Didn't you listen to what I just said?" Vin demanded.

"I did," Yomen said calmly. "And do not forget that you are a prisoner here—one who is very close to death."

Vin forced herself to be quiet.

"You find my words ridiculous?" Yomen said. "More ridiculous than your own? Think of how I see you, claiming to have slain a man I *know* to be God. Is it not plausible that he wanted this to happen? That he's out there still, watching us, waiting . . ."

That's what this is all about, she realized. *Why he captured me, why he's so eager to speak with me. He's convinced that the Lord Ruler is still alive. He only wants to figure out where I fit into all of this. He wants me to give him the proof that he's so desperately wishing for.*

"Why don't you think you should be part of the skaa religion, Vin?" Ruin whispered.

She turned, trying not to look directly at him, lest Yomen see her staring into empty space.

"Why?" Ruin asked. "Why don't you want them worshipping you? All of those happy skaa? Looking toward you for hope?"

"The Lord Ruler *must* be behind all of this," Yomen mused aloud. "That means that he wanted the world to see you as his killer. He wanted the skaa to worship you."

"Why?" Ruin repeated. "Why be so uncomfortable? Is it because you know you *can't* offer them hope? What is it they call him, the one you are supposed to have replaced? The Survivor? A word of Preservation, I think."

"Perhaps he intends to return dramatically," Yomen said. "To depose you and topple you, to prove that faith in him is the only true faith."

Why don't you fit? Ruin whispered in her head.

"Why else would he want them to worship you?" Yomen asked.

"*They're wrong!*" Vin snapped, raising hands to her head, trying to stop the thoughts. Trying to stop the guilt.

Yomen hesitated.

"They're wrong about me," Vin said. "They don't worship me, they worship what they think I should be. But I'm not the Heir of the Survivor. I didn't do what Kelsier did. He freed them."

You conquered them, Ruin whispered.

"Yes," Vin said, looking up. "You're searching in the wrong direction, Yomen. The Lord Ruler won't return."

"I told you that—"

"No," Vin said, standing. "No, he's not coming back. He doesn't need to. *I* took his place."

Elend had worried that he was becoming another Lord Ruler, but his concern had always seemed flawed to Vin. He hadn't been the one to conquer and reforge an empire, she had. She'd been the one who made the other kings submit.

She'd done exactly as the Lord Ruler had. A Hero had risen up, and the Lord Ruler had killed him, then taken the power of the Well of Ascension. Vin had killed the Lord

Ruler, then taken that same power. She'd given up the power, true, but she'd filled the same role.

It all came to a head. The reason why the skaa worshipping her, calling her their savior, felt so wrong. Suddenly her real role in it all seemed to snap into place.

"I'm not the Survivor's Heir, Yomen," she said sickly. "I'm the Lord Ruler's."

He shook his head dismissively.

"When you first captured me," she said, "I wondered why you kept me alive. An enemy Mistborn? Why not simply kill me and be done with it? You claimed you wanted to give me a trial, but I saw through that. I knew you had another motive. And now I know what it is." She looked him in the eyes. "You said earlier that you planned to execute me for the Lord Ruler's murder, but you just admitted that you think he's still alive. You say that he'll return to topple me from my place, so you can't kill me, lest you interfere with your god's plans."

Yomen turned away from her.

"You *can't* kill me," she said. "Not until you're certain of my place in your theology. That's why you kept me alive, and that's why you risk bringing me in here to talk. You need information only I can give—you have to get testimony from me in a trial of sorts because you want to know what happened that night. So you can try to convince yourself that your god still lives."

Yomen didn't respond.

"Admit it. I'm in no danger here." She stepped forward.

And Yomen moved. His steps suddenly became more fluid—he didn't have the grace of pewter or the knowledge of a warrior, but he moved just *right*. She dodged instinctively, but his atium let him anticipate her, and before she could so much as think, he'd thrown her to the floor, holding her pinned with a knee against her back.

"I may not kill you yet," he said calmly, "but that hardly means that you're in 'no danger,' Lady Venture."

Vin grunted.

"I want something from you," he said. "Something more

than what we've discussed. I want you to tell your husband to send his army away."

"Why would I do that?" Vin said, her face pressed against the cold stone of the floor.

"Because," Yomen said, "you claim to want my storage cache, yet you claim to be good people. You now know that I will use the food in it wisely, to feed my people. If your Elend really is as altruistic as you claim, he certainly won't be so selfish as to throw away lives just so you can steal our food and use it to feed your own."

"We need it to grow crops," Vin said. "We get enough light in the Central Dominance, while you don't. The seed stock you have will be useless to you!"

"Then trade me for it."

"You won't *talk* to us!"

Yomen stepped back, releasing the pressure on her spine. She rubbed her neck, sitting up, feeling frustrated. "It's about more than the food in that cache, Yomen," she said. "We control the other four of them. The Lord Ruler left clues in them. There is something to the whole group that can save us."

Yomen snorted. "You were down there all that time, and you didn't read the plaque that the Lord Ruler left?"

"Of course I did."

"Then you know that there *is* nothing more in those caches," Yomen said. "They're all part of his plan, true. And for some reason that plan requires that men think he is dead. Regardless, you know now what he said. So why take the city from me?"

Why take the city from me? The real reason itched at Vin. Elend had always found it an unimportant one, but to her, it held powerful appeal. "You know full well why we have to take the city," Vin said. "As long as you have *it,* we have reason to conquer you."

"It?" Yomen asked.

Ruin stepped forward, curious.

"You know what I mean. The atium. The Lord Ruler's supply."

"That?" Yomen asked, laughing. "This is all about the atium? Atium is worthless!"

Vin frowned. "Worthless? It's the single most valuable commodity in the Final Empire!"

"Oh?" Yomen said. "And how many people are there around to burn it? How many noble houses remain to play petty politics and vie for power by showing how much atium they can leech from the Lord Ruler? The value of atium was based in the economy of an empire, Lady Venture. Without the trappings of a reserve system and an upper class giving the metal implied worth, atium has no real value." Yomen shook his head. "To a starving man, what is more important—a loaf of bread, or an entire jar of atium he can't use, eat, or sell?"

He waved for the guards to take her. They pulled her to her feet, and she struggled, holding Yomen's eyes.

Yomen turned away from her once more. "Those lumps of metal do me no good, save perhaps to keep you in check. No, the food was the real resource. The Lord Ruler left me the riches I required to establish his power again. I only need to figure out what he wants me to do next."

The soldiers finally succeeded in pulling her away.

I don't wonder that we focused far too much on the mists during those days. But from what I now know of sunlight and plant development, I realize that our crops weren't in as much danger from misty days as we feared. We might well have been able to find plants to eat that did not need as much light to survive.

True, the mists did also cause some deaths in those who went out in them, but the number killed was not a large enough percentage of the population to be a threat to our survival as a species. The ash, that was our real problem. The smoke filling the atmosphere, the black flakes covering up everything beneath, the eruptions of the volcanic Ashmounts . . . Those were what would kill the world.

61

"ELEND!" HAM CALLED, RUSHING UP to him. "You're back!"

"Surprised?" Elend asked, reading his friend's expression.

"Of course not," Ham said, a little too quickly. "The scouts reported your approach."

My arrival may not surprise you, Elend thought tiredly, *but the fact that I'm still alive does. Did you think I'd run off to get myself killed, or did you think that I'd simply wander away and abandon you?*

It wasn't a line of reasoning he wanted to pursue. So he smiled, resting a hand on Ham's shoulder and gazing toward the camp. It looked strange, bunkered down as it was, ash piled up outside it. It seemed like it was dug into the ground several feet. There was so much ash. . . .

I can't worry about everything at once, Elend thought with determination. *I just have to trust. Trust in myself and keep going.*

He had pondered the mist spirit for the rest of his trip. Had it really told him not to attack Fadrex, or was Elend misinterpreting its gestures? What had it wanted him to learn by pointing at his vial of metals?

Beside him, Ham was regarding the mass of new koloss. By the army, Elend's other koloss sat—still under his control. Though he had grown increasingly adept at keeping a hold on the creatures, it was nice to be back close to them. It made him feel more comfortable.

Ham whistled quietly. "Twenty-eight thousand?" he asked. "Or at least that's what the scouts say."

Elend nodded.

"I hadn't realized how large the group was," Ham said. "With that many . . ."

Thirty-seven thousand total, Elend thought. *More than enough to storm Fadrex.*

He began to walk down the incline, toward the camp. Though he hadn't needed much pewter to help him through the hike, he was still tired. "Any news of Vin?" he said hopefully, though he knew that if she'd managed to escape, she would have already found him.

"We sent a messenger into the city while you were gone," Ham said as they began to walk. "Yomen said a soldier could come and confirm that Vin was still alive, so we complied in your name, thinking it best if Yomen thought you were here."

"You did well," Elend said.

"It's been a while since then," Ham said. "We haven't heard anything of her since."

"She's still alive," Elend said.

"I believe so too."

Elend smiled. "It's not just faith, Ham," he said, nodding toward the koloss that had remained behind. "Before she was captured, I gave a thousand of those to her. If she'd died, then they would have gone out of control. As long as she lives—whether or not she has metals—she will remain bonded to them."

Ham paused. "That . . . would have been something good to tell us earlier, El."

"I know," Elend said. "It's too easy to forget how many I'm controlling—I didn't even think that not all of those are mine. Post scouts, keep an eye on them. I'll take them back if they go wild."

Ham nodded. "Could you contact her through them?"

Elend shook his head. How did he explain? Controlling the koloss wasn't a subtle thing—their minds were too dull for much beyond simple commands. He could order them to attack, or to freeze, or to follow and carry things. But he couldn't direct them precisely, couldn't tell them to speak a message, or instruct them *how* to accomplish a goal. He could only say "Do this" and watch them go.

"We've had scout reports from the Central Dominance, El," Ham said, voice troubled.

Elend looked at him.

"Most of our scouts didn't return. Nobody knows what happened to Demoux and the men you sent—we hope they reached Luthadel, but the capital is in bad shape. The scouts who have returned bear frustrating news. We've lost many of the cities you conquered during this last year. The people are starving, and a lot of villages are empty save for the dead. Those who can, flee to Luthadel, leaving trails of corpses on the road, buried in ash."

Elend closed his eyes. But Ham wasn't done.

"There are tales of cities swallowed by the rumbling earth," Ham said, voice almost a whisper. "King Lekal and his city fell to lava from one of the Ashmounts. We haven't heard from Janarle in weeks; his entire retinue seems to have vanished, and the Northern Dominance is in chaos. The entire Southern Dominance is said to be burning. . . . Elend, what do we do?"

Elend continued to stride forward, walking onto an ash-free pathway and then into the camp proper. Soldiers were gathering about, whispering, staring at him. He didn't know how to answer Ham's question. What did he do? What *could* he do?

"We'll help them, Ham," he said. "We won't give up."

Ham nodded, looking slightly bolstered. "Though before you do anything else, what you should probably do is go change your clothes."

Elend glanced down, remembering that he was still wearing the black uniform, bloodied from killing koloss, then stained by ash. His appearance caused quite a stir in the men. *They've only seen me in the pristine white outfit. Many have never seen me fight—never seen me bloodied or dirtied by ash.*

He wasn't certain what bothered him about that.

Ahead, Elend could see a bearded figure sitting in a chair by the pathway, as if out for an afternoon repose. Cett eyed him as he passed. "More koloss?"

Elend nodded.

"We're going to attack, then?" Cett asked.

Elend stopped.

The mist spirit apparently didn't want him to attack. But he couldn't be certain what it had wanted him to know or think—he didn't even know if he should trust it. Could he base the future of his empire on vague impressions he got from a ghost in the mists?

He had to get into that cache, and he couldn't afford to wait in siege—not any longer. Plus, attacking seemed the best way to get Vin back safely. Yomen would never return her—Elend either had to sit around and wait, or he had to attack, hoping that in the chaos of battle Yomen would leave her in a dungeon somewhere. True, attacking risked her execution, but letting Yomen use her as a bargaining chip seemed as dangerous for her.

I have to be the man who makes the hard decisions, he told himself. *It's what Vin was trying to teach me at the ball—that I can be both Elend the man, and Elend the king. I took these koloss for a purpose. Now I need to use them.*

"Inform the soldiers," Elend said. "But don't have them form ranks. We attack in the morning, but do so in surprise—koloss first, breaking through their defenses. The men can form up after that, then go in and seize control."

We'll rescue Vin, get into that cavern, then get to Luthadel with the food supplies.

And survive as long as we can.

I suspect that Alendi, the man Rashek killed, was himself a Misting—a Seeker. Allomancy, however, was a different thing in those days, and much more rare. The Allomancers alive in our day are the descendants of the men who ate those few beads of Preservation's power. They formed the foundation of the nobility, and were the first to name Rashek emperor.

The power in those few beads was so concentrated that it could last through ten centuries of breeding and inheritance.

62

SAZED STOOD OUTSIDE THE ROOM, looking in. Spook lay in his bed, still swaddled in bandages. The boy had not awakened since his ordeal, and Sazed wasn't certain he ever would. Even if he did live, he'd be horribly scarred for the rest of his life.

Though, Sazed thought, *this proves one thing. The boy doesn't have pewter.* If Spook *had* been able to burn pewter, then he would have healed far more quickly. Sazed had administered a vial of pewter just in case, and it had made no difference. The boy hadn't mystically become a Thug.

It was comforting, in a way. It meant that Sazed's world still made sense.

In the room, Beldre sat at Spook's side. She came every day to spend time with the lad. More time than she spent with her brother, Quellion. The Citizen had a broken arm and some other wounds, but nothing lethal. Though Breeze ruled in Urteau, Quellion was still an authority, and he had grown far more . . . civil. He now seemed willing to consider an alliance with Elend.

It was strange to Sazed that Quellion would become so accommodating. They had entered his city, sown chaos, and nearly killed him. Now he listened to their offers of peace? Sazed was suspicious, to be sure. Time would tell.

Inside, Beldre turned slightly and noticed Sazed at the doorway. She smiled, standing.

"Please, Lady Beldre," he said, entering. "Don't stand."

She seated herself again as Sazed walked forward. He leaned over and surveyed his bandage work on Spook, then checked the young man's condition, comparing notes taken from the medical texts in his copperminds. Beldre watched quietly.

Once he was finished, he got up to leave.

"Thank you," Beldre said. She glanced at Spook. "Do you think . . . I mean, has his condition changed?"

"I am afraid that it has not, Lady Beldre. I cannot promise anything in regard to his recovery."

She smiled faintly, turning toward the wounded lad. "He'll make it," she said.

Sazed frowned.

"He's not just a man," Beldre said. "He's something special. I don't know what he did to bring my brother back, but Quellion is his old self—the way he was before all of this insanity began. And the city. The people have hope again. That's what Spook wanted."

Hope . . . Sazed thought, studying the young woman's eyes. *She really does love him.*

In a way, it seemed silly to Sazed. How long had she known the boy? A few weeks? During that time, Spook had not only earned Beldre's love, but had become a hero to the people of an entire city.

She sits and hopes, having faith that he will recover, Sazed thought. *Yet upon seeing him, the first thing I thought of was how relieved I was that he wasn't a Pewterarm.* Had Sazed really become that callous? A year and a half ago, he had been willing to fall hopelessly in love with a woman who had spent most of her life chastising him. A woman with whom he'd had only a few precious days.

He turned and left the room.

Sazed walked to his quarters that formerly belonged to an obligator. It was nice to have ordinary walls and steps again, rather than endless shelves bounded by cavern walls.

On his desk lay the open portfolio, its cloth-wrapped coverboard stained with ash. One stack of pages sat to its left and one to its right. There were only ten pages left in the right stack.

Taking a deep breath, Sazed approached and sat down. It was time to finish.

It was late morning the next day before he set the final sheet onto the top of the left stack. He'd moved quickly through these last ten, but he'd been able to give them his undivided attention, not being distracted by riding or other concerns. He felt that he'd given each one due consideration.

He sat for a time, feeling fatigued, and not merely from lack of sleep. He felt . . . numb. His task was done. After a year's work, he'd sifted through each and every religion in his stack. And he'd eliminated every one.

It was odd, how many common features they all had. Most claimed ultimate authority, denouncing other faiths. Most taught of an afterlife, but could offer no proof. Most taught about a god or gods, yet—again—had little justification for their teachings. And every single one of them was riddled with inconsistencies and logical fallacies.

How did men believe in something that preached love on one hand, yet taught destruction of unbelievers on the other? How did one rationalize belief with the lack of proof? How could they honestly expect him to have faith in something that taught of miracles and wonders in the far past, but carefully gave excuses for why such things didn't occur in the present day?

And then, of course, there was the final flake of ash on the pile—the thing that each and every faith had, in his opinion, failed to prove. All taught that believers would be blessed. And all had absolutely no answer as to why their gods had allowed the faithful to be captured, imprisoned, enslaved, and slaughtered by a heretic known as the Lord Ruler.

The stack of pages sat face down on the desk before him. They meant that there was no truth. No faith that would bring Tindwyl back to him. Nothing watching over men, contrary to what Spook had affirmed so strongly. Sazed ran his fingers across the last page, and suddenly the depression he'd been fighting—barely holding at bay for so long— was too strong for him to overcome. The portfolio had been his final line of defense.

It was pain. That was how the loss felt. Pain and numbness at the same time; a barb-covered wire twisting around his chest combined with an absolute inability to do anything about it. He felt like huddling in a corner, crying, and just letting himself die.

No! he thought. *There must be something. . . .*

He reached under his desk, trembling fingers seeking his sack of metalminds. He didn't pull one of them out, but instead removed a book. He put it on the table by his portfolio, then opened it to a random page. Words written in two different hands confronted him. One was careful and flowing. His own. The other was terse and determined. Tindwyl's.

He rested his fingers on the page. He and Tindwyl had compiled this book together, deciphering the history, prophecies, and meanings surrounding the Hero of Ages. Back before Sazed had stopped caring.

That's a lie, he thought, forming a fist. *Why do I lie to myself? I still care. I never stopped caring. If I'd stopped caring, then I wouldn't still be searching. If I didn't care so much, then being betrayed wouldn't feel so painful.*

Kelsier had spoken of this. Then Vin had done the same. Sazed had never expected to have similar feelings. Who was there that could hurt him so deeply that he felt betrayed? He was not like other men. He acknowledged that not out of arrogance, but out of simple self-awareness. He forgave people, perhaps to a fault. He wasn't the type to feel bitter.

So he'd assumed that he would never have to deal with these emotions. That was why he'd been so unprepared to be betrayed by the only thing he couldn't accept as flawed.

He couldn't believe. If he believed, it meant that God—or the universe, or whatever it was that watched over man—had failed. Better to believe that there was nothing at all. Then all of the world's inadequacies were mere chance. Not caused by a god who had failed them.

Sazed glanced at his open book, noticing a little slip of paper sticking out between its pages. He pulled it free, surprised to find the picture of a flower that Vin had given him, the one that Kelsier's wife had carried. The one she'd used to give herself hope. To remind her of a world that had existed before the coming of the Lord Ruler.

He glanced upward. The ceiling was of wood, but red sunlight—refracted by the window—sprayed across it. "Why?" he whispered. "Why leave me like this? I studied everything about you. I learned the religions of *five hundred* different peoples and sects. I taught about you when other men had given up a thousand years before.

"Why leave *me* without hope, when others can have faith? Why leave *me* to wonder? Shouldn't I be more certain than any other? Shouldn't my knowledge have protected me?"

Yet his faith had made him more susceptible. *That's what trust is,* Sazed thought. *It's about giving someone else power over you. Power to hurt you.* That was why he'd given up his metalminds. That was why he had decided to sort through the religions one at a time, trying to find one that had no faults. Nothing to fail him.

It made sense. Better to not believe than to be proven wrong. Sazed looked back down. Why did he think to talk to the heavens? There was nothing there.

There never had been.

Outside in the hallway, he could hear voices. "My dear doggie," Breeze said, "surely you'll stay for another day."

"No," said TenSoon the kandra, speaking in his growling voice. "I must find Vin as soon as possible."

Even the kandra, Sazed thought. *Even an inhuman creature has more faith than I.*

But how could they understand? Sazed closed his eyes tight, feeling a pair of tears squeeze from the corners. How could anyone understand the pain of a faith betrayed? He had *believed.* Yet when he had needed hope the most, he had found only emptiness.

He picked up the book, then snapped closed his portfolio, locking the inadequate summaries within. He turned toward the hearth. Better to burn it all.

Belief . . . He remembered a voice from the past. His own voice, speaking to Vin on that terrible day after Kelsier's death. *Belief isn't simply a thing for fair times and bright days, I think. What is belief—what is faith—if you don't continue in it after failure?*

How innocent he had been.

Better to trust and be betrayed, Kelsier seemed to whisper. It had been one of the Survivor's mottos. *Better to love and be hurt.*

Sazed gripped the book. It was such a meaningless thing. Its text could be changed by Ruin at any time. *And do I believe in that?* Sazed thought with frustration. *Do I have faith in this Ruin, but not in something better?*

He stood quietly in the room, holding the book, listening to Breeze and TenSoon outside. The book was a symbol to him. It represented what he had once been. It represented failure. He glanced upward again. *Please,* he thought. *I want to believe. I really do. I just . . . I just need something.*

Something more than shadows and memories. Something real.

Something true. Please?

"Farewell, Soother," TenSoon said. "Give my regards to the Announcer." Then Sazed heard Breeze thump away. TenSoon padded down the hallway on his quieter dog's feet.

Announcer . . .

Sazed froze.

That word . . .

Sazed stood stunned for a moment. Then he threw open his door and burst into the hallway. The door slammed against the wall, making Breeze jump. TenSoon stopped at the end of the hallway, near the stairs. He turned back, looking at Sazed.

"What did you call me?" Sazed demanded.

"The Announcer," TenSoon said. "You are, are you not, the one who pointed out Lady Vin as the Hero of Ages? That, then, is your title."

Sazed fell to his knees, slapping his book on the floor before him. He flipped through the pages and located one in particular, penned in his own hand. *I thought myself the Holy First Witness,* it said, *the prophet foretold to discover the Hero of Ages.* They were the words of Kwaan, the man who had originally named Alendi the Hero. From these writings, which were their only clues about the original Terris religion, Sazed and the others had gleaned what little they knew of the prophecies about the Hero of Ages.

"What is this?" Breeze asked, leaning down, scanning the words. "Hum. Looks like you've got the wrong term, my dear doggie. Not 'Announcer' at all, but 'Holy First Witness.' "

Sazed looked up. "This is one of the passages that Ruin changed, Breeze," he said. "When I wrote it, it read differently—but Ruin altered it, trying to trick me and Vin into fulfilling his prophecies. The skaa had started to call me the Holy First Witness, their own term. Ruin retroactively changed Kwaan's writings so that they seemed to prophetically reference me."

"Is that so?" Breeze asked, rubbing his chin. "What did it say before?"

Sazed ignored the question, instead meeting TenSoon's canine eyes. "How did you know?" he demanded. "How do you know the words of the ancient Terris prophecies?"

TenSoon fell back on his haunches. "It strikes me as odd, Terrisman. There's one great inconsistency in all this, a problem *no one* has ever thought to point out. What happened to the packmen who traveled with Rashek and Alendi up to the Well of Ascension?"

Rashek. The man who had become the Lord Ruler.

Breeze stood up straight. "That's easy, kandra," he said, waving his cane. "Everyone knows that when the Lord Ruler took the throne of Khlennium, he made his trusted friends into noblemen. That's why the nobility of the Final Empire were so pampered—they were the descendants of Rashek's good friends."

TenSoon sat quietly.

No, Sazed thought with wonder. *No . . . that couldn't be!* "He *couldn't* have made those packmen into nobles."

"Whyever not?" Breeze asked.

"Because the nobility gained Allomancy," Sazed said, standing. "Rashek's friends were *Feruchemists*. If he'd made them into noblemen, then . . ."

"Then they could have challenged him," TenSoon said. "They could have become both Allomancers and Feruchemists as he was, and had his same powers."

"Yes," Sazed said. "He spent ten centuries trying to breed Feruchemy *out* of the Terris population—all in fear that someday someone would be born with both Feruchemy and Allomancy! His friends who went to the Well with him would have been dangerous, since they were obviously powerful Feruchemists, and they knew what Rashek had done to Alendi. Rashek would have had to do something else with them. Something to sequester them, perhaps even kill them . . ."

"No," TenSoon said. "He didn't kill them. You call the Father a monster, but he was not an evil man. He didn't kill his friends, though he did recognize the threat their powers posed to him. So he offered them a bargain, speaking directly to their minds while he was holding the power of creation."

"What bargain?" Breeze asked, clearly confused.

"Immortality," TenSoon said quietly. "In exchange for their Feruchemy. They gave it up, along with something else."

Sazed stared at the creature in the hallway, a creature who thought like a man but had the form of a beast. "They gave up their humanity," Sazed whispered.

TenSoon nodded.

"They live on?" Sazed asked, stepping forward. "The Lord Ruler's companions? The very Terrismen who climbed to the Well with him?"

"We call them the First Generation," TenSoon said. "The founders of the kandra people. The Father transformed every living Feruchemist into a mistwraith, beginning that race. His good friends, however, he returned to sapience with a few Hemalurgic spikes. You've done your work poorly, Keeper. I expected that you'd drag this out of me *long* before I had to leave."

I've been a fool, Sazed thought, blinking away tears. *Such a fool.*

"What?" Breeze asked, frowning. "What's going on? Sazed? My dear man, why are you so flustered? What do this creature's words mean?"

"They mean hope," Sazed said, pushing into his room, hurriedly tossing some of his clothing into a travel pack.

"Hope?" Breeze asked, peeking in.

Sazed looked back toward where Breeze stood. The kandra had walked up, and stood behind him in the hallway. "The Terris religion, Breeze," Sazed said. "The thing my sect was founded for, the thing my people have spent lifetimes searching to discover. It lives on. Not in written words that can be corrupted or changed, but in the minds of men who actually practiced it. *The Terris faith is not dead!*"

There was one more religion to add to his list. His quest was not yet over.

"Quickly, Keeper," TenSoon said. "I was prepared to go without you, since everyone agreed that you had stopped caring about these things. But if you will come, I will show you the way to my Homeland—it is along the path I must travel to find Vin. Hopefully you will be able to convince the First Generation of the things I have not."

"And that is?" Sazed asked, still packing.

"That the end has arrived."

Ruin tried many times to get spikes into other members of the crew. Though some of what happened makes it seem that it was easy for him to gain control of people, it in fact was not.

Inserting a spike in precisely the right place—at the right time— was incredibly difficult, even for as subtle a creature as Ruin. For instance, he tried very hard to spike both Elend and Yomen. Elend managed to avoid it each time, as he did on the field outside the small town that contained the next-to-last storage cache.

Ruin did manage to get a spike into Yomen once. Yomen, however, removed the spike before Ruin got a firm grip on him. It was much easier for Ruin to get a hold on people who were passionate and impulsive than it was for him to hold on to people who were logical and prone to working through their actions in their minds.

63

"WHAT I DON'T UNDERSTAND," VIN said, "is why you chose me. You had a thousand years and hundreds of thousands of people to choose from. Why lead *me* to the Well of Ascension to free you?"

She was in her cell, sitting on her cot—which now lay legless on the floor, having collapsed when she removed the screws. She'd asked for a new one. She'd been ignored.

Ruin turned toward her. He came often, wearing Reen's body, still indulging himself in what Vin could only assume was a kind of gloating. As he often did, however, he ignored her question. Instead he turned to the east, his eyes seeming to look directly through the cell wall.

"I wish you could see it," he said. "The ashfalls have grown beautiful and deep, as if the sky has shattered, raining down shards of its corpse in flakes of black. You feel the ground tremble?"

Vin didn't respond.

"Those quakes are the earth's final sighs," Ruin said. "Like an old man moaning as he dies, calling for his children so that he can pass on his last bits of wisdom. The very ground is pulling itself apart. The Lord Ruler did much of this. You can blame him, if you wish."

Vin perked up. She didn't draw attention to herself by asking more questions, but instead let Ruin ramble on. Again she noted how *human* some of his mannerisms seemed.

"He thought he could solve the problems himself," Ruin continued. "He rejected me, you know."

And that happened exactly a thousand years ago, Vin thought. *A thousand years have passed since Alendi failed in his quest; a thousand years since Rashek took the power for himself and became the Lord Ruler. That's part of the answer to my question. The glowing liquid at the Well of Ascension—it was gone by the time I finished freeing Ruin. It must have disappeared after Rashek used it too.*

A thousand years. Time for the Well to regenerate its power? But what was that power? Where did it come from?

"The Lord Ruler didn't really save the world," Ruin continued. "He merely postponed its destruction—and in doing so, he helped me. That's the way it must always be, as I told you. When men think they are helping the world, they actually do more harm than good. Just like you. You tried to help, but you only ended up freeing me."

Ruin glanced at her, then smiled in a fatherly way. She didn't react.

"The Ashmounts," Ruin continued, "the dying landscape, the broken people—those were all Rashek's. The twisting of men to become koloss, kandra, and Inquisitor, all his . . ."

"But you hated him," Vin said. "He didn't free you—so you had to wait another thousand years."

"True," Ruin said. "But a thousand years is not much time. Not much time at all. Besides, I couldn't refuse to help Rashek. I help everyone, for my power is a tool—the sole tool by which things can change."

It's all ending, Vin thought. *It really is. I don't have time to sit and wait. I need to do something.* Vin stood, causing Ruin to glance toward her as she walked to the front of the cell. "Guards!" she called. Her voice echoed in her own chamber. "Guards!" she repeated.

Eventually she heard a thump out in the hall. "What?" a rough voice demanded.

"Tell Yomen that I want to deal."

There was a pause.

"Deal?" the guard asked.

"Yes," Vin said. "Tell him I have information that I want to give him."

She wasn't certain how to read the guard's response, since it was simply more silence. She thought she heard him walking away, but without tin she couldn't tell.

Eventually, however, the guard returned. Ruin watched her, curious, as the door unlocked and then opened. The customary troop of soldiers stood outside.

"Come with us."

As Vin entered Yomen's audience chamber, she was immediately struck by the differences in the man. He looked much more haggard than he had the last time they'd met, as if he'd gone far too long without sleep.

But . . . he's Mistborn, Vin thought with confusion. *That means he could burn pewter to keep that fatigue out of his eyes.*

Why doesn't he? Unless . . . he can't burn it. Unless there's only a single metal available to him.

She'd always been taught that there was no such thing as an atium Misting. But more and more, she was realizing that the Lord Ruler perpetuated a lot of misinformation to keep himself in control and in power. She had to learn to stop depending on what she'd been *told* was true, and focus on the facts as she found them.

Yomen watched as she entered, guards surrounding her. She could read the expectation of a trick in his eyes—yet as always he waited for her to act first. Hovering close to the edge of danger seemed his way. The guards took stations at the doors, leaving her standing in the middle of the room.

"No manacles?" she asked.

"No," Yomen said. "I don't expect you to be here long. The guards tell me that you've offered information."

"I have."

"Well," Yomen said, arms clasped behind his back, "I told them to bring you to me if they so much as suspected a trick. Apparently they didn't believe your pleas that you want to deal. I wonder why." He raised an eyebrow toward her.

"Ask me a question," Vin said. To one side, Ruin walked through the wall, stepping with an idle, unconcerned gait.

"Very well," Yomen said. "How does Elend control the koloss?"

"Allomancy," Vin said. "Emotional Allomancy, when used on a koloss, will bring them under the Allomancer's control."

"I find that hard to believe," Yomen said flatly. "If it were that simple, someone other than you would have discovered it."

"Most Allomancers are too weak to manage it," Vin said. "You need to use a metal that enhances your power."

"There is no such metal."

"You know of aluminum?"

Yomen hesitated, but Vin could see in his eyes that he did. "Duralumin is the Allomantic alloy of aluminum," Vin said. "Where aluminum dampens the power of other metals, duralumin enhances them. Mix duralumin and zinc or brass, then Pull or Push on the emotions of a koloss, and he will be yours."

Yomen didn't dismiss her comments as lies. Ruin strolled forward, walking around Vin in a circle.

"Vin, Vin. What is your game now?" Ruin asked, amused. "Lead him on with little tidbits, then betray him?"

Yomen apparently came to the same conclusion. "Your facts are interesting, Empress, but completely unprovable in my present situation. Therefore they are—"

"There were five of these storage caverns," Vin said, stepping forward. "We found the others. They led us here."

Yomen shook his head. "And? Why should I care?"

"Your Lord Ruler planned something for those caverns—you can tell that much from the plaque he left here in this one. He says that he came up with no way to fight what is happening to us in the world, but do you believe that? I feel there has to be more, some clue hidden in the text of all five plaques."

"You expect me to believe that *you* care what the Lord Ruler wrote?" Yomen asked. "You, his purported murderer?"

"I couldn't care less about him," Vin admitted. "But Yomen, you *have* to believe that I care what happens to the people of the empire! If you've gathered any intelligence about Elend or me, you know that is true."

"Your Elend is a man who thinks far too highly of himself," Yomen said. "He has read many books, and assumes that his learning makes him capable of being a king. You . . . I still don't know what to think about you." His eyes showed a bit of the hatred she had seen in him during their last meeting. "You claim to have killed the Lord Ruler. Yet . . . he couldn't really have died. You're part of all this, somehow."

That's it, Vin thought. *That's my in.* "He wanted us to meet," Vin said. She didn't believe it, but Yomen would.

Yomen raised an eyebrow again.

"Can't you see?" Vin said. "Elend and I discovered the other storage caverns, the first one under Luthadel. Then we came here. This was the *last* of the five. The end of the trail. For some reason, the Lord Ruler wanted to lead us here. To you."

Yomen stood for a few moments. To the side, Ruin mimed applause.

"Send for Lellin," Yomen said, turning toward one of his soldiers. "Tell him to bring his maps."

The soldier saluted and left. Yomen turned to Vin, still frowning. "This is not to be an exchange. You will give me the information I request, then I will decide what to do with it."

"Fine," Vin said. "But you yourself said that I'm connected to all of this. It's *all* connected, Yomen. The mists, the koloss, me, you, the storage caverns, the ash . . ."

He flinched slightly as Vin mentioned that last one.

"The ash is getting worse, isn't it?" she asked. "Falling more thickly?"

Yomen nodded.

"We were always worried about the mists," Vin said. "But the ash, it's going to be what kills us. It will block the sunlight, bury our cities, cover our streets, choke our fields. . . ."

"The Lord Ruler won't let that happen," Yomen said.

"And if he really is dead?"

Yomen met her eyes. "Then you have doomed us all."

Doomed . . . The Lord Ruler had said something similar right before Vin killed him. She shivered, waiting in awkward silence, suffering Ruin's smiling stare until a scribe scuttled in, bearing several rolled maps.

Yomen took one of the maps, waving the man away. He spread it out on a table, waving Vin forward. "Show me," he said, stepping clear to keep out of her reach as she approached.

She picked up a piece of charcoal, then began to mark the locations of the storage caverns. Luthadel. Statlin City. Vetitan. Urteau. All five that she had found—all near the Central Dominance, one in the center, the other four forming a box around it. She put a final X by Fadrex City.

Then, with charcoal gripped in her fingers, she noticed something. *Sure are a lot of mines shown on this map around Fadrex*, she thought. *A lot of metal in the area.*

"Step back," Yomen said.

Vin moved away. He approached, scanning the map. Vin stood in silence, thinking. *Elend's scribes could never find a pattern to the cache locations. Two were in small cities, two in large ones. Some near canals, others not. The scribes claimed that they didn't have a large enough set from which to determine patterns.*

"This seems completely random," Yomen said, echoing her thoughts.

"I didn't make up those locations, Yomen," she said, folding her arms. "Your spies can confirm where Elend has taken his armies and sent his emissaries."

"Not all of us have the resources for extensive spy networks, Empress," Yomen said flatly. He looked back at the map. "There should be some pattern. . . ."

Vetitan, Vin thought. *The place where we found the cavern before this one. It was a mining town as well. And Urteau too.*

"Yomen?" she said, looking up. "Does one of those maps list mineral deposits?"

"Of course," he said distractedly. "We *are* the Canton of Resource, after all."

"Get it out."

Yomen raised an eyebrow, indicating what he thought of her giving him orders. However, he waved for his scribe to do as she had requested. A second map overlaid the first, and Vin walked forward. Yomen immediately shied away, keeping out of reach.

He has good instincts, for a bureaucrat, she thought, slipping the charcoal out from underneath the map. She quickly made her five marks again. With each one, her hand grew more tense. Each cavern was in a rocky area, near metal mines. Even Luthadel bore rich mineral deposits. Lore said that the Lord Ruler had constructed his capital in that location *because* of the mineral content in the area, particularly the groundwater. That much the better for Allomancers.

"What are you trying to imply?" Yomen asked. He'd edged close enough to see what she'd marked.

"This is the connection," Vin said. "He built his storages near sources of metal."

"Or it was simple chance."

"No," Vin said, looking up at Ruin. "No, metal equals Allomancy. There's a pattern here."

Yomen waved her away again and approached the map. He snorted. "You've included marks near each of the most productive mines in the inner empire. You expect me to believe that you're not playing me for a fool, offering some phantom evidence that these really are the locations of the storage caverns?"

Vin ignored him. *Metal. The words of Kwaan were written in metal, because he said they were safe. Safe. Safe from being changed, we assumed.*

Or did he mean safe from being read?

The Lord Ruler had drawn his maps on metal plaques.

So, what if Ruin couldn't find the storages on his own because of the metal shielding them? He would have needed someone to lead him. Someone to visit each one, read the map it contained, then lead him on . . .

Lord Ruler! We've made the same mistake again! We did exactly what he wanted. No wonder he's let us live!

However, instead of feeling ashamed, this time Vin felt herself growing angry. She glanced over at Ruin, who stood there with his air of cosmic wisdom. His knowing eyes, his fatherly tone, and his deific arrogance.

Not again, Vin thought, gritting her teeth. *Now I'm on to him. That means I can trick him. But . . . I need to know why. Why was he so interested in the storages? What is it he needs before he wins this battle? What is the reason he's waited so long?*

Suddenly the answer seemed obvious to her. As she examined her feelings, she realized that one of her main reasons for searching out the caches had repeatedly been discredited by Elend. Yet Vin had continued to pursue the caches, searching for this one thing. She'd *felt,* for reasons she couldn't explain, that it was important.

The thing that had driven the imperial economy for a thousand years. The most powerful of Allomantic metals.

Atium.

Why had she been so infatuated with it? Elend and Yomen were both right—atium was of little importance in the current world. But her feelings denied that. Why? Was it because *Ruin* wanted it, and Vin had some unexplained connection to him?

The Lord Ruler had said Ruin couldn't read her mind. But she knew that he could affect her emotions. Change how she regarded things, push her forward. Drive her to search out the thing he wanted.

Examining the emotions that had affected her, she could see Ruin's plan, the way he had manipulated her, the way he thought. Ruin wanted the atium! And with a chill of terror, Vin realized that she had led him straight to it. *No wonder he was so smug before!* Vin thought. *No wonder he assumed that he'd won!*

Why would a godlike force be so interested in such a simple thing as an Allomantic metal? The question made her doubt her conclusions slightly. But at that moment, the doors to the chamber burst open.

And an Inquisitor stood beyond them.

Immediately, Yomen and the soldiers each fell to one

knee. Vin took an involuntary step backward. The creature stood tall, like most of its kind, and still wore the grey robes of its pre-Collapse office. The bald head was wrinkled with intricate tattoos, mostly black, one stark red. And of course there were the spikes driven point-first through its eyes. One of the spikes had been pounded in farther than the other, crushing the socket around the spikehead. The creature's face, twisted by an inhuman sneer, had once been familiar to Vin.

"Marsh?" Vin whispered in horror.

"My lord," Yomen said, spreading his hands out. "You have finally come! I sent messengers, searching for—"

"Silence," Marsh said in a grating voice, striding forward. "On your feet, obligator."

Yomen hastily stood. Marsh glanced at Vin and smiled slightly, but then pointedly ignored her. He did, however, look directly at Ruin and bow his head in subservience.

Vin shivered. Marsh's features, even twisted as they were, reminded her of his brother. Kelsier.

"You are about to be attacked, obligator," Marsh said, sweeping forward, throwing open one of the large windows along the side wall. Through it, from the building's vantage atop a rise, Vin could see over the rocky shelves to where Elend's army camped beside the canal.

Except there was no canal. There were no rocky shelves. Everything was just a uniform black. Ash filled the sky, as thick as a snowstorm.

Lord Ruler! Vin thought. *It's gotten so bad!*

Yomen hurried over to the window. "Attacked, my lord? But they haven't even broken camp!"

"The koloss will attack in surprise," the Inquisitor said. "They don't need to form up ranks—they will simply charge."

Yomen froze for a second, then turned to his soldiers. "Hasten to the defenses. Gather the men on the forward rises!"

Soldiers scuttled from the room. Vin stood quietly. *The man I know as Marsh is dead,* she thought. *He tried to kill Sazed, and now he's fully one of them. Ruin has . . .*

Has taken control of him . . .

An idea began to spark in her mind.

"Quickly, obligator," Marsh said. "I did not come to protect your foolish little city. I've come for the thing you discovered in that cache."

"My lord?" Yomen said, surprised.

"Your atium, Yomen," the Inquisitor said. "Give it to me. It *cannot* be in this city when that attack comes, in case you fall. I shall take it someplace safe."

Vin closed her eyes.

"My . . . lord?" Yomen finally said. "You are, of course, welcome to anything I possess. But there was no atium in the storage cache. I had only the seven beads I had gathered, held as a reserve for the Canton of Resource."

Vin opened her eyes. *"What?"*

"Impossible!" Marsh roared. "But you told the girl earlier that you had it!"

Yomen paled. "Misdirection, my lord. She seemed convinced that I had some wealth of atium, so I let her think that she was right."

"NO!"

Vin jumped at the sudden yell. But Yomen didn't even flinch—and a second later she realized why. Ruin was the one who had shouted. He had become indistinct, losing Reen's form, his figure blossoming outward in a tempest of whirling darkness. Almost like mist, only far, far blacker.

She'd seen that blackness before. She'd walked through it, in the cavern beneath Luthadel, on her way to the Well of Ascension.

A second later, Ruin was wearing Reen's image again. He folded his arms behind his back and didn't look at her, as if trying to pretend that he had not lost control. In his eyes, however, she could see frustration. Anger. She edged away from him—edging *closer* to Marsh.

"You fool!" Marsh said, walking away from her, speaking to Yomen. "You idiot!"

Damn, Vin thought in annoyance.

"I . . ." Yomen said, confused. "My lord, why do you

care for atium? It is worthless without Allomancers and house politicians to pay for it."

"You know nothing," Marsh snapped. Then he smiled. "But you are doomed. Yes . . . doomed indeed . . ."

Outside there was a lull in the ashfall, and she saw Elend's army breaking camp. Yomen turned back to the window, and Vin edged closer, ostensibly to give herself a better look. Elend's forces were gathering—men and koloss. Most likely they had noticed the buildup of city defenses, and had realized that they'd lost any opportunity for surprise.

"He's going to ravage this city," Ruin said, stepping up beside Vin. "Your Elend is a good servant, child. One of my finest. You should be proud of him."

"So many koloss . . ." Yomen whispered. "My lord, there is no way we can fight so many. We need your help."

"Why should I help you?" Marsh asked. "You who fail to deliver to me what I need?"

"But I've remained faithful," Yomen said. "When all others abandoned the Lord Ruler, I have continued to serve him."

Marsh snorted. "The Lord Ruler is dead. He was an un-profitable servant as well."

Yomen paled.

"Let this city burn before the wrath of forty thousand koloss," Marsh said.

Forty thousand koloss, Vin thought. He'd found more somewhere. Attacking seemed the logical thing to do—he could finally capture the city, perhaps giving Vin a chance to escape in the chaos. Very logical, very smart. Yet suddenly, Vin became sure of one thing.

"Elend won't attack," she announced.

Six eyes—two steel, two flesh, two incorporeal—turned toward her.

"Elend won't loose that many koloss upon the city," she said. "He's trying to intimidate you, Yomen. And you should listen. Would you still obey this creature, this Inquisitor? He disdains you. He wants you to die. Join with us instead."

Yomen frowned.

"You could fight him with me," Vin said. "You're an Allomancer. These monsters *can* be defeated."

Marsh smiled. "Idealism from you, Vin?"

"Idealism?" she asked, facing the creature. "You think it's idealistic to believe I can kill an Inquisitor? You know I've done it before."

Marsh waved a dismissive hand. "I'm not talking about your foolish threats. I'm talking about *him*." He nodded toward the army outside. "Your Elend belongs to Ruin, just as I do—just as you do. We all resist, but we all bow before him eventually. Only then do we understand the beauty there is in destruction."

"Your god does not control Elend," Vin said. "He keeps trying to claim that he does, but that simply makes him a liar. Or perhaps something of an idealist himself."

Yomen watched, confused.

"And if he *does* attack?" Marsh asked with a quiet, eager voice. "What would that mean, Vin? What if he does send his koloss against this city in a blood frenzy, sends them to slaughter and kill, all so that he can get what he *thinks* he needs so badly? Atium and food couldn't get him to come in . . . but you? How would that make you feel? You killed for him. What makes you think that Elend won't do the same for you?"

Vin closed her eyes. Memories of her assault upon Cett's tower returned to her. Memories of wanton killing, Zane at her side. Memories of fire, and death, and an Allomancer loosed.

She had never killed like that again.

She opened her eyes. Why wouldn't Elend attack? Attacking made so much sense. He knew he could take the city easily. However, he also knew he had trouble controlling the koloss when they reached too great a frenzy. . . .

"Elend won't attack," she said quietly. "Because he's a better person than I am."

One might notice that Ruin did not send his Inquisitors to Fadrex until after Yomen had—apparently—confirmed that the atium was there in the city. Why not send them as soon as the final cache was located? Where were his minions in all of this?

One must realize that Ruin considered all people his minions, particularly those whom he could manipulate directly. He didn't send an Inquisitor because they were busy doing other tasks. Instead he sent someone who, in his mind, was the exact same thing as an Inquisitor.

He tried to spike Yomen and failed, and by that time Elend's army had arrived. So he used a different pawn to investigate the cache for him and discover if the atium really was there or not. He didn't commit too many resources to the city at first, fearing a deception from the Lord Ruler. I still wonder, as Ruin did, if the caches were in part intended for just that purpose—to distract him and keep him occupied.

64

". . . AND THAT'S WHY YOU ABSOLUTELY *must* get that message sent, Spook. The pieces of this thing are all spinning about, cast to the wind. You have a clue that nobody else does. Send it flying for me."

Spook nodded, feeling fuzzy. Where was he? What was going on? And why did everything suddenly hurt so much?

"Good lad. You did well, Spook. I'm proud."

He tried to nod again, but everything was fuzz and blackness. He coughed, prompting some gasps from a place far off. He groaned. Parts of him hurt sharply, though others only tingled. Still others . . . well, those he couldn't feel at all, though he thought he *should* have been able to.

I was dreaming, he realized as he slowly came to consciousness. *Why have I been asleep? Was I on watch? Should I go on watch? The shop . . .*

His thoughts trailed off as he opened his eyes. There was someone standing above him. A face. One . . . quite a bit uglier than the face he'd hoped to see.

"Breeze?" he tried to say, though it came out as a croak.

"Ha!" Breeze said, with uncharacteristic tears in his eyes. "He *is* waking!"

Another face hovered over him, and Spook smiled. *That* was the one he'd been waiting for. Beldre. "What's going on?" Spook whispered.

Hands brought something to his lips—a water skin. They poured carefully, giving him a drink. He coughed, but got it down. "Why . . . why can't I move?" Spook asked. The only thing he seemed able to twitch was his left hand.

"Your body is being held in casts and bandages, Spook," Beldre said. "Sazed's orders."

"The burns," Breeze said. "Well, they aren't *that* bad, but . . ."

"To hell with the burns," Spook croaked. "I'm alive. I wasn't expecting that."

Breeze looked up at Beldre, smiling.

Send it flying . . .

"Where is Sazed?" Spook asked.

"You should really try to rest," Beldre said, rubbing his cheek softly. "You've been through a lot."

"And slept through more, I expect," Spook said. "Sazed?"

"Gone, my dear boy," Breeze said. "He went off west with Vin's kandra."

Vin.

Feet clomped across the floor, and a second later Captain Goradel's face appeared beside the other two. The square-jawed soldier smiled broadly. "Survivor of the Flames indeed!"

You have a clue that nobody else does. . . .

"How is the city?" Spook asked.

"Mostly safe," Beldre said. "The canals flooded, and my brother organized fire brigades. Most of the buildings that burned weren't inhabited anyway."

"You saved it, my lord," Goradel said.

I'm proud. . . .

"The ash is falling more thickly, isn't it?" Spook asked.

The three above shared looks. Their troubled expressions were enough of a confirmation.

"We're getting a lot of refugees into the city," Beldre said. "From surrounding cities and villages, some as far as Luthadel . . ."

"I need to send a message," Spook said. "To Vin."

"All right," Breeze said soothingly. "We'll do that as soon as you are better."

"Listen to me, Breeze," Spook said, staring up at the ceiling, unable to do much more than twitch. "Something was controlling me and the Citizen. I *saw* it—the thing that Vin released at the Well of Ascension. The thing that's bringing the ash down to destroy us. It wanted this city, but we fought it off. Now I need to warn Vin."

That was what he'd been sent to do in Urteau. Find information, then report it back to Vin and Elend. He was only just beginning to understand how important a duty that could be.

"Travel is difficult right now, my boy," Breeze said. "These are hardly ideal conditions for sending messages."

"Rest some more," Beldre said. "We'll worry about it when you're healed."

Spook gritted his teeth in frustration.

You must *get that message sent, Spook. . . .*

"I'll take it," Goradel said quietly.

Spook looked at him. Sometimes it was easy to ignore

the soldier, with his simple, straightforward manner and his pleasant demeanor. However, the determination in his voice made Spook smile.

"Lady Vin saved my life," Goradel said. "The night of the Survivor's rebellion, she could have left me to die at the hands of the mob. She could have killed me herself. But she took the time to tell me she understood what I'd been through, and convinced me to switch sides. If she needs this information, Survivor, then I *will* get it to her, or die trying."

Spook tried to nod, but his head was held tight by the bandages and wrappings. He flexed his hand. It seemed to work . . . or at least work well enough.

He met Goradel's eyes. "Go to the armory and have a sheet of metal pounded thin," Spook said. "Then return here with something I can use to scratch the metal. These words must be written in steel, and I cannot speak them aloud."

In those moments when the Lord Ruler held the power at the Well but was feeling it drain away from him, he understood a great many things. He saw what Feruchemy could do, and rightly feared it. Many of the Terris people, he knew, would reject him as the Hero, for he didn't fulfill their prophecies well. They'd see him as the usurper he was—the one who killed the Hero they sent.

I think, over the years, Ruin would subtly twist him to do terrible things to his own people. But at the beginning, I suspect his antagonism toward them was motivated more by logic than by emotion. He was about to unveil a grand power in the Mistborn.

I suppose he could have kept Allomancy secret and used Feruchemists as his primary warriors and assassins. However, I think he was wise to choose as he did. Feruchemists, by the nature of their powers, have a tendency toward scholarship. With their incredible memories, they would have been very difficult to control over the centuries. Indeed they were difficult to control even when he suppressed them. Allomancy not only provided a spectacular new ability without that drawback, but it offered a mystical power he could use to bribe kings to his side.

65

ELEND STOOD UPON A SMALL rock outcropping to look over his troops. Below, the koloss stalked forward, stomping a pathway in the ash for his humans to use after the initial koloss assault.

Elend waited, Ham standing a few steps lower.

I wear white, Elend thought. *The color of purity. I try to represent what is good and right. For my men.*

"The koloss should have no trouble with those fortifications," Ham said quietly. "They can leap to the top of city walls; they'll be able to climb those broken stone ridges."

Elend nodded. There probably wouldn't be any need for the human soldiers to attack. With his koloss alone, Elend had the numerical advantage, and it was unlikely Yomen's soldiers had ever fought the creatures before.

The koloss sensed a fight. He could feel them getting excited. They strained against him, wishing to attack.

"Ham," he said, glancing down. "Is this right?"

Ham shrugged. "This move does make sense, El," he said, rubbing his chin. "Attacking is our only real chance of saving Vin. And we can't hold the siege—not any longer." Ham paused, then shook his head, and his tone of voice took on that uncertain quality it always did when he considered one of his logic problems. "Yet loosing a group of koloss on a city does seem immoral. I wonder if you'll be able to control them, once they begin to rampage. Is saving Vin worth the possibility of killing even one innocent child? I don't know. Then again, maybe we'll save more children by bringing them into our empire. . . ."

I shouldn't have bothered to ask Ham, Elend thought. *He never has been able to give a straight answer.* He looked out over the field, blue koloss against a plain of black. With tin, he could see men cowering on the tops of the Fadrex City ridges.

"No," Ham said.

Elend glanced down at the Thug.

"No," Ham repeated. "We shouldn't attack."

"Ham?" Elend said, feeling a surreal amusement. "Did you actually come to a *conclusion*?"

Ham nodded. "Yes." He didn't offer an explanation or rationalization.

Elend looked up. *What would Vin do?* His first instinct was to think that she'd attack. But then he remembered when he had discovered her over a year before, after she'd assaulted Cett's tower. She'd been huddled up in a corner, crying.

No, he thought. *No, she wouldn't do this thing. Not to protect me. She's learned better.*

"Ham," he said, surprising himself. "Tell the men to pull back and disassemble camp. We're returning to Luthadel."

Ham looked at him, startled—he clearly hadn't expected Elend to come to the same conclusion he had. "And Vin?"

"I'm not going to attack this city, Ham," Elend said. "I won't conquer these people, even if it is for their own good. We'll find another way to get Vin free."

Ham smiled. "Cett's going to be furious."

Elend shrugged. "He's a paraplegic. What's he going to do? Bite us? Come on, let's get down off this rock and go deal with Luthadel."

"They're pulling back, my lord," the soldier said.

Vin sighed in relief. Ruin stood, expression unreadable, hands folded behind him. Marsh stood with one hand claw-like on Yomen's shoulder, both of them watching out the window.

Ruin brought in an Inquisitor, she thought. *He must have grown tired of my efforts to get the truth out of Yomen, and instead decided to use someone he knew the obligator would obey.*

"This is very odd," Ruin finally said.

Vin took a breath, then gambled. "Don't you see?" she asked quietly.

Ruin turned toward her.

She smiled. "You really don't understand, do you?"

This time, Marsh turned as well.

"You think I didn't realize?" Vin asked. "You think I didn't know you were after the atium all along? That you were following us from cavern to cavern, Pushing on my emotions, forcing me to search it out for you? You were so obvious. Your koloss always drew close to a city only *after* we discovered that it was the next in line. You moved in to threaten us and make us go more quickly, but you never got your koloss there *too* fast. The thing is, we knew all along."

"Impossible," Ruin whispered.

"No," Vin said. "Quite possible. Atium is metal, Ruin. You can't see it. Your vision gets fuzzy when too much of it is around, doesn't it? Metal is your power; you use it to make Inquisitors, but it's like light to you—blinding. You never saw when we actually discovered the atium. You just followed along with our ruse."

Marsh let go of Yomen, then rushed across the room and grabbed Vin by the arms.

"*WHERE IS IT!*" the Inquisitor demanded, lifting her, shaking her.

She laughed, distracting Marsh as she carefully reached for his sash. The shaking was too strong, however, and her fingers couldn't find their mark.

"You will tell me where the atium is, child," Ruin said calmly. "Haven't I explained this? There is no fighting me. You think yourself clever, but you really don't understand. You don't even know what that atium is."

Vin gritted her teeth. "You think I'd actually lead you to it?"

Marsh shook her again, rattling her. When he stopped, her vision swam. She could barely make out Yomen watching with a frown. "Yomen," she said. "Your people are safe now—can you not finally trust that Elend is a good man?"

Marsh tossed her aside. She hit hard, rolling.

"Ah, child," Ruin said, kneeling down next to her. "Must I *prove* that you cannot fight me?"

"Yomen!" Marsh said, turning. "Prepare your men. I want you to order an assault!"

"What?" Yomen said. "My lord, an assault?"

"Yes," Marsh said. "I want you to take all your soldiers and have them attack Elend Venture's position."

Yomen paled. "Leave behind our fortifications? Charge an army of *koloss*?"

"That is my order," Marsh said.

Yomen stood quietly for a moment.

"Yomen . . ." Vin said, crawling to her knees. "Don't you see that he's manipulating you?"

Yomen didn't respond. He looked troubled. *What would make him consider an order like that?*

"You see," Ruin whispered. "You see my power? You see how even their faith serves me?"

"Give the order," Yomen said, turning from Vin to face his soldier captains. "Have the men attack. Tell them that the Lord Ruler will protect them."

"Well," Ham said, standing beside Elend in the camp. "I didn't expect that."

Elend nodded slowly, watching the flood of men pour through the Fadrex gateway. Some stumbled in the deep ash; others pushed their way forward, their charge hampered to a slow crawl.

"Some stayed back," Elend said, pointing up at the rocky shelves. Not having tin, Ham wouldn't be able to see the men who lined the top, but he'd trust Elend's words. Around them, Elend's human soldiers were breaking camp. The koloss still waited silently in their positions, surrounding the camp.

"What is Yomen thinking?" Ham asked. "He's throwing an inferior force against an army of koloss?"

Like we did, attacking the koloss camp in Vetitan. Something about it made Elend very uncomfortable.

"Retreat," Elend said.

"Huh?" Ham asked.

"I said sound the retreat!" Elend said. "Abandon position. Pull the soldiers back!"

At his silent command, the koloss began to charge away from the city. Yomen's soldiers were still pushing their way through the ash. Elend's koloss, however, would clear the way for his men. They should be able to stay ahead.

"Strangest retreat *I've* ever seen," Ham noted, but went to give the orders.

That's it, Elend thought in annoyance. *It's time to figure out what the hell is going on in that city.*

Yomen was crying. They were small, quiet tears. He stood straight-backed, not facing the windows.

He fears that he's ordered his men to their deaths, Vin thought. She moved up to him, limping slightly from where she'd hit the ground. Marsh stood watching out his window. Ruin eyed her curiously.

"Yomen," she said.

Yomen turned toward her. "It's a test," he said. "The Inquisitors are the Lord Ruler's most holy priests. I'll do as commanded, and the Lord Ruler will protect my men and this city. Then you will see."

Vin gritted her teeth. Then she turned and forced herself to walk up beside Marsh. She glanced out the window—and was surprised to see that Elend's army was retreating away from Yomen's soldiers. Yomen's force wasn't charging the foe with much conviction. Obviously they were content to let their superior enemy flee before them. The sun was finally setting.

Marsh did not seem to find Elend's retreat amusing. That was enough to make Vin smile—which made Marsh grab her again.

"You think you have won?" Marsh asked, leaning down, his uneven spikeheads hanging right before Vin's face.

Vin reached for his sash. *Just a little farther . . .*

"You claim to have been playing with me, child," Ruin said, stepping up next to her. "But you are the one who has been played for a fool. The koloss who serve you, they get their strength from *my* power. You think that I would let you control them if it weren't for my eventual gain?"

Vin felt a sudden chill.

Oh no . . .

Elend felt a terrible *ripping* sensation. It was as if a part of his innards had been suddenly and forcibly pulled away from him. He gasped, releasing his Steelpush. He fell through the ash-filled sky, and landed unevenly on a rock shelf outside Fadrex City.

He gasped, breathing in and out, trembling.

What in the hell was that? he thought, standing up, holding his thumping head.

And then he realized it. He couldn't feel the koloss anymore. In the distance, the massive blue creatures stopped running away. And then, to Elend's horror, he watched them turn around.

They began to charge his men.

Marsh held her. "Hemalurgy is *his* power, Vin!" he said. "The Lord Ruler used it unwittingly! The fool! Each time he built an Inquisitor or a koloss, he made another servant for his enemy! Ruin waited patiently, knowing that when he finally broke free, he'd have an entire army waiting for him!"

Yomen had moved to the other side window. He gasped quietly, watching. "You did deliver my men!" the obligator said. "The koloss have turned to attack their own army!"

"They'll come after your men next, Yomen," Vin said, dizzily. "Then they'll destroy your city."

"It is ending," Ruin whispered. "Everything needs to fit into place. Where is the atium? It's the last piece."

Marsh shook her. She finally managed to reach his sash—and slipped her fingers into it. Fingers trained by her brother, and by a lifetime on the street.

The fingers of a thief.

"You can't fool me, Vin," Ruin said. "I am God."

Marsh raised one hand—releasing her arm—then swung

one hand toward her. He moved with power, Allomantic pewter clearly burning within him.

Vin flipped her hand up and downed the vial of metals she'd stolen from his sash.

Marsh froze, and Ruin fell silent.

Vin smiled.

Pewter flared in her own stomach, restoring her to life. Marsh swung his hand toward her again, but she shifted aside, then yanked him off balance by yanking her other arm, which he still held. He hung on, barely, but when he turned to face Vin, he found her holding her earring in one hand.

And she duralumin-Pushed it directly into his forehead. It was a tiny bit of metal, but it tossed up a drop of blood as it struck, ripping through his head and passing out the other side.

Marsh dropped, and Vin was thrown backward by her own Push. She crashed into the wall, causing soldiers to scatter and yell, raising weapons. Yomen turned toward her, surprised.

"Yomen!" she said. "Order your men to return! Fortify the city!" Ruin had disappeared in the chaos of her escape. Perhaps he was out overseeing the control of the koloss.

Yomen seemed indecisive. "I . . . No. I will not lose faith. I must be strong."

Vin gritted her teeth, climbing to her feet. *Nearly as frustrating as Elend is at times,* she thought, scrambling over to Marsh's body. Reaching into his sash, she pulled out the last vial he had stored there, then downed it, restoring the metals she'd lost to duralumin.

Then she hopped up on the windowsill. Mist puffed around her—the sun had not yet set, but the mists were arriving earlier and earlier. She saw Elend's forces beleaguered by rampaging koloss on one side, Yomen's soldiers not attacking—yet blocking retreat—on the other. She moved to jump out and join the fight, and then she noticed something.

A small group of koloss. A thousand in number, small

enough to apparently have been ignored by both Elend's forces and Yomen's. Even Ruin appeared to have paid them no heed, for they simply stood in the ash, partially buried, like a collection of quiet stones.

Vin's koloss. The ones that Elend had given her, Human at their lead. With a devious smile, she ordered them forward.

To attack Yomen's men.

"I'm telling you, Yomen," she said, hopping off the windowsill and back into the room. "Those koloss don't care which side the humans are on—they'll kill anyone. The Inquisitors have gone mad, now that the Lord Ruler is dead. Didn't you pay any attention to what this one said?"

Yomen looked thoughtful.

"He admitted that the Lord Ruler was dead, Yomen," Vin said with exasperation. "Your faith is commendable. But sometimes you just have to know when to *give up and move on*!"

One of the soldier captains yelled something, and Yomen spun back toward the window. He cursed.

Immediately Vin felt something *Pulling* on her koloss. She cried out as they were yanked away from her, but the damage had been done—Yomen had seen them attack his soldiers. Troubled, he stared into Vin's eyes, silent for a moment. "Tell them to retreat into the city!" he finally yelled to his captains. "And order the men to allow Venture's soldiers refuge inside as well!"

Vin sighed in relief. And then something grabbed her leg. She looked down with shock as Marsh climbed to his knees. Her earring had sliced through his brain, but the amazing Inquisitor healing powers had dealt even with that.

"Fool," Marsh said, standing. "If Yomen turns against me, I can kill him, and his soldiers will follow me. He's given them a belief in the Lord Ruler, which devolves to me as chief among his priests."

Vin took a deep breath, then hit Marsh with a duralumin-fueled Soothing. If it worked on koloss and kandra, why not Inquisitors?

Marsh stumbled. Vin's Push lasted a brief moment, but during it she *felt* something. A wall like she'd felt the first time she'd tried to control TenSoon or the first time she'd taken control of a group of koloss.

She *Pushed* with everything she had. In a burst of power, she came close to seizing control of Marsh's body, but not close enough. The wall within his mind was too strong, and she had only one vial's worth of metal to use. The wall shoved her back. She cried out in frustration.

Marsh reached out, growling, and grabbed her by the neck. She gasped, her eyes widening as Marsh began to grow in size. Getting stronger, like . . .

A Feruchemist, she realized. *I'm in serious trouble.*

People in the room were yelling, but she couldn't hear them. Marsh's hand—now large and beefy—gripped her throat, strangling her. Only flared pewter was keeping her alive. She flashed back to the day years ago when she'd been held by another Inquisitor. Standing in the Lord Ruler's throne room.

On that day, Marsh had saved her life. It seemed a twisted irony that he was now the one who would end it.

Not. Yet.

The mists began to swirl around her.

Marsh started, though he continued to hold her.

Vin drew upon the mists.

It happened again. She didn't know how or why, but it just *happened.* She breathed the mists into her body, as she had on that day so long ago when she'd killed the Lord Ruler. She somehow pulled them into her and used them to fuel her body with an incredible surge of Allomantic power.

And with that power, she *Pushed* on Marsh's emotions.

The wall inside him cracked, then burst. For a moment, Vin felt a sense of vertigo. She saw things through Marsh's eyes—indeed, she felt like she *understood* him. His love of destruction, and his hatred of himself. And through him, she caught a brief glimpse of something. A hateful, destructive thing that hid behind a mask of civility.

Ruin was *not* the same thing as the mists.

Marsh cried out, dropping her. Her strange burst of power dissipated, but it didn't matter, for Marsh fled through the window and Pushed himself away in the mists. Vin picked herself up, coughing.

I did it. I drew upon the mists again. But why now? Why, after all the trying, did it happen now?

There was no time to consider it at the moment—not with the koloss attacking. She turned to the baffled Yomen. "Continue to retreat into the city!" she said. "I'm going out to help."

Elend fought desperately, cutting down koloss after koloss. It was difficult, dangerous work, even for him. These koloss couldn't be controlled—no matter how he Pushed or Pulled on their emotions, he couldn't bring a single one of them under his power.

That only left fighting. And his men weren't prepared for battle—he'd forced them to abandon camp too quickly.

A koloss swung, its sword whooshing dangerously close to Elend's head. He cursed, dropping a coin and Pushing himself backward through the air, over his fighting men and into camp. They'd managed to retreat to the positioning of their original fortification, which meant they had a small rise for defense and didn't have to fight in ash. A group of his Coinshots—he had just ten—stood launching wave after wave of coins into the main bulk of the koloss, and archers loosed similar volleys. The main line of soldiers was supported by Lurchers from behind, who would Pull on koloss weapons and throw them off balance, giving the regular soldiers extra openings. Thugs ran around the perimeter in groups of two or three, shoring up weak spots and acting as reserves.

They were still in serious trouble. Elend's army couldn't stand against so many koloss any more easily than Fadrex could have. Elend landed in the middle of the half-disassembled camp, breathing heavily, covered in koloss blood. Men yelled as they fought a short distance away, holding the camp perimeter with the help of the Allomancers. The bulk of the koloss army was still bunched around the northern section of camp, but Elend couldn't pull his men back any farther toward Fadrex without exposing them to Yomen's archers.

Elend tried to catch his breath as a servant rushed up with a cup of water for him. Cett sat a short distance away, directing the battle tactics. Elend tossed aside the empty cup and moved over to the general, who sat at a small table. It held a map of the area that hadn't been marked on. The koloss were so close, the fighting happening mere yards away, that there was little point in keeping an abstract battle map.

"Never did like having those things in the army," Cett said as he downed a cup of water himself. A servant moved over, leading a surgeon, who pulled out a bandage to begin working on Elend's arm which up until that moment he hadn't noticed was bleeding.

"Well," Cett noted, "at least we'll die in battle rather than of starvation!"

Elend snorted, picking up his sword again. The sky was nearly dark. They didn't have much time before—

A figure landed on the table in front of Cett. "Elend!" Vin said. "Retreat to the city. Yomen will let you in."

Elend started. "Vin!" Then he smiled. "What took you so long?"

"I got delayed by an Inquisitor and a dark god," she said. "Now, hustle. I'll go see if I can distract some of those koloss."

Inquisitors had little chance of resisting Ruin. They had more spikes than any of his other Hemalurgic creations, and that put them completely under his domination.

Yes, it would have taken a supreme will for anyone to resist Ruin even slightly while bearing the spikes of an Inquisitor.

66

SAZED TRIED NOT TO THINK about how dark the ash was in the sky, or how terrible the land looked.

I've been such a fool, he thought as he rode. *Of all the times that the world needed something to believe in, this is it. And I wasn't there to give it to them.*

He hurt from so much riding, yet he clung to the saddle, still somewhat amazed at the creature who ran beneath him. When Sazed had first decided to go west with TenSoon, he had despaired at making the trip. Ash fell like the snows of a blizzard, and it had piled terribly high in most places. Sazed had known travel would be difficult, and he'd feared slowing TenSoon, who could clearly travel far more quickly as a wolfhound.

TenSoon considered this concern, then had ordered a horse and a large hog to be brought to him. TenSoon first ingested the hog to give himself extra mass, then molded his gelatinous flesh around the horse to digest it as well. Within an hour, he'd formed his body into a replica of the horse—but one with enhanced muscles and weight, creating the enormous, extra-strong marvel which Sazed now rode.

They'd been running nonstop since then. Fortunately, Sazed had some wakefulness he'd stored in a metalmind a year ago, after the siege of Luthadel. He used it to keep himself from falling asleep. It still amazed him that Ten-Soon could enhance a horse's body so well. It moved with ease through the thick ash, where a real horse—and certainly a human—would have balked at the difficulty. *Another thing I've been a fool about. These last few days, I could have been interrogating TenSoon about his powers. How much more is there that I don't know?*

Despite his shame, however, Sazed felt a peace within. If he'd continued to teach about religions after he'd stopped believing in them, then he would have been a true hypocrite. Tindwyl had believed in giving people hope, even if one had to tell them lies to do so. That was the credit she had given to religion: lies that made people feel better.

Sazed couldn't have acted the same way—at least he couldn't have done so and remained the person he wanted to be. However, he now had hope himself. The Terris religion was the one that had taught about the Hero of Ages in the first place. If any contained the truth, it would be this one. Sazed needed to question the First Generation of kandra and discover what they knew.

Though if I do find the truth, what will I do with it?

The trees they passed were stripped of leaves. The landscape was covered in a good four feet of ash. "How can you keep going like this?" Sazed asked as the kandra galloped over a hilltop, shoving aside ash and ignoring obstructions.

"My people are created from mistwraiths," TenSoon explained, not sounding winded in the least. "The Lord Ruler turned the Feruchemists into mistwraiths, and they began to breed true as a species. You add a Blessing to a mistwraith, and they become awakened, turning into a kandra. One such as I, created centuries after the Ascension, was born as a mistwraith but became awakened when I received my Blessing."

". . . Blessing?" Sazed asked.

"Two small metal spikes, Keeper," TenSoon said. "We

are created like Inquisitors or koloss. However, we are more subtle creations than either of those. We were made third and last, as the Lord Ruler's power waned."

Sazed frowned, leaning low as the horse ran beneath some skeletal tree branches.

"What is different about you?"

"We have more independence of will than the other two," TenSoon said. "We only have two spikes in us, while the others have more. An Allomancer can still take control of us, but free we remain more independent of mind than koloss or Inquisitors, who are both affected by Ruin's impulses even when he isn't directly controlling them. Did you never wonder why both of them are driven so powerfully to kill?"

"That doesn't explain how you can carry me and all our baggage, and still run through this ash."

"The metal spikes we carry grant us gifts," TenSoon said. "Much as you gain strength from Feruchemy, or Vin does from Allomancy, my Blessing gives strength to me. It will never run out, but it isn't as spectacular as the bursts your people can create. Still, my Blessing—mixed with my ability to craft my body as I wish—allows me a high level of endurance."

For a while, Sazed returned to his thoughts. They continued to gallop.

"There isn't much time left," TenSoon noted.

"I can see that," Sazed said. "It makes me wonder what we can do."

"This is the only period in which we could succeed," TenSoon said. "We must be poised, ready to strike. Ready to aid the Hero of Ages when she comes."

"Comes?"

"She will lead an army of Allomancers to the Homeland," TenSoon said, "and there will save all of us—kandra, human, koloss, and Inquisitor."

An army of Allomancers? "Then . . . what am I to do?"

"You must convince the kandra how dire the situation is," TenSoon explained, slowing to a halt in the ash. "For there is . . . something they must be prepared to do. Something very difficult, yet necessary. My people will resist it, but perhaps you can show them the way."

Sazed nodded, then climbed off the kandra to stretch his legs.

"Do you recognize this location?" TenSoon asked, turning to look at him with a horse's head.

"I do not," Sazed said. "With the ash . . . well, I haven't really been able to follow our path for days."

"Over that ridge, you will find the place where the Terris people have set up their refugee camp."

Sazed turned with surprise. "The Pits of Hathsin?"

TenSoon nodded. "We call this the Homeland."

"The *Pits*?" Sazed asked, shocked. "But . . ."

"Well, not the Pits themselves," TenSoon said. "You know that the entire area has cave complexes beneath it?"

Sazed nodded. The place where Kelsier had trained his original army of skaa soldiers was a short trip to the north.

"One of the cave complexes is the kandra Homeland. It abuts the Pits of Hathsin—in fact, several of the kandra passages run into the Pits, and had to be kept closed off, lest workers in the Pits find their way into the Homeland."

"Does your Homeland grow atium?" Sazed asked.

"Grow it? No, it does not. I suppose that is what separates the Homeland from the Pits. In any case, the entrance to my people's caverns is right there."

Sazed turned with a start. "Where?"

"That depression in the ash," TenSoon said, nodding his large head toward it. "Good luck, Keeper. I have my own duties to attend to."

Sazed nodded, amazed they had traveled so far so quickly, and untied his pack from the kandra's back. He left the bag containing bones—those of the wolfhound, and another set that was human. Probably a body TenSoon carried to use should he need it.

The enormous horse turned to go.

"Wait!" Sazed said, raising a hand.

TenSoon looked back.

"Good luck," Sazed said. "May . . . our god preserve you."

TenSoon smiled, a strange expression on an equine face, then took off galloping through the ash.

Sazed turned to the depression in the ground. Then he hefted his pack—filled with metalminds and a solitary book—and walked forward. Moving even that short distance in the ash was difficult. He reached the depression and—taking a breath—began to dig his way into the ash.

He didn't get far before he slid into a tunnel. It didn't open straight down, fortunately, and he didn't fall far. The cavern around him led up at an incline, opening to the outside world in a hole that was half pit, half cave. Sazed stood up in the cavern, then reached into his pack and pulled out a tinmind. With this, he tapped eyesight, improving his vision as he walked into the darkness.

A tinmind didn't work as well as an Allomancer's tin—or rather it didn't work in the same way. It could allow one to see great distances, but it was of far less help in poor illumination. Soon, despite the tinmind Sazed was walking in darkness, feeling his way along the tunnel.

And then he saw light.

"Halt!" a voice called. "Who returns from Contract?"

Sazed continued forward. A part of him was frightened, but another part was only curious. He knew a very important fact.

Kandra could not kill humans.

Sazed stepped up to the light, which turned out to be a melon-size rock atop a pole, its porous material coated with some kind of glowing fungus. A pair of kandra blocked his path. They were easily identifiable as such since they wore no clothing and their skins were translucent. They appeared to have bones carved from rock.

Fascinating! Sazed thought. *They make their own bones. I really do have a new culture to explore. A whole new society—art, religion, mores, gender interactions . . .*

The prospect was so exciting that for a moment, even the end of the world seemed trivial by comparison. He had to remind himself to focus. He needed to investigate their religion first. Other things were secondary.

"Kandra, who are you? Which bones do you wear?"

"You are going to be surprised, I think," Sazed said as gently as he could. "For I am no kandra. My name is Sazed, Keeper of Terris, and I have been sent to speak with the First Generation."

Both kandra guards started.

"You don't have to let me pass," Sazed said. "Of course, if you don't take me into your Homeland, then I'll have to leave and tell everyone on the outside where it is. . . ."

The guards turned to each other. "Come with us," one of them finally said.

Koloss also had little chance of breaking free. Four spikes, and their diminished mental capacity, left them open to domination. Only in the throes of a blood frenzy did they have a taste of true autonomy.

Four spikes made them easier for Allomancers to control. In our time, it required a duralumin Push to take control of a kandra. Koloss, however, could be taken by a determined ordinary Push, particularly when they were afraid.

67

ELEND AND VIN STOOD ATOP the Fadrex City fortifications. The rock ledge had once held the bonfires they'd watched in the night sky; the blackened scar from one of them lay to her left.

It felt good to be held by Elend again. His warmth was a comfort, particularly when looking out of the city, over the field that Elend's army had once occupied. The koloss army was growing. It stood silently in the blizzard of ash, thousands strong. More and more of the creatures were arriving each day, amassing into an overwhelming force.

"Why don't they attack?" Yomen asked with annoyance. He was the only other one who stood on the overlook; Ham and Cett were down in the city, seeing to the army's preparation. They'd need to be ready the moment the koloss launched their assault.

"He wants us to know just how soundly he's going to beat us," Vin said. *Plus,* she added in her mind, *he's waiting. Waiting on that last bit of information.*

Where is the atium?

She'd fooled Ruin. She'd proven that it could be done. Yet she was still frustrated. She felt like she'd spent the last few years of her life reacting to every wiggle of Ruin's fingers. Each time she thought herself clever, wise, or self-sacrificing, she discovered that she'd been doing his will the entire time. It made her angry.

But what could she do?

I have to make Ruin play his hand, she thought. *Make him act, expose himself.*

For a brief moment back in Yomen's throne room, she had felt something amazing. With the strange power she'd gained from the mists, she'd touched Ruin's own mind—via Marsh—and seen something therein.

Fear. She remembered it, distinct and pure. At that moment, Ruin had been afraid of her. That was why Marsh had fled.

Somehow she'd taken the power of the mists into her, then used them to perform Allomancy of surpassing might. She'd done it once before, when fighting the Lord Ruler in his palace. Why could she only draw on that power at random unpredictable times? She'd wanted to use it against

Zane, but had failed. She'd tried a dozen times during the last few days, as she had during the days following the Lord Ruler's death. She'd never been able to access a hint of that power—

A *crack* like a thunderclap.

The massive, overpowering quake rolled across the land. The rock ledges around Fadrex broke, some of them tumbling to the ground. Vin remained on her feet with the help of pewter, and she barely snatched Yomen by the front of his obligator robes as he careened and almost fell from their ledge. Elend grabbed her arm, reinforcing her as the quake continued to shake the land. In the city, several buildings fell.

Then all went still. Vin breathed heavily, her forehead slicked with sweat, Yomen's robes clutched in her grip. She glanced at Elend.

"That was far worse than the previous ones," he said, cursing quietly to himself.

"We're doomed," Yomen said, forcing himself to his feet. "If the things you say are true, then not only is the Lord Ruler dead, but the thing he spent his life fighting has now come to destroy the world."

"We've survived this long," Elend said firmly. "We'll make it yet. Earthquakes may hurt us, but they hurt the koloss too—look and you'll see that some of them were crushed by toppling rocks. If things get rough up here, we can retreat into the cavern."

"And will it survive quakes like that one?" Yomen asked.

"Better than the buildings up here will. None of this was built for earthquakes—but if I know the Lord Ruler, he anticipated the quakes and picked caverns that were solid and capable of withstanding them."

Yomen seemed to take little comfort in the words, but Vin smiled. Not because of what Elend said, but because of how he said it. Something about him had changed. He seemed confident in a way he'd never been before. He had some of the same idealistic air he'd expressed when he'd been a youth at court—yet he also had the hardness of the man who'd led his people in war.

He'd found the balance at last. Oddly enough, it had come from deciding to retreat.

"He does have a point, Vin," Elend said in a softer tone. "We need to figure out our next step. Ruin obviously intended to defeat us here, but he has been pushed back at least for a time. What now?"

We have to trick him, she thought. *Perhaps . . . use the same strategy Yomen used on me?*

She paused, considering the idea. She reached up, fingering her earring. It had been mangled after its trip through Marsh's head, but it had been a simple matter to have a smith bend it into shape.

The first time she'd met with Yomen, he'd returned the earring to her. It had seemed a strange move, giving metal to an Allomancer. Yet in a controlled environment, it had been clever. He'd been able to test and see if she had any hidden metals—all the while reserving the fact that he could burn atium and protect himself.

Later he'd been able to get her to reveal her hand, to attack and show him what she was planning, so that he could undermine it in a situation where he was in power. Could she do the same to Ruin?

That thought mixed with another one. Both times when the mists had helped her, they had come in a moment of pure desperation, as if they reacted to her need. So, was there a way to put herself in a situation where her need was even greater than before? It was a thin hope, but—mixed with her desire to force Ruin's hand—it formed a plan in her head.

Put herself in danger. Make Ruin bring his Inquisitors, placing Vin in a situation where the mists *had* to help her. If that didn't work, maybe she could get Ruin to play his hand or spring any hidden traps he had waiting for her.

It was incredibly risky, but she could feel that she didn't have much time. Ruin would win soon—very soon—unless she did *something.* And this was all she could think of to do. But how could she make it happen without explaining it to Elend? She couldn't speak of the plan, lest she reveal to Ruin what she was doing.

She looked up at Elend, a man she seemed to know better than herself. He hadn't needed to tell her that he'd reconciled the two halves of himself; she'd simply been able to tell it from looking at him. With a person like that, did she really need to speak her plans? Perhaps . . . "Elend," she said, "I think there's only one way to save this city."

"And that is?" he said slowly.

"I have to go get *it*."

Elend frowned, then opened his mouth. She peered into his eyes, hoping. He hesitated.

"The . . . atium?" he guessed.

Vin smiled. "Yes. Ruin knows that we have it. He'll find it even if we don't use it. But if we bring it here, at least we can fight."

"It would be safer here anyway," Elend said slowly, his eyes showing confusion, but also trust. "I'd rather have an army between those riches and our enemies. Perhaps we could use it to bribe some local warlords to help us."

The ruse felt flimsy to her. Yet she knew that was because she could see Elend's confusion, could read his lies in his eyes. She understood him, as he understood her. It was an understanding that required love.

And she suspected that was something that Ruin would never be able to comprehend.

"Then I need to leave," she said, embracing him tightly, closing her eyes.

"I know."

She held him close for a few moments longer, feeling the ash fall around her, blowing against her skin and cheek. Feeling Elend's heart beat beneath her ear. She leaned up and kissed him. Finally she pulled back, then checked her metals. She met his eyes, and he nodded, so she jumped down into the city to gather horseshoes.

A few minutes later, she was shooting through the ashy

air toward Luthadel, a maelstrom of metal around her. Elend stood silently behind on the rock ledge, watching her go.

Now, she thought to Ruin, who she knew was watching her carefully, although he hadn't revealed himself since she'd drawn upon the mists. *Let's have a chase, you and I.*

When the Lord Ruler offered his plan to his Feruchemist friends—the plan to change them into mistwraiths—he was making them speak on behalf of all the land's Feruchemists. Though he changed his friends into kandra to restore their minds and memories, the rest he left as nonsapient mistwraiths. These bred more of their kind, living and dying, becoming a race unto themselves. From these children of the original mistwraiths, he made the next generations of kandra.

However, even gods can make mistakes, I have learned. Rashek, the Lord Ruler, thought to transform all of the living Feruchemists into mistwraiths. But he did not think of the genetic heritage left in the other Terris people, whom he left alive. So it was that Feruchemists continued being born, if only rarely.

This oversight cost him much, but gained the world so much more.

68

SAZED WALKED IN WONDER, LED by his guards. He saw kandra after kandra, each with a more interesting body than the one before. Some were tall and willowy, with bones made of white wood. Others were stocky, with bones thicker than any human's. All kept to generally human body shapes, however.

They used to be *human,* he reminded himself. *Or at least their ancestors were.*

The caverns around him felt old. The pathways were worn smooth, and while there were no real buildings, he passed many smaller caverns, varied drapery hanging across their openings. There was a sense of exquisite craftsmanship to it all, from the carved poles that held the fungus lights, to the very bones of the people around him. It wasn't the detailed ornamentation of a nobleman's keep, for there were no patterns, leaves, or knots carved into the stonework or bones. Instead, things were polished smooth, carved with rounded sides, or woven in broad lines and shapes.

The kandra seemed afraid of him. It was a strange experience for Sazed. He had been many things in his life: rebel, servant, friend, scholar. However, never before had he found himself an object of fear. Kandra ducked around corners, peeking at him. Others stood in shock, watching him pass. Clearly, news of his arrival had spread quickly, otherwise they would have assumed him to be a kandra wearing human bones.

His guards led him to a steel door set into a large cavern wall. One of them moved inside, while the other guarded Sazed. Sazed noticed shards of metal twinkling in each of the kandra's shoulders. They appeared to be spikes.

Smaller than Inquisitor spikes, Sazed thought. *But still sufficient. Interesting.*

"What would you do if I were to run?" Sazed asked.

The kandra started. "Um . . ."

"Can I assume from your hesitance that you are still forbidden to harm, or at least kill, a human?" Sazed asked.

"We follow the First Contract."

"Ah," Sazed said. "Very interesting. And with whom did you make the First Contract?"

"The Father."

"The Lord Ruler?" Sazed asked.

The kandra nodded.

"He is, unfortunately and truly, dead. So, is your Contract no longer valid?"

"I don't know," the kandra said, looking away.

So, Sazed thought, *not all of them are as forceful of personality as TenSoon. Even when he was playing the part of a simple wolfhound, I found him to be intense.*

The other soldier returned. "Come with me," he said.

They led Sazed through the open metal doors. The room beyond had a large metal pedestal about a foot in height. The guards did not step on it, but led Sazed around it toward a place before a group of stone lecterns. Many of the lecterns were empty, though kandra with twinkling bones stood behind two of them. These creatures were tall—or at least they used tall bones—and very fine-featured.

Aristocrats, Sazed thought. He had found that class of people easy to identify, no matter the culture or—apparently— species.

Sazed's guards gestured for him to stand before the lecterns. Sazed ignored the gestures, walking in a circle around the room. As he expected, his guards didn't know what to do—they followed, but refrained from putting their hands on him.

"There is metal plating surrounding the entire chamber," Sazed noted. "Is it ornamental, or does it serve a function?"

"We will be asking the questions here, Terrisman!" said one of the aristocratic kandra.

Sazed paused, turning. "No," he said. "No, you will not. I am Sazed, Keeper of Terris. However, among your people I have another name. The Announcer."

The other kandra leader snorted. "What does an outsider know of such things?"

"An outsider?" Sazed said. "You should better learn your own doctrine, I think." He began to walk forward. "I am Terris, as are you. Yes, I know your origins. I know how you were created—and I know the heritage you bring with you."

He stopped before their lecterns. "I announce to you that I have discovered the Hero. I have lived with her, worked with her, and watched her. I handed her the very spear she used to slay the Lord Ruler. I have seen her take command of kings, watched her overcome armies of both men and koloss. I have come to announce this to you, so that you may prepare yourselves."

He paused, eyeing them. "For the end is here," he added.

The two kandra stood quietly for a few moments. "Go get the others," one finally said, his voice shaking.

Sazed smiled. As one of the guards ran off, Sazed turned to the second soldier. "I shall require a table and chair, please. Also something with which to write."

A few minutes later, all was ready. His kandra attendants had swelled from four to over twenty—twelve of them being the aristocratic ones with the twinkling bones. Some had set up a small table for Sazed, and he seated himself as the kandra nobles spoke together in anxious whispers.

Carefully, Sazed placed his pack on the table and began to remove his metalminds. Small rings, smaller earrings and studs, and large bracers soon lined the table. He pushed up his sleeves, then clasped on his copperminds—two large bracers on the upper arms, then two bracers on the forearms. Finally he removed his book from the pack and set it on the table. Some kandra approached with thin plates of metal. Sazed watched curiously as they arranged them for him, along with what appeared to be a steel pen, capable of making indentations in the soft writing metal. The kandra servants bowed and withdrew.

Excellent, Sazed thought, picking up the metal pen and clearing his throat. The kandra leaders turned toward him.

"I assume," Sazed said, "that you are the First Generation?"

"We are the Second Generation, Terrisman," one of the kandra said.

"Well, I apologize for taking your time then. Where can I find your superiors?"

The lead kandra snorted. "Do not think that you have us quelled merely because you were able to draw us together. I see no reason for you to speak with the First Generation, even if you can blaspheme quite accurately."

Sazed raised an eyebrow. "Blaspheme?"

"You are not the Announcer," the kandra said. "This is not the end."

"Have you seen the ash up above?" Sazed said. "Or has it stopped up the entrances to this cavern complex so soundly that nobody can escape to see that the world is falling apart?"

"We have lived a very long time, Terrisman," one of the other kandra said. "We have seen periods where the ash fell more copiously than others."

"Oh?" Sazed asked. "And you perhaps have seen the Lord Ruler die before as well?"

Some of the kandra looked uncomfortable at this, though the one at the lead shook his head. "Did TenSoon send you?"

"He did," Sazed admitted.

"You can make no arguments other than those he has already made," the kandra said. "Why would he think that you—an outsider—could persuade us, when he could not?"

"Perhaps because he understood something about me," Sazed said, tapping his book with his pen. "Are you aware of the ways of Keepers, kandra?"

"My name is KanPaar," the kandra said. "And yes, I understand what Keepers do—or at least what they did before the Father was killed."

"Then," Sazed said, "perhaps you know that every Keeper has an area of specialty. The intention was that when the Lord Ruler finally did fall, we would already be divided into specialists who could teach our knowledge to the people."

"Yes," KanPaar said.

"Well," Sazed said, rubbing fingers over his book, "my specialty was religion. Do you know how many religions there were before the Lord Ruler's Ascension?"

"I don't. Hundreds."

"We have record of five hundred and sixty-three," Sazed said. "Though that includes sects of the same religions. In a more strict count, there were around three hundred."

"And?" KanPaar asked.

"Do you know how many of these survived until this day?" Sazed asked.

"Nonc?"

"One," Sazed said, holding up a finger. "Yours. The Terris religion. Do you think it a coincidence that the religion you follow not only still exists, but also foretells this exact day?"

KanPaar snorted. "You are saying nothing new. So my religion is real, while others were lies. What does that explain?"

"That you should perhaps listen to members of your faith who bring you tidings." Sazed began to flip through his book. "At the very least, I would think that you'd be interested in this book, as it contains the collected information about the Hero of Ages that I was able to discover. Since I knew little of the true Terris religion, I had to get my information from secondhand accounts—from tales and stories, and from texts written during the intermediate time.

"Unfortunately," Sazed continued, "much of this text was changed by Ruin when he was trying to persuade the Hero to visit the Well of Ascension and set him free. Therefore, it is quite corrupted and tainted by his touch."

"And why would I be interested?" KanPaar asked. "You just told me that your information is corrupt and useless."

"Useless?" Sazed asked. "No, not useless at all. Corrupt, yes. Changed by Ruin. My friend, I have a book here filled with Ruin's lies. You have a mind filled with the original truths. Apart, we know little. However, if we were to *compare*—discovering precisely which items Ruin changed—would it not tell us exactly what his plan is? At the very least, it would tell us what he didn't want us to focus on, I think."

The room fell silent.

"Well," KanPaar finally said, "I—"

"That will be enough, KanPaar," a voice said.

Sazed paused, cocking his head. The voice hadn't come from any of those beside the pedestals. Sazed glanced around the room, trying to discover who had spoken.

"You may leave, Seconds," another voice said.

One of the Seconds gasped. "Leave? Leave you with this one, an outsider?"

"A descendant," one of the voices said. "A Worldbringer. We will hear him."

"Leave us," said another voice.

Sazed raised an eyebrow, sitting as the Second Generationers—looking rattled—left their lecterns and quietly made their way from the room. A pair of guards pushed the doors shut, blocking the view of those kandra who had been watching outside. Sazed was left alone in the room with the phantoms who had spoken.

Sazed heard a scraping sound. It echoed through the steel-lined chamber, and then a door opened at the back of the room. From this came what he assumed was the First Generation. They looked . . . old. Their kandra flesh visibly hung from their bodies, like translucent tree moss drooping from bone branches. They were stooped, clearly more aged than the other kandra, and they didn't walk so much as shuffle.

They wore simple robes with no sleeves, but the garments still appeared odd on the creatures. In addition, beneath their translucent skin he could see that they had white, normal skeletons. "Human bones?" Sazed asked as the elderly creatures made their way forward, walking with canes.

"Our own bones," one of them said, speaking with a tired near-whisper of a voice. "We hadn't the skill or knowledge to form True Bodies when this all began, so we took our original bones again when the Lord Ruler gave them to us."

The First Generation appeared to have ten members. They arranged themselves on the benches. Out of respect, Sazed moved his table so that he was seated before them, like a presenter before an audience.

"Now," he said, raising his metal scratching pen. "Let us begin—we have much work to do."

The question remains, where did the original prophecies about the Hero of Ages come from? I now know that Ruin changed them, but did not fabricate them. Who first taught that a Hero would come, one who would be an emperor of all humankind, yet would be rejected by his own people? Who first stated he would carry the future of the world on his arms, or that he would repair that which had been sundered?

And who decided to use the neutral pronoun, so that we wouldn't know whether the Hero was a woman or a man?

69

MARSH KNELT IN A PILE of ash, hating himself and the world. The ash fell without cease, drifting onto his back, covering him, yet he did not move.

He had been cast aside, told to sit and wait. Like a tool forgotten in the field, slowly being covered in snow.

I was there, he thought. *With Vin. Yet . . . I couldn't speak to her. Couldn't tell her anything.*

Worse, he hadn't wanted to. During his entire conversation with her, his body and mind had belonged to Ruin completely. Marsh had been helpless to resist, hadn't been able to do anything that might have let Vin kill him.

Except for a moment. A moment near the end, when she'd almost taken control of him. A moment when he'd seen something within his master—his god, his *self*—that gave him hope.

For in that moment, Ruin had feared her.

And then Ruin had forced Marsh to run, leaving behind his army of koloss—the army that Marsh had been ordered to let Elend Venture steal and bring to Fadrex. The army that Ruin had eventually stolen back.

And now Marsh waited in the ash.

What is the point? he thought. His master wanted something . . . needed something . . . and he feared Vin. Those two things gave Marsh hope, but what could he do? Even in Ruin's moment of weakness, Marsh had been unable to take control.

Marsh's plan—to wait, keeping his rebellious sliver secret until the right moment, then pull the linchpin spike from between his shoulder blades and kill himself—seemed increasingly foolish. How could he hope to break free for that long?

Stand.

The command came wordlessly, but Marsh reacted instantly. And Ruin was back, controlling his body. With effort, Marsh retained some small control of his mind, though only because Ruin seemed distracted. Marsh started dropping coins, Pushing off them, using and reusing them in the same way Vin used horseshoes. Horseshoes—which had far more metal—would have been better, for they would have let him Push farther with each one. But he made coins work.

He propelled himself through the late-afternoon sky. The air was unpleasantly abrasive, so crowded with ash. Marsh watched it, trying to keep himself from seeing beauty in the destruction without alerting Ruin that he wasn't completely dominated.

It was difficult.

After some time—after night had long since fallen—Ruin commanded Marsh to the ground. He descended quickly, robes flapping, and landed atop a short hill. The ash came up to his waist, and he was probably standing on a few feet of packed ash underneath.

In the distance, down the slope, a solitary figure pushed

resolutely through the ash. The man wore a pack and led an exhausted horse.

Who is this? Marsh thought, looking closer. The man had the build of a soldier, with a square face and balding head, his jaw bearing several days' worth of beard. Whoever he was, he had an impressive determination. Few people would brave the mists—yet this man not only walked through them, but forged his way through ash that was as high as his chest. The man's uniform was stained black, as was his skin. Dark . . . ashen . . .

Beautiful.

Marsh launched himself from the hilltop, hurtling through the mist and ash on a Push of steel. The man below must have heard him coming, for he spun, reaching anxiously for the sword at his side.

Marsh landed atop the horse. The creature cried out, rearing, and Marsh jumped, placing one foot on the beast's face as he flipped over it and landed in the ash. The soldier had worn a path straight ahead, and Marsh felt as if he were looking down a narrow corridor.

The man whipped his sword free. The horse whinnied nervously, stamping in the ash.

Marsh smiled, and pulled an obsidian axe from the sheath by his side. The soldier backed away, perhaps trying to clear room in the ash for a fight. Marsh saw the worry in the man's eyes, the dreadful anticipation.

The horse whinnied again. Marsh spun and sheared off its front legs, causing it to scream in pain. Behind, the soldier moved. And surprisingly, instead of running, he attacked.

The man rammed his sword through Marsh's back. It hit a spike, veering to the side, but still impaled him. Marsh turned his head, smiling, and tapped healing to keep himself standing.

The man reached toward Marsh's linchpin spike, obviously intending to try to pull it free. Marsh burned pewter and spun, ripping away the soldier's weapon.

Should have let him grab the spike . . . the free sliver thought, struggling, yet useless.

Marsh swung for the man's head, intending to take it off with a single sweep of the axe, but the soldier rolled and whipped a dagger from his boot, swiping it in an attempt to hamstring Marsh. A clever move, which would have left Marsh on the ground, healing power or not.

However, Marsh tapped speed. He suddenly moved several times faster than a normal person, and he easily dodged the slice, instead planting a kick in the soldier's chest.

The man grunted as his ribs cracked. He fell, rolling and coughing, blood on his lips. He came to a stop, covered in ash. Weakly, he reached for his pocket.

Another dagger? Marsh thought. However, the man pulled out a folded sheet. Metal?

Marsh had a sudden and overpowering desire to grab that sheet of metal. The soldier struggled to crumple the thin sheet, to destroy its contents, but Marsh screamed and brought his axe down on the man's arm, shearing it off. Marsh raised the axe again, and this time took off the man's head.

He didn't stop, the blood fury driving him to slam his axe into the corpse over and over. In the back of his head, he could feel Ruin exulting in the death—yet he could also sense frustration. Ruin tried to pull him away from the killing, to make him grab that slip of metal, but in the grip of the bloodlust, Marsh couldn't be controlled. Just like koloss.

I can't be controlled . . . That's—

He froze, Ruin taking command once again. Marsh shook his head, the man's blood rolling down his face, dripping from his chin. He turned and glanced at the dying horse, which screamed in the quiet night. Marsh stumbled to his feet, then reached for the severed arm, pulling free the sheet of metal the soldier had tried to destroy with his dying strength.

Read it!

The words were distinct in Marsh's mind. Rarely did Ruin bother to address him—it just used him as a puppet.

Read it aloud!

Marsh frowned, slowly unfolding the letter, trying to give himself time to think. Why would Ruin need him to read it? Unless . . . Ruin couldn't read? But that didn't make sense. The creature had been able to change the words in books.

It *had* to be able to read. Then was it the metal that stopped Ruin?

He had the flap of metal unfolded. There were indeed words scratched into its inner surface. Marsh tried to resist reading the words. In fact, he longed to grab his axe from where it had fallen, dripping blood in the ash, then use it to end his own life. But he couldn't manage. He didn't even have enough freedom to drop the letter. Ruin pushed and pulled, manipulating Marsh's emotions, eventually getting him so that . . .

Yes. Why should he bother disagreeing? Why argue with his god, his lord, his self? Marsh held the sheet up, flaring his tin, steel, and iron to get a better look at its contents with an Inquisitor's strange metallic sight.

"'Vin,'" he read. "'My mind is clouded. A part of me wonders what is real anymore. Yet one thing seems to press on me again and again. I must tell you something. I don't know if it will matter, but I must say it nonetheless.

"'The thing we fight is real. I have seen it. It tried to destroy me, and it tried to destroy the people of Urteau. It got control of me through a method I wasn't expecting. Metal. A little sliver of metal piercing my body. With that, it was able to twist my thoughts. It couldn't take complete control of me, like you control the koloss, but it did something similar, I think. Perhaps the piece of metal wasn't big enough. I don't know.

"'In any case, it appeared to me, taking the form of Kelsier. It did the same thing to the king here in Urteau. It is clever. It is subtle.

"'Be careful, Vin. Don't trust anyone pierced by metal! Even the smallest bit can taint a man.

"'Spook.'"

Marsh, again completely controlled by Ruin, crumpled the metal up until its scratchings were unreadable. Then he tossed it into the ash and used it as an anchor to Push himself into the air. Toward Luthadel.

He left the corpses of horse, man, and message lying in the ash, slowly being buried.

Like forgotten tools.

Quellion actually placed his spike himself, as I understand it. The man was never entirely stable. His fervor toward following Kelsier and killing the nobility was enhanced by Ruin, but Quellion already had the impulses. His passionate paranoia bordered on insanity at times, and Ruin was able to prod him into placing that crucial spike.

His spike was bronze, and he made it from one of the first Allomancers he captured. That spike made him a Seeker, which was one of the ways he was able to find and blackmail so many Allomancers during his time as king of Urteau.

My point here is that people with unstable personalities were more susceptible to Ruin's influence, even if they didn't have a spike in them. That is likely how Zane got his spike.

70

"I STILL DON'T SEE WHAT good this does," Yomen said, walking next to Elend as they passed Fadrex's gates.

Elend ignored the comment, waving a greeting to a group of soldiers. He stopped at another group—not his, but Yomen's— and inspected their weapons. He gave them a few words of encouragement, then moved on. Yomen watched quietly, walking at Elend's side as an equal, not as a captured king.

The two had an uneasy truce, but the field full of ko-loss outside was more than enough of a motivation to keep them working together. Elend had the larger army of the two, but not by much —and they were growing increasingly outnumbered as more and more koloss arrived.

"We should be working on the sanitation problem," Yomen continued once they were out of the men's earshot. "An army exists on two principles: health and food. Provide those two things, and you will be victorious."

Elend smiled, recognizing the reference. Trentison's *Supplying in Scale*. A few years earlier, he would have agreed with Yomen, and the two would probably have spent the afternoon discussing the philosophy of leadership in Yomen's palace. However, Elend had learned things in the last few years that he simply hadn't been able to get from his studies.

Unfortunately, that meant he really couldn't explain them to Yomen—particularly not in the time they had. So instead he nodded down the street. "We can move on to the infirmary now, if you wish, Lord Yomen."

Yomen agreed, and the two turned toward another section of the city. The obligator had a no-nonsense approach to nearly everything. Problems should be dealt with quickly and directly. He had a good mind, despite his fondness for making snap judgments.

As they walked, Elend was careful to keep an eye out for soldiers—on duty or off—in the streets. He nodded to their salutes, met their eyes. Many were working to repair the damages caused by the increasingly powerful earthquakes. Perhaps it was only in Elend's mind, but it seemed that the soldiers walked a little taller after he passed.

Yomen frowned slightly as he watched Elend do this. The obligator still wore the robes of his station, despite the little bead of atium at his brow that he used to mark his kingship. The tattoos on the man's forehead almost seemed to curl toward the bead, as if they had been designed with it in mind.

"You don't know much about leading soldiers, do you, Yomen?" Elend asked.

The obligator raised an eyebrow. "I know more than you ever will about tactics, supply lines, and the running of armies between distinct points."

"Oh?" Elend said lightly. "So you've read Bennitson's *Armies in Motion,* have you?" The "distinct points" line was a dead giveaway.

Yomen's frown deepened.

"One thing that we scholars tend to forget about, Yomen, is the impact *emotion* can have on a battle. It isn't solely about food, shoes, and clean water, necessary as those are. It's about hope, courage, and the will to live. Soldiers need to know that their leader will be in the fight—if not killing enemies, then directing things personally from behind the lines. They can't think of him as an abstract force up on a tower somewhere, watching out a window and pondering the depths of the universe."

Yomen fell silent as they walked through streets that, despite being cleaned of ash, had a forlorn cast to them. Most of the people had retreated to the rear portions of the city, where the koloss would go last, if they broke through. They were camping outside, since buildings were unsafe in the quakes.

"You are an . . . interesting man, Elend Venture," Yomen finally said.

"I'm a bastard," Elend said.

Yomen raised an eyebrow.

"In composition, not in temperament or by birth," Elend said, smiling. "I'm an amalgamation of what I've needed to be. Part scholar, part rebel, part nobleman, part Mistborn, and part soldier. Sometimes I don't even know myself. I had a devil of a time getting all those pieces to work together. And just when I'm starting to get it figured out, the world up and ends on me. Ah, here we are."

Yomen's infirmary was a converted Ministry building—which in Elend's opinion showed that Yomen was willing to be flexible. His religious buildings weren't so sacred to him that he couldn't acknowledge that they were the best facilities for taking care of the sick and wounded. Inside they found physicians tending those who had survived the initial clash with the koloss. Yomen bustled off to speak with the infirmary bureaucrats—apparently he was worried about the number of infections that the men had suffered. Elend walked over to the section with the most serious cases, and began visiting them, offering encouragement.

It was tough work, looking at the soldiers who had suffered because of his foolishness. How could he have missed seeing that Ruin could take the koloss back? It made so much sense. Yet Ruin had played its hand well—it had misled Elend, making him think that the Inquisitors were controlling the koloss. Making him feel the koloss could be counted on.

What would have happened, he thought, *if I'd attacked this city with them as originally planned?* Ruin would have ransacked Fadrex, slaughtering everyone inside, and *then* turned the koloss on Elend's soldiers. Now the fortifications defended by Elend and Yomen's men had given Ruin enough pause to make it build up its forces before attacking.

I have doomed this city, Elend thought, sitting beside the bed of a man who had lost his arm to a koloss blade.

It frustrated him. He knew he'd made the right decision. And in truth, he'd rather be in the city—almost certainly doomed—than be out there besieging it, and winning. For he knew that the winning side wasn't always the right one.

Still, it came back to his continuing frustration at his inability to protect his people. And despite Yomen's rule of Fadrex, Elend considered its people to be his people. He'd taken the Lord Ruler's throne, named himself emperor. The entirety of the Final Empire was his to care for. What good was a ruler who couldn't protect a single city, let alone an empire full of them?

A disturbance at the front of the infirmary room caught his attention. He cast aside his dark thoughts, then bade farewell to the soldier. He rushed to the front of the hospital, where Yomen had already appeared to see what the ruckus was about. A woman stood holding a young boy, who was shaking uncontrollably with the fits.

One of the physicians rushed forward, taking the boy. "Mistsickness?" he asked.

The woman, weeping, nodded. "I kept him in until today. I knew! I knew that it wanted him! Oh, please . . ."

Yomen shook his head as the physician took the boy to a bed. "You should have listened to me, woman," he said firmly. "Everyone in the city was to have been exposed to the mists. Now your son will take a bed that we may need for wounded soldiers."

The woman slumped down, still crying. Yomen sighed, though Elend could see the concern in the man's eyes. Yomen was not a heartless man, just a pragmatic one. In addition, his words made sense. It was no use hiding someone inside all of their lives, simply because of the possibility that they might fall to the mists.

Fall to the mists . . . Elend thought idly, glancing at the boy in bed. He had stopped convulsing, though his face was twisted in pain. It looked like he hurt so much. Elend had been in that much pain only once in his life.

We never did figure out what this mistsickness was all about, he thought. The mist spirit had never returned to him. But perhaps Yomen knew something.

"Yomen," he said, walking up to the man, distracting him from his discussion with the surgeons. "Did any of your people ever figure out the reason for the mistsickness?"

"Reason?" Yomen asked. "Does there need to be a reason for a sickness?"

"There does for one this strange," Elend said. "Did you realize that it strikes down exactly sixteen percent of the population? Sixteen percent—to the man."

Instead of being surprised, Yomen shrugged. "Makes sense."

"Sense?" Elend asked.

"Sixteen is a powerful number, Venture," Yomen said, looking over some reports. "It was the number of days it took the Lord Ruler to reach the Well of Ascension, for instance. It figures prominently in Church doctrine."

Of course, Elend thought. *Yomen wouldn't be surprised to find order in nature—he believes in a god who ordered that nature.*

"Sixteen . . ." Elend said, glancing at the sick boy.

"The number of original Inquisitors," Yomen said. "The number of Precepts in each Canton charter. The number of Allomantic metals. The—"

"Wait," Elend said. "What?"

"Allomantic metals."

"There are only fourteen of those."

Yomen shook his head. "Fourteen we know of, assuming your lady was right about the metal paired to aluminum. However, fourteen is not a number of power. Allomantic metals come in sets of two, with groupings of four. It seems likely that there are two more we haven't discovered, bringing the number to sixteen. Two by two by two by two. Four physical metals, four mental metals, four enhancement metals, and four temporal metals."

Sixteen metals . . .

Elend glanced at the boy again. Pain. The only time Elend had known such pain was the day his father had ordered him beaten. Beaten to give him such pain that he thought he might die. Beaten to bring his body to a point near death, so that he would Snap.

Beaten to discover if he was an Allomancer.

Lord Ruler! Elend thought, shocked. He dashed away from Yomen, pushing back into the soldiers' section of the infirmary.

"Who here was taken by the mists?" Elend demanded.

The wounded regarded him with quizzical looks.

"Did any of you get sick?" Elend asked. "When I made you stand out in the mists? Please, I must know!"

Slowly, the man with one arm raised his remaining hand. "I was taken, my lord. I'm sorry. This wound is probably punishment for—"

Elend cut the man off, rushing forward, pulling out his spare metal vial. "Drink this," he commanded.

The man paused, then did as asked. Elend knelt beside the bed eagerly, waiting. His heart pounded in his chest. "Well?" he finally asked.

"Well . . . what, my lord?" the soldier asked.

"Do you feel anything?" Elend asked.

The soldier shrugged. "Tired, my lord?"

Elend closed his eyes, sighing. *It was a silly—*

"Well, that's odd," the soldier suddenly said.

Elend snapped his eyes open.

"Yes," the soldier said, looking a bit distracted. "I . . . I don't know what to make of *that*."

"Burn it," Elend said, turning on his bronze. "Your body knows how, if you let it."

The soldier's frown deepened, and he cocked his head. Then he began to thump with Allomantic power.

Elend closed his eyes again, exhaling softly.

Yomen was walking up behind Elend. "What is this?"

"The mists were never our enemy, Yomen," Elend said, eyes still closed. "They were only trying to help."

"Help? Help how? What are you talking about?"

Elend opened his eyes, turning. "They weren't killing us, Yomen. They weren't making us sick. They were *Snapping* us. Bringing us power. Making us able to fight."

"My lord!" a voice suddenly called. Elend turned as a frazzled soldier stumbled into the room. "My lords! The koloss are attacking! They're charging the city!"

Elend felt a start. *Ruin. It knows what I just discovered—it knows it needs to attack now, rather than wait for more troops. Because I know the secret!*

"Yomen, gather every bit of powdered metal you can find in this city!" Elend yelled. "Pewter, tin, steel, and iron! Get it to anyone who has been stricken by the mists! Make them drink it down!"

"Why?" Yomen said, still confused.

Elend turned, smiling. "Because they are now Allomancers. This city isn't going to fall as easily as everyone assumed. If you need me, I'll be on the front lines!"

There is something special about the number sixteen. For one thing, it was Preservation's sign to humankind.

Preservation knew, before he imprisoned Ruin, that he wouldn't be able to communicate with humankind once he diminished himself. So he left clues—clues that couldn't be altered by Ruin. Clues that related to the fundamental laws of the universe. The number was meant to be proof that something unnatural was happening, and that there was help to be found.

It may have taken us long to figure this out, but when we eventually did understand the clue—late though it was—it provided a much-needed boost.

As for the other aspects of the number . . . well, even I am still investigating that. Suffice it to say that it has great ramifications regarding how the world and the universe itself works.

71

SAZED TAPPED HIS PEN AGAINST the metal sheet, frowning slightly. "Very little of this last chunk is different from what I knew before," he said. "Ruin changed small things—perhaps to keep me from noticing the alterations. It's plain that he wanted to make me realize that Vin was the Hero of Ages."

"He wanted her to release him," said Haddek, leader of the First Generation. His companions nodded.

"Perhaps she was never the Hero," one of the others offered.

Sazed shook his head. "I believe that she is. These prophecies still refer to her—even the unaltered ones that you have told me. They talk of one who is separate from the Terris people, a king of men, a rebel caught between two worlds. Ruin merely *emphasized* that Vin was the one, since he wanted her to come free him."

"We always assumed that the Hero would be a man," Haddek said in his wheezing voice.

"So did everyone else," Sazed said. "But you said your-self that all the prophecies use gender-neutral pronouns. That had to be intentional—one does not use such language in old Terris by accident. The neutral case was chosen so that we wouldn't know whether the Hero was male or female."

Several of the ancient Terrismen nodded. They worked by the quiet blue light of the glowing stones, as they sat in the chamber with the metal walls—which from what Sazed had been able to gather was something of a holy place for the kandra.

He tapped his pen, frowning. What was bothering him? *They say I will hold the future of the entire world on my arms. . . .* Alendi's words, from his logbook written so long ago. The words of the First Generation confirmed that was accurate.

There was still something for Vin to do. Yet the power at the Well of Ascension was gone. Used up. How could she fight without it? Sazed looked at his audience of ancient kandra. "What *was* the power at the Well of Ascension anyway?"

"We are not certain of that, young one," Haddek said. "By the time we lived as men, our gods had already passed from this world, leaving the Terris with only the hope of the Hero."

"Tell me of this," Sazed said, leaning forward. "How did your gods pass from this world?"

"Ruin and Preservation," said one of the others. "They created our world, and our people."

"Neither could create alone," Haddek said. "For to pre-serve something is not to create it—and neither can you create through destruction alone."

It was a common theme in mythology—Sazed had read it in dozens of the religions he'd studied. The world being created out of a clash between two forces, sometimes rendered as chaos and order, sometimes named destruction and protection. That bothered him a little. He was hoping to discover something *new* in the things these men were telling him.

And yet . . . simply because something was common, did that make it false? Or could all of those mythologies have a shared, true root?

"They created the world," Sazed said. "Then left?"

"Not immediately," Haddek said. "But here is the trick, young one. They had a deal, those two. Preservation wanted to create men—to create life capable of emotion. He obtained a promise from Ruin to help make men."

"But at a cost," one of the others whispered.

"What cost?" Sazed asked.

"That Ruin could one day be allowed to destroy the world," Haddek replied.

The circular chamber fell silent.

"Hence the betrayal," Haddek said. "Preservation gave his life to imprison Ruin, to keep him from destroying the world."

Another common mythological theme—the martyr god. It was one that Sazed himself had witnessed in the birth of the Church of the Survivor.

Yet . . . this time it's my own religion, he thought. He frowned, leaning back, trying to decide how he felt. For some reason, he had assumed that the truth would be *different*. The scholarly side of him argued with his desire for belief. How could he believe in something so filled with mythological clichés?

He'd come all this way believing he'd been given one last chance to find the truth. Yet now that he studied it, he found it shockingly similar to religions he had rejected as false.

"You seem disturbed, child," Haddek said. "Are you that worried about the things we say?"

"I apologize," Sazed said. "This is a personal problem, not related to the fate of the Hero of Ages."

"Please, speak," one of the others said.

"It is complicated," Sazed said. "For some time now, I have been searching through the religions of humankind, trying to ascertain which of their teachings were true. I had begun to despair that I would *ever* find a religion that offered the answers I sought. Then I learned that my own religion still existed, protected by the kandra. I came here hoping to find the truth."

"This is the truth," one of the kandra said.

"That's what *every* religion teaches," Sazed said, frustration mounting. "Yet in each of them I find inconsistencies, logical leaps, and demands of faith I find impossible to accept."

"It sounds to me, young one," Haddek said, "that you're searching for something that cannot be found."

"The truth?" Sazed said.

"No," Haddek replied. "A religion that requires no faith of its believers."

Another of the kandra elders nodded. "We follow the Father and the First Contract, but our faith is not in him. It's in . . . something higher. We trust that Preservation planned for this day, and that his desire to protect will prove more powerful than Ruin's desire to destroy."

"But you don't know," Sazed said. "You are offered proof only once you believe, but if you believe, you can find proof in anything. It is a logical conundrum."

"Faith isn't about logic, son," Haddek said. "Perhaps that's your problem. You cannot disprove the things you study, any more than we can prove to you that the Hero will save us. We simply must believe it, and accept the things Preservation has taught us."

It wasn't enough for Sazed. However, for the moment he decided to move on. He didn't have all the facts about the Terris religion yet. Perhaps once he had them, he would be able to sort this all out.

"You spoke of the prison of Ruin," Sazed said. "Tell me how this relates to the power that Lady Vin used."

"Gods don't have bodies like those of men," Haddek said. "They are . . . forces. You could say they *are* the powers. Preservation's mind passed, but he left his power behind."

"In the form of a pool of liquid?" Sazed said.

The members of the First Generation nodded.

"And the black smoke outside?" Sazed asked.

"Ruin," Haddek said. "Waiting, watching, during his imprisonment."

Sazed frowned. "The cavern of smoke was much larger than the Well of Ascension. Why the disparity? Was Ruin *that* much more powerful?"

Haddek snorted quietly. "They were equally powerful, young one. They were *forces,* not men. Two aspects of a single power. Is one side of a coin more powerful than the other? They pushed equally upon the world around them."

"Though," one of the others added, "there is a story that Preservation gave too much of himself to make mankind, to create something that had *more* of Preservation in them than they had of Ruin. Yet it would be only a small amount in each individual. Tiny . . . easy to miss except over a long, long time . . ."

"So why the difference in size?" Sazed asked.

"You aren't seeing, young one," Haddek said. "The power in that pool, that wasn't Preservation."

"But you just said—"

"It was *part* of Preservation, to be sure," Haddek continued. "But he was a force—his influence is everywhere. Some of it was concentrated into that pool. The rest is . . . elsewhere and everywhere."

"But Ruin, his mind was focused there," another kandra said. "And so his power tended to coalesce there. Much more of it than that of Preservation."

"But not all of it," another one said, laughing.

Sazed cocked his head. "Not all of it? It too was spread out across the world, I assume?"

"In a way," Haddek said.

"We now speak of things in the First Contract," one of the other kandra warned.

Haddek paused, then turned, studying Sazed's eyes. "If what this man says is true, then Ruin has escaped. That means he will be coming for his body. His . . . power."

Sazed felt a chill. "It's here?" he asked quietly.

Haddek nodded. "We were to gather it. The First Contract, the Lord Ruler named it—our charge in this world."

"The other children had a purpose," another kandra added. "The koloss, they were created to fight. The Inquisitors, they were created to be priests. Our task was different."

"Gather the power," Haddek said. "And protect it. Hide it. Keep it. For the Father knew Ruin would escape one day. And on that day, he would begin searching for his body."

The group of aged kandra looked past Sazed. He frowned, turning to follow their eyes. They were staring toward the metal dais.

Slowly, Sazed stood and walked across the stone floor. The dais was large—perhaps ten feet across—but not high. He stepped onto it, causing one of the kandra to gasp. Yet none of them called out to stop him.

There was a seam down the middle of the circular platform, and a hole the size of a large coin at the center. Sazed peered through the hole, but it was too dark to see anything.

He stepped back.

I should have a little left, he thought, glancing toward his things on the table. *I refilled that ring for a few weeks before I gave up on my metalminds.*

He walked over quickly, selecting a small pewter ring off the table. He slipped it on, then looked up at the members of the First Generation. They turned from his querying gaze.

"Do what you must, child," Haddek said, his aged voice echoing in the room. "We could not stop you if we wished."

Sazed returned to the dais, then tapped his pewtermind for the strength he had stored in it over a year ago. His body immediately grew several times stronger than normal, and his robes suddenly felt tight. With hands now thick with muscles, he reached down and—bracing his feet on the rough floor—shoved one side of the disc.

It ground against stone as it moved, uncovering a large pit. Something glittered beneath.

Sazed froze, his strength—and body—deflating as he released his pewtermind. His robes became loose once more.

The room was silent. Sazed stared at the half-covered pit, and at the enormous pile of nuggets hidden in the floor.

"The Trust, we call it," Haddek said with a soft voice. "Given for our safekeeping by the Father."

Atium. Thousands upon thousands of beads of it. Sazed gasped. "The Lord Ruler's atium stockpile . . . It was here all along."

"Most of that atium never left the Pits of Hathsin," Haddek said. "There were obligators on staff at all times—but never Inquisitors, for the Father knew that they could be corrupted. The obligators broke the geodes in secret, inside a metal room constructed for the purpose, then took out the atium. The noble family then transported the empty geodes to Luthadel, never knowing that they didn't have any atium in their possession at all. What atium the Lord Ruler did get and distribute to the nobility was brought in by the obligators. They disguised the atium as Ministry funds and hid the beads in piles of coins so that Ruin wouldn't see them as they were transported to Luthadel in convoys of new acolytes."

Sazed stood, dumbstruck. *Here . . . all along. Only a short distance from the very caves where Kelsier raised his army. A short journey from Luthadel, completely unprotected all these years.*

Yet hidden so well.

"You worked for atium," Sazed said, looking up. "The kandra Contracts, they were paid in atium."

Haddek nodded. "We were to gather all of it we could. What didn't end up in our hands, the Mistborn burned away. Some of the houses kept small stockpiles, but the Father's taxes and fees kept most of the atium flowing back to him as payments. And eventually, almost all of it ended up here."

Sazed looked down. *Such a fortune,* he thought. *Such . . . power.* Atium never *had* fit in with the other metals. Every one of them, even aluminum and duralumin, could be mined or created through natural processes. Atium, however, had only ever come from a single place, its appearance mysterious and strange. Its power had allowed one to do something unlike anything else in Allomancy or Feruchemy.

It let one see the future. Not a thing of men at all, more . . . a thing of gods.

It was more than just a metal. It was condensed, concentrated power.

Power that Ruin would want. Very badly.

TenSoon pushed toward the crest of the hill, moving through ash so high that he was glad he had switched to the horse's body, for a wolfhound could never have moved through piles so deep.

I will never make it to Fadrex at this rate, he thought with anger. Even pushing his massive equine body hard, he was moving too slowly to get far from the Homeland.

He finally crested the hill, his breath coming in puffing snorts out the horse's snout.

At the top of the hill he froze, shocked. The landscape before him was burning.

Tyrian, closest of the Ashmounts to Luthadel, stood to the south in the near distance, half of its top blown free from a violent eruption. The air seemed to burn with tongues of flame, and the broad plain to the west of TenSoon was clogged with flowing lava. It was a vivid, powerful red. Even from a distance, he could feel the heat pushing against him.

He stood for a long moment, deep in ash, gazing upon a landscape that had once contained villages, forests, roads, and the northern part of Lake Tyrian. All was now gone, burnt away. The earth had cracked in the distance, and more lava was spilling out of it.

By the First Contract, he thought with despair. He could detour to the southeast all the way around where Lake Tyrian should have been, continue on to Fadrex as if he'd come in a straight line from Luthadel, but for some reason he found it hard to get up the motivation.

It was too late.

Yes, there are sixteen metals. I find it highly unlikely that the Lord Ruler did not know of them all. Indeed, the fact that he spoke of several on the plaques in the storage caches meant that he knew at least of those.

I must assume that he did not tell humankind of them earlier for a reason. Perhaps he held them back to give him a secret edge, much as he held back the single nugget of Preservation's body that made men into Mistborn.

Or perhaps he decided that humankind had enough power in the ten metals they already understood. Some things we shall never know. Part of me still finds what he did regrettable. During the thousand-year reign of the Lord Ruler, how many people were born, Snapped, lived, and died never knowing that they were Mistings, simply because their metals were unknown?

Of course, this did give us a slight advantage at the end. Ruin had a lot of trouble giving duralumin to his Inquisitors, since they'd need an Allomancer who could burn it to kill before they could use it. And since none of the duralumin Mistings in the world knew about their power, they didn't burn it and reveal themselves to Ruin. That left most Inquisitors without the power of duralumin, save in a few important cases—such as Marsh— where they got it from a Mistborn. This was usually considered a waste, for if a Mistborn was killed with Hemalurgy, only one of their sixteen powers could be drawn out and the rest would be lost. Ruin deemed it much better to try to subvert them and gain access to all of their power.

72

IT BEGAN RAINING JUST BEFORE Vin reached Luthadel. A quiet, cold drizzle that wetted the night, but did not banish the mists.

She flared her bronze. In the distance she could sense Allomancers. Mistborn. Chasing her. There were at least a dozen of them homing in on her position.

She landed on the city wall, bare feet slipping slightly on the stones. Beyond her stretched Luthadel, even now proud in its sprawl. Founded a thousand years before by the Lord Ruler, it was built atop the Well of Ascension. During the ten centuries of his reign, Luthadel had grown, becoming the most important—and most crowded—place in all of the empire.

And it was dying.

Vin stood up straight, looking out over the vast city. Pockets of flame flared where buildings had caught fire. The flames defied the rain, illuminating the various slums and other neighborhoods like watchfires in the night. In their light, she could see that the city was a wreck. Entire swaths of the town had been torn apart, the buildings broken or burned. The streets were eerily vacant—nobody fought the fires, nobody huddled in the gutters.

The capital, once home to hundreds of thousands, seemed empty. Wind blew through Vin's rain-wetted hair and she felt a shiver. The mists, as usual, stayed away from her—pushed aside by her Allomancy. She was alone in the largest city in the world.

No. Not alone. She could feel them approaching—Ruin's minions. She had led them here, made them assume that she was bringing them to the atium. There would be far more of them than she could fight. She was doomed.

That was the idea.

She launched off the wall, shooting through the mist, ash, and rain. She wore her mistcloak, more out of nostalgia than utility. It was the same one she'd always had—the one that Kelsier had given her on her very first night of training.

She landed with a splash atop a building, then leaped again, bounding over the city. She wasn't certain if it was poetic or ominous that it was raining this night. There had been another time when she had visited Kredik Shaw in the rain. A part of her still thought she should have died that night.

She landed on the street, then stood upright, her tasseled mistcloak falling around her, hiding her arms and chest. She stood quietly, looking up at Kredik Shaw, the Hill of a Thousand Spires. The Lord Ruler's palace, location of the Well of Ascension.

The building was an assemblage of several low wings topped by dozens of rising towers, spires, and spines. The awful near-symmetry of the amalgamation was only made more unsettling by the presence of the mists and ash. The building had been abandoned since the Lord Ruler's death. The doors were broken, and she could see shattered windows in the walls. Kredik Shaw was as dead as the city it once had dominated.

A figure stepped up beside her. "Here?" Ruin said. "This is where you lead me? We have searched this place."

Vin remained quiet, gazing up at the spires. Black fingers of metal reaching up into a blacker sky.

"My Inquisitors are coming," Ruin whispered.

"You shouldn't have revealed yourself," Vin said, not looking toward him. "You should have waited until I retrieved the atium. I'll never do it now."

"Ah, but I no longer believe that you *have* it," Ruin said in his fatherly voice. "Child . . . child. I believed you at first—indeed, I gathered my powers, ready to face you. When you came here, however, I knew that you had misled me."

"You don't know that for certain," Vin said softly, voice complemented by the quiet rain.

Silence. "No," Ruin finally said.

"Then you'll have to try to make me talk," she whispered.

"*Try*? You realize the forces I can bring to bear against you, child? You realize the power I have, the destruction I represent? I am mountains that crush. I am waves that crash. I am storms that shatter. I am *the end*."

Vin continued to stare up into the falling rain. She didn't question her plan—it wasn't her way. She'd decided what to do. It was time to spring Ruin's trap.

She was tired of being manipulated.

"You will never have it," Vin said. "Not while I live."

Ruin screamed, a sound of primal anger, of something that *had* to destroy. Then he vanished. Lightning flared, a wave of power moving through the mist. It illuminated robed figures in the blackened rain, walking toward her. Surrounding her.

Vin turned to face a ruined building a short distance away, and watched as a figure climbed over the rubble. Now lit only faintly by starlight, the figure had a bare chest, a stark rib cage, and taut muscles. Rain ran down his skin, dripping from the spikes that sprouted from his chest. One between each set of ribs. His face bore spikes in the eyes—one of which had been pounded farther into his skull, crushing the socket.

Normal Inquisitors had ten or eleven spikes. Marsh appeared to have upward of twenty. He growled softly.

And the fight began.

Vin threw back her cloak, spraying water from the tassels, and Pushed herself forward. Thirteen Inquisitors hurtled through the night sky toward her. Vin ducked a flurry of axe swings, then slammed a Push toward a pair of Inquisitors, burning duralumin. The creatures were flung away by their spikes, and Vin accelerated in a sudden lurch to the side.

She hit another Inquisitor, feet against his chest. Water sprayed, flecked with ash, as Vin reached down and grabbed the spike in the Inquisitor's left eye. Then she Pulled herself backward and flared pewter.

She lurched, and the spike came free. The Inquisitor screamed, but did not fall dead. It looked at her, the left side of its face a gaping hole, and hissed. Apparently, removing one eye-spike wasn't enough to kill.

Ruin laughed in her head.

The spikeless Inquisitor reached for her, and Vin Pulled herself into the sky, yanking on one of the metal spires of Kredik Shaw. She downed the contents of a metal vial as she flew, restoring her steel.

A dozen figures in black robes sprang up through the falling rain to follow. Marsh remained below, watching.

Vin gritted her teeth, then whipped out a pair of daggers and Pushed herself back down—directly toward the Inquisitors. She passed among them, surprising several who had probably expected her to jump away. She slammed directly into the creature she'd pulled the spike from, spinning him in the air, ramming her daggers into his chest. He gritted his teeth, laughing, then slapped her arms apart and kicked her toward the ground.

She fell with the rain.

Vin hit hard, but managed to land on her feet. The Inquisitor hit the cobblestones back-first, her daggers still in his chest. But he stood up easily and tossed the daggers aside, shattering them on the cobblestones.

Then he moved suddenly. *Too* quickly. Vin didn't have time to think as he splashed through the misty rain and grabbed her by the throat.

I've seen that speed before, she thought as she struggled. *Not only from Inquisitors. From Sazed. That's a Feruchemical power. Just like the strength Marsh used earlier.*

That was the reason for the new spikes. These other Inquisitors didn't have as many as Marsh, but they clearly had some new powers. Strength. Speed. Each of these creatures was essentially another Lord Ruler.

You see? Ruin asked.

Vin cried out, duralumin-Pushing against the Inquisitor, tearing herself out of his grasp. The move left her throat bleeding from his fingernails, and she had to down another vial of metals—her last—to restore her steel as she skidded across the wet ground.

Feruchemical storages run out, she told herself. *Even Allomancers make mistakes. I can win.*

Yet she wavered, breathing heavily as she came to a rest, one hand to the ground, up to the wrist in cold rainwater. Kelsier had struggled fighting one Inquisitor. What was she doing fighting thirteen?

Sodden-robed figures landed around her. Vin kicked, slamming a foot into an Inquisitor chest, then Pulled herself off to spin away from another one. She rolled across the slick cobblestones, an obsidian axe nearly taking off her head as she came up and kicked two pewter-enhanced feet at the knees of an opponent.

Bones crunched. The Inquisitor screamed and fell. Vin pushed herself to her feet with one hand, then Pulled on the spires above, throwing herself up about ten feet to dodge the multitude of swings that came after her.

She landed on the ground, grabbing the handle of the fallen Inquisitor's axe. She swung it up, spraying water, her skin stained with wet ash as she blocked a blow.

You cannot fight, Vin, Ruin said. *Each blow only helps me. I am Ruin.*

She screamed, throwing herself forward in a reckless attack, shouldering aside one Inquisitor, then slamming her axe into the side of another. They growled and swung, but she stayed a step ahead, barely dodging their strikes. The one she had knocked down stood up, his knees healed. He was smiling.

A blow she didn't see took her in the shoulder, throwing her forward. She felt warm blood running down her back, but pewter deadened the pain. She threw herself to the side and regained her feet, clutching her axe.

The Inquisitors stalked forward. Marsh watched quietly, rain dripping down his face, spikes protruding from his body like the spires of Kredik Shaw. He did not join the fight.

Vin growled, then Pulled herself into the sky again. She

shot ahead of her foes and bounded from spire to spire, using their metal as anchors. The twelve Inquisitors followed like a flock of ravens, leaping between spires, robes flapping, each taking different paths than she. She lurched through the mists, which continued to spin around her in defiance of the rain.

An Inquisitor landed against the spire she was aiming for. She yelled, swinging her axe in an overhand blow as she landed, but he Pushed off—dodging her swing—then Pulled himself back immediately. She kicked at his feet, sending both her and her opponent sprawling into the air. Then she grabbed his robe as they fell.

He looked up, teeth clenched in a smile, and knocked her axe out of her hand with an inhumanly strong arm. His body began to swell, gaining the unnatural bulk of a Feruchemist tapping strength. He laughed at Vin and grabbed her neck. He didn't seem to notice as Vin Pulled them both slightly to the side as they fell through the air.

They struck one of the lower spires, the metal piercing the surprised Inquisitor's chest. Vin wrenched herself out of the way to one side, but hung on to his head, her weight pulling him down the spire. She didn't watch as it ripped through his body, but when she hit the ground below, she was holding only a head. A disembodied spike splashed into an ashen puddle beside her, and she dropped the dead creature's head by it.

Marsh bellowed in anger. Four more Inquisitors landed around her. Vin kicked at one, but it moved with Feruchemical speed, catching her foot. Another seized her by the arm and yanked her to the side. She cried out, kicking her way free, but a third one grabbed her, its grip enhanced by both Allomantic and Feruchemical strength. The other three followed, holding her with clawlike fingers.

Taking a deep breath, Vin extinguished her tin, then burned duralumin, steel, and pewter. She Pushed outward with a sudden wave of power, and the Inquisitors were tossed away by their spikes. They sprawled, falling to the ground, cursing.

Vin hit the cobblestones. Suddenly the pain in her back and her throat seemed impossibly strong. She flared tin to clear her mind, but still stumbled, woozily, as she climbed to her feet. She'd used up all of her pewter in that one burst.

She moved to run, and found a figure standing in front of her. Marsh was silent, as another wave of lightning lit the mists.

Bleeding from a wound that probably would have killed anyone else, with no pewter to heal it, she was truly desperate.

Okay. Now! she thought as Marsh slapped her. The blow threw her to the ground.

Nothing happened.

Come on! Vin thought, trying to draw upon the mists. Terror twisted within her as Marsh loomed, a black figure in the night. *Please!*

Each time the mists had helped her, they had done so when she was most desperate. This was her plan, weak though it seemed: to put herself in more trouble than she'd ever been in before, then count on the mists to help her. As they had twice before.

Marsh knelt over her. Images flashed like bursts of lightning through her tired mind.

Camon, raising a meaty hand to beat her. Rain falling on her as she huddled in a dark corner, her side aching from a deep gash. Zane turning toward her as they stood at the top of Keep Hasting, one of his hands dripping a slow stream of blood.

Vin tried to scramble away across the slick, cold cobblestones, but her body wasn't working right. She could barely crawl. Marsh slammed a fist down on her leg, shattering the bone, and she cried out in shocked, icy pain. No pewter tempered the blow. She tried to pull herself up to grab one of Marsh's spikes, but he snatched her leg—the broken one—and her own effort only made her scream in agony.

Now, Ruin said in his kindly voice, *we will begin. Where is the atium, Vin? What do you know of it?*

"Please . . ." Vin whispered, reaching toward the mists. "Please, please, please . . ."

Yet they remained aloof. Once they had swirled playfully around her body, but now they pulled away instead. As they had for the entire last year. She was crying, reaching for them, but they puffed away. Shunning her like a victim of the plague.

It was the same way the mists treated the Inquisitors.

The creatures rose, surrounding her, silhouettes in the dark night. Marsh yanked her back to him, then reached for her arm. She heard her bone snap before she felt the pain. Then it came, and she screamed.

It had been a long time since she'd known torture. The streets had not been kind, but during the last few years she'd been able to repress most of those experiences. She'd become a Mistborn. Powerful. Protected.

Not this time, she realized through the haze of agony. *Sazed won't come for me. Kelsier won't save me. Even the mists have abandoned me. I'm alone.*

Her teeth began to chatter, and Marsh raised her other arm. He looked down at her with spiked eyes, expression unreadable. Then snapped the bone.

Vin screamed again, more from the terror than the pain.

Marsh watched her scream, listening to its sweetness. He smiled, then reached down for her unbroken leg. If only Ruin weren't holding him back. Then he could kill her. He strained against his bonds, lusting to do her more harm.

No . . . a tiny piece of him thought.

The rain fell, marking a beautiful night. The city of Luthadel lay bedecked in its funereal best, smoldering, some parts still burning despite the rain. How he wished he'd arrived in time to see the riots and the death. He smiled, the passionate love of a fresh kill rising in him.

No, he thought.

He somehow knew that the end was very near. The ground trembled beneath his feet, and he had to steady himself with one hand before continuing his work, snapping Vin's other leg. The final day had arrived. The world would not survive this night. He laughed gleefully, fully in the throes of a blood frenzy, barely controlled as he broke Vin's body.

NO!

Marsh awakened. Though his hands still moved as ordered, his mind rebelled. He took in the ash and the rain, the blood and the soot, and it disgusted him. Vin lay nearly dead.

Kelsier treated her like a daughter, he thought as he broke her fingers one at a time. She was screaming. *The daughter he never had with Mare.*

I've given up. Exactly as I did with the rebellion.

It was the great shame of his life, giving up leadership of the skaa rebellion only one year before it—with Kelsier at its head—at last overthrew the Final Empire. Marsh had been its leader, but had lost hope mere months before the victory.

No, he thought as he broke the fingers on her other hand. *Not again. No more giving up!*

His left hand moved up to her collarbone. And then he saw it. A single bit of metal glittering in Vin's ear. Her earring. She'd explained it to him once.

I don't remember it, Vin's voice whispered to him from the past. From when he had sat with her on a quiet veranda at Mansion Renoux, watching Kelsier organize a caravan below, right before Marsh left to infiltrate the ranks of the Steel Ministry.

Vin had spoken of her insane mother. *Reen said that he came home one day and found my mother covered in blood,* Vin had said. *She'd killed my baby sister. Me, however, she hadn't touched—except to give me an earring . . .*

Don't trust anyone pierced by metal. Spook's letter. *Even the smallest bit can taint a man.*

The smallest bit.

As he peered closer, the earring—though twisted and chipped—looked almost like a tiny spike.

He didn't think. He didn't give Ruin time to react. Amid his Inquisitor servant's thrill at killing the Hero of Ages,

Ruin's control was weaker than it had ever been. Summoning all the will he had remaining, Marsh reached out.

And ripped the earring from Vin's ear.

Vin's eyes snapped open.

Ash and water fell on her. Her body burned with pain, and the echoing screams of Ruin's demands still reverberated in her head.

But the voice spoke no further. It had been stifled mid-sentence.

What?

The mists returned to her with a snap. They flowed around her, sensing the Allomancy of her tin, which she still burned faintly. They spun around her as they once had, playful, friendly.

She was dying. She knew it. Marsh was done with her bones, and was obviously growing impatient. He screamed, holding his head. Then he reached down and grabbed his axe from the puddle beside him. Vin couldn't have run if she'd wanted to.

Fortunately, the pain was fading. Everything was fading. It was black.

Please, she thought, reaching out to the mists with one final plea. They felt so familiar all of a sudden. Where had she felt that feeling before? Where did she know them?

From the Well of Ascension, of course, a voice whispered in her head. *It's the same power, after all. Solid in the metal you fed to Elend. Liquid in the pool you burned. And vapor in the air, confined to night. Hiding you. Protecting you.*

Giving you power!

Vin gasped, drawing in breath—a breath that sucked in the mists. She felt suddenly warm, the mists surging within her, lending her their strength. Her entire body burned like metal, and the pain disappeared in a flash.

Marsh swung his axe for her head, spraying water.

And she caught his arm.

I have spoken of the Inquisitors' ability to pierce copperclouds. As I said, this power is easily understood when one realizes that many Inquisitors were Seekers before their transformation, which meant their bronze became twice as strong.

There is at least one other case of a person who could pierce copperclouds. In her case, however, the situation was slightly different. She was a Mistborn from birth, and her sister was the Seeker. The death of that sister—and subsequent inheritance of power via the Hemalurgic spike used to kill that sister—left her twice as strong at burning bronze as a typical Mistborn. And that let her see through the copperclouds of lesser Allomancers.

73

THE MISTS CHANGED.

TenSoon looked up through the ash. He lay, exhausted and numb, atop the hill before the field of lava that barred his path westward. His muscles felt lethargic—a sign that he had been pushing too hard. The Blessing of Potency could do only so much.

He stood, forcing his horse body to rise, looking at his nighttime surroundings. Endless fields of ash extended behind him; even the track he had worn to the top of the hill was close to being filled in. The lava burned ahead of him. However, something seemed different. What?

The mists flowed, moving about, swirling. Generally the mists had a chaotic pattern. Some parts would flow one way, while others would spin about in other directions.

There were often rivers of motion, but they never conformed to one another. Most often they followed the wind; this night the wind was still.

Yet the mist seemed to be flowing in one direction. As soon as he noticed it, TenSoon found it one of the most singularly strange sights he had ever beheld. Instead of swirling or spinning, the mists moved together in a seemingly purposeful flow. They coursed around him, and he felt like a stone in a huge, incorporeal river.

The mists flowed toward Luthadel. *Perhaps I'm not too late!* he thought, regaining some of his hope. He shook himself from his stupor, and took off in a gallop back the way he had come.

"Breezy, come see this."

Breeze rubbed his eyes, looking across the room to where Allrianne sat in her nightgown, gazing out the window. It was late—too late. He should have been asleep.

His eyes returned to his desk, and the treaty he had been working on. It was the sort of thing Sazed or Elend should have had to write, not Breeze. "You know," he said, "I distinctly remember telling Kelsier that I did *not* want to end up in charge of anything important. Running kingdoms and cities is work for fools, not thieves! Government is far too inefficient to provide a suitable income."

"Breezy!" Allrianne said insistently, Pulling on his emotions quite blatantly.

He sighed, rising. "Very well," he grumbled. *Honestly, how is it, of all the qualified people in Kelsier's little crew, that* I *end up the one leading a city?*

He joined Allrianne at the window, peeking out. "What is it exactly I'm supposed to see, dear? I don't . . ."

He trailed off, frowning. By him, Allrianne touched his arm, seeming concerned as she looked out the window.

"Now that *is* strange," he said. The mists flowed past outside like a river—and they seemed to be accelerating.

The door to his room slammed open. Breeze jumped,

and Allrianne squeaked. They spun to find Spook standing in the doorway, still half covered in bandages.

"Gather the people," the boy croaked, holding the door-frame to keep from collapsing. "We need to move."

"My dear boy," Breeze said, unsettled. Allrianne took Breeze's arm, holding on quietly, yet tightly. "My dear boy, what is this? You should be in bed!"

"Gather them, Breeze!" Spook said, suddenly sounding very authoritative. "Take them to the storage cavern. Pack them in! Quickly! We don't have much time!"

"What do you make of it?" Ham asked, wiping his brow. Blood immediately oozed from the cut again, running down the side of his face.

Elend shook his head, breathing deeply—almost in gasps—as he leaned back on a shelf of a jagged rock out-cropping. He closed his eyes, fatigue making his body shake despite his pewter. "I don't really care about mists right now, Ham," he whispered. "I can barely think straight."

Ham grunted in agreement. Around them, men screamed and died, fighting the endless waves of koloss. They had some of the creatures bottled up in the natural stone corridor leading into Fadrex, but the real fights were happening on the rugged rock formations that enclosed the city. Too many koloss, tired of waiting outside, had begun crawling up to attack from the flanks.

It was a precarious battlefield, one that often demanded Elend's attention. They had a large number of Allomancers, but most of them were inexperienced—having been unaware of their powers until this very day. Elend was a one-man reserve force, bounding across the defensive lines, plugging holes while Cett directed tactics.

More screams. More death. More metal hitting metal, rock, and flesh. *Why?* Elend thought with frustration. *Why can't I protect them?* He flared pewter, taking a deep breath and standing up in the night.

The mists flowed overhead, as if pulled by some invisible force. For a moment, exhausted as he was, he froze.

"Lord Venture!" someone shouted. Elend spun, looking toward the sound. A youthful messenger scrambled up the rock outcropping, wide-eyed.

Oh no . . . Elend thought, tensing.

"My lord, they're retreating!" the lad said, stumbling to a halt before Elend.

"What?" Ham asked, standing.

"It's true, my lord. They pulled back from the city gates! They're leaving."

Elend immediately dropped a coin, shooting himself into the sky. Mist flowed around him, its tendrils a million tiny strings being yanked eastward. Below, he saw the hulking dark forms of the koloss running away in the night.

So many of them, he thought, landing on a rock formation. *We'd never have beaten them. Even with Allomancers.*

But they were leaving. Running at an inhuman speed. Moving . . .

Toward Luthadel.

Vin fought like a tempest, spraying rainwater in the dark night as she threw Inquisitor after Inquisitor.

She shouldn't have been alive. She'd run out of pewter, yet she felt it flaring inside, burning brighter than it ever had before. She felt like the bleeding sun blazed within her, running molten through her veins.

Her every Steelpush or Ironpull slammed against her as if flush with the power of duralumin. Yet the metal reserves within her did not vanish. Instead they grew stronger. Vaster. She wasn't certain what was happening to her. However, she *did* know one thing.

Suddenly, fighting twelve Inquisitors at once did not seem such an impossible task.

She cried out, slapping an Inquisitor to the side, then ducking a pair of axes. She crouched, then jumped, leaping in an arc through the rain, coming down by Marsh, who still lay stunned from where she had thrown him after her rebirth.

He looked up, finally seeming to focus on her, then cursed and rolled away as Vin punched downward. Her fist shattered a cobblestone, throwing back a ripple of dark rainwater, splashing her arms and face, leaving black specks of ash behind.

She looked toward Marsh. He rose to his feet, barechested, his spikes glistening in the darkness.

Vin smiled, then spun on the Inquisitors rushing her from behind. She yelled, dodging a swinging axe. Had these creatures ever seemed quick to her? Within the embrace of limitless pewter, she seemed to move as the mist did. Light. Quick.

Unchained.

The sky spun in a tempest of its own as she attacked, moving in a swirling frenzy. The mists whirled around her arm in a vortex as she punched one Inquisitor in the face, throwing him backward. The mists danced before her as she caught the fallen Inquisitor's axe, then sheared the arm off another of the creatures. She took his head next, leaving the others stunned with the speed of her motion.

That's two dead.

They attacked again. She bounded away, Pulling herself toward the spires above. The trail of ravens launched after her, their robes snapping in the wet darkness. She hit a spire feet-first, then launched upward and Pulled on an Inquisitor's spikes, something that was easy to do with her new power. Her chosen quarry lurched upward ahead of his companions.

Vin shot downward, meeting the Inquisitor in the air. She grabbed him by the eye-spikes and pulled, ripping them out with her newfound strength. Then she kicked off the creature and Pushed against the spikes in his chest.

She shot upward in the air, leaving a corpse flipping end over end in the rain beneath her, gaping holes in its head where the spikes had been. They could lose some spikes and live, she knew, but the removal of others was deadly. Losing both eye-spikes appeared to be enough to kill them.

Three.

Inquisitors hit the spire she had Pushed off of, and they leaped up to follow her. Vin smiled, then threw the spikes she still carried, catching one of the Inquisitors in the chest with them. Then she Pushed. The unfortunate Inquisitor was thrown downward, and he hit a flat rooftop so violently that it pushed several of his spikes up out of his body. They sparkled and spun in the air, then fell by his immobile corpse.

Four.

Vin's mistcloak fluttered as she shot upward in the sky. Eight Inquisitors still pursued, reaching for her. Crying out, Vin raised her hands toward the creatures as she began to fall. She *Pushed.*

She hadn't realized how strong her new powers were. They were clearly akin to duralumin, since she could affect the spikes inside an Inquisitor's body. Her overpowering Push forced the whole flock of them downward, as if they'd been swatted. In fact, her Push also hit the metal spire directly beneath her.

The stone architecture holding the spire in place exploded, spraying chips and dust outward as the spire crushed the building beneath it. And Vin was thrown upward.

Very quickly.

She blasted through the sky, mists streaking past her, the force of her Push straining even her mist-enhanced body with the stress of sudden acceleration.

And then she was out. She emerged into the open air, like a fish leaping from the water. Beneath her, the mists covered the nighttime land as an enormous white blanket. Around her was open air. Unsettling, strange. Above her, a million stars—normally visible only using tin-enhanced sight—watched her like the eyes of those long dead.

Her momentum ran out, and she spun quietly, whiteness below, light above. She noticed that she'd trailed a line of mist up out of the main cloud. This hung like a tether ready to pull her back down. In fact, all the mists were spinning slightly in an enormous weather pattern. A whirlpool of white.

The heart of the whirlpool was directly beneath her.

She fell, plummeting toward the earth below. She entered the mists, drawing them behind her, breathing them in. As she fell, she could feel them surging about her in a massive, empire-wide spiral. She welcomed them into herself, and the vortex of mist around her grew more and more violent.

Instants later, Luthadel appeared, a massive black welt upon the land. She fell, streaking toward Kredik Shaw and its spires, which seemed to be pointing toward her. The Inquisitors were still there—she could see them on a flat rooftop amid the spires, looking up. Waiting. There were only eight, not counting Marsh. One lay impaled on a nearby spike from her last push; the blow had apparently torn the center spike out of his back.

Five, Vin thought, landing a short distance from the Inquisitors.

If a single Push could propel her up so far she passed out of the mists, then what would happen if she Pushed outward?

She waited quietly as the Inquisitors charged. She could see desperation in their movements. Whatever was happening to Vin, Ruin was apparently willing to risk every one of the creatures in the hopes that they would kill her before she was complete. Mists pulled toward her, moving more and more quickly, drawn into her like water being sucked down a drain.

When the Inquisitors had almost reached her, she *Pushed* outward, throwing metal away from her with all the force she could muster, while at the same time strengthening her body with a massive flare of pewter. Stone cracked. Inquisitors cried out.

And Kredik Shaw exploded.

Towers toppled from their foundations. Doors ripped free from their frames. Windows shattered. Blocks burst, the entire structure torn to pieces as its metals lurched away. She screamed as she Pushed, the ground trembling beneath her. Everything—even the rock and stone, which obviously contained residual traces of metal ore—was thrown violently back.

She gasped, stopping her Push. She drew in breath, feeling the rain splatter against her. The building that had been the Lord Ruler's palace was gone, flattened to rubble that spread out and away from her like an impact crater.

An Inquisitor burst from the rubble, face bleeding from where one of his spikes had ripped free. Vin raised a hand, Pulling and steadying herself from behind. The Inquisitor's head lurched, his other eye-spike pulling out. He toppled forward, and Vin caught the spike, Pushing it toward another Inquisitor who was rushing her. He raised a hand to Push it back at her.

And she drove it forward anyway, ignoring his Push with a quick Push behind her for stability. He was thrown away and slammed into the remnants of a wall. The spike continued forward, Pushed like a fish darting through water, ignoring the current. The spike slammed into the Inquisitor's face, crushing it, pinning his head against the granite.

Six and seven.

Vin stalked across the rubble, mists storming. Overhead they swirled furiously, forming a funnel cloud with her at its focus. It was like a tornado, but with no air currents. Only impalpable mists, painted on the air. Spinning, swirling, coming to her silent command.

She stepped over an Inquisitor corpse that had been crushed by the rubble; she kicked his head off to make certain he was dead.

Eight.

Three rushed her at once. She shouted, turning, and Pulled on a fallen spire. The massive construction of metal—nearly as big as a building—lurched into the air, spinning at her command. She slammed it into the Inquisitors like a club, crushing them. She turned, leaving the enormous iron pillar resting atop their corpses.

Nine. Ten. Eleven.

The storm broke, though the mists continued to swirl. The rain let up as Vin walked across the shattered building, eyes searching for blue Allomantic lines that were moving. She found one trembling before her, and she picked up and tossed aside an enormous marble disc. An Inquisitor groaned beneath; she reached for him, and realized that her hand was leaking mist. It didn't just swirl around her, it came from her, smoking forth from the pores in her skin. She breathed out and mist puffed before her, then immediately entered the vortex and was pulled in again.

She grabbed the Inquisitor, yanking him up. His skin began to heal as he used his Feruchemical powers, and he struggled, growing stronger. Yet even the awesome strength of Feruchemy made little difference against Vin. She pulled his eye-spikes free, tossed them aside, then left the corpse slumping in the rubble.

Twelve.

She found the last Inquisitor huddled in a pool of rainwater. It was Marsh. His body was broken, and he was missing one of the spikes from his ribs. The spike hole was bleeding, but that one apparently wasn't enough to kill him. He turned his pair of spikeheads to look up at her, his expression stiff.

Vin paused, breathing deeply, feeling rainwater trail down her arms and drip off her fingers. She still burned within, and she looked up, staring into the vortex of mists. It was spinning so powerfully, twisting down. She was having trouble thinking, for all the energy that coursed through her.

She looked at the Inquisitor again.

This isn't Marsh, she thought. *Kelsier's brother is long dead. This is something else. Ruin.*

The mist swirled in a final tempest, the circular motion growing faster and tighter as the last wisps of mist spun down and were pulled into Vin's body.

Then the mists were gone. Starlight shone above, and flecks of ash fell in the air. The night landscape was eerie in its stillness, blackness, and clarity. Even with tin—which let her see at night far better than a normal person could—the mists had always been there. To see the night landscape without them was . . . wrong.

Vin began to tremble. She gasped, feeling the fire within her blaze hotter and hotter. It was Allomancy as she had never known it, and she now knew she had never understood it. The power was far greater than metals, than mere Pushes and Pulls. It was something awesomely more vast. A power that men had used, yet never comprehended.

She forced her eyes open. There was one Inquisitor left. She had drawn them to Luthadel, forced them to expose themselves, laying a trap for someone far more powerful than her. And the mists had responded.

It was time to finish what she had come for.

Marsh watched limply as Vin fell to her knees. Shaking, she reached for one of his eye-spikes.

There was nothing he could do. He'd used up most of the healing in his metalmind, and the rest would do him no good. Stored healing worked by way of speed. He could either heal himself a small amount very quickly, or wait and heal himself slowly yet completely. In any case, he was dead as soon as Vin pulled those spikes free.

Finally, he thought with relief as she grabbed the first spike. *Whatever I did . . . it worked. Somehow.*

He felt Ruin's rage, felt his master realizing his mistake. In the end, Marsh had mattered. In the end, Marsh hadn't given up. He'd done Mare proud.

Vin pulled the spike free. It hurt, of course—hurt far more than Marsh would have thought possible. He screamed—both in pain and in joy—as Vin reached for the other eye-spike.

And she hesitated. Marsh waited expectantly. She shook, then coughed, cringing. She gritted her teeth, reaching toward him. Her fingers touched the spike.

And then Vin vanished.

She left behind the misty outline of a young woman. That dissipated and was soon gone too, leaving Marsh alone in the wreckage of a palace, head blazing with pain, body covered in sickly, sodden ash.

She once asked Ruin why he had chosen her. The primary answer is simple. It had little to do with her personality, attitudes, or skill with Allomancy.

She was merely the sole child Ruin could find who was in a position to gain the right Hemalurgic spike—one that would grant her heightened power with bronze, which would then let her sense the location of the Well of Ascension. She had an insane mother and a sister who was a Seeker, and was herself Mistborn. That was precisely the combination Ruin needed.

There were other reasons, of course. But even Ruin didn't know those.

74

DAY BROKE WITH NO MISTS.

Elend stood atop the rocky heights in front of Fadrex City, looking out. He felt far better with a night's rest behind him, though his body ached from fighting, his arm throbbed where he'd been wounded, and his chest hurt where he'd carelessly allowed a koloss to punch him. Another man would have been crippled, but he bore no more than a massive bruise.

Koloss corpses littered the ground before the city, piled

particularly high in the corridor leading into Fadrex. The whole area smelled of death and dried blood. Far more often than Elend would have liked, the field of blue corpses was broken by the lighter skin of a human. Still, Fadrex had survived—if only because of the last-minute addition of several thousand Allomancers and the eventual retreat of the koloss.

Why did they leave? Elend wondered, thankful yet frustrated. *And perhaps more importantly, where are they going?*

Elend turned at the sound of footsteps on rock and saw Yomen climbing the rough-hewn steps to join him, puffing slightly, still pristine in his obligator's robes. No one had expected him to fight. After all, he was a scholar, not a warrior.

Like me, Elend thought, smiling wryly.

"The mists are gone," Yomen said.

Elend nodded. "Both day and night."

"The skaa fled inside when the mists vanished. Some still refuse to leave their homes. For centuries, they feared being out at night because of the mists. Now the mists disappear, and they find it so unnatural that they hide again."

Elend turned away, looking back out. The mists were gone, but the ash still fell. And it fell hard. The corpses of those who had been slain during the night hours were nearly buried.

"Has the sun always been this hot?" Yomen asked, wiping his brow.

Elend frowned, noticing for the first time that it *did* seem hot. It was still early morning, yet it already felt like noon.

Something is still wrong, he thought. *Very wrong. And worse.* The ash choked the air, blowing in the breeze, coating everything. And the heat . . . shouldn't it have been getting *colder* as more ash flew into the air, blocking the sunlight? "Form crews, Yomen," Elend said. "Have them pick through the bodies and search for wounded among that mess down there. Then gather the people and begin moving them into the storage cavern. Tell the soldiers to be ready for . . . for something. I don't know what."

Yomen frowned. "You sound as if you're not going to be here to help me."

Elend turned eastward. "I won't."

Vin was still out there somewhere. He didn't understand why she had said what she had about the atium, but he trusted her. Perhaps she had intended to distract Ruin with lies. Elend suspected that the people of Fadrex owed her their lives. She'd drawn the koloss away—she'd figured something out, something that he couldn't even guess at.

She always complains that she's not a scholar, he thought, smiling to himself. *But that's only because she lacks education. She's twice as quick-witted as half the "geniuses" I knew among the nobility.*

He couldn't leave her alone. He needed to find her. Then . . . well, he didn't know what they'd do next. Find Sazed perhaps? In any case, Elend could do no more in Fadrex. He moved to walk down the steps, intending to find Ham and Cett. However, Yomen caught his shoulder.

Elend turned.

"I was wrong about you, Venture," Yomen said. "The things I said were undeserved."

"You let me into your city when my men were surrounded by their own koloss," Elend said. "I don't care *what* you said about me. You're a good man in my estimation."

"You're wrong about the Lord Ruler though," Yomen said. "He's guiding all this."

Elend merely smiled.

"It doesn't bother me that you don't believe," Yomen said, reaching up to his forehead. "I've learned something. The Lord Ruler uses unbelievers as well as believers. We're all part of his plan. Here."

Yomen pulled the bead of atium free from its place at his brow. "My last bead. In case you need it."

Elend accepted the bit of metal, rolling it over in his fingers. He'd never burned atium. For years, his family had overseen its mining—but by the time Elend had become Mistborn, he'd already either spent what he'd been able to obtain, or had given it to Vin to burn.

"How did you do it, Yomen?" he asked. "How did you make it seem you were an Allomancer?"

"I *am* an Allomancer, Venture."

"Not a Mistborn," Elend said.

"No," Yomen said. "A Seer—an atium Misting."

Elend nodded. He'd assumed that was impossible, but it was hard to rely on assumptions about *anything* anymore. "The Lord Ruler knew about your power?"

Yomen smiled. "Some secrets, he worked very hard to guard."

Atium Mistings, Elend thought. *That means there are others too . . . gold Mistings, electrum Mistings . . .* Though as he thought about it, some—like aluminum Mistings or duralumin Mistings—would be impossible to find because they couldn't use their metals without being able to burn other metals.

"Atium was too valuable to use in testing people for Allomantic powers anyway," Yomen said, turning aside. "I never found the power all that useful. How often does one have both atium and the desire to use it up in a few heartbeats? Take that bit and go find your wife."

Elend stood for a moment, then tucked the bead of atium away and went down to give Ham some instructions. A few minutes later, he was streaking across the landscape, doing his best to fly with the horseshoes as Vin had taught him.

Each Hemalurgic spike driven through a person's body gave Ruin some small ability to influence them. This was mitigated, however, by the mental fortitude of the one being controlled.

In most cases—depending on the size of the spike and the length of time it had been worn—a single spike gave Ruin only minimal powers over a person. He could appear to them, and could warp their thoughts slightly, making them overlook certain oddities—for instance, their compulsion for keeping and wearing a simple earring.

75

SAZED GATHERED HIS NOTES, CAREFULLY stacking the thin sheets of metal. Though the metal served an important function in keeping Ruin from modifying—or perhaps even reading—their contents, Sazed found them a bit frustrating. The plates were easily scratched, and they couldn't be folded or bound.

The kandra elders had given him a place to stay, and it was surprisingly lush for a cave. Kandra apparently enjoyed human comforts—blankets, cushions, mattresses. Some preferred to wear clothing, though those who didn't declined to create genitals for their True Bodies. That left him wondering about scholarly sorts of questions. They reproduced by transforming mistwraiths into kandra, so genitals would be redundant. Yet the kandra identified themselves by gender—each was definitely a "he" or a "she." Why? Did they choose arbitrarily, or did they actually know what they would have been, had they been born human rather than as a mistwraith?

He wished he had more time to study their society. So far, everything he'd done in the Homeland had been focused on learning more of the Hero of Ages and the Terris religion. He'd made a sheet of notes about what he'd discovered, and it sat at the top of his metallic stack. It looked surprisingly—even depressingly—similar to any number of sheets in his portfolio.

The Terris religion, as one might have expected, focused heavily on knowledge and scholarship. The Worldbringers—their word for Keepers—were holy men and women who imparted knowledge, but also wrote of their god, Terr. It was the ancient Terris word for "to preserve." A central focus of the religion had been the histories of how Preservation—or Terr—and Ruin had interacted, and these included various prophecies about the Hero of Ages, who was seen as a successor to Preservation.

Aside from the prophecies, the Worldbringers had taught temperance, faith, and understanding to their people. They had taught that it was better to build than to destroy, a principle at the core of their teachings. Of course there had been rituals, rites, initiations, and traditions. There were also lesser religious leaders, required offerings, and codes of conduct. It all seemed good, but hardly original. Even the focus on scholarship was something shared by several dozen other religions Sazed had studied.

That, for some reason, depressed him. It was just another religion.

What had he expected? Some astounding doctrine that would prove to him once and for all that there was a god? He felt like a fool. Yet he also felt betrayed. This was what he'd ridden across the empire, elated and eager, to discover? This was what he'd expected to save them? These were only more words. Pleasant ones, like most in his portfolio, but hardly compelling. Was he supposed to believe them simply because it was the religion his people had followed?

There were no promises here that Tindwyl still lived.

Why was it that people had followed this, or any, of the religions? Frustrated, Sazed dipped into his metalminds, dumping a group of accounts into his mind. Writings the Keepers had discovered—journals, letters, other sources from which scholars had pieced together what had once been believed. He looked through them, read them, pondered them.

What had made these people so willing to accept their religions? Were they merely products of their society, believing because it was tradition? He read of their lives, and tried to persuade himself that the people were simpletons, that they hadn't ever truly questioned their beliefs. Surely they would have seen the flaws and inconsistencies if they'd taken the time to be rational and discerning.

Sazed sat with closed eyes, a wealth of information from journals and letters in his mind, searching for what he expected to find. But as the time passed, he did not discover what he sought. The people did not seem fools to him. As he sat, something began to occur to him. Something about the words, the feelings, of the people who had believed.

Before, Sazed had looked at the doctrines themselves. Now he found himself studying the people who had believed, or what he could find of them. As he read their words over again in his mind, he began to see something. The faiths he had examined couldn't be divorced from the people who had adhered to them. In the abstract, those religions were stale. However, as he read the words of the people—really *read* them—he began to see patterns.

Why did they believe? Because they saw miracles. Events one person took as happenstance, a person of faith took as a sign. A loved one recovering from disease, a fortunate business deal, a chance meeting with a long lost friend. It wasn't the grand doctrines or the sweeping ideals that seemed to make believers out of people. It was the simple magic in the world around them.

What was it Spook said? Sazed thought, sitting in the shadowy kandra cavern. *That faith was about trust. Trusting that somebody was watching. That somebody would make it all right in the end, even though things looked terrible at the moment.*

To believe, it seemed, one had to *want* to believe. It was a conundrum, one Sazed had wrestled with. He wanted someone, something, to force him to have faith. He wanted to have to believe because of the proof shown to him.

Yet the believers whose words now filled his mind would have said he already had proof. Had he not, in his moment of despair, received an answer? As he had been about to give up, TenSoon had spoken. Sazed had begged for a sign, and received it.

Was it chance? Was it providence?

In the end, that was up to him to decide. He slowly returned the letters and journals to his metalminds, leaving his specific memory of them empty—yet retaining the feelings they had prompted in him. Which would he be? Believer or skeptic? At that moment, neither seemed a patently foolish path.

I do want to believe, he thought. *That's why I've spent so much time searching. I can't have it both ways. I simply have to decide.*

Which would it be? He sat for a few moments, thinking, feeling, and—most important—remembering.

I sought help, Sazed thought. *And something answered.*

Sazed smiled, and everything seemed a little brighter. *Breeze was right,* he thought, standing and organizing his things as he prepared to go. *I was not meant to be an atheist.*

The thought seemed too flippant for what had just happened to him. As he picked up his metal sheets and prepared to meet with the First Generation, he realized that kandra passed outside his humble little cavern, completely oblivious to the important decision he'd made.

That was how things often went. Some important decisions were made in public, on a battlefield or in a conference room. But others happened quietly, unseen by others. That didn't make the decision any less important to Sazed. He would believe. Not because something had been proven to him beyond his ability to deny. But because he chose to.

As, he realized, Vin had once chosen to believe and trust in the crew. Because of what Kelsier had taught her. *You taught me too, Survivor,* Sazed thought, moving out into the stone tunnel to meet with the kandra leaders. *Thank you.*

Sazed made his way through the cavern corridors, suddenly eager at the prospect of another day interviewing the members of the First Generation. Now that he had covered most of their religion, he planned to find out more about the First Contract.

As far as he knew, he was the only human other than the Lord Ruler to have ever read its words. The members of the First Generation treated the metal bearing the contract with noticeably less reverence than the other kandra. That had surprised him.

Of course, Sazed thought, turning a corner, *it does make sense. To the members of the First Generation, the Lord Ruler was a friend. They remember climbing that mountain with him—their leader, yes, but not a god. Much like the members of the crew, who had trouble seeing Kelsier in a religious light.*

Still lost in thought, Sazed wandered into the Trustwarren, whose broad metallic doors were open. He paused, however, just inside. The First Generation waited in their alcoves, as was common. They wouldn't come down until Sazed closed the doors. But oddly, the members of the Second Generation stood at their lecterns, addressing the crowds of kandra—who, despite being far more reserved than a similar group of humans would have been, still displayed an air of anxiety.

". . . does it mean, KanPaar?" one lesser kandra was asking. "Please, we are confused. Ask the First Generation."

"We have spoken of this thing already," said KanPaar, leader of the Seconds. "There is no need for alarm. Look at you, crowding together, murmuring and rumormongering as if you were humans!"

Sazed moved up to one of the younger kandra, who stood gathered outside the doorway to the Trustwarren. "Please," he whispered. "What is the source of this concern?"

"The mists, Holy Worldbringer," the kandra—a female, he thought—whispered back.

"What of them?" Sazed asked. "The fact that they are staying later and later in the day?"

"No," the kandra woman replied. "The fact that they're *gone*."

Sazed started. *"What?"*

The kandra nodded. "Nobody noticed it until early this morning. It was still dark out, and a guard walked by to check one of the exits. He says there was no mist at all outside, despite it being night! Others went out too. They all agree."

"This is a simple matter," KanPaar said to the chamber. "We know that it was raining last night, and sometimes rain disperses the mists for a short time. They will return tomorrow."

"But it's not raining now," one of the kandra said. "And it wasn't raining when TarKavv went out on patrol. There have been mists in the morning for months now. Where are they?"

"Bah," KanPaar said, waving his hand. "You worried when the mists started staying in the mornings, and now you complain that they are gone? We are *kandra*. We are eternal—we outwait everything and anything. We don't gather in rowdy mobs. Go back to what you were doing. This means nothing."

"No," a voice whispered into the cavern. Heads turned up, and the entire group hushed.

"No," Haddek—leader of the First Generation—said from his hidden alcove. "This is important. We have been wrong, KanPaar. Very . . . very wrong. Clear the Trustwarren. Leave only the Keeper behind. And spread the word. The day of the Resolution may have come."

This comment merely served to agitate the kandra further. Sazed stood frozen with wonder; he had never seen such a reaction in the normally calm creatures. They did as they were told—kandra appeared to be particularly good at that—and left the room, but there were whispers and debates. The Seconds slunk out last, looking humiliated. Sazed watched them go, thinking about KanPaar's words.

We are eternal—we outwait everything and anything. Suddenly the kandra began to make more sense to Sazed. How easy it would be to ignore the outside world if one were immortal. They had outlasted so many problems and predicaments, upheavals and riots, that anything occurring on the outside must have seemed trivial. So trivial, in fact, that it was possible to ignore the prophecies of one's own religion as they started to come true.

Eventually the room was empty, and a pair of beefy members of the Fifth Generation pushed the doors closed from the other side, leaving Sazed alone on the floor of the room. He waited patiently, arranging his notes on his desk as the members of the First Generation hobbled from their hidden stairwells and joined him on the floor of the Trust-warren.

"Tell me, Keeper," Haddek said as his brothers seated themselves, "what do you make of this event?"

"The departure of the mists?" Sazed asked. "It does seem portentous—though admittedly I cannot give a specific reason why."

"That is because there are things we have not yet explained to you," Haddek said, looking toward the others. They seemed very troubled. "Things relating to the First Contract, and the promises of the kandra."

Sazed readied a metal writing sheet. "Please continue."

"I must ask that you not record these words," Haddek said.

Sazed paused, then set down his pen. "Very well—though I warn you. The memory of a Keeper, even without his metalminds, is quite long."

"That cannot be helped," said one of the others. "We need your counsel, Keeper. As an outsider."

"As a son," another whispered.

"When the Father made us," Haddek said. "He . . . gave us a charge. Something different from the First Contract."

"To him, it was almost an afterthought," one of the others added. "Though once he mentioned it, he implied it was very important."

"He made us promise," Haddek said. "Each of us. He told us that someday, we might be required to remove our Blessings."

"Pull them from our bodies," one of the others added.

"Kill ourselves," Haddek said.

The room fell silent.

"You are certain this would kill you?" Sazed asked.

"It would change us back to mistwraiths," Haddek said. "That is the same thing, essentially."

"The Father said we would have to do it," another said. "There wasn't a 'might' about it. He said that we would have to make certain the other kandra knew of this charge."

"We call it the Resolution," Haddek said. "Each kandra is told of it when he or she is first birthed. They are given the charge—sworn and ingrained—to pull their Blessings free, should the First Generation command it. We have never invoked this charge."

"But you're considering it now?" Sazed asked, frowning. "I do not understand. Simply because of the way the mists are acting?"

"The mists are the body of Preservation, Keeper," Haddek said. "This is a *very* portentous event."

"We have been listening to our children discuss it all morning," another said. "And it troubles us. They do not know all that the mists represent, but they are aware of their importance."

"Rashek said that we'd know," another said. "He told us. 'The day will come when you have to remove your Blessings. You'll know when it arrives.' "

Haddek nodded. "He said that we'd know. And . . . we are extremely worried."

"How can we order the deaths of our entire people?" another asked. "The Resolution has always bothered me."

"Rashek saw the future," Haddek said, turning. "He held the power of Preservation and wielded it. He is the sole man ever to have done so! Even this woman of whom the Keeper speaks did not *use* the power. Only Rashek! The Father."

"Then where are the mists?" another asked.

The room fell silent again. Sazed sat, pen held in his hand, yet not writing anything. He leaned forward. "The mists are the body of Preservation?"

The others nodded.

"And . . . it has disappeared?"

More nods.

"Does this not mean that Preservation has returned?"

"That is impossible," Haddek said. "Preservation's power remains, for power cannot be destroyed. His mind, however, was all but destroyed—for this was the sacrifice he made to imprison Ruin."

"The sliver remains," another reminded. "The shadow of self."

"Yes," Haddek said. "But that is not Preservation, merely an image—a remnant. Now that Ruin has escaped, I think we can assume that it too has been destroyed."

"I think it is more," another began. "We could—"

Sazed held up his hands, getting their attention. "If Preservation has not returned, then has someone else perhaps taken up his power to use in this fight? Is that not what your teachings say will happen? That which has been sundered must again begin to find its whole."

Silence.

"Perhaps," Haddek said.

Vin, Sazed thought, growing excited. *This is what it means to be the Hero of Ages! I am right to believe. She* can *save us!*

Sazed took a sheet of metal and began to scribble down his thoughts. At that moment, the doors to the Trustwarren burst open.

Sazed paused, turning with a frown. A group of rock-boned Fifth Generationers clomped into the room, followed by the willowy members of the Second Generation. Outside, the cavern hallway was empty of its earlier crowd.

"Take them," KanPaar said furtively, pointing.

"What is this!" Haddek exclaimed.

Sazed sat where he was, pen held in his fingers. He recognized the urgent, tense posture in the figures of the Second Generationers. Some looked frightened, others de-

THE HERO OF AGES 685

termined. The Fifth Generationers moved forward quickly, their movements enhanced by the Blessing of Potency.

"KanPaar!" Haddek said. "What is this?"

Sazed slowly stood up. Four Fifth Generationers came over to surround him, bearing hammers as weapons.

"It's a coup," Sazed said.

"You can no longer lead," KanPaar said to the First Generation. "You would destroy what we have here, polluting our land with outsiders, letting the talk of revolutionaries cloud kandra wisdom."

"This is not the time, KanPaar," Haddek said, the members of the First Generation crying out as they were prodded and grappled.

"Not the time?" KanPaar asked angrily. "You spoke of the Resolution! Have you no idea the panic this has caused? You would destroy *everything* we have."

Sazed turned calmly, looking at KanPaar. Despite his angry tone, the kandra was smiling slightly through translucent lips.

He had to strike now, Sazed thought, *before the First Generation said more to the common people—making the Seconds redundant. KanPaar can stuff them all away somewhere, and then prop up dummies in the alcoves.*

Sazed reached for his pewtermind. One of the Fifths snapped it away with a too-quick grab, and two others took Sazed by the arms. He struggled, but his kandra captors wielded inhuman strength.

"KanPaar!" Haddek yelled. The First's voice was surprisingly strong. "You are of the Second Generation—you owe obedience to me. We created you!"

KanPaar ignored him, directing his kandra to bind the members of the First Generation. The other Seconds stood in a cluster behind him, looking increasingly apprehensive and shocked at what they were doing.

"The time for the Resolution may indeed be here!" Haddek said. "We must—" He cut off as one of the Fifths gagged him.

"That is exactly why I must take leadership," KanPaar

said, shaking his head. "You are too unstable, old one. I will not trust the future of our people to a creature who could, at a whim, order them to kill themselves."

"You fear change," Sazed said, meeting the kandra's eyes.

"I fear instability," KanPaar said. "I will make certain the kandra people have a firm and immutable leadership."

"You make the same argument as many revolutionaries," Sazed said. "And I can see your concern. However, you *must* not do this thing. Your own prophecies are coming to a head. I understand now! Without the part the kandra are to play, you could inadvertently cause the end of all things. Let me continue my research—lock us in this room if you must—but do not—"

"Gag him," KanPaar said, turning.

Sazed struggled, with no success, as his mouth was bound and he was pulled from the Trustwarren, leaving the atium—the body of a god—behind, and in the hands of traitors.

I've always wondered about the strange ability Allomancers have to pierce the mists. When one burned tin, he or she could see farther at night through the mists. To the layman this might seem natural—tin, after all, enhances the senses.

The logical mind, however, may find a puzzle in this ability. How exactly would tin let one see through the mists? As an obstruction, they are unconnected with the quality of one's eyesight. Both the nearsighted scholar and the long-sighted scout would have the same trouble seeing into the distance if there was a wall in the way.

This should have been our first clue. Allomancers could see through the mists because the mists were composed of the very same power as Allomancy. Once attuned by burning tin, the Allomancer was almost part of the mists. And therefore they became more translucent to him.

76

VIN . . . FLOATED. SHE WASN'T ASLEEP, but she didn't feel awake either. She was disoriented, uncertain. Was she still lying in the broken courtyard of Kredik Shaw? Was she sleeping in her cabin aboard the narrowboat with Elend? Was she in her palace quarters in Luthadel, the city under siege? Was she in Clubs's shop, worried and confused by the kindness of this strange new crew?

Was she huddled in an alleyway, crying, her back hurting from another of Reen's beatings?

She felt about her, trying to make sense of her surroundings. Her arms and legs didn't seem to work. In fact, she couldn't focus on them. The longer she floated, however, the clearer her vision became. She was . . . in Luthadel. After killing the Inquisitors.

Why couldn't she feel anything? She tried to reach down, to push herself to her knees, but the ground seemed strangely far away. And she saw no arms in front of her. She simply continued to float.

I'm dead, she thought.

Even as that occurred to her, she woke up a bit more. She could see, though it was as if through a blurry, distorting pane of glass. She felt . . . a power buzzing within her. A strength unlike that of limbs, but more versatile.

Vin managed to turn, getting a sweeping view of the city. And halfway through her turn, she came face-to-face with something dark.

She couldn't tell how far away it was. It seemed close and distant at the same time. She could view it with detail—far more detail than she could see in the actual world—but she couldn't touch it. She instinctively knew what it was.

Ruin no longer took on Reen's appearance. Instead he manifested as a large patch of shifting black smoke. A thing without a body, but with a consciousness greater than that of a simple human.

That . . . is what I've become, Vin realized, her thoughts becoming clearer.

Vin, Ruin said. His voice was not that of Reen, but instead something more . . . guttural. It was a vibration that washed across her, like an Allomantic pulse.

Welcome, Ruin said, *to godhood.*

Vin remained silent, though she reached out with her power, trying to get a sense of what she could do. Understanding seemed to open to her. It was as before, when she'd taken the power at the Well of Ascension. She immediately *knew* things. Only this time the power was so vast—the understanding so great—that it seemed to have shocked her mind. Fortunately that mind was expanding, and she was growing.

Awakening.

She rose above the city, knowing that the power spinning through her—the core of her existence—was simply a hub. A focus for power that stretched across the entire world. She could be anywhere she wished. Indeed, a part of her was in all places at once. She could see the world as a whole.

And it was dying. She felt its tremors, saw its life ebbing. Already most of the plant life on the planet was dead. Animals would go quickly—the ones that survived were those that could find a way to chew on dead foliage now covered by ash. Humans would not be far behind, though Vin noted with interest that a surprising percentage of them had found their way down into one or another of the storage caverns.

Not storage caverns . . . Vin thought, finally understanding the Lord Ruler's purpose. *Shelters. That's why they're so vast. They're fortresses for people to hide in. To wait, to survive a little longer.*

Well, she would fix that. She felt energized with power. She reached out and plugged the Ashmounts. She soothed them, deadened them, smothered their ability to spray ash and lava. Then she reached into the sky and wiped the smoke and darkness from the atmosphere, as a maid might wipe soot from a dirty window. She did all of this in a matter of instants; not more than five minutes would have passed on the world below.

Immediately the land began to burn.

The sun was amazingly powerful—she hadn't realized how much the ash and smoke had done to shield the land. She cried out, spinning the world quickly so that the sun moved to its other side. Darkness fell. And as soon as she did that, tempests began to swoop across the landscape. Weather patterns were disrupted by the motion, and in the sea a sudden wave appeared, enormously large. It rolled toward the coast, threatening to wipe away several cities.

Vin cried out again, and reached to stop the wave. And something blocked her.

She heard laughter. She turned in the air and looked to where Ruin sat as a shifting, undulating thundercloud.

Vin, Vin . . . he said. *Do you realize how like the Lord Ruler you are? When he first took the power, he tried to solve everything. All of man's ills.*

She saw it. She wasn't omniscient—she couldn't see the entirety of the past. However, she could see the history of the power she held. She could see when Rashek had taken it, and she could see him, frustrated, trying to pull the planet into a proper orbit. Yet he pulled it too far, leaving the world cold and freezing. He pushed it back again, but his power was too vast—too terrible—for him to control properly at that time. So he again left the world too hot. All life would have perished.

He opened the Ashmounts, clogging the atmosphere, turning the sun red. And in doing so he saved the planet—but doomed it as well.

You are so impetuous, Ruin thought. *I have held this power for longer than you can imagine. It takes care and precision to use it correctly.*

Unless, of course, you just want to destroy.

He reached out with a power Vin could feel. Immediately, without knowing how or why, she blocked him. She threw her power up against his, and he halted, unable to act.

Below, the tsunami crashed into the coast. There were still people down there. People who had hidden from the koloss, who had survived on fish from the sea when their crops failed. Vin felt their pain, their terror, and she cried out as she reached to protect them.

And again was stopped.

Now you know the frustration, Ruin said as the tsunami destroyed villages. *What was it your Elend said? For every Push, there is a Pull. Throw something upward, and it will come back down. Opposition.*

For Ruin, there is Preservation. From time immemorial!

For eternity! And each time I push, YOU push back. Even when dead, you stopped me, for we are forces. I can do nothing! And you can do nothing! Balance! The curse of our existence.

Vin suffered as the people below were crushed, washed away, and drowned. *Please,* she said. *Please just let me save them.*

Why? Ruin asked. *What is it I told you before? Everything you do serves me. It is out of kindness that I stop you. For if you were to reach your hand out for them, you would destroy more than you preserve.*

That is always the way it is.

Vin hung, listening to the screams. Yet a part of her mind—now so vast, now capable of many thoughts at once—dissected Ruin's words.

They were untrue. He said that all things destroyed, yet he complained about balance. He warned that she would only destroy more, but she could not believe he would stop her out of kindness. He wanted her to destroy.

It couldn't be both ways. She knew herself as his opposite. She *could* have saved those people, if he hadn't impeded her. True, she probably didn't have the accuracy to do it yet. That wasn't the power's fault, however, but hers. He had to get in her way so that she wouldn't learn, as the Lord Ruler had, and become more capable with the power.

She spun away from him, moving back toward Luthadel. Her awareness was still expanding, but she was confused by something she saw. Bright points of light dotting the landscape, shining like flares. She drew closer, trying to figure out what they were. Yet the same way it was difficult to look directly at a bright lantern and see what was emitting the light, it was difficult to discern the source of this power.

She figured it out as she reached Luthadel. A large glow was coming from the broken palace. Most of the light was shaped vaguely like . . .

Spires. Metal. *That* was what caused the glowing power.

I was right. Metal is power, and it's why Ruin couldn't read things written in steel. Vin turned away from a brightly shining spire. Ruin was there, as always, watching her.

I was surprised when Preservation said he wanted to create you, Ruin said, a bit of curiosity in his voice. *Other life is ordered by way of nature. Balanced. But Preservation . . . he wanted to create something intentionally unbalanced. Something that could choose to preserve at some times, but to ruin at others. Something in the form of that which we'd seen before. It was intriguing.*

I find it odd that he expended so much of himself to create you. Why would he weaken himself, eventually giving me the strength to destroy the world, simply to place human beings on his world? I know that others call his death to imprison me a sacrifice, but that *wasn't the sacrifice. His sacrifice came much earlier.*

Yes, he still tried to betray me—to imprison me. But he could not stop me. He could only slow me. Forestall. Delay. Since the day we created you, there has been an imbalance. I was stronger. And he knew it.

Vin frowned—or at least she felt as if she were frowning, though she no longer had a body. His words . . .

He says he's stronger, Vin thought. *Yet we are equally matched. Is he lying again?*

No . . . he didn't lie. Looking back with her ever-expanding mind, she saw that everything Ruin said, he *believed.* He truly thought that whatever she did helped him. He saw the world through the lens of destruction.

He wasn't lying about being more powerful than she. Yet they were obviously matched at the moment. Which meant . . .

There's another piece of Ruin out there, Vin thought. *Preservation* is *weaker because he gave up a piece of himself to create humankind. Not his consciousness—that he used to fuel Ruin's prison—but an actual part of his power.*

What she had suspected before, she now knew with certainty. Ruin's power was concentrated, hidden somewhere by Preservation. *The atium.* Ruin *was* stronger. Or he would be, once he recovered the last part of his self. Then he would be able to destroy completely—they would no longer be balanced.

She swung about in frustration, a glowing white aura of mist with wispy tendrils expanding across the entire world. *There's so much I still don't know,* Vin thought.

It was an odd thing to acknowledge, with her mind broadening to include so much. Yet her ignorance was no longer that of a person. Her ignorance was related to experience. Ruin had such a huge head start on her. He had created for himself servants who could act without his direction, and so she could not block them.

She saw his plan manifesting in the world. She saw him subtly influencing the Lord Ruler a thousand years ago. Even while Rashek held the power of Preservation, Ruin had whispered in his ear, directing him toward an understanding of Hemalurgy. And Rashek had obeyed without realizing it, creating minions—armies—for Ruin to take when the time was right.

Vin could see them—the koloss—converging toward Luthadel.

I will give you credit, Vin, Ruin said, hovering nearby. *You destroyed my Inquisitors. All but one, at least. They were very difficult to make. I . . .*

She stopped focusing on him with most of her mind. Something else drew her attention. Something moving into Luthadel, flying on spears of light.

Elend.

Looking back, we should have been able to see the connection among the mists, Allomancy, and the power at the Well of Ascension. Not only could Allomancers' vision pierce the mists, but there was the fact that the mists swirled slightly around the body of a person using any type of Allomancy.

Perhaps more telling was the fact that when a Hemalurgist used his abilities, it drove the mists away. The closer one came to Ruin, the more under his influence, and the longer one bore his spikes, the more the mists were repelled.

77

ELEND STOOD IN THE RUBBLE of Kredik Shaw, mind numb as he contemplated the destruction.

It seemed . . . impossible. What force could have leveled such an enormous, majestic building? What could have caused such destruction, breaking apart buildings and flinging rubble several streets away? And all of the destruction was focused here, at what had once been the center of the Lord Ruler's power.

Elend skidded down some rubble, approaching the center of what looked like an impact crater. He turned around in the dark night, gazing at the fallen blocks and spires.

"Lord Ruler . . ." he swore, unable to help himself. Had something happened at the Well of Ascension? Had it exploded?

Elend turned and looked across his city. It appeared to

be empty. Luthadel, largest metropolis in the Final Empire, seat of his government. Empty. Much of it in ruins, a good third of it burned, and Kredik Shaw flattened as if pounded by the fist of a god.

Elend dropped a coin and shot away, heading along his original path toward the northeastern section of the city. He'd come to Luthadel hoping to find Vin, but had been forced to take a slight detour to the south in order to get around a particularly large swath of lava burning the plains around Mount Tyrian. That sight, along with the sight of Luthadel in ruin, left him very disturbed.

Where was Vin?

He jumped from building to building. He kicked up ash with each leap. Things were happening. The ash was slowly trickling away—in fact, it had mostly stopped falling. That was good, but he remembered well a short time ago when the sun had suddenly blazed with an amazing intensity. Those few moments had burned him enough that his face still hurt.

Then the sun had . . . dropped. It had fallen below the horizon in less than a second, the ground lurching beneath Elend's feet. Part of him assumed he was going mad. Yet he could not deny that it was now nighttime, even if his body—and one of the city clocks he had visited—indicated that it should have been afternoon.

He landed on a building, then jumped off, Pushing against a broken door handle. He shivered as he moved in the dark, open air. The stars blazed uncomfortably above, and there was no mist. Vin had told him that the mists would protect him. What would protect him now that they were gone?

He made his way to Keep Venture, his palace. He found the building to be a burned-out husk. He landed in the courtyard, staring up at his home—the place where he had been raised—trying to make sense of the destruction. Several guards in the white and brown colors of his livery lay decomposing on the cobblestones. All was still.

What in the hell happened here? he thought with frustration. He poked through the building, but found no clues. All had been burned. He left via a broken window on the top floor, then paused at something he saw in the rear courtyard.

He dropped to the ground. And there, beneath a patio canopy that had kept off much of the ash, he found a corpse in a fine gentlemen's suit lying on the cobbles. Elend rolled it over, noting the sword thrust through its stomach and the posture of a suicide. The corpse's fingers still held the weapon. *Penrod,* he thought, recognizing the face. Dead, presumably by his own hand.

Something lay scrawled in charcoal on the patio floor. Elend wiped away the drifted ash, smudging the letters in the process. Fortunately, he could still read them.

I'm sorry. Something has taken control of me . . . of this city. I am lucid only part of the time. Better to kill myself than to cause more destruction. Look toward the Terris Dominance for your people.

Elend turned toward the north. Terris? That seemed an odd place in which to seek refuge. If the people of the city had fled, then why would they have left the Central Dominance, the place where the mists were the weakest?

He eyed the scribbles.

Ruin . . . a voice seemed to whisper. *Lies . . .*

Ruin could change text. Words such as Penrod's couldn't be trusted. Elend bade a silent farewell to the corpse, wishing he had the time to bury the old statesman, then dropped a coin to Push himself into the air.

The people of Luthadel had gone *somewhere.* If Ruin had found a way to kill them, then Elend would have found more corpses. He suspected that if he took the time to search, he could probably find people still hiding in the city. Likely the disappearance of the mists—then the sudden change from day to night—had driven them into hiding. Perhaps they had made it to the storage cavern beneath

Kredik Shaw. Elend hoped that not many had gone there, considering the damage that had been done to the palace. If there were people there, they would be sealed in.

North . . . the wind seemed to whisper. *Pits . . .*

Ruin usually changes text so that it's similar to what it said before, Elend thought. *So . . . Penrod probably did write most of those words, trying to tell me where to go to find my people. Ruin made it sound like they went to the Terris Dominance, but what if Penrod originally wrote that they went to the Terris people?*

It made good sense. If he'd fled Luthadel, he would have gone there—it was a place where there was already an established group of refugees, with herds, crops, and food.

Elend turned north, leaving the city, cloak flapping with each Allomantic bound.

Suddenly, Ruin's frustration made more sense to Vin. She felt she held the power of all creation. Yet it took everything she had to get even a few words to Elend.

She wasn't certain whether he'd heard her or not. She knew him so well, however, that she felt a . . . connection. Despite Ruin's efforts to block her, she felt some part of her had been able to get through to some part of Elend. Perhaps in the same way Ruin was able to communicate with his Inquisitors and followers?

Still, her near-impotence was infuriating.

Balance, Ruin spat. *Balance imprisoned me. Preservation's sacrifice—that was to siphon off the part of me that was stronger, to lock it away, to leave me equal with him again. For a time.*

Only for a time. And what is time to us, Vin?

Nothing.

It may seem odd to those reading this that atium was part of the body of a god. However, it is necessary to understand that when we said "body" we generally meant "power." As my mind has expanded, I've come to realize that objects and energy are composed of the very same things, and can change state from one to the other. It makes perfect sense to me that the power of godhood would manifest within the world in physical form. Ruin and Preservation were not nebulous abstractions. They were integral parts of existence. In a way, every object that existed in the world was composed of their power.

Atium, then, was an object that was one-sided. Instead of being composed of half Ruin and half Preservation—as, say, a rock would be—atium was completely of Ruin. The Pits of Hathsin were crafted by Preservation as a place to hide the chunk of Ruin's body that he had stolen away during the betrayal and imprisonment. Kelsier didn't truly destroy this place by shattering those crystals, for they would have regrown eventually—in a few hundred years—and continued to deposit atium, as the place was a natural outlet for Ruin's trapped power.

When people burned atium, then, they were drawing upon the power of Ruin—which is perhaps why atium turned people into such efficient killing machines. They didn't use up this power, however, but simply made use of it. Once a nugget of atium was expended, the power would return to the Pits and begin to coalesce again—as the power at the Well of Ascension would slowly return there after it had been used.

78

THIS IS, SAZED THOUGHT, *WITHOUT a doubt, the oddest dungeon I have ever been in.*

Granted, it was only the second time he had been imprisoned. Still, he had observed several prisons in his lifetime, and had read of others. Most were like cages. This one, however, consisted only of a hole in the ground with an iron grate covering the top. Sazed crouched down inside it, stripped of his metalminds, his legs cramped.

It was probably built for a kandra, he thought. *One without bones perhaps?* What would a kandra without bones be like? A pile of goo? Or perhaps a pile of muscles?

In any case, this prison had not been meant to hold a man—particularly not one as tall as Sazed. He could barely move. He reached up, pushing against the grate, but it was secure. A large lock held it in place.

He wasn't certain how long he had been in the pit. Hours? Perhaps days. They still hadn't given him anything to eat, though a member of the Third Generation had poured some water on him. Sazed was still wet with it, and he had taken to sucking on the cloth of his robes to slake his thirst.

This is silly, he thought, not for the first time. *The world is ending, and I'm in prison?* He was the final Keeper, the Announcer. He should be above, recording events.

Because, truth be told, he was beginning to believe that the world would not end. He had accepted that something, perhaps Preservation itself, was watching over and protecting humankind. He was more and more determined to follow the Terris religion—not because it was perfect, but because he would rather believe and have hope.

The Hero *was* real. Sazed believed that. And he had faith in her.

He had lived with Kelsier and had helped the man. He had chronicled the rise of the Church of the Survivor during the first years of its development. He had researched the Hero of Ages with Tindwyl and taken it upon himself to announce Vin as the one who fulfilled the prophecies. But it was only recently that he'd started to have faith in her. Perhaps it came of his decision to be someone who saw miracles. Perhaps it was the daunting fear of the ending that seemed to loom ahead. Perhaps it was the tension and anxiety. Regardless, somehow from the chaos he drew peace.

She would come. She would preserve the world. However, Sazed needed to be ready to help. And that meant escaping.

He eyed the metal grate. The lock was of fine steel, the grate itself of iron. He reached up tentatively, touching the bars, draining a bit of his weight and putting it into the iron. Immediately his body grew lighter; the metal of the grate was pure enough to hold a Feruchemical charge. It went against his instincts to use it as a metalmind—it wasn't portable, and if he had to flee he'd leave behind all of the power he'd saved. Yet what good would it be to merely sit in the pit and wait?

He reached up with the other hand, touching the steel lock with one finger. Then he began to fill it as well, draining his body of speed. He instantly began to feel lethargic, his every motion—even his breathing—becoming more difficult. It was as if he had to push through tar each time he moved.

He stayed that way. He had learned to enter a kind of meditative trance when he filled metalminds. Often he would fill many at once, leaving himself sickly, weak, slow, and dull-minded. When he could, it was better to simply . . .

Drift.

He wasn't certain how long the meditation lasted. Occasionally the guard came to pour water on him. When he heard the guard approach, Sazed would let go and huddle down, pretending to sleep. But as soon as the guard withdrew, he would reach back up and continue to fill the metalminds.

More time passed. Then he heard sounds. Sazed huddled

down again, then waited expectantly for the shower of water.

"When I brought you here to save my people," a voice growled, "this wasn't what I had in mind."

Sazed popped his eyes open, glancing upward, and was surprised to see a dog's face looking through the grate. "TenSoon?" Sazed asked.

The kandra grunted and stepped away. Sazed perked up as another kandra appeared. She wore a delicate True Body of wood, willowy and almost inhuman. And she held keys.

"Quickly, MeLaan," TenSoon growled with his dog's voice. He had apparently switched to the wolfhound, which made sense. Moving as a horse through the sometimes steep and narrow tunnels of the Homeland would have been difficult.

The female kandra unlocked the grate, then pulled it back. Sazed eagerly climbed free. In the room, he found several other kandra wearing deviant True Bodies. In the corner, the prison guard lay bound and gagged.

"I was seen entering the Homeland, Terrisman," Ten-Soon said. "So we have little time. What has happened here? MeLaan told me of your imprisonment—KanPaar announced that the First Generation had ordered you taken. What did you do to antagonize them?"

"Not them," Sazed said, stretching his cramped legs. "It was the Second Generation. They have taken the Firsts captive, and plan to rule in their stead."

The woman—MeLaan—gasped. "They would never!"

"They did," Sazed said, standing. "I fear for the safety of the Firsts. KanPaar may have been afraid to kill me because I am human. However, the Firsts . . ."

"But," MeLaan said, "the Seconds are kandra. They wouldn't do something like that! We're not that kind of people."

TenSoon and Sazed shared a look. *All societies have people who break the rules, child,* Sazed thought. *Particularly when power is concerned.*

"We have to find the Firsts," TenSoon said. "And recover the Trustwarren."

"We will fight with you, TenSoon," one of the other kandra said.

"We're finally throwing them off!" another said. "The Seconds, and their insistence that we serve the humans!"

Sazed frowned at this. What did humans have to do with this conflict? Then he noticed how the others regarded Ten-Soon. *The dog's body,* he realized. *To them, TenSoon is a revolutionary of the highest order—all because of something Vin ordered him to do.*

TenSoon met Sazed's eyes again, opening his mouth to speak. Then he paused. "They're coming," he said, and cursed, his dog's ears flattening.

Sazed spun with concern, noticing shadows on the rock wall of the corridor leading into the prison chamber. The chamber was small, with six or so pit cells in the floor. There were no other entrances.

Despite their brave words, TenSoon's companions immediately shied away, huddling against the wall. They were plainly not accustomed to conflict, particularly with their own kind. TenSoon shared none of their timidity. He charged forward as soon as the group of Fifths entered the room, ramming his shoulder into one's chest, howling and clawing at another.

There is a kandra who fits in with his people as poorly as I do with my own, Sazed thought, smiling. He stepped backward, moving up onto the top of the prison grate, touching its metals with his bare feet.

The Fifths had trouble fighting TenSoon—he was apparently quite confident in his canine body. He kept moving, knocking them over. However, there were five of them, and only one TenSoon. He was forced to retreat.

The wounds in his body close as he orders them, Sazed noticed. *That must be why the guards usually carry hammers.*

Which made it fairly obvious how one had to fight kandra. TenSoon retreated beside Sazed. "I apologize," the dog growled. "This isn't much of a rescue."

"Oh, I don't know," Sazed said, smiling as the Fifths surrounded them. "You needn't give up so quickly, I think."

The Fifths charged, and Sazed tapped iron from the grate beneath his bare feet. Immediately his body grew several times heavier than normal, and he grabbed a kandra guard by the arms.

Then fell on him.

Sazed always said he wasn't a warrior. However, the number of times he'd said that, then been forced to fight anyway, made him think he was losing that excuse. The truth was that he'd been in far more battles over the last few years than he felt he had any right to have survived.

In any case, he knew some rudimentary moves—and with both Feruchemy and surprise to aid him, that was about all he needed. Tapping weight increased the density of his body and of his bones, keeping him from damaging himself as he collapsed on top of the soldier. Sazed felt a satisfying crack as they hit the grate, Sazed's greatly increased weight crushing the kandra guard's bones. They used stone True Bodies, but even that wasn't enough.

Sazed released the metalmind, then began to fill it instead, making his body incredibly light. He touched his foot to the steel lock and tapped speed. Suddenly he was faster than any man had a right to be. He stood up as the other four guards turned toward him in surprise.

He stopped filling his ironmind and regained normal weight, then reached with a blurring speed to pick up the hammer of the fallen soldier. He didn't have enhanced strength, but he had speed. He slammed the hammer down on a kandra shoulder, growing heavier to add to the momentum of his blow.

The kandra's bones shattered. Sazed snapped his foot on the lock and tapped the remaining speed. He crouched, pivoting, and slammed his hammer into the knees of two kandra who were trying to attack him with their own hammers.

They cried out, falling as Sazed's speed ran out.

He stood up straight. TenSoon was sitting atop the final guard, pinning him to the ground. "I thought you were a scholar," the dog noted, his captive squirming.

Sazed tossed aside the hammer. "I am," he said. "Vin

would have fought her way free from this prison days ago. Now, I believe we should deal with these . . ." He waved toward the fallen Fifths, who seemed to have quite a bit of trouble moving with their bones broken.

TenSoon nodded. He motioned for some of his friends to help him with the one he was sitting on. They held the captive tentatively, but there were enough of them to keep the prisoner still.

"What have you done here, FhorKood?" TenSoon demanded of the captive. Sazed kept an eye on the other Fifths, and was forced to slam a mallet against one of them, breaking more bones as he tried to sneak away.

FhorKood spat. "Dirty Third," he muttered.

"*You* are the traitor this time," TenSoon said, smiling slightly. "KanPaar brands me a Contract-breaker, then he overthrows the First Generation? If the world weren't ending, I'd find that far more amusing. Now, speak!"

Sazed paused as he noticed something. The other cells in the floor were occupied. He leaned down, recognizing something about the muscles he saw inside. They were . . . discolored, and a bit deformed. Like . . . hanging moss.

"TenSoon!" he said, glancing up. "Perhaps the First Generation *is* still alive. Come here."

TenSoon moved over, then looked down at the pit, frowning with canine lips. "MeLaan! The keys!"

She rushed over, unlocking the grate. With some consternation, Sazed was able to determine that there were multiple sets of squirming muscles in the pit, each of a slightly different color.

"We need bones," TenSoon said, standing.

MeLaan nodded, rushing from the room. Sazed shared a gaze with TenSoon.

"They must have killed the other kandra in these cells," TenSoon said softly. "Traitors to our kind, imprisoned endlessly. It was to have been my fate. It's clever—everyone thinks that these cells hold dire criminals. It wouldn't be odd for the Fifths to continue feeding them, and nobody would suspect that the occupants had been replaced with the First Generation, assuming they didn't look too closely at the color of the muscles."

"We need to keep moving," Sazed said. "Get to Kan-Paar."

TenSoon shook his head. "We won't get far without the Firsts to tell our story, Terrisman. Go and store more of your Feruchemy. We may need it."

With that, TenSoon moved, crouching over their captive. "You have two options, FhorKood," he said. "Either relinquish those bones, or I'll digest your body and kill you, as I did OreSeur."

Sazed frowned, watching. The captured kandra seemed terrified of TenSoon. The Fifth's body liquefied, and he moved sluglike away from the granite bones. TenSoon smiled.

"What is that for?" Sazed asked.

"Something Zane taught me," TenSoon said, his dog's body beginning to melt, the hair falling out. "Nobody expects a *kandra* to be an impostor. In a few moments, FhorKood here will return to the Second Generation and tell them that the traitor TenSoon has been captured. I should be able to stall long enough for the Firsts to regenerate—they will take far longer than I do to make bodies."

Sazed nodded. MeLaan returned a short time later with a large sack full of bones, and TenSoon—having re-created FhorKood's body with incredible speed—moved out of the chamber on his mission.

Then Sazed sat down, removing the lock and holding it to use as a metalmind, an iron hammer in the other hand to store weight. It felt odd to just sit there, but apparently the Firsts would need a few hours to regenerate their bodies.

There really isn't a rush, is there? Sazed thought. *I have the First Generation here—they're the ones I needed. I can continue to question them, learn what I want. TenSoon will have KanPaar distracted. It doesn't matter that the Seconds will be in charge for a few more hours.*

What harm could they possibly do?

I believe that the mists were searching for someone to become a new host for them. The power needed a consciousness to direct it. In this matter, I am still confused. Why would power used to create and destroy need a mind to oversee it? Yet it seems to have only a vague will of its own, tied to the mandate of its abilities. Without a consciousness to direct it, nothing could be created or destroyed. It's as if the power of Preservation understood that its tendency to reinforce stability was not enough. If nothing changed, nothing would ever come to exist.

That makes me wonder who or what the minds of Preservation and Ruin were.

Regardless, the mists—the power of Preservation—chose someone to become their host long before all of this happened. She, however, was immediately seized by Ruin and used as a pawn. He must have known that by giving her a disguised Hemalurgic spike, he would keep the mists from Investing themselves in her as they wished.

The three times she drew upon their power, then, were the three times when her earring had been removed from her body. When she had fought the Lord Ruler, his Allomancy had Pushed it away. When fighting Marsh in Fadrex, she had used the earring as a weapon. And at the end, Marsh ripped it out, freeing her and allowing the mists—now desperate for a host, since Preservation's last wisp was gone—to finally pour into her.

79

SOMETHING CHANGED.

Vin arose from her contemplation of the world. Something important was happening. She didn't have enough experience to tell what it was immediately, but she did see Ruin's nexus suddenly shoot away.

She followed. Speed wasn't an issue. In fact, she didn't really feel like she was moving. She "followed" because that was how her mind interpreted the experience of instantly moving her consciousness to the place where Ruin had focused his.

She recognized the area. The Pits of Hathsin, or a place nearby. As a portion of her mind had noticed earlier, the Pits had become a massive refugee camp, the people there quickly consuming the resources that the Terris had carefully stored. A part of her smiled. The Terris gave of their goods freely, helping those who had fled Luthadel. The Lord Ruler had worked to breed the Terris to be docile. However, had he expected that in making his perfect servants, he would also create a thoughtful, kindly people who would give of their last flocks to help those who were starving?

What she'd noticed earlier didn't have to do with the Terris or their guests. She saw it as she drew closer. A shining blaze of . . . something. Powerful, more mighty than the sun to her eyes. She focused on it, but could see little. What could shine so magnificently?

"Take this," a voice said. "Find humans, and trade for weapons and supplies."

"Yes, Lord KanPaar," a second voice said. They were coming from the center of the shining area. It was to the side of the Pits, only a few minutes' travel from the refugees.

Oh no . . . Vin thought, feeling a sudden dread.

"The foolish Firsts have sat on this treasure for far too long," KanPaar said. "With these riches, we could be *ruling* the humans rather than serving them."

"I . . . thought we didn't want to change things?" the second voice said.

"Oh, we won't. Not quickly at least. For now, just this small amount needs to be sold . . ."

Hidden beneath the ground, Vin thought, her heightened mind making the connections. *In a place that already shines because of the large number of metal deposits. Ruin would never have been able to know where the atium was.*

The depth of the Lord Ruler's strategies amazed her. He had held on for a thousand years, maintaining such an amazing secret, keeping the atium safe. She imagined obligators communicating only on metal plates, giving instructions for the operations at the Pits. She imagined caravans traveling from the Pits, carrying atium mixed with gold and coins to hide where it was moving and what exactly was going on.

You don't know what I do for mankind, the Lord Ruler had said.

And I didn't, Vin thought. *Thank you.*

She felt Ruin surge with power, and she blocked him. But just as she had been able to get a tendril of power past Ruin to Elend, Ruin was able to get the tiniest thread through. It was enough, for the one who had spoken was tainted with Hemalurgy. A spike in each shoulder drew Ruin's power and allowed him to speak to their bearer.

A kandra? Vin thought, her senses finally managing to peer through the atium glare to see a creature with a translucent body standing in a cavern, barely beneath the ground. Another kandra was crawling out of a hole nearby, carrying a small pouch of atium.

Ruin seized control of the kandra KanPaar. The creature stiffened, his metal spikes betraying him.

Speak of this, Ruin said to KanPaar, Vin feeling his words as they pulsed into the kandra. *How much atium is there?*

"Wha . . . who are you?" KanPaar said. "Why are you in my head?"

I am God, the voice said. *And you are mine.*
All of you are mine.

Elend landed outside the Pits of Hathsin, tossing up a puff of ash. Oddly, some of his own soldiers were there guarding the perimeter. They rushed forward, spears held anxiously, then halted when they recognized him.

"Lord *Venture?*" one of the men asked with shock.

"I know you," Elend said, frowning. "From my army at Fadrex."

"You sent us back, my lord," the other soldier said. "With General Demoux. To help Lord Penrod in Luthadel."

Elend glanced up at the night sky, speckled with stars. Some time had passed during his travel to the Pits from Luthadel. If time was now passing normally, the night was half-way through. What would happen when the sun rose again?

"Quickly," Elend said. "I need to speak with the leaders of this camp."

The return of the First Generation was accomplished with as much flair as Sazed had hoped. The old kandra, now wearing larger bodies, still bore the distinctive colorings and aged skin of their generation. He had feared that the ordinary kandra would not recognize them. But he hadn't taken into account the long life spans of the kandra people. Even if the Firsts emerged only once every century, most of the kandra would have seen them several times.

Sazed smiled as the group of Firsts moved into the main kandra chamber, continuing to cause shock and surprise in the others. They proclaimed KanPaar had betrayed them and imprisoned them, then called the kandra people to assemble. Sazed stayed behind MeLaan and the others, watching for snags in their plan.

From the right, a familiar kandra approached.

"Keeper," TenSoon said, still wearing the body of a Fifth. "We need to be careful. There are strange things afoot."

"Such as?" Sazed asked.

Then TenSoon attacked him.

Sazed started, and his moment of confusion cost him dearly. TenSoon—or whoever it was—got his hands around Sazed's throat and began to choke him. They fell backward, drawing the attention of the surrounding kandra. Sazed's assailant— bearing bones of rock—weighed far more than Sazed, and was easily able to roll to the top, his hands still on Sazed's neck.

"TenSoon?" MeLaan asked, sounding terrified.

It's not him, Sazed thought. *It can't be. . . .*

"Keeper," his assailant said between clenched teeth. "Something is very wrong."

You're telling me! Sazed tried to gasp for breath, reaching toward the pocket of his robe, struggling to grab the metalmind lock inside.

"I can barely keep myself from crushing your throat right now," the kandra continued. "Something has control of me. It wants me to kill you."

You're doing a pretty good job! Sazed thought.

"I'm sorry," TenSoon said.

The Firsts had gathered around them. Sazed was barely able to focus, panic controlling him as he fought a much stronger, much heavier foe. He grabbed hold of his impromptu steelmind, but only then realized that speed would do him little good when he was being held so tightly.

"Then it has come," whispered Haddek, leader of the Firsts. Sazed barely noticed as one of the other Firsts began to shake. Kandra were crying out, but the blood thumping in Sazed's ears kept him from hearing what they were saying.

Haddek turned away from the gasping Sazed. And then, in a loud voice, yelled something. "The Resolution has come!"

Above him, TenSoon jerked. Something within the kandra seemed to be fighting—tradition and a lifetime of training warred against the control of an exterior force. TenSoon released Sazed with one hand, but kept choking him with the other. Then, with his free hand, the kandra reached toward his own shoulder.

Sazed blacked out.

The kandra people always said they were of Preservation, while the koloss and Inquisitors were of Ruin. Yet the kandra bore Hemalurgic spikes like the others. Was their claim, then, simple delusion?

No, I think not. They were created by the Lord Ruler to be spies. When they said such things, most of us interpreted that as meaning he planned to use them as spies in his new government, because of their ability to imitate other people. Indeed, they were used for this purpose.

But I see something much more grand in their existence. They were the Lord Ruler's double agents, planted with Hemalurgic spikes, yet trusted—taught, bound—to pull them free when Ruin tried to seize them. In Ruin's moment of triumph, when he'd always assumed the kandra would be his on a whim, the vast majority of them immediately switched sides and left him unable to seize his prize.

They were of Preservation all along.

80

"THE TERRISMEN DID A GOOD job here, my lord," Demoux said.

Elend nodded, walking through the quiet nighttime camp with hands clasped behind his back. He was glad he'd stopped to change into a fresh white uniform before leaving Fadrex. As it was meant to, the clothing attracted attention. The people seemed to take hope simply from seeing him.

Their lives had been cast into chaos—they needed to know that their leader was aware of their situation.

"The camp is enormous, as you can see," Demoux continued. When the general had discovered that Penrod was dead and that most of Luthadel's population was at the Pits, he'd decided to keep his men there to help. "Several hundred thousand people now live here. Without the Terrismen, I doubt that the refugees would have survived. As it is, they managed to keep sickness to a minimum, to organize crews to filter and bring fresh water to the camp, and to distribute food and blankets."

He hesitated, glancing at Elend. "Food is running out," he said.

They passed another campfire, and the people there rose. They watched Elend and his general with hope. At this campfire, Demoux halted as a young Terriswoman approached and handed him and Elend some warm tea. Her eyes lingered fondly on Demoux, and he thanked her by name. The Terris people were affectionate toward Demoux, perhaps grateful to him for bringing soldiers to help organize and police the mass of refugees.

The people needed leadership and order in these times. "I shouldn't have left Luthadel," Elend said softly.

Demoux didn't respond immediately. The two of them finished their tea, then continued on, walking with an honor guard of about ten soldiers, all from Demoux's group. The general had sent several messengers to Elend in Fadrex, but they had never arrived. Perhaps they hadn't been able to get around the lava field. Or perhaps they had run afoul of the same army of koloss Elend had passed on his way to Luthadel.

Those koloss . . . Elend thought. *The ones we drove away from Fadrex, plus more, are coming directly here. There are more people here than at Fadrex. And they don't have a city wall, or many soldiers, to protect them.*

"Have you figured out what happened in Luthadel, Demoux?" Elend asked quietly, pausing in a darkened area between campfires. It still felt strange to be out with no mists to obscure the night. He could see so much farther—yet oddly the night didn't seem as bright.

"Penrod, my lord," Demoux said in a low voice. "They say he went mad. He began finding traitors in the nobility and his own army. He divided the city, and it turned into another house war. Almost all the soldiers killed one another, and the city half burned down. The majority of the people escaped, but they have little protection. A determined group of bandits could wreak havoc on this whole group."

House war, Elend thought with frustration. *Ruin using our own tricks against us. That's the same method Kelsier used to seize the city.*

"My lord . . ." Demoux said tentatively.

"Speak," Elend said.

"You were right to send me and my men away. The Survivor is behind this, my lord. He wanted us here for some reason."

Elend frowned. "What makes you say that?"

"These people, they fled Luthadel because of Kelsier. He appeared to a pair of soldiers, then a group of people. They say he told them to be ready for disaster, and to lead the people out of the city. It's because of them that so many escaped. Those two soldiers and their friends had supplies prepared, and they had the presence of mind to come here."

Elend's frown deepened. Yet he had seen too much to reject even so strange a story. "Send for these men," he said.

Demoux nodded, waving for a soldier.

"Also," Elend said, remembering that Demoux and his men had been sick from the mists, "see if anyone here has any Allomantic metals. Pass them out to your soldiers and have them ingest them."

"My lord?" Demoux said, confused, as he turned.

"It's a long story, Demoux," Elend said. "Suffice it to say that your god—or somebody—has made you and your men into Allomancers. Divide your men by the metal it turns out they can burn. We're going to need all of the Coinshots, Thugs, and Lurchers we can get."

Sazed's eyes fluttered open, and he shook his head, groaning. How long had he been out? Probably not long, he realized, as his vision cleared. He'd passed out from lack of air. That kind of thing usually left one unconscious for only a short time.

Assuming one woke up at all.

Which I did, he thought, coughing and rubbing his throat, sitting up. The kandra cavern glowed with the soft light of its blue phosphorescent lanterns. By that light, he could see that he was surrounded by something strange.

Mistwraiths. The kandra's cousins, the scavengers that hunted at night and fed on corpses. They moved about Sazed, masses of muscle, flesh, and bone—but with those bones combined in strange, unnatural ways. Feet hanging off at angles, heads connected to arms. Ribs used as legs.

Except these bones were not bone at all, but stone, metal, or wood. Sazed stood up solemnly as he looked over the remnants of the kandra people. Littered across the floor, among the jumbled mass of mistwraiths—who oozed about like giant translucent slugs—were discarded spikes. Kandra Blessings. The things that had brought them sapience.

They had done it. They had held to their oath, and had removed their spikes rather than be taken over by Ruin. Sazed gazed upon them with pity, amazement, and respect.

The atium, he thought. *They did this to stop Ruin from getting the atium. I have to protect it!*

He stumbled away from the main chamber, regaining his strength as he made his way to the Trustwarren. Sounds from that direction made him pause, and he peeked around a corner to look down the corridor through the open Trustwarren doorway. Inside it a group of kandra—perhaps twenty in number—worked to push back the plate on the floor that covered the atium.

Of course they didn't all become mistwraiths, he

thought. Some would have been too far away to hear the Firsts, or wouldn't have had the courage to pull their spikes free. In fact, as he thought about it, he was that much more impressed that so many *had* obeyed the command from the First Generation.

Sazed easily recognized KanPaar directing the work. The kandra would take the atium and deliver it to Ruin. Sazed had to stop them. But it was twenty against one—with Sazed having only one small metalmind. It wasn't good odds.

Then Sazed noticed something in the corridor: a simple cloth sack, of little note save for the fact that he recognized it. He'd carried his metalminds in it for years. They must have tossed it there after taking Sazed captive. It lay about twenty feet down the corridor from him, near the doorway into the Trustwarren.

In the other room, KanPaar looked up, staring directly toward Sazed's position. Ruin had noticed him.

Sazed didn't pause to think further. He reached into his pocket, grabbed the steel lock, and tapped it. He rushed through the corridor on inhumanly quick feet, snatching his sack from the ground as kandra began to cry out.

Sazed snapped open the sack and found a collection of bracelets, rings, and bracers within. He dumped them out, spilling the precious metalminds to the floor, and grabbed two particular ones. Then, still moving at blurring speed, he dashed to the doors.

His steelmind ran out. One of the rings he'd grabbed was pewter. He tapped it for strength, growing in size and bulk. Then he slammed the doors to the Trustwarren closed, and the kandra now trapped inside cried out in shock. Next he tapped the other ring—this one iron. He grew several times heavier, making himself into a doorstop, holding the massive metal doors to the Trustwarren closed.

It was a delaying tactic. He stood, holding the doors shut, his metalminds depleting at an alarming rate. They were the same rings he'd worn at the siege of Luthadel. He'd replenished them following the siege, before he'd given up

Feruchemy, but they were small and would not last long. What would he do when the kandra got through the door? He searched desperately for a way to bar or block the portal, but could see nothing. And if he let go for even a moment, the kandra would burst free.

"Please," he whispered, hoping that—like before—the thing that listened would give him a miracle. "I'm going to need help. . . ."

"I swear it was him, my lord," said the soldier, a man named Rittle. "I've believed in the Church of the Survivor since the day of Kelsier's passing, my lord. He preached to me, converted me to the rebellion. I was also there when he visited the caves and had Lord Demoux fight for his honor. I'd know Kelsier like I'd know my father. It *was* the Survivor."

Elend turned to the other soldier, who nodded in agreement. "I didn't know him, my lord," said this man. "However, he matched the descriptions. I think it was really him, I do."

Then Elend glanced at Demoux, who nodded. "They described Lord Kelsier accurately, my lord. He *is* watching over us."

Elend . . .

A messenger arrived and whispered something to Demoux. The night was dark, and in the torchlight, Elend studied the two soldiers who'd seen Kelsier. They didn't look like highly reliable witnesses—he hadn't exactly left his best soldiers behind when he'd gone campaigning. Still, others had reportedly seen the Survivor too. He needed to speak with them.

He shook his head. And where in the world was Vin?

Elend . . .

"My lord," Demoux said, touching his arm, looking concerned. Elend dismissed the two soldier witnesses. Accurate or not, he owed them a great debt—they had saved many lives with their preparation.

"Scouts' report, my lord," Demoux said, face illuminated

by a pole-top torch flickering in the night breeze. "Those koloss you saw, they *are* heading this way. Moving quickly. Scouts saw them approaching in the distance from a hill-top. They . . . could be here before the night is over."

Elend cursed quietly.

Elend . . .

He frowned. Why did he keep hearing his name on the wind? He turned, looking into the darkness. Something was pulling him, guiding him, whispering to him. He tried to ignore it, turning back to Demoux. Yet it was there in his heart.

Come . . .

It seemed like Vin's voice.

"Gather an honor guard," Elend said, grabbing the torch by its pole, then throwing on an ashcloak and buttoning it down to his knees. Then he turned toward the darkness.

"My lord?" Demoux said.

"Just do it!" Elend said, striding off.

Demoux called for some soldiers, following in a hurry.

What am I doing? Elend thought, pushing his way through the waist-deep ash, using the cloak to keep his uniform some-what clean. *Chasing at dreams? Maybe I'm going mad.*

He could see something in his mind. A hillside with a hole in it. A memory perhaps? Had he come this way be-fore? Demoux and his soldiers followed quietly, looking ap-prehensive.

Elend pushed onward. He was almost—

He stopped. There it was, the hillside. It would have been indistinguishable from the others around it, except there were tracks leading up to it. Elend frowned, pushing for-ward through the deep ash, moving to the point where the tracks ended. There he studied the hole in the ground, lead-ing down.

A cave, he thought. *Perhaps . . . a place for my people to hide?*

It likely wouldn't be big enough for that. Still, the caves Kelsier had used for his rebellion were large enough to hold some ten thousand men. Curious, Elend poked down into the cave, walking down its steep incline, and threw off the cloak. Demoux and his men followed with curiosity.

The tunnel went down for a bit, and Elend was surprised to find that there was light coming from ahead. Immediately he flared pewter, growing tense. He tossed aside his torch, then burned tin, enhancing his vision. He could see several poles that glowed blue at the top. They appeared to be made of rock.

What in the world . . . ?

He moved forward quickly, motioning for Demoux and his men to follow. The tunnel led to a vast cavern. Elend stopped. It was as large as one of the storage caverns. Larger perhaps. Down below, something moved.

Mistwraiths? he realized with surprise. *Is this where they hide? In holes in the ground?*

He dropped a coin, shooting himself through the poorly lit cavern to land on the stone floor a distance away from Demoux and the others. The mistwraiths weren't as large as others he had seen. And . . . why were they using rocks and wood in place of bones?

He heard a sound. Only tin-enhanced ears let him catch it, but it sounded distinctly unlike a sound a mistwraith would make. Stone on metal. He waved sharply to Demoux, then moved carefully down a side corridor.

At its end, he stopped in surprise. A familiar figure stood against a pair of large metal doors, grunting, apparently trying to hold them closed.

"*Sazed?*" Elend asked, standing up straighter.

Sazed looked up, saw Elend, and was apparently so surprised that he lost control of the doors. They burst open, throwing the Terrisman aside, revealing a group of angry, translucent-skinned kandra.

"Your Majesty!" Sazed said. "Do not let them escape!"

Demoux and his soldiers clanked up behind Elend. *That's either Sazed or a kandra who ate his bones,* Elend thought. He made a snap decision. He'd trusted the voice in his ear. He would trust that this was Sazed.

The group of kandra tried to get past Demoux's soldiers.

However, the kandra were poor warriors, and their weapons were made of metal. It took Elend and Demoux all of about two minutes to subdue the group, breaking their bones to keep them from healing and escaping.

Afterward, Elend walked over to Sazed, who had stood up and dusted himself off. "How did you find me, Your Majesty?"

"I honestly don't know," Elend said. "Sazed, what is this place?"

"The Homeland of the kandra people, Your Majesty," Sazed said. "And the hiding place of the Lord Ruler's atium hoard."

Elend raised an eyebrow, following Sazed's pointed finger. There was a room beyond the doors, and a pit in the floor.

Great, Elend thought. *Now we find it.*

"You don't look too excited, Your Majesty," Sazed noted. "Kings, armies, Mistborn—even Kelsier—have been searching for this cache for years."

"It's worthless," Elend said. "My people are starving, and they can't eat metal. This cavern, however . . . it might prove useful. What do you think, Demoux?"

"If there are any other chambers like that first one, my lord, it could hold a substantial percentage of our people."

"There are four large caverns," Sazed said. "And four entrances that I know of."

Elend turned to Demoux. He was already giving orders to his soldiers. *We have to get the people down here before the sun rises,* Elend thought, remembering the heat. *At the very least, before those koloss arrive.*

After that . . . well, they would have to see. For now, Elend had only one goal.

Survival.

Snapping has always been the dark side of Allomancy. A person's genetic endowment may make them a potential Allomancer, but in order for the power to manifest, the body must be put through extraordinary trauma. Though Elend spoke of how terrible his beating was, during our day, unlocking Allomancy in a person was easier than it had once been, for we had the infusion of Preservation's power into the human bloodlines via the nuggets granted to nobility by the Lord Ruler.

When Preservation set up the mists, he was afraid of Ruin escaping his prison. In those early days before the Ascension, the mists began to Snap people as they did during our time—but this action of the mists was one of the only ways to awaken Allomancy in a person, for the genetic attributes were buried too deeply to be brought out by a simple beating. The mists of that day created Mistings alone—there were no Mistborn until the Lord Ruler made use of the nuggets.

The people misinterpreted the mists' intent, as the process of Snapping Allomancers caused some—particularly the young and the old—to die. This hadn't been Preservation's desire, but he'd given up most of his consciousness to form Ruin's prison, and the mists had to be left to work as best they could without specific direction.

Ruin, subtle as ever, knew that he couldn't stop the mists from doing their work. However, he could do the unexpected and encourage them. So he helped make them stronger. That brought death to the plants of the world, and created the threat that became known as the Deepness.

81

VIN TURNED TOWARD RUIN, PROJECTING a smile. The cloud of twisting black mist seemed agitated.

So, you can influence a single minion, Ruin snapped, turning upon itself, rising in the air. Vin followed, streaking up to loom over the entire Central Dominance. Below, she could see Demoux's soldiers rushing to the camp, waking the people, organizing them to flight. Already some of them were making their way along the tracks in the ash toward the safety of the caverns.

She could feel the sun, and knew that the planet was far too near it to be safe. Yet she could do nothing more. Not only would Ruin have stopped her, but she didn't understand her power yet. She felt as the Lord Ruler must have—almighty, yet clumsy. If she tried to move the world, she would just make things worse.

But she had accomplished something. Ruin had his koloss pounding toward them at breakneck speed, but they still wouldn't arrive at the Pits for several hours. Plenty of time to get the people to the caverns.

Ruin must have noticed what she was studying, or perhaps he sensed her smugness. *You think you've won?* he asked, sounding amused. *Why, because you managed to stop a few kandra? They were always the weakest of the minions the Lord Ruler created for me. I have made a habit of ignoring them. In any case, Vin, you cannot really think that you have beaten me.*

Vin waited, watching as the people fled to the relative safety of the caverns. Even as the bulk of them arrived—soldiers separating them into groups, sending them to the different entrances—her good humor began to fade. She had managed to get through to Elend, and while it had seemed a great victory at the moment, she could now see that it was little more than another stalling tactic.

Have you counted the koloss in my army, Vin? Ruin asked. *I've made them from your people, you know. I've gathered hundreds of thousands.*

Vin focused, enumerating instantly. He was telling the truth.

This is the force I could have thrown at you at any time, Ruin said. *Most of them kept to the Outer Dominances, but I've been bringing them in, marching them toward Luthadel. How many times must I tell you, Vin? You can't win. You could never win. I've merely been playing with you.*

Vin pulled back, ignoring his lies. He hadn't been playing with them—he'd been trying to discover the secrets that Preservation had left, the secret that the Lord Ruler had kept. Still, the numbers Ruin had ultimately managed to marshal were awe-inspiring. There were far more koloss than there were people climbing into the caverns. With a force like that, Ruin could assault a well-fortified position. And by Vin's count, Elend had fewer than a thousand men with any battle training.

On top of that was the sun and its destructive heat, the death of the world's crops, the tainting of water and land with several feet of ash . . . And the lava flows, which she had halted, were beginning again, her plugging of the Ashmounts having provided only a temporary solution. Even a bad one. Now that the mountains couldn't erupt, great cracks were appearing in the land, and the lava, the earth's burning blood, was boiling out that way.

We're so far behind! Vin thought. *Ruin had centuries to plan this. When we thought we were being clever, we fell for his plots. What good is it to sequester my people beneath the ground if they're just going to starve?*

She turned toward Ruin, who billowed and shifted upon himself, watching his koloss army. She felt a hatred that seemed incompatible with the power she held. The hatred made her sick, but she didn't let go of it.

This thing before her would crush everything she knew,

everything she loved. It couldn't understand love. It built solely to destroy later. At that moment, she reversed her earlier decision. She'd never again call Ruin a "him." Humanizing the creature gave it too much respect.

Seething, watching, she didn't know what else to do. So she attacked.

She wasn't certain how she did it. She threw herself at Ruin, forcing her power up against its power. There was friction between them, a clash of energy, and it tormented her divine body. Ruin cried out, and—mixing with Ruin—she knew its mind.

Ruin was surprised. It didn't expect Preservation to be able to attack. Vin's move smacked too much of destruction. Ruin didn't know how to respond, but it threw its power back at her in a protective reflex. Their selves crashed, threatening to dissolve. Finally Vin pulled away, lacerated, rebuffed.

Their power was too well matched. Opposed, yet similar. Like with Allomancy.

Opposition, Ruin whispered. *Balance. You'll learn to hate it, I suspect, though Preservation never could.*

"So, *this* is the body of a god?" Elend asked, rolling the bead of atium in his palm. He held it up next to the one Yomen had given him.

"Indeed, Your Majesty," Sazed said. The Terrisman looked eager. Didn't he understand how dangerous their situation was? Demoux's scouts—the ones who had returned—reported that the koloss were mere minutes away. Elend had ordered his troops posted at the Homeland's entrances, but his hope—that the koloss wouldn't know where to find his people—was a slim one, considering what Sazed had told him about Ruin.

"Ruin can't help but come for it," Sazed explained. They stood in the metal-lined cavern called the Trustwarren, the place where the kandra had spent the last thousand years gathering and guarding the atium. "This atium is *part* of him. It's what he's been searching for all this time."

"Which means we'll have a couple hundred thousand koloss trying to climb down our throats, Sazed," Elend said, handing back the bead. "I say we give it to him."

Sazed paled. "Give it to him? Your Majesty, my apologies, but that would mean the end of the world. Instantly. I am certain of it."

Great, Elend thought.

"It will be all right, Elend," Sazed said.

Elend frowned up at the Terrisman, who stood peacefully in his robes.

"Vin will come," Sazed explained. "She is the Hero of Ages—she will arrive to save this people. Don't you see how perfect this is? It's arranged, planned. That you would come here, find me, at this exact moment . . . That you'd be able to lead the people to safety in these caverns . . . Well, it all fits together. She'll come."

Interesting time for him to get his faith back, Elend thought. He rolled Yomen's bead between his fingers, thinking. Outside the room he could hear whispers. People—Terris stewards, skaa leaders, a few soldiers—stood listening. Elend could hear the anxiety in their voices. They had heard of the approaching army. As Elend watched, Demoux carefully pushed his way through them and entered the room.

"Soldiers posted, my lord," the general said.

"How many do we have?" Elend asked.

Demoux looked somber. "The three hundred I brought with me," he said. "Plus about five hundred from the city. Another hundred ordinary citizens that we armed with those kandra hammers, or spare weapons from our soldiers. And we have four different entrances to this cavern complex that we need to guard."

Elend closed his eyes.

"She'll come," Sazed said.

"My lord," Demoux said, pulling Elend aside. "This is bad."

"I know," Elend said, exhaling softly. "Did you give each of the men metals?"

"What we could find," Demoux said quietly. "The people

didn't think to bring powdered metal with them when they fled Luthadel. We've found a couple of nobles who were Allomancers, but they were only Copperclouds or Seekers."

Elend nodded. He'd bribed or pressed the useful noble Allomancers into his army already.

"We gave those metals to my soldiers," Demoux said. "But none could burn them. Even if we had Allomancers, we could not hold this location, my lord! Not with so few soldiers, not against that many koloss. We'll delay them at first, because of the narrow entrances. But, well . . ."

"I realize that, Demoux," Elend said with frustration. "But do you have any other options?"

Demoux was silent. "I was hoping you'd have some, my lord."

"None here," Elend said.

Demoux's face grew grim. "Then we die."

"What about faith, Demoux?" Elend asked.

"I believe in the Survivor, my lord. But . . . well, our outlook is bleak at best. I've felt like a man waiting his turn before the headsman ever since we spotted those koloss. Maybe the Survivor doesn't want us to succeed here. Eventually, death must come to all."

Elend turned away, clenching and unclenching his fist around the bead of atium. It was the same problem, the same trouble he always had. He'd failed during the siege of Luthadel—it had taken Vin to protect the city. He'd failed in Fadrex City—only Ruin ordering the koloss army to attack elsewhere had rescued him there.

A ruler's most basic duty was to protect his people. In this one area, Elend continually felt impotent. Useless.

Why can't I do it? Elend thought, his frustration building. *I spend a year searching out storage caverns to provide food, only to end up trapped with my people starving. I search all that time for the atium—hoping to use it to buy safety for my people—and then I find it too late to spend it on anything. Too late . . .*

He paused, glancing back toward the metal plate in the floor.

Years searching for . . . atium.

None of the metals Demoux had given his soldiers had worked. Elend had assumed that Demoux's group would be similar to the other mistfallen in Fadrex—that they'd be composed of all kinds of Mistings. Yet there had been something *different* about Demoux's group. They had fallen sick for far longer than the others.

Elend pushed forward, rushing past Sazed to grab a handful of beads. A vast wealth, unlike anything any man had ever possessed. Valuable for its rarity. Valuable for its economic power. Valuable for its *Allomancy.*

"Demoux," he snapped, rising and tossing a bead to him. "Eat this."

Demoux frowned. "My lord?"

"Eat it," Elend said.

Demoux did as asked. He stood for a moment.

Three hundred men, Elend thought. *Sent away from my army because of all the ones who fell sick, they were the most sick. Sixteen days.*

Three hundred twenty-seven men. One-sixteenth of those who fell sick. One out of sixteen Allomantic metals.

Yomen had proven that there was such a thing as an atium Misting. If Elend hadn't been so distracted, he would have made the connection earlier. If one out of sixteen who fell sick remained that way the longest, would that not imply that they'd gained the most powerful of the sixteen abilities?

Demoux looked up, his eyes widening.

And Elend smiled.

Vin hovered outside the cavern, watching with dread as the koloss approached. They were already in a blood frenzy, thousands upon thousands of them. The slaughter was about to begin.

Vin cried out as they drew closer, throwing herself at Ruin again, trying to drive her power to destroy the thing. As before, she was rebuffed. She felt herself screaming, trembling as she thought about the impending deaths below. It would be like the tsunami deaths on the coast, only worse.

For these were people she knew. People she loved.

She turned back toward the entrance. She didn't want to watch, but she wouldn't be able to do anything else. Her self was everywhere. Even if she pulled her nexus away, she knew that she'd still feel the deaths—that they would make her tremble and weep.

From within the cavern, echoing, she sensed a familiar voice. "Today, men, I ask of you your lives." Vin hovered down, listening. Though she couldn't see into the cavern because of the metals in the rock, she could still hear. If she'd had eyes, she knew she would have been crying.

"I ask of you your lives," Elend said, his voice echoing, "and your courage. I ask of you your faith and your honor— your strength and your compassion. For today, I lead you to die. I will not ask you to welcome this event. I will not insult you by calling it good, or just, or even glorious. But I will say this.

"Each moment you fight is a gift to those in this cavern. Each second we fight is a second longer that thousands of people can draw breath. Each stroke of the sword, each koloss felled, each breath earned is a victory! It is a person protected for a moment longer, a life extended, an enemy frustrated!"

There was a brief pause.

"In the end, they will kill us," Elend said, his voice loud, ringing in the cavern. "But first, they shall *fear* us!"

The men yelled at this, and Vin's enhanced mind could pick out over three hundred distinct voices. She heard them split, rushing toward the different cavern entrances. A moment later, someone appeared from the front entrance near her.

A figure in white slowly stepped out into the ash, brilliant white cape fluttering. He held a sword in one hand.

Elend! she tried to cry at him. *No! Go back! Charging them is madness! You'll be killed!*

Elend stood tall, watching the waves of koloss as they approached, trampling down the black ash, an endless sea of death with blue skin and red eyes. Many carried swords, and the others just bore rocks and lengths of wood. Elend was a tiny white speck before them, a single dot on an endless canvas of blue.

He raised his sword high and charged.

ELEND!

Suddenly, Elend burst with a brilliant energy, so bright that Vin gasped. He met the first koloss head-on, ducking beneath the swinging sword and decapitating the creature in one stroke. Then instead of jumping away, he spun to the side, swinging. Another koloss fell. Three swords flashed around him, but all missed by a hair. Elend ducked to one side and took a koloss in the stomach, then whipped his sword around—his head barely passing beneath another swing—and lopped off a koloss arm.

He still didn't Push himself away. Vin froze, watching as he took down one koloss, then beheaded another in a single fluid stroke. Elend moved with a grace she had never seen from him—she had always been the better warrior, yet at this moment he put her to shame. He wove between koloss swords as if taking part in a rehearsed stage fight, body after body falling before his gliding blade.

A group of soldiers in Elend's colors burst from the cavern entrance, charging. Like a wave of light, their forms exploded with power. They also moved into the koloss ranks, striking with incredible precision. Not a single one of them fell as Vin watched. They fought with miraculous skill and fortune, each koloss blade falling a bare moment too late. Blue corpses began to pile up around the glowing force of men.

Somehow Elend had found an entire army who could burn atium.

Elend was a god.

He'd never burned atium before, and his first experience

with the metal filled him with wonder. The koloss around him all emitted atium shadows that moved before they did, showing Elend precisely what they would do. He could see into the future, if only a few seconds. In a battle, that was exactly what one needed.

He could feel the atium enhancing his mind, making him capable of reading and using all of the new information. There was no need to pause and think. His arms moved of their own volition, swinging his sword with awesome precision.

He spun amid a cloud of phantom images, striking at flesh, feeling almost as if he were in the mists again. No koloss could stand against him. He felt energized—he felt amazing. For a time he was invincible. He'd swallowed so many atium beads he felt like he'd throw up. For its entire history, atium had been a thing that men had needed to save and hoard. Burning it had seemed such a shame that it had been used only sparingly, in instances of great need.

Elend didn't need to worry about any of that now. He just burned as much as he wanted. And it made him into a disaster for the koloss—a whirlwind of precision strikes and impossible dodges, always a few steps ahead of his opponents. Foe after foe fell before him. And when he began to get low on atium, he Pushed himself off a fallen sword back to the entrance. There, with plenty of water to wash it down, Sazed waited with another bag of atium.

Elend downed the beads quickly, then returned to the battle.

Ruin raged and spun, trying to stop the slaughter. Yet this time Vin was the force of balance. She blocked Ruin's every attempt to destroy Elend and the others, keeping it contained.

I can't decide if you're a fool, Vin thought toward it, *or if you simply exist in a way that makes you incapable of considering some things.*

Ruin screamed, buffeting against her, trying to destroy her

as she had tried to destroy it. However, once again their powers were too evenly matched. Ruin was forced to pull back.

Life, Vin said. *You said that the sole reason to create something was so that you could destroy it.*

She hovered by Elend, watching him fight. The deaths of the koloss should have pained her. Yet she did not think of the slaughter. Perhaps it was the influence of Preservation's power, but she saw only a man struggling, fighting when hope seemed impossible. She didn't see death; she saw life. She saw faith.

We create things to watch them grow, Ruin, she said. *To take pleasure in seeing that which we love become more than it was before. You said that you were invincible—that all things break apart. All things are Ruined. But there are things that fight against you—and the ironic part is, you can't even understand those things. Love. Life. Growth.*

The life of a person is more than the chaos of its passing. Emotion, Ruin. This is your defeat.

Sazed watched anxiously from the mouth of the cavern. A small group of men huddled around him. Garv, leader of the Church of the Survivor in Luthadel. Harathdal, foremost of the Terris stewards. Lord Dedri Vasting, one of the surviving Assembly members from the city government. Aslydin, the young woman whom Demoux had apparently come to love during his few short weeks at the Pits of Hathsin. A smattering of others, important—or faithful—enough to get near the front of the crowd and watch.

"Where is she, Master Terrisman?" Garv asked.

"She'll come," Sazed promised. his hand resting on the rock wall. He wore his metalminds—all of them with any charge remaining, including his rings from the battle at Luthadel, in case the tunnel was breached. His copperminds rested on his arms, ready for recording every detail of the Hero's arrival.

The men fell quiet. Soldiers—those without the blessing

of atium—waited nervously with them, knowing they were next in line should Elend's assault fail.

She has to come, Sazed thought. *Everything points toward her arrival.*

"The Hero *will* come," he repeated.

Elend sheared through two heads at once, dropping the koloss. He spun his blade, taking off an arm, then stabbed another koloss through the neck. He hadn't noticed that one approaching, but his mind had seen and interpreted the atium shadow before the real attack came.

Already he stood atop a carpet of blue corpses. He did not stumble. With atium, his every step was exact, his blade guided, his mind crisp. He took down a particularly large koloss, then stepped back, pausing briefly.

The sun crested the horizon in the east. It started to grow hotter.

They had been fighting for hours, yet the army of koloss still seemed endless. Elend slew another koloss, but his motions were beginning to feel sluggish. Atium enhanced the mind, but it did not boost the body, and he'd started to rely on his pewter to keep him going. Who would have known that one could get tired—even exhausted—while burning atium? Nobody had ever used as much of the metal as Elend had. But he had to keep going.

His atium was starting to run low. He turned back toward the mouth of the cavern, in time to see one of his atium soldiers go down in a spray of blood.

Elend cursed, spinning as an atium shadow passed through him. He ducked the swing that followed, then took off the creature's arm. He beheaded the one that followed, then cut another's legs out from beneath it. For most of the battle, he hadn't used fancy Allomantic jumps or attacks, just straightforward swordplay. His arms were growing tired, however, and he was forced to begin Pushing koloss away from him to manage the battlefield. The reserve of atium—of *life*—within him was dwindling. Atium burned so quickly.

Another man screamed. Another soldier dead.

Elend began to retreat toward the cavern. There were just *so many* koloss. His band of three hundred had slain thousands, yet the koloss didn't care. They kept attacking, a brutal wave of endless determination, resisted only by the clusters of atium Mistings protecting each of the entrances to the Homeland.

Another man died. Their atium was running out.

Elend bellowed, swinging his sword about him, taking down three koloss in a maneuver that never should have worked. He flared steel and Pushed the rest away from him. *The body of a god, burning within me,* he thought. He gritted his teeth, attacking as more of his men fell. He scrambled up a pile of koloss, slicing off arms, legs, heads. Stabbing chests, necks, guts. He fought on, his clothing long since stained from white to red.

Something moved behind him, and he spun, raising his blade, letting the atium lead him. Yet he froze, uncertain. The creature was no koloss. It stood in a black robe, one eye socket empty and bleeding, the other bearing a spike that had been crushed into its skull. Elend saw straight into the empty eye socket, through the creature's head and out the back.

Marsh. He had a cloud of atium shadows around him—he was burning the metal too, and would be immune to Elend's own atium sight.

Human led his koloss soldiers through the tunnels. They killed any person in their path.

Some had stood at the entrance. They had fought long. They had been strong. They were dead now.

Something drove Human on. Something stronger than anything that had controlled him before. Stronger than the little woman with the black hair, though she had been very strong. This thing was stronger. It was Ruin. Human knew this.

He could not resist. He could only kill. He cut down another human.

Human burst into a large open chamber filled with other little people. Controlling him, Ruin made him turn away and not kill them. Not that Ruin didn't want him to kill them. It simply wanted something else *more*.

Human rushed forward. He crawled over tumbled rocks and stones. He shoved aside crying humans. Other koloss followed him. For the moment, all of his own desires were forgotten. There was only his overpowering desire to get to . . .

A small room. There. In front of him. Human threw open the doors. Ruin shouted in pleasure as he entered this room. It contained the thing Ruin wanted.

"Guess what I found," Marsh growled, stepping up, Pushing against Elend's sword. The weapon was ripped from his fingers, flying away. "Atium. A kandra was carrying it, looking to sell it. Foolish creature."

Elend cursed, ducking out of the way of a koloss swing, pulling his obsidian dagger from the sheath at his leg.

Marsh stalked forward. Men screamed—cursing, falling—as their atium was used up. Elend's soldiers were being overrun. The screams tapered off as the last of his men guarding this entrance perished. He doubted the others would last much longer.

Elend's atium warned him of attacking koloss, letting him dodge—barely—but he couldn't kill them effectively with the dagger. As the koloss took his attention, Marsh struck with an obsidian axe. The blade fell and Elend leaped away, but the dodge left him off balance.

Elend tried to recover, but his metals were running low—not just his atium, but his basic metals. Iron, steel, pewter. He hadn't been paying much attention to them, since he had atium, but he'd been fighting for so long now. But that was no advantage over Marsh—and without basic metals, Elend would die.

An attack from the Inquisitor forced Elend to flare pewter to get away. He cut down three koloss with ease, his atium still helping him, but Marsh's immunity was a serious challenge. The Inquisitor crawled over the fallen bodies of koloss, scrambling toward Elend, his single spikehead reflecting the too-bright light of the sun overhead.

Elend's pewter ran out.

"You cannot beat me, Elend Venture," Marsh said in a voice like gravel. "We've killed your wife. I will kill you."

Vin. Elend didn't believe it. *Vin will come,* he thought. *She'll save us.*

Faith. It was a strange thing to feel at that moment. Marsh swung.

Pewter and iron suddenly flared to life within Elend. He didn't have time to think about the oddity; he simply reacted, Pulling on his sword, which lay stuck into the ground a distance away. It flipped through the air and he caught it, swinging with a too-quick motion, blocking Marsh's axe. Elend's body seemed to pulse, powerful and vast. He struck forward instinctively, forcing Marsh to retreat across the ashen field. Koloss backed away for the moment, shying from Elend as if frightened. Or awed.

Marsh raised a hand to Push on Elend's sword, but nothing happened. It was . . . as if something deflected the blow. Elend screamed, charging, beating back Marsh with the strikes of his silvery weapon. The Inquisitor looked shocked, blocking with the obsidian axe, his motions too quick for even Allomancy to explain. Yet Elend still forced him to retreat, across fallen corpses of blue, the ash stirring beneath a red sky.

A powerful peace swelled in Elend. His Allomancy flared bright, though he knew the metals within him should have burned away. Only atium remained, and its strange power did not—could not—give him the other metals. But it didn't matter. For a moment, he was embraced by something greater. He looked up, toward the sun.

And he saw—just briefly—an enormous figure in the air right above him. A shifting, brilliant personage of pure white. Her hands held to his shoulders with her head thrown back, white hair streaming, mist flaring behind her like wings that stretched across the sky.

Vin, he thought with a smile.

Elend looked back down as Marsh screamed and leaped forward, attacking with his axe in one hand, seeming to trail something vast and black like a cloak behind him. Marsh raised his other hand across his face, as if to shield his dead eyes from the image in the air above Elend.

Elend set alight the last of his atium, flaring it to life in his stomach. He raised his sword in two hands and waited for Marsh to draw close. The Inquisitor was stronger and was a better warrior. Marsh had the powers of both Allomancy and Feruchemy, making him another Lord Ruler. This was not a battle Elend could win. Not with a sword.

Marsh arrived, and Elend thought he understood what it had been like for Kelsier to face the Lord Ruler on that square in Luthadel. Marsh struck with his axe; Elend raised his sword in return and prepared to strike.

Then Elend burned duralumin with his atium.

Sight, Sound, Strength, Power, Glory, Speed!

Blue lines sprayed from his chest like rays of light. But those were all overshadowed by one thing. Atium plus duralumin. In a flash of knowledge, Elend felt a mind-numbing wealth of information. All became white around him as knowledge saturated his mind.

"I see now," he whispered as the vision faded, and along with it his remaining metals. The battlefield returned. He stood upon it, his sword piercing Marsh's neck. It had gotten caught on the spikehead jutting from Marsh's back, between the shoulder blades.

Marsh's axe was buried in Elend's chest.

The phantom metals Vin had given him burned to life within Elend again. They took the pain away. However, there was only so much that pewter could do, no matter how high it was flared. Marsh ripped his axe free, and Elend stumbled backward, bleeding, letting go of his sword.

Marsh pulled the blade free from his neck, and the wound vanished, healed by the powers of Feruchemy.

Elend fell, slumping into a pile of koloss bodies. He would have been dead already, save for the pewter. Marsh stepped up to him, smiling. His empty eye socket was wreathed in tattoos, the mark that Marsh had taken upon himself. The price he had paid to overthrow the Final Empire.

Marsh grabbed Elend by the throat and pulled him up. "Your soldiers are dead, Elend Venture," the creature whispered. "Our koloss rampage inside the kandra caverns. Your metals are gone. You have lost."

Elend felt his life dripping away, the last trickle from an empty glass. He'd been here before, back in the cavern at the Well of Ascension. He should have died then, and he'd been terrified. This time, oddly, he was not. There was no regret. Only satisfaction.

Elend looked up at the Inquisitor. Vin, like a glowing phantom, still hovered above them both. "Lost?" Elend whispered. "We've won, Marsh."

"Oh, and how is that?" Marsh asked, dismissive.

Human stood at the edge of the pit in the center of the cavern room. The pit where Ruin's body had been. The place of victory.

Human stood, dumbfounded, a group of other koloss stepping up to him, looking equally confused.

The pit was empty.

"Atium," Elend whispered, tasting blood. "Where is the atium, Marsh? Where do you think we got the power to fight? You came for that atium? Well it's *gone*. Tell your master that! You think my men and I expected to kill all of these koloss? There are tens of thousands of them! That wasn't the point at all."

Elend's smile widened. "Ruin's body is gone, Marsh.

We burned it all away, the others and I. You can kill me, but you'll *never* get what you came for. And that is why we win."

Marsh screamed in anger, demanding the truth, but Elend had spoken it. The deaths of the others meant that they had run out of atium. His men had fought until it was gone, as Elend had commanded, burning away every last bit.

The body of a god. The power of a god. Elend had held it for a moment. More importantly, he'd destroyed it. Hopefully that would keep his people safe.

It's up to you now, Vin, he thought, still feeling the peace of her touch upon his soul. *I've done what I can.*

He smiled at Marsh again, defiantly, as the Inquisitor raised his axe.

The axe took off Elend's head.

Ruin raged and thrashed about, furious and destructive. Vin just sat quietly, watching Elend's headless body slump into the pile of blue corpses.

How do you like that! Ruin screamed. *I killed him! I Ruined everything you love! I took it from you!*

Vin floated above Elend's body, looking down. She reached out with incorporeal fingers, touching his head, remembering how it had felt to use her power to fuel his Allomancy. She didn't know what she had done. Something perhaps akin to what Ruin did when it controlled the koloss. But opposite. Liberating. Serene.

Elend was dead. She knew that, and knew that there was nothing she could do. That brought pain, true, but not the pain she had expected. *I let him go long ago,* she thought, stroking his face. *At the Well of Ascension. Allomancy brought him back to me for a time.*

She didn't feel the pain or terror that she had known before, when she'd thought him dead. Now she felt only peace. These last few years had been a blessing—an extension. She'd given Elend up to be his own man, to risk himself as he wished, and perhaps to die. She would always love him. But she would not cease to function because he was gone.

The contrary, perhaps. Ruin floated directly above her, throwing down insults, telling her how it would kill the others. Sazed. Breeze. Ham. Spook.

So few left of the original crew, she thought. *Kelsier dead so long ago. Dockson and Clubs killed at the Battle of Luthadel. Yeden dead with his soldiers. OreSeur taken at Zane's command. Marsh, fallen to become an Inquisitor. And the others who joined us, now gone as well. Tindwyl, TenSoon, Elend . . .*

Did Ruin think she would let their sacrifices be for nothing? She rose, gathering her power. She forced it against the power of Ruin, as she had the other times. Yet this time was different. When Ruin pushed back, she didn't retreat. She didn't preserve herself. She drove onward.

The confrontation made her divine body tremble in pain. It was the pain of cold and hot meeting, the pain of two rocks being smashed together and ground to dust. Their forms undulated and rippled in a tempest of power.

And Vin drove on.

Preservation could never destroy you! she thought, almost screaming it against the agony. *He could only protect. That was why he needed to create humankind. All along, Ruin, this was part of his plan!*

He didn't give up part of himself, making himself weaker, simply so that he could create intelligent life! He knew he needed something of both Preservation and Ruin. Something that could both protect and destroy. Something that could destroy to protect.

He gave up his power at the Well, and into the mists, giving it to us so that we could take it. He always intended this to happen. You think this was your plan? It was his. His all along.

Ruin cried out. Still she drove on.

You created the thing that can kill you, Ruin, Vin said.

And you just made one huge final mistake. You shouldn't have killed Elend.

You see, he was the only reason I had left to live.

She didn't shy back, though the conflict of opposites ripped her apart. Ruin screamed in terror as the force of her power completely melded with Ruin's.

Her consciousness—now integrated and saturated with Preservation—moved to touch that of Ruin. Neither would yield. And with a surge of power, Vin bade farewell to the world, then pulled Ruin into the abyss with her.

Their two minds puffed away like mist under a hot sun.

Once Vin died, the end came quickly. We were not prepared for it—but all of the Lord Ruler's planning could not have prepared us for this. How did one prepare for the end of the world itself?

82

SAZED WATCHED QUIETLY FROM THE mouth of the cavern. Outside, the koloss raged and stomped about, looking confused. Most of the men who had been watching with Sazed had fled. Even most of the soldiers had retreated into the caverns, calling him a fool for waiting. Only General Demoux—who had managed to crawl back to the entrance after his atium ran out—remained, a few steps into the tunnel. The man was bloody, his arm ending in a tourniquet, his leg crushed. He coughed softly, waiting for Aslydin to return with more bandages.

The sun rose into the sky. The heat was incredible, like an oven. Cries of pain echoed from deep in the cavern behind Sazed. Koloss were inside.

"She'll come," Sazed whispered.

He could see Elend's body. It had slid down the pile of koloss corpses. It was stark, bright white and red against the black and blue of the koloss and ash.

"Vin will come," Sazed said insistently.

Demoux looked dazed. Too much blood lost. He slumped, closing his eyes. Koloss began to move toward the cavern mouth, though they didn't have the direction or frenzy they'd displayed before.

"The Hero *will* come!" Sazed said.

Outside a figure appeared, forming from mists, then slumped down among the bodies next to Elend's corpse. It was followed immediately by a second figure, which also fell motionless.

There! Sazed thought, scrambling out of the cavern. He dashed past several koloss who swung for him, but he tapped a steel ring and dodged their attacks. Sazed ran quickly through the mass of confused-looking koloss, climbing over bodies, moving up to the scrap of white cloak that marked Elend's resting place. His corpse was there, headless.

A small body lay beside his. Sazed fell to his knees, grabbing Vin by the shoulders. Near her, atop the pile of koloss, lay another body—of a man with red hair whom Sazed did not recognize, but he ignored it.

For Vin was not moving.

No! he thought, checking for a pulse. There was none. Her eyes were closed. She looked peaceful, but very, very dead.

"This can *not* be!" he yelled, shaking her body again.

He glanced upward at that rising sun. It was getting hard to breathe for the heat. He felt his skin burning. By the time the sun reached its zenith, it would likely be so hot the land would be set afire.

"Is this how it ends?" he screamed toward the sky. "Your

Hero is dead! Ruin's power may be broken, the koloss may be lost to him as an army, but *the world will still die!*"

Ash had killed the plants. The sun would burn away all that remained. There was no food. Sazed blinked at tears, but they dried on his face.

"This is how you leave us?" he whispered.

And then he felt something. He looked down. Vin's body was smoking slightly. Not from the heat. It seemed to be leaking something . . . or, no. It was connected to something. The twists of mist he saw, they led to a vast white light. He could just barely see it.

He reached out and touched the mist, and felt an awesome power. A power of stability. To the side, the other corpse— the one he didn't recognize—was also leaking something. An inky black smoke. Sazed reached out with his other hand, touching the smoke, and felt a different power—more violent. The power of change.

He knelt, stunned, between the bodies. And only then did it start to make sense.

The prophecies always used the gender-neutral form, he thought. *So that they could refer to either a man or a woman, we assumed. Or . . . perhaps because they referred to a Hero who wasn't really either one?*

He stood up. The sun's power overhead felt insignificant compared to the twin—yet opposite—powers that surrounded him.

The Hero would be rejected of his people, Sazed thought. *Yet he would save them. Not a warrior, though he would fight. Not born a king, but would become one anyway.*

He looked upward again.

Is this what you planned all along?

He tasted the power, but drew back, daunted. How could he use such a thing? He was a mere man. In the brief glimpse of the forces he touched, he knew that he'd have no hope of using them. He lacked the training.

"I can't do this," he said through cracked lips, reaching to the sky. "I don't know how. I cannot make the world as it was—I never saw it. If I take this power, I will do as the

Lord Ruler did, and will only make things worse for my trying. I am simply a man."

Koloss cried out in pain from the burning. The heat was terrible, and around Sazed trees began to pop and burst into flames. His touch on the twin powers kept him alive, he knew, but he did not embrace them.

"I am no Hero," he whispered, still reaching to the sky.

His arms twinkled, golden. The copperminds on his forearms reflected the light of the sun. They had been with him for so long. His companions. His knowledge.

Knowledge . . .

The words of the prophecy were very precise, he thought suddenly. *They say . . . they say that the Hero will bear the future of the world on his arms.*

Not on his shoulders. Not in his hands. On his arms.

By the Forgotten Gods!

He slammed his arms into the twin mists and seized the powers offered to him. He drew them in, feeling them infuse his body, making him burn. His flesh and bones evaporated, but as they did, he tapped his copperminds, dumping their entire contents into his expanding consciousness.

The copperminds, now empty, dropped with his rings to the pile of blue remains beside Vin and Elend's bodies, and Ruin's nameless corpse. Sazed opened eyes as large as the world, drawing in power that latticed all of creation.

The Hero will have the power to save the world. But he will also have the power to destroy it.

We never understood. He wouldn't simply bear the power of Preservation. He needed the power of Ruin as well.

The powers were opposites. As he drew them in, they threatened to annihilate each other. Yet because he was of one mind on how to use them, he could keep them separate. They could touch *without* destroying each other, if he willed it. For these two powers had been used to create all things. If they fought, they destroyed. If they were used together, they created.

Understanding swelled within him. Over a thousand

years, the Keepers had collected the knowledge of humankind and stored it in their copperminds. They had passed it down from Keeper to Keeper, each man or woman carrying the entire bulk of knowledge, so that he or she could pass it on when necessary. Sazed had it all.

And in a moment of transcendence, he understood it all. He saw the patterns, the clues, the secrets. Men had believed and worshipped for as long as they had existed, and within those beliefs, Sazed found the answers he needed. Gems hidden from Ruin in all the religions of humanity.

There had been a people called the Bennet. They had considered mapmaking to be a solemn duty; Sazed had once preached their religion to Kelsier. From their detailed maps and charts, Sazed discovered how the world had once looked. He used his powers to restore the continents and oceans, the islands and coastlines, the mountains and rivers.

There had been a people known as the Nelazans. They had worshipped the stars, had called them the Thousand Eyes of their god, Trell, watching them. Sazed remembered well offering the religion to the young Vin while she had sat, captive, undergoing her first haircut with the crew. From the Nelazans, the Keepers had recovered star charts, and had dutifully recorded them—even though scholars had called them useless, since they hadn't been accurate since the days before the Ascension. Yet from these star charts, and from the patterns and movements of the other planets in the solar system they outlined, Sazed could determine exactly where the world was supposed to sit in orbit. He put the planet back into its old place—not pushing too hard, as the Lord Ruler once had, for he had a frame of reference by which to measure.

There had been a people known as the Cazzi who had worshipped death; they had provided detailed notes about the human body. Sazed had offered one of their prayers over the bodies they had found in Vin's old crew hideout, back when Kelsier had still lived. From the Cazzi teachings about the body, Sazed determined that the physiology of humankind had changed—either by the Lord Ruler's intention or by simple evolution—to adapt to breathing ash and eating brown plants. In a wave of power, Sazed restored the bodies of humans to the way they had been before, leaving each person the same, yet fixing the problems that living for a thousand years on a dying world had caused. He didn't destroy the people, warping and twisting them as the Lord Ruler had when he'd created the kandra, for Sazed had a guide by which to work.

He learned other things too. Dozens of secrets. One religion worshipped animals, and from it Sazed drew forth pictures, explanations, and references regarding the life that should have lived on the earth. He restored it. From another—Dadradah, the religion he had preached to Clubs before the man died—Sazed learned about colors and hues. It was the last religion Sazed had ever taught, and with its poems about color and nature, he could restore the plants, sky, and landscape to the way they had once been. Every religion had clues in it, for the faiths of men contained the hopes, loves, wishes, and lives of the people who had believed them.

Finally, Sazed took the religion of the Larsta, the one that Kelsier's wife, Mare, had believed in. Its priests had composed poetry while meditating. From these poems—and from a scrap of paper that Mare had given to Kelsier, who had given it to Vin, who had given it to Sazed—he learned of the beautiful things that the world had once held.

And he restored flowers to the plants that had once borne them.

The religions in my portfolio weren't useless after all, he thought, the power flowing from him and remaking the world. *None of them were. Not one had the whole truth.*

But they all had truth.

Sazed hovered over the world, changing things as he felt he must. He cradled the hiding places of humankind, keeping the caverns safe—even if he did move them about—as he reworked the world's tectonics.

The koloss he altered so they could choose to rejoin humanity or form their own separate society. The kandra held no desire to be human, so to these he restored their Blessings—but he also implemented a mortality trigger that those who felt the weight of the centuries could discover.

Finally he exhaled softly, his work finished. Yet the power did not evaporate from him as he had expected it to.

Rashek and Vin only touched small pieces of it at the Well of Ascension, he realized. *I have something more. Something endless.*

Ruin and Preservation were dead, and their powers had been joined together. In fact, they belonged together. How had they been split? Perhaps someday he would discover the answer to that question.

Somebody would need to watch over the world, care for it, now that its gods were gone. It wasn't until that moment that Sazed understood the term Hero of Ages. Not a Hero that came once in the ages.

But a Hero who would span the ages. A Hero who would preserve humankind throughout all times. Neither Preservation nor Ruin, but both.

God.

Vin was special.

Preservation chose her from a very young age, as I have mentioned. I believe that he was grooming her to take his power. Yet the mind of Preservation was quite weak at that point, reduced only to the fragment that we knew as the mist spirit.

What made him choose this child? Was it because she was a Mistborn? Was it because she had Snapped so early in life, coming to her powers as she suffered the pains of the unusually difficult labor her mother went through to bear her?

Vin was unusually talented and strong with Allomancy, even from the beginning. I believe that she must have drawn some of the mist into her when she was still a child, in those brief times when she wasn't wearing the earring. Preservation had mostly gotten her to stop wearing it by the time Kelsier recruited her, though she put it back in for a moment before joining the crew. Then she'd left it there at Kelsier's suggestion.

No one else could draw upon the mists. I have determined this. Why were they open to Vin and not others? I suspect that she couldn't have taken them all in until after she'd touched the power at the Well of Ascension. It was always meant, I believe, to be something of an attuning force. Something that, once touched, would adjust a person's body to be able to accept the mists.

Yet she did make use of a small crumb of Preservation's power when she defeated the Lord Ruler, more than a year before she began hearing the thumping of the power's return to the Well.

There is much more to this mystery. Perhaps I will tease it out eventually, as my mind grows more and more accustomed to its expanded nature. Perhaps I will determine why I was able to take the powers myself. For now, I wish to make a simple acknowledgment of the woman who held the power right before me.

Of all of us who touched it, I feel she was the most worthy.

EPILOGUE

SPOOK AWOKE FROM THE NIGHTMARE, then sat up. The cavern around him was dark, lit only by candles and lamps.

He stood, stretching. Around him, people gasped. He walked past them, seeking out his friends. The cavern was packed—holding everyone from Urteau who had been willing to come and hide. As such, it was difficult for Spook to pick his way through the shuffling, coughing, chatting bodies. As he walked, the whispers grew louder, and people stood, following.

Beldre came running up to him, her white dress flapping. "Spook?" she asked with wonder. "What . . . what happened?"

He just smiled, putting his arm around her. They made their way to the front of the cavern. Breeze sat at a table—of course *he* would have furniture, while pretty much everyone else sat on the rock floor. Spook nodded at him, and the Soother raised an eyebrow.

"You seem well, my boy," Breeze said, taking a drink of his wine.

"You could say that," Spook said.

"That's all you're going to say?" Beldre said to Breeze. "Look at him! He's been healed!"

Breeze shrugged, putting down his wine and standing. "My dear, with all the oddities that have been happening lately, young Spook's appearance doesn't measure up. A simple healing? Why, that's rather mundane if you ask me."

Breeze winked, catching Spook's eye.

"Shall we, then?" Spook asked.

Breeze shrugged. "Why not? What do you think we'll find?"

"I'm not sure," Spook admitted, stepping into the antechamber beyond the cavern. He started to climb the ladder.

"Spook," Beldre said warily. "You know what the scouts said. The entire city was burning from the heat of the sun."

Spook looked up, noting the light shining between the cracks of the trapdoor. He smiled, then pushed it open.

There was no city outside. Just a field of grass. *Green* grass. Spook blinked at the strange sight, then crawled onto the soft earth, making room for Breeze. The Soother's head popped out, then cocked to the side. "Now *there's* a sight," he said, crawling out next to Spook.

Spook got to his feet in the grass. It came up to his thighs. Green. Such a strange color for plants.

"And . . . the sky," Breeze said, shading his eyes. "Blue. Not a hint of ash or smoke. Very odd. Very odd indeed. I'll bet Vin had something to do with this mess. That girl never *could* do things the proper way."

Spook heard a gasp from behind, and turned to see Beldre climbing from the cavern. He helped her step up onto the ground, and then they walked in silent wonder through the tall grass. The sun was so bright overhead, yet it wasn't uncomfortably hot.

"What happened to the city?" Beldre whispered, holding Spook's arm.

He shook his head. Then, however, he heard something. He turned and saw motion on the horizon. He walked forward, Beldre at his side, Breeze calling down for Allrianne to come up and see.

"Are those . . . people?" Beldre asked, finally seeing what Spook had. The people in the distance saw them too, and as soon as they drew close, Spook grinned and waved at one.

"Spook?" Ham called. "Kid, is that you?"

Spook and Beldre hurried forward. Ham stood with others, and behind them Spook could see another trapdoor in the middle of the grassy meadow floor. People he didn't recognize—some wearing uniforms from Elend's army—were climbing out. Ham rushed over and grabbed Spook in an embrace.

"What are you doing here?" Ham asked, letting go.

"I don't know," Spook said. "Last I knew, I was in Urteau."

Ham looked up at the sky. "I was in Fadrex! What happened?"

Spook shook his head. "I don't know if the places we used to know have meaning anymore, Ham."

Ham nodded, turning as one of the soldiers pointed. Another batch of people was emerging from a hole a short distance away. Spook and Ham walked forward—at least until Ham saw someone in the other batch of people. Spook vaguely recognized her as Ham's wife, who had been back in Luthadel. The Thug let out a cry of excitement, then rushed forward to greet his family.

Spook made his way from hole to hole. There appeared to be six of them, some well populated, others not so much. One stood out. It wasn't a trapdoor like the others, but a slanted cave entrance. Here he found General Demoux speaking with a small group of people, a pretty Terriswoman holding his arm.

"I was in and out of consciousness for it," Demoux was saying, "but I saw him. The Survivor. It *had* to be him—hanging in the sky, glowing. Waves of color moved through the air, and the ground trembled, the land spinning and moving. He came. Just like Sazed said he would."

"Sazed?" Spook spoke up, Demoux noticing him for the first time. "Where is he?"

Demoux shook his head. "I don't know, Lord Spook." Then he paused. "Where did you come from anyway?"

Spook ignored the question. The openings and holes formed a pattern. Spook walked through the thick grass, leading Beldre, and made his way to the very center of the pattern. The wind blew softly, the stalks of grass undulating in waves. Ham and Breeze rushed to catch up to him, already arguing about something trivial, Ham with a child on one arm, his other around his wife's shoulders.

Spook froze as he caught sight of a bit of color in the grass. He held up a hand, warning the others, and they stepped forward more quietly. There, in the center of the grass, was a field of . . . somethings. Growing from the ground, with tops like bright-colored leaves. They were in the shape of upside-down bells, perched on long straight stalks, the petals open toward the sun. As if reaching for its light and gaping to drink it in.

"Beautiful . . ." Beldre whispered.

Spook stepped forward, moving among the plants. *Flowers,* he thought, recognizing them from the picture Vin had carried. *Kelsier's dream finally came true.*

At the center of the flowers, he found two people. Vin lay wearing her customary mistcloak, shirt, and trousers. Elend was in a brilliant white uniform, complete with cape. They were holding hands as they lay amid the flowers.

And they were both dead.

Spook knelt beside them, listening to Ham and Breeze cry out. They examined the bodies, checking for vital signs, but Spook focused on something else almost hidden in the grass. He picked it up—a large leather tome.

He opened it, reading the first page.

I am, unfortunately, the Hero of Ages, read the delicate, careful letters. Spook thought he recognized the handwriting. As he flipped through the book, a slip of paper fell out. Spook picked it up—one side had a faded drawing of a flower, the very picture he'd been thinking about moments before. On the other side was a note scrawled in the same handwriting as the book.

Spook,

I tried to bring them back, but apparently fixing their bodies doesn't return their souls. I will get better at this with time, I expect. However, be assured that I have spoken with our friends, and they are quite happy where they are. They deserve a rest, I think.

The book contains a short record of the events that led up to the world dying and being reborn, along with some musings I have made about the history, philosophy, and science of recent occurrences. If you look to your right, you will find a much larger group of books in the grass. These contain all of the knowledge— transcribed verbatim—that was contained in my metalminds. Let the knowledge of the past not be forgotten.

Rebuilding will be difficult, I think—but likely far easier than living beneath the Lord Ruler or surviving Ruin's attempt to destroy the world. I think you'll be surprised at the number of people who fled to the storage caverns. Rashek planned very well for this day. He suffered much beneath Ruin's hand, but he was a good man who ultimately had honorable intentions.

You did well. Know that the message you sent via Captain Goradel saved us all, in the end. The people will need leadership in the years to come. Likely they will look to you. I'm sorry that I cannot be there in person to help you, but know that I am . . . around.

I have made you Mistborn, and healed the damage you did to your body by flaring tin so much. I hope you don't mind. It was actually Kelsier's request. Consider it a parting gift from him.

Watch over them for me.

P.S. There are still two base metals and their alloys that no one knows about. You might want to poke about and see if you can figure out what they are. I think they'll interest you.

Spook looked up, staring at the strangely empty blue sky. Beldre came over and knelt beside him, glancing over his paper, then gave him a quizzical look.

"You're troubled," she said.

Spook shook his head. "No," he said, folding up the little slip of paper and putting it in his pocket. "No, I'm not troubled. In fact, I think that everything is going to be all right. Finally."

ARS ARCANUM

Find extensive author's annotations of every chapter of this book, along with deleted scenes and expanded world information, at brandonsanderson.com.

TABLE OF ALLOMANTIC METALS

METAL	ALLOMANCY	FERUCHEMY	HEMALURGY
☾ *Iron*	Pulls on Nearby Metals	Stores Physical Weight	Steals Strength
⚒ *Steel*	**Pushes on Nearby Metals**	Stores Physical Speed	Steals Physical Allomancy
☉ Tin	Increases Senses	Stores Senses	Steals Senses
☉ **Pewter**	**Increases Physical Abilities**	Stores Physical Strength	Steals Physical Feruchemy
♋ *Zinc*	Riots Emotions	Stores Mental Speed	Steals Emotional Fortitude
♆ *Brass*	**Soothes Emotions**	Stores Warmth	Steals Cognitive Feruchemy

⚘ Copper	Hides Allomantic Pulses	Stores Memories	Steals Mental Fortitude
⚘ **Bronze**	**Reveals Allomantic Pulses**	Stores Wakefulness	Steals Mental Allomancy
⚘ *Atium*	See Other People's Futures	Stores Age	Steals Any Power
⚘ *Malatium*	**See Other People's Pasts**	Unknown	Unknown
⚘ Gold	See Your Own Past	Stores Health	Steals Hybrid Feruchemy
⚘ **Electrum**	**See Your Own Future**	Unknown	Steals Enhancement Allomancy
⚘ **Aluminum**	**Destroys Allomantic Reserves**	Stores Identity	Removes All Powers
⚘ **Duralumin**	**Enhances Next Metal Burned**	Stores Connection	Steals Connection & Identity

External metals have been italicized. Pushing metals have been bolded.

ALLOMANCY ALPHABETICAL REFERENCE

ALUMINUM (INTERNAL ENHANCEMENT PULLING METAL)   Once known only to the Steel Inquisitors, this metal, when burned, depletes all of an Allomancer's other metal reserves.

ATIUM (EXTERNAL TEMPORAL PULLING METAL)   A strange metal formerly produced in the Pits of Hathsin. It collected inside small geodes that formed in crystalline pockets in caves beneath the ground. A person burning atium can see moments into the future, represented by shadows moving ahead of people and objects.

BRASS (EXTERNAL MENTAL PUSHING METAL)   A person burning brass can Soothe another person's emotions, dampening them and making particular emotions less powerful. A careful Allomancer can Soothe away all emotions but a single one, essentially making a person feel exactly as they wish. Brass, however, does not let that Allomancer read minds or even emotions. A Misting who burns brass is known as a Soother.

BRONZE (INTERNAL MENTAL PUSHING METAL)   A person burning bronze can sense when people nearby are using Allomancy. Allomancers burning metals nearby will give off "Allomantic pulses"—something like drumbeats that are audible only to a person burning bronze. A Misting who can burn bronze is known as a Seeker.

COINSHOT   A Misting who can burn steel.

COPPER (INTERNAL MENTAL PULLING METAL)   A person burning copper gives off an invisible cloud that protects anyone within it from the senses of a Seeker. While within one of these "copperclouds," an Allomancer can burn any metal they wish, and not worry that someone will sense their Allomantic pulses by burning bronze. As a side effect, people burning copper are themselves immune to any form of emotional Allomancy (Soothing or Rioting). A Misting who can burn copper is known as a Smoker.

DURALUMIN (INTERNAL ENHANCEMENT PUSHING METAL)   The Allomantic alloy of aluminum with four percent copper. If an Allomancer burns duralumin, the next metal (or metals) they burn will be given explosive power, at the cost of burning away all at once every bit of that metal inside the Allomancer.

ELECTRUM (INTERNAL TEMPORAL PUSHING METAL)   The Allomantic alloy of gold. A person burning this metal can see moments into their own future, represented by a shadow of their body's movement. Sometimes known as "poor man's atium," it allows the Allomancer to counteract the effects of a foe burning atium.

GOLD (INTERNAL TEMPORAL PULLING METAL)   A person burning gold can see a past version of themselves, or possibly an alternate version of themselves had their past gone differently.

IRON (EXTERNAL PHYSICAL PULLING METAL)   A person burning iron can see translucent blue lines pointing to nearby sources of metal. The size and brightness of the line depends on the size and proximity of the metal source. All types of metal are shown, not just sources of iron. The Allomancer can then mentally yank on one of these lines to Pull that source of metal toward them. A Misting who can burn iron is known as a Lurcher.

LURCHER   A Misting who can burn iron.

MALATIUM (EXTERNAL TEMPORAL PUSHING METAL)   The metal discovered by Kelsier, often dubbed the Eleventh Metal. Nobody knows where he found it, or why he thought it could kill the Lord Ruler. It did, however, eventually lead Vin to the clue she needed to defeat the emperor. A person burning malatium can see a past version of others, or possibly an alternate version of them had their past gone differently.

MISTBORN   An Allomancer who can burn all of the Allomantic metals.

PEWTER (INTERNAL PHYSICAL PUSHING METAL)   A person burning pewter enhances the physical attributes of their body. They become stronger, more durable, and more dexterous. Pewter also enhances the body's sense of balance and ability to recover from wounds. Mistings who can burn pewter are known as both Pewterarms and Thugs.

PEWTERARM   A Misting who can burn pewter.

RIOTER   A Misting who can burn zinc.

SEEKER   A Misting who can burn bronze.

SMOKER   A Misting who can burn copper.

SOOTHER   A Misting who can burn brass.

STEEL (EXTERNAL PHYSICAL PUSHING METAL)   A person burning steel can see translucent blue lines pointing to nearby sources of metal. The size and brightness of the line depends on the size and proximity of the metal source. All types of metal are shown, not just sources of steel. The Allomancer can then mentally Push on one of these lines to send that source of metal away from them. A Misting who can burn steel is known as a Coinshot.

THUG   A Misting who can burn pewter.

TIN (INTERNAL PHYSICAL PULLING METAL)   A person burning tin gains enhanced senses. They can see farther and smell more keenly, and their senses of touch and hearing become far more acute. This has the side effect of letting them pierce the mists, allowing them to see much farther at night than even their enhanced senses should let them. A Misting who can burn tin is known as a Tineye.

TINEYE   A Misting who can burn tin.

ZINC (EXTERNAL MENTAL PULLING METAL)   A person burning zinc can Riot another person's emotions, enflaming them and making particular emotions more powerful. It does not let one read minds or even emotions. A Misting who burns zinc is known as a Rioter.

THE STORMLIGHT ARCHIVE®

The Way of Kings, Words of Radiance, Oathbringer

With more than ten years spent in research, world-building, and writing, The Stormlight Archive is a true epic in the making, a multi-volume masterpiece in the grand tradition of The Wheel of Time®.

THE MISTBORN® SAGA

Mistborn, The Well of Ascension, The Hero of Ages

This modern fantasy classic dares to ask a simple question: What if the hero of prophecy fails, and the Dark Lord takes over? What follows is a story full of surprises and political intrigue, driven by a memorable heist crew.

The Alloy of Law, Shadows of Self, The Bands of Mourning

Three hundred years after the events of the Mistborn trilogy, the world is on the verge of modernity, but one scion returning from the Roughs discovers that the civilized world isn't as civilized as he'd thought.

BRANDON SANDERSON

OTHER WORKS

Elantris

Fleet, fun, and full of surprises, this is a rare epic fantasy debut that doesn't recycle the classics. A city and people go from blessed to bewitched, but when the latest outcast arrives, he brings something new—hope.

Warbreaker

By using Breath and the color in everyday objects, miracles and mischief can be accomplished—and are. But it will take considerable quantities of each for two sisters and a Returned God as they face the challenges ahead.

The Rithmatist

While Joel's mind for figures would make him a genius with the magic of Rithmatics, he doesn't have the spark. But he could be the only one able to protect the other students when they start disappearing. A new favorite of YA readers, this fantasy has lively and feisty characters as well as an inventive and detailed magic system.

FOLLOW TOR BOOKS 🄵 🄴 🄾 t TOR-FORGE.COM

Sign up for author updates at: tor-forge.com/author/brandonsanderson

Note: Within series, books are best read in listed order.